THE
SHIPWRIGHT
AND THE
SHROUDWEAVER

THE
SHIPWRIGHT
AND THE
SHROUDWEAVER

RAFAEL TORRUBIA

First published in Great Britain in 2025 by Gollancz
an imprint of The Orion Publishing Group Ltd
Carmelite House, 50 Victoria Embankment
London EC4Y 0DZ

An Hachette UK Company

The authorised representative in the EEA is Hachette Ireland,
8 Castlecourt Centre, Dublin 15, D15 XTP3, Ireland (email: info@hbgi.ie)

1 3 5 7 9 10 8 6 4 2

A CIP catalogue record for this book is
available from the British Library.

ISBN (Hardback) 978 1 3996 2366 7
ISBN (Export Trade Paperback) 978 1 3996 2367 4
ISBN (Ebook) 978 1 3996 2369 8
ISBN (Audio) 978 1 3996 2370 4

Typeset by Input Data Services Ltd, Bridgwater, Somerset
Printed in Great Britain by Clays Ltd, Elcograf, S.p.A

MIX
Paper | Supporting
responsible forestry
FSC
www.fsc.org   FSC® C104740

www.gollancz.co.uk

For my father, who could not sail the ship,
but will greet it on the far shore.
For my mother, who is the lighthouse that calls me home.
For Rowan, who is the sea, and the sun, and the fairest wind.

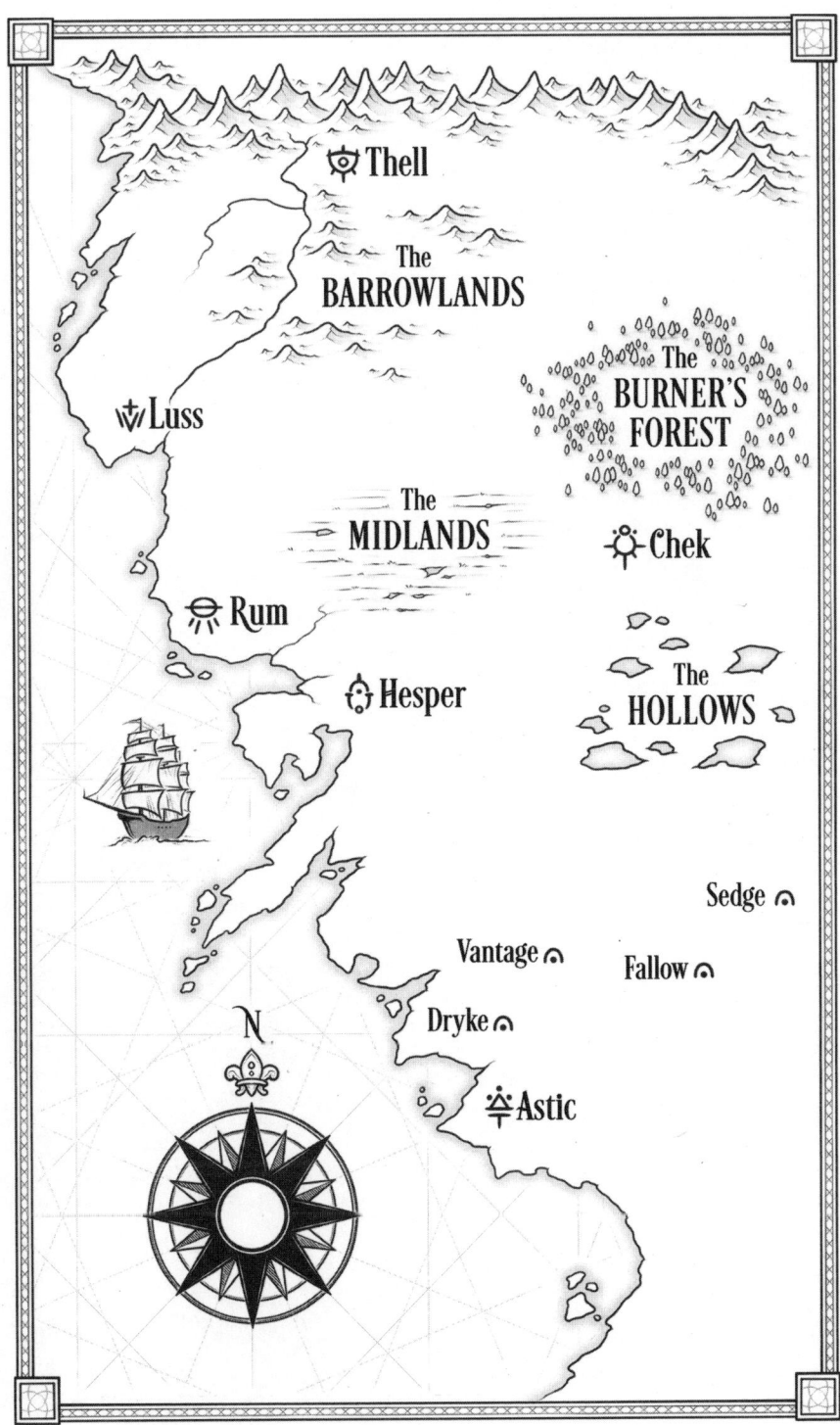

I

first light
dawn
water moving onto water

Shipwright's hands.

Coarse, heavy things.

Fit for spars and oars and swallowing skies.

Shroudweaver's hands.

Thin things, light-boned as a bird.

Fit for cerements, the twisting and weaving of linen, brief touches on shoulder blades.

Both bent to their tasks with quiet focus. Each living in the hush of their own heads, the ship pitching and bucking in a ceaseless swell.

The ocean rocks the wet timber like a wolf at the door, seeking gaps and weaknesses. The Shipwright feels it under her as she stands on the deck, feels it run up her legs, a slow rhythmic push in her muscles. A gentle, hungry flexing. The first whispers of a challenge. She drives and hammers pegs, splits wood, retwists twine with raw fingers. She's quiet as she works, letting the sea fill the spaces in her mind. Above, clouds ravel like skeins of old wool, spitting the first few drops of new rain. She raises her head, sticks out a dry tongue and catches the cool water. The ship rocks, the sea waits, the crew watch, callow and listless. She splits wood, strings sail, slops tar in silence.

The Shroudweaver stands below decks, a slip of a man, his body built from forgotten pieces and then trimmed by a life in lightless places, by years spent in the hollow of other lives, gently shaping and weaving and sending forth. He feels the sea against the hull, sees its slow salting into the barnacle gaps, hears its dripped-out irregular rhythms, feels its predator sway. He works efficiently, binding and parcelling, making swift stitches and careful knots to hold what remains of the spirit within the body under his fingers. Much of it is likely lost already; the man has come to him late in the day. A lesser worker would have given up long ago, but Shroudweaver is practiced and stubborn and knows the ways to carve a god from a man.

Heavy boots sound on the stairs down, the hatch thumps, and Shipwright joins him, broad-shouldered in the drip-down light.

'This war's too fucking hungry,' she says, and the curl in her lip stretches the scars on her face as she glances down at the corpse.

He's a light thing, slim, roughly hewn. Ribbon threading his fingers, neat red stitching on his eyes and lips strangely out of place on a face that looks fresh off a mason's block.

'Did he come in on West Tide?' she asks.

He doesn't look like a West Tide boy. Too raw-boned – skin clear of ash – his teeth still straight and proud in his head.

Shroudweaver purses his lips, shakes his head, slowly darns and stitches. 'I don't think so. He floated in at dawn with a few others. Kisser's been hunting again.'

The needle moves, silver swift.

'Too emptied. I couldn't do anything for them.'

If there's a frown there, it fades like breath on a mirror. She claps him on the shoulder. 'I'm going to take a look topside.'

The deck greets her listlessly. What remains of the crew tend their tasks with quiet persistence. This close to land, even the great ships are vulnerable. She reaches the rail in measured strides and scans the shoreline with a spyglass.

Despite the distance, as the shingle gives way to scree and scrub, she can see that they've hung up gallowswatchers – limp-fleshed, their stretched necks craning ceaselessly, the hollows of their sockets filled with a bright hungry light. Dead men dancing a salt-jig, as their eyes comb the coastal paths. No one is making it out of the port of Astic tonight, not without attracting their stares. It's not worth running the gauntlet to get out to open sea.

The ship is dubious shelter at best, despite her efforts. She shifts her wide hips uneasily, plants her feet more securely against the shuck and roll. She's done what she can, Shroudweaver too.

The rig spirits are tightened, lashed steadily to spinning copper bearings which whine gently in the stiffening wind. Whether it'll be enough – that's another question. This voyage has been long, sucking life from the spinners like meat from a bone.

On the grey coast, the port spits out a flock of questing crows. They wheel drunkenly.

Magic is being worked ashore. She can taste it on her tongue, bitter as burnt sugar. Staying here is a fool's game.

There's only one thing for it. Shipwright fills lungs built from bellows–brass and gives the order.

'Raise sails!'

Shroudweaver hears the shout thunder above decks, watches the corpse's fingers stiffen. Even in death, a sailor wants to sail. He leans low over the dead man's cool skull and rubs saltpetre into its temples. A little touch of the soil to soothe the spirit. His long fingers move with exaggerated care, his thin heart flutters like a bird in a paper cage.

The raising of gods is a dicey business. Decades he's been doing it now, with a catch in his throat every time. He still hears his teacher's voice in his head. Red thread for binding. Holding the scraps of the soul in the body long enough for him to push them together into something new. Old notes reused for a new song. Stale air slipped into fresh lungs.

Above, the gunshot snap of canvas as the sails unfurl. The cries of the crew given sudden life. More distantly he senses the hot toffee taste of magic, a flash of crow wings, and stifles a frantic fear of being torn asunder.

Shroudweaver finishes his preparations and, inside the body of the dead man, a small god begins to sing. A halting thing, at first, for the god is fragile and unreal. Stitched from scraps of spirit and nested in a dead man's chest. Yet it sings as it grows, its fledgling body stretching through meat and muscle. Filling dead flesh with golden light.

The song filters up through straining timbers and curls around Shipwright like a cat. The crew's backs straighten and the sails fill with a wind hung with spices.

The ship is brightest in motion. Shipwright's face is split by a broad grin and she throws back her whipcord arms to greet the freshening wind. Shroudweaver appears by her shoulder, his thin grey hair spidering in the breeze. She drops the grin on him, broad white teeth and sharp eyes.

'Nice work,' she says.

He shrugs diffidently. 'I had good materials.'

The ship kisses the ocean, the tops of the waves a brief press against her surging bow.

'We couldn't move like this without you.'

Another shrug. 'You couldn't move like this without the god.'

She cuffs him around the head. 'And who makes the gods?'

This time, with the shrug, a sly smile.

2

the body chases the flame of first creation
the name burns like tinder
the mouth still holds the song

Eventually they stop running, the crows far behind, the last gilded breath fading from the sails. They've both left the rail by the time the last swell subsides, sprawled around a bottle of wine in Shipwright's cabin.

She takes a deep draw of her pipe and speaks through the smoke.

'How long can we keep this up?'

Shroudweaver waves a hand loose with drink.

'There'll be gods as long as there's corpses.'

Shipwright coughs, spits.

'We can run a while yet then. Up to Hesper at least.'

She stretches, shoulders popping. 'We need to do something more than just harry her though. Our luck can't hold, not with the north locked down.'

Shroudweaver pours, marvels at the steadiness of his hands. Amazing what a drop of something good can do. 'Locked down? Is that what we're calling it? Last I talked to Fallon he said they were' – he sips, adopts an enraged expression – '"Pissing over everything between hill and coast", by which I think he meant, getting a bit more aggressive about their borders.'

'Hard to tell with Fallon,' Shipwright says. 'He's so understated.' Shroudweaver raises an eyebrow and clinks her glass. Shipwright leans back, crosses her legs, drinks deep. It *is* good, this one. Nabbed out the hold of some unlucky merchantman a few days back. A bit opportunistic, perhaps, but if Kisser was sinking ships, there was no reason to let the wine drown as well. She swills it a little as she wriggles her toes to warm them up. 'I think aggressive is putting it mildly. Some of the caravels that used to run north have given up entirely. Trade routes are all locked down from the coast on in. Heard tell there's towns burning there that haven't been touched by Kisser.'

Shroudweaver's expression is perplexed. 'Why would they?'

'Why do people do anything these days? Fear. There are still the remains of temples up there, still pilgrim routes that might pull people north. It's clear they have no interest in that. Not in money, not in the war. Thell wants one thing, to be left the fuck alone.'

She sips again. 'I can sympathise'.

After a moment, she takes her glass to the cabin window and looks out across the waves to the shore. She watches distant, small lights bob as patrols of people who want to kill her tread the coastline, waiting for any ship stupid enough to court the rocks.

'Ah, no peace for us until we finish this.' She reaches up with a hand, pulls the curtain against the growing chill, turns the lamplight down softer, before she sits back on the bench, arching a spine grown weary from standing.

Shroudweaver's breath catches in his throat and he rubs his brow with tired fingers.

Shipwright sees the movement and her smile is softer than her face should allow.

'It's alright,' she says. 'I'm not quite done yet.'

'We're getting closer though,' he says.

Her rough hand is heavy on his knuckles and when she leans in to kiss his forehead she smells of tar, split wood, and sweat.

'Close isn't done,' she says and there's steel in it.

She pours more wine, raises the glass.

'Kicking and screaming?' she says.

Shroudweaver's smile could light lamps.

3

other temples
whalebone arch
willow bower
lover's arms
mother

In the city on the shore, the crows return. She waits for them, watches their wings beat over lamp-lit streets, between smoke-stained buildings.

People are avoiding the curfew, she notices, in small defiant clumps. Tiny rebellions. Irritating.

The crows descend, in ones and twos, pressing themselves against her body, clustering on the pale branches of her arms. Their small insistent hearts hammering with secrets.

She opens her mouth and they crawl inside, sharp claws on her lips and tongue, small bones crunching under her teeth.

She swallows feathers and blood, feels them wriggle down her throat and settle in her stomach. Their quiet cawing threads through her muscles. Their knowledge fills her brain.

She swallows the flock piece by piece, as the lamps wink out and the streets are filled by loyal men with sharp blades.

The ship is long gone, sped across the sea, its body mended and its sails filled with a new god. She'd almost had them, Shipwright and Shroudweaver both. That would have been a thing, an end to at least one annoyance. She couldn't move anything up the coast because of Hesper and the remnants of her bastard fleet; couldn't move anything overland while the republic in Thell was marking its borders in bronze and blood. So she stayed here – her *people* stayed here – slowly starving.

She steps to the side of the room, pours a pitcher of water and begins to wash herself. The water darkens with swirls of blood and feather.

It takes some time for her hands to scrub clean. The blood has worked in deep, under the nails, dark against her skin. She works studiously, precisely, like a surgeon, feeling her throat contract as the last scraps of bone and flesh wriggle downwards.

The Crowkisser seems small in this room, as if it were designed for someone larger, bolder. She could get lost in the shadows of the great pillars. Her thin hair could be pulled by the wind that howls through the shattered panes and be lost.

When she straightens and stands her spine is picked out in the moonlight like a half-finished carving. The harshness of her breathing is the only sign that she might be anything less than utterly calm.

Inside her skull, her mind runs like a rat. Testing out theories. Scurrying to conclusions. None of it made sense. She'd won; *had* won for three years now. Three years where her enemies had refused to die, and where she'd been kept penned in the south by a mountain of fundamentalists, and a handful of ships' captains.

She swirls water, spits redly. One ship the worst of them, ruddy as the dawn, and pushed along by some foreign magic she barely understood. Sails always bright against the dark rocks of the coast. Every one of its damned voyages heralded by the lighting of the signal beacons. Great piles of bleached wood, coughing flame up into the sky.

The Teeth, the people of this city called them. The people of Astic. Her people, looking up at her over cups or across scattered maps and shaking their heads ruefully.

'When the Teeth spit fire, the sea burns.'

And wasn't that the truth? She sits, straightens the coarse line of her skirts, half spattered with blood, feather, other darknesses.

As long as the ship remained on the sea, she would never truly have won. Faster than the rest. Stronger. Worse than that, a symbol.

As long as that pair remained aboard the ship, that symbol

actually held meaning. The last Shroudweaver. Perhaps the last Shipwright.

Her fingers run over the map before her, digging in.

Patience. She needs patience. Patience and a drink of water. And him, much though she hates to admit it.

As if the shadows hear her, he approaches from behind. Soft-booted in the half-light, announced only by the faint clink of harness and clasp, he steps lightly over tilted flagstones, strewn with the bones of small creatures and wet with the insistent, driving rain.

She steps quietly backwards into his opening arms and he pulls her towards him until she rests on her heels and can flick her eyes up precariously to meet his.

'Long night, Crowkisser?' he says, his lips grazing her neck as his fingers tighten against her ribs.

She opens her mouth to reply but her first words are feather and gristle. She coughs and wriggles free self-consciously.

'Yeah, too long,' she says, and her fingers flick anxiously at the corners of her lips, brushing away the ghosts of birds.

He steps towards her again, and staggers. Beneath his jacket, under the armour, there's blood, ragged and spreading.

'You're hurt,' she says, and it's an accusation.

He shrugs apologetically, lopsidedly. 'They got lucky.'

Crowkisser shakes her head tersely and walks towards him.

'No,' she says. 'I got lucky. Which means you, you get to stay alive. And be safe.' Each point punctuated by a prodding finger in the middle of his chest.

He winces and nods, slower than she is, less confident.

'Fine, fine. I hear, I obey. Help me off with this, will you?'

The rifle over his shoulder is almost as tall as he is. She slips behind him and unclasps buckles that retract back into the weapon with a satisfied hiss. He stands clear, and Crowkisser does something quick and clever with her fingers. The rifle clicks, folds, collapses, until it's no more than a sullen, wrought, jagged spike in her hands, a foot long, if that. It smells acrid and she sucks at her gums subconsciously.

'Who was aboard?'

Another shrug. The Slickwalker is full of them tonight.

'More of Fallon's diehards,' he mutters. 'Change is hard for some people.'

Crowkisser purses her lips. 'They shouldn't take it out on you.'

For a second, his face flickers into something sharper, more remorseful.

'They're paid to. Besides, who else are they going to take it out on?' He raises his arms in exasperation, 'We pulled the trigger. We . . . we set all this in motion.'

His shoulders slump, the anger flows out of him like water. He holds her at arm's length, runs a finger along the proud, sharp jaw he's known since they were kids, remembering her jutting defiance at children twice her size, at anyone who said no.

'We did this, Crowkisser. We can't step back from that.'

Her eyes flick up to meet his and he flinches back in shock at their flat hardness.

'We set them free.' Crowkisser's voice is the first stones of the landslide. 'We set them all free.' She pitches and cracks, boulders crashing in the mountain heights. 'Every. Single. One. Of. Them.' Her eyes are black fire and her voice is the roll of distant thunder.

He barely sees the slap coming, but feels the whip-crack sting on his cheek, spits blood into the dust and bones.

'Every. Single. One.' She repeats and her voice is hollow as the high valleys.

'Every one,' she says, in the husk of a whisper. He pulls her close with aching arms and feels her heart hammer against his chest.

'Every one,' and her breath lurches ragged and wet.

'Oh gods,' she breathes.

Slickwalker rocks her like a baby.

'No,' he says. 'Not anymore.'

4

on anatomising the hearts
we found them strange
nacreous, rigid,
ringing like a struck bell

—*Excursions in the Near Wreck*, Wicktwister

Dawn rises shyly off the Hesperian coast, East Tide retreating from the beaches where grey gulls sweep, cackle and war with fat green crabs over the bounty of last night's swell.

Four or five fresh bodies, bloated and scoured by the sea. Shroudweaver watches them. Shipwright watches Shroudweaver.

Her arms enfold him from behind and she murmurs in his ear. 'Recognise them?'

Shroudweaver squints and his mind falls into a quieter space, rattles and hums with detail. The weave of cloth, the cut of boots.

'Wreck of the *Volante*,' he says and feels Shipwright's arms stiffen. His sharp eyes scan cuts, abrasions, peeled-back grimaces, and the crabs squabbling over charred fingertips.

'She went down to something big and noisy. Maybe guns. Maybe magic. Maybe sabotage.' He rolls his shoulders. 'Lots of fire. Not quick. Not pretty.'

Shipwright snarls, 'Fucking Crowkisser.' She ruffles Shroudweaver's thin hair. 'No offense, but your daughter's a cunt.'

She turns to the crew.

'Bring us in.'

A few minutes later and they're standing knee-deep in the surf, watching the broken boards of the *Volante* make their way to land for the last time. The crabs have retreated to a safe distance, their slick bodies jostling in oily, boisterous heaps.

The crew fan out, searching for salvage, and more importantly, for bodies. Names and faces to bring home to the widows on shore. Scoured fingers to break fathers' hearts and salted hair to be clasped in lockets and shaking hands.

Shipwright squats on the tideline, an ache in the small of her back, and a harder ache in her heart. Never too many drowned young faces for the sea. She fishes around, pulls up a shattered plank, its edges burnt and curved smooth as glass. She sniffs it – lemon and grease – and bites her cheek to stop her breakfast from coming up.

'Slickwalker. He's getting better.'

Shroudweaver turns. He's shivering already, the cold of the water stealing up his thin legs.

'He shouldn't even be able to get aboard. I thought you fitted the remaining ships with spinners?'

She nods, sloshes towards him to push him gently out of the water and up the beach.

'That I did. Stay dry.'

He pulls his hood higher, tightens a scarf against the wind. 'I'll try.'

His eyes wander up the cliffs, lingering on the distant spike of a gallowswatcher against the skyline. Closer, one of the Teeth smoulders. 'We shouldn't hang about. Any clue on the spinners?'

Shipwright rolls her eyes, hikes her trousers and heads back to the swelling scurf of the wreck. She lets her fingers sink into the waves, reading their rhythm, and trying to feel the hum of a spinner somewhere amid it all.

'Nothing.'

Up the beach, one of the crewmen yelps, trips, flounders in the surf and dark sand. Shipwright glances across, down at his feet and sees it buried, just at toe height. Fairly rough and ready as spinners go, but she'd been working fast, and the smiths in Hesper hadn't seen one for years.

When she draws closer, the problem is obvious – half the facing torn off, that same lemony stink.

'The bastard shot them off,' she calls.

Shroudweaver turns. '*Shot* them. From where?'

She shrugs. 'The shore, I'd guess. I should have seen that coming.'

Shroudweaver's eyes scan the distance between shore and deep sea. 'You have to be kidding me,' he mutters.

'What?' she shouts.

He walks closer. 'What did she do to him that he can do that?'

She shrugs, pockets the spinner. 'A mystery for another day.' Then, rubbing a hand across her brow, asks, 'Can we go? This is breaking my heart. And Fallon needs to know.'

He nods, places a hand gently in the small of her back.

'Of course.'

From the gangplank, they look back at the shore as the ship casts off.

Shipwright's eyes are narrow against the wind, her hair pulled across her face.

'One of the last,' she says.

'Last what?' he asks

'Last of the great ships.' Her hands tighten on the rail. 'One of the last to sail south with us. One of the last still standing. One of the last with a crew still breathing. I should have seen this coming.' The tears on her cheek are dragged by the wind. 'She'll come for all of them, eventually. Then us.'

He turns her face towards his. 'We won't let that happen.'

'They took me in,' she says.

He frowns, 'Who?'

'The *Volante*'s crew, when I first got here. Not a damn crew would turn their head. Afraid of me, afraid of the ship.' She smiles wistfully. 'Not the *Volante* though. It was two minutes of bristling then days of drinking something red and foul.'

'Buckwater,' Shroudweaver mutters, and grimaces.

She nods. 'That was it. Tasted like burning goat's piss.' Her face softens. '*They* didn't care that I wasn't from here; that they'd never seen a ship like mine.' She snorts. 'I mean, they offered to sell their captain to me in trade for it, but I don't think they were serious.'

Her face clouds again. 'Wish I could remember his name. Poor sod never lived long enough to take a new one. I suppose he's just blowing ash somewhere in the south now.' She shakes her head. 'Last of the great ships.'

Shroudweaver taps her arm, 'Wait here.'

The shore pulls up to the horizon before he returns with two leather cups and a bladder that reeks like a drunkard's nightmare.

She stares at him.

'That isn't?'

He grins, 'I got the taste for it a while back, on the voyage down.'

He leans on the rail and pours, passes her a cup. Turns to the sea, and raises it.

'To the *Volante*.'

She mirrors him, 'The *Volante*. Those shabby bastards. The sea's too good for them.'

5

every map different
every river returning to
the same source

A few hours later and the *Volante*'s unlucky crew are just more bodies in their wake. Shroudweaver sucks on hard tack and looks at Shipwright with narrowed eyes as she buffs the scratches out of her thick deck-boots. Her broad lips curl as she spits and polishes, and he falls in love again. Almost twenty years now. Always the same motions when she's worried. Boots polished and socks darned. Small repairs. Always the same motions. Probably the same boots, come to think of it.

He waves the biscuit pointedly. 'Old habits, huh?'

She nods, tongue on teeth.

He grins. 'So, what's the plan?'

There's barely a beat before she replies. 'Two more days up the coast to Hesper. We see what's left of their fleet, we talk to Fallon and we take on who we can. Get the civilians up the coast some before Crowkisser comes to stir up trouble. She'll head for Hesper next.'

Shroudweaver frowns, tips his head. 'And then?'

Shipwright snorts, slips thick grey socks on her broad feet and buckles up. 'Then we find out if anyone else is as pissed off as we are, and we start to dream up some really inventive ways to fuck her shit up.' When Shroudweaver laughs it's dry as sand swilling around a glass.

'Poetry,' he says. 'Pure poetry. Maybe just a hair short on ideas though.'

She sets the boot down, fixes him with a look. 'We have thirteen fresh bodies in the hold. I'm a little light on ideas.'

He picks sand out from between his toes. 'Me too. Well, I have one or two, but it depends on Fallon. And I don't know if he can be depended on.'

She watches him. 'That's a little . . . off-putting.'

He flicks with a nail. 'Sorry. Sandals.'

She shakes her head despairingly. 'It's just as well you're cute. Do you think Fallon'll be happy to see us?'

Shroudweaver shrugs and looks out to the coast. 'I think so. We're all he has left at this point, since the north shut its gates. Since Riss, and then Quickfish.'

She follows his gaze to where white-bellied birds wheel around the headland. 'Time was we would have run north first. We had that heroic glow about us. A bit of cred to lean on.'

He snorts, but she continues. 'Now, I wouldn't set foot up there without someone watching my back. Too much god-stink clinging to our boots. Then after the fleet burnt, after we lost the ships, after the south . . .'

'Hard to hold your head high', he finishes

'Hard to hold your head high.'

She moves closer to him, undoes a strap, starts rubbing the blood back into his feet.

'I really thought it would work, you know? Time was, I thought there was nothing the three of us couldn't achieve.'

He sighs, half relief, half regret. 'We're bad losers, that's our problem.'

She tries to hold back a smile, fails. 'Among other things, maybe.'

He wriggles his toes. 'Can you do the other one?'

She taps her thigh. 'Yes. Bring me your manky feet. Something I can actually handle.'

Her tone's light enough, but he'd have to be an idiot to miss the edge on her words. Eighteen months of skirmishing and running fraying at the edge of her smile. Crowkisser hadn't sat meekly in Astic while they starved her out.

'I think,' he says, 'that it's partly our fault.'

She rolls her eyes. 'Thanks for that. Very uplifting.'

Above them, a spinner whines like a wet cat. A wave breaks over the side of the ship, salt water sliding down the curve of the spinner's vibrations, leaving the deck untouched.

He smiles. 'You know what I mean. We were cocky. We'd won one war already. Liberated Thell. Founded the Republic. Defeated a monster.'

She dries off his foot, slips the sandal back on. 'Do you ever think we were a bit rusty? Decades between saving the Republic and sailing south.' A bitter laugh. 'I remember sitting with Declan and his wife. Before' – she waves a hand – 'all of it. And we were *laughing*.'

She puts her head in her hands. 'I remember her saying to me . . . she was holding that battered sword of his, and she turned and she said to me, "how much damage can one girl do?"' She winces again as the spinners whine, and the whole ship bucks. 'I guess we all found out the answer to that.'

Shroudweaver says nothing, re-straps his sandals quietly. The ship cants again, and she sways. 'I guess we're still finding out.'

She reaches into a pouch, digs out some shards of metal and starts whittling, bending them gently with her hands. 'Gods. What were we thinking?'

He watches her hands move over the brass. 'That we had an alliance of the biggest cities on this side of the world? That we, somehow, had Hesper and the whole of the Republic at our back. That we'd had more than fifteen years of peace. Tenuous peace, but real peace. Growing peace, farming peace.' Her fingers tighten. Metal snaps and she curses. 'Didn't save us.'

He takes her hands, checks them for cuts. 'What are you working on?'

She gestures up at the spinner. 'That one's off by a tone. Ten, twenty more big waves and we're getting wet.'

He follows her finger up to the tiny brass sphere strung impossibly high above. 'They still amaze me.'

She clenches her jaw. 'They didn't save us either. We all sailed down there. That big beautiful fleet. All those people.' She breathes deep. 'They didn't save us either.'

Shroudweaver brushes faint flecks of metal from Shipwright's hands, takes her face and pulls it down to his shoulder. 'You know why though, love?'

She settles into the curve of his neck. 'No. Hair, please.'

He starts moving his fingers through it, teasing out the burrs and snags, and wishes he could hold the world there for a while, with just her slowly relaxing breath, and the rock of the ship under them. The world had never seemed interested in waiting for them.

He kisses the top of her head. 'Nothing would have saved us. We sailed down looking to win a war. Instead, we got the end of the world.'

Her voice is sleepy with the rhythm of the sea, the rhythm of his fingers. Her hand snakes around his ribs. 'Not yet.'

He brushes the salt from her hair. 'What, love?'

'Not the end of the world yet.'

6

What does the sea take
But everything
But everything
But everything?
Everything
  but light.

—Burial litany, Heron Halls

The ship takes on water at night, and they bail during the day. Salt moves into the skin, and into the blood. Shipwright feels herself aching with every swing of the bucket, a tiredness burning deeper than muscle.

It's dark down in the bilges. What little sun there is has been snagged in the rigging and spilt over the deck boards, as the ship noses her way up the coast.

Hesper waits. Distant, still, but sat in her mind like a toad in a well. A great, grey body hauled atop the stark cliffs by pure pride, a city with money in its bones. Once fat on trade from the South, now wasting away, as this war that is not a war drags out, year on year. The city hollowing out, building by building; any life that's left sparkling like fever in the eyes of a corpse.

She stoops, scoops, tosses.

In Hesper, the Fallons are the only named lords left: Declan and his wife. And beneath them, a guddle of guildmasters and ships' captains; the dark jars of the Glass Archive and the hammering fire of the forges. Hesper was a body built from smaller bodies, guilds and captaincies, fraternities and consanguinities.

She stoops, scoops. The water is black in the bucket, shot with small, silvered fish dancing within, barely fry. Little scraps of flesh and electric movement, swept up by the waves and driven here. What must it be like for them? The world so dark, huge and irresistible.

She dips her fingers in the bucket and lets them nibble at her skin, feeling the tingle of their energy against her palm. As if their bodies had tiny spinners nestled amid their soft bones, their thrumming hearts.

Unexpectedly, she feels like weeping. Instead, she murmurs a small blessing and tips them over the side into the wider, drowning dark of the sea.

Her fingers are numbing, but she persists. Stoops, scoops.

Hesper was a body built from smaller bodies, and stitched together with lies. The reason the Fallons stayed on top of the pile was that they knew who was lying, and why.

'Nothing wrong with it,' Fallon had said, before they last sailed out. 'Human nature.' This as he pored over charts and ledgers of debts owed, every inch the responsible businessman.

He had to be responsible. With Arissa gone, Hesper scented weakness like sharks chased blood, and for a while, after the South fell, Shipwright had felt a stirring of something dangerous; rats looking to climb to the top of the pile. Fallon had responded as he always had, by looking at those with debts due; by finding the strings wound tight around half the city's worthies, and then yanking them until they choked.

Fallon was many things, but he was not shy to wield the knife. The days were long gone when he had needed to do it personally, although Shipwright had seen what that could do.

She stooped again, letting her hands sit in the black water, feeling the salt pick at the cuts in her palms. No, these days, she was the knife.

She had brought it on herself, of course. She had come here, and she had made herself useful. Young enough to view the whole coast as a basket of opportunities ripe for the plucking, with a heart full of hot blood and ambition, and a love for that wild, howling sea. The trouble was, the sea was attached to the land

and she'd quickly realised that what this country needed wasn't a shipwright, but a surgeon.

Even before the South burnt, a host of petty rivalries and ancient grudges boiled up and down the continent, and she had followed like a good dog, year falling on year as plagues raged, and cities fell.

She'd done a lot of good, she knew it – even if you were a knife, you could choose how to strike. Amid it all, somehow, she'd made friends. Some of them on the crew, others stowed inland, tucked away in the Burners' forest and along the trade roads wending through the Green.

Easy to make friends, and easier still to stay with the friends that had found you. It had been painless working for the Fallons after the war for the Republic. Hard to imagine it any other way, in fact. How could you leave the side of someone who had walked through fire with you? And after Arissa was lost, how could she have left Declan to pick up the pieces by himself?

She scoops again. Bangs her knuckles on the edge of the bucket. Curses.

That was the rub of it, really. Too many years piled on top of each other, and too many people who it would hurt to leave. So she stayed as Fallon's knife; against the Herons when they tried to lock down Serpent. When the plague hit Errant. When Crowkisser burnt the South.

And that last one was killing them all. Nothing to fight. Nothing to save. A nightmare so vast she still struggled to comprehend it. A disaster that had split the seams between Hesper and Thell wide open. That purple sky stooped over the South as a reminder that the wound wasn't healed, but growing, festering into new and dangerous shapes. It wouldn't close until Crowkisser was done. And she wouldn't be done without the application of a little corrective force.

Shipwright was trying to stitch the world, and Crowkisser was a half-step behind, ripping at the seams. Sometimes it felt like crafting a spinner. You made something you hoped would work, and when it began to spin erratically, you hammered it back to true. So, she did what she could, harried supply lines and chased down spies. Always Fallon's first choice because her ship was bigger, faster. Because she made people afraid.

Again, she feels like weeping. Something filling up her chest, salt water in the hold of her heart.

She could let it go. She could begin to do the work. She knows what drowns inside her ribs. Another life, where she was not a knife. Where she moved by her own tides. She'd like to see it, some day.

Not now though. Not with the wolf at the door. She hears her father's voice, down here, rocked by the creak and swill of the ship, 'Try to drink the sea all at once, and you'll choke.'

So, drop by drop, she bends her aching back, swallows the salt inside her, and bails.

7

some rivers open wide
deer step in them
some rivers, you can see clear to the bottom
still drown in them

—*Proverbs of the Burning Forest*, Heartshamer

Three days and a stiff salt wind later, and the Grey Towers of Hesper are visible on the horizon, cut against the coast like an old scar.

Hesper is barely changed from the first time Shipwright sailed into port with a heart full of hope and a hold full of spice, her hands jittery on the ship's wheel. Then, the city had welcomed her like a surly lover, the massive barques of the other captains sliding past her as their crews alternately jeered, catcalled or cheered. The savviest waiting in silence, eyes wide at the sight of a ship from the East in all its long-beamed glory. Requests for boarding hollered and signalled. Ratlines helpfully tossed. Clods of shit. Bottles of rum. Arcs of piss. A mixed welcome.

Nudging into the lowest loop at the bottom of the cliffs, where the city finally dared to let her toes touch the sea. Above, the switchbacks and twists that brought up the smaller ships into the belly of the port, through the canals and straight to where the money was.

No room for her ship, even in those massive engineered channels, she needed more depth. Besides, Shipwright had thought, it was good to make an entrance. A few quick twists to the mechanisms at the base of the main masts, and the spinners atop roared to life, bigger than anything else she'd ever worked with, the size of a small globe, or a man's skull. A little cocky, a little dangerous; a little exciting.

Their hum spread down the spars, shivering the whole ship and Shipwright along with it. Spinner magic disregarding the boundaries between bone and board, threading her muscles until she thrummed like a barely chained dog, wild with energy.

Out across the water, the ship began to sing. The sound flattened the tops of the waves, and lifted her bow. The speed with which she moved cut the rim of the ocean, sending waves of spume over the howling crews of the barques, spinning the latch boats and tugs that had come to greet her.

Her crew crowded the rails, shinned up the masts and opened their mouths to the song of the spinners, an old eastern shanty, one Shipwright had only heard in quiet whispers around the deck fires and mess tables before. Here, held in harmony by thirty voices, it sounded entirely different, the burr of the spinners a ceaseless bass. Beyond that copper twang, the cries of the sailors hit the water with force, the shout at the end of each verse almost a physical thing.

She felt the eyes of Hesper's captains on her, and beyond that, attention from the shore. It didn't take her long to find the source.

A busy port, Hesper, labourers and merchants and counters and cutters, hand over fist. All of them curious, some panicked at the speed of the approaching ship. A scurry of tar-boys with lines and no plan. A docksman shouting at them to get their worthless arses back.

At the heart of them all stood a great grey charger, motionless as stone. Atop it, back straight as a spear, a woman who put all the ships' figureheads to shame. Tall as a tree, slender as a mountain ash, her back straightened by armour of sculpted steel. A grey cape settled across her shoulders like a cormorant's wing, a sword at her hip. Lady Arissa Fallon, Lady of the Grey Towers.

Shipwright should have been humble – she knew nobility when she saw it. But she was the best captain on this sea, and she helmed the best ship. Humble could wait.

She wrenched the wheel and kicked the spinners into a flying hold. The ship turned, skewed broadside and kept thundering towards the docks, the wave building before it now like the skirts of a sea god, thrashed with kelp and fish and flotsam.

She watched the onlookers flinch back. All but Arissa. Thousands of tonnes of roiling, singing wood and water, and all she did was sit up a little straighter yet, something in her eyes, perhaps the shadow of a smile on her face.

Shipwright left it to the last moment, the docks reaching out for her like the mouth of a startled drunk. All that ship under her hands and only the faintest movement from her fingers to swing the spinners into a ghost hang. Two feet from the docks, from the yelling traders and scrambling guards, the ship simply stopped.

She felt the stress of the spinners in the back of her skull as they took all that forward weight and stored it. The faintest pine in their pitch, and then, still. She dropped them to silence with a gesture.

For the first time in months, the docks of Hesper hung quiet.

Held it for a second, two, and then erupted into cheers, hollering from the cobbles and the flung-wide windows; salt-wives corpsing into their baskets and old sailors pushing up from their lobsterpot perches.

A whip-thin gangplank out, and the crowd swarmed forwards. Shipwright set foot on the rail and waited a moment, watching the faces in front of her, the whitewashed stretch of the city above, its reddened roofs, its arches. Above it all, the bulk of those great grey towers.

The air split with sound as either side of that massive horse, soldiers pealed out on silvered trumpets. The crowd melting grudgingly from the foot of the gangplank, encouraged on by the hafts of pikes across thighs and backs.

The horse and its rider approached, hooves striking echoes from the wet stone.

Closer up, the Lady of the Grey Towers was still dignified, but more human, her cloak spattered with the spray. A wariness in her eyes, and something else; a lick of humour that Shipwright could stand to see more of.

She tilted down the plank, jumped the last few feet.

Down on the cobbles, Arissa Fallon seemed less approachable. The horse holding her up against the sky, and the cut of her shoulders framed against the scudding clouds. The wind pulling at her cloak, at her hair in its severe ponytail. Beautiful. Shipwright felt a brief twitch in her stomach, tried to stay professional.

The cobbles slicked with fish guts and bird shit. It wasn't easy.

'Lady, I am . . .'

'Shipwright. I know.' Her voice was filed glass. Dark and crisp. 'I've heard of you. You ran the blockade at Serpent. That was brave. And you were the first ship into Errant during the plague. That was . . . interesting. No profit in that one.'

'Last one out,' Shipwright muttered.

'What?'

She crossed her arms. 'I was the last one out. Of Errant. With half her people.'

Arissa unknotted her dark hair, letting it fall down her back before it was caught by the wind.

'From what I heard, half her people was all she had left.'

'That's true, Lady.'

'So why risk it? I can't imagine they had coin. The plague hit the guildhalls first, as I heard.'

'No coin, Lady.'

She dismounted in one fluid step, 'Why then?'

'No one deserves that death, Lady. Not just because they're too poor to run.'

Arissa watched her, her eyes the blued grey of the clouds.

'Interesting. My cousin married a fisherman in Errant. Family hated him, but she loved that man. Do you know what she told me about you?'

Shipwright shook her head.

'No, Lady. I couldn't put names to all the faces, I'm afraid.'

Arissa waved a gloved hand, 'She said you didn't sleep for the whole four days it took to get them into safe harbour.'

'True, Lady.'

'Said you sailed that ship alone some nights, so your crew wouldn't have to go near the sick.'

'True, Lady.'

'Said you gave near half your cargo when you pulled into Visage, to get cure to them all.'

'Also true.'

Arissa stepped forwards, until she was barely an inch or two away from Shipwright's face.

'Interesting.'

Her breath was sweet. Like flowers. Or aniseed.

'My cousin said, Shipwright, that you never sickened, nor tired.' A faint smile, the briefest line of teeth, 'Also true?'

'Yes, Lady.'

A gloved hand settled on Shipwright's shoulder, another, startlingly, snaked around her waist. A shiver ran down her spine from the suddenness of the touch.

'I think I can use you, Shipwright. I think this city can use you.'

'I hope so, Lady.' She caught herself. This was hardly driving a bargain. Her cheeks were too hot. She couldn't focus.

'Why did you come here, Shipwright?'

Did the fingers around her waist tighten, for just a moment?

'I wanted to help people. Talk on deck is that you do right by your own.'

Arissa pulled her in close, her lips the barest brush against her ear. Not a hope of hiding the slyness in her voice.

'Also true. Welcome to Hesper, Shipwright.'

Shipwright rolls her shoulders, shakes herself back to the present. Over her head gulls scream, and the ship rocks on the cusp of a wave.

Arissa was long gone. Pulled down into nothing by Crow-kisser. Defiant, sly, caring to the last. Her best friend. Almost . . . almost her lover. Her breath still catches at the thought.

With Arissa's fall, Hesper had stumbled too. Her husband, never the most sociable of rulers, grew suddenly reclusive beyond reason. Apparently, he'd thrown himself into his work, because the wheels kept turning, but the towers grew as quiet as they could.

Gradually, Hesper's trade dwindled. The bold, brutal captains were gone, deceived into thinking that joining the great fleet sailing south would crown their careers and send their barques and bosuns home covered in glory and gold. Packed off and provisioned by the guild heads, who had slid into their still-warm bunks and cradled their coffers with startling speed.

Almost all those great ships were sunk now, sundered at the bottom of the sea, along with their crews, their captains, their cheers and their piss. When you sailed into Hesper now, the silence created itself.

Shipwright wanted to mourn it all, or cut loose of it all, but she couldn't. High in those grey towers, her best friend still lay. Heart still beating. Lungs still breathing. Nothing to shake her out of it, for all she had tried.

Oh, how she'd tried. The last of her gold, the most precious pieces of her cargo that she'd squirreled away over the years had bought her nothing but disappointment. Arissa was gone. Only her body remained. That smile, that wit, that fierce kindness, had fled to somewhere no ships sailed.

Shipwright could leave Hesper, could go if she wanted, but the city remained just like Arissa, a whisper of what it had been, a shadow on her heart with just enough of the shape of something she loved to keep her coming home.

8

Hey now mill wheel,
hey now furrow,
hey now the high ice,
hey the sleeping barrow

—Harvest song, Millet

The hill held the tomb and the shadow of the tomb held the town. That's how the story went. The people of Millet drawn by the gentle curve of the river and the rolling fields of dark earth that spilt out on either side like a dowager's skirts, brought their rickety wagons from Hesper's walls and made a little town in the crook of the water, got fat on fish and grain.

Quickfish could hear his mother's voice telling the story, could see the silhouette of her body framed against the lamplight. His childhood bedroom, a world and twenty years ago. The lines of her hands miming fish and grain. The flicker of the flame. He is seven, maybe eight. Enough of a boy to crave the terror of the outside; enough of a child to want to hear about it in bed, at home. The grey walls of his tower bedroom cradle him, the sheets white canvas for the tale, as Arissa spins it onwards.

The shadow of the tomb held the town. Night would fall, and the lights of Millet would cluster in the dark of the hill, against the kiss of the wind.

The people of Millet were simple people, good people, as much as all people are good. They locked their doors, and stoked their fires, and slept in each other's arms.

And if the wind ran strangely over the hill, they marked it not. And if the mouth of the tomb whispered, they marked it not.

And this was their undoing. For although the good people of

Millet had built well above the ground, in the crook of the river, they had forgotten to fear what slept below the earth.

Arissa's hands slipping under the covers. Hunching into fearsome shapes that crept towards her boy. He'd wriggled higher, pressed against the headboard. Chest fluttering with excitement as he watched those hands move, and imagined what crawled beneath his very feet.

Worms, yes, and other animals. But what else? Bones? Bodies? Magic?

The next bit of the story had been his favourite, his mother pulling the lantern close against her chest, so flame licked her throat and the stark planes of her face. Her eyes black hollows against the softness of the light. Enunciating every word, playing with the sounds of the tale. Shooting a sly smile over her shoulder at his Da who watched by the door.

The hill held the tomb. And the shadow of the tomb held the town. But the tomb had been here long before the town. For the people of Millet were not the first to feel the call of that dark soil and the bright curve of the river.

Long ago, the mountains had coughed forth warriors. Bold warriors, sharp-toothed and bronze-bladed. Conquerors, pouring from a city that lived in the stone, like a maggot lived in the wound, or a worm slept in the soil.

Thell. And her voice dipped and rumbled enough, that for a second, he wondered if that really was his mother sat at the foot of the bed, this black-eyed shade licked by light.

Warriors of an empire which slept in the shadow of glaciers. Followers of an Emperor who craved blood. Times past, they had pushed far south from the mountain, almost to the gates of Hesper itself.

She creeps up the bed as she says this, the lamplight swaying, just enough of a smile on her face that he doesn't scream. His Da's muffled laughter fluttering round the side of a whisky glass.

And as Thell's warrior had conquered, they'd died. And they had built homes for their dead. Great tombs beneath the earth. But those dead slept lightly, for their Emperor lived in their blood and always called them, called them, called them back to war.

And here was Millet, sleeping in the shadow of one such tomb. And when the good people of Millet slept, and dreamt, the old ghosts of those warriors crept down the hill on the night wind, soft as wending. Skulked through alleys and rapped on windows. Waited for the one house with an unlatched door, the one window without a light to guard it.

And when the lock was loose and the light was dimmed, they would strike. Dragging a child from its bed and back up the dark hill on the cusp of the wind. Stifling its screams and pulling it down into the black below until they could slit its throat, slake their thirst and finally, sleep again. Red with blood, quiet as the grave.

Quickfish had barely moved. Pressed back against the wood, breath stilled in his chest as he imagined dead fingers on his throat, dead mouths drinking hot blood. And of course, his mother had pounced, pulling him tight against her breast. Soft cloth and strong bone. The warmth of her like nothing else. The smell of her; herbs and cooking oil, perfume and steel.

And she'd reassured him that the warriors were long gone and the Emperor dead. And he knew it was true, because his own mum and dad had done it. She had shown him the sword she swung, and the armour she wore.

There were no monsters anymore, because his mother had killed them all. She had repeated this as she kissed his cheeks and tucked him back in. Tight as a shroud, she'd said. Ruffled his hair, kissed his forehead again, held on it. Said his name, which does not exist anymore. Which slips through the memory like an oiled absence, and vanishes.

Quickfish remembers the touch of her lips though, and the feel of her hands. The callus where the sword grip had rested. The way the killing she had done to keep him safe had marked her body. The way her smile lingered in lamplight as she kissed him. The way she shrank back into the dark bulk of his Da's body, tipping her head for a different kiss. The pair of them against the light. Solid as shadow. Fading as his memory slips back to the present.

To the curve of a river, to the hill above a town. To a tomb upon the hill. Millet had survived the stories, but there was enough truth to them that he had been pulled out of Hesper to chase the shape of the tale. Roofkeeper dutifully plodding ahead of him, broad shoulders set against a fine rain, axe swinging loose at his side.

The tomb on the hill was real. And Thell was real. The Empire had been real. And perhaps their magic had been real. That magic that called the dead back simply for the memory of blood. The hunger for life.

Quickfish had read about it in the tower's small library, and when that was exhausted and insufficient, taken himself to the street of small saints, and when that had given only rumours, he'd visited the Glass Archive, and paid the price for some real knowledge.

And what they had told him was simple: that Thell was an empire which had defeated death. Until it was itself defeated. His mum and dad had killed the monsters he now needed to find, and put the Republic in their place.

The connection was clearest in what the sources didn't say, be they book or back alley or archive. The Republic was not so distant from the Empire it had overthrown. Something of that Empire still lived on in Thell. Which meant that magic might still sleep there. Like a maggot in the wound, like a worm in the soil.

And if there was any hope of bringing his mother back into the light, Quickfish would take it. Even if it meant stepping into the place of his childhood nightmares.

Ahead, Roofkeeper has stopped to chat with a miller working by the lock, with two children who are very hale, and not at all starved of blood. He looks back and beckons.

'Got a bed for the night, and some food too if we don't mind bending our backs to the wheel.'

Quickfish smiles at this man who has left house and home with him. Because of love. Because of hope that something can still be saved.

And maybe Quickfish had stopped believing that, at points. And maybe he needed to see that face, with its honest brow and firm bones. He catches up with Roofkeeper and kisses him on the forehead. Lingers on it for a second. Smiles at the kids as they go to chase ducks down the eddies.

'Time to earn your supper, your majesty,' Roof mutters, and Quickfish kicks him.

'Time to mind your tongue.'

Roof holds his eye as he hefts a sack of flour. 'I thought that was your job.'

And Quickfish doesn't mean to blush, but the blood is in his cheeks before he knows it. Roof's laughter cutting the rill of the mill water.

'Come on, come on. Town's not so bad after all, is it?'

Quickfish hefts a second sack, and looks at Millet as it shelters in the river's bend. At his back, the Grey Towers of Hesper still limn the sky. In the tallest tower, his mother, and all the stories she ever told. If he's going to get her back, he's going to need to go Thell.

Perhaps it's like Roofkeeper says. Perhaps the stories are just stories. Perhaps there is only enough magic left to fix the world, not break it again.

Shoulders set and cheeks aglow, Quickfish steps into the town, into the shadow of the hill, and the shadow of that tomb.

9

These berks are so superstitious
they shit into their own shadows.

—Caskheart, first mate of the *Pride of the Forests*

The docks of Hesper embrace the water in long, lazy loops, switchbacks of solid stone, creating a series of calmer pools, a brief breathing space between the city's ships and the ceaseless pull of East Tide.

A trade city from the very shape of it. Smaller ships and boats could make their way up the canals that climbed the cliffside, levered up on lock and muscle, and follow the waterways right out to the whitewashed merchant houses, with their low loading docks and broad, beautiful doors which opened with slowness, stillness, onto the sluggish waters. Shipwright could still remember the merchants carefully stepping down slick canal steps, lifting the trimmed hems of their gowns and robes free of the algae, running broad, confident fingers over wares which came from all corners of the world. Fruits shelled in hard black spikes, silks and linens and perfume. The bigger barges bringing the real trade; iron and brass and powder.

She could still remember the thrill of the mornings, floating markets flung wide, their owners crying out their newly arrived wares in a looping, liquid shout that was part song, part prayer, part auctioneer's block. Browsing wares and delicacies in those low-arched salerooms, their roofs crisscrossed with geometric patterns that seemed to reflect and refract the water lapping inches from her feet.

Each shop had its own smell, a mix of the produce and incense, the sweat of the sellers and the pomade in their dark hair. She

34

missed their confident, soft hands, offering up treats with a glint, a soft word, taking her money with twice the speed.

A good hustle, with everyone in on the con. And then break-fast on the canal's edge, feet dangling above the water, stripping rind and spitting pips at the mouthy barge boys below. Behind her, that half-song, half-sale, growing and ebbing in the morning light. It almost felt like being home.

The ship's sails snap uncertainly in the seaport's breeze, jerking her loose from the soft grip of memory. Their sail-god is dying, a guttering pulse of buttery light in the struggling canvas.

Below decks, Shroudweaver holds the body of a dead man and weeps as he feels him buck and writhe. The last shreds of his existence burnt and cindered to feed the god that got them here. Shipwright wants to join him down there, but there's no time. There hasn't been time for months.

Above the looped entrails of her port, the Free City of Hesper squats like a vulture on a fresh kill. The talons of her grey towers spear into the twitching body of the city, their massive flanks writhing with rope and men. Once upon a time whitewashed and beautiful, perhaps; now stained by the smoke from a million foundries. The whole city stinking with the filth of war.

Shipwright watches her crew unload; barrels and bales, oilcloth swaddled blades bobbing and weaving their way down ropes and hawsers into the guts of the city. After that, thirteen long boxes, each bound with red ribbon by Shroudweaver. Proof against any final indignities for the crew of the *Volante*. The men and women were mostly quiet as they worked, focused on the task beyond what was necessary.

There had been precious little chat since the fall of Astic. The last of the border towns swallowed up by the grey tide of Crow-kisser's army. A few ragged survivors arriving in Hesper with tales that were too bloody familiar. Wild-eyed dissenters with their names peeled loose, fraying like chewed skin. Mad within a week, dead within two. And they were the lucky ones. Many of them hadn't run fast enough. The sea and shore between Astic and Hesper were studded with bodies reeking of lemon and rot. Slickwalker ranging ahead of Crowkisser's armies, burning through shadow and twilight to keep the exodus slim. How he did it, she didn't know, but it chilled her blood. Almost as much as the other tales. Not spoken as loudly, no froth of ale or madman's roil to muddy them. The tales that Fallon's scouts told, that Astic had welcomed Crowkisser in. That even now, warm lights burnt in that little fisher town, and its people gave themselves over to the new regime, so long as the boats still sailed, and their nets still pulled fish. Shipwright hadn't mentioned that to Shroud, not yet. Scared to, if truth be told. Could be that's how this war would be won. Folk got tired of fighting.

She looked at her crew, and marked the strain of it on them, the shadowed eyes and shaking hands. Too much time taken up with running and hiding, even if they called it raiding. Crowkisser hunted the ship like a coursing dog, and her crew were run ragged. Almost all of them new fish, brought aboard after the last disastrous sally towards the south. Shipwright barely knew their faces, much less their names.

She cracks her knuckles methodically. Ah, well. Time enough for that if they survive.

As the last barrel bellies off into the depths of the city, Shipwright beckons her first mate towards her. Sandy haired, wide-faced and blue-eyed, scarred along the collarbone where something hot and hungry has tried to put an end to him. Slickwalker's blasted gun, most likely. Makes him distinctive though. Let's her hang onto his name.

He dips his head respectfully. She smiles.

'Ropecharmer. All swinging steady?'

'Yes, ma'am,' he says, 'Smooth and easy.'

Gods, she thinks, *he's fucking enjoying himself.* Maybe it was easier, when you were young. She stifles a twinge of envy and steadies a hand on his shoulder. 'OK, Rope. Take the rest ashore. Get them fed, get them laid, get them drunk. I don't care but get them out from under my feet. I need you back by first swell, but no sooner.'

Her eyes slide up to the city's writhing talons.

'Shroud and I have to go see the boss.'

IO

the shepherd knows truths the sailor does not
that every byre is a fiction
that old heifers only rest in the teeth of dogs

A few hours later Shipwright and Shroudweaver stand in front of the High Lord of Hesper.

A decanter arcs lazily over their heads and bursts against the wall, spattering a room which looks like an antiquary's wet dream. In the middle of it all, Declan Fallon, moustache bristling, arm in a sling and looking less than positive.

'The *Volante*! That skinny fucking bitch. That pallid, dead-eyed slut. I'll take her apart bone by fucking bone and never mind that ratshit lover of hers. I'll shove his fancy fucking gun so far down his throat he'll be shitting lead for years.'

Another wave of the arm that had sent the decanter to a better place.

'That. Fucking. Slit. I'll end her, see if I don't.'

Shipwright rocks back on her heels. That was what someone like Fallon expected, all noise and bluster, flapping his mouth because he'd found a problem that his money and his cock couldn't solve.

It might have worked on her once, a decade ago, two decades ago.

She glances at Shroudweaver to see if he is similarly impressed. The fingers of his left hand flash a quick response in Katkani tip-speak.

Let the bag empty itself.

She chokes down a smile and turns back to Declan. 'We agree the problem is serious.'

The large man's face purples in rage. 'Serious? No. Serious is

37

when the crops are slow. Serious is when the rifles run out of bullets. Serious is maybe, *maybe* when my feckless son disappears two ruddy months before our fucking chat here. Serious is when my wife can't . . .'

Shipwright lets it all flow over her like the tide.

'How is your wife?' she asks quietly.

Fallon deflates like a sodden bellows.

'She's . . .' His voice falters, fades into emptiness. 'She . . . is. I suppose.'

For a moment, Declan Fallon is not the Lord of the Grey Towers, he's something smaller, more delicate. If Crowkisser could see him now, Shipwright thinks, she'd break him into a thousand pieces.

Perhaps she can. Shipwright's eyes flick over the shadows in the room. Shroud's right. This isn't a war anymore. She doesn't really know what it is. Somewhere between a losing battle and a reluctant surrender.

She watches Declan shrink in on himself. Three years ago, he'd been planting trailing vines over the high balconies. Getting drunk mid-day. Talking about another kid, maybe. Three years ago, Shipwright had been thinking about a life on land. What it might be like to dig the earth. She hadn't thought about children, but she'd dreamt spaces where they might be.

Now, she watched the shadows, and waited for the hammer to drop.

I I

Mind your mother's words boy
Mind your father's tongue
Mind the trade in liars' coin
Beneath the turning sun

—Tannery kids' kick song, Hesper

Fallon watches Ship and Shroud leave. Pathetic. He knows how it looks. He can't make it look any another way. Grief hangs on him like whaler's tarp and their sympathy is a finger in the wound.

He'd liked that decanter. He'd liked running this wild dog of a city. Riding home with his wife after the Revolution like the land itself had been carved for him. A proper victor's return, stomping stallions and tossing banners.

A bit of peace after that. The world luring him in, letting him get soft. Arissa finally untensing and revealing the girl that lived inside the soldier, inside the diplomat. Quick smiles and soft touches, kisses in the stairwell that ran straight to his hips.

Mornings dicing and dickering with all the squabs and vultures that made up the shape of the city, Quickfish at his elbow, learning the trade. How to spot a bastard. How to slip a lie between two sheets of paper. How to hang a smile on your face and leave it clear of your heart.

Hesper had disagreed with herself since her founding. Founded by a guddle of captains rich enough and lazy enough to crave a big house on high cliffs, and just smart enough to realise they could run coin through their fingers from tariffs and trade, give their sword arms a rest, turn their criminal brains to more mercantile pursuits.

Brilliant idea. A potage of colossal egos and miserly cunts. That had been before his time of course. Over the years, all those captains and corsairs had fucked hard and brewed up a whole passel of mewling babes that craved not just money but legitimacy. So they had stopped calling themselves captains, and stopped sailing forth. Put down roots, hard, like a vine twining the throat of a tree, moving into all the trades that kept Hesper's blood pumping. Forges, tanners and bilge-merchants. Cutters, crossers and crooks, the lot of them. Guilds. With guildmasters to lead them. Every one of them snakes in sharp coats, but wielding real coin, and wearing big, flashy hats, so impossible to ignore. The city needed money to turn, and Fallon needed the city to turn to keep his hand on the wheel. It was exhausting. Hard to believe he'd married into this. Stepped in that nest of snakes. All for her hand. For her smile. For Arissa.

The loss of the *Volante* would worsen things. The captain had been insufferable, a real preening prick, but he'd known what side his bread was buttered. And he'd survived the South.

That was how it was these days. Your friends were just those folk who'd stayed alive. Couldn't be pickier than that, unless you were down in the Archive kissing glass.

Precious few friends for Declan Fallon, High and Knackered Lord of Hesper. Ship and Shroud, he'd grant. They'd stuck to him like barnacles on a bilge pump, even after the South burnt to glass and Crowkisser boiled up from her rancid nest with a pile of grey-cloaked, sharp-eyed menaces. Loyal to a fault, both of them, even when it cost them time together. Or space to breathe. Now, even that loyalty was showing cracks. Arissa lying between them all like a corpse in the wedding bed.

He knew everyone could smell it on him. The stink of grief. And he didn't mind Ship or Shroud clocking it. He could wash off that shame with a few swigs of something amber and warm. But the other vultures squatting on Hesper's corpse could see it too, and for them it was like chum in the water.

That's why he'd held off going cap in hand to the guilds. Courting them was weakness. They came to him. He flattered himself that he was still the last word, despite it all. No one twitched in Hesper without his say.

Or so he hoped. He'd wound enough gilded chains around the worthies of the city to keep them to heel, but even he could feel a tension. The odd exploratory tug. This sorry excuse for a war had made everyone fractious. No clear victories, and Crowkisser's grim little flock pecking at the edges of what little control he had left.

He hung on. For all Hesper's newly minted guildmasters styled themselves as respectable men of business, they were only a few births and burials down from those pirate captains, and that corsair's urge for control still stirred their blood. So, he let their pride and hunger run them into traps baited with good deals and firm handshakes. Balanced their urges and egos with ledgers, and threats. Debts due and debts owed. The red columns and the black.

He could feel the squeeze though. If Kisser kept up her current pace, she was going to swallow every wretched little hamlet that still clung to the black crust of the southern border. Something strange was happening there, a swing in the weather vane that didn't quite add up. Resistance had been fierce to begin with, after the South burnt, and Hesper's fleet had limped back to port. Terror had quickly turned to fury, and fury had kept the forges lit for a while, even the most callow entrepreneurs among Hesper's grasping classes realising that to stay atop the pile, there needed to be a pile to climb.

When Crowkisser had taken her victory as a chance to stretch her claws northwards, the little southern towns scattered in her path had fought tooth and nail, panic lending steel to their spines. He'd run men and supplies out for months, until he ran out of men, and the towns ran out of living mouths and able hands.

Now, his scouts were whispering another, shittier story. Crowkisser and her shadow-walking hunting dog rolling up on those towns and being greeted with, if not open arms, then arms open enough for a boot and a gun barrel to be jammed between them. All those little southern villages choosing bowing heads over digging graves. A pragmatism that was impressive, but deadly to Fallon. For every town that realised that submission to the crow-witch was easier, the wall of free folk around the south crumbled. Every one of them a drop in the bucket, but enough drops, and that bucket would spill dross all over his boots.

The southern towns were just sprats though. The real twist of the knife had been Thell. Years they'd fought for that bastard lump of rock. He still had a hot pain above his hip where little shards of some jade mace ground against the bone, reminding him of his bad decisions. He should've known better. Thell had left quicker than a scalded cat when the world burnt, and stones piss on them for that.

Kinghammer and the rest of them tucking themselves away from the world, as if that seclusion wasn't just a dangerous indulgence. He glances over the map to where the Stump lurked in the mountains. A fat little blot of selfish ink. A new capital for a new age that wanted precisely fuck all to do with the folk who had bled and died for it.

He'd understood it when they wanted to be left to themselves. A whole fledgling nation brutalised by what they'd fought through. Except, they weren't bloody keeping to themselves anymore.

He takes some chalk and sketches, irritated, down the map. Crowkisser's fuckery in the south had put the wind up Kinghammer, clearly. Just days later, and all roads north had been sealed. Villages cleared, livestock and people pulled up and into the shadow of the mountain and all of it done with the same clinical economy that had won Thell's freedom.

Of course, when the scale of what Kisser had done became clear, as names fell like leaves and the prayers of hosts went unanswered, Thell had stepped its operations up a gear. Now, Hesper was squeezed between the hammer and the anvil. All their efforts to keep Crowkisser penned in the south fraying, as the southern villages tired, and great ships like the *Volante* slowly sank to the bottom of the sea.

The crow-witch nipping at his arse cheeks, and from the north, Thell sent patrol after patrol of harsh-eyed young warriors, hands sweaty on their leaf-bladed spears. Guarding the roads, so they claimed. Turning back every rider that tried to canter towards the mountain.

He scratches his stubble and sighs. Doing a damn sight more than that, he suspected. Thin columns of smoke kissing the Midlands sky. Some of his scouts had seen enough before they were turned homewards, riding back with warnings that Thell was marking its borders with blood and ash. Those tight patrols of lithe young killers alighting in villages which had hosted temples, seeking the god-touched, seeking hosts. Fallon was surprised they had found any worth marking. Most towns with temples had turned quick enough when the south burnt. As the sky split and ran, those poor folk playing host to the gods had felt the full effects, half their body clinging to the earth, and the other half boiling loose and fleeing to the heavens.

Easy enough to find scapegoats when they were stumbling through the streets, hair aflame, jaws loosening with stellar fire.

Not all the hosts had fallen in that first flash though. The divine had left them, of course. Broken, golden things spilling out of the first available hole, and writhing helpless in the streets until their scales and sinew twitched into the space between stars and air.

Without their gods, the hosts were a broken lot. Either in mind, or in body. The land round here had long been a good home for the broken though, and its people had picked up the pieces often enough that a few more wild-eyed mouths were no great hardship.

So some towns had kept their hosts, or husks, or whatever they were now that the gods had fled. Some pulled their weight, and some simply took up an attic cot and wept, singing songs their mothers had sung.

Fallon pours a splash of something fierce, swills it around his teeth. Thell was doing exactly what he would do in their place. He admired Kinghammer for it, the wall-toothed sod. They were hunting hosts. Burning out the god-touched, root and branch. And if every temple set alight took the town along with it, that seemed a price they were willing to pay.

He taps the glass on the centre of the map. A damp circle marking the worst of it. If Thell kept burning southwards, and Crowkisser kept pushing northwards, it didn't matter how daintily Hesper hiked her skirts, she was getting fucked either way.

There had been other options, briefly. Nothing with enough clout, though. And he knew that for a fact, because he hadn't been sitting on his hands while Ship and Shroud roamed the coast. He'd sent a skiff to Errant, but she was locked down after the famine, and there was rumour of a strangeness among her rulers. Some feral madness skulking across tile and trellis, blossoming in the bone. Fallon had skipped the details, he was already up to his neck in weird shit.

He'd sought out the Heron Halls as well, sent bird after blasted bird west across the waves, and heard nothing. Perhaps their cities were moving again, the current pushing them further than wings and hollow bones could reach. The best he'd got out of it was a few quiet nights in the aviary, and a sill covered in exotic, redolent excrement.

Birds and skiffs and messengers, a hundred fractured hopes tossed out into the wind. And what had it got him? A few polite lads from the Burners wringing their sooty hands and tugging their caps, muttering that the Forest sought only to weather the storm. Some well-meaning Midlands coin-kissers who had half a brain between them, and barely twice as many swords. A smattering of other soldiers of misfortune. It was embarrassing.

And always, Thell on the horizon. The great chain of mountains that held the new Republic stitching the far hem of the sky on clear days, just close enough to mock him with its distant, cloud-laced seclusion.

Thell's soldiers were active and lethal, carrying torch and spear through the Midlands, but none of it to help Hesper. Fallon had toyed with going north himself, to rattle Kinghammer's thick neck and ask what he thought he was playing at.

He sits down heavily, drains the glass. He'd rather stick his fist in a furnace. Hesper had bled enough for Thell, and if they wanted to snap at the fingers of any outstretched hand, let the rock take them. He had some pride still.

At his back the sounds of the city rolled against the towers. The songs of the canal workers, the canary clamour of the markets; the hot ring of forges, and the stench of tanneries. The answer was there for him, rising in his mind with the acrid reek of gunpowder, and the distant flash of blades on the walls.

He had to ask the guilds. Cap in hand. Which meant he needed something in the shape of a cap. And he had it, nestled there in his ledgers of account. Red debts which could be flipped to black, and black debts which could fall to red, with the barest nudge of his pen. The invisible weight hung around the guildmasters of Hesper. Something to trade that he was loath to give. And which he *had* to give. Which meant he needed another drink. He moves to fill the glass, then finishes the bottle, orange fire coating the back of his throat.

Was it really such a sacrifice? A few imaginary numbers for the bodies and blood to push Crowkisser into the sea?

The whisky swills around his teeth, acrid, burning, hard to swallow. Midlands grain lighting little fires on his tongue.

Still, it's not that which chokes him, in the end.

12

On the Dancing of Bones
On the Infusion of Smoke into Blood
On the Cost of Negligence

—Chapter headings, *Archivist's Primer,*
for Transparencies I–III

Hesper, the great city by the sea, offers a whitewashed tower room that smells faintly of gull, and a thin cot with roughened sheets.

To Shroudweaver, it's paradise. He hasn't slept much since the war began, especially not aboard ship, where the rocking and stretching of the boat makes him feel like a ratty squirrel clinging to a slim branch over the boundless sea.

Here, the stone is solid, and the covers, though rough, are pleasant. The linen lets in the lamplight, filtering it as he pulls them over his head.

He's never craved the softer things. Life in the Aestering had been gentle, but it was a simple place, built of simple things. Rough textures and uneven edges suited him fine.

He's slept enough in sailcloth and sheepcloth, under tarp and straw. This is, if not luxury, something close.

The thin mattress creaks as Shipwright slips in beside him, the weight of her bowing the bed, before the warmth of her stomach lines his back as she slips an arm around his shoulders. She smells of the port, a faint glisten of spice and oil. He kisses her wrist, her forearm, lets his lips linger on the thin white scars of lash lines and splinters that have healed into sailors' silver.

Every time they climb aboard the ship, she exacts her toll of blood in a thousand small cuts. The ship herself is sleeping in the deep dock of Hesper, Ropecharmer pacing the deck like a cat, tying off and stowing to.

The docks are far from here. The city spilling from the towers in a ruck of tile, staggering merrily over the grid of canals that pull Hesper's life through her sluggish body. Arched bridges and low porticos where the bargemen can pull to and trade in all the little scraps of sense-memory that make up this city. Thick-rinded fruit that stains the fingers and mouth, scraps of forgotten songs that have bubbled up over the Halls and been caught in their nets. Lean blades of copper, and fine-worked shawls that have come all the way from the mountains, from Thell.

The docks are far from here, and Thell is further still. Hesper sinks into the night like a bone into broth, and Shroudweaver lets himself sink with it. That thin mattress opens up to the softness of sleep. Shipwright's breathing at his back stronger than the sea, soft and steady. The push of her stomach, the brush of her thigh as she settles closer.

Her hair falls over his face, and he keeps it like a curtain. The warmth of her skin is held in it, and a lightness from the herbs she washes with. She kisses his neck gently. 'Stop smelling me.'

'Can't help it,' he murmurs. And even those words come from a long way away, falling through the tiredness that pulls him down to dreaming.

Sleep like weaving, the soul unlatching from the world, and lifting to hover over dreaming bones. Night becoming a nest of breath and pulse. Sleep like the spaces between, where his magic lives. A weaving not his own. The world reaching for him. For the threads that connect him to the rest of the earth.

The docks are far from here. Thell is far from here. Even Crowkisser, dark and feathered, is far from here. There is only the solid wall of the Shipwright, and the halter of her arm.

He can rest. The world is far from here. His world is right here. There are no lines between far and near. He is a weight on the threads of the world, and time and distance fold under him like a sheet. He feels Shipwright's fingers move through his hair and across his shoulders, and he falls into sleep.

The scholars of the Glass Archive refer to sleep as the dancing of bones. Bodies twitching in dream and nightmare, sketching a map of the roads that their minds run.

Does the world feel the Shroudweaver when he dreams? Does the world recognise the mind that slips into the dark?

Something marks him perhaps. Marks him like the fish feel the shadow of the heron. The dreaming world opens up paths for him. The world opens paths for the Shroudweaver, and he chooses one. As much as we choose anything. Like a deer chooses the forest, or an arrow chooses the heart.

In that small tower room, Shipwright holds him as he shivers and twitches. The man she loves, shaking like a dying leveret, a beached fish. It doesn't worry her. This is how the evenings go, and have gone, and will go.

The scholars of the Glass Archive will have you believe our bodies are nothing more than the metronome of our souls. Do not confuse the instrument for the song, they will say.

The Shroudweavers knew the truth was more complicated, and the last Shroudweaver is about to find this out.

For he sleeps, and worse he dreams. With all the logic that his mind has left.

And in his dream, the broken earth is singing. Lowing like a calf just born.

And in his dream, he can go to the earth and place his hands upon it. He ties his red right hand to the soil, and digs deep.

And there is sense to this. For this is how he has always been able to work his magic. By the touching and binding of things.

And in this dream, the song of the earth is a chorus. The earth a composite of all the little lives that burrow within it. The lives of worm and beetle. The earth a composite of all the great energies that move above it. The weight of the glaciers, and the immense, heartless whirl of the stars. The earth itself vast, porphyritic. The past embedded within it, and moving through it. Great distant caverns where water falls unseen in the black. Hidden tombs where blind life is born and dies far from the touch of the sun.

The earth's song is the wind moving through hollows and over hills. It whips him like a bird in a storm. Rips his hands from the skin of the world and hurls him into the air. Still there are threads here. His red right hand trails the red of binding, and his left begins to spark with the silver of sending.

The earth follows the red, and the air takes the silver, spinning him higher.

He laughs in the dream, and in the bed, Shipwright laughs too, as she feels his chest twitch. This is new. There is usually little joy in Shroudweaver's dreams. But she does not see what he sees, the vast unrolling of the land, the shadows of forests and the blue cut of rivers, the black sink of the Midland swamps and the smudged trees of the Burner's groves.

The earth's song holds here, for he cradles the earth in his red right hand. Dark clods and red threads. The sky's song joins it, and for a second, his heart feels light. He is a boy again. Beneath the Aestering grove, watching birches dance in the summer light. He relaxes, and the dream has him.

The land unspools below him. He can see the scars on it. He does not look south, he cannot, but even here the earth has seen too much. Not just the wars of Thell's rebellion, but the smaller conflicts before and between. The bladedrinkers. Thriceflower. The land is green with grass and the grass is thick with barrows.

He is pulled faster in the dream. Northwards, with the song of the wind. He is a brother to geese and swans. Smooth, wild cuts of feather and noise barrelling through the stripped clouds.

He is pulled northwards, along what were once pilgrim roads, over the ruins of towns that held temples, market squares scoured empty, nursing only ash and mangy dogs.

Further north still, the grey of the air falling to blue with ice, and then purple with the growing cold. The shadow of mountains stretching over the land.

And here the towns are small things, and at their heart there are shrines, cold and empty. No candles, no meat, no offerings. The people left living in the shadow of the Barrowlands draw close to each other as darkness falls, and leave their shrines to the night, stroked by the calls of owls.

The scholars of the Glass Archive will have you know that every dream is a wealth of symbols, and that the body crawls through their meanings as the evening unravels.

The Shroudweaver would instead tell you this, were he awake: your soul will go where it is needed, pulled and bound.

By the time he realises where he is headed, it is too late. His dream-self greets it with fatalism, folding his body into the curve of the wind, and plunging downwards.

Sleet licks his skin, and the mountains open up to take him.

The land outside of Thell much as he remembers. Scattered now with cattle-fold and firepit, a few smaller, softer signs of life.

Thell remains the same. This Thell, which his mind has built. A composite of memory, and map ink. A dark line that cuts the sky like an absence. The white light of glaciers hanging on its far edge, like the whole chain of mountains might be a mouth waiting to unveil sharper teeth.

His mind does not panic, but his body does. In that thin tower cot, Shipwright grumbles as his ankles kick, and his brow sweats. Resignedly, she pours water from a pitcher, straightens the covers, sips.

Here, in the Thell of times gone, Shroudweaver falls towards the heart of it all – the Stump. Rock piled upon stone, battlements and hollow windows, and the flicker of red flags, bright tongues of flame in the dark.

The threads he holds unravel. The wind takes them.

He falls lower. The great escarpments loom, socketed and waiting. There is an impression of armour, of spears, but the dream does not care for this.

Instead, he falls towards a brazier that gutters against the cold. That spits as the sleet falls into the flame. As night pushes against the light, again and again.

The figure at the brazier is hooded, wrapped in rags of red and yellow. They smile, and the movement cuts the shadow of their face.

'Weaver.' A familiar voice; a familiar hand that passes a cup of spiced cider, thick and wild on the tongue.

'You're dreaming, Weaver.'

Shroudweaver answers in the voice of geese, of the snow.

The figure laughs. 'Oh dear. You're *really* dreaming'.

Shroudweaver answers in the song of the land. His hands scatter threads of red and silver into the flame.

The figure adjusts its robes, scratches its side. 'I think this is supposed to be a prophecy, Shroud.' They shrug. 'Of course, it's broken. Because the gods are dead.'

They scratch their ribs again, and the brazier flares. 'You're trying to dream a way to stop the godkiller, Weaver.' The figure leans in, cloves and spice on their breath. 'You're trying to save your daughter while you sweat your skin off in a Hesper bed.'

Shroudweaver answers in the bark of a fox, juddering out of his jaw.

The figure by the fire starts. 'Hm. Let's sort this before it gets any worse. Do you want an omen?'

Shroudweaver does not answer. The ice is dancing on his skin in patterns of silver flame.

The figure's voice deepens, their tan hands stretching against the fire. 'I'm the omen, Shroud. Thell is an omen you made for yourself. If you want to stop a godkiller, you need to build a god.'

They stand and walk to the edge of the escarpment where the wind bites the skin. Their robes bowing back against the night, red and yellow and red again.

'Do you remember how to build gods, Shroud?'

And Shroudweaver does, deep in his heart. But he waits for the answer anyway.

'You build a god the same way you kill an empire – piece by bloody piece.'

The figure beckons him to the edge of the mountain, where the wind howls like a mourner.

Their arm is warm along Shroudweaver's shoulders, where ice flickers in gouts of pale fire.

'This is why the dream carried you here, Weaver. If you want a god to stop the godkiller, you need a composite. You need the biggest god-stitching your pallid hands have ever seen.'

They push on Shroudweaver's shoulders until he is leaning out over the edge of the scoured field beneath the Stump. It opens up below him like a mother's arms. The grass and roots falling away into pits of dark earth that writhe with bones.

'We put them all here, Shroud. You and I. If you want to build a god, come to Thell.'

Their voice lowers. 'We have all the pieces you will ever need.'

Shroudweaver tries to answer, but his voice emerges in that tower room, clipped with sleep.

Shipwright shushes him, holds him close, and in his dream, the figure does too. Their lips are dry and warm against his, their arms strong and firm.

The wind howls, and the clouds part to spill the light of the moon across their face.

And it is gold, and it is broken, and it is familiar. It has one eye, then two, then none. It smiles at him with the face of a friend, and an enemy, then kisses him again, as you might kiss a child, or a corpse.

'Come to Thell and build me a god, Weaver.' Its strong arms wrap around him, and the push is stronger still, sending Shroudweaver out, over the battlements and down into the bone-filled dark.

The song of the earth rises to meet him, and he screams, so much louder in that small, whitewashed tower room, that smells of gull and sweat, and Shipwright. He is sitting, wrapped tight in sheets and white as chalk. He tries to speak, but his mouth is full of the memory of bones, the dry weight of earth.

Softly, firmly, she places a cup of cool water in his hands.

'Take it easy, skinny. Just a dream.'

He looks at her and she flinches, sees something in him that scares her. And he watches as she kills it, packs it away, and puts her arm around him.

'Not just a dream, eh?' she sighs. 'Well, under the circumstances, I can probably let you take another huff.'

She leans her head into him. Her hair falls over his face like a curtain and he breathes deep. And for the second time that night, even as distant geese kiss the rim of the moon, he sleeps.

13

the power of the gun doesn't lie in powder, barrel or stock
it fires from the flicker in your heart as you thumb the trigger.

—*Drill Hall Maxims*, Coglifter

They wait for him in a quiet room. It is unprepossessing, in the way that only men desperately concerned with status can make a room unprepossessing.

A servant closes the door behind him with a soft click. Even the latch doesn't want to make a fuss.

Fallon wants to make a fuss, to ripple the water. Instead, he stands in the wan light from the bullseye glass that frames the hall and waits.

There is a low curved table and six chairs. The leather on some worn near to fading and on others, ruddy as blood. He marks the spacing between the chairs, marks the carving on their backs, and the less official marks where daggers and nails have scratched boredom into the wood.

They file in soon after. Two of them, hooded, and masked. Like he doesn't know every line of them; he could tell them in the dark just by their stink; good targets for a little hard trading.

Hammershy squats on the far chair like a rookery gargoyle, thighs wide and hands clasped, the reek of the forges rolling off him, burnt hair and salver's grease. His eyes beneath the hood are wide, lucid. A dangerous man, all peace and steadiness until the time comes to break bones and collect dues. The face beneath the mask is a blunt thing, unworked ore thick with stubble.

He catches Fallon's eye and grunts, lifts a finger. Somebody is feeling gracious today. A couple of seats down, Rookspit slides into a barely touched chair, thin bones hovering over the leather, like a little comfort might be caustic.

They have barely bothered with hood or mask. The rind of their smile slips out from behind the cloth, and thin, soft hair spills like thistledown across the blistered bone of their cheeks. The pale prince of catchpoles and thimbleriggers dances their toes on the threadbare carpet as if at the end of a gallows' rope.

'Gentlemen,' Fallon says, and there's barely any venom in it. 'I have an offer.'

Hammershy snorts again, 'Of course, Fallon. We have eyes and ears.'

Declan smiles, and he can feel the muscles in his face start to thrum as he holds them carefully, politely still. 'I'm hoping you have brains, too, Shy. This war is turning the screws on us. Kisser's turning the screws on us. We need money, we need bodies, and we need them fast.'

Hammershy leans back, a gold chain glinting in the thick net of hair that curls disrespectfully through the front of his robe. 'You need money, Fallon. Your pretty wife's sleeping, and you can't dip her pockets no more.'

Rookspit snickers at this, and it turns into a snorting, hacking cough that flecks the table. 'Do you miss dipping her pockets, Fallon?'

Declan feels a fire light in him. Decades on this earth and he's never got any better at being talked down to. He lets it burn to ashes in his gut, because this is politics. This is what Arissa taught him to do.

'I'll keep it quick. You are both in deep with me. Shy, after that nonsense your crew pulled after-hours in the Dogloop foundry, you'll be lucky if you see another contract before the winter snow.'

Hammershy opens his mouth, and Declan barrels on. 'Yes, yes, I know. Exuberant lads, boys will be boys, but it takes *months* to chip slag off the bottom of the canals, and it's my men doing it, and my waterways clogged with that idiot spill.' He turns to Rookspit, who is watching him rather like a frog might watch a windmill, wide-eyed and gormless.

'And as for you, there are currently two ships short crew because you traded them in for bounties. The diggers outside of Twelvebarrow keep talking about ghosts, but I bloody know it's you from the description, and you owe me at least six port bells which have "accidentally" fallen from their belfries and split into unstamped currency in your shoddy little clipping dens.'

Rook twines a coil of hair around their finger, then pulls it loose with a hiss.

'Sailors shouldn't be misbehavin' under the silver moon. And I am only a ghost when it is required of me. As for your bells,' they shrug expressively. 'I needed some quick cash, mighty Lord.'

Fallon paces. This was how they liked to play it. Hammershy the stolid obstacle, Rook all twists and lip. It was an act; two different coloured sheaths for two very sharp knives.

He glances at the window, thin light falling from the day. 'I'll keep this quick. I will scrub the debts you owe. Lock and stock, root and branch, and I will feign stupidity if I get any hard questions on that topic. Two nice clean slates.'

Hammershy has a poor poker face, on occasion. 'And in exchange?'

'In exchange I want your best. Men, and blades and enough coin to send them roving to the blasted arse of the world if required. Enough to split Crowkisser's lip and buy us some time. Let's say a two-month lease.'

The two guildmasters look at each other. A bluebottle plinks against the sun-warmed glass, before bumbling downwards to die.

Hammershy shifts, drums thick fingers together. 'Well, that seems . . .'

Rookspit holds up a pale, loose hand. Amazingly, Hammershy stops and leans back, like his mother has just walked in to collect him from school.

Spit takes their time, lowers the hand, rolls their shoulders. Theatre, theatre, bloody theatre.

'Got something you want to say, Spit?' Fallon asks. A little push.

Rookspit's eyebrows raise, pale as milk worms on the soft bone of their face. 'Shall I, Hammer?'

Hammershy shrugs. 'You are your own creature, Rook.'

Another laugh at that, limp and spidery. From the floor above, muffled voices. The thump of something heavy hitting the floor.

Hammershy glances up. 'Pick it up Rook, we have other engagements.'

Fallon nods. 'Like your colleague said, what's on your mind Spit? It's a good deal.'

Rookspit shrugs. Rookspit shuffles their feet. Rookspit leans forwards, runs an exploratory finger up a nostril.

'Found a snail in my boot today, Fallon. Found him with my toe.'

Hammershy laughs despite himself. 'How'd a snail get in your boots, Rook?'

The look Rookspit shoots him is pitying.

'Left them behind when I was scurrying up by Teller's Bell, didn't I? Came back after I'd cut a slice or two from the Malker's lot, and there he was tucked into the tip, quite the thing. Little idiot. Found him with my big toe, Fallon. My foot was the last thing he ever felt falling from on high.'

Their palm arcs toward the wood, miming. Rookspit cranes closer, their long lean fingers reaching over the table.

'First the crunch of his little walls, then all the goo and juice of him spurting up between my toes.'

Hammershy grunts.

Rookspit laughs, thin and looping. 'Too messy for you Hammer? Not enough steel and scorch, eh?' One lean finger makes an obscene gesture, and even Fallon smiles.

The grin falls off Rookspit's face like a dropped curtain.

'I need to know if I'm the snail Fallon, no matter how much you're offering.'

Hammershy straightens at this, listening.

'Me and my broad-beamed associate here are holding up a lot of your precious city. Even if we have taken the odd liberty in the process. In fact, we've got it cupped top to bottom, roofs to rats, and so we have to be real careful.'

Their hands move fluidly, flicking a small ball of something unpleasant down the table. 'Everything we move from one place, has to come from another place.'

Rook looks up, their eyes the green of pond scum. 'Everything we give to you has to be paid for from somewhere else. I ain't saying we don't like what you're offering. You could swing our red columns black with a stroke of the pen, and starlings' shins if that wouldn't open up some options for me, never mind old Hambone over the table.'

Hammershy snorts, but nods. 'They're right. Irritating, but right.'

'But it ain't just about the columns. We are *committed*, meat and bone and coin. Everything we have is going to keeping this old girl turning, because we are more easily shaved than we have ever been.'

Long fingers trace the grooves of the table, sharp nails picking at the joins. 'All it takes is a promise from the little crowkissing girl, and a village that used to send piss to the tanners is singing holy holy shag-a-fishy. And what's piss you say? Well piss is money, and piss is half a walk towards armour, and armour keeps you half a step from death.'

Hammershy opens his mouth, but Rook is in full flow. Fallon watches their hands wave. 'And sure, OK, you cuts my red columns in half and you gives me new black columns, but my pisspots are still empty, and the young lads that used to run scopes up on the Cheapskin way have left, and where are we going to find them?'

Spit's eyes flash. 'One of them puts on a grey hood and starlings' tongues! Now he's singing shag-a-fishy with the rest of Crowkisser's lot, and one of them, he runs west over the sea, and the last we see of him he's lining the plushy guts of a whale. And the *last* one, he steals my horse, *my* beautiful palfrey, the one with the white neck and he rides north towards Thell, and maybe there's something in him that sets off those stone-lickers from the mountain. Eyes a little too gold, or maybe he smiles when the sky is bare and they decide he is host-holding! God-tainted! And bang, his ribs are split with a spear, neat as old Hammerhonk splits the withy and the steel.'

Hammershy finally gets a word in edgeways. 'What Rook is saying is that numbers are just numbers without bodies and matter underneath. We are running out of able bodies, and we are running out of material. Port's not pulling like she used to and the land is dry. We can't trade what we don't have.'

Rookspit leans forwards and there is something lean in them now, like an alley cat. And Fallon remembers where this man came from, and who disappeared to get him there. Those green eyes flash, the skin at their sides flaking, pale.

'Hammer's right for his one allotted time per day, so listen up, we need more than promises. We can't give you no more, because it'd be like taking blood from one lush organ to flush another. Heart thrums, lungs die. Lungs puff, guts shit. You follow me?'

Rookspit frowns. 'Frankly, the others ain't here because they already feel like you're bouncing on our necks like a five-day rope, and they're shit-sick of it.' They smile again, that wet rind of teeth. 'But Hammer and I, we are practical and honest and we wanted you to know that it ain't a no 'til the worms eat birds, it's a no until you get some new blood into the system.'

That sallow face is flat, serious. 'Corpses or coin, meat or money, we need men and we need funds, Fallon. Get them from somewhere other than us, split sky above, because we are running out of time.'

'And?' Hammershy rumbles.

Rook looks at him like the interruption is a hot poker down the shirt. '*And* we don't know enough about what's going on.'

They lean further forwards still now, their knees brushing the edge of the table, feet on the chair, sticky boots neatly balanced. 'This is weird shit, Dec. *Weird* shit. The Grey Lady's gone and Hammer and I, we respect you, you know, in fact, I guess all the guilders do, but you ain't her, and you weren't born to it, you're a . . .'

'Shepherd's son,' Hammer grumbles.

'Sheep fucker,' Rookspit finishes, smiling.

Fallon tries not to rise to it, but he feels the bile choke him. Same old story, like all of them weren't a few steps down from pirates and vagabonds, vermin of the seas. But he was worse. He was land vermin, and he'd worked his way in through love, rather than at the point of a sword.

The room feels close, stuffy, the wan light washing over the thunder in his temples. Maybe things could change. Maybe the sword diplomacy could start now. No. Stupid. Ship and Shroud are depending on him. Hesper depends on him. He breathes, long and ragged. In through the nose, out through the mouth, like Arissa taught him.

As if reading the room, Hammer raises his hands. 'Look, leadership or provenance disputes aside, it doesn't change the brute facts. We need the bodies. We need the money. From outside Hesper. We need new blood.'

'And,' Rookspit says, eyes savage now, like flint struck on emerald. 'And, I need to know if I'm the goddamn snail.'

Fallon snaps at that, steps forwards, and gods it's good to see them both flinch. Even if it's just a little, even if it's quickly hidden.

'What is your point, Spit?'

Rookspit steadies themself, those lean fingers adjusting a belt beneath that ragged robe. Their dangling mask swings now, the grey cut of his chin sharp as he speaks.

'My point is, Fallon, that them as hides themselves away sometimes survives, and sometimes they get squashed by toes they never even imagined. My point is that I don't know where the crow-witch gets her shit from. It's weird. My point is that there are bigger forces at play then we can even see. And I'm wondering – is we the snail? Or is we the foot?'

They crawl forwards on to the table until Fallon can smell them, the acrid snap of lockpicker's acid, and the mildewed damp of hours spent on the belfries and roofs.

'My point is are we the snail, or are we the toe? Because we sure as shit ain't the *boot*.'

Hammershy says nothing, already standing. The meeting over for him. Fallon's lost them both. Rookspit follows him, scampering along the table. They cast a look over their shoulder, a flash of sour green as the mask is drawn back below their eyes.

'I need to know, Dec, I need to know what we're dealing with. I'm not moving until I know the shape of the boot, and that's the all of it.'

Hammershy holds open the door graciously for Rookspit, who tumbles off the table, and brushes themself down.

As he moves to pull the door closed, the forge-master catches Fallon's eye, and the two huge men regard each other for a moment. Dust hangs in the yellow light.

'New blood would mean a tighter grip, Fallon.'

Fallon nods.

'You need a tighter grip, Fallon.'

Fallon nods.

Hammershy tips his head. 'Otherwise, well.' And he taps something at his hip beneath his robes that rings with steel. 'Otherwise, we'll forge something new.'

The door clicks softly closed.

Fallon walks to the bullseye window, to that yellow light, grubby and old with filth and flies in the corners, for all it seems grand. Beyond that, distant, like another smudge across the skyline, the great mountain kingdom. The unspoken weight pressing down everyone on both sides of this war.

His last benighted resort.

Thell.

14

there is a deer who has come by the cairn in recent years.
a pale deer, and alone
its eye frozen on the line of birches
it sees nothing
not shadow, not new grass
not ancient blood

—*Lament for the Back of the Land,* excerpt

They reconvene in the port tower at evening bell. A carillon running across the roofs of Hesper as windows are flung and kitchens
sizzle with the tang of meat and spice. Tonight, Declan Fallon
has set a more sober table. Shipwright can read his mood in the
cringing of the servants who do their very best to fade into the
walls, or dissolve into the dust that coats the tower floor. Fallon
has not been entertaining very much.

The man himself is already present, sat on the long side of the
table, a half-drained mug by one hand, a sheaf of papers in the
other. He looks up as she enters, and waves pointedly at the seat
opposite.

'Just you?'

She shrugs, which is enough to send the serving boy at her
shoulder scurrying.

'Shroud'll be along. He slept like shit.'

She waves her own empty glass at the nervous boy. 'Please, lad,
I think I'll need it.'

He pours a slug of some bitter black ale straight into fine gilded
stemware. And if that doesn't tell her the state of things, what
would?

She sips. 'Should we wait?'

Fallon snorts. 'We should.'

Silence falls. The city rumbles along outside the window, cat squall and birdsong falling to the first tipsy shanties rolling up the walls from early starters taking shore leave.

Shipwright rearranges the cutlery and sips again, casting a plaintive look at the serving staff who studiously avoid her eyes. She stops drumming her fingers on the table when Fallon glances up from the papers; jigs her leg on the floorboards instead.

'Widow's tits, are you going to dance a full hornpipe for me, Ship?'

Shipwright sinks the ale, and straightens the forks again. 'I'm not in the mood, Dec. It was a long voyage, and a longer night after.'

Something in Fallon softens for a second, then he turns back to the papers. 'Your beau better get a shift on.'

As if on cue, Shroudweaver enters, ragged as an owl in an aviary, something feral in his gaze. His robe askew, with wisps of red, cindered thread trailing from his wrist. He sees their eyes on him, and seems to realise he is expected to speak.

'There was a dream. I mean. Last night. And then this morning, I was experimenting. Trying to get a hold of it.' He waves his right hand casually. Something stinks of saltpetre.

Fallon says nothing, just motions the servants to bring trays, salvers, platters filled with an excess of good food. Tense as she is, Shipwright's mouth waters.

Shroudweaver settles next to her with a faint air of embarrassment, but there's something worse beneath it. He's thrumming like a violin string, taut with worry. She leans in, fixes his robes, tucks a particularly wispy strand of hair behind his ear.

'Let's just ride this out.'

Shroudweaver nods and makes a pretence of fussing with his cuffs. A splash of some pleasant fizz, and a little grilled bird wallowing in butter steadies him somewhat. She watches him start to come back together as he gently peels the meat from the bone. Good – she needs an ally.

Before Fallon even opens his mouth, Shipwright knows this

is going to be a long dinner. The old bull's weighed down with the kind of misery that slides into spite. He starts holding forth, the cup waving in his hand, his fingers stabbing at the papers fluttering in the other. Shipwright lets it wash over her, admiring the patterns on the glassware. She'd picked these out with Arissa in a little trinket shop, a long, long time ago. They were passé even then, but there's something in the cut of them that reminds her of home.

The thought of home holds her for a while. Fallon says something about the *Volante* and she nods. He curses out the guilds of the city for being stretched too thin to help, and she nods. He ticks a litany of dead ends off on his fingers – Errant, the Heron Halls, the Burners.

She nods.

Half of them Shipwright had already chalked up as lost. She's sailed farther by far than Fallon over the past little while, but she knows he needs to strike them off his list, to balance the sheets. She also knows that every fleck of spit, every slammed fist and dancing plate, every palpitation that runs through the staff is cover for something worse.

This table is set for three, when there should be four.

Arissa's absence is a palpable, crushing thing. Not just for Fallon, for her too. It doesn't quite floor her, but it almost does. Her fingers tighten on the glass. Beside her, Shroudweaver's hands skip a quiet, fluttering dance.

Beware the shards of a broken pot. A wrist twist, a shoulder dip. *Hawks most fear an empty nest.*

And with that, Shipwright notices the other ghost at the feast. Quickfish, not long gone, but so dear to Fallon's heart that the stupid man hasn't spoken of him since.

She flicks a quick message back across the table.

Pups run and hounds howl.

Shroudweaver's answering shrug is fluid.

Katkani is too poetic for this room, for this space that Declan fills with rage so they won't notice the sour stench of his grief, or trace it in his rumpled clothes, his shadowed eyes, the yellowing of his large horse teeth. She half expects Shroud to step in, but something else is tugging at his attention, his pale eyes flicking from Declan to the table and back. This theatre of attention, she knows it all too well. He's running some calculations neither of them are in on, rolling something else around in the bone box of his skull. She's on her own.

Thankfully, Declan blows himself out after a time. He slumps in the chair, one leg slung baldly over the arm, the curve of his belly clasped under strong hands, like an old wolf woken in the wrong season.

Not brought to bay yet though. Shipwright has sailed and failed with Declan more times than she can count, and she knows every movement that signals him limping back to the fray. He strokes his moustache with thick brown fingers, slurps from the mug. Shipwright can see his thoughts marshal themselves, and watches the confession bubble up like marsh gas.

'Look, I don't want to be the one to say it.'

She can see that he does, as if some perverse imp's goading him on. She laughs. At least it's humour, at least it's something.

'I don't want to be the one to say it,' he continues, as she rolls her eyes. 'But I have begged and bartered and run every last rat road I can to get us the bodies and blood we need to push Kisser back properly.'

He flaps the papers. 'I have offered favours and forbearances and things I should not even have considered. I have done everything possible save bending myself over the table and pulling down my breeches, but the fact of it is, I am down to one miserable option. It's shaped like my worst bloody nightmare, and filled with fickle fucks I haven't seen in years.'

Shipwright looks at Shroudweaver. Shroudweaver looks at Shipwright. She can see the shape of that great, black mountain reflected in his eyes.

'Thell,' she says, the sound of it on her tongue like a stone down a well.

'Aye, Thell,' Fallon agrees.

Shipwright waits for Shroudweaver, for some comfort. He

puts a hand on hers, but his smile is thin, absent. He's seen this coming, and those numbers are still running in his head.

'Thell's a big risk, Dec,' she says. 'Worse than a risk. A millstone.'

Fallon sniffs. 'Right again. Plus, there's him.'

'Him?' Shipwright says, even though she already knows. Another ghost loping into the room.

Fallon sinks lower, mournfully ripping apart a quail.

'Kinghammer.' He sucks grease from a thumb.

Shipwright smiles weakly. 'He's not been returning your letters?'

It's a bad joke that falls as flat as it deserves.

Fallon's face twists as he works around a lump of gristle. 'Worse than that. Keeping one toe just the right edge of hostile. And after what the rebellion cost us?' The stripped leg waves expressively. 'His weeping Republic is mortared with Hesper blood.' He snaps, sucks marrow. 'With my wife's blood, Ship.'

Shipwright reaches for some fruit, digs in with her thumb. The juice stings.

'Let's not get ahead of ourselves, then. For the sake of your heart, if nothing else.'

The look Fallon shoots her is venomous, but she ignores him, breathes deep.

'What do we have left?'

Shroudweaver twitches, but Fallon answers.

'Scraps. That slit shredded us good. The *Volante* was one of the best we had.'

'What do we have *left*?' Shipwright repeats, using the tone she saves for cabin boys. Arissa always responded well to that one.

Fallon picks at the skin on his lip. 'The *Hart's Pride*, the *Maiden of the Forests*.'

She waits.

'You,' he finishes lamely.

'Shit,' she says, her mind a mess of half-remembered faces. 'We can't keep Crowkisser penned in with three ships.'

Fallon's fingers idly trace the table, running over a map of shipping routes, currents inked in blue and green and black. 'There were a few others. They sailed north and west a while ago. It's not their fight, and I didn't have the money to keep them.' He laughs. 'I only have the *Hart* and the *Maiden* because they're in too deep to leave without collecting.'

Shipwright shakes her head. 'Never thought I'd see you happy to have creditors.'

She glances down at the map, at the couple of hundred miles of coast between Hesper and Astic further south.

Declan watches her with dark eyes. She can feel him waiting for a miracle, for her to be a clever, useful knife.

She shakes her head, and watches his shoulders drop.

'Starving her out was a nice idea, but it's out the window now. If we had the full fleet . . .'

He slumps back down, digging a finger in his ear. '*If.* But most of the ships on this side of the world are at the bottom of the sea. We can rebuild, but it takes time, takes money. Worse than money, it takes boots on the ground.'

He slaps the papers on the table. The staff recoil. 'Money, I have, for a little longer. Arissa's father was a parsimonious prick, and I've always been good at stretching it. Boots are trickier.'

Shipwright opens her mouth, but he holds up a finger.

'People keep dying, Ship. And the ones we have left are looking after their own. No matter how hard I tug on the gilded hooks.'

She says nothing, drumming her foot under the table as the blood starts to sing in her ears. She glances at Shroudweaver for a bit of back up. Finally, he surfaces from whatever thought is holding him, his voice quiet, tired.

'So it's coming to a fight?'

Fallon scratches. 'Might do. We're fine here. We've got the walls. The guns. What we don't have, like I said, is the people.' His lip curls. 'Most of them are growing weed down south with my fucking ships. And the rest are tied britches-and-bollocks to the guilds, who have no interest in burning bodies against that little witch. So, no people.'

'I don't think she has the people either,' Shroudweaver mutters.

Fallon's face is sceptical. 'You know that?'

Shroudweaver shakes his head. 'Not for sure, but you saw what happened.' He presses his lips into a thin line. 'I'd say at best, she's got the northern line of towns. Astic, of course, but that was a stroke of luck.' He ticks them off on his hands. 'Sedge, Fallow, Vantage, Dryke.' Holds up five fingers. 'It's not much.'

Fallon sucks his teeth. 'Not much for now, but we didn't expect Astic to fall so fast. That bitch is persuasive when she wants to be.'

Shipwright takes her eyes from the map. 'There's another problem.'

'Oh good.' Fallon waves a hand. 'Go on. Keep shitting on my doorstep.'

She makes a face. 'Thanks, Declan.' Her fingers sketch a route on the map, from Astic, up the coast, and past Hesper.

'She doesn't need to come here, she just needs to push past us. If she can get far enough north or east, she'll open up new supply routes, at the very least. More likely, she'll roll up a few more villages into her loving arms. Tips the numbers against us even more.'

Fallon purses his lips. 'Do you really think those Midlands swamp-lickers will fall for her shtick?'

Shipwright shrugs. 'Maybe not. I can't guarantee it though.'

Fallon tuts. 'There's not enough of them to make a difference. There's nothing big enough to give her the bodies she needs, unless she makes a run right up to the mountains and the Republic.' He raises an eyebrow, pointedly.

Shipwright blanches. 'She wouldn't?' Just the thought of it chokes her. That mountain. That war. The blood hammers in her throat.

Shroudweaver looks between the two of them. 'Just because we haven't? She might, if she was desperate enough.'

Fallon pinches the bridge of his nose. 'If for example, she'd been starved out by a ragged-arse naval blockade for the last two and a half years?'

He stabs the point of his knife into some unlucky squab.

'Which brings me back to my original, miserable option. We

have to beat her to it, to Thell. We need them back onboard before we get squeezed between north and south like a nut in a vice.'

Shipwright and Shroudweaver glance at each other. Shipwright shifts awkwardly.

'When was the last time you were up there?' Shroudweaver asks, gently.

Fallon walks his fingers up the map. 'Fuck knows. Ten, fifteen years. It's over five hundred weeping miles.'

'Exactly,' Shroudweaver says. 'We haven't seen them since the fall of the Empire. Near enough twenty years. Who knows what they're doing up there? Heaven knows we didn't leave reeking of glory.'

'Dog piss,' Fallon says. 'They only chased you out because you saved them. Nobody likes owing their life to someone. And fucking nobody likes their saviour popping in every couple of weeks.'

He uncorks a fresh bottle of something amber and acrid and swills it morosely.

'Those bloody-lipped stone-fuckers crave independence like mother's milk and your skinny little arse reminds them they'd still be dancing on the Emperor's ragged strings if it wasn't for you.'

Shroudweaver grimaces. 'That might all be true, but we're a generation down from any good we ever did. Skinpainter's the only real friend we have left up there, and they can't tell half of what they saw. Kinghammer's grateful, I've no doubt, but he's ambitious too. I don't fit his plans. And his kids have had decades to hear tall tales about me. The problems I caused. The hands I forced.' He twines a loose hair, pulls. 'We might find allies up there. We might get a spear between the ribs.'

Fallon leans in. 'I get it, but we have a window. Kisser won't get a warm welcome up there either. Not from what I've heard. Tight lips and tight borders. Scared of the gods, and of what killed them. That's why Kinghammer's closed himself up tighter than a spinster's clam. That's why half my scouts are riding back with damp breeks and lame horses.'

Shipwright pushes aside the thrum of her own pulse and fumbles for the glass. 'It's too much of a risk.'

Fallon's eyes narrow. 'Since when did you run scared of a little risk?'

'Since I fished the crew of the *Volante* out a cold sea, Fallon. If we go back to Thell, we have no idea what we are walking into. They have done everything to push us away. And nothing to invite us.'

She looks to Shroud, beseeching. 'Tell him, love. Tell him that we can't go through that again.' And he, more than anyone should know. This should be the easiest sell.

Except she sees his fingers stiffen, and his shoulders set, and she knows that secret he's been hiding is about to slink forth. All those unspoken equations finally adding up.

'I had a dream,' he says, and there's a dry humour to it, because he knows how stupid it sounds. And of course, she remembers the dream, and his shaking, twitching bones, but he hadn't said *anything*, just sipped his water and gone back to sleep.

Fallon clocks it though. He sees the shift, and practiced politician that he is, moves in.

'A dream?' Careful, considered. It'd be easy to mock this, but Fallon knows when to play it close, play it kind.

'Shroud,' Ship says, but he waves her away. His fingers flutter again.

the heart like breathing, the truth like breath

And it isn't fair for him to say that. But she loves him, so she chokes down the fear coiling in her lungs and waits.

Shroudweaver speaks, and the way he holds himself, you'd think his entire body was trying to move away from the words. 'If we want to stop a godkiller, we need to build a new god.'

'Bloody shit,' Fallon says. He holds his hands out in front of him, palms out. 'OK, give me a damn second. I was expecting a gunshot and you fired a broadside.'

Shipwright watches them both and tries to nail them to their chairs with sheer willpower. She wraps her fingers around the delicate stem of that pretty glass and tries to stop the world from turning. It fails, like it always does, catastrophe rolling in on the riptide again.

Fallon levers himself up, swearing and carping. He walks around the table until they are all on the same side, until he's close enough to shove himself between Ship and Shroud, close enough to lay a meaty hand on the weaver's thin shoulders.

'What are you saying to me, Shroud? Could we hit her with one of your gods then? A sucker punch? If we find a body fresh enough and strong enough, could one of those little golden bastards blow a hole through that feathered bitch?'

Shipwright watches Shroudweaver compose himself, the tiny pulse in his neck the only sign of his racing mind.

He shakes his head slowly, chews his lip. When he speaks, his words click into place like the tumblers of a lock.

'No. No, I don't think so. Whatever she's done, she's changed the rules.'

He pauses, turns, stretches fingers through worried hair.

'Or at least, she's changed the rules as I understand them. Calling gods. It's . . . not what it was. It costs more. They burn out faster. The fuel required is . . . unimaginable. Even little gods cinder quick.'

He breathes, thin and shuddering. 'Perhaps though, if it was big enough. There's only once place we could get the bodies for it. Only one place where enough of the dead will linger long enough.'

Fallon frowns. 'I don't follow.'

Shroudweaver glances up at him, then takes his hand. Traces his fingers over scar and callus as he talks.

'Calling a god. It's like striking a light. Building a home. Making a body into tinder and kindling. *Building* a god? That's like taking every light you could have struck, and stitching them into a sun. Everything burns. And the light of its burning takes on a life of its own.'

His fingers tighten. 'I can't begin to describe the scale of it. The cost of it. It took years for me to grasp it, even though they hammered it into us day after day. The cost of creation. The howling flame of gathered fire. The forging of a new god. A composite thing.'

Shroudweaver drops Fallon's hand, the blood leaving his face. 'Put it this way, Declan. Only Thell has seen enough death. The death it was born in, the death we caused. The death that came before.'

Fallon's eyes are wide. Shipwright can sympathise. He's touching on the wild edge of the world where only a Shroudweaver walks. That kind of talk does strange things to the heart.

Shroud himself is oblivious, running the numbers again. He coughs and dabs at his lips. 'I think if we can beat Crowkisser to Thell then I can summon something that will be strong enough to stop her.' He pauses. 'If she gets there first? At best she takes the city; at worst she finds allies. We can't let her do that. We won't survive that.'

There's something else in his tone there. Shipwright sees it for a second, like a grey fish dipping under grey water, another lie slipping beneath the first. She grips the stem of the glass hard enough that it creaks. Now is not the time.

Shroud is still talking, leaning into Fallon's arm, his irritatingly attentive head.

'Stopping her though. That needs something that can knock her flat. That needs a composite. A gathered flame. I can do that.'

His voice quietens, drops into his chest, emerges cold, and thin. 'I've become the kind of person that could do that.'

The admission knocks something out of him and he shrinks in on himself.

Shipwright watches Declan. She's expecting a clever line or some brutal sentence that still gets him what he wants, but that stupid, bullish man surprises her again.

Shroudweaver flinches when Fallon puts an arm around him and pulls him tight. It feels genuine. She desperately wants it to be genuine. They stand like that for a moment, his slim frame held close to Fallon's broad chest, his forehead light against his ribs. Shipwright wants to hold on to the fury inside her, to nurse it until it's a knife that will cut away the half-truths still clouding the air. But the *look* of them, the pair of them – a wounded deer and a ruined house.

Shipwright watches Shroudweaver unravel, and when he begins to cry, she feels something hard break inside her. Something that's been inside her since Astic. Since Crowkisser. Since the end of the world.

That knife she wants to keep hold of crumbles into nothing. And Declan Fallon, that big, drunk, arrogant prick, he puts one broad hand on Shroudweaver's shaking shoulders and he kisses the top of his frail head.

'It's OK,' he murmurs. 'It's OK. We'll put it all back together. You and me and Ship.'

Shroudweaver shakes quietly. And Declan Fallon, Lord of the Grey Towers, Warden of the Free City of Hesper, holds him as he cries.

Shipwright smiles softly, despite herself. When Declan beckons her with one broad arm, she joins them, and it almost feels like coming home. It almost feels like coming home, even though the blood thunders in her head, and her palm aches from the pressure of near-shattered glass.

15

there are men in the far sea
who swim up rivers
the sea unzips their spines
lays salt into their bones

—*The Blue Beyond the Halls*, Hallowfeather

Afterwards, the sun sets over the great grey towers, quieted now by the oncoming night. Shipwright looks down at Shroudweaver, asleep again, covered with thin cotton, his chest rising and falling with a steady, child-like rhythm. For the first time in weeks, she lets herself relax.

He needs the rest, and so does she. She sits on the corner of the bed and unclasps her boots, peels back thick socks and stretches her toes with an audible sigh.

Shroudweaver mutters in his sleep, and she watches his bone-spun body writhe as she runs her hands through her braids, unpicking them one by one, setting the pins to one side. There's never enough time, every day a little wearier. Her fingers linger on a pin, carved from the shell of one of the turtles that used to cluster around the pillars of her house, red as a low fire. She turns it once, twice, fingers catching a little jagged edge she hadn't noticed before.

The knock on the door startles her. He's standing there, filling the frame.

'Hello, Declan,' she says.

He smiles and waves a bottle at her. 'Thought I'd keep you company. Apologise a bit, for earlier.' He glances at Shroudweaver. 'How's he doing?'

Shipwright pops the cork, swigs, purses her lips. 'Better now. He's been pushing himself too hard. Holding too much.'

Declan settles down on the bed which creaks in protest. 'He always did.'

She sees him try to form Shroudweaver's old name on his lips, watches his tongue slip and choke on it.

He ducks his head back apologetically. 'Sorry, Ship.'

She passes him the bottle. 'No need for apologies. We're all in the same weird boat.'

He laughs at that, drinks deep. 'Fair enough. Old habits, Ship.'

The bottle changes hands.

'So,' she says over the rim. 'How is she, really?'

Declan frowns, his thick thumbs plucking at his jawline. 'It feels longer, doesn't it? Longer than three years.'

He rolls his massive shoulders. 'Do you know what normally happens in three years? Next to nothing. The guilds raise their dues. A few people turn up dead. Some deals fall through; some don't. We build a little, we tear down a little. We hold our own.'

He pushes his thumbs into the corner of his eyes wearily. 'Last three years, the world's ended. And, do you know what the stupidest thing is?'

Shipwright holds out her cup, and he pours.

'Everyone still wants paid. The bills still come due. Everyone still gets pissed off about their own little things. And up there, she's sleeping. Through all of it.'

The bottle lingers on the rim of her cup. Clinks a little as his hand shakes.

'So the world carries on, it's just my world that's ended.' His hand lingers on the sheets for a moment. Thick chipped nails, grimed down to the beds.

'I visit her as much as I can. Read. The boy used to sing to her.'

Shipwright nods at that. 'Good. Keep her anchored. Where is Quickfish? You said he disappeared?'

Declan kneads the sheets. 'Aye, gone. Left a couple of months ago without a word. Took a horse and his boyfriend and left.'

He sinks his great head into the cup of his hands. 'What did I do to raise a kid like that, huh? Junking his own goddamn name. Leaving his own damn mother.'

Shipwright steadies herself on her hands, yawns. 'Really? Put yourself in his shoes. Your mother's comatose, because she kept her damn name. Because she pissed off a crow-eating warlord. Your father's a temperamental prick. The gods you loved are dead. Hell, Declan, I'd leave you too, and you're like a brother to me.'

He winces at that, and she wonders if she's pushed too hard. She strikes flint into the bowl of her pipe, takes a draw to give him time to recover. When he meets her eyes, there's a bit of that grey stone she'd missed. 'You always did keep me straight Ship. I just worry about the kid.'

She cups his cheek. 'Look at it this way, if he headed north, then he's headed away from Kisser and Walker and all that brood. Best place for him. Plenty little Midlands villages from him to get a little peace out from under your thumb.' She grins. 'We can pick him up once we've kicked her scrawny ass out of Astic.'

Fallon laughs at that full-throated, but it trails off with speed.

Shipwright wriggles until she's got him fixed properly in her stare. For a second, she lets the words hang and he watches her warily, with the bottle between them.

'Don't get coy on me Ship. Out with it.'

She licks her lips and asks the question that's been on her mind since that long night of blood and bone, when their names burnt away on the wind. 'Why did you keep your name, Fallon?'

His smile is crooked, wistful. 'What else was I going to do Ship? It's who I am.'

She rests her head on his shoulder, lights her pipe.

'But you know?'

He glances down, tucks his chin. 'What she can do to me? Of course. We all walked out the south together. And my wife's right up there.'

Shipwright glances up to the roofbeams, waves a line of smoke. 'So why then? Why risk it? Crowkisser won't hesitate, you know.'

Declan frowns, the plates of his face shifting slowly. 'Because' – he pauses, swallows – 'because when she killed the gods, she took away the things that defined us. And then when she tried to take our names, she hooked the things that *make* us. And she doesn't get that. Not from me. Not at any price.'

He smiles merrily. 'Stupid fucking slit.'

Shipwright grins. 'You're such a fucking ass, Declan.'

The Lord of the Grey Towers pats her shoulder companionably, and lets rip a thunderous fart.

'I know, I know. But you love me.'

16

Twice sang the mother to her pretty baby
Twice cried the baby in the crib so cold
Once came a rider, chasing bitter weather
Blood spilt and bones split, all for hate of gold

—*Merryweather's Lament*

Some towns sat on the earth like they were ashamed to be there. Squat, ill-favoured things. Clusters of cottages and byres that had come together on soft Midlands soil for no other reason than water was available, or this was where the thin roads crossed, or this was where their founder had set down sword and shield, and fell to his bloody knees.

Quickfish was happy to see even the miserable ones. They weren't in the Midlands proper yet, just hauling across the scattered roads and sighing grass that split the world that still lived from the devastation to the south.

A glance over his shoulder is enough. Something always burning against the sky, and the sky always the sullen colour of a bruise.

'What's even left to burn?'

Roofkeeper's voice is shooting for cheerful, but dying before it gets there.

The weight of his arm on Quickfish's shoulder is comforting; the smell of his body, the scratch of his shirt. Fish leans in and kisses a bicep lightly where it sits against his chest.

'Plenty, I suppose. They say Kisser's still hunting stragglers. Even after the border towns were burnt out.'

Roof scans the treeline, the sallow fringe of hills brooding to the south. 'We should keep moving, we're too exposed up here.

77

Might get better shelter at the next town. There should be one just over the rise.'

Roofkeeper says this with a map in front of him. He turns and twists it as if that changes where the roads might lie.

'Give me that,' Quickfish says. 'For a lad that spends most of his time on the tops of buildings you're terrible on the ground.'

'I hate the ground,' Roof says. 'I only come down for you.'

Quickfish raises an eyebrow. 'Smooth today.'

'I get one day a month. Come on. We really have to move.' This said with a glance southwards. Distantly, a copse of trees coughs up a flock of feathers that wheel, and move towards the smoke colouring the sky. Evening is falling faster than he would like.

They turn and track up the next hill along a path carved by goats as much as people, twisting with a shepherd's logic up the crown and turning underfoot at every chance. Stones skitter away down green flanks, pocked with rabbit warrens and their liberally gifted shit.

'We'll be lucky not to break a leg before we find a bed.'

And of course, as soon as he says it, his legs go, a strange dizziness rising to meet him, like the ground singing. The lines of the world fall away for a second, just enough to turn his ankle, and leave him teetering on the edge of the track.

Roof is there. Not that there's anything more dangerous down below than gorse and sheep skulls, but he's there, and his grip is strong on Quickfish's wrist. He's light-headed for a second, and not just from the dizziness. But from the intimacy of it, the tightness.

'Again?' Roof says, and he means the seizure.

Quickfish tries to focus. There's a strange light creeping around the edges of his vision, as if the air is burnished and twitching. He blinks, and it clears.

'Again,' he says, his voice more pathetic than he would like.

There's no judgement in Roof's face, just the same soft lines he's grown to love over the days they've been on the run, and in the years before that – the sharp twist of his jaw where it broke as a child and the way the stubble shadows under it.

He knows how it feels against his skin. Part of him wants it now, to burrow into that hollow like a rabbit pulling against the cold of the night.

'How many times now?' Roof says, as Quickfish's vision steadies. The feeling is fading like a dream, like the echoes of a small spell. He scratches at his palm.

'Five? Six maybe?'

'Worse since we left Hesper?'

Quickfish thinks of the nights before that, when he'd been awoken by the feel of the night pressing on his chest, by sweat dancing on his skin. Too many to count.

The lie is easier. 'Worse. Maybe just . . . adjusting to the road.'

Roof frowns, 'Worry does strange things to a body, Quick. If you need to stop, or turn back?'

'No.' And there's the voice he wants to find, strident and commanding. He regrets it immediately as Roof's expression slumps. Tries to prop it up again with a smile and a shrug.

'What I mean is . . . there's no time. The Teeth are burning. Signal fires all along the coast. Crowkisser is moving, and we have— *I* have run out of options.'

Roofkeeper opens his mouth to say something, and Quick stops it with a kiss. He lingers for a second then pulls away.

'Trust me. You don't know how hard I've searched. *Everyone* washes up in Hesper. Quacks and cursers and healers of every stripe under the sun, and none of them have been able to help her.'

He puts a hand on Roof's throat, just below the chin. 'I have to help her, Roof. I'm all she's got.'

'Your father,' he says, and Quickfish winces. 'Declan's . . . not reliable when it comes to my mother.'

'And they will be?' Roof can't quite keep the scorn from his tone. It's to be expected, he was raised near the south, and all the ghouls of his childhood live in the wild north.

'Thell will be,' Quickfish says.

Which isn't to say he wasn't nervous. He hadn't even thought of Thell for years, save for when another messenger failed to return and his Da cursed the mountain city to the bottom of a bottle.

Not many folk knew what happened up there, especially since the rebellion. Quick had picked up a little as he grew, first playing beneath the tables while the guild heads bickered and carped, later finding the gaps behind the walls and tapestries where he could peek out and glimpse the pirate finery of Fallon's confidants as they complained.

And if Roofkeeper was sometimes hiding with him, and if he sometimes forgot to concentrate, what of it? It was basically a bunch of adults telling each other ghost stories anyway.

The empty mountain; rumours of a deposed king; a new leader with the unsubtle name of Kinghammer; a leader disinclined to play the usual games of copper and compliments. Thell had had its revolution, and it wanted to be left alone.

Things had got worse since the south burnt. If Thell had been standoffish before, it was actively hostile now, patrolling its borders with enough vitriol to send the odd unlucky plaintiff home feathered in a pine box.

It isn't worth dwelling on, not with his head still ringing six bells. They have more pressing problems.

The last few feet are a scramble to a twisted thorn tree clinging grimly to the crown of the hill, desperate for rain. Beyond that, a gentle course down the valley, to where the town should be.

Roof's breath hisses between his teeth, and Quickfish steps to join him. Even from this distance, it's clear the town is gone, little left except charred wood and broken stone; dark marks on the land like blood under the skin. Whatever has passed through here has been merciless.

Even the small stable is shattered, the bleached bones of its last horse sinking slowly into the earth. A few echoes remain of what might have been here – the stone shaft of a well, the pillars of something slightly grander behind.

Quickfish hates that he isn't surprised. These little towns have never been particularly safe, shielded only by the lee of softer hills, the goodwill of the landholders, and the billhooks of a few second cousins and energetic uncles who drink too much cider at the weekends.

The world had hardened since the south burnt, and these gentle little towns had been caught up in the wave. Some hit by bandits, some by famine, several by Crowkisser as she ranged out from the south to make sure her curse had stuck. He knew this because Hesper had traded blows with her for a while, running militia out to vulnerable towns and trying to train the farmers to scan the sky for crows and sharpen their blades.

Hesper, and his father, had lost their taste for that pretty quickly. Hesper fought best on the sea; on land, Crowkisser sent home one too many soldiers for morale to hold. He'd glimpsed one, once, hustled to the infirmary after delivering a report, clutching a hole in his arm the size of a fist, burnt clean to the marrow and stinking of lemon and rot.

So the little towns die, and the maps are slow to update. But they are still here, and night is still falling.

Quickfish takes Roof's hand. 'Come on, let's find somewhere out of the wind, at least.'

They find more than that.

The death of the village unveils itself in a series of small sadnesses – the discarded weapons at what would have been the west gate; the bones that would have comprised a few second cousins and uncles, if the dogs hadn't had their way with them, before they too died.

The whole town clustered around a well, which still ran clear, mercifully, fed by some natural spring deep below, sluicing away whatever petty murder had occurred up here.

Roofkeeper rinses his hands and scrubs his face.

'This is fucking awful,' he says. 'What happened here?' Quickfish hears him, but he's already a little way from the well, climbing the steps of that pillared structure beyond. It's a little familiar to him. Smaller, cruder, but familiar. Memories of holidays in the south with his mother, his Da off betting on horses or staking a fortune on *calcio*. And in some sun-kissed plaza, a half-remembered temple, pillars like this, steps like these.

The gods liked their homes to conform to certain shapes.

He turns back to Roof, calls out over the blasted square. 'I think there was a temple here.'

Roofkeeper picks his way across the rubble to join him.

'A temple? Like, hosts, gods, the works?'

Quickfish shrugs. 'Maybe? Certainly shaped like it. It might explain how they survived out here as long as they did.' He scratches at his palm. 'Might explain why they died.'

Roof spits, not one of his better habits. 'I don't want to sleep here, we should just keep going. Rest tomorrow. Don't want to lay my head where the god-sick were splitting their skulls.'

Quickfish shakes his head. 'Not . . . exactly how it worked, love. 'Sides, I'm done in. There's enough of this place still standing that it'll keep the weather off. A quick sleep, and back to it. Captain's nap, that's what my da used to call it.'

Roofkeeper eyes him sceptically. 'Aye, aye Cap'n'. The loose corner of a smile makes it all worthwhile.

A short bit of work sees a lean-to and a fire, and some hides to keep off the cold. Quickfish tucks himself into an alcove, and eyes Roof across the flames. 'One of your best features.'

Roof grins, long and easy, and pokes the fire with a stick. 'My hair? My eyes?'

Quickfish shakes his head. 'Nah. Your packing skills.'

Roof snorts. 'You cosy over there, Captain?'

Quickfish laughs. 'Not as cosy as I could be.'

The rest of the night passes like their nights usually do. The fire dips to embers, and the cold spike of the stars holds the night.

When Quickfish wakes, the air is clearer, the soft gold of morning slanting between the pillars and crumbled stone. He stands and stretches. Walking the night's stiffness off, first around the edge of the temple grounds, where the hosts would have taken offerings, then stepping into the bowl of the temple, where they would have opened their minds to the sky.

All of it gone now, save for a few stark markers. It's good for a brisk walk though, clears the head.

The crunch under his foot is less pleasant. Old stone, he thinks at first, a bit of flaked marble, but stone does not have the curve, or that symmetry. He kneels and digs a little. Ribs, and beneath that a spine, and then the rest.

'What have you got there, Fish?' he hears Roofkeeper call. He ignores him. There's a glint amid the bones. And it should feel wrong, should feel morbid, but his hand is already in there, searching.

So when Roof reaches him, he's already holding what killed the people of this town. The tip of a spear, flattened and leaf-shaped. Beautiful. He's seen it before, of course, in his dreams, in the bodies of those unlucky scouts. There's only one city on this whole continent that makes spears like that, thin enough to move the wind.

He turns it over in his hands, and for a moment, he can see it. The patrol coming from the north, wild and paranoid after the burning of the south. Best to stop the rot before it draws Crow-kisser's attention; take out the hosts and their gods with them.

And really, how much defence could this little town muster? Not with Thell's young bucks already out for blood. All it takes is a loud voice in command. Maybe a panicked movement by one of the temple guards. Maybe a scream.

Then the spears fly, and the bodies fall. And once a host body dies, the god leaves. And once the gods leave, well, best to make sure of the others. Best to run the blade in twice. Best to set light to the thatch. In case they hid up there, in case they take root somewhere.

Burn it out. Cut it out. Burn it out.

He realises he's shaking. The edge of the spear-point bites a thin red line across his palm that flows like ruddy gold in the morning light.

'Tower and turn, Fish. What have you been doing?' And Roof is there, unclenching his fingers, cleansing, bandaging.

'Any deeper and you'd need stitches.'

'Sorry,' Fish says, and it's exactly as pathetic as he deserves.

Roof crouches next to him. The bones stretch between them,

sun slatting between the ribs, between the temple pillars. 'Do I need to be worried, Fish?'

Quickfish smiles at him. His hand aches, but the sun is warm on his back. He feels bathed in gold.

'No, never.'

Roof's brows furrow.

'Sure?'

Quickfish straightens and kisses the top of his head. He smells of sand and sun.

'Sure. Let's shake a leg.'

They turn and pull northwards again, leaving the skeleton of the town to the sun, to the shadow, to the soft shape of bones.

17

a strand of muscle the texture of salmon skin,
descending from the neck,
the manipulation of which can cause the body to move
in strange ways.

—*Simple Anatomical Explanations for the Rational Mind,*
Wicktwister

When Shroudweaver wakes, it's morning. The light is pale and clean, and the air of Hesper is as dry as he remembers. He inhales the smells of the street, the chatter and the bustle, the hum and the clash of her. Hesper is a corpse, of course, a relic of the older wars, wars that were about smaller, more human things. But, like all the corpses he works with, she has a strange and beautiful life to her.

He swings his feet out from under the covers and presses them flat against the cool stone of the floor. His legs from the knee down are a mess of thin, bright scars. A memento from the south. As he runs his hands over them, he marvels at how thin his skin has become, stretched over the sticks and scaffolds of his fingers like a poorly wrapped gift.

The shroudweaving is taking its toll. He had softened the blow for Declan. It's not just that souls burn brighter and faster now, like dust before a flame. His own body burns a little, each time. His veins are black with ritual silt, and there's an ache between his ribs where the cries of dying gods have lodged and crusted.

It was so much easier, once. Before Crowkisser, yes, before the south, but even before that, when he was younger. Before even the war against the Empire and the rising of the Republic. Before he met Shipwright. When he was *young*.

He could still see the light-woven branches of the Aestering, the Shroudweavers' place of learning. He could still hear the chatter and murmur of the birch trees as they leant against each other. Not a building in the traditional sense, but a light-filled forest, bent and guided by staves and bindings, by ribbons strung thickly from tree to tree, pulling them into paths and bowers and shaded places over the space of years. The whole college had been shaped as much as the people inside it, as much as they would learn to shape, and bind and connect. He remembered how easy he'd found it all, laughing, giggling with his classmates as they spun the soul of a frog into the blossom of a flower, and they wove the life of the flower into the hairs of a rabbit.

Hearts in mouths, they had egged each other on to greater heights, stranger combinations. How restrictive he'd found it all. All those stern-faced masters; men and women as light and shadowed as the birches around them, moving gloved fingers and hands as they spelled out the rules, the most basic bindings, the never-to-be-broken.

A closed fist. 'Red for binding.' An open fist. 'Silver for sending.'

He'd followed their movements, and the souls had flowed through him like water. Tiny gods of wind and light and earth and worms falling from his fingertips, curling into the waiting bodies of foxes or birds, or babies. Bringing them to life, or making their own lives stronger.

It seemed like every soul had burnt for a long time then, even the smallest. He had held life in his hands, made it, shared it and breathed it out into the world.

Of course, that was before he had questioned what lay beyond the bounds of the Aestering, what lay outwith the rules and beyond the ribbons. Before he had truly understood, before the Aestering had burnt and those silvered trees had wept smoke and ash.

Things are, perhaps unsurprisingly, harder now.

He swallows, coughs and slides himself into his robes, cleaned and folded at the foot of his bed. He can smell Shipwright on them, and it's like soft armour. As the collar strings the back of his neck, he feels the ghost of Declan's fingers, and the warmth that goes with them.

Funny how you could miss someone so completely and not realise until you saw them in front of you. The things the three of them had shared and seen, from the walls of Luss in the north to the burning south.

He shivers, and steps into the sun by the window. In front of his sleep-tired eyes, Hesper spills down to the sea, full of life and lustre. Worth fighting for.

Worth killing his daughter for?

The stone is rough on his tightening fingers. How many daughters out in Hesper today? How many fathers? And beyond the city, how many countless more, strewn in the path of Crow-kisser?

The breeze freshens on Shroudweaver's face and he sucks teeth grown thin and pale from hunger.

He can feel her out there. He could let her find him, if he chose. But if he does, she turns her gaze to Hesper, and if she does that, people begin to die.

With a short, frustrated sigh, Shroudweaver turns from the window and finishes dressing.

Breakfast first.

18

every sleep is a truce
between the world
and the mind behind the world

—Aestering Knotsong, No. 3

She barely fills the bed. A thin scrap of grey against the sheets. The slow rise and fall of her chest a half-glimpsed movement. The High Lady of the Grey Towers. Everything that remains of his wife.

Declan steps closer and bends to twist the lamp into life, the soft glow sliding across her face like a caress. The rest of the room is thrown into sharp relief and he becomes painfully conscious of its contours and its filth, the sharp sting of piss rising from the sheets and beneath it, the sweet, thick stink of a body emptied of purpose. He steps quietly to the edge of the bed and begins unwrapping her.

She fights him feebly, making small wet noises in the back of her throat, but there's no strength left in her. Declan flips her with the ease of long practice, peeling back sheets foul with her waste. Another servant to flog bloody.

Within minutes she lies thin and naked. Slowly, methodically, he soaps his hands and cleans her. As he does, he sings to her, the low, wordless songs he remembers his father singing in high pastures and damp byres, as the rain lanced downwards and he softly coaxed new life into the world.

She sighs raggedly as he works, tense muscles scored and straightened by seizures loosening under his touch. Before he was Lord of Hesper, these hands were the centre of his work and his world. They know bodies well, whether beast or man.

He wants to call her name as he works, but of course, he can't. It's vanished, taken by Crowkisser. He can feel his tongue slip around the space where the syllables used to be. For a moment, his fingers tighten involuntarily on her shoulders and she flinches in pain.

His hands jump back instantly, cradling her head, smoothing the furrows of her brow.

'I'm so sorry, love.' Again, that slip where her name would be, the feel of something thick and oily in his mouth.

Every time he sees her, he remembers the night it happened. The pair of them, laughing over dinner. Was it something she'd said? Or something Quickfish had said? He forgets. No, it was when they'd found Quick in the stables, trying to pretend that carpenter boy wasn't in there with him. His breeches half drawn up and misbuttoned – the belt of his trousers clanging like a watch bell every time he moved.

'He'd almost pulled it off until the hay bale sneezed,' she'd said, and they'd collapsed into laughter.

One of those evenings he can barely remember now, because it seems impossible. Impossible to have laughed that much, to have held her in his arms; impossible to have turned wine in crystal glasses that caught the light and eaten food that tasted of anything. He could remember her favourites, those little birds that thronged the fields outside of Hesper, herbed and buttered; some kind of red syrup that fizzed up in the glass and tasted like morning. That's what she'd said, anyway, it tasted like fruit to him. But good fruit. He could remember the food she'd eaten, but he couldn't say her name, the crow-witch's magic keeping it locked somewhere in the crumbling pit of his brain.

He curses. That whole evening lurks in the back of his mind like a rat in a rotten attic, filling his head as he turns the pillows and takes herbs from the bedside drawer. He crushes them between his fingers, holding them to his nose for a second before placing them underneath her head.

She'd smelt the same on the night it happened, almost two years ago. She was never one for perfume, but that bag of herbs was always in her drawer. He'd hated it at first, its scent cloying and thick. He hadn't even really liked it that night, as they danced, his face buried in the curve of her neck, her fingers tight around the small of his back. They were out on the balcony of one of the Towers, just the two of them and the night, with the lights of the city spread out below. The sky was a low red, fading to purple as the last of the sunlight burnt off into the dark.

He'd spun her then, which was tricky, but she'd ducked accommodatingly under his upstretched hand, flashed a smile, and turned.

It was when she'd turned that the crow hit, a ragged ball of feather and muck falling out of the twilight, moving faster than anything had a right to. She'd shuddered, coughed, doubled over. He'd run to her, cradled her heaving back, her writhing spine, even as he called for a cutter, and a physicker. Her hands clawing at her mouth, her stomach moving in great retching gasps.

He'd seen it tunnelling down her throat, bowing out her rib-cage. He could swear he remembered hearing her bones creak. She'd screamed, wet and wordless, blood on her lips, the shape of it still burrowing under her skin, moving downwards.

He'd taken his knife from his belt, said a useless prayer, and stabbed.

He had caught her before she hit the cobbles, and felt something wriggling away from under the blade, tearing into shreds, dissolving in gobbets of black feather, briefly wrapped with something silver that faded like morning mist.

Her eyes turned back in her skull, her breath soft and scurrying, all the strength flown out of her. He'd held her in his arms and tried to call her name.

It hadn't come. The physickers had, eventually, following the sound of his voice trying to make a noise it no longer could. They had taken her, eventually, after a few broken noses and blackened eyes and dosed him with something so he slept.

Had dosed her too, with everything under the sun.

She'd never awoken; would never awaken. Now she moved

only in that last dance, where he'd hated the smell of her against his skin.

He rubbed the leaves between his palms again, bent forwards, and kissed his wife's sweat-cold brow.

'I miss her.'

The voice slides out of nowhere, the body holding it coalescing out of the dark corners, solid only in the corner of the eye.

'I miss her,' the voice says again, and Declan is moving even as his head turns, one hand snatching the lamp from the bedside, the other pulling back into a fist.

The figure in the corner flickers, and one arm extends in a series of fluid clicks, a gun barrel unfurling like a forgotten petal to touch lightly against his sternum.

'No, Declan,' the voice says.

Declan stops. He can still feel the oily taste of forgetting on his lips as he mouths the words. 'Slickwalker.'

The body in the corner inclines itself briefly.

'I suppose I am now.' Slickwalker tips his head towards the bed. 'I mean it though, I do miss her.'

Declan's eyes flick to the barrel resting against his chest.

Slickwalker smiles slightly, a grey ripple in the shadows. 'No, Declan,' he says.

Declan spits. 'No what, you ratshit?'

Slickwalker pushes the gun forwards slightly. It whines hungrily. 'No, you're not fast enough.' Slickwalker shrugs. 'Anyway, I'm not here to fight.'

Declan sets the lamp down and flexes his shoulder.

'Just here to reminisce about the time your slit girlfriend sucked the soul out of my wife?' He grins, all teeth and gums, 'If you breathe wrong for an instant, I'll rip out your throat. Just so we're clear.'

Slickwalker shrugs again, fluidly. 'Perfectly. Like I said, I'm not here to fight. What you do . . . well, I can't do anything about that.'

He tilts the gun barrel slightly. 'Can I get this out of the way though?'

Declan tips his head. 'I suppose.'

The gun coils back in on itself like a well-fed snake. Slickwalker shudders and his outline solidifies into the tall, lean man that Declan recognises. *Almost* recognises.

'Oh dear, ratshit. Shacked-up life not agreeing with you?'

Slickwalker smiles ruefully and runs a hand through short-cropped hair now frosted with grey. 'Oh, this?' His laugh is loose and easy. 'Perils of the job. I can't always look like me. This is,' – he tilts a hand – 'a familiar mode.'

Declan curls a lip derisively, 'Can't look like yourself. Can't show yourself. Can't fuckin' name yourself. What *are* you, exactly?'

Slickwalker smiles again and glances down at the shadow of a woman in the bed. 'Content, mostly. Which is more than I can say for you. It's a pity you both acted the way you did. It's not too late though.' He tugs at his earlobes. 'I'd vouch for you, you know, if it came to that. Crowkisser'd stop all of this. We could bring Hesper into the fold. You'd be safe. Your wife would be safe. Your son would be safe.'

Declan's voice is slow and hot when he speaks. 'Where. Is. My. Son?'

Slickwalker shrugs like a long-boned cat. 'I wish I knew. We'd be as delighted as you to see young Quickfish returned.'

Slickwalker runs a hand through the sleeping woman's hair. 'You could at least give her a new name you know? I admit it's closing the stable door after the horse, but these things have power.' He glances towards Declan, runs his gaze over the man's flat, narrow eyes. 'It'd give her something, at least.'

Fallon's fist hits from the right, and Slickwalker feels his cheekbone shatter even as he falls to the floor. The boot that comes after would catch him, but he's up and moving, flowing into the shadows of the room as easy as breathing.

He watches Declan spin and search, running a hand over the bones of his face even as he feels them start to wriggle and knit together. 'God, old man. You *are* fast. And brutal. No one's hit me in years.'

Scanning the shadows, Declan snarls, 'Maybe if they'd started a damn sight earlier, we wouldn't be in this situation.'

Slickwalker smiles and reforms as easy as an exhalation. 'Maybe, maybe. But we are where we are. And I am *not* here to fight.' He raises a hand in warning, fingers splayed, dropping them one by one. 'If I was, you'd be gone. Your wife, your son, gone. Your city, gone. No one wants that.'

Declan laughs. 'Kisser's already on the way. You think I don't know that? I've been fighting wars like this longer than you've been alive.'

For a second, Slickwalker seems genuinely irritated. He spins, arms wide. 'You think we want this? Do you? Do you think we enjoy blood? Enjoy killing? Do you know what the *Volante* sounded like when it went down?'

He sinks a weary head into his hands. 'The world changed, Fallon, and you forgot to move with it. Don't hate us for that. We're the same people we were before.'

Declan takes a step towards Slickwalker, a cold smile on his face. 'If only I'd known. I would have killed you sooner.'

He spreads his arms mockingly, mirroring Slickwalker's loose-limbed style.

'Still, seeing as that's apparently not on the cards, how do I get you out of my fucking house?'

Slickwalker raises his head and considers him levelly. For a moment, Declan feels like nothing more than the shadow of a mouse before a very big, very old cat.

'Hand them over,' Slickwalker says, his voice numb and empty. 'Hand them over. If they're not here already, they'll be coming to you soon, and if you let them in, all the gods they could ever build will not be enough to save this city.'

Slickwalker stretches out shadowed arms pleadingly.

'Two people. Two people against a whole city. Against your *family*.'

Declan studies the face in front of him. The first beginnings of crow's feet, the shadows of sleepless nights. More familiar than he'd like to admit. He glances down at the bed and feels the name of his wife slip off his tongue, oily and flat.

It takes a while for him to get the words out. 'Family is important.'

He stretches a hand tentatively out to Slickwalker, who clasps it firmly. The relief on the younger man's face is palpable.

'Family is so important,' Declan repeats, and he watches Slickwalker nod slowly in response.

'The only problem,' he continues, 'is that you godkilling fucks have no idea what the word even means.'

He watches Slickwalker's eyes widen even as he pulls tight on his clasped hand, bringing the man's startled face down and in to meet his rising left palm.

Slickwalker's face breaks with a comforting, wet sound, only matched by his hiss of pain as Declan flattens out his right hand and chops into his throat. The tall man staggers back gasping, and Declan sees the shadows reach out for him, pulling him to safety. A heartbeat quicker, his shoulder hits Slickwalker square in the chest and throws them both against the wall. Ribs break like commemorative gunshots.

Fallon throws in a headbutt out of sheer pleasure, his teeth wide and bloody with delight. Wrapping a thick hand around Slickwalker's struggling neck, he whispers fiercely into his ear, flecking him with spit and rage.

'You were right, Slick, I am fast. Always have been. And maybe, maybe the only good thing about having your life ripped out from under you is that it gives you plenty of time to practice getting faster.'

Slickwalker's eyes widen, and laughter lurches up out of his broken throat, bubbling and wet. Fallon's fingers tighten as the laughter slides down and down, into a damp, shuddering rhythm that flows through Slickwalker's twitching body. He squeezes harder, his thumbs closing around the last scraps of air, close enough that he can watch Slickwalker's wide pupils suddenly split and sunder, sending tendrils of black spidering through the whites of his eyes.

Then there's nothing beneath his fingers except a few drifting wisps of darkness.

When Slickwalker speaks, his voice slides from every shadow, doubled and repeated, looped and layered, and *angry*. 'Not fast enough, Declan. Never fast enough.'

Declan thinks about turning even as he feels the barrel of the gun kiss his neck. His skin smoulders.

Slickwalker's voice is a low curl of heat in the still room. 'I wasn't lying, you know. I don't know where your son is . . .' The pause stretches, lengthens, fills the room with indrawn breath. '. . . but I can find out. Think about it, Declan. Two of them. Just the two of them. Against a family. Against a city.' His voice lowers. 'Don't make this harder than it has to be. Please.'

Declan lets his shoulders slump, feels the pressure on his neck slacken ever so slightly.

He can hear his wife's breath sliding in and out, hear the slow wicking of the lamp as it fills the room with light. Between the breaths, in the light, there is space.

His arm moves with the inhalation. When his fingers grab the gun barrel it burns, but he's expecting that. He pulls before the next exhalation and feels Slickwalker stagger forwards, stumbling over her body as his knees hit the edge of the bed.

The gun goes off with a noise like a cat burning. Declan feels the heat of the bullet pass along his palm as he pulls and lifts. Slickwalker isn't stupid. He lets go, but the momentum is enough. Declan spins, and the stock of the gun hits the reeling man across the temple with enough force to knock him to the floor. His blood scatters across the shadowed walls.

Declan lets the gun fall from his blistering fingers and steps backwards. The arms that enfold him are barely there, thin things of shadow and blood. And in his ear, Slickwalker hisses. 'Never fast enough.'

Declan feels the air driven out of his lungs. The world darkens with shocking speed and there's a red thunder in his head, like an insistent tide, a thick, fading drumbeat.

He struggles, but the arms around him are strong as steel. As the darkness wraps itself around him, he looks across at his dreaming wife, and for the briefest of seconds, he feels nothing but relief.

The last thing he experiences before he loses consciousness is a wash of golden light, a wind hung with spices and a voice like bellows-brass.

19

other halos
the barley crown
dawn across the sea
the hills before rain
the light that comes after

Shipwright takes the stairs three at a time. Her hair is pale gold, electric, haloed around the shout on her face. A few steps behind, Shroudweaver watches in delight. His lips move rapidly and quietly, his fingers flying in front of him, laced with silver thread, spinning a cat's cradle of incredible complexity. His heart is thick with elation, the thrill of real magic, strong magic.

A true weaving, the first he's done in years.

In the streets of Hesper, the dead bodies of the canals burst from the thick water and hang in confusion as their scoured limbs are wrapped in threads of golden light. Giving up the last dregs of their sodden souls, lending them to Shroudweaver. They blaze as they are harvested. Bone, weed, barnacle and tooth consumed as they're rendered down into the light that moved them. The hastier the binding, the hotter it burns.

The Grey Towers of Hesper are suffused in gold, a sunrise of dead men.

Shroudweaver had felt Slickwalker arrive like a knife pressing on the inside of his tongue, all his old bruises aching as the blood in them fought to escape. Arrogant boy. Stupid boy. Did Slickwalker really think he could hound them for near on a year and they would never learn to look for him?

He knew his daughter, knew what she might teach a lover, or a stupid, heart-struck acolyte. A hundred ways of moving swiftly, beyond lock and bar.

He feels another shudder of activity from somewhere near Arissa's rooms, exploding like rotten fruit on his tongue. He spits, wrenches, the red-wrapped fingers of his right hand closing into a fist, falling into the silvered threads of his open left palm. Shreds of souls gathered, then reflowed into a single stream, aimed upwards at Shipwright's heart. Old corpses were the trickiest, barely offering a scrap of energy. Hesper burnt most of its dead. The only recourse was the canals – the lost, the drowned, the unmourned. He is scavenging the dregs, bottom-feeding.

It's tempting to take too much. Hesper is a hungry city and her disregarded dead are legion. Their bodies spin slowly above choked, reed-thick waterways, bleached white from lack of light, hung with leeches.

And they glow. How they glow. He pulls the light from them with studied care, piece by piece, their bodies falling to ash and ruin as the brightness leaves them.

Even these discarded shells have a kick. He's lifted by it, almost physically. There's a lightness in his bones, like they were taken from a bird. Later there will be pain, the slow crusting of residue around his ribs, dull as old heartache. For now, high over the loops of the city, the light of the weaving scorches the shadows into sharpness. The streets slow to a crawl as drunkards, dockers and soldiers stop and gaze open-mouthed. The skies of Hesper are birthing gods. Pulses of new, pure, thundering energy that run silver lines of light and loss straight to the tower, to the steps, into the body of the Shipwright.

The stolen light hammers into her with increasing speed, a crescendo of brightness and beauty. And vengeance.

Raising a god in a living body is a dangerous thing. Worse still if that god was stitched together from the scavenged shards of a thousand souls, a swill of barely formed memories and lives jockeying for existence, a tattered sack of power slammed into a host body, for a few brief moments. Gods lingered, though. Fragments were always left in the muscle, the bone, like hedgerow burrs waiting to blossom.

Still, needs must.

Shroudweaver opens his left hand, and pushes outwards.

Above, Shipwright keeps climbing. She's not sure how she got here or when she started, but she knows that Fallon's in danger. Shroudweaver's magic is like a fish lure in her lip, pulling her upwards.

Stranger things there with it, hammering into her back, her shoulders, a series of soft concussions. Each one like a shot of strong spirit. Her legs are lit with cold fire and her lips are sticky with remembered sweetness, teeth sharp.

All the spaces left in her filled with fire.

Her boots crack the stones. When she hits the door at the top of the stairs, it vaporises.

Fallon's in the room, on the floor, and over him stands a thing of shadow, blood and murder.

She hits it from the side like a thunderbolt.

It tears in half from the impact, its torso scrabbling for purchase on the unforgiving boards. Shroudweaver reaches the door in time to watch Shipwright as she grabs Slickwalker's echo by the hair and dashes his skull against the window frame, where it bursts into sticky threads, writhing over the walls.

There is a brief space, a void of furious light around her. The fleeing darkness sizzles. Shroudweaver watches it as his fingers dip and weave, picking atoms from the air, opening paths, switching channels, keeping the energy within Shipwright as stable as he can. His mind is frantically cataloguing the risks involved in stitching so many souls into a single body. He's seen where a single mistake can lead.

She can handle it though. Right now, he's sure she can handle anything.

At the heart of the roaring light, Shipwright is laughing, her face wet with tears. Shreds of shadow slip from her fingers and are burnt away like mist in the dawn. So much for Slickwalker.

Shroudweaver starts laughing too. The light and the love are infectious. Shipwright blazes with golden warmth. Beneath her feet, slowly, painfully, Declan begins to drag himself towards the door, lungs rattling like loose stones.

Shroudweaver would help him; should help him. The boards are slick with blood. Shadow flows and drips from holes scored deep into the man's neck and arms. When it hits the light, it burns with a smell like sweet spice.

Shroudweaver should help him, but the weave cannot be neglected. His fingers twist and spin, closing off divine arteries, silencing songs. Newborn gods want to grow. Inexorably, unstoppably. They need a firm hand.

In the heart of the light, Shipwright turns to look at him. Her eyes are hot amber, her hair floating in unseen winds.

He knows how it feels, the rush of multiplying, stretching beyond the possible. The thrum in your body, the sweetness on your lips. The taste of other lives.

At his feet, Declan reaches up a bloody hand.

Shroudweaver methodically splices, cuts, silences. Ends. Feels a pressure on his wrist, red fingers. Red fingers.

Declan's face white from shock, his broad mouth working in fury. 'Help me, damn you!'

Declan pulls harder on his wrist, and Shroudweaver's arm slips. The rhythm stutters. The red threads run slack.

Shipwright staggers, falls to her knees.

Shroudweaver feels the weaving slide loose. Screaming, he slaps Declan across the face, and pulls his arm free even as he runs forwards.

Shipwright is stooped in front of him, her broad shoulders shaking with each perforating pulse of light. Shroudweaver presses his lips into a thin line, and begins to stitch, deftly and confidently. He can feel the pressure of the weaving against his fingers. Births generally move only in one direction. There's an inevitability to these things. This god wants to be born.

When Shipwright raises her head again, her eyes are clear and, for a second, he relaxes, lets the threads fall. Before he's even realised his mistake, Shroudweaver watches the god take hold.

Shipwright's body stiffens, her lips peeling back into a grin of savage joy. She becomes more solid in heartbeats, the lines of her sharpening against the rest of the useless, soft room.

That doesn't matter. Nothing else matters now she's here, properly here, not the imitation he has been loving these past years. If you can call it love. She demands something stronger now, a fiercer affection, a purer offering.

Without thinking, Shroudweaver falls to his knees and raises his head for benediction.

She looms above him, a thousand feet tall. She is gold, and brass and fire. She is love and the sea and the end of things.

His lips move, forming new prayers. Distantly, Declan screams himself hoarse, but Shroudweaver doesn't notice. Declan's a voice on the wind, and he's gazing into the heart of the storm. When the big man's body slumps to the floor, he barely sees it.

The storm reaches out her hands to him and where she touches him he feels the shadows of the last twenty years slip away. She's light and life, she's the salt in the waves and the cry of a clear canvas sky.

Shroudweaver gives himself over to her. Her light spreads through him, bone and marrow, warm and hungry. He feels himself dissolving into it. He's never been so grateful.

Then like the snap of a finger, the light goes out. Shadow flows into the room like a river and from the shadow, Slickwalker, his face a mask of fury. 'Really? *Really*?! Not this again. How many times?' He raises a shaking hand, and makes a quick chopping motion.

Groggily, Shroudweaver watches something small, black and twisted fray between Slickwalker's fingers. A thread? No, couldn't be.

'No more. Enough.' Slickwalker's lips are black with anger, even as he reels backwards against the wall, wincing in pain.

As the light of the weaving vanishes, Shipwright gutters, sputters, and drops. In an instant, Shroudweaver's head clears. He lurches forwards, breaking her fall as best he can, before he turns back to Slickwalker.

He's naked, a livid purple bruise circling his stomach, but the cold smile on his face is the same as ever. He waves a hand languidly. 'Apologies, Shroud. You don't catch me at my best.'

Already pulling himself together. Composure returning as worms of shadow stitch the rents in his flesh. He tentatively feels the remnants of the fading scar around his midsection. 'Everyone hits harder than I remembered,' he mutters, and laughs.

Shroudweaver ignores him, runs a finger along Shipwright's sweat-slick neck and finding a pulse, straightens. Fingerprints still red on his wrist, he looks down at Fallon's curled body. 'Declan?'

Slickwalker snorts. 'It'll take more than me to kill that old prick.' As he talks, the shadows crawl over him like solicitous snakes, weaving clothes onto his body.

Slickwalker grins. 'Of course, killing him was never on the agenda. I even told him that. As if I'd really do that to . . .' His mouth twists awkwardly. A flicker of shadow nudges at his lips.

Shroudweaver makes a soft, sad noise. 'Hard, isn't it? When you want to call them by their names?'

Slickwalker flashes him a sharp look. 'Preferable to the alternative. Although, I don't think there's much point us debating that right now.'

Shroudweaver nods. 'So, why are you here?'

Slickwalker drums his fingers against his temples. 'C'mon, old man. Kisser always talks about how you're so damn smart. I'm not seeing it.'

Shroudweaver looks around the room, at the blood and the wreckage, and then at the people in it. 'Oh.'

Slickwalker smiles like a lazy wolf. 'Give the man a prize.' He points. 'It's very simple. I needed to know if Fallon was hiding you two. But we can't touch either of you without you' – he sweeps an arm to encompass the room – 'without you reacting as expected.' The arm ends in a spear of shadow, which becomes the gun. 'So, we tug on Declan. And, well, here you are.'

Shroudweaver bends to straighten Shipwright's arms. 'I didn't think you'd force a confrontation so soon.'

Slickwalker laughs. 'A confrontation? This isn't a confrontation. This is my last attempt to make sure my wife doesn't kill her father.'

Shroudweaver stops his fussing, and stares at the rise and fall of Shipwright's chest. 'I don't want to hurt her.'

Slickwalker is behind him in an instant, his voice low and soft in his ear. 'A bit late for that, I think. The only way you can hurt her now is by forcing her hand.' Tight fingers on his shoulder. 'I'm not going to let you do that. She's been through enough.'

Ignoring the grip, Shroudweaver dips into his pockets and begins smearing salve on Shipwright's lips and fingers. 'What do you suggest?'

Slickwalker walks around Shipwright's body, his toes nudging at her thick boots, her splayed legs. He crouches down opposite Shroudweaver and fixes him with a stare.

'Turn yourselves in. I'll give you a week.' He twists his fingers into Shipwright's hair and tugs thoughtfully. 'If you don't, then I take your head and hers back in a sack. And I leave that fat pig nailed to the gate for the crows.' He taps Shroudweaver on the forehead. 'Think about it.'

Shroudweaver closes his eyes. 'I feel sorry for you, Slickwalker.'

Slickwalker snorts. 'Don't feel sorry for me, old man. I won a long time ago.' He stands, dusts himself off, 'The sooner you both accept that, the sooner we can stop all this. But, I should go.'

Shroudweaver nods, 'Yes, the guards will be here soon.'

Slickwalker turns as he walks away, shadow peeling his body into nothingness.

'No, Shroud. They've been dead for hours. Like I said, the fight's long over.'

He turns, points his index finger, and drops the thumb like a hammer.

'Be seeing you.'

20

I will tuck you in like a wood dove
I will settle you down
kiss your hair
light the auburn flame of love

—Postscript, letter found at Dryke, hand unknown

Warmth is the first thing he feels. That steady, heavy warmth that lets you know someone you love is nearby. He turns his face, meets soft hair, rough lips, kisses them groggily. The kiss is returned and a strong hand loops around his shoulders, pulling him tight. He makes himself comfortable on a steadily rising chest, and falls back into sleep.

The dream is the same as before. A city in ruins. Clouds scud overhead, unnaturally fast. The air stinks of burnt sugar, the streets are aggressively silent.

He's naked, smoke-stained. Shattered paving stones sharp under his bare feet. He coughs from split lips and walks towards the square. He knows what lives there. He knows what it will say, but this is a dream and his feet don't care what he's afraid of.

The square opens up before him like a cauterised wound. Ragged wrecks of buildings frame a plaza slick as melted glass. The echoes of shop signs offer goods he'll never see. His feet slip and roll on small hard objects that skitter away across the polished, crazed stone. Teeth and bones, some human some not; birds, maybe.

It waits for him in the remains of the fountain, circling endlessly. Its wings are broken, and trail a sticky golden light behind it, shuffling foot after shuffling foot.

He'd been afraid to approach it, in the first dream. In the second, they had talked. This is the third dream.

It looks up as he approaches and lets out a high, burbling cry. He smiles in response and sits on the edge of the fountain, trailing a hand down into the empty reservoir. It butts against his fingers enthusiastically, its teeth nibbling, sharp and insistent as a kitten.

'Hello, you,' he says and waits for its reply.

The words fall into his head with beautiful precision, filling spaces he hadn't known were empty.

Quickfish. Hello. Bright-heart. Great happiness.

Quickfish smiles nervously. What do you say to a dream-creature in a ruined city?

'How are you?' he adds lamely, and snorts at his own predictability.

Bright-hunger. Great emptiness. Missed you.

Quickfish runs a finger along its jaw and feels the slack pulse.

'You want fed, huh? You're as predictable as me.'

It shudders excitedly, runs a hot tongue across his palm.

Quickfish frowns, pulls his hand away. Distantly, he can hear his father's voice. Don't hold your hand out to anyone unless they're filling it first.

He bites his lip. 'OK, food. But first a question.'

It chirrups curiously, its glow pulsing steadily.

Quickfish turns to look at the blasted ruins of the city. 'What happened here?'

It's quiet for a second or two, and he watches it think, its ruined face surprisingly animated. It might have been beautiful once.

Great-hurt. Sky fell. Crows-eat. Eat-meaning.

Quickfish frowns. Of course the dream creature is a cryptic little thing. He turns back to it. 'So why bring me here?'

It snorts unhappily, its skin writhing over its bright bones.

Quickfish presses his lips tight. 'Tell me.'

Two-questions. Small-sneak. Two-questions, two-food.

He nods curtly. 'Sure, two food. Answer me.'

It squirms uncomfortably, a faint buzz building within its body.

Hello-Quickfish. Because-Quickfish. Not-brought. Returned-love. Back-birthed.

Quickfish squints down at it. It's hard to see now, blurring as the dream begins to end.

'Fine. Two food. Here.' He dips his arm back into the bowl of the fountain and it scurries towards him eagerly. Its teeth are so sharp he barely notices them. It purrs contentedly as it feeds and for just a moment he sees it straighten, a little less broken, a little less fragile.

Around them the buildings still send smoke into the scudding sky, the air thick and sweet. The plaza starts to spin as he wakes, the lines and certainties blurring into something softer.

As he pulls away, it protests faintly and he feels a brief pang of guilt.

He can feel a warm chest under him now, a strong arm around his shoulders. The real world is reasserting itself. He glances back at the fountain as he's pulled away and sees someone else watching him.

The fountain creature hasn't noticed her.

She's slight, pale, crooked, her black hair drifting out from a skull more angles than curves. She meets his eyes and raises a finger to lips lifted by a faint smile.

Quickfish wakes to the sound of beating black wings.

21

as you move north, the landscape becomes
not wilder, but looser
the flowers leashed haltingly to the cliffs
the cliffs only reluctantly touching the sky

—*What Is Born Beyond Blades*, Heartshamer

Strong arms around him. The scratch of stubble on his cheek, and somewhere nearby, the sound of running water.

A clear sky, blue with the first hints of northern ice and a familiar voice in his ear. 'Bad dreams again Fish?'

Quickfish sits up, rolls his neck, feels fingers start working at the knots and twists in his muscles. He turns to look over one shoulder and smiles.

'Not bad. Just lively.' As he says it, he feels his palm ache. Roofkeeper, kneading his shoulders with all the practiced firmness of his stable hand days, smiles a broad, white smile, like the first cut into a new tree.

'Must be the only time you're lively then.' The fingers stop, flick dark hair out of laughing eyes lined with creases, and Quickfish thinks again how very lucky he is.

'Hold up and I'll brew up some kind of potion to wake sleepy fish.'

Quickfish scratches his own mousey hair and yawns. 'Thanks Roof.'

Roofkeeper moves to the remains of their fire and works his magic. A few soft, precise movements and the embers cough out a hot glow. He sets a tin can over the flames, fills it with water from the stream and crushes herbs rapidly between his palms. The smell is incredible, sharp and fresh. Quickfish watches him as he works, his sharp jaw thick now with a good few weeks of road beard, a strong back hunched with care over the bubble and simmer.

Levering himself up from the grass, he walks across and runs his fingers down the thick curve of Roofkeeper's spine. 'Put a top on, slut.'

The taller man laughs, spins, tackles him to the grass and kisses him furiously.

'Typical highborn. Always telling us commoners what to do.'

Roofkeeper grins again, swift and easy. Pins Quickfish under his legs and looks down mockingly. 'How else may I serve you, Lordling of the Grey Towers?'

Quickfish laughs, a little, but it dies in his throat.

Roofkeeper bites his lip and looks away, out into the forests that sketch the first stage of their climb, a pang of regret skirling around his mind. 'I'm sorry, Fish. Me and my mouth.'

Quickfish shakes his head, forces a smile on to the lank sadness he feels in his head.

'No, no. It's fine. I just . . . miss them.' A pause, a sly smile. 'Besides, I *like* your mouth.'

Roofkeeper bends, kisses his neck, speaks along the collarbone. 'Do you think your dad'll come for us?'

Quickfish wriggles, only half-pleasurably.

'I hope not. How long have we been on the road now? A month? More? Hopefully we got him good and pissed enough that he won't think to come chasing after us for a while. Safer for him. And Mum.'

Roofkeeper stands, stretches, heads to the fire and gets two mugs from their packs. 'Do you honestly think we can find someone to help her?'

Quickfish shrugs himself into a shirt, and buttons it thoughtfully. 'I hope so. We've got a better chance the further we get from Astic. And you know, there's stories about the mountains.'

Roofkeeper strolls across, sipping pensively. 'There's always stories about the mountains, Fish. No one would bloody go there otherwise.'

Quickfish snorts in exasperation. 'Well, if nothing else, we're a step ahead of the mess brewing back home.'

Roofkeeper sits next to him, cups the mug to his chest. 'You sure of that?'

Quickfish's arm takes in the river, the trees, the sky. 'You see any fucking crows around here?'

Roofkeeper laughs. 'Point taken. Drink your tea, love.'

22

the blessed song, the blessed life
the lightest touch of bloody knife

—*Paean to the Gold*

Crowkisser cuts the meat from the bone in small, precise strokes. The scrape of blade against scapula, then sharp, savage cuts loosening tendon and cartilage. She works quickly, deft fingers peeling shreds of flesh loose and threading them wetly through the ropes which nest just above her head. The crows watch her quietly, hopping two-legged along the spans, chucking quietly to themselves.

Crowkisser cuts the meat from the bone, and the body beneath the blade gets whiter as she works.

Outside in the streets of Astic, the city stirs to life under a sluggish grey sky.

She turns to the bowl beside her, steeps her elbows in cool water which flushes red.

The crows alight on the scraps, worry at the meat with bright eyes and dull beaks.

She watches them as they move in feathered formation, and slowly, surely, prophecy starts to move on the edge of their wings. She can feel her mind loosening in her skull, ready to travel. She dreams constellations in front of her waking eyes.

A quick dip of her hand in the bowl, bloody water smeared across brow, lids and lips. The room is blurring. The soft-feathered shuffling growing in intensity until it's a solid hiss in her head. She is a thinly tethered thing, haltingly bound to her own meat and bone.

Her eyes roll back to kiss the inside of her skull and she can see.

The uplands, a few dozen miles out from the Republic. The jagged, flint-streaked bones of the foothills incongruous amid swathes of wide green grass, where the first flowers of spring battle the thawing ice for space. Some she recognises, Burners' Bridle and Hollowcrown. The earth is dark and rich and hard. Small, hot lives burrowing in it, skittering through it. Hawks stooping and hunting.

And two men. Two young men asleep around the remains of a campfire, tucked in the bend of a river, twined around each other. The smaller one she recognises, sandy-haired like a half-blown dandelion. Quickfish takes after his mother. The larger man she doesn't know. He's young, dark haired. She smiles. Handsome.

Quickfish dreams. Something swirling in his skull like a storm or sickness. Hands twitching fitfully, like a sleeping dog, adorable. She lets her consciousness dip lower, hooking onto the edges of his dream. It smells familiar, has a familiar feel, like burnt glass. She briefly wants to recoil as she feels it sliding over her skin, but she takes a hold of herself. As always, the curiosity overwhelms the pain. She touches down on canted stones. She is in the city, in the south. It's still burning. She recognises the melted curve of the plaza, the broken snag of the fountain where she made the first cut. Her fingers clench reflexively. Her breathing is speeding up. The pressure of the memory is too much for her. She can feel the panic growing in her chest, like suffocating; like a clot.

She shouldn't be back here. She shouldn't be back here.

Then she sees Quickfish, and the curiosity takes hold again. He . . . he shouldn't be here at all.

He's never been here. He wasn't here three years ago. And he can't be here now. And yet, here he is, sitting on the edge of the fountain, trailing his hand into the bowl like some debutante.

She edges closer and tries not to think about the feel of melted stone under her feet. Tries not to breathe in the air that still smells of terror, somehow. Tries not to remember that moment when the world fell into itself, when sounds became thick and solid and flesh, and caught fire, and you could breathe in the ash of peoples' screams as they burnt.

She digs her nails into the palms of her hands. Focus. That is not now. She is *not* here, not really. She is an interloper in a runaway boy's dream. Nothing more.

She edges closer. Something stirs in the fountain. She stiffens and stops. Every muscle in her body tight, her nerves alight.

Impossible. She can only make out the kiss of gold light around the rim, watching the buttery, liquid glow wax and wane. Impossible. But then, there's only one thing that casts light like that.

She tastes blood in her mouth and realises she's bitten through her lip. She is back in her body, back in the temple. This is a strong seeing, maybe a stronger dream. She needs to be careful.

More than that though, she needs to get closer.

As she moves, Quickfish talks to the thing in the fountain. She hears nothing in reply, but he seems amused, friendly even. He leans over further, exposes his palm, winces. She rushes forwards, setting her toes carefully around the scraps of seared glass and bone. She can remember the shapes of them all. She can remember the moment she set it all in motion.

She digs deeper and almost screams with the pain. Focus.

Her arched feet bring her up just shy of the fountain's opposite lip where it crouches, drinking from the palm of Quickfish's outstretched hand like a grateful dog.

She barely manages to choke down the outraged scream in her throat. Barely. Instead, she lets herself run butcher's eyes over its body. It is broken in ways she had never realised something could be broken. Joints and wings twisted and torn at such impossible angles. And yet when it moved, it was still, almost, beautiful. She fights the urge to find a rock, a sharp shard, something with which to crush and bleed it back into stillness.

But there's no point. She is not really here, just a passenger in the dream of a stupid boy.

Instead, she watches it like a child watching a wasp with a crushed wing, flinching at its every pulse, wanting to kill it, but not daring to get close. Hoping for its own quiet death.

A living god. Impossible. The unfairness of it. The offense of it.

She watches it feed, desperate and hungry. It's weak, and alone, the very last, perhaps.

Something in her thrills at that thought.

She hovers on the edge of the fountain until it has drunk its fill. Quickfish withdraws his arm, rubs at the palm where the needle-marks of teeth even now close over. As he raises his head, he meets her eyes.

Crowkisser smiles, raises a finger to her lips and then pushes him out of the dream. As he leaves, she does too, the world dissolving around her, back into the formless space of seeing, back into the between. She reorients herself and lets her shadow fall down on the land, on the couple below.

As she watches, they wake, rise, kiss, talk. Barely disturbed by the dream, if at all. They are altogether too perfect. Quickfish has done well for himself.

In Astic, in the temple, Crowkisser throws her head back far enough to make her spine crack; the crows bicker and scuff, and the blood in her throat pulses. The landscape unravels before her, the men shrink to a point and she can see the road in front of them. Another two, three days and they'll be on the outskirts of the Republic, of the mountain city. Of Thell.

She can see it now, crouched in the shadow of the mountains like a low cat. She hasn't forgotten Thell, or its people. She lets her eye run over the stooped dwellings, the smithies and stables woven among the cairns. The people outside of the mountain liked to live close to their dead, their doors hung with bone and dark wood.

Above the fringes of Thell lies the Stump, hewn into the mountain itself, its endless hollows open to the biting wind, the dark sockets in its stone corpse alight with fire, and metal and the ceaseless march of men.

Thell is preparing for war. News travels fast and even in the broken north, there are rumours of what has happened in Astic. Men's tongues are loose things and they spit secrets faster than a ship sails. They're afraid of her, of what she's achieved.

She watches them gather themselves on the battlements, tall

men, old men, young men, broad-shouldered women, fierce-faced girls.

Jostling each other, wheeling, cursing. Painting each other in bright geometric patterns, inked into the skin and brushed onto the bone.

She smiles at that, and crooks her fingers. Above her head, the crows grow in volume, their black beaks plucking at bloody scraps.

In the deep sockets of the Stump, the people grip their weapons tighter.

Cold winds blow in the north and riding the edge of them, the promise of war. Beyond that, the promise of freedom, real freedom – if she gets her way, and she will.

So, two days to Thell for the lovers. Two days until they slip inside the Stump and things get complicated. She can't catch Quickfish now, not before he bolts into Thell like a mouse. So be it, she'll take him when she takes the whole of the mountain.

Crowkisser pulls her gaze back from the brutal canker of the citadel, out across the cairns, windblown, threaded with stubborn, long-bladed grass. She lets her mind's eye run along the upper edge of the Barrowlands.

The dead of Thell sleep uneasily. This has always been the way in the north. They're a people who find it hard to stay buried, a legacy of the old Empire, and its Emperor's peculiar gifts. So her father used to say, and he would know. Her eye is drawn to the symbols on the stones, harsh and angular beneath the scudding clouds, a little echo of mountain paint.

The dead of Thell, stacked in their barrows. *Stay asleep*, she thinks. The living have enough trouble as it is.

She's pulled back into herself by a sudden feeling of loss. Her mind hits the meat of her body with bruising force, and she staggers, leans on the table for support. The world spins and the crows above her head explode into the sky in a cawing frenzy.

There's a voice in the room, a voice not her own. A voice between the pillars of the halls, soft and sibilant.

'. . . Kisser.'

The echoes fall thick around her, licking the stone at her back, pushing against the blood in her temples.

'. . . Kiss kiss kisssssssss-errrrrr.'

Ragged flesh moves under her hands. The soft grind of bone against bone. The drip of thick blood. Until the meat on the bone speaks, ragged and hoarse, the words forcing themselves up from a torn throat, sockets of red ruin twisting and searching for her face.

'Kisssser.'

Crowkisser moves with the speed of terror. She can feel her lizard brain screaming at her to run. But she's never been a runner, and the knife is close. It fits neatly into the palm of her hand like an old, heavy friend.

The first cut slashes the vocal cords. The second the tendons of the wrist. The third the tendons of the feet. Neither walk, nor hold, nor speak.

This is how the dead are bound. Her father taught her this. The corpse's empty eyes meet hers and for a second she hears something. Something that comes from beyond lips and tongues and falls into her brain like a shard of ice.

Crowkisser screams in rage, and drives the knife downwards to cut the meat from the bone.

Down and down and down again.

The blade doesn't drop from her hands until her arm is too sore to move.

23

the bare mountain
the ice house
death's hold
old Blood-belly
ever-hunger
witherfell
heartbarrow

—Travellers' names for the Republic of Thell (trans.)

The three of them sit around the table.

The fire is going, as it always is at this time of year, cooking the cold out of the stones, swallowing logs away into itself. Soot scorches the breast of the chimney, where a fire was laid yesterday, and the day before, and almost all the days before that. The chill creeps in under every door this close to the mountains.

A small crowd tonight, but a good one. All the usual faces, Tapshuck at the bar, pulling draughts of something bitter and fine. The dog is at his feet, farting up a storm and cadging what it can. Dampstrand's got her feet up on the table already, boots caked with river mud. She's still red at the wrists from gutting the catch, but already winkling and salting all the little molluscs that have sat at the bottom of the net. They go nice with a sharp pint, those. A lick of butter and a sniff of pepper, and you're set.

So she's sprinkling all over the plates, and there's Thinshanks next to her, leaner than he used to be, ruddy at the nose where the hill winds have picked the skin off the bone. He's trying hard to catch his crumbs, and harder to catch her eye. It's been that way since Damp was widowed, and Thinshanks is nothing if not an optimist. You have to be, to tend sheep this close to the mountains.

He laughs as he talks, widemouthed and flat toothed. And if there's a knife by his side, they all know why it's there.

And the last of them, of course. All the best crews come in threes, and Rustneck's been the top of this triangle for a long time now, for she's the only one with the nerve to go delving the barrows. That's how she got the name, of course, from years of stooping below those low lintels and grubbing in the dirt for all the tarnished treasures of the barrow folk, and the mountain. It's slicked her shoulders with a thick brown line, like a half-caulked boat. She's peacocking it tonight, letting her shirt slip down as she fleeces Damp at another round of dice, reminding everybody who the real thrill-seeker in this town is.

Town, such as it is; a village, if that, contracting in on itself, after the wars and the south. Flinching inwards like a snail in the shell, abandoning the high roads, because Thell is marching them, the horizon lined with brass. It's better to stay home.

So, the town's become a village, and the village has become a huddle of little cottages, with the tavern at the heart of it, and busy every night, because no one wants to be alone, not this close to the mountains.

Thinshanks has heard rumours from the other herders, the ones that don't stick to a little clump of shonky houses, that take their flocks roving over the thin clay soil of the Barrowlands. The herders that sometimes let those flocks graze on the thick, green grass nearer Thell, lush as it is in those places where battles were fought, and where the dead push up the roots and shoots.

Thinshanks has been hearing rumours, and this is what he says through half a loaf of bread, the spatter of crumbs toasting in the fire as it stretches over the hearth.

'There's a drover told me they scooped the hill out like an egg. Sucked all the blood and spirits out of it. Sent in their witches to drain the whole thing, 'til it couldn't support its own weight.'

Rustneck's unconvinced, having seen her share of crumbling

holes, but she's enjoying the performance. She leans forwards and fills his cup. 'Scooped it out?'

Shanks nods emphatically. 'Like an egg, they said, all hollow, and the stone itself flaking away, crick crack.' He sups meaningfully. 'That was good masonry too. I laid some of the blocks myself. Frogbreath's father did the slab stone but I did the littler bits, hammer and chisel, fiddly fiddly.'

Damp snorts. 'Sounds like the usual clip-clop bollocks. Pass the nuts would you? My stomach thinks my throat's been cut.'

Rust slides them over, palms a few for herself. Split and sat in the embers of the fire, they'll make good eating when the night has wound on.

'Something's up though. Half the barrows I used to dip are sealed now. And professional like. Pulled the capstones down and piled on new earth.' She shoots a look at Shanks.

'Plus, they're up on the hills. Which is what's driven you down here so often, to nest in our armpits.'

Shanks laughs and calls to Tap for another round. Both barkeep and dog answer, the latter padding over to push its thick wiry skull against all these familiar hands. Damp pats its flank and pulls her hand away sticky. She sniffs it, licks it and looks at Tapshuck. 'Dog's bleeding Tap.'

Tap bends down to the beast, gentles its shoulders. The cuts aren't obvious, beneath all that shag, but they're there, a day or two old, maybe, scabbing and rusting down to black.

'Where did you get these, lad?' The dog doesn't answer, more interested in the scraps of jerky that Shanks is waggling like sprats on a line.

Damp tuts, wipes off her hands and searches a little more carefully. There's not just blood on the fur, but the stink of incense and other sour herbs.

'Your dog's been running where he shouldn't, Tap. Put a stave behind the bar and leash him, I've told you often it.'

Tapshuck grumbles. 'He likes his wandering.'

Damp looks up, furrows her thick brows. 'That's as may be, but it was me coaxed him from a pup and gave him to your lumpy arse. So you do as you're told. This old fella's been digging in graves marked by the Republic, sure as shit sticks.'

Rust spits into the fire, stretches, yawns. '*Thell*. The ways we talk about them, you'd think they were all wights.' She massages her wrists, shoots a sympathetic look at the dog. 'I've been in their barrows. They silt down to dust just like the rest of us.'

Damp grins. 'Don't talk like that, my lovely, you with that big ol' vein pulsing in your throat there, they'll come right down that chimney and drink you up.'

She elbows Shanks, cackling, but gets little back.

It's plain Thinshanks is less convinced. His face is flicked with shadow as he gazes into the fire. 'They say the port folk in Mither nail gannet skulls to the chimney breast, just in case. Stops souls slipping down. Maybe we should put up some wards. I'd fence the sheepfold, if I thought it would make a blind bit of difference.'

Damp snorts, takes a fresh drink, and looks him dead in the eye. 'The only thing I want nailed to my breast is a strapping young man with an empty head, Shanks.' She pats him on the shoulder, and he flinches.

'We can't go jumping at every shadow that rolls down from those blasted mountains.'

The door opens with a slam, and all three of them jump. A squall of rain chases in from outside, with a flash of moonlight, like the edge of a knife.

The man in the doorway has an axe, but he also has a pack, and a look about him that says he's not in the mood for any more weather. His face bears a scrub of beard, and cheekbones that make Damp think she's got her wish for a second.

He's joined by another young lad who slips an arm around his waist, and she rinses the hope out of her head like swill-water.

The younger lad wipes plastered hair from his face, and says in a sweet burr of a voice, 'Got room for two?'

Tapshuck looks at them both. The dog growls, and shows its last few teeth. The trio look too, mostly because they haven't seen travellers since the apple moon turned.

Eventually, Damp comes to her senses, and pulls Shanks up the bench. 'Make room.'

Rust stands, and gestures something that might be grand, might be courtly, if her shirt wasn't still smudged with grave dust and toasted nuts. 'Join us lads, it's a bitter night.'

'You drinking?' Tap says, more of a statement than a question really. The bearded man nods, and slips him a couple of coins that brighten his lump of a face considerably.

Damp knows that coin, for the husband she buried was a Hesper boy, and something in her softens at the memory.

'Settle lads. It's bitter right enough. A cat-creep night, and the dead are out looking for flame. Not a good one to be abroad.'

They settle, as much as young men settle. Taking a cup of ale, and even trying some of her little winkled delights. Introducing themselves like polite lads: Quickfish and Roofkeeper.

The evening slinks by in small talk. A few new faces is nice enough, after all. Even if Tapshuck spends most of his time with the dog, and polishing the brass that's already glimmered.

Rust lets the fire sink, and coaxes the lamps in the windows to spill a little buttered flame against the dark. The talk gets looser, as sleep and drink settle on the group like an old coat. And if the roof creaks a little, well, the building is old. And if the sheep scatter on the hill, well, they are wont to do that, wild little things.

The tavern closes itself for the night. Tap bars and bolts the door, and bids the trio goodnight. Takes the dog up to bed for some heat, and plants a little two-fingered kiss on the stair charm as he passes. Just another little brass thing in a pub full of brass things, but it gives him comfort.

The creak of him settling stretches the rafters for a while, and Damp makes a foul joke. Shanks is next to go. There's still not enough fat on him to hold the drink, and he slides first to her shoulder, and then her lap. She adjusts her kirtle to pillow his head, and strokes his hair. Because he's not so bad, when you get down to it. And not when the night is so dark, so cold, so close to the mountain.

Weariness weights her eyes like merchants' lead, the fire blurs and the faces around it swim. Shadows of flame dance on the chimney breast, bouncing off brass and tack. And if something moves there, then it's just light and heat; ash becoming flame and flames falling to ash.

The new folks are tiring too, falling into each other like lobsters into the creel. And isn't that how it should be? Shanks's head is warm across her thighs, and all her friends are here. Dampstrand sleeps.

So there's just Rustneck, and she's stretched out by the fire, because the ale's stronger than she remembers, and the cold fiercer, creeping in every crack of this little place that feels like home. She sleeps too, but fitful, a doze pulled back and forth by the aches in her shoulders where she's dug and turned the dark soil.

She wakes in the small hours when the fire has fallen to black, and all her friends are dreaming. The rain pushes the thin panes of glass like breath, and the eaves tick with the feet of rats. And she thinks she sees something. The two young men are asleep in one of the corner chairs, twined like mice in the skirting. And the younger one is twitching, dancing. His fingers moving in a world she does not see, his lips muttering something she cannot hear.

Rust ignores it. She has made a living ignoring things that scare her. She ignores it until the light blossoms. A spatter of rain and wind pushes against the thatch, and in the same moment, a welter of gold light washes over that young man. His palm. His lips. His eyes.

He speaks again, and she steps closer, tries to make it clear, just a single word. The gold light washes her bones, brighter than fire. And she can feel something on the edge of it, like digging out something buried deep. She can almost feel the glint and turn of it. She can almost hear her own name.

She steps closer. That small parlour is washed with gold as she puts her ear to Quickfish's lips, and makes out just one word.

'Thell.'

The gold flares, and Rustneck dreams.

When she wakes, it's morning, the hearth cold. Damp and

Shanks are already up, rubbing some life back into aching muscles, and pouring grease into a skillet to greet some eggs.

The young men are nowhere to be seen.

The light nowhere to be seen.

Rust thinks about saying something, about sharing what she felt, for that one moment. The touch of that light, the whisper of Thell.

But she's made a living keeping her mouth shut. Her friends don't deserve the worry.

So she sits at the table, and runs that Hesper coin through her fingers, wondering just what else those young lads will be buying. And just how much it will cost.

24

Being a city of startling prospect and prosperity, proceeding from a stark elevation through a number of close-hung districts, suitable for the lower sorts.

—*An Exile's Guide to the Cities of the Chalk Shore,*
Chapter 4, Hesper (The Vulture)

He takes the usual route, off the main canal and into the smaller streets that twitch their way between the regular grids of waterway and plaza. Ropecharmer looks up as he walks. Hesper is a strange city. From the grey towers high on the hill, past the porticos and pillars of the old merchant homes, and down to the sprawl of waterways that pulls commerce into the heart of the port.

The canals themselves are broad. Sometimes he crosses them on sculpted bridges, the carved faces of their benefactors slowly sifting into the water below. Sometime he hops, from barge to barge, wobbling the cargo and collecting curses. Not too hard. He's a light lad, a thin thing.

Between the canals, Hesper stretches upwards. Apartments and galleries of fine façade nestled against lean-tos and add-upons. Little penthouses fit only for rats, and the spark-eyed kids who run errands, glimming the streets. That could have been him once, without the luck he'd had, the friends he'd made.

Into another snarl of streets. Cats sloping the gutters watch him with affront. The smell of life clings to the walls, kitchen windows spitting grease, and café porters swapping slander over a smoke.

Ropecharmer looks up. If you have a good eye, you can see the scars, the spots on a building where there used to be a shrine, or the rough stone where the mascarons of gods were ripped from the plaster. They are shiny and strangely healed, like a burn.

The gaze of the gods wasn't welcome in Hesper anymore. Not since the south, since Fallon's wife had fallen.

Rope had adored Arissa Fallon once. He'd seen her at the parades, always on the biggest horse, bucking beneath banners that snapped like a ship at sail, tossing sweets and favours to the crowd, and always to the little sprats like Rope who crowded the edges of the processional. There had been nights where those little favours had made the difference between sleeping hungry and sleeping full, and he had been grateful. He had sketched her face and her horse in his books, when he was supposed to be outlining rigging and knots.

Now, Crowkisser had put paid to Arissa, and Ropecharmer was done begging for scraps.

He walks onwards, to the streets where laundry spans the skyline, where little ladders and passthroughs were dropped between windows. Everyone knows each other here. Everyone knows if you don't belong. Rope belongs.

He collects smiles and nods as he goes. For wasn't he a good lad? And hadn't he dealt with a lot, with his parents and all? And hadn't he done well to sign on with the Shipwright? Running the rigging on a great ship, not the sorry scows and scuttlers that clogged the canals round here.

The door he wants is at the end of the alley, nestled under a little turret that used to be part of the old draper's shop here. Coglifter had cannibalised the house much as she cannibalised any old bits and bobs, keeping what was useful, and grafting on where it was needed. The latest addition was a little belvedere squatting on the roof, windows enough for delicate work, and air to let the fumes out, he suspects.

The door itself is unassuming, a little split-hinge thing, some of that red eastern wood that shines almost brassy. She takes good care of it, keeps a little hatch in it, so she can scry whoever comes knocking, and a little bell above it to announce their presence.

There's more to it than that, but nothing Rope needs to fuss about. He's welcome. He's expected.

He doesn't even need to knock today. The door opens as he approaches. Another guest is leaving. He sees a familiar face in a heavy cowl, arms tight around one of Cog's deliveries. Rope gets a nod, a little muttered assurance, which he returns in kind.

Cog's stood behind him in the doorway, sleeves rolled up and apron on. The cloth one, which means she's cooking, which is the best news Rope's had all day. His stomach says hello before she does and she grins.

'You hungry sprat? Never enough meat on those bones.'

She stretches out an arm to welcome him in, a length of lean muscle sprinkled with wiry grey hair, and the ghost of old burns. It's as scarred as the buildings round here. She lays it heavy over his shoulders, her strong fingers pulling him into the hall and towards the kitchen where already the smell of toasting spice calls to him.

She busses his cheek lightly. 'Course you're hungry.'

Cog never takes no for an answer, so he doesn't argue. She smells as she always does, of her powders and acids, of onion and butter.

The kitchen is small and the table smaller. He takes his usual seat, folding himself on a stool half his size. Coglifter shifts to the stove and agitates a skillet which hisses with salt and sugar, coaxing those onions down into something sweeter.

She sucks her thumb and shoots him a look.

'Saints, does the wind whip it off you when you're shimmying up the rigging? Thinner than I've ever seen you.'

She cracks the oven, and little waves of heat lap at his ankles.

'Here. Start with this. No time to lose.'

A little loaf of bread, light and crisp. Cog's hands are delicate, when they need to be.

She slaps it in front of him with little ceremony. Pointedly nudges a crock of butter over too. 'Dig in, you limpet.'

Rope does, and forgets how to speak, his mouth flooded with warmth and salt.

She tuts as he eats. 'Skin and bone lad, and the skin's giving up the ghost.'

She turns back to the range, and a board laid with legs of poultry. She splits the skin and shanks the bones with quick, economical movements. The flesh is impaled on a skewer and set over a low flame. The bones are put to broth, with some onion and dark roots.

She cracks a bottle open on the edge of the counter and eyes him thoughtfully as she slowly turns the skewers, fat hissing into fire.

'How are you finding it Rope? Walking that line?'

He shrugs, sucks butter off a thumb. 'Can't say as I love it, but I know it's necessary.'

Cog nods, scrapes at her chin. 'Practical boy. Keep that head and we'll come out of this just fine.'

She crosses to the table and sets a second bottle down for him. 'Drink. These brewed up well.'

He does. She's not wrong. A thick slick of sour, syrupy ale, tinged with sweetness and fizz. Something sparky on the edge of it. 'New botanicals?' he says.

She grins. 'New chemicals. One of the stone-melters from the last dig. Just a drop or two and you get the zing.'

He frowns. 'That safe?'

Cog pats his hand companionably. Her palm is callus over callus. 'Course it is sprat, I still need you.'

She flips the birds, shakes the shit out the skillet and sits next to him for a spell.

'So, this is a joy, but I know it ain't just a social. Handsome lad like you has better places to be.' She elbows him. 'You seeing anyone? Charming more than ropes? Raising more than sails?'

He snorts.

'That's not all I've got lad. Plumbed any depths? Found any new harbours?'

'Gods above, Cog, that's enough.'

She clinks his bottle. 'Gods are gone, sprat, they can't save you from me.'

Ropecharmer says nothing, just stares at the grain on the table while Cog busies herself setting plates and cutlery, lighting a few candles against the coming night.

The table is smooth. It has been sanded and varnished over, and over again to remove the marks of Coglifter's work, to banish stubborn stains. Yet still the grain persists, something deep in the wood that can't be scrubbed out. He runs a finger over it, trying to shape the question in his head.

At the stove, Cog doesn't turn her head, but she sets down the skewers and sighs. 'Just spit it out lad, I can see it hanging on your shoulders like a tick on a dog.'

Rope coughs and takes another swig. 'I've been hearing things, Cog. Seeing bits of things I don't rightly understand. I've been buying drinks for people in the Towers instead of plumbing depths, as you put it, and the folk I buy drinks for are telling me stuff I can't square away.'

Cog shutters the flames and leaves the birds to crackle. Turning from the stove, she fixes him with those sharp eyes, like a blackbird running over a hedgerow. 'What sort of stuff, lad? Out with it.'

Rope picks at the bread. 'About the Shipwright. And the Shroudweaver.'

Coglifter sucks her teeth. 'More about him though, I bet.'

He nods. She stirs the bones in their broth and waits.

'Something went down with Fallon. The scullions and stable hands are too skittish to say much but there's a couple that like me.'

Cog waggles her eyebrows.

'Salt and spit, Cog. Relax. We've done each other a few favours. They need stuff brought in, medicines, kit. I pick it up when we're out with Ship and charge it to Fallon's tab.'

'Proper accounting lad, s'good. He pays the bills, even the ones we don't tell him about.'

She rests the ladle in the crook of the pot. 'So, what happened?' She already knows, of course, but it's a good little habit to see if Rope's staying true, like running your thumb along the edge of a knife.

Rope scrapes at the table with his nail. 'Some kind of assassination attempt. Crowkisser's dog, most folk think. The one that crawls through shadows.' He straightens, rubs a finger over the scar on his neck, 'The weaver foiled it apparently, with gold magic – god magic.'

This much she knows, but he's not done.

'One of the girls that works the ropes on the Cattongue canal says she saw bodies hanging over the water. Says she woke up choking like someone was pouring scalded syrup down her mouth, and there were bodies there, lit up like morning, burning to ash and gold.'

Cog nods as she agitates the broth. It's catching a little where the meat hits the metal. 'There'll be some folk glad to see the last of the evidence gone, I bet. Lot of sins swimming around down there.'

Ropecharmer runs his hands through his hair. It's short-cropped, pale as death along the side where Slickwalker's last shot came too close.

'I don't get it, Cog. All this shit because the gods are dead. And yet the weaver's running around doing . . . what, exactly? Because it sure looks like god magic to me.'

Cog sighs. 'I know, lad. If it looks like a duck and quacks like a duck and all that. But sometimes it's just a bastard dressed as a duck.'

Rope seems unconvinced, so she beckons. 'Come over here. Get off your arse for once.'

He laughs at that, levers himself up and joins her by the stove. This close the smell is nearly crippling, garlic, butter, spice and herbs dancing on iron. Chicken fat rendering into that crunch he's loved since he was a little boy.

'Close your mouth or the flies'll get in, lad, I'm trying to educate you.'

Cog jabs at the broth where a chicken carcass rolls like a submerged lugger, a slick of fat and flavour slowly boiling from the bone.

'Gods are like soup. Or god-magic is, at any rate. Least far as I can tell, and I've had some very serious conversations with some serious folk about it.'

'The hosts? The temples? They were begging for what they got. Asking, not taking. Getting the odd spoonful of grace and power, in return for the right offerings and mumbo-jumbo' – she waves the ladle – 'but the pot was elsewhere. Out there. In the sky or the stars, or whatever, doesn't matter. Distant. Got to ask for every spoonful. Some of the hosts, they went further, dressed themselves up as bowls to make themselves seem more appealing to the soup. Kept little bits of the gods inside themselves, brewing up stock in their bones, so they could offer a more consistent supply of *grace* to their parishioners.'

She smacks her lips. 'Repulsive.' She breaks up a carrot into softer chunks and flips the meat again. It's getting close.

'You following?'

Rope nods. 'Amazingly, yes.'

Cog smiles. He notices there are some new scars on her forearms, like she was working with something sharp. He says nothing.

She damps the coals beneath the griddle, and turns back to the stock.

'Weaver magic, I don't fully scan. A lot of it was kept pretty close to the chest even when there was more of them. Now? The way they talk about him? You'd think he was a god himself.'

She coats the back of the spoon, lets it drip. 'He's not, just another sack of bones carrying more power than he should.'

'Here, try.' She shoves the spoon in Rope's face, and he sips, obediently.

'Good?'

'Great,' he says, and it is, thick and salty and humming with flavour.

'Flatterer,' she says. 'I'll kiss the pan with it once the birdies are done, and then we'll eat proper. What was I saying? Aye, Shroudweaver. Prick. Powerful prick at that. Fallon's always happily sat on his hand and got diddled, but we need him out of the picture if we're ever going to get anything done.'

She scrapes the pot. 'That magic of his? The god stuff? He's been throwing enough of it around pissing about on Dec's errands that I think I get the rough shape of it.'

She moves to the table and adjusts the place settings, all two of them. 'Two kinds, basically. One folks have seen, the other I just hear sots and tremblers talking about every time that ship sails into harbour. Your floating corpses? All that gold light? That's making soup from raw stock. Not asking for it. Boiling it up yourself from whatever's been left lying around. Sure, maybe the gods put the base material in our souls, in our hearts, way back when' – she pats her chest – 'but it's like ore. It needs to burn to become usable. Once it does, you get all that slinky, sugary, gold power which you can hammer into anything you like. A ship, a gun. A body.'

Ropecharmer stirs the stockpot, the bones cresting and subsiding. 'Seems dangerous.'

Cog nods as she politely elbows him out the way, and does the same thing, but better. 'You bet your tits it's dangerous. Doubt he cares though. Or more like, he'll convince himself every time that there's no other choice.'

She kills the fire beneath the pot. 'That's what they all do, lad. Tell themselves every day that they're the ones making the smart decisions.'

Rope helps her tilt the pan and strain.

'So if that's the first kind of god-magic, what's the second?'

Bones, roots and gristle catch in the mesh. Cog grinds it all mercilessly against the wire.

'Well, depends who you talk to, but the *official* term is "composite". Dry as a bone. Like when they call all the lads that die in battle "losses". It's god-building, lad.'

She thumps down the sieve full of split bone and skin.

'Starts the same as the other kind, stealing from all the scraps of life that are lurking in the world since the gods put them there. Except it doesn't just cinder them up and shove the energy into something else, no.'

She tips the strained sauce over the birds, where the glaze sweetens and clings.

'No, some clever shit back in shroudweaving school obviously thought too damn hard about how far they could push things. Isn't that always the way? Can't just have power. Got to see how much power you can have, how far it will take you.'

She flips the skewers a final time. 'Well, it took them far enough. There's talk that weavers could build a god from nothin'. Burn up enough souls and mash them together into something stronger than the sum of its parts.'

She pokes the skin of a bird, and sucks her thumb. 'Think of it this way. All my little leavings and choppings and marrow renderings? All of them sit together and the thing they make is finer than it ever should be. Same idea for these gods they build.'

Rope watches as she licks the last bits of nail clean.

Cog takes a thin knife and slips the birds off the skewers onto the plates.

'Except, you make a thing that big, that powerful? The weight of it distorts the world.' She pairs the birds with another round of soft bread and some oil flecked with spice.

'So the weavers outlawed it. Told themselves it was too far, and that they were too good and kind and just to ever do it. And then almost all of them had the grace to die before the world found how much their promises were worth.'

She snorts. 'So now there's only one left, with his back to the wall, and what do powerful people with their backs to the wall do? What did Crowkisser do?'

'Desperate things,' Rope says, holding a chair out for her.

She sits and pats his hand as it rests on her back. Her grip is strong, the knuckles stark against the skin.

'Aye, my boy. Desperate things.'

She sighs, follows it with a smile. 'Which is why we do what we do.' She glances at the carcass lying in its bed of peelings and clippings. 'Removing the stuff that's not good for us. Leaving something finer behind.'

He sits opposite her, and they clink bottles.

She holds his gaze after, her eyes bright as a surgeon.

'Eat up lad. You'll need every scrap of strength for what comes next.'

25

the world initiates you in its rituals
the short ones; the breath, the sleep
the longer; the death, the birth

—Aestering Knotsong, No. 35

'Be you free men and unnamed?'

She stands tall atop one of the boundary cairns, her chin jutting down the tip of a flat-bladed spear which hovers warningly in front of Quickfish's widening eyes. Her hair is drawn high on her head, shaved short at the sides. The geometrics on her face mean *something* – he forgets.

Behind her a few of Thell's other border guards are equally direct, equally wary.

The spear-point flicks at his face like a snake.

'Are you slow, pup? Answer the question!'

Quickfish feels Roofkeeper shift beside him, muscles tensing, and the words pour out of him in a hurried mess.

'Free, yes, and unnamed. I'm Quickfish. This is Roofkeeper.'

Her eyes narrow and her lips twist like wire. The spear doesn't move.

'I don't know you. And I wasn't expecting you. Where have you stumbled up from?'

The crowd behind her mutters, and a ripple of laughter passes through them.

Quickfish feels their eyes on him, and his cheeks flush hot.

'What I mean is. I'm Quickfish. Quickfish of Hesper. Of the Grey Towers.'

'Hesper? They haven't had the stones to knock on our door

for years.' His interrogator wrinkles her nose warily, 'Are you Fallon's kid?'

Quickfish sighs. 'Among other things.'

Her posture shifts. The spear withdraws and she leans on it quizzically. 'Fallon's kid?' She snorts. 'You?' Another ripple of laughter.

Roofkeeper rumbles next to him. 'I can vouch for him.'

She snorts again, a smile fighting the official frown. 'Oh. This is too much. You're adorable. Vouch for him?'

She moves down the hill with sudden speed, heavy solid foot-falls that bring her face to a stop an inch from Roofkeeper's open mouth. He can smell her breath, sweet and slightly spiced. 'You know how much we value your words here, pup?' – a twist of the head, a spit, a two-fingered stab in the chest – 'This is *Thell*, you wet-eared nit. We value stone and steel and bone.'

Roofkeeper swallows.

She grins wide as a shark. 'Cute little pups are always a plus though. Especially if Fallon's dribbled them out.'

She steps back and bows mockingly, arms stretching to encom-pass the cairns, the buildings, the mountain fortress which looms at her back.

'Welcome to Thell, pup of the Grey Towers. I'm Icecaller. And we're like nothing you've ever seen.'

26

the body can be enumerated in several ways
by the crenelations of the teeth
by the wet tumuli of vein and artery

—*Redwork and Bonework*, Wicktwister

Quickfish's first few hours in Thell prove how inadequate a statement that is.

Icecaller is an unforgiving tour guide, seemingly taking great delight in hurrying them through a whirl of unfamiliar sites with nothing but a few cryptic remarks flung over her shoulder.

They crest the low-slung mounds that hide Thell's dead, marked with intricate boundary posts and hung with brightly coloured flags which snap and bite in the freshening wind. The land stretches out for miles to east and west, peppered with small homesteads, framed by raised cairns with deep defiles between, where the grass lingers dark and weak, mixed with never-quite-thawed ice.

The buildings become sturdier the closer they draw to the mountain. Squat, scalloped structures, that might be forges or tanneries, and some that he doesn't recognise, their walls slashed with broad strokes of paint in deep red, burnt black.

'Inkworks,' Icecaller says, unhelpfully, gesturing to great pots which seem to roil ceaselessly over stretched fire pits. The air above their rims is thick with fumes. His eyes sting.

The inhabitants of the cottages watch them pass with flat eyes. Their hands twisting the necks of speckled mountain birds, plucking feathers from their breasts with quick, practiced movements, driving their fingers down the throat to remove guts, innards. The most wretched scraps are tossed to the animals that root around the mire of the cairns, squat as houses, bigger and wider than a cat, their shoulders and hips armoured with some kind of cartilage that shifts and clacks as they waddle about industriously. The cottagers chuckle as their striped jaws wrap around old bones, cracking down into the marrow, and pulling it out with strong, black tongues.

That morbid little feast merits more comment.

'Bonebadgers,' Icecaller says, toeing one out of the way to a chorus of yips. 'Ornery little shits.'

She stoops, throws a scapula low, underhand, and watches them race off, grinning. 'My sister loves them.'

She wipes her bloody hands on her trousers. 'You'll see why. Come on. A ways to go.' Quickfish tries to hang onto the brief enthusiasm in her smile as he slips over the half-thawed mud. Behind him, meat is skinned and the air simmers.

Even the geography of Thell leaves him feeling like an outsider.

The curves of the outbuildings fade back into the hills as they grow closer. The scent of ice is sharper as they thread their way higher, towards a brutal edifice that clings to the mountain like a scab on a wound. Pocked with shadowed chambers and walkways, it looms imperious; a ravaged, many-eyed face looking down on the dreaming dead.

'The Stump,' Icecaller says, her blue eyes bright and fierce. 'This is where the magic happens. And I mean that very fucking literally.'

She laughs a thin, sniggering laugh as she looks at their blank faces.

'No? I'm wasted on you, pups. You'll see. That's Skinpainter's thing. They basically' – her fingers wriggle – 'made it all up.'

She cocks her head, pouts. 'It's cooler than it sounds. Just you wait.'

Roofkeeper finally finds his voice. 'Don't they need you on the perimeter? We probably shouldn't take you away from your post.'

She raises an eyebrow at that. 'My post? Oh, southerners. I'm on the Council for the next three years. As long as I don't stab anyone or fuck anyone over, I can pretty much work where I please.'

More blank faces. Icecaller throws her hands up in exasperation, her spear whistling unnervingly through the air.

'God, what do they teach you down there? We're a me-rit-o-cracy, pups. Ever since the birth of the Republic. If you can pull your weight, and everyone knows it, you get into power. Just you, not your spawn. Minimises a prevalence of cunts in charge.'

She smiles.

'Not like you savages with your manycockracy. Inheritances, titles, power based on who you've come inside? Uh. No thanks.'

She shrugs, and her spear waggles. 'No offense, pup. I'm sure you're a perfectly adequate little spunkpocket.'

The next hour passes in much the same fashion, Quickfish and Roofkeeper speaking in a code of shared glances and rueful looks, Icecaller throwing sentences which explode in a series of barbs that seem half-affectionate, half-serious.

As they enter the shadow of the Stump, their guide holds up a hand. 'Wait, wait. Hold up. Come see this.'

Icecaller ducks into a jagged crack at the mountain's base. They leave its dark body stretching far overhead, slipping down a flaw in the rock lit with softly glowing panels, that pick out the jut of the stone. As they walk, Quickfish begins to hear noises – sharp cracks, yelps of pain, shouting. He throws another worried glance to Roofkeeper and receives another shrug in response.

In short order, the twisting path opens up into a low curved cavern, shot with light which filters down from high above. The mountain must be huge. Quickfish can distantly make out galleries filled with laughter and movement, spanning heights that make him dizzy. Most of the space below is taken up with a tiled circle marked precisely with blood-red geometrics. A few of Thell's great and good stand around the edges, watching the events inside with quiet interest, save for the occasional whoop of victory or shouted encouragement.

Inside the circle, two small bodies move and spar with sharp, fierce precision. A boy and girl, maybe six or seven, their heads and cheeks tattooed, brightly coloured hair clinging to their half-shorn scalps like the flags clung to the cairns. Their dark skin catches the light as they duck and turn.

As Quickfish watches, the boy dashes in, arms swinging wildly, small teeth split on the edge of a smaller battle cry.

The girl meets him with a wide stance, her palms open wide.

As he swings, she ducks, her right palm hitting him squarely between the legs, the left catching his jaw, sending him up and over her dropped shoulder. The boy hits the ground with a wet slap and a ragged burst of air. Quickfish winces.

Next to him, Icecaller whoops and punches the air.

'Yes! Get him, Nigh! Rip his nuts off!' She smiles broadly at Quickfish. 'That's my little sister. She's a nutter.'

In the circle, Nigh stops, looks down at the writhing boy.

The circle goes very quiet.

Her foot swings forwards with violent speed, and stops just short of the boy's recoiling chin, one scuffed toenail tapping lightly on his lip. A sniggering, snorting belly laugh falls out of Nigh, even as she helps the boy to his feet. She shoots a glance at her sister, and sticks out a small pink tongue.

Quickfish looks at his guide. 'What the fuck was that?'

Icecaller shrugs. 'What was what? We're at war, Pocket. You use what you've got.'

27

the naked work of the heart
follows raw rhythm
and we follow the rhythm
to better run the working heart

—Aestering Knotsong, No. 17

Shipwright looks down at the body on the bed, bandages wet with blood. Beside her, Shroudweaver slips his fingers into her broad palm. She squeezes tight, but doesn't look at him.

'We fucked up.' It's not an accusation, just an observation. She licks her lips, sucks at her gums. The faint taste of something sweet and spicy lingers.

She feels Shroudweaver nod.

'Will he make it?' It comes out drier than she meant, rasping the words. Her throat feels like a shaved plank.

'Perhaps. I'm better at corpses.' Shroudweaver's voice is soft, rational. He sounds tired. He *is* tired. Long hours spent with Fallon, mending the great rips in the man's body, salving the burns that crawled over his skin.

Working where the old bull had fallen.

She can read the guilt in his bones, in his wide eyes, his shallow breaths, his bird-cage ribs. He knows what's coming. Best to get it over with.

'You put a god in me.'

He nods. 'I did. More or less. Something small, something hasty.'

The guilt hangs in his eyes like mist. 'Borrowing a bit of power from the dead.'

Her ribs hold more than a borrowing. She feels fractured inside, filled with brittle glass and wet light.

She smiles sadly, sucks her gums again. That sugary taste lingers. 'I thought you said raising a god burnt out everything it touched.'

Shroudweaver winces. 'A controlled burning. A few scraps of dead soul. We were desperate. I would never,' his shoulders slump. 'I would never.'

'Seems like you already did.' A little cruel, that, but she can't help it. When she turns her head, someone else's ghosts dance across her vision.

'What was I like?' she asks, curious, in spite of the fire on her tongue. Slipping the words through that golden hum in her ears and over the electric feeling skirting the edge of her teeth.

He runs shaking fingers through his hair. A few strands drift loose and waft slowly to the floor.

'Terrifying. Beautiful. Perfect.'

She puts a hand on his shoulder, pulls him close. 'I never want to be perfect.' She's impressed by how steady she sounds. Inside her chest, someone's screaming. Not her own voice. Not even close.

His reply is quiet, muffled by the weight of her body. 'Do you forgive me?'

Does she? What's she forgiving, exactly? Nothing worse than the years before this. She knew what she signed up for. And despite what Fallon says, she has never flinched from a fight.

She holds him tighter, her fingers exploring his shoulder blades, his spine. 'Always, dearest. Always and ever.'

And even if it's not easy, it's true, and it's what he needs. She sees him come loose, and fall into her. There. Was that so hard?

She tightens the hug, 'You can't be perfect either. Deal?'

His voice is quiet, reflective. 'Perhaps.'

He's not really picked up on the imperative. She wonders whether to push it.

There's a pause as she feels the guilt curl in his brain, stretching its little sharp teeth. 'I'm a long way from perfect. Other end of the scale, I think,' he says. 'Do you know what they would have done to me, in the Aestering? For what I just suggested?'

She turns as Declan coughs raggedly and holds a cloth to his lips, catching the thick black clots, cleaning the corners of his mouth. She knows.

'Do you think he understands the cost? The bodies? The risk?'

Shroudweaver's voice seems far away. 'We left a lot of dead up there. And they all need to burn.'

Shipwright bites her tongue and fights down a flare of annoyance. She doesn't look at him as she brushes hair away from Declan's sweat-slick head. 'Of course he understands. He's squared it already.' She laughs dryly. 'Anything that stops that *slit* right?' She turns to face him. 'Except we both know she's a lot more than that.'

Shroudweaver moves closer to her. He lifts Fallon's lips and pushes his gums, watching the blood flush back. 'We do. But I have to stop her. For her sake. Before she goes any further.'

She flashes him a dark glance. 'She's gone a fair road already, love.'

The room stinks of copper and rot. She cracks a window, listening to the sound of the port flood in. The sea isn't far, not far at all.

Turning back to face Shroudweaver, she says 'We can't lead her here? You're sure? We've pulled her and Slick a pretty dance before.'

'No,' Shroudweaver muses. 'Not here, not Hesper. She knows we're here. She'll be expecting us to lure her in, find some way to force her to make a stand. And even if the guilds are leery of sallying out, they'll fight like cornered rats for their home. For their purses.'

Shipwright adjusts the covers, rubs contorted muscles. 'So, you're taking me back. To Thell. Both of us.'

She runs a critical eye over Fallon's scorched body as she kisses the taste of burnt sugar from her teeth. 'Like we didn't have enough problems.'

Shroudweaver looks up at her, one eyebrow raised. 'Where else do you suggest we go? The Halls are far and roaming. The Burners are all held under root and briar. We need something to end this. We need some*where* to end this.'

His voice drops. 'This needs to end.'

Shipwright sighs. 'Don't take that tone with me.'

Shroudweaver smiles sadly. 'Love. Salt-hair sweetheart. We knew it would come to this.'

'You knew,' she says, and there's that knife again like a hot blade turning in her heart, cutting hope from under her ribs. '*You* knew. And you said nothing.'

'I'm sorry, Ship. I am. I didn't think I had it in me. That she would push us this far.'

She stands, pushes her hair back. Below her, Fallon twists in the bed and moans. That sound, ragged and wordless, almost stops her throat. Almost.

'You *knew*. You've always had it in you. And I've loved you for it. You don't back down. Not even when you should. But you should have told me.

'You should have told me.' Again, and fiercely.

Shroudweaver places a hand on either side of her hips. 'I should have. I did.'

She pushes his hands away. 'Not in front of fucking Fallon. Not spilt out over some maudlin breakfast in the same wretched tower where my best friend fights for every spit-flecked breath.'

Her voice shakes. Worse, it burns. 'Not when we are going back there. To the blood, and the dark.'

His answer is weak. He doesn't even convince himself. 'We survived it before.'

Shipwright shakes her head. Feels tears burning at the back of her eyes. 'Not all of us. Barely any of us. Never *enough* of us.'

He moves into her again, kisses her chest along the sternum, up the collarbone. 'It's different now. We're different now.'

She winces. 'We might be, but are they? Do you remember the last time we were there? Do you remember their faces? Probably not. You were watching our friends. Our allies.'

She shifts uncomfortably, moving to swipe the cloth across Fallon's stubbled jaw. 'Me, I was watching your back. Which meant I was watching the rest of them.'

She moves her hand across the covers to take his. 'Do you know what I saw, love?'

His says nothing. His mind focused on diagnosis and remedy, on spittle and blood. So she says it for him.

'Rage, love. Rage and hunger. We ran with a wolf and we pulled it back right before the kill.'

He slides his hand loose. 'It wasn't that bad.'

She feels the anger inside her and handles it, like she always does, pushing it down until it barely frays the edge of her voice.

'If it wasn't that bad, then why have we never gone back? Three wretched years getting harried from pillar to post. Three years of drownings, deaths and burials, and we have never once gone back.'

'No need,' he murmurs. 'We still had options. There was still a chance.'

She almost thumps the covers, but stops herself short of Fallon's chest.

'No need? Sure. Then why no messages from our *allies* after the south melted to howling glass? I mean, Kinghammer always feared you. You were a shade too close to his enemies for any-thing else. But Skinpainter too? Quiet as a mouse for three whole years?'

She takes his shoulders, makes him look at her.

'They never asked because they never wanted to see us again. And we never went, because we were scared of what we might find.' She catches her breath, blowing a strand of hair clear of her face. 'Admit it.'

Shroudweaver's voice is quiet, clipped. 'You're right. I don't find it particularly charming, but you're right.'

Shipwright snorts. 'Well, you've had years of charm. A little truth won't kill you. But now' – she gestures vaguely northwards – 'now you want to go back. For the dead. For Fallon's bloody composite.'

'There's no place like it,' he says. 'What happened there, what we did there? There's more bodies in the fields of Thell than anywhere else.' He rubs at tired eyes. 'And the world's thinner there. I can reach through easier, bind them tighter. And . . .'

'And we're desperate enough now,' she finishes.

He pulls her a little closer. 'Yes, we are. But not done, right?'

She tries to hold herself stiff, tries to keep some of that anger against her lips. Because he lied and he might well lie again. Yet, there's his face, held in the light from the window, those same clean lines, and bright bones, those hollow cheeks. Those pale eyes watching her, waiting for the answer that will keep him going; that will keep them both going. One last light against the dark. Her anger drains like spring rain.

'Not done, love. Not yet.' And it's still true, it still feels good to say. She steels herself, then pulls him close, lays her lips on the top of his head, breathes him in. 'OK. This is going to happen, isn't it? Again.'

He nods against her, his cheekbone pushing her shirt against her skin. 'It has to. I'm out of ideas. Out of time.'

She holds him at arm's length. 'Thell, then.'

Shroudweaver's smile could bury bodies. 'Thell.'

28

the morrow
  the barrow
the sorrow
  the harrow

Thell. Shipwright had never even heard the name when she arrived in Hesper near enough two decades ago. Some godforsaken mountain city. The people here talked about it like something out of a folktale, or a nightmare.

'Heart of the Empire,' one old man had said, waggling a finger at her, his beard and tongue wet with drink. 'Barely human, most of them. Never mind that cabal of wights at the top.'

She'd nodded politely, moved her seat further along the bar.

'And him!' His hand insistent on her shoulder. She'd shrugged it off but he didn't seem to notice.

'Him. He's the worst of the lot. Foul southern magics. He raises the dead.'

She'd smiled, and turned her back. At least, until he had moved his hand to her wrist and pulled her round.

'He gave me this,' the man said, pulling his shirt at the neck.

A scar on his jugular, two livid purple crescents, touching at the tips.

'Leave the lady alone,' the barkeep had said, but nothing she'd done could put the old sot off. He'd spun his tale from spit-flecked lips, and more than that. He'd called the man, the Emperor, by his name. By his real name. He'd probably called Shipwright by hers too, not that she'd ever be able to remember.

Whatever name-stealing magic Crowkisser had used in the south had somehow reached back into her memories, ripping names loose like stitches along a wrenched thread. Shipwright could recall most things, not with utter clarity, but with enough to get by. Yet every scrap of memory she had was scoured of names.

She could still feel them in her mind, the space they should take up oily, and slick.

Funny how you got used to it.

The drunk hadn't left her alone. He'd retreated to the corner to mutter and glower about the dangers of foreigners, their magics, their strange food, their pretty hair. Then lurched into her in the alley afterwards, at least until the *Volante*'s captain had broken his wrist and his nose.

The *Volante*'s captain, too, used to have a name, used to exist, beyond memories. She could remember the cut of his hair, the gap in his teeth. She could remember the way he laughed higher than you'd think and the way he swung that big brutal sword; even the colours of his shirts, bright blue and gold.

It had been his fault she'd stayed, mostly. A few weeks arrived from the east and already her heart had been bursting for home. She'd been more or less ready to turn around, to see the end of this strange city, and its stranger people. Until she'd met the *Volante*'s captain, and his crew.

They'd run the place once, he'd told her, his arms waving with the assured confidence of every drunk man that'd ever given a tour of his city to a pretty girl. Every whitewashed loop given up to the greatest ship's captains. Even once they were dead and gone, and their skulls, as he'd put it, 'gone to glass', the loops had kept their names. Bitterhaven. Mirestem.

It had been the *Volante*'s captain who had first taken her to Thell.

Too busy with his own schemes, maybe a little too pleased with himself, he'd brought her along to a meeting with a bear of a man, broad like a bull was broad, with hair black as sea-rock, and an easy smile under a loud, ridiculous moustache.

Declan Fallon, she now knew. He hadn't changed much. Not that she'd ever thought he'd be such a constant in her life. Big enough to be an anchor, as he'd put it the one time she'd tipsily, stupidly brought it up.

Back then, twenty years ago, she'd been young enough and

new enough to think him just another lord of another big city. A fan of himself. Looking to make a mark on the world, by hitting it hard and often.

But if Declan loved himself, he loved his wife more. He held her close during his councils, kept her stood at his side, like a pillar, and stopped everything the moment she spoke to listen her advice. That, more than anything else, had won Shipwright over. Both Declan and Ship sat in the shadow of Arissa Fallon, the Lady of the Grey Towers. Not just that stern dockside figurehead, but the real power in Hesper, the actual noble blood. Shipwright had pegged that the moment she saw the pair of them together, watching Declan with his loud mouth and busy hands, while Arissa stayed quiet as a still pond, eyes reading the room with ceaseless precision.

It had been Arissa that had looked her up and down, like a drover reading horseflesh. Leant into Fallon's ear, and murmured. 'This is the one I told you about.'

He'd straightened up at that, focused in on Shipwright in a way that moved fast beyond courtesy. He obviously knew plenty about her, she didn't doubt that, but all he'd said, as he fixed her with an appraising look was, 'My wife says you have the most incredible ship.'

They needed a fleet, he said. But before that they needed a few good captains. Ships to run up the coast into the forbidding north. Word had come of this city, this Thell and its Emperor. It was, somehow, on the march.

The details, Fallon said with a swig and a smile, were vague.

That was where she would come in.

Not to sail so far as Thell, oh no, because who would ask that of her, and who would sail to a mountain, anyway?

Laughter. Some real, some forced.

No, with a bottle wave, just up the coast to the city of Luss, a big city, a proud city, and most of all, a rich city. A city dear to Hesper, and dear to Fallon's heart in the same breath.

The *Volante*'s captain was already committed, he had contracts, and gold that pulled him north surer than any lodestone.

Would she, they asked sweetly, consider coming along?

29

where that fire touched the world, the sky
flushed a darker blue
like a bruise
like light seen inside the lid, when the eye is closed

—*On Swallowing Gold*, Heartshamer

'Thell?!'

Slickwalker throws his arms up in exasperation. 'Why the fuck would we march on Thell?'

Crowkisser pours from the copper kettle and watches the leaves split and bleed into the water. 'Because Fallon's son is there.' She strains, blows, sips, then smiles.

Slickwalker throws himself down opposite her and begins worrying at his bootstraps. 'So? *Fallon's* in Hesper. Along with his *army*. And Shroud and Ship.' He peels off a boot, taking the sock with it, and winces.

'Stones below, my feet are raw.' He looks up. 'I did mention that right? Shroud and Ship. Both. In Hesper. With Fallon. Who nearly killed me.'

Crowkisser watches his worried face, its clean, dark lines. She smiles again. 'Yes, you did. But they won't stay there.'

He rolls his eyes. 'They're there *now*. Am I making sense?' He holds his hands out.

'Kiss, we finally, *finally* know where they are. We drew them out.' He rubs at his jaw. 'Not without some cost, at that. They hit hard.'

She glances across. 'I noticed that. I'm glad you're OK. But like I said, they're not staying. They're going to push north to where my father can work some meaningful magic. They need the dead. They need Thell.'

He scratches at his chin. 'You're sure of it?'

She nods curtly, crushing some herbs into her cup.

He watches them settle on the surface.

'How are the shakes?'

She sips, grimaces. 'Fine.'

He tilts his head. 'Seriously, Kiss? You can do better.'

She sips again, holding his gaze. 'They're fine.'

He shrugs out of his jacket. 'OK, I'll buy it. And the voices?'

She waves her fingers. 'Fine too. I'm just tired.'

He nods slowly, wearily, and starts working at the bones of his left hand with the fingers of his right. 'I'm not an idiot, Kisser. You're not as a good a liar as you think you are.'

She drains the cup. 'I'm as fine as I need to be, Slick. Don't make me explain it. You don't know the first thing about prophecy.'

He feels a surge of irritation. Bites his tongue. 'Obviously, or I wouldn't be out there risking my skin to find out something you'd apparently already heard.' He pauses, glances at the scurrying, squawking roof. 'From the *birds*.'

'You were never in any danger,' she says. 'The shadow protects you.'

He grits his teeth. 'In danger, Kiss? I was in *pieces*.' He wiggles his jaw experimentally. 'I can still feel it grinding.'

She steps closer, plants a foot either side of his thighs. Takes his chin, turns it. 'No permanent damage. Don't worry. I won't allow it. The shadow doesn't permit it.'

He bats her hand away. 'Do you ever think that maybe you don't know everything?'

She looks at him, baffled expressions flitting across her face. Confusion, then fury.

Slickwalker stands. 'Of course not. My mistake.' He glances up at the ceiling, at the twisted ropes, the charms, the rotten meat and bone. The ceaseless shuffle of the crows. 'This place is starting to stink.'

The shadows begin to tear at him as he walks away.

He half turns to look at her. The faintest shake in his voice.

'Tell me next time, Kisser.'

She watches his face and steps forwards, catching his wrist before it fades totally into the dark. Marvels again at the feel of the shadow on his skin, like silk, or driest snake-skin.

When she pulls him close he resists only a little. She runs a finger along his side, draws him in, guides him back to the chair.

Pushing him gently down she frowns, just enough for effect. 'Slick, the prophecies only show one pattern. The birds only see what birds see. It all needs corroborating.'

She turns back to the kettle, returning it to the flame and begins ordering cups, jars, herbs, everything back to its place. 'I wouldn't be much of a leader if I only acted on my own hunches. The more patterns I can see, the more eyes I have, the smarter I'll be.'

She licks honey off a spoon, smiles sweetly. 'I needed to put the cat among the pigeons, see which way they'd jump.' She grins wider, as she steps in and ruffles his hair. 'You were my cat.'

Crowkisser can tell that he enjoys her touch, even though he wants to push her off. She runs her nails lightly over the back of his scalp, watches even that small resistance crumble. 'I'm new at this too, Slick. It's not easy.' She feels the truth of that in her heart as it comes out, takes it, uses it to hook into him.

He responds almost immediately, takes her hand. Such nice fingers. He squeezes. 'I'm sorry. I shouldn't mouth off. I some-times forget how quickly all of this unfurled.' A flicker of sadness touches his eyes. 'Sometimes I can still see the trees in the south. Those big branches.' He grabs her waist. 'Thicker round than you.' He laughs. He does have a good laugh.

She wriggles free slowly, letting the folds of her dress linger against his fingers, and eyes him critically.

'This is a poor attempt at undressing. Sort yourself out so we can make up properly.'

Slickwalker salutes, wriggles his toes and starts working at the second boot. 'Can I get some of that tea?'

She touches her palm to the copper, just warm enough. She can feel his eyes on her back as she pours, stirs in honey and reaches across to set the cup by him. As she leans in, he grabs her hip and pulls her down to his lips.

'Am I being insufferable?' His words are muffled by her skin, his tongue light against her teeth.

She nods. He kisses down her neck, running his hands over her sides. 'How do you cope with me?'

She wriggles, bringing her mouth close to his ear, smells metal and sharpness and blood.

'How do I cope?' She lets the question hang, runs her tongue along his jaw.

'How, do, I, cope?' With every word, a bite as punctuation. 'Persistence. Affection. Inertia.'

She sits back, stares him in the eye. 'Plus, I really, really enjoy fucking you.'

Slickwalker laughs. A proper laugh, his eyes light. A rare thing. He wriggles an arm free, grabs the tea, cups it between them. 'I'm too cold to fuck. Ask anyone.'

She pouts. 'That won't do. You can't survive tangling with that pair and not get fucked. That's just unfair.'

He sips the tea, regarding her over the rim. 'Is that so? That's the rule is it?'

She nods confidently. 'Definitely.'

His face hardens. 'Do one thing for me first.'

Crowkisser tips his head, runs her nails through his hair, 'What?'

'Tell me why Fallon's kid is so important.'

She shrugs. 'Because if Fallon thinks he's safe, he'll fight. Fight hard. And that'll cost us. If he knows he's dead, or that we have him, Hesper'll open up like a nut. We can crack its gates without ever seeing the walls.' She unbuttons his shirt, kisses down his stomach. 'Make sense?'

Slickwalker nods as he watches her dark hair sink down his body. It feels so pleasant, it almost takes the sting out of the lie. He catches her hair. 'And the kid's in Thell?'

She nods, kisses him lightly.

He tugs. 'And that's why we need to march on the mountain?'

She smiles, slyly. 'Not convinced?'

He snorts. 'Of course not.'

She moves her hands down again, and he stops them, gently. 'Explain.'

She pouts. 'I'm not sure you're really getting on board with this.'

For once, he holds his ground. 'Explain. I need to know.'

She straightens, resting her elbows on his thighs. 'Dad's not just going to Thell for the dead.' She pauses. 'Well, he might think he is, but there's another reason.'

Slickwalker tucks a curl of wild hair behind her ear. 'What's that?'

'He's going back to the last place he won. The last place he has anything close to friends. He wants to feel confident again.'

Slickwalker twists his lips sceptically. 'Did the crows tell you that?'

She sticks her tongue out. 'Nah, I just know my da. He likes to feel like he's on the right side of history. Plus,' she says, fingers tracing lines in the dark hair of his calves. 'Thell's the biggest city around after Hesper. The Republic's a real power. They've done well for themselves.'

He catches her hands, traces the fingers one by one. 'So, aren't we just picking a bigger fight? If we march all the way to Thell, we'll tear ourselves ragged if we have to fight Fallon.'

'That's not going to happen. We're getting into Thell.'

His fingers stop. 'Into that mountain? It'll tear us apart.'

She shakes her head. 'We're getting in.'

He laughs resignedly. 'How do you know that?'

She grins triumphantly. 'The crows told me, of course.'

30

Spitethorn (perennial), being those flowers which first arose among the Spires. Preternaturally hardy, of sweet flavour. Rumoured to be drawn to sorrow and blood.

—*Lockstep's Botany Primer* (2nd ed.)

None of the legends of Thell had mentioned tea, or a copper kettle, leaves dancing in the pot. Legends left that kind of stuff out. You never heard about the choice of tapestries in the princess' tower, or the care taken in cutting the rushes that covered the floor.

Quickfish was enjoying the real Thell as it shucked off the husk of stories, as its people thawed a little, and the strangeness of every new sight shifted from terror to wonder. The more he saw, the more he realised how little he had seen, how sheltered his parents had kept him in Hesper and how much those high walls had hidden. And here he was with Roof, hundreds of miles away, seeing things no Hesper lad had ever seen before.

He squeezes Roofkeeper's hand at the thought, and the taller man turns to him, eyebrows raised.

'What?' he says, a smile on his lips, for once.

'Nothing. Just you. This. Here.'

A step or two ahead, Icecaller stops. She's kept up a fierce pace, an urgency in her step that Quickfish doesn't quite understand. The look she shoots back at him is the same as the other glances she's been stealing as they marched deeper into the Stump. Half pity, half curiosity, like she's looking at a dog who can dance. Her little sister perches on her shoulders like a rosy cheeked gargoyle, dismantling small, sticky fruit, and watching him with dark, flashing eyes.

Ahead, the passageway curves to an antechamber where coats and hats hang above stitched boots and a few scattered toys.

'Wipe your feet,' Ice mutters, and pushes aside a curtain at the far end of the chamber. Clacking bronze and beads announce their arrival. Beyond, Icecaller carries Nigh into a small room, and Quickfish watches as her entire body changes into something softer.

She sets the little girl down on a rug strewn with cushions and crosses to the woman by the kettle, snakes her arms around her waist, and plants a soft kiss on her shoulder.

'Right on time, love.'

Her voice is dark, steady, like rain on wood. She is a little shorter than Icecaller, but broader at the shoulders, her hair a soft brown, her eyes shadowed and her fingers flecked red and black with ink. Her belt hung with needle, scalpel and gauze. The marks of Thell's trade in tattoos. Skin magic. Blood magic. The sort of stuff that might save his mum.

The woman catches him staring and smiles, crooked teeth flashing.

'Oh, we have company.'

Ice settles another kiss on her cheek and slides into a chair.

'We certainly do. Steel, this is Quickfish and Roofkeeper. They're Hesper boys. Hesper boys, this is the best girl in Thell, Steelfinder.'

Steelfinder sketches a little bow. 'Welcome, welcome. Nice to have some new blood. Grab a seat, there'll be tea, there might be something to go with it if I'm left in peace long enough.'

She shoots a glance at Ice, who shrugs innocently. 'I'm just here as a chaperone for these two.'

'Mmhm. Honey as usual?' Steel waves the ladle.

'Yes, love.'

'What about you lads? It's nothing fancy, petals and spices. A little bit of heat and sugar to keep the cold off.'

Quickfish has settled in a chair that looks big enough for two, but isn't. Roofkeeper is balanced awkwardly on the arm.

'Sounds essential. Thank you.'

The cups are small, sweet things, hammered copper that catches the light and sends little pulses of warmth through his fingers.

Steelfinder hands a cup to Roofkeeper too, then joins Icecaller opposite them.

'So, what brings you to Thell?'

Icecaller snorts. 'They are being very fucking coy about that, love. Aren't you boys?'

Quickfish feels his chest tighten, feels Roof stiffen a little next to him too. It all seems friendly enough here, and there was no tea in the legends. But the legends were not kind, and visitors did not walk out of them.

Roof squeezes his hand and leans down. 'We didn't come this far . . .'

Quickfish nods, but there's a catch on his tongue, a little latch of fear. His palm itches, and he rubs the cup against it absently.

Ice leans forwards, Steelfinder's hand on her back.

'Look, you can tell us. In fact, I think you want to tell us. I know it's a big old scary place and my da's a shit-your-britches story for you Hesper kids, but I've known him since before he had grey in his beard and he's softer than you think.'

Quickfish frowns and sips. 'It's good.'

Ice smiles. A genuine smile. Not pretty, a bit weird on her stark face, but the first real flash of joy he's seen from her.

'Course it's good. It'll put a bit of fire in you.'

She toasts him. 'You've come too cold, to a cold place, Quickfish, but that doesn't mean there's no hope.'

Steelfinder crosses to where Nigh is playing and takes her by the wrist, bringing her back to the group, tucking her between Ice's legs and her own and stroking her hair softly.

'You can trust us, Quickfish. I know they all say that, but you've come a long way to keep your own counsel. Besides' – she elbows Ice – 'you have a line to the top in this one.'

Quickfish drinks again, holding the sweetness on his tongue, and swallows.

'Why would you help me? You've been pretty . . .'

'Obnoxious?' Steel finishes. 'That's her style. She thinks it's charming.' She nudges Icecaller. 'We haven't really cured her of that yet.'

'I'm unsalvageable,' Ice says. 'But I'll tell you why you can trust me, Quick. I am impatient, I am bored and I am way too ambitious to moulder away in this cold rock for my whole life.'

She sets her cup down and leans further forwards still. 'If we help you, we're back in the world whether my da likes it or not. Which means we get to go out in the world, and we have a chance to *do* something decent out there.' She waves a hand. 'Look at this! Pretty. Cosy. Dark. Unchanging. We need out if we're going to survive. Or some of us do, at least.'

Quickfish feels a pang of sympathy as he thinks again of those grey towers and those high Hesper walls.

Icecaller looks almost guilty for a second, then bats the thought away.

'We bottled ourselves up in here because my da, and the rest of them, waded through blood to get us free. And then we've . . . stayed bottled up in here because the South burnt, and the waves from that splashed us, even here. Where we thought we were safe.'

There's a shake to her voice. Steelfinder rubs her back a little more softly.

'And it's *stupid*. Because if the world can get us like that, what is the point of rotting in the dark? When we could go out and do something?'

'What would you do?' Roofkeeper asks.

Ice rolls her eyes. 'I don't *know*. Because I don't know what's out there, because I've never bloody been. But I've got a good spear arm, and half a brain, and I think I'm not a total cunt, so I'm pretty sure we could do something.' She sinks her head into her hands and scratches at her scalp.

'Look, I'm tired, *we're* tired of being locked away. There's a world out there, and it might be fucked or it might not be, but I know in my bones we can see it and still protect our folk here. It doesn't have to be either or. No matter what my da says.'

Quickfish laughs, and that little latch eases. 'Well, you are looking at the crown prince of ignoring your dad.'

Ice blinks. 'Did you say clown prince?' She snorts. 'Well, aye, welcome to the club. My da's a good man, but he fought for most of his life. He can't think of a peaceful world, or a road to it.'

She sips, swirling the tea around her mouth.

'He struggles to see it, they all do. They fought too hard and too long to risk what they've made, but Steel and I, we want more. Lot of folks here do.'

She glances down. 'And Nigh, she deserves better. Wider, wilder. This mountain isn't big enough for her.'

She kisses the top of her head. 'Is it, you little snot?'

Steelfinder gestures at the small girl. 'Look at her, she's got a world to conquer.'

Nigh burps and smiles at Quickfish, who holds his arms out reflexively. She walks across, climbs into his lap, and drums inquisitively on his collarbone.

'She's talking to you,' Steel says. 'That's how she talks. Learnt it from the Singers after she couldn't do anything else.'

Quickfish smiles. The little girl is surprisingly heavy, but she leans back against his stomach contentedly. 'What's she asking?'

Ice grimaces. 'Well, she *was* asking if you were a friend, but as usual, she's made her own mind up, without waiting for anyone else's opinion.'

She sets the tea down, fixing him again with that more familiar, harder look.

'So *are* we friends Quickfish? Are you going to tell me what you want? Have I bared enough of my soul to you, or do you need another bloody little piece?'

For a moment he returns her hard look in kind, but what's the point? He's come too far, and he's too desperate. His mum's still shrivelling in a starched seaward bed, and his pride isn't going to save her.

'I'm hoping there's someone here that can help my mum. Someone that understand blood and body. She's been lost since the South. Since Crowkisser came for her.'

'Lost?' Steelfinder says, skewering the evasion.

'Coma.' Quick says, and even saying it feels like lifting the stone on something that shouldn't see light.

'Shit,' they both say. 'I'm sorry,' Ice adds, and there's no hardness in it.

She sits for a second, thoughts running across her face like foxes over a field.

'Might be we can help you. Our resident warlock does things with bodies that I've never seen done, and Steel's no slouch herself.'

Steelfinder nods modestly.

'We could come with you even, if we get my da to agree.'

Icecaller pauses, exhales. 'I should go talk to him. Before you bring this before everybody. If it goes to Council first, and someone sticks their oar in . . .' She puffs out her cheeks. 'Then you're fucked. Or we're at this for months, which is worse than being fucked.'

Quickfish's head swims. 'Resident warlock?'

Ice nods. 'Skinpainter. Old as my da, I think. Doesn't look it. Was there back in the day when your mum came to fight for us, and brought half the western coast with her. I think it's safe to say that they're a safe bet.' She drums her fingers on Steelfinder's thigh. Realisation creeping across her face. 'Shit. If I can get my daddy dearest to agree, we could actually take a crack at helping you, at helping her. Tits on a snake, we could finally fucking *do* something.'

She wriggles her leg free of Nigh, and stands. 'You trust me with this, Fish? You're a wet nit, right enough, but I can do this for you. For us.'

She holds out a hand. 'Go on, skinny. Take a chance.'

Quickfish shakes her hand. It's warm, firm, the bones beneath the skin smooth and long. She holds him for a second, her fingertips kissing the pulse of his wrist. Her eyes are bright, shivering.

'I'm taking a chance', he says. She grins.

'Pretty and smart, eh? Maybe not a total disappointment to your big daddy just yet.'

She leans in and plops a kiss on his forehead. Laughs with her lips against his skull.

'Steel, I'm going now. I'll catch Da while his farts are still cooking. Look after the maggot and these two.'

She turns at the curtain, and smiles again. That warm, soft smile that's only escaped twice now. 'Something new at last, lads. Let me go piss of my dad so we can wake up your mum.'

It's quieter after she leaves. Steelfinder fusses with Nigh, adding some more honey to the kettle. Quickfish leans into the crook of Roofkeeper's arms and breathes. For the first time in months the weight in his chest shifts. Something else is stirring there, a little bird of hope fluttering in the dark. He lets himself rest for a second as he takes in the soft light of the room, the curls behind Nigh's ears, the clunk of the ladle against the rim of the kettle. Steelfinder's fingers move delicately as she crushes herbs and makes small talk. He drains the last of his cup and listens to the mountain. There is water running somewhere. He stands, lets his mind and his feet follow the sounds, crossing over soft rugs, to the dark curve of the walls, finding little green hollows where meltwater courses behind the stone, dipping into carefully carved cups, that hold plants, dark earth, pale blossoms.

The ice doesn't seem to touch them. Steel catches him looking and smiles. 'You like them?'

He leans in and sniffs, inhaling the lightest sweet scent, rising like morning. 'Very much.' Saying it cracks that stone in his heart and tears pool hot behind his eyes.

The young woman moves to stand with him, putting a hand lightly on his shoulders. 'Spitethorn. Terrible name for a lovely wee thing. Never understood it. No thorns on the damn thing.' She strokes the thin green shoots. 'They only really grow around here, over the top of the mountain and in the slopes of the glacier. Amazing. The bulb generates its own heat. Here, see.'

She takes his finger and sticks it in the earth. Distant, faintly, he feels a soft warm glow. She must see his smile, because she laughs. 'I know, right? Stubborn bugger. Melts its way right through the frost, the cold. It just wants to grow. It's burning to grow.'

She brushes the earth off his fingers. 'All it needs is a little space. A little time. Then something beautiful arrives.'

As she moves back to the kettle and the herbs, Quickfish turns to look at the small room, Roofkeeper dozing on the cushions, Nigh playing on the rug.

Perhaps that really is all that's needed. A little more space. A little more time.

Until something beautiful arrives.

31

neither thigh crack, nor ice
so long as the blood thrums

—Inscribed handbell, found in the ruins of Luss

The ice was always thickest in the morning. Barely visible in the heights of the mountain, more a blue haze that crept downwards over the rock, congealing into sleek, black sheets that limned the stone.

Bitter cold. Even beneath layers of fur and wool, bitter. Big as he was, bitter. Even with another body in the bed. Even with a few other bodies in the bed.

Thell's cold ate through everything it touched, the mountain bowing with the weight of the glacier. It was worse today, because Kinghammer was alone. And he was thinking. There were no soft legs twined over his hips, no arms over his chest. He'd needed space, needed time. Needed a little quiet for once. Thell would sit in his lap all year if he let it, and he couldn't think like that.

So he was alone, in bed, shivering like a skinned sprat.

A dull ache pulsed in the back of his head, and a hotter ache matched it by his hip, the result of a few mistimed thrusts on the practice ground, and later. He was showing his age, the machine of his body slowing down, beginning to fray at the edges. Little tears spidering into torn seams, a burning on the inside, as the heat of his life sputtered and sparked.

He snorts. Indulgent shit. If anyone else brought this whining to him, he wouldn't give them the time of day.

The world carried on, bigger waves of pain moving across the land. He stretches, and his back pops. A chill breeze steals beneath the covers.

One of those waves was breaking on his own shores, as if he'd not been working these past three years to keep Thell high and dry from all the other chaos. Tired young bucks walking endless patrols along tight closed borders. Skinpainter run ragged with the weight of it all, slapping ink and charm on every road leading to the Stump, and bindings on every barrow.

When that wasn't enough, Kinghammer applied a little violence; a few calculated burnings. Those border towns were mostly ghost villages anyway, hollowed out after Crowkisser's great fuckery. It was a small price to pay for peace, and didn't Thell deserve some peace, after all they had been through? Didn't *he* deserve some? A little quiet? A hand off the hammer?

He shivers again. That was all sifting to dust now. War inexorably arriving on the slim shoulders of a dandelion-haired boy and his young lover. He could see a little of Fallon in Quickfish, in the cut of his jaw, the set of his shoulders. He saw more of Arissa though, that flash in the eyes, like steel drawn underwater. The boy looked soft, but there was something inside him that wasn't built for breaking. And that scared him, the spirit of that woman come back to haunt Thell again.

He rolls over and buries his face in the pillow, muttering a curse his grandfather taught him. Fucking Fallon. *Fallons.* All of them. Stormriders, black dogs, cursed family.

And yet, he owes them, whether it sits in his guts like a goose egg or not. He'd bet rats to ribbons that Quick has come to collect, even if the boy doesn't know it.

Whatever he wants, it's going to pull Thell back into Hesper's orbit, and back into Crowkisser's shortly after that.

Kinghammer shivers again. Bitter, bitter cold. It'll get worse before it gets better. The morning sun hauling itself across the mountain takes a long time to bounce its way down into the dark.

He can feel the stubble speckling his jaw like spoil in the field – fuck it, a shave at least, a good way to start.

Right, feet on the cold stone. Chipped nails and blue veins. Old man's feet, his grandfather's legs stuck on his own aching hips. It's a miracle he can talk anyone into warming his bed.

He stands, and makes a noise like an old bellows, and a few other noises that don't bear mentioning. He steps to the bowl, the polished bronze of the mirror. There's enough of the man he recognises in the reflection to take the edge off. The Kinghammer still looks back at him, shoulders as broad as an ox, ribs like temple beams, and all the scars of all the wars he's ever fought and won.

Thell's free now, but it's freedom balances on the thump of a skittish heart, and he knows that better than most. Fretting. Pointless.

A shave then; the badger-hair brush, and the soap that Ice gave him, all sharp herbs and something musky beneath. She must have traded a pretty penny for that, listening to tattles and twits down in the Still Market.

He splinters the crust of ice in the bowl with the back of the brush, watching the little floes disappearing as he dips and soaps. The blade itself is the same one he's had for a long, long time. It's shaved a lot of throats, and slit a few too, in the early days. When he was desperate, before he'd properly learnt to fear the spilling of blood.

A pull, a scrape. The dipping of the blade. The movement of the ice. Water sliding across water. Silence rising to fill the room, threading the great cracks that lead to the mountain and the high ice.

Peace. Water splashed across the face. Bitter cold. Fingers through his hair, shivers along the scalp. Peace.

He hears her coming before she arrives, but it's still not enough time to prepare.

'You absolute feral little stoat! Give it back.'

Nigh enters a scuttling length ahead of her sister and positions herself neatly behind Kinghammer's legs. He ruffles her hair affectionately, accidentally dripping soap on her head. Icecaller is a beat behind, red-faced, wheezing.

She skids to a stop and glares at Nigh, who leans around her dad's thighs and shakes a necklace clutched in one grubby fist.

Kinghammer laughs. 'Morning, girls.'

Icecaller hisses. 'Dad, she . . . I . . . that little *rat*.' She stops, takes in the scene. 'Father dearest, everything in the shop front's on display.'

He grunts. 'Wasn't expecting company this early, was I? I should know better with you too.'

He slopes to the bed, dragging Nigh with him on one leg like a lead weight. Militantly slips some breeches on by unpeeling her fingers one by one, freeing the necklace at the same time and tossing it back to Ice.

'Thank you *very* much', she grins, sticking a tongue out at Nigh. Kinghammer lifts the little girl to sit next to him on the bed. 'Get me her brush would you, Ice? She looks like she's been wrestling a fox.'

Icecaller pulls the brush from a drawer, a pretty little tortoise-shell thing, with a stylised dog on it.

'Good fucking luck with that tangle of vines.' She sits next to Nigh on the bed and taps a few quick gestures on her shoulders and hands, laughs and kisses her neck as she coories in to her sister.

Kinghammer smiles. 'You two friends again?'

Ice nods. 'Aye, for now. A truce with the stoat.'

'Thank all that's good. I have enough fracturing alliances today without adding one more to the list'.

He brushes Nigh's hair with all the practice of years. 'Stone's teeth, Nigh, this is like wire.'

She giggles, and he pulls her to sit in his lap. 'Prison for you until you look more presentable.'

Ice laughs. 'You not gonna do mine, Da?' She tilts her shaved scalp towards him.

'Spit and polish would do you, you scruff.' He puts his free arm around her and squeezes.

'So, what are they like?'

Icecaller pouts. '"Morning darling daughter, so nice to see you, what an unexpected surprise when my raggedy old cheeks are still catching the breeze." No? None of that?'

Kinghammer pins back Nigh's hair and starts on another section. 'None of that. You know it all already.'

'I do, but I like to hear it.'

'Fine, beloved daughter, sweetest little eagle that ever flew the coop, what are they like? What do you think?'

Icecaller's face goes still as she looks up. High above, the light is beginning to cut through the cold. Thell is waking.

'I think they're trouble, whether they know it or not. They probably don't. Quickfish seems . . . wet. He wouldn't survive up here. His mama's ghost is sitting on his shoulders.' She slowly re-fastens the necklace around her neck, settles it on her collarbone. 'That's what he's here for. One last swing at bringing mum home, using our mysterious mountain ways.' She smooths the beads of the necklace, garnet glistening against the skin.

Kinghammer nods, picks something out of Nigh's hair. 'What the fuck is this? Fish skin?' He waves it at Icecaller. She takes it between finger and thumb. 'Bit of old lizard, I think. They're moulting down in the low galleries, and little Miss Maggot here thinks they are cute.'

Kinghammer smiles. 'We should get her one. Might do her good, having a wee thing to care for.'

Ice looks at her sister ruefully. 'Can't say as it did me much good.' She elbows her father and he kisses the top of her head.

'I'm trying to figure out which way to jump, Ice. It's a big risk.'

She nods. 'It is. And you've been awfully shy of risk the past while. Why is that?'

Kinghammer looks at her flatly. 'Think, beloved.'

Ice rolls her eyes. 'We are big enough and ugly enough, Da.'

He tuts. 'You might be. She isn't.'

He adds another burnished clip to Nigh's hair, gives her a toy to tinker with. A square of beautiful, polished little tiles that slide and click.

'That used to be mine,' Ice says.

'Yeah, and you were too daft to solve it,' he grumbles.

She mimics his tut, pulling a face. 'I can solve this for you though.'

His glance is sceptical. 'Can you, aye?'

'I can.' She crosses her legs. 'Look, I understand how it's been.

We were fresh out of a war, last thing we needed was a whole new catastrophe crawling onto our doorstep to die. We'd lost enough. *You'd* lost enough. Wee monkey-nuts there needed some peace to grow up in. All the kids in this echoing madhouse needed a bit of breathing space.'

'No arguments here'. Kinghammer ties off Nigh's hair with a few twists of ribbon, and sets her down. She squats and watches her sister, fiddling with the click and shift of tile.

Icecaller leans forwards. 'Get ready to argue, father mine. I get it, but it was a mistake. We built all this because of them. Because they got off their arse and helped us when no one else would. Were they slow? Sure. Did it all go quite to plan? No. But they were *there*. They showed up. The Fallons showed up, and that spooky pair you barely even mention. Shipwright. Shroudweaver.'

He opens his mouth and she holds up a finger. 'Ah! Be patient. Don't think I haven't seen how you, Skin, Bell, and the singing twins all carefully dance around the subject when we're planning for the future. And I get it. But we can't sail a ship over a reef by pretending it's not there. We need to know the shape of it. Where it will cut. Where we need to make ourselves strong.'

Kinghammer's expression changes, and he keeps his mouth shut.

'And Quickfish? This isn't even official. This is a boy who lost his mother, and aren't we in some kind of position to feel a shaved hair of sympathy towards that? Stone and spit, we might even be able to do something about it. I've seen Skin work. I've seen what Steel can do with ink, and she's still just learning.'

'It's a . . .'

'Risk,' she finishes. 'It is, but I'll tell you what's riskier. Sitting with our fingers up our holes until the rest of the world comes knocking.'

She slips an arm around his shoulders. 'Think of it this way. Think how grateful they will all be if we help that boy. Quickfish is the only thing Fallon has left. A puff-headed, undergrown hope for the future. We don't even need to succeed. We just have to try.'

She taps his temple. 'We owe it to them. We owe it to our-selves. And it's the smart thing to do.'

Kinghammer sighs. Nigh echoes him, for fun. 'I raised you smart after all, eh? Too smart.'

Icecaller's grin is wide and unrepentant. 'Just smart enough to take over from you when your last marble finally rolls onwards.'

Kinghammer stands, stretches, goes back to the bowl and mirror to finish up. Nigh traipses after him. He pulls on a loose shirt, and then a heavy jacket to keep out the chill. He talks to Icecaller's rippled reflection as he works.

'I take your point, but we can't have this out in open council. There's too many unknown quantities. If this *is* what Quickfish wants, there has to be no surprises. No dissenters. We need them all on board.'

Icecaller stands, scoops Nigh up en route. 'Oh, easy then. No strong personalities in this mountain at all. Not like you're cheek by jowl with a couple of wild sorcerers and two auld biddies who see the future in each other's farts.' She kisses him on the cheek. 'We do have to help though. So we can sleep at night.'

He grunts noncommittally as she sits Nigh onto her shoulders and backs towards the door. 'Good luck, mighty Kinghammer. Smack 'em into line. What's one old bellringer and a couple of tooth-suckers anyway?'

She steps on the toe first, then stumbles into legs, a long torso, and robes clacking with cold, black wood. The skin underneath is barely different, lean and hard.

Belltoller puts a hand on her shoulder, and gently steadies her. 'What indeed, young Icecaller?'

Ice looks up. Belltoller's hair falls over her brow, and a thin, dark smile cuts the long bones of her face. 'I rather suppose we will find out.'

'I . . . yeah . . . because, I mean. Nigh and I . . .'

'You can go,' Belltoller says. Icecaller shoots a strangled look at her da, but he's no use, already pivoting to face this new intrusion.

She shrugs helplessly, and Nigh waves cheerily as the pair retreat into the corridor that'll pull them back into less judgemental areas of the Stump.

As Icecaller turns the corners of the dark rock, two slight shadows flick past her, heads bowed, beads rattling. The Deadsingers are headed in exactly the same direction Belltoller just stalked, cutting through the half-light of the Stump's passageways like slinky little minnows in the wake of a shark. Ice winces and taps Nigh's feet. 'Shall we let the old folks tear each other to pieces, maggot?'

Nigh plants a damp kiss right on her sister's scalp, and she retches.

'Feels like a wet little agreement to me. Let's get breakfast, and go see the new kids, while Da breaks some eggs.'

A little away, Belltoller watches the pair go with faint amusement. She stands perfectly still, but her robes rise and fall, as if with some small unseen air. Her hands are folded neatly in front of her, deep lines and strong wrists. The heavy braids of her hair frame a face that is sharp, stark, amused.

'How bad indeed?'

She watches Kinghammer as he composes himself, all the familiar lines hardening. This isn't their first disagreement, and it won't be their last.

He starts to speak, and she raises a finger. 'Wait. The sisters are coming.'

The Deadsingers arrive shortly after, flanking Belltoller where she stands.

Kinghammer's eyes narrow. 'Ladies. Do you want to sit?'

'No,' Belltoller says. 'This won't take long.'

The Deadsingers nod in unison.

Kinghammer pinches the bridge of his nose. 'I've just had Caller and the kid barracking me, so can this wait?'

'No,' Belltoller says. A flicker of a smile plays over her face.

Kinghammer sighs. 'Right then. Let's get it over with. Say your piece.'

Belltoller glances down at the other two women. 'If you'll allow, sisters?'

They nod.

'Hammer, you'll forgive me being direct. We are both too old to be anything but. The current course of action is unsound.'

He laughs at that, and she frowns.

'Unsound? I thought it was a joke. You know? Bells?'

Belltoller's eyes are like two slips of agate set in a damp log. 'Hilarious. I mean the boys. The Southerners. Fallon's son, and the other attachment.'

Kinghammer nods. 'Popular topic this morning. Everyone wants to state their case before I have both legs in my breeches.'

The Deadsingers chuckle, a single, soft slither of mirth.

Belltoller doesn't. She steps closer, almost silent, the soft boots of her trade barely scuffing the stone.

'Every second we have them here is a risk. It draws eyes to us. First Hesper, then her.'

'I know that, Bell. I was thinking that myself. Ice says the boy is here to try and save his mother.'

Belltoller hisses between her teeth. 'Of course. That's all little boys ever think about. Mum and Dad can't die, because they are the *world* and the centre.'

She waves an arm, the wood charms at her wrist clashing. 'We have a mountain of mothers and fathers, Hammer. A mountain that we need to keep safe. We don't do that by pulling them into another war.'

'Scared of a fight, Bell?'

Her face drops, the composure broken for a second, before that glacial calm reasserts itself. 'Of course I am. You should be too. And don't you dare imply I'm a coward. After what I did for you? For this city? For our people?'

Kinghammer raises his hands like he's gentling a horse. 'Easy, we're still on the same side. We want the same things.'

'Do we, Hammer? Or do you want to be something impossible? You cannot be a ruler *and* a father *and* a friend. No matter what we owe the Fallons or anyone else, that is *done*. That kind of sympathy is weakness. It's water in the rock – the slightest shock and we'll shatter.'

He grimaces. 'Ice says we owe it to them. That we can't not help, not if we want to keep our conscience clear.'

Belltoller's eyes flash, the agate running with hill lightning. 'My conscience is clear. I will see the rest of the world break before we put our people into danger.'

She runs her hands through her hair and sucks her teeth. 'This is precisely the problem. Icecaller is too soft for the work and you are becoming too gentle for it. Peace has dulled your edge.'

'Careful, Bell.'

'Careful? The time for careful is long past. We need action. We need to put ourselves first. You need to remember where the centre lies.'

'It's a big world, Bell.'

'Don't fucking patronise me. Pay attention to what that world is doing to us. We are already tainted by what happened in the South. What's your name, Kinghammer? What's the name of your daughter? Either one?'

She raises an eyebrow, and waits. He does search for it, reflexively, but finds only the hole which swallowed the words, oily and slick in his mind.

She sees it on his face. 'Exactly. The world has come for us already, and that was *with* our borders sealed.'

'Shattering,' the singers say. 'The falling of one into another, and the making of a third. The breaking of the gold, and the singing of the dark. The mother, and the eye, and the sweet thread of sorrow.'

Kinghammer snarls. 'Spare me.'

'Sorry, my lord,' the left Singer says. 'It comes unbidden.'

'Sorry my lord,' the right Singer says, then softer. 'Amethyst. Cat bone. Flint.'

'What?' Both Belltoller and Kinghammer, briefly united in confusion.

'I said apologies, my lord,' the right Singer smiles. The geometrics on her hands seem to twist in the morning light as it crawls down the wall.

Kinghammer snorts. 'I suppose these two mystic coots agree with you?'

Belltoller nods. 'The singers have listened. To the wind, the dead, the things that move between the dead. They can see the path we are being pulled down. They tell me it has death at the end of it.'

The twins chatter like mice in the walls. 'Death coming to meet you, death coming to move you, to make you dance. To be a poor father, a headless mother.'

Kinghammer slams his hand down. The mirror rattles.

'Enough. By the binding and the blood, *enough*. We are not so faint and cowardly as to shy from helping one boy and his mother. His mother, who fought for us. Who lifted the blades when no one else would.'

'The past will not save you for honouring your debts, Hammer.' Belltoller's face is forlorn. 'The present is here, and the future will eat us alive if we do not take care.'

She steps forwards again, puts a hand on his shoulder. 'I say this because I am your friend, and I have been your friend longer than anyone in this cold rock. Do not welcome them in.'

Kinghammer looks at her hand. The neatly manicured nails. The deep seams of work.

'We can argue like this in private, Bell, but we can't do this in open Council.' He takes her hand and removes it, gently. 'That goes for you two as well. If you're worried about cracks, then the four of us butting heads in front of every pot-boy and rat-wrangler is going to send a clearer message than anything we do with Quickfish.'

He looks Belltoller dead in the eye. Her breath runs fast beneath the robes, her heart hammering. There's a tightness in his own chest. 'I need you on my side, Bell. The Singers too. We need to help this kid. It's a little thing. An easy kindness.'

Belltoller steps back. 'There are no easy kindnesses, Kinghammer. Any ease we ever had drowned in the depths of this mountain. We do not get it back. We cannot earn it back. You'll see. I can feel it. Like a black dog on my neck. This will doom us.'

He nods, resigned. 'So it's a no?'

'It's a no, Hammer. It has to be.'

Kinghammer sighs. 'And from you too?'

The Singers look at each other, then nod. 'No doors for the bloodwind, my lord. No bones for dog teeth.'

He looks at the three of them. 'Clear as I'll get, I suppose. Get out.' It's quiet, but he means it. Belltoller still stands uncertainly, and the last shred of his patience frays. 'Get out. Give me some air. I need to think.'

The trio leave as softly as they came.

In his bedchamber, the Kinghammer sinks onto the edge of the bed, and tilts his gaze to the blue ice high above, to a glimmer of something there.

Maybe light. Maybe fire. Maybe the hunger of the glaciers creeping downwards once again.

32

Better loose hands than an ill-tethering.

—Burner saying, last heard at the signing of
the Black Accord

Belltoller leaves with a hammering in her heart. Unconsciously, she stretches her hands out to either side. The Deadsingers take one each, leaning their heads consolingly against her arms. They smell as they always do, of fur and smoke, cider and blood.

The trio take a path back towards the heart of the Stump. A little food might help. Stone knows she doesn't want to split the Council over one wayward lad, but this risk? It's too much. The Singers are some comfort, though rarely do they speak up. Theirs is a life of ritual and reassurance, they don't take to disruption easily.

A little food, she thinks, and a stiff drink. Perhaps there is a way through this.

She almost doesn't notice her new company as they emerge from the shadows. One of the mountain's innumerable alcoves disgorges ragged robes fluttering red, yellow and red again. Skinpainter's amber eyes catch hers and the Deadsingers flinch, shrinking into her shadow. Belltoller stands tall, but she can still feel the pulse crawling in her throat.

'Painter.'

'Ladies. What a pleasant coincidence.'

Skinpainter's smile is light as a knife in the darkness of their hood. 'Been breakfasting with the Kinghammer?'

'He hasn't eaten yet,' Belltoller replies. Like that's relevant. She's off-balance.

'Really? Rather you than me then. The old bear gets twitchy

when his blood runs cold.' They match her stride as they continue through the Stump. A group of young soldiers hurries past, late for training. They smile at Skinpainter, flicking their tattoos in quick salute. Belltoller notices the eddy they leave around the Singers and her own tired feet.

'All well though, I trust?' Skinpainter's voice is warm, friendly, like a banked fire. 'Strange times, with new visitors. Little stray dogs that Icecaller's brought in.'

'Strange times indeed,' she concurs.

'Good to be able rely on one's old friends, when the world shifts.'

Belltoller makes a noncommittal noise.

'Times like these, we remember how much we owe to each other. Wouldn't you agree?'

She turns to look at them. The warlock is always bigger than she remembers, something strange about their shape in that robe. The sense of something being held back. Like staring into one of the deep caves, and only too late noticing the spoor of wolves or bear.

'I have a good memory, Painter. Better than most.'

They nod, smile softly again. Their warm voice like honey heated and stirred. 'Of course, then you will remember Twice-fallow, and the sound it made when it broke. You will remember what was almost lost there. And you will remember who brought it back.'

Warm words that slide ice into her heart. She moves to step away, but their hand is on her wrist. Such strong fingers, honed from the work of moving ink and blood.

'You do remember, Bell? Do you remember that high sound in that dark night? Do you remember what followed after?'

'I can never forget, Painter. What is your point?'

'My point, old friend, is that sometimes, a little change can scare us, but when we remember how we have overcome adversity together in the past, than a little change seems small weather for our sturdy boat.'

Skinpainter waits. They watch the Deadsingers, whose eyes

flash in the half-light. They have paused just before the passage opens up into a warmer cavern. Food, and drink; laughter and light just beyond.

Skinpainter waits. Belltoller's hand twitches. For a second, she brushes the metal curve of the bell beneath her robes, watching as Skinpainter's own fingers move, just a little, in response.

'Are we rowing in the same direction, Bell? Or will we be swept away like the good people of Twicefallow, who made one resounding mistake?'

Their amber eyes hold her like a moth trapped in resin. She matches it, for a time, then slumps.

'You want my assent in Council.'

Skinpainter inclines their head. 'If you are offering it so freely, who am I to refuse?'

Her lips set in a hard line. She fights the urge to spit. 'In re-membrance of our time in Twicefallow then.'

Skinpainter's voice is soft, pleased, like a cat. 'I am glad to hear it old friend. For truly, is that not the burden of your name, and your trade? Shall we focus on the sound of the bell, and forget the toll?'

'I think not,' she says, clipped, furious.

'Then I look forward to your assent when young Quickfish brings forth his petition.'

Belltoller steps forward. For a moment it seems as though Skin-painter will not move, but they bow graciously, and wave her past. She storms outwards, towards the smell of frying venison, towards some honest light.

The Deadsingers move to follow, but Skinpainter is there again, red and yellow flickering in the dark of the passageway. Their smile sharper than before.

'Singers. I require your assent, in addition.'

The pair look at each other. The left mutters something, and the right amplifies. 'No debts to pay to your double-flesh.'

Skinpainter actually laughs. Light and easy.

'Of course not, ladies. No debts. For you have always stayed clean and clear. Reading the wind, and the songs, the murmurs of the dead and those moving towards death. Ah, I understand how soothing it must be.'

The warlock steps closer. The Singers look at them. Elderly women in the end. Small. Slight. Frail.

'How soothing it must be,' Skinpainter says. 'And how quickly these things can change. If we don't take care, tomorrow, the very wind might fall still. The dead could finally find peace. Silence would descend on you both. Like a shroud.'

The pair say nothing, but step closer together. Skinpainter laughs again. 'Of course, we do not need to worry. We will remain united. We will support our friends. And we will prevent harm coming to one another. Yes?'

The question hangs in the half-light. Eventually, the leftmost sister nods.

'Yes', says the rightmost.

'Excellent,' Skinpainter purrs. And their voice is softened butter, and the hearth of home. 'I'll go and tell Kinghammer that this misunderstanding has melted away like ice before spring. Take care, dearest ladies.'

They step into the shadows again, turning towards Kinghammer's chambers.

Alone now, the Singers look at each other. They say nothing, but the song flows between them. Moving in breath, in the flicker of an eye, in the blush of skin. The dead and the living singing. The pulse of blood keeping time. The metre of the mountain, and the high notes. The flourish of hawks, and the thrum of change.

Two women, elderly, slight and frail. Staring into each other's eyes, and seeing in that reflected light the split between the world that might have been, and the world that must now inevitably come.

33

Mark the stock precisely on the brow and tongue
if grazing the higher pastures, place a tar-salt brand
on the rightmost foot.

—*Practicalities of the Longer Years*, Softcatch, herder

'. . . and let no man do you harm.'

Swift, precise strokes, brush and needle working over skin like a feeding bird.

The echo of the crowd like celebrants.

do you harm.

The broad honeycomb of the Stump above their heads, its paths worn smooth by the feet of generations, its caverns roiling with the echoes of the ritual.

Quickfish stands amid the gathered people of Thell and feels deeply alone. Distantly there is the sound of bells, doubled and discordant. The needle dips, spits, colours. Geometrics of stunning intricacy, black on red on white. The colours of the city; blood and bone and stone.

A half-stripped man sits on raised steps, the crowd clustered around him young and old alike, but almost all of them lean, hard as mountain rock. The tattooist works over his shoulders, weaving a right-angled web, her head dipped low in concentration. Her short brown hair is marked with ritual scars, laced with charms that rattle softly with each twist and turn. At her side stands a small cup of some clear spirit that she swirls around her mouth every time she licks the needle clean of ink. Her lips are tight against his cheek, whispering words to him that he needs to echo back. With every square completed, he repeats the refrain.

'Know the dead. Honour the dead. Let them be still in you.

And as they are you . . . let no man do you harm.' A pause in the incantation as the tattooist's head dips, as her teeth skirt shoulder blades and bite deep. Blood flows, pools in the corners and lines of the forming geometrics, fills them precisely. Not a drop escapes.

The lights above hiss and spit, fuelled by the same bright energy that pulses through the rest of the Stump, some kind of sorcery that Quickfish has never seen worked before. Under their glare, the blood stiffens and hardens. Over and over the process is repeated, the hall filled with soft, insistent call and response, the voices of the crowd as steady and regular as the patterns that gradually thread over the man's shoulders and spine.

By the time they are finished, the man's back is a sea of squares. He moves, stretches, and the geometrics shift softly, riding against muscle and tendon.

The tattooist staggers as she inks the final line, falls, is caught by willing, ready hands. She disappears into the shadows of the Stump. In the distance, a bell tolls.

Quickfish glances across at Roofkeeper. He looks vaguely sick, fingers tugging at his beard, like there's a thought in his head that he doesn't like.

Quickfish leans across, runs his chin against his cheek. 'Go on then.'

Roofkeeper smiles. 'That obvious? OK, fine. I miss Hesper. I'm not sure we should have come here. I don't think these people can help us.' He pauses, coughs out the incense-thick air. 'Or want to help us. You've seen what Icecaller's like. We're a joke to her.'

Quickfish sucks at his teeth, slips his fingers into Roofkeeper's hand. 'Maybe. Maybe. I don't see what other choice we have right now.'

Roofkeeper watches as the crowd disperses, flowing up and down into the other levels of the Stump. They hadn't been allowed to explore much yet, but he'd quickly figured out that the portion of the city which jutted out from the mountain was just a sliver of something much larger. Multiple storeys, running up and down, maybe even into the bedrock, or the caverns beneath.

He could feel them under his feet, a sense of something vast and echoing.

A little like those moments on the very edge of a roof. Hanging by nothing but a few feet of rope and harness. Your belly clutched by the wind, and acres of hurling air between you and the ground.

All these people had to go somewhere; there were a couple of hundred in this room at least. Factor that up by the size of the mountain, and Thell was holding two, three thousand. Somewhere. None of them particularly helpful.

He turns to Quickfish. 'Just because this might be our only option doesn't mean I have to like it. How long have we been here now? Two days? Three? What do we actually know about these people? What have they actually offered us, other than insults and' – he waves his hand after the crowd – 'whatever that was.'

He watches Quickfish's mouth open to correct him. Holds up a finger.

'A minute, Fish.'

He waits, bless him.

'I've been thinking. I'm not even sure this is our only option. My granddad always said, the Burners . . .'

Quickfish butts in. Roofkeeper wonders if he got that from his dad.

'The Burners are hedge magic. Nothing of theirs works for long out of the forest.' He laughs, 'Dad bought a present for Mum one time. Spent a fortune on it, if you believed him. Some kind of bird, made of blossoms. It'd sing every morning when the light hit it.' He smiles at the memory. 'For a couple of weeks, at least. Then the flowers all started to wither, and the branches of its little cage thing turned to dust.'

Roofkeeper grins, despite himself. 'What happened to it?'

Quickfish can barely keep a straight face, 'It stopped singing sweetly. Escaped up into the rafters. Would only respond to the moon.' He cracks up. 'Every night at midnight, we'd hear it screaming around up there, like a wasp in a cowbell.'

He stops, gets his breath. 'I guess it died, after a while. Not soon enough for Dad though. He didn't trade with the Burners for months.'

He steadies himself on Roofkeeper's arm as they wind their way downwards. 'What I'm trying to say is, I get your point, but can we just give this a bit more of a chance? There might be someone here who can help Mum, and, well, at least we know they've got some really strange stuff going on.'

Roofkeeper nods. 'Strange is right.'

Quickfish takes his hand and leads him back towards where he thinks Icecaller might be.

'Roof, I love you, but we come from a city where we put dead people in glass urns so the earth won't take them. We throw ourselves off the Towers for sport. We drink in *most* of Hesper's dockside pubs. We are not allowed to call other people strange.'

Roofkeeper snorts. 'But that's *our* strange, Quick.' He catches a look. 'Fine, fine. A good point, smugly made.'

Quickfish smiles. 'I take after my folks sometimes.' He thinks. 'Actually, they might be a bit stranger here, but there's reasons for it. My dad always said the folks in Thell were different after the Empire fell. Something about keeping to themselves for safety. I don't think they were allowed to do much together, back in the bad old days.' He shrugs. 'Dad was never much for history. Even the stuff he was involved in.'

'Rich people,' Roofkeeper murmurs. Quickfish jabs him in the ribs.

He follows it with a soft kiss on the cheek. 'Let's see how it shakes out, please?'

Roofkeeper turns his jaw with a hand, kisses him back deeply. 'You're such a terrible optimist. I'm doomed.'

'He's right you know.' Icecaller's voice cuts in. They've walked to the edge of one of the stepped tunnels that slopes through the mountain. Her legs dangle from the alcove above as she looks down at them with a wry smile twisting her raw-boned face.

Quickfish tries to smile politely. 'Right?'

Icecaller shrugs. 'Right. You're probably doomed.' She slides down until she's sitting opposite them, cross-legged, long fingers twisting expressively.

'I mean,' she says, rolling her neck. 'Look at the facts. Your dad runs Hesper. Everyone knows he's a problem.'

Quickfish's face darkens like a spring storm. She holds up a pacifying hand, palm out. 'A problem to that skinned nit of a girl in Astic anyway.'

She tips her head. 'Or maybe, maybe, more of a challenge.' She points at Quickfish, 'Your big pappy kept his name, right? That takes, fuck, I dunno . . . Guts. Stupidity. Both. He kept his *name*, and he kept his city. That's got to sting. Hesper's not pretty, but it's got clout.'

Quickfish catches Roofkeeper's brief smile.

Icecaller continues, oblivious. 'Clout, yeah. And. *Annnnd*. And he used to hang out with that mad sailor cunt, back before the Republic was a thing, fuckin' yeaars ago.'

Quickfish nods. 'Shipwright. Yeah, they've been friends for ages. As long as I've been alive, at least.'

'What did they even do?' Icecaller asks. 'Other than set us up in our big stone home?' She slouches. 'I've never been very clear on the rest. Something spooky with Skinpainter. Then, what, dicking around at politics and proxy wars for two decades and change until they sailed a big old fleet down south a few years ago? I remember hearing *something* about that. Not much. Didn't end well.'

Quickfish shrugs. 'Dad doesn't like to talk about it. I hear bits sometimes. Something happened in the south. Something big. It changed things, I think. My dad, Shipwright, Shroudweaver. They all tried to stop it. It didn't work.'

Icecaller watches closely, all the nervous energy drained from her, still and cool as her namesake. 'Changed things how?'

Roofkeeper coughs, clears his throat. 'Changed the . . . what would you call them? The rules, the fundamentals.'

Icecaller picks her teeth with an old tattoo needle. 'Rules of what, vagueboy?'

Roofkeeper purses his lips. 'Magic, I think. Religion, definitely. That's when the gods went. And our names.'

Icecaller examines the end of the needle. 'Wow. That's a lot.'

Quickfish nods. 'Yeah. From what I can figure all *this* . . .' – with a despairing sweep of an arm – 'all this is fallout from that. Where Crowkisser comes in, I don't know.'

Icecaller smiles, picks at the muck between the crazed tiles of the alcove. 'I can hazard a guess. I gotta theory. Want to hear it?'

Quickfish waits.

'OK then, so think on this. Your dad, and Shipwright, and the other one. The skinny bloke.'

'Shroudweaver,' Roofkeeper supplies.

She waves dismissively. 'Yeah, that guy. So the three of them get this big old fleet. We've all heard the stories. Golden sails, amber winds. The burnished armour of the brave people of Hesper. The first show of any fucking unity since any dusty old cock can remember.' She frowns, 'Or since they helped us out, at least.'

She pauses, grabs a passing wrist, kisses it, slaps the ass of the man who owns it. 'All of them, all of them sail down to this mysterious southern place. That big old city that must have existed, and none of us can bloody remember. And we don't know what they do down there. But . . .' and here she raises a finger. 'But who comes back? Three people, and one ship. And a story about a ragged girl that does supremely unsettling shit with birds. The rest of us kicking our heels up here, we don't know anything. Except, if you read the records, what does it say?' She grins toothily at Roofkeeper. 'Go on, you say it. I'd like to hear it come out your sweet wee lumberjack face.'

Roofkeeper winces. 'The books say . . .'

Icecaller widens her eyes and paints her face with excitement.

Roofkeeper sighs.

'The books say, that on the last day, before the Shipwright and the Shroudweaver came to the city in the south, that the sky grew sick, that the clouds fled like sheep before a wolf, the sun and the moon split and ran and that the roof of the world peeled open.'

Icecaller claps excitedly. 'Go on, this is my favourite bit.'

Roofkeeper scratches at his beard. 'The way we tell it, it wasn't an accident. The way we tell it, the daughter of crows peeled the roof of the world open, so that the eye of the heavens was turned full on us and the stars fell into the south. And ever since, the rules have changed. But no one knows how. Not exactly. Depends who you talk to. Some things are harder, but I've heard that you can do stuff now that wasn't even possible before.' He coughs, 'People agree on some of it. There's no gods. There's no hosts. There's no names.'

Icecaller grins delightedly. 'Except your fuckbuddy's dad. Always a wrinkle. Still, you're well-informed for a . . . whatever you are.' She looks at Roofkeeper quizzically.

'Carpenter,' he mutters.

'Carpenterrrr,' she draws the word out, lets it hang thickly on her lips. 'The wayward spunkpocket of a famous war hero. And a carpenter.' She snorts. 'This is getting interesting.'

Quickfish smiles. 'What's your theory then? Before the compliments overwhelm me.'

Icecaller doesn't bat an eye. 'Yeah, *so*, all this goes down in the south. And we know it's true right because it's in books and when have they ever lied to us?' She rolls her eyes. 'OK, so the fleet sails down. With your dad, Shipwright, Shroudweaver. Then, somehow, the sky falls. Seems safe to assume everyone in the south dies. But,' she grins. 'Where the fuck does she come from? Crowkisser. Where. The. Fuck. Does. She. Come. From?'

Quickfish and Roofkeeper glance at each other, puzzled.

Icecaller's face splits wide with satisfaction. 'It's simple, pups. Armies don't fuck shit up that badly. Allies don't fuck shit up that badly. Friends don't fuck shit up that badly.' She holds up her fingers and ticks them off. 'There's only two things in the world that can fuck shit up that badly. Families.' She fixes them with a hard stare. 'Families. And lovers.'

It hangs in the air between them for a moment, before she pats them both on the cheek. 'Speaking of which, let's go and meet mine.'

34

No sweet bread baked from sour grain.

—*A Litelle Marchaunts' Almanac*, excerpt

On reflection, Roofkeeper thought, the Stump wasn't really that strange. Or rather it was, but only because it was so new. He'd expected the north to *conform*, to fit the stories he'd heard as a child. A fierce people. Hardy. Stoic. Resilient. Building their chill Republic in the heart of the mountains.

The north had not conformed. If there was a sound that defined Thell, it was laughter. Echoing down the halls, triumphantly, cruelly, affectionately. The people of Thell laughed as they talked, as they ate, as they fought and fucked. It was growing on him.

Laughter, and after that, the sound of the bells. Those distant off-key tones he'd been hearing ever since they arrived. Resonating aquatically through the scoured corridors of the Stump. He'd found it unsettling at first, but now they faded into the background wash of the city – mostly. Sometimes, the tones would shudder disharmoniously, and he'd feel the hair on his neck rise.

He'd glanced at Icecaller the first time that happened. She'd responded with her usual chattiness. 'Tolling for the dead,' she'd said. Then again. 'For. The. Dead.' Repeating it slowly and carefully, as you would for a slow child.

She was an interesting one. He could see that Quickfish thought it too, although, he, in his sweet, affable way, was clearly burning to impress her. Or if not to impress her, at least to thaw her a bit, to find some crack beneath the put-downs and the swagger. What little softness she had shown with Steelfinder was shuttered and barred as they stalked through the more public areas of the mountain.

Roofkeeper, for his part, enjoyed the severity, her hacked back hair, her stalking walk. The blood-red geometrics that thronged her temples and cheekbones.

She'd caught him watching her a while ago and stared back levelly. Something had passed between them briefly and he'd risked a half-smile. When she smiled back it didn't feel like a connection. It *did* feel like a victory.

She was taking them to the council chamber now, confident that she'd softened her father enough that Quickfish's plea wouldn't fall on deaf ears. Roofkeeper hoped she was right. Petitioning the council meant forging through the heart of the Stump. Anatomising the life of the mountain. With Icecaller at their head, they pushed into places that no one from Hesper had seen in years, if ever.

Roofkeeper was reminded of his early days working on the tiles and turrets of Hesper. Peeling back thatch, pin and beam to gaze into abandoned attics and ruined rooms which hadn't been touched for decades, places which had sunk off plans, and maps. And of course, nowhere that looked empty really was. In Hesper, those hidden spaces had been filled by orphans and gutter rats, criminals and spies, traders in things that couldn't been sold under clear sky.

Peel off the roof of the mountain, and Thell was crammed with life. The legends had offered a fell king, perhaps a strange warlock or a cursed daughter. The reality was a thriving city that was part barracks, part bazaar, part cathedral. The halls rolling with the sound of bells and the drift of incense. The sizzle of oil and the clink of tankards. It could have been chaos. It had *felt* like chaos, to begin with, but the city's founders had carved out something with purpose. The city was more organised than at first blush. He could see workshops, smithies, artificers as they walked. Everything had its place, and everything pulsed with life.

The more he saw, the less alien the Stump became. Less alien, but no less strange. A better sense of its geography helped. Some-where, hundreds of feet above, were the tops of ancient glaciers, the beginnings of the utmost north. Somewhere, hundreds of feet below, were deep caverns. Artesian wells pushing springs up into the body of the mountain to be channelled, diverted and pooled.

Sandwiched in between, eleven or so levels of interwoven tunnels, housing the growing throng of the Republic, not nearly as inaccessible or as insular as he might have believed. Roofkeeper was surprised to find himself relaxing. Here, of all places. Now, of all times. He wasn't the sort of man to turn down a little grace though. He slipped his hand into Quick's, and squeezed softly, was rewarded with a smile in return. Icecaller glanced back at them and made little kissy noises before picking up the pace. He risked another smile in her direction, was rewarded with an eye-roll. Progress, progress.

As Icecaller led them onwards they moved into a broad cavern with stalls haphazardly racked up the walls, pushing through a swelling holler of voices in a welter of dialects and accents. The clatter steadied his heart further. A little hint of home, something of the burly tone of Hesper in these merchants' voices. He could see Quick felt it too, watching his eyes light on stall after heaped stall. It shouldn't have surprised him that Thell survived on trade. He couldn't imagine the slopes of the mountain producing much, beyond a scattering of hardy, brutal little sheep.

Amid all that bartering and bickering, finally, a bit of breathing space. Icecaller was too far ahead to mind them, glad-handing stallholders and street rats with seemingly equal enthusiasm. Still, the clamour was almost too much to take in. The skirling sounds of some kind of flute crashing into a stringed instrument whose player kept half a hand on the music, half on turning a great spit of crackling meat which smelt mouth-wateringly good.

Roofkeeper tugged Quickfish's elbow, pointing. A sprawl of tents marked the stalls of the semi-nomadic people from the north, elaborately painted in swirling designs of white, blue, orange. Their wares arranged with utter precision. Layered and stamped hides; dried bunches of powerful herbs, Elsta's Folly, Slipwort, others he didn't even dare guess at.

A few steps down from them, a burly woman lay atop massive

sacks of salt, one leg cocked up as she scanned the crowds and rubbed her raw palms off on her scarves.

'It's like a circus,' Quickfish whispered. Roofkeeper could only nod in agreement as they passed under raised stalls with swinging scales where moustached workers from the Midlands weighed out crops and grain, sifting the seeds between their hands, purple and red and dark brown.

Opposite them, a wiry man worked a clay oven, turning out breads studded with the same grains, that smelt soft and rich as an autumn morning.

Quickfish's heart leapt a little at the sight of traders from the Burners' forest. Soft pelts spread with intricately worked amber; charcoal, for painting, sketching. Their bright eyes, perpetually smudged faces, and quick hands offering charms made of beetle-shell and nut, woven with thorns. Haggling back and forth, lithe young men listening intently to elderly women bent and gnarled over the details of a brooch, a hilt, a blood channel.

More and more, in bewildering profusion, until he was almost grateful to watch Icecaller disentangle herself from a wide-eyed young man in a threadbare cloak, and swan across to them.

'Try one,' she says, thrusting out two skewers. Some kind of pastry, glazed with sugar that puffs hot steam into their mouths as they bite in.

She watches them as they chew. 'You like it?'

Roofkeeper nods. 'They're good.'

'Yeah,' she says. 'Kids love them.'

He decides to let that one slide, though he tries a barb in return. 'I can see why Crowkisser might be afraid of you.'

She cocks her head at him, lips half stuck with sugar. 'What?'

Quickfish turns, his face frantically miming a shut up, but Roofkeeper doesn't much feel like it. 'I said, I can see why she's scared of you.' He gestures at the market. 'All of this. The deep wells. The community spirit. The army.'

He sucks the stick, throws it in a passing pail.

'It'd take years to crack this place, if it ever fell. You'd need to hit it from both sides at once, and there's no way she can pull that off. It's really . . .'

He trails off as he sees Icecaller watching him like a drenched cat. Quickfish over her shoulder, slowly straining an agonised expression through his fingers.

She walks up to him, puts sticky fingers on his chest. 'For some reason, I don't totally hate you. I think it's because you're pretty. But you better keep that talk to *yourself* when we speak to the council. Makes you sound a lot like a filthy foreign spy.' She chews the last words like they are still sticky with sugar.

Icecaller reaches behind her, dragging Quickfish forwards by his wrist, and leaning in conspiratorially.

'Wouldn't it be really, really awkward if I had to kill your boyfriend?'

He inhales sharply, face whitening to a ghost before she bursts out laughing. 'Oh. Why are you southern boys so *easy*?'

Another arm drags Roofkeeper into a sticky huddle.

'Come on stupid boys. More sightseeing later. If we take any longer, my father'll have my tits.'

Easy for her to say. It was hard to hurry, when Thell was suddenly opening itself up like the intricate, twisting clusters of gears that spun behind the great carillons of Hesper. All the machinery of life thundering in these dark vaults. Echoing caverns swelling with a holler of voices in a welter of dialects and accents. Deep redoubts where mushrooms grew in upsetting profusion and thick, luminous algae sat in colossal, creaking tanks. Brighter passages housing what might have been drinking halls, or taverns, with long rock tables, channels cut in the centre, piled with fruits and meats, and banked fires smouldering gently below. Small horn cups filled with something fierce, and all around them people, most of them boisterous, in close contact. Light touches, hugs, kisses in passing. A few held apart on the edges of rooms. Strong hands resting gently on spears, bright and alert.

The honeycomb of the Stump rose in easy inclines and as they climbed the life of the fortress pushed past them in carts, in groups of joking soldiers, in the occasional glimpse of a tattooist tracing geometric shapes and muttering softly.

War was everywhere in Thell. Roofkeeper could taste it in the air. But this was not Hesper's war. In Hesper, the city lashed in frenzy. The walls were raised and strengthened. The foundries dripped hot streams of bullets and blades into a populace itching to raise them.

Hesper was a sea city and she fought like a pirate. Brutal and ragged and bloody.

He hadn't seen Thell in action yet, but he could guess from the way the city moved, she would hit hard. Perhaps only once. Whatever was left would be . . . dismantled, at best. And if the truth of the city was intimidating, the legends were worse.

Stories first spun at his father's knee had been fattened by the rumours he'd heard as he walked north with Quickfish. Of the dead of Thell. The endless, restless, dead. Some old, paranoid legacy from the days of the Empire, though they seemed pretty restful to him. Barrows and cairns pockmarked the foothills for miles around, but within the Stump, there was no sign of anything beyond the living.

Icecaller was quiet on the subject and Roofkeeper had only ever heard the word mentioned in ritual. It didn't seem smart to pry.

It didn't seem like superstition, exactly, but there was something in the way that people avoided mention of the dead, in the space they left around them, that made Roofkeeper uneasy. He wondered what Shroudweaver would make of it, if he ever came here. The stories said he was close to the dead. Too close, Roofkeeper's father had muttered, too close by half.

The sound of Quickfish's voice pulled him out of his own head. He was talking animatedly to Icecaller, commenting on the carvings on the walls, asking questions about the Republic. She responded with steady, laconic patience and the occasional eye roll.

Roofkeeper watched them both, and remembered meeting Quickfish for the first time. Five years ago now. He had been much like this. Full of energy and questions, slipping from one topic to another like, well, like his namesake.

Standing in the stable yard of the Towers, frustrated and sweaty from trying to tame the massive bastard of a horse his father had saddled him with, his dandelion-shock hair pulled high by the movement of his fingers.

Roofkeeper sometimes wished their first meeting had been more romantic. More storybook. He had to admit Icecaller was right. The fledgling lord and the carpenter. It had a ring to it. But even then, especially then, he'd mostly been thinking about fucking him. There was something about Quick, something about the way he moved, the jut of his hips, the curve of his ribs, the lines of him that filled Roofkeeper's head whenever he saw him.

So, they'd fucked and fucked often. Face down and gasping in the stables, his hands tight in Quick's light hair, pulling his teeth down onto his neck. Running his lips down his stomach, falling hot and sticky into one another with the city clattering its pirate-song outside.

What had surprised him then, what surprised him now, was how quickly that first hot fire had transformed into something fiercer. The lust never went. He felt it even now. A desire to push him against the wall, to taste him on his lips, but beyond that there was something else. There was something about Quick that made Roofkeeper want him nearby. He got restless when they weren't together. His mind replayed their conversations, selected out his laugh, his tired voice, his slow, easy smile.

It had taken Roofkeeper a little while to realise just how in love he was. It had all seemed a bit stupid. Fallon's son and the boy that pulled the ticks off the horses. Afterwards though, he threw himself into it with complete abandon. The shape of his days changed as he made space for Quick, brought him as near and close as possible.

When Quickfish's mother had her name taken by Crowkisser, he'd held him in the night. He'd found him naked in the kitchen, shaking, staring into the fire. He'd found him drunk on the battlements, one foot already in space. He'd held him as all the loss and the confusion tried to swallow him. He'd fought it with everything he had.

At some point, he'd won. Quickfish came back from the grey places and started to smile. It was a sadder smile than before, with death at its edges, but it was there, and Roofkeeper counted it a victory.

A pity then, about Fallon. If his mother's loss had hit Quick hard, it had destroyed his father. When Quick needed him, he was gone. In wine, or in war, or in trade, Declan Fallon had responded to the loss of his wife by trying to work himself out of the world.

He wasn't cruel to Quick. There was never a harsh word between them, not a scrap of judgement. He was just gone, inaccessible. Striding the boards of a trade ship, or spitting curses at Crowkisser from the top of the Grey Towers.

Roofkeeper wondered what Fallon was doing now. If he was looking for his son – his *only* son. He wondered what Fallon thought of the man who had persuaded his son to leave.

Part of him hoped they were being hunted. It would show interest, at least.

Part of him thought they weren't. Roofkeeper had become good, long ago, at moving through places without leaving much trace. There was no real art to it, just an eye for detail and a relentless precision. Hesper's guilds always needed someone to get goods to and fro without much fuss, and roofkeepers had always been respected for the work they did.

When they left Hesper a couple of months ago, they had done so as ghosts, from the dawn gate, perfectly legally. No one was expecting them to leave, so no one thought to stop them.

The journey north had been similar. No frantic flight. Weeks of steady, measured progress, always inwards, away from the coast. Away from ships. One eye on the sky perhaps, trying to pick out the daggers of crows as they spun and wheeled.

It was hard to stay tense though, with the world opening up to the first warmth of spring. The woods and coppices rattling with the hollow tock of woodpeckers, strung with the smoke of charcoal burners, and in the evenings, around the fire-sucked embers, bitter beer and the slow chat of dark-eyed men.

Beyond the Midlands villages which fed Hesper's appetites, they'd followed the rivers which cut down from the foothills, slicked across the landscape by some lazy cartographer, meandering across broad fields, spilling over scattered scree, stabbed with the beaks of kingfishers, herons. Only sometimes pushing the scoured shadow of bones to the surface, whitened by water and time, echoing the fields where dark humps spoke of the graves from the last great war. The southernmost edge of the Empire. And before that, the other, countless battles that had scarred the earth and the soul of the Midlands.

Roofkeeper's grandfather had told him sometimes of the old wars, when a plough had turned a shattered blade or caught in the empty sockets of a sleeping skull. When he was younger, the markets of Hesper had been scattered with the occasional carts of treasure seekers, amateur archaeologists who poured forth scraps of dented armour, teeth, and finger bones like the gems from some dragon-haunted hoard.

He remembered the feel of them against his fingers, rough and sharp and smooth over and over. Crumbs from the dead, his grandfather had called them, as he rubbed the scarred space between his second and fourth fingers. After that, over spiced rum, he'd talk a little of cities that were familiar, but strangered by time.

Errant, Serpent, Hesper, Thell. The last survivors among the great cities. Names that sat heavy on the tongue, heavy on the heart. His hand shaking as he wrapped thick fingers around a clay mug, waved it slowly, conducting a symphony of the friends he'd lost.

In all of them shadows thronged the rise of the bladedrinkers, the seven-day war, the battle of the stolen heart, tales that sounded, from a distance, beautiful, desirable. And woven into them echoes of places less familiar, promises of stories beyond stories.

Rom, Luss, Chek. Ruins even in their own tales, unformed ghosts. Warnings. Dreams. Relics of the war against the Empire, that great coming together of the cities of the western coast to tear down the tyrant that used to exist within this very mountain. The way his grandfather had told it, it had been a desperate war, against an enemy that seemed never to sleep, or tire. That could move troops from mountain shadow to shore in the breadth of a night.

Barely a thing that could be won, he'd said. But, sometimes, there were fights you fought because not fighting was worse. The sour scour of his stubble curling around the scars on his face as he smiled.

Because they had won, because the Lord of the Grey Towers and his Lady had taken the field. And they had brought allies.

His grandfather would talk about the Fallons like he talked about storms. Something unstoppable. Sometimes he even talked about the people who became the Shipwright and the Shroudweaver, and he scratched his ruined hand, even as a half-smile balanced on his jaw.

And sometimes, beyond those, his grandfather would talk of the south. Of the fleet, and the opening sky. Of sending his son away on the promise of another righteous war. Of cursing his own injuries that wouldn't let him join the golden fleet.

Of seeing his heroes at the prow of a wondrous ship.

Of days on the dockside, watching the salt sea.

Of watching the light that blossomed in the south. Of smelling the sky burn and watching it blacken with the burnt bodies of crows.

Of seeing the Shipwright, the Shroudweaver, Fallon limp home alone.

Of course, after Crowkisser took his only child, he talked of nothing, until weeks of quiet ended in a long drop and a sharp stop.

It takes Roofkeeper a second to feel Quick's fingers on his arm. 'We're here.' A buzz of tension in his voice.

Roofkeeper meets his gaze, smiles. 'Yeah, sorry.'

Icecaller shoots him a glance, her hard eyes lingering on his for a long time. 'Daydreaming of building, were you?'

She turns before he can answer, flicking her fingers dismissive-ly over her shoulder.

Roofkeeper puts a hand on Quickfish's shoulder, steers him forwards. 'Keep your head, OK? I've got you.'

Quickfish nods, but Roof can see the breath flickering in his chest.

The room they enter is narrow, but impossibly tall. Seats and benches carved into its dark rock, winding one above the other, losing themselves in the shadows at some point before the light filters down from a ragged hole far above.

An old volcanic vent perhaps, Roofkeeper thinks, but sculpted and worked beyond anything he's ever seen.

On its lowest ranks are a scattering of wary looking men and women.

In the centre, a beast of a man, stoop-shouldered, his eyes flat-lidded under heavy brows, hands clasped in front of him.

He watches the three of them enter with studied care.

Icecaller keeps her voice low. 'That's father dearest. The King-hammer. We've had a chat.'

'A chat?' Quickfish hisses.

She fixes him with a flat look. 'Yes, as we discussed, over tea. Like civilised people.' The words sliding out between gritted teeth. 'Pay attention. You need to know who you're dealing with.'

Next to Kinghammer, a lean woman, her skin like burnished wood, one hand toying fitfully with a web of beads which clack softly as she rolls them over her knuckles.

Icecaller's chapped lips brush Quickfish's ear. 'Belltoller.'

Belltoller seems anxious. Her dark eyes track Quickfish as he walks closer, like an oarsman watching a shark cut through water. He wants to say something, speak up. A little spark of his mother's fire lighting in his soul. He feels Roof's hand tighten on his shoulder and thinks better of it. Icecaller flicks a glance at him, mouthing one word. 'Good.'

On Belltoller's left, two other women. Old, sharp-boned, their grey hair pulled back from the broad planes of their faces by bright ribbons, their right hands thick with stark, black geometrics.

They watch Quickfish enter with sharp eyes, passing whispers between each other like gifts.

Icecaller's hand grips his arm, her fingers tight and hard. 'The Deadsingers.'

Quickfish nods, watching the Singers' hands dance. Little flurries of bird-like movement. He's old enough to know he's being weighed, parcelled, assessed. He pulls his eyes back to the council, to the others, blood rushing in his temples. A red push like the sea.

To the right of Icecaller's father, a man sits slumped. At least, Quickfish assumes they're a man. They are swathed in so many layers of coloured fabric that there is only the briefest suggestion of a body beneath.

Ragged yellow and red strands flutter as they move, bringing two broad hands forwards to rest on their knees. Quickfish has seen the pose before, many times, in the stables with Roofkeeper. Watching the old hands scan horseflesh as it shivered in front of them.

In the hollow of their hooded face, a pair of eyes catch the light briefly.

Icecaller's fingers dig deep, the message obvious. 'There they are. Skinpainter. Knew your mother. Owes your mother.'

Quickfish glances at her, and she flicks her fingers expectantly at the row of waiting bodies. 'Time to shine, pup.' Then softer. 'Got your back.'

Nice words. It doesn't feel like it. The dark walls of the council chamber stretch up and out, thronged with the shadows of strangers. People who don't know him at all. Or worse, people who think they do, and fear him for it.

It's just him though. And he's a Fallon, whatever that means.

He takes a small, shuddering breath. It means he can see the stark line of his mother's bones whenever he closes his eyes. It's just him. And this is her only chance.

When he speaks, his voice feels thin and naked in the stomach of the mountain. 'Greetings, my lords, ladies.'

Stupid. Empty. He can do better. He has to do better.

They watch impassively. Icecaller leaves his side on soft feet and slides behind her father's brooding shoulders, words skirting the edge of his ears. Doing what she can. He's pathetically grateful. He has to try.

Quickfish clears his throat. 'I'm . . .'

'Fallon's kid.' When Icecaller's father speaks, he seems an easy part of the mountain. Dusty, deep, forceful. His smile when it comes, is like his daughter's, bright with a cutting edge. 'We know who you are, Quickfish. Everything filters down into the depths of the mountain. And we remember your father. Your mother.' He sits on that for a second. Glances to his right, at the Belltoller.

She stiffens. Barely. Enough that Quickfish can read it. He's seen it in the horses, back in Hesper. Roof taught him to look for it. That tension that runs through the bones when stray dogs are sniffing round the stables. That widening of the eyes that speaks to the promise of teeth. Or fire.

Quickfish watches her face. She's looking at him. She's deliberately *not* looking at Kinghammer.

Quickfish wants to say something kind, but he has no idea what that would mean to her. So he waits.

Not for long. Something shifts in her body. Just the faintest twitch in the fold of her dress, until her face focuses on him fully, her dark eyes running the length of him. He can feel the pressure of her gaze. Deep, black water. He tries to hold his nerve. Tries to keep breathing.

Eventually, Belltoller tips her head at him. The gesture feels grudging, somehow, but her voice is strong and clear, 'We remember your father. Your *mother*. We remember what they did. And there are many debts owed to them. The question is: why are *you* here?'

More interest than he'd expected. More of a hearing, at that. Maybe there is a chance. He has to be careful, has to think back to all those days spent with half an ear on the diplomacy of the sea rolling behind the tapestries while he fumbled with Roof and kissed the salt of his neck. There's a language for this; he can use it.

Quickfish nods respectfully. 'A fair question. I need help for my mother. There's no other help to be found. She was taken a while ago. By Crowkisser.'

Belltoller nods. 'I know the witch.'

Skinpainter laughs. 'We all do.'

Icecaller squeezes in next to her dad as they talk. The Deadsingers shuffle ruefully aside as she wriggles her hips. She shoots Quickfish a stealthy thumbs up. Mouths, 'Keep going.'

Quickfish coughs. 'Thing is. Crowkisser's magic. It takes names. And when it can't take the name, well, things go wrong.'

He clears his throat. He can feel the panic rising. 'My da stopped her. But . . .'

His shoulders drop. 'But she's gone, beyond the physickers and the saltwitches, and anyone else my da could find.'

He looks at Belltoller's long face, at Skinpainter's golden eyes. 'But maybe not beyond you.'

'Maybe not,' Belltoller says. 'Why is your father not here though?'

'Because he respects our boundaries,' Skinpainter cuts in. 'Fallon can take a cue.'

'Maybe that,' Quickfish nods, surprising himself. 'But he doesn't know I'm here.' He smiles, 'Wouldn't like it, I suspect.'

Belltoller smiles back. A half-moon, but a smile. She leans towards him. 'Just you. All this way?'

Quickfish turns. 'And Roofkeeper. My partner.' He blushes, a little.

Icecaller makes kissy faces again.

Belltoller's eyebrows raise. 'It's a long way. And we have made it clear that we do not welcome visitors.'

Quickfish nods, 'Yep. I got that. Lots of spears. Lots of warnings.' He straightens a little. 'But it's my mum. And there's nothing else. Nowhere else.'

Belltoller taps her fingers on the haft of something beneath her robes. Glances at Kinghammer, Skinpainter, then the Deadsingers.

'Fine.'

Kinghammer looks at her, and even Quickfish catches the flash of surprise, like a salmon in a river. It's gone quickly. Caught and beaten on the rock of his expression. Icecaller takes a second longer, but the grin she shoots him is wild. No one saw this coming.

Kinghammer senses the momentum, and rolls with it. 'Well, if Bell is willing, so am I. I've been waiting for your mother to come collect for a long time.' He pauses. 'It figures she'd find some awkward way to do it.'

Quickfish breathes, a little. 'Thank you. Thank you.'

Kinghammer raises a hand. 'We're not done, lad. There's more than me here.'

He looks at Ice and she shrugs.

There's a pause then. Mutterings from the higher seats as the folk of Thell confer among themselves. Quickfish knows that noises. Not *sold*. Not yet. He doesn't know what's needed though. That panic flutters again.

Below Kinghammer, Skinpainter stretches. Offers a small wrapped twist to the Deadsingers. A sweet? Now? Quickfish almost laughs, but watches as the leftmost takes it. Pockets it. The pair turn to Quick, twin heads sliding like owls on a farmhouse gate.

The sisters speak as one, spider-soft, fluting. 'Your father was a good man.'

Skinpainter's voice is loud in the silence. 'Is. You addled hags.'

They ignore the interruption. 'Your father was a good man, and your mother was the grey of the sea. She was the sword unsheathed and the hawk of morning. Your father is a good man, and he is the heart of dusk. He is the lord of fire and brass. Your mother is the gold of dawn, and she is the song restitching itself.'

They wait. They seem to expect a response.

Quickfish has nothing. Nothing but the image of a dream, and the logic of that dream fading faster than he can hold it.

The Deadsingers laugh, a hollow, stripped little sound that scurries between them. 'And you, beggar-child, you are twilight, the gold not yet burnt and the fire not yet dimmed, you are the edge of the blade and the untipped coin. And you come here! To the city that sings blood to blood and death to death, you come here asking us to wake the dawn, to call your mother like the chorus again?'

There's enough for Quickfish to hang onto, and so he replies, 'Yes. Please. Help her, if you can.'

The Singers glance at each other. 'Help is an unlocking of the sealed door. Help is adding a new voice to the chorus and hoping for harmony. Help is calling to the dark, and hoping the sun remembers.'

Their eyes flicker over his face, to Skinpainter, and back. 'We will help, if we can. We will see if we remember the songs to wake the dawn. We will sing them if the rest of the chorus permits.'

They glance upwards at the serried ranks of the council chamber, where the people of Thell watch and wait. There is a muttering again, the low thrum of the body politic deciding upon itself, more dissonant now. Quickfish knows that sound too, strands of persuasion weaving themselves into once hardened hearts. He allows himself a splinter of hope, sharp and bright. Just some other little push needed.

Consternation flits over Kinghammer's face again, unexpected developments. He leans in and mutters something to Ice, who laughs. Quickfish hangs onto that laugh. Maybe this is working.

As the murmur from the stalls subsides, the Deadsingers still watch him. A slow hiss builds behind their teeth like rain on the fields.

As Skinpainter rises, it deepens, before the warlock flashes a look to the pair, and the two old women tuck their heads to their chests, mumming and fumbling with the ribbons and beads about their necks.

When Skinpainter stands, it is slowly, awkwardly. They walk towards Quickfish on lurching legs, rags and ribbons trailing in their wake. Their voice is low, warm. Muted. It runs between their lips and Quickfish's ears like a little fox. Quickfish can see the others straining to hear as Skinpainter speaks.

'Quickfish. Look at you. I can see the pair of them in you.

Your father *and* your mother.' They laugh. 'Family is the strangest thing. You stand just like her when you are waiting for an answer. She stood like that in front of me, not so many years ago.'

They pause. 'It's good to see her again. To meet you. I am so curious as to what tides have brought you here and brought you *now*.'

Their voice drops lower still. 'But then, you have heard about me, of course. That's why you're looking at me like a flame that learnt to talk.'

They bow. 'Here I am. The dread warlock of the bitter mountain. Blood mage. Ink-twister. Painter of the high ice. Did your mother tell you about me?'

Quickfish looks into the depths of the hood and sees the faintest wriggle of a smile. 'A little,' he says carefully.

Skinpainter nods, reaches out a hand to Quickfish. It feels light on his shoulder.

'I understand,' they whisper. 'It's no easy thing to ask for help. It took me longer than it should have. To find your mother, the Shipwright, the Shroudweaver. I think you are driven by the same fear that drove me. To be out of options. To see death on the one hand, and desperation on the other.'

Quickfish wants to stay strong. The eyes of a whole city are on him. Hard men and women. Survivors of an awful war.

But the tremor won't leave his voice. He keeps it low, at least. 'She's my mother, Skinpainter. She hasn't woken up since. Not for anything. This is my last chance. *You* are my last chance.'

Skinpainter's reply is soft, reassuring. The frayed edges of their hood brushing against his face. 'I'm that for a lot of people, lad. I've become used to it. And I can't lie, I'm very good with things that exist on the boundary, between here and there. If your mother hasn't crossed over we might yet save her.'

A shudder of relief runs through Quickfish. He frames a reply as Skinpainter catches his wrist, and pulls him in tighter. 'We might not, boy. You have to be prepared for that.'

They glance back at Kinghammer, Icecaller. The lean scratch of Belltoller watching them like a hawk on a post. 'There will be a cost, for this. For Thell, for us. You will drag us back into the burnt world whether we succeed or not.'

Their breath is hot against Quickfish's cheek. Roofkeeper leans back to give them space. 'You carry Crowkisser on your shoulders. She has followed your family ever since they dared to sail against her. She won't rest until that's never going to happen again.'

Quickfish nods, surprised at how little the thought scares him, compared to the alternative. 'She's my mum, Skinpainter. Whatever it takes. Whatever I owe you. Or them.' He tilts his chin at the ranks of the council chamber who are beginning to shift restlessly as the hushed conversation rolls on.

Skinpainter smiles again, that sharp flash of white in the dark. 'The cost has already been paid by your mother, Quickfish. I remember what she did for us, at Luss, and after. The others' – they tut – 'needed a little reminding of cost and consequence, but I took the liberty of doing that ahead of your visit.'

They pat Quickfish's shoulders. 'Crowkisser has turned her eye on the mountain in recent weeks. I've felt her crawling all over me.'

They glance at Roofkeeper, back to Quick. 'Have you ever had to convince a child to take their medicine? Often times, it's best to make it seem like it was their idea.' Quickfish smiles quizzically. 'Other times of course,' Skinpainter says, 'You must hold their nose and force it down their throat. The Council is about to agree to your demands. Don't let that show on your face just yet.'

They press closer still. Quickfish is reminded of his father, for a moment. Beneath the robes, Skinpainter's frame is angular, strong.

'That' – they gesture at the council – 'is politics. This' – they place their fingers on his chest – 'is family.' Skinpainter holds their hand steady for a moment. Quickfish can feel the drum of his heart. An answering thrum in Skinpainter's fingers.

'No one has ever returned from being stripped of a name. No one has ever been audacious enough to try.' They drum their fingers against his ribs. 'Imagine, if we succeed. Crowkisser will curse us until the end of time.'

The laughter in their voice is barely concealed. 'Wouldn't that be fun?' They pause for a moment, their lungs rasping. 'I need you to know though. We may well fail. We will likely fail. So tell me, Quickfish. If you can't have recovery, will you take revenge?'

Quickfish glances across to Roofkeeper, who shrugs sympathetically. 'I don't want Crowkisser to hurt anyone else.'

The grip around his wrist releases. 'Neither do I, young man. And your current audience will be much more likely to bite if we slake their lips with the taste of blood.'

Skinpainter turns back to the lords and ladies of Thell, spreads their ragged arms wide.

Their voice swells upwards, rich and round into the depths of the mountain, 'Brothers and sisters. We always knew this day would come. We have known since the south burnt that those responsible would turn their eyes north, eventually. So I ask you now, will we abandon our oldest allies? Will we abandon the son of the man who helped birth our Republic? Who helped us cast down the Emperor?'

They turn, point at Quickfish. 'This boy has travelled many miles to seek our aid. From Hesper, the city that sailed when no other would. All he asks is that we bring his mother back from the darkness into which the crow-witch has cast her. That we return what she has stolen. That we honour the blood that she spilt in our name. For our city. For our freedom.'

There's a pause. A murmur from the walls where the members of the Republic council bow their heads like ghosts in a rookery.

Icecaller is watching the performance like an old, familiar play. Next to her Kinghammer seems nervous. It's an odd look on his face. He keeps glancing at Quickfish like he's about to speak, then choking it down.

On his right, Belltoller's face is impassive, but her knuckles are white around the handle of an iron bell she has slipped from her robes. A little further down, the Deadsingers have entwined hands, their nails sinking into the soft flesh of each other's wrists.

The entire chamber holds its breath. Quickfish looks at Roofkeeper, who narrows his eyes. They know this energy. A big room of people, just waiting to be told which way to jump. The question is, who has their hand on the tiller? And what price has been paid to keep it there?

Quickfish watches Kinghammer, notices the brief tilt in Skinpainter's hood. The fleeting question in their stance. His answering, minute, nod. That settles that, then.

Skinpainter's voice rises again. 'We can do better, friends. We who suffered for centuries under the tyranny of the undying Emperor. Will we allow a new tyrant to grow? Will we allow her to take our friends, our allies, our home?'

The chorus swells gradually at first, mutterings of assent that flit down from the high seats like bats. Lower, the Deadsingers stand. Their voices coil like drowsy snakes.

'The painter is right. We stand on the edge of a great blackness. The dead are restless. The old songs have changed. The chorus turns on itself. We have seen the future, the future. Daughters of Thell leaving the mountain. Leaving the shadow of death. Embraced in light, and blood. We cannot step out of this tide.' This last said with resignation. A fatalism that doesn't match the prophetic tone. One of the old women catches Quickfish's eye and shrugs sadly. He smiles reflexively, and her eyes flash.

She composes herself, and pulls her sister down to sit, before they, turn their heads to gaze expectantly at Belltoller.

There is no confusion in Belltoller's face. No sympathy. When she rises, she unfolds like a tree bent by winter, tall and black and slender. She runs her hands through her long hair before she speaks.

'I have seen nothing. I do not have my sisters' gifts. But I know madness when I see it. I can smell it in the south, in the crow-girl. And I know how to cut it out.'

She sits without prompting. Her throat flexes like she's swallowed a dagger.

Kinghammer shoots her a look as he levers himself up. His face doing the same complex dance that Declan's used to as it read the room, and compensated on the fly. Turning first to the assembled crowd, stalking back and forth in front of them like a caged bear.

Tasting the murmurs swilling around the chamber, the cries of assent growing louder and louder.

He raises his hand. They fall quiet. The echoes drop away.

Good theatre. The politics of control.

When he speaks, his voice is low as summer thunder. Rich and assured.

'Brothers, sisters. When we took back our home, we carved it from the heart of tyranny. We reached into the ribs of that old Empire and we pulled out something fresh and strong and new. I promised myself then, even in the first days when everything was still blood and bone and chaos, I promised myself then that we would be beholden to no one. That our fresh start would genuinely be a birth, a new birth for our city, our people.'

His back moves with his gestures, bone swimming slowly under muscle.

When he turns to face Quickfish, there's a half-smile hung on his face. 'I also promised myself that we'd be good people. That we'd look after our friends. That we would pay our debts when they came due, whatever the cost. Perhaps I needed reminding of that.'

His feet loud on the echoing stone as he steps closer

'Your father, your mother, Shipwright, Shroudweaver. They were the first ones, the only ones, to put their reputations, their cities, their bodies on the line for us. We wouldn't be free without them. This mountain would still be quiet as the grave, and the Emperor would still be on his throne. If Crowkisser comes for them, she comes for us.'

And it all sounds true, sounds genuine. Yet Quickfish can see Skinpainter's hands dance in the background, can see the minute shifts in body and bone, as the song they want to play is sung by Kinghammer.

The big man moves like he is in charge, but his path is already set. Even as he puts a hand on Quickfish's shoulder. Even as he says, 'I don't know if we can help your mother, Quickfish. That's Skinpainter's world, and their sorcery has always been beyond me. But we've kept out of this for too long. We're stronger now.

I don't know if your father was smart enough to let you run here, to seek an alliance without risking the journey himself. Or if you're just a very brave, slightly stupid young man.'

He squeezes. 'I do know that I remember your mother. She was a warrior. She deserves another fight. And if she brings us along with her?' He rolls his shoulders. 'So be it. A safer world with Crowkisser in the ground. An end to it.'

Quickfish says nothing, and round his head runs the idea that his father might have let him do this. Might have had it in his plans all along.

He doesn't get the chance to reply.

Skinpainter shoulders between the muttering pair, raises their voice to the throng, 'There you have it, brothers and sisters. Such a nice boy to bring war to our gates. But war we have. Do we have your assent?'

The roar is deafening. The rookery bursts to life as the council throws itself to its feet, stamping and applauding.

Quickfish can't help but feel that he's just watched something huge be cut loose.

As the cacophony grows, Skinpainter's voice thunders out above it. Their arms outstretched like a prophet, the rags at their sides flaring red and yellow and red again.

'Steel time, my good friends, steel and blood and the dead. Go kiss your lovers while you can. Tomorrow we plan for the killing of crows.'

The council answers with a single shout that boils up the sides of the mountain.

Skinpainter lets the echoes fall back to lap at their feet, waits a moment, then moves to Kinghammer's side, murmurs a few soft words in his ear, and departs. Icecaller's father turns, beckons to Quickfish and Roofkeeper.

There's a sad smile on his face, even as his heavy lips grind the words like stones. 'You're just like your father, y'know. You bring blood behind you.'

35

The red of binding and the silver of sending?
Developed theory for a simpler truth,
that of exerting an inexorable pull.

—Meditations on the Vanished Arts, lecture series

Shroudweaver remembers the sound of the hills.

Thell was built on the sound of granite and gravel, on the slow death of mountains.

He remembers a lot about Thell. More than he would like. It seems relatively innocuous on a map, a thick line of ink-stained grey to the north. Five small letters framed by Fallon's blunt fingers.

He meets the old bull's shadowed gaze. It's a miracle he's standing really, but then, Declan had never been one for listening to reality.

Weeks of recovery had stripped the fat from his frame. Days more of intensive attention by the physickers and drill sergeants had fed the muscle underneath.

Declan Fallon. Probably the only man to stare death in the eye and come out looking ten years younger.

On the surface, at least. Something is lingering in his old friend's demeanour since the attack that's hard to put his finger on. A nervousness; an uncertainty. Covered up with layers of bluster, but there, like a tremor in the bone.

Shroudweaver hasn't seen him this way since the south burnt.

Still Fallon though. Still sharp. His reddened eyes catch Shroudweaver's gaze and his broad, ugly moustache twitches. 'Reminiscing, Shroud?'

Shroudweaver twists his lips, sips tea to wash down the unpleasant taste. 'More than I'd like.'

Declan sits back, picks at his teeth. 'You know, I wonder if everyone else tries to forget. I wonder if *they* try to forget.' He glances out of the window, at a sky filtered with the shouts of workers, the ring of hot steel. 'Thell before the *glorious* revolution. Thell before the Republic.'

Shroudweaver tightens his grip on the mug.

'The Empire of the Dead.' Fallon turns his eyes to the map, runs a calloused finger thoughtfully over its borders. 'How many years was it, Shroud?'

'Coming up on twenty.'

'Twenty. Twenty long hard years. Remember when they were at the gates of Luss? Do you remember those things? Those paint-ed, eyeless things?'

Shroudweaver chews his lips. 'Hard to forget.'

Fallon laughs. 'You understated fuck. I still have nightmares. Still,' he grins. 'Everything burns. Reassuring that.'

He grabs a bottle, slops it into a glass, drinks deep. 'They're not going to be pleased to see you back in Thell.'

Shroudweaver shakes his head. 'Now, *that's* an understatement.'

Another belly laugh. 'Well, you did turn their world upside down.'

Shroudweaver frowns. 'I did worse than that.'

Fallon shrugs, winces as stitches stretch. 'What else were we going to do, let the Emperor's fucking revenants eat everything between the hills and the sea? You put them down. Sorry, you put the *Empire* down. The Republic owes you. And now look at them, all civilised.' He coughs, spits. 'It's cute.'

Shroudweaver lets the air out his lungs. 'I wonder if it was the right thing to do. I know the Republic and the Empire are tides apart. I know they'd skin me alive for even drawing a line between them, but, sometimes, the way they treat the dead now, I wonder if . . .'

Fallon smiles. 'You gave them a new religion, Shroud. Who wouldn't love that? One that doesn't eat their children. Doesn't press them into service to . . . whatever the Emperor believed in. It's made them a lot more tolerable.'

Shroudweaver shrugs. 'How do we know that? Really? Years without a whisper. They're tolerable if silence is tolerable. And I burnt my line of credit getting out of there. Only the old guard even remember me, and not all of them kindly. As for the kids . . .' he winces. 'Do you remember what we were like at that age?'

Shroudweaver takes a small sip of something strong, coughs. 'I have a feeling our coin's worth a lot less these days. Heroes or no.'

Fallon snorts. 'Don't beat yourself for backing the right horse. It's the only reason we're still alive.' Another wince. 'Mostly.'

He picks at his lunch, congealing slowly on a plate.

'Like treating with the Empire was ever an option after we saw what they'd done in Luss.'

His fingers drum flatly on the map, grease stains pockmarking the mountain. 'The Republic. Fah. A meritocracy, they say? Give it a generation of nepotism, and that place'll make a hornet's nest look peaceful.'

'Always my sunshine, Fallon.' Shipwright's voice cuts the air as she joins them, boots up on the table. 'Personally, I'm all for a city where everyone has a use.' She shoots him a look. 'Although I can see why that might unnerve you. Emptying cellars isn't really a vocation.'

The joke falls a little flat, but Fallon still smiles thinly as he fills her tankard, 'Come on then, let's make you a hypocrite.' He sips. 'Join us in reminiscing about the glorious revolution, the fall of the Empire.'

Shipwright frowns, 'I'd rather not.'

Fallon stretches pointedly. 'Well, seeing as you left me bleeding on the floor to play Pretty Magic Glow Princess, I think you owe me a few seconds' catharsis.'

That thin smile hangs on his face, but there's not much light under it.

Shipwright sucks at her gums, 'I'm not going to get to forget that, am I?'

Fallon shakes his head. 'Oh no. But you did save my life, so I'll keep it restrained. I won't even ask questions yet, because I've got a dead dog of a headache.'

'Too kind.'

Declan turns to Shroudweaver. 'So this meritocracy. Still the same people we helped put in power?'

Shroudweaver nods, gesturing at the sigils surrounding Thell on the map. 'I think so, although unnamed now. Whatever Crowkisser did, the mountain wasn't proof against it.'

Fallon winkles gristle from his teeth. 'What have they been up to? I never hear a peep. The north's locked down tighter than a spinster's mousehole. Which suited me, up to a few years ago. Until I ran out of better options.'

Shroudweaver shrugs. 'I don't know much more than you. Only what we picked up from traders moving south. Seems like they kept to themselves mostly. Rebuilding, trading. Picking a few easy fights. More sense than some.'

Fallon waves his hand. 'Ha bloody ha. Slay me.' He wipes a hand down his stubble, pulls his face long. 'So, who are we going to be dealing with?'

Shroudweaver ticks them off on long fingers. 'I'd guess King-hammer, Belltoller, the Deadsingers, Skinpainter. All known faces. And all the problems that brings with it.'

Fallon listens. 'Yeah, I remember Kinghammer. That big sack of shit. They all must be getting on a bit now though. They have babies up in Thell or do they just fuck rocks?'

Shipwright cuts in. 'Oh they have babies. Seen 'em coming down the high trade routes since last spring. You know the type. Strong, confident.'

'Faintly homicidal,' Fallon mutters.

She grins. 'To you? Definitely.'

Shroudweaver grimaces. 'Fairly unequivocally now, from scuttlebutt. Lots of crews won't push inland for fear of bronze blades.'

Fallon flicks his fingers at him. 'OK, so these old bastards, who no doubt are deeply fucking conscious of just how much they owe us, and this new contingent of bright-eyed mountain death-babies. That's who we're dealing with? That's who we're expecting to pull my city out of the fire?'

Shipwright and Shroudweaver nod.

There's a pause as Fallon drains the bottle.

'And remind me, these revolutionaries, when they finally threw down the Emperor, what did they do with him? When they had him cowering at their feet?'

Shipwright flashes a glance at Shroudweaver, who rubs his temples wearily.

'They ate him.'

36

what the sea brings sits in the bone
what the land brings sleeps in the soul

—*Proverbs of the Burning Forest*, Heartshamer

Those words hang in Shroudweaver's head for the rest of the day. He can't quite shake them loose. He takes to the streets for a while, trying to drown them in noise. He walks the loops of the city, through the bustling apartments of Mirestem, their windows pulled up like a widow raising her skirts, then higher, into the broader curves of Bitterhaven, where the rock that holds the Grey Towers pushes above the city, forest spilling down its flanks, cut into for parks and estates. Half of them are empty now, the ghost homes of Hesper's old captain-gentry. Most of them dead, or gone, moved on to other cities, on other continents. Writing this one off as a dead loss. Or just dodging the spectres of their vanished friends around every corner.

Shroudweaver would give a lot to see a few old ghosts these days. He used to dream about getting rich enough to buy one of those cliffside mansions, up high on one of the sea-facing hills, where the balconies caught the sun, and the hot sap smell of the pines would rise in the evening. Declan had promised to gift him one, a hundred times over, after the war. Somewhere for him to sit and grow old and stiff with Shipwright, for them to recline in chairs that would soften to the shape of their bodies and bleach from the sun off the sea.

Those dreams had died a long time ago, hollowed-out like those great mansions, as desiccated as the soil that blew from the roots of the trees and swept in muddy curls down East Tide towards Astic.

Yet even so, he still felt a pang in his heart when he looked at them.

They'd been standing on the balcony of one of those great mansions when the news about Luss first came. He had forgotten who the owner was; that memory had faded along with their stolen name. But he did remember standing between the great pillars, lined with some stone that caught the brazier's light, leaning into a wind that swirled scented herbs off into the greater dark of the ocean, which even then was alive with the bobbing watch-lights of ships flying back and forth.

That was before he'd even met Shipwright, as inconceivable as that seemed now. Just a naïve young Shroudweaver, fresh out of the Aestering. Kitted out and sent north to Hesper on his first placement, to study there, ostensibly to learn the rules of the city, their strange treatment of the dead in their shrines of clear glass. In reality, there to make friends among the great and good, most particularly the Fallons, but also the city's hosts, those strange god-touched prophets who lived dual lives, uneasy with their symbiotes, roaming the streets in a welter of odd configurations.

Nowhere bred hosts like Hesper, and no one ruled a city like the Fallons. The Aestering had wanted a piece of both, and as the youngest and brightest of his year, he was a natural choice as both diplomat and confidante. Or alternately, as observer and spy. Shroudweavers had always been political pieces. Too powerful an institution to be entirely unaffiliated, the Aestering was smart enough to keep a toe in every camp, a finger in every pie. With each shroudweaver's magic bound so inextricably to his own body, they became agents almost impossible to co-opt or subvert.

Nowadays, with all the shroudweavers gone but one, that balance was ruined. He almost missed it. Nowadays, there was just him. For good or ill, and he felt like he was losing the ability to tell which.

Back then, twenty years ago, with the trees rustling gently on the darkened hills and the spice of the braziers mixing with the wine in his head, he'd been glad to be part of the web.

When the news first came that he'd be headed out of the city on a diplomatic assignment, he hadn't known how to take it. He'd sipped wine out of a crystal glass, and watched as Arissa Fallon outlined the scope of his mission. North, on a specially sequestered ship, to discover what had befallen the city of Luss and, if possible, to find out whether this had anything to do with the strange and mysterious Empire filling the outriders' tales.

Growing from the heart of a mountain she'd said, but Shroudweaver already knew of the Empire before it crossed Arissa's lips in the evening light. The Empire of the Quiet Men, some called it, others the Stilled Mountain. He preferred its most prosaic title, the one that had first caught his interest. The one, he suspected, that might have motivated the Aestering's sending him here. The Empire of the Dead.

He'd kept that to himself as Arissa and he had talked. Nibbled on canapés of some large insect, dried and spiced, crunching a little unnervingly. He'd choked at one point, utterly failing to arrest it with an overlarge draught of wine. Right at the moment that Arissa had gestured to the ship's captain who would take him north.

When he'd first set eyes on Shipwright, he could barely breathe. His mouth a mess of legs and half-swallowed wine. She'd always pretended she didn't remember him like that, but the laughter in her eyes gave it away every time.

He remembered her exactly as she had been. Leaning awkwardly against the balcony, a glass clutched deathly in one hand, trying to watch the guests move and mingle at the party, more often letting her eyes fall back to the sea.

Always outside the circle of light.

His gaze held on her for a long time, a strange anticipation in his heart. Half the soft heat of the wine stealing through his body, half the dancing shadows from the suspended flames. The sound of the sea just beyond, pushing rhythmically up against the shore. Her head had raised, her eyes caught his, and she had held him there for a span, until Arissa's voice buzzed back into his consciousness.

'She's incredible, Shroudweaver.'

Odd how his brain recast it all. Letting Arissa's name swim in his head, even though it remained locked behind his teeth, twenty years later. His own name scoured cleaner still, not even the shadow of it on his mind. Not a ghost of it in Arissa's remembered words. Even in memory, he could see her lips move in the lee of the pillars. They didn't make the shape of his old name. In fact, it was as if they never had.

'Just incredible,' she'd continued. Her voice as clipped and precise as always, like hooves on granite, but softened ever so slightly by the wine.

'I'd heard of her before she arrived of course. No one like that could escape us for long. The agents I have . . . understated the case though. When she arrived at the docks' – she took his arm in an uncharacteristically close gesture – 'you would not have believed, Shroud. Come on, let me introduce you.'

He'd been steered across the intervening space with efficiency, around waiters and entertainers, the distant raucous howl of Fallon's laugh spilling out over the terrace. Shipwright had watched him arrive, eyes widening in faint horror, but before anything could be done, he was standing in front of her.

Arissa had continued, mercilessly. 'Shipwright, this is Shroudweaver, of the southern Aestering. Up to study the glass archive, and to make some friends. He is, I understand, at the very pinnacle of his profession. He will be accompanying you north.'

She'd nudged Shroudweaver forwards with a hand in the small of his back and brought Shipwright close in the same moment. 'Shroudweaver, this is Shipwright. She has recently arrived from the east and entered our service. She has the most incredible ship.' Arissa stopped, caught herself, smiled. 'And she is proving, day on day, to be a most interesting young lady.'

A dazzling smile flashed at Shipwright, a blush rising on her cheeks.

'I'll leave you both to get acquainted,' she'd said, and before either one could object, had swirled back into the light of the party.

Out in the dark of the balcony, they were silent. The sea shadowed back and forth beneath.

'It'll be good to work with you,' he'd ventured.

'Any friend of Arissa's is a friend of mine,' she'd replied.

'I'm not really . . .' he'd started. Stopped, turned to her. 'I'm useless at this, sorry. And a bit drunk. This was sprung on me.'

She smiled then, soft and genuine, her head tipped down. Her hair just catching the edge of the fading light. 'Oh, me too. That . . . uh. . .' she glanced over her shoulder. 'That seems to be how they do things here.'

He laughed. 'Oh, yes, absolutely. A very Hesper thing. So, we could exchange professional pleasantries?' He smiled, 'I'm sure we could do it if we tried.'

She blanched a little.

'Or,' he said, gesturing up at the forest behind them, 'there is another option . . .'

She raised an eyebrow. 'What's that?'

He turned, took a bottle from a discarded tray, and waggled it in what he hoped was an enticing manner. 'We could go somewhere a lot quieter and get a little drunker.'

She looked at him for a second, the sharp bones of his face in the firelight, the wind from the sea pulling his long, dark hair across his eyes. 'I think this might work out after all.'

After that, the party fell away behind them, and they climbed the winding hill in the gathering dark, beneath the gently buzzing branches, until the forest, the sea, and the city left them alone with each other.

37

not all flames may be extinguished
some burn perpetual, as is the way of the world
all matter trending inexorably towards fire.

—Archivist Splitwater

Declan sits in the room at the top of the tower for a long time after Shipwright and Shroudweaver have left. He watches the dust move in the light, watches the shadows shift over the map as the sun ticks slowly over the sky, hot against the fly-blown windows.

He tries to ignore that feeling in his chest, like a burnt stone. Foreboding. Deep and heavy as a well.

He doesn't really want another war; never really expected one. Two should be enough for any lifetime.

'One won, one lost. Same mess at the end of it all.'

He smiles bitterly at the thought, walks to the window and looks at the city, gathering speed as the day gathers light. Already the shouts and songs of Peacock's Rest filling the air, as the bars and brothels spill tempting shade out into the warming streets. The distant pop and shimmer of fireworks. Some noble brat's birthday party, most like. He hated them, the way they scared the animals. Scared him, if he admitted it. Always just too close to the sound of war. Altogether too many people around him fond of blowing things up.

That thought rustles his memory and he walks back to the table, stretching his hands out over the map. Vivid still, if food-stained and wine-spattered. Things couldn't be kept pretty if you used them.

Amazing how much it had changed in a span of years. Redrawn twice over. First to expunge the black stain of the Empire in the north, then again to scratch the remains of the city Crowkisser killed into the burnt mess of the south. His fingers lingered there. That whole southern stretch just a ragged line below the villages of the Rim. Nothing to sketch in. Nothing rebuilt. No one able to go there to see what, if anything, remained.

He reaches for his desk drawer, finds the bottle and pours. It was early, but somehow, it was always early these days. Pours, drinks, and swills the sour taste of his own teeth around his head.

Somewhere beneath his chest, the fading bruises of Slickwalker's fists press against his gut. He takes another pull, half to dull the pain, half to try and put a little fire back into his bones.

Tallest walls on the whole Western seaboard and that ratshit had waltzed in like it was nothing, holding his wife's name in his mouth as he beat him bloody. He'd be bits and brains on the flagstones now if it wasn't for Shipwright, and even that truth stunk. The pair of them rolling in, old as they were, bowed as they were, still with power pulsing at their backs. Silver thread and spinner brass.

And what did he have? An ego, and enough money to back it up. A strong sword arm that got weaker by the day. A hip and a shoulder that ached with slow fire in the mornings and cold fire at nights.

He could stave it off, of course. He was old enough and smart enough to strike the pose and hurl the bluster. But it was all dance. All smoke and mirrors.

He ran on fire and spite these days, and even that fire was a guttering flame, death growing in the bone.

But that wasn't what they saw. It wasn't what he *let* them see. If he faltered, Hesper faltered, and he'd be gone to glass before he let that happen.

He'd always kept the watch. Always held the fort. Even when that meant being alone in the night, with an ache in the bone and another empty bottle.

And here he was holding down the fort again. That seemed to be what he did these days. Hold the fort while the fleet sails north. Watch your friends, your wife, disappear over the horizon.

Hear nothing of use from bastard scouts for months. Field requests from captains and guilds and traders, all jockeying like sharks in a shrinking tank.

Climb the seawall and watch the ocean painted with the bright flags of ships, hating every one for not being the one you want to see. Then welcome them all, somehow, miraculously back. Manage to build a life, in the aftermath, beyond the celebrations. Have a kid. Watch it grow. Hear its words and wipe its snot and dry its tears and watch it grow. Into a person. A man.

Start to dream of another life. Of peace, and simple things.

Then catch rumours of something wrong. Storms in the south. Ships lost in unseasonable drownings. The wind stinking of sulphur and dark earth. The air carrying the sound of something vast, cracking and rolling across the sky. Crows. Flocks upon flocks of crows arrowing down through the grey rain, skimming the fallow fields, bowing the branches and crowding the battlements as they rested before flying onwards, ever south.

Hearing your dearest friend warn you that something terrible was brewing, resolving to go yourself this time, because she's got the baby and she shouldn't travel, and anyway, wasn't that what men did, what a real man would do?

Marshalling a smile on your face and trading all your goodwill like coin. Pulling the other cities behind you into a great fleet that stroked the surface of the water like an Emperor's ego.

And finally, finally sailing south.

For a second, Fallon's fingers linger on the map's ragged southern scar, and he feels a similar, poorly healed itch in his mind.

No, not today. Today he would hold down the fort again while his friends once again went north, to seek allies, this time. Maybe to win this third war before it started; maybe, just maybe, to get them all enough peace to stretch them to the grave.

And wouldn't that be a mercy.

38

the rotted barns,
the fallow fields,
the piping call of lean birds
legacy, legacy, legacy

—*What Is Born Beyond Blades*, Heartshamer

Morning. A horse thunders across the square, trailing half a cart behind it, its owner an arm-span behind. Shipwright watches it go with a flicker of amusement. Hesper.

The dip of the horse's spine masks Fallon for the briefest second as he descends the tower stairs into the courtyard. Not looking too bad, all in all, broad shoulders rolling in the shadow and a blackwood cane just enough of a sop for the physickers' clucking. Never handsome, but just sometimes, he was so *much* that you couldn't help but admire him.

The bubble bursts as he sways at the bottom of the stairs. She hurries forwards and offers an arm. He takes it and pulls her in with surprising strength, planting a kiss on her cheek. 'My smooth moves worked, I see.'

She sticks her tongue out at him. 'Your moves have never worked. And they've never been smooth.'

He nods cheerfully. 'Still got myself a good one.'

She smiles wistfully. 'That you did.' Only the briefest pang in her heart today. 'How is she this morning?'

'Resting,' he replies, his eyes scanning the courtyard. 'Like I'm supposed to be. Fuck happened here?'

'Stray cart,' Shipwright says. 'Overexcited horse.'

Fallon tuts. 'I'm in bed two weeks and the city literally falls apart.' He walks over, pushes the debris with his cane.

'Overexcited my arse, that's a horny stallion. You can smell it in the piss. This time of year, all they want to do is mount something.' He picks up a shattered urn, sniffs. 'Not pull carts of sour Midlands wine.'

'Reminds me of someone,' Shipwright murmurs.

He grins. 'Because you're such a shy violet. How do you not break that skinny little ghost?'

She taps the side of her nose. 'Trade secrets.'

He laughs and she smiles. It feels good to talk shit again.

She claps an arm around his shoulders, 'So what are we up to this morning? Other than adding hot air to this hot air?' She fans herself, pointlessly.

'Sweaty as a boar's tit, isn't it? I thought you and Shroud might want the tour. It's been a few years since you were here after all. Plus, we should get you fitted out if you're heading north. Then maybe lunch? There's a place I want you to check out.'

She frowns. 'What kind of a dive is this? Knives out?'

He shakes his head. 'Arses out at worst. It's practically civilised.'

She waits as he stops to speak with the stable hand who has stopped, doubled over, a while down the road. Some coin changes hands, and Fallon thumps him on the back consolingly. The man's legs buckle a little.

She watches him with a smirk as he rejoins her. 'You soft-hearted old man.'

He taps the cane on the back of her legs. 'I prefer benevolent ruler, thanks.'

'I call it like I see it, Declan. You never change.'

He rolls his eyes. 'Part of my ineffable charm.'

The street widens as they exit the square, pushing down through the forested slopes of Bitterhaven and the hillsides dotted with pillared houses, their empty windows looking out to sea.

Shipwright feels a tug in her heart as she remembers an evening of firelight, dark sea and strong drink among the pines.

'Emptier than last time I was here.'

'So what? I like the quiet.'

'No, you don't.'

'Fine, I don't, but don't push me on this, Ship. Do you have any idea how hard it is to sell real estate at the moment?'

He slips a coy expression on his face. 'So *beautiful*, so *spacious*. So *regal*. And what happened to the previous owners?' His voice changes. 'Oh, they were rendered into strips by a psychopath bitch made of crows.' He mimes horror. 'Perhaps we'll look elsewhere.'

Shipwright frowns. 'I'm sorry Declan.'

He rolls his shoulders. 'I'm not. One day those houses are going to be full of drunk idiots and noisy fucking and fat babies, and I'll be drinking out her skull. I'm a patient man. I can wait.'

39

Trade it to an honest man
trade it fast, in kind
but never sell a confidence
go deaf, go dumb, go blind

—Glimmer's skelf-song

Fallon walks on, his pace a little brisker, back a little stiffer, hiding the worst of it, prideful sod. He pauses as they pass a darkened arcade. The latticed roof thick with bird-shit and the scorched walls lined with sheets of dusty glass, clouded with spiders. Hints of broken furniture behind the panes, split chairs and shattered tables. A memory of shouting voices, torches, an evening of flame.

He notices Shipwright watching him. 'You remember what this used to be?'

She shakes her head, running a critical eye over the soot-blacked stone.

'The Street of Small Saviours.'

Shipwright turns an eye to him, shrugs blankly.

Fallon sighs. 'Little traders. Curios. Antiques. And one host. A banker. A securities man. Styled himself the Gutgod.'

Shipwright grimaces. 'That doesn't sound good.'

'Could store anything for you. Seal it away inside himself. Uncrackable, incorruptible. Expensive as sin. A little wet, a little sticky on extraction, but that was a small price to pay.' He smiles grimly. 'Time was he must have had half the secrets of the guilds and captains tucked up under his ribs.'

Fallon picks at his stubble, flicks something into the street. 'A principled entrepreneur, they'd thought. Using the powers of his god for good. Slicing himself open with barely a hissed complaint, letting its gold light stitch him back together, with his latest commissions safely stowed inside.'

He scrapes idly at some blistered paint. 'Of course, when the south burnt, we discovered his . . . storage system. Screams coming up from the cellar. And down there, all these street kids, linked together. Flesh to bone. Must have been a king's ransom inside them, and suddenly they could feel it all, every coin, every gem, every secret cutting into them. All the pain flooding back in as his god died.'

His face pales. 'We should have realised sooner. Should have figured there was no way one man could hold the secrets of a city inside himself. But he was easy. Convenient. We would never have known, if it wasn't for Crowkisser. I suppose I owe her for that.'

Shipwright's eyes are wide, her voice thick with horror. 'What happened to him? To the Gutgod?'

Fallon's eyes go flat, as he glances at a series of dark scars on his knuckles. 'I beat him bloody myself when I found out. Right there in the street.' He looks down at the blackened stones. 'And all through it, he was so startled to be *feeling*. So surprised his body wasn't pulling itself back together. That his god had left him.' He laughs. 'Prick.'

Shipwright twists her mouth in disgust. 'Declan . . . what did you do with him?'

He shrugs. 'I gave what was left to the guilds, after they'd razed the street to ash. They treated him pretty much as I expected.'

Shipwright raises an eyebrow.

Declan grins. 'As far as I know, the Gutgod's currently on display in seven different gilded cases around the city. If the gods ever return, he's going to have a very harsh awakening.'

Shipwright chokes down bile as she surveys the wreckage of the arcade.

Fallon claps her on the shoulder. 'Anyway, wasn't I supposed to be taking you shopping?'

Shipwright rolls her eyes. 'You're a monster, Fallon.'

He shoots a glance at the broken street over her shoulder. 'Mm, when I need to be.'

His eyes linger on the hollow windows for a moment longer. 'Where's your better half meeting us?'

'Down by the lock. He said he had some errands to run first.'

The city thickens up as they fall out of the curves of Bitterhaven into Mirestem. Lines of clothes stretch over rat-ways built of planks and rigging slung to and fro, houses raised high above the canals, the streets ringing with voices and the water pocked with detritus falling from above.

Gangs of urchins swing from roof to roof, feet light on the tiles, arcing above the hubbub on long poles that bend precariously. Shipwright watches them with delight.

Shuttered windows are flung open, heads hollering at Fallon. An old man with an eye patch tosses a velvet sack which he catches with aplomb.

'For you and the Grey Lady.'

Behind his stooped back, a cacophony of birds sing in small, mismatched cages.

Shroudweaver waits for them by the lock that lowers the water down into Peacock's Rest. He's barefoot, sandals at his side, hood pushed back and the sleeves of his robes unwound to the shoulder. Head tipped, at peace for a moment, enjoying the sun on his skin, a hand trailing in the water.

Shipwright points him out to Fallon. He winks back at her. 'You'll rot your fingers off if you do that,' he yells.

Shroudweaver leaps like a scalded cat, teetering on the edge. A gaggle of boatmen yell warnings.

Fallon catches his wrist and pulls him steady, just about hiding a grimace of pain. 'Morning, skinny. Sightseeing?'

Shroudweaver dusts himself off. 'That was earlier, I was just warming my bones. In peace.'

Fallon nods, oblivious. 'Warm them later. We've got things to do.' He slings an arm around them both. 'Does it feel good to be home?' He sees their expressions. 'Well, as near to home as you two get.' The big man pulls Shroudweaver's cheeks. 'We're going to have some fun. Remember that?'

Shroudweaver yawns. 'Well, this is the place for it.'

They walk onwards and downwards as the business of pleasure carries on in Peacock's Rest, in its shaded courtyards, with their cobbled stones crowded with patterns and their fountains thick with lilies. Geckos on the porticos, scuttling between the tiled tables and the softly steaming urns of tea.

Heads turn to watch them pass; hooded figures in rich robes, others with hats like the chewed ear of a rat. Fallon sees Shipwright following their stares.

'Guildsmen. Squabbling like gulls every morning. It's guilds all the way down, these days. Got their hands in all the important trade. For better or worse.'

'Are they a problem?' Shroudweaver asks.

'Not yet,' Fallon replies. 'Wait until the war bites. Then we'll see.'

Past another courtyard, another clutch of lidded stares. A tall, dark-skinned woman lingers in an archway, a massive hat pulled low over eyes, a single long feather sprouting from the band. She tugs it respectfully as Fallon passes, flashing an eerily bright smile.

'Morning, Brim,' Fallon says.

She smiles wider, sparkling. 'Nice to see the old gang back together, Declan.'

He hustles them past. 'It's a delight. Can't stop though. We've got appointments.'

They round a corner, taking a set of small, staggered steps to the bottom of the loop, stepping over fruit peel and broken glass.

'Can't stop, eh, Declan?' Shroudweaver's face is sceptical.

Fallon leans on the edge of a water fountain, rubs his stitches. 'Partially true. Truer that we don't have time for Brim.'

'Don't fuss with those,' Shipwright cuts in. 'Why not?' She splashes her face, wipes grit from her eyes. 'She's still a great-ship captain, right?'

Fallon nods, gargles, spits. 'One of the best. And one of the last, of course. Sailed with us at Luss, if you remember. Not a captain then. The old one had to die first.'

'That didn't take long once we were through the gates,' Shipwright mutters, glancing over her shoulder.

'What's with her teeth these days?' Shroudweaver asks.

Fallon grins. 'Sharp eyes. Filed them down herself. Capped them off with little shards of pearl.' He shivers. 'Spooky bitch.'

'I always liked her hat,' Shipwright says, drying her hands on the edge of her shirt. 'Can I get a hat, Declan?'

She leans across to Shroudweaver. 'Maybe that's our appointment? A nice new hat.' She smiles sweetly at Fallon, 'Is it?'

He rolls his eyes, and leads them downslope through a maze of alleys that press one against the other. They can still hear the canals, distantly, but even the light is muted here, coloured awnings strung across the close-leaning streets, cutting the shadow into stripes of red, orange, purple.

'Two places we're due today,' Fallon says. 'Anything look familiar?' Shroudweaver scans the street more closely, takes in the swinging signs, the windows fronted with wooden boards that doubled as stall fronts arrayed with curios, some strung out with quiet precision, others in heaps of indiscriminate value. Metal and bone and chain and gem.

'Thriftglow,' he says. 'The Ghostmarket.'

He remembers it more clearly now. It's not much changed from his first time there, with its doorways hung with bunches of herbs, its slowly rattling chimes moving in the dust spirals and heat. The stallholders impassive behind their wares, their eyes bright as hunting hawks. The customers quiet – sifting through their offerings, judging by touch as much as sight.

Declan grins as they look around. 'You need supplies, right?'

Shipwright frowns. 'Ropecharmer'll take care of all that stuff, Dec.'

He waves a hand dismissively, narrowly missing a delicate charm of hanging arrowheads. 'Not that dull shit. Hard tack and rope and crab tar, or whatever the hell you sailors use. I'm talking the real deal. Brass and copper. Thread and powder. Magic, dipshits.'

Shroudweaver laughs. 'Is that our new codename? He's right, Ship. I'm almost dry. Thread's near burnt through and my powders are just dust and spit at this point. And you said yourself the spinners are stressed.'

Shipwright rubs the bridge of her nose. 'Me and the spinners both. Declan, do we have time for shopping trips?'

The grin on his face steadies. 'Ship, I don't know magic. I don't want to know it. How you do what you do can die with you. And certainly Shroud's kit gives me the crawling shivers.' He picks up a bowl, turns it critically, sets it down. 'But I know war. And you don't send anyone off to war without kit. Get your kit. Do this right. Stay safe.'

The other shoppers melt away as unobtrusively as possible, clocking the Lord of the Towers rolling down the street. A few brief, furtive exchanges follow, gloved hands brushing silk and the barest glimmer of coin. The proprietors adjust their wares and wait patiently. The street quietens to the yowl of cats, the chirping of the bright-plumed birds which fret in their stall-side cages.

Shipwright feels curiosity light in her like it hasn't for years, but tries to play it cool. 'How do you even know they'll have what we need, Declan?'

Fallon taps his nose. 'I've got a woman. She scoped it out. These guys have everything. This is where the weirdness of the city ends up. All the artefacts, the charms, the occult bits and bollocks; it all sifts down to Thriftglow eventually.'

If he notices the stallholders bristle slightly, he says nothing.

He sighs. 'Just . . . let someone else handle it, for once, OK? You control freak.'

Shipwright beams at him, smiles wider still at Shroudweaver's laugh. 'Fine, fine. You got me. Fine.' Holds her hands up in surrender.

'Good,' Fallon grins. 'You need to head four doors down, talk to that man there, the one that looks like a snake in a fur wrap.' He points to a man who watches flatly, eyes lizard-lidded, fingers adjusting a belt hung with thin, sharp tools.

'They all love me down here.' He turns. 'Shroud, come with me, we're going to see Smokesister.'

Shroudweaver starts. 'She's still alive?'

Fallon laughs. 'I think she's too mean to die.' He pulls Shroud in close. 'Why, do you still have a crush on her?'

40

there are sympathetic tendencies in all things
the bird seeks the cage
the hawk seeks the bird
the sky seeks the hawk.

—Meditations on the Vanished Arts, lecture series

The snake-eyed man waits for her in the half-darkness of his shop. His skin is leaf-thin, the veins blue as ice beneath. His laboured breathing rustles like a stack of dropped papers. He beckons her to a seat as she enters.

His voice is quiet, almost lost in the soft sound of his settling robes.

'The Shipwright herself. An honour.' A thin smile, but his eyes are bright above it, like sparks struck in the lamp of his tall skull. A few brief wisps of hair cling to either side of his head.

'Thank you,' she replies. 'That's not . . . I mean. I'm sorry, I don't know your name.'

He smiles again, like a flipped switch. 'Wicktwister; the lord keeps me on for my services, my stock.'

He busies himself to the back of the shop where a massive apothecary's cabinet looms. Its drawers are opened and closed with speed, his head still half-turned to Shipwright as he works.

'Tell me what you need. Your magic is alien to me, and the lord is . . .' his smile flickers. 'Not magically inclined.' He brings forth a selection of thin, metal sheets on a small wooden tray and offers it across to her.

'I find it . . . I find *you* fascinating.' His fingers linger on the metal, then guide Shipwright's hands towards it. 'A whole new magic. So foreign to our shores. Imagine, the things you must have seen. The things that must seem foreign to you!' That smile again. 'What a delight.'

He opens more drawers, brings small, precise tools, tongs and hammers. 'But I digress. You are a craftsman, as well as a sorcerer. That I know, that I understand better than *anyone* in this city.' He leans in close. 'In this, city, on this earth, if I dare say.' His breath smells of aniseed, faintly medicinal. He leans back, fans the tools out.

'Teach me, an ignorant, eager student. Which of these will make your magic sing?'

Shipwright lets her fingers drift over the samples and sighs gently. Alloys of the finest sheen. Metal that bruises like butter, that bends like willow.

'These are amazing,' she breathes.

Wicktwister dips his head. 'Too kind. But not too kind, really. Rarities, the finest of my collection. Worked and layered and smelted, just so.'

He fans out a selection, and she watches the calluses and burns dance on the tips of his fingers.

'See, here – coast ore – it sucks up the salt in the rocks – marvellous conductive. Heat, lightning. An obliging metal.' Pats it approvingly, holds up a finger. 'But, weak. No friend to a fire.' He smiles proudly. 'But marry it to iron, keep it held over embers for days, and it will learn to like the heat.' His head slides inquiringly. 'You follow?'

She nods. 'I think so. This is fascinating. I've only ever used copper, brass.'

He nods. 'So it needs to be malleable, yes. But the durability? An issue? At sea, great stresses on the toughest materials.'

He begins to make some notes. Stops, scratches a line through them. Sets the quill down.

'First principles. Tell me how it works. I need to know the system before I can help you build the machine.'

She flicks a glance at the door.

Wicktwister raises a calming hand.

'No trade secrets required.' His head bobs. 'Not that I would betray such. I am sworn to the archive, mouth, hand and bone.'

He pulls his lip revealing a scar like a stretched crescent on his gum; shows her the mirror of the same on his hand. It doesn't mean much to her.

She starts sorting the metals, weighing them in her hand, discarding them by feel. 'The archive?'

He murmurs in agreement. 'Not a full-fledged archivist, no, not me. Methods too direct, too physical. A consultant only.' He catches himself, slows. 'The archive keeps the secrets of the city. Its dead, once they have gone to glass.' Tips his hand back and forth. 'Secrets, dead. There is much overlap. The ramifications for you? I do not share a syllable without consent.'

Shipwright scratches her chin thoughtfully. 'Good enough for me. I've never met anyone else that could do this anyway, other than my parents.'

She opens her mouth. Shuts it. 'I've never tried to explain this before. Bear with me.'

Wicktwister nods encouragingly. 'Of course. Water? Tea?'

Shipwright demurs. 'This won't take long.'

She leans forwards, separates her hands. 'Everything I do starts with spinners. Have you seen one?'

He shakes his head, slowly. 'Heard tales. Read reports.'

She digs into her satchel, takes out a small brass sphere that hums and whirrs.

The spinner sits on the table where it rotates gently under its own momentum; a buzzing sphere of beaten metal, folded like the petals of a flower, or the segments of an orange.

Shipwright points to it. 'The folded metalwork's not usual, but it's my style. Helps the vibrations.'

Wicktwister moves towards it, glances up for permission. She nods. 'Sure, it's harmless.'

He picks it up, lets it dance across his knuckles like a drowsy bee. 'Wondrous.'

Shipwright laughs. 'Hardly, to me. Can you feel inside? The loops that intersect? The hum?'

Wicktwister cups it gently, waits, nods as the vibration spills gently through his bones.

Her heart warms at the joy on his face. 'Lovely, isn't it?'

He grins. 'Lovely, yes, but lovely will not teach me which metals you need, which hammers must beat upon this beautiful bird's egg. Basic principles, Shipwright.'

He holds the spinner up between them. 'This is the tool of your will. What is your will?'

A good question. She waits a quiet moment, but for the slow tick of a clock, the muffled murmur of shoppers outside. An elderly grey cat limps through the room pausing to butt its head against Wicktwister's ankles. He scratches absently between its ears. Shipwright leans across and pats its flanks. 'She's lovely.'

Wicktwister chucks the cat's snaggle-toothed chin fondly. 'She is an old faulty machine. I keep her around for warmth, for love. Too much sentiment in my heart for simple things, for this cat.'

Shipwright runs her hand over the cat's bones, stroking the purr down her spine. 'What's her name?'

'Nubbin,' Wicktwister replies with a laugh.

Shipwright lifts Nubbin gently onto her lap, where she settles down in short order, nose under tail. She shifts her legs gently, before she looks back to Wicktwister.

'Spinner magic's about two things. Stasis and speed. Increasing one at the expense of the other, usually. Sometimes, on rare occasions, creating stasis for speed to work within.'

She strokes the cat, fends off its rough little tongue.

'Where I come from, it's not common, but it's known. We're told about it as children. The brass magic, the magic that pins the world.'

Wicktwister raises a set of tongs, examines them critically. 'Pins?'

She nods. 'My people. And me, I suppose, we believe that the world exists in layers.' She moves her hands until they're atop one another, palms flat.

'Spinner magic,' she interlocks her fingers. 'Spinner magic holds the layers of the world together.'

Wicktwister retrieves the quill and writes softly. 'Continue.'

'The top layer' – she wiggles her hands – 'above the sky, that's gods, or where the gods used to be. Flux. Momentum. Good change. The middle, that's us. The real world. Earth and sea and stone. Below that' – she lowers her hands – 'Death. Destruction. Chaos. Dissolution.'

Wicktwister raises an eyebrow. 'You believe this?'

She shrugs. 'I was raised with it. It's more complicated than that though. Above us, that's also like . . . the future. Below us, that's the past. And everything gets associated with everything else. The past is death. The sky is momentum.'

She strokes Nubbin and rubs her eyes. 'It sounds a bit mad when you explain it all at once.'

Wicktwister shakes his head. 'Hesper does not believe in mad. Only the unknown not yet comprehended. Continue.'

Slightly surprised, she does. 'So, if you believe all that, change is the natural state of things. Onwards or downwards. Spinner magic either arrests that, or speeds it up.'

Wicktwister's pen dots a line, stops. 'It sounds fearsome. How are we not all your humble slaves? You could rule worlds with this.'

Nubbin stretches, yawns pinkly. Shipwright waits before she continues. 'No. See, it can do a lot. It can shield you from other magics, so long as the spinner lasts. It can keep things going, machines. Ships.' She smiles. 'Even people, though that last is dangerous.'

'But it's all localised. One spinner only stretches so far. A room. A body. An object. I don't know how anyone could ever make one big enough to affect more than that.'

Wicktwister looks sceptical, 'No one has ever tried?'

She rolls a hammer over her palm. 'Of course. We have stories about those people. Rooms, bodies torn apart by a mistuned vibration. Buildings lost, people disappeared. We've found shards of things that might have been spinners once. Old, ragged, long as your arm.' She points the hammer. 'Anything larger than an orange, and things get weird. It's hard to regulate the vibrations.'

Wicktwister glances up at her. 'And a broken spinner? What cost?'

Shipwright thinks. 'Small stresses can be repaired, if they're caught quick enough. After that, damage can mess with the balance. With time, with the substance of things. Fray away at objects, bodies.'

Wicktwister makes a few more notes, draws a graph and annotates it. 'You said localised? How localised?' He crosses to the other side of a room. 'I am a spinner, here. Can I affect you?'

She smiles. 'Yes, most likely, but it depends on your position. Are you held in a hand? Are you hung from the ceiling? Atop a mast? A tower?'

He nods. 'Understood. I am now atop a Thriftglow apartment. Can I affect you? The district?'

She shakes her head. 'The room, most likely.'

He turns to a work bench, jiggers open a can with sharp, swift movements, decants some oily fish into a bowl. 'I begin to understand.'

He sets the food down. Nubbin stirs herself, and hirples slowly to the bowl.

'Here the limitations, then.' He checks them off. 'Materials, size, position, duration and task. Correct?'

She nods. 'Seems about right. We could add in location, speed, interference.'

He does. Nudges the cat towards some missed scraps with his foot.

'You mentioned a danger. Spinners. Bodies. A bad combination?'

Shipwright takes her own small spinner back. 'Not necessarily. I use them. To speed up my reactions. Watch.' With the spinner in one hand, she takes a shard of metal and dances it between her fingers, faster and faster, until there is only the briefest blur.

Wicktwister grins. 'Useful, I imagine, in a confrontation. In all sorts of ways. Again, please.' She obliges, and he makes notes. 'Fascinating. An interface on the muscular level, perhaps. On the firing of the nerves. Guiding the lightning of the body to new, unexpected efficiencies.'

He watches the spinner slow again as she sets it down.

'Vulnerabilities, obvious now. Damage the spinner, detriment the effect. One cannot encase, in armour say, or other protection, because thus the vibrations would be affected.' He sketches as he talks. 'Further, one imagines the risks involved in bodily use. Fatigue of the muscles, fitting, seizures, ruptures and sundering of the major organs, likely death.'

She pales, a little. 'Don't tell Shroud.'

Wicktwister taps his lips with the quill. 'Not a syllable, never fear.'

She fights a surge of relief. 'Does that help?'

He nods. 'There is the omitted component, of course.'

She laughs. 'I'm impressed. How did you know?'

'I am a craftsman. As are you.' He looks at his notes. 'Some motive force, non-mechanical, likely sorcerous or spiritual. Not derivative of the gods, for they, alas, are dead and gone. Thus, some other force, but one not limited by your home geography. One which you can perceive with relative ease, but which others, perhaps, cannot.'

Shipwright watches him in amazement. 'How did you?'

Wicktwister shrugs. 'Extrapolations. Reading the not-said as much as the said. I would surmise something in the vibrations. Perhaps a sensitivity. An ability to harness or find something amid them. To capture, cage, inject or sublimate it as needed.'

She starts to reply and he brushes a finger lightly against her lips. 'No need. I have enough to assist, and the safest secret is the one unshared.'

He closes his notebook. 'Make your selections. I shall have a package delivered, with materials, tools, instructions.'

He taps the tip of the quill on the book's cover. 'Would you allow me to produce a few prototypes, according to your design? I would like to experiment. You then might test them in the field . . . for efficacy.'

Shipwright thinks. 'I don't see why not.'

Wicktwister's eyes light. 'Excellent. After all, it is only metal without you.' He glances at the shelves. 'But what metal it shall be.' He stands, brushes his robes. 'Enough of your time, I suspect.

And a genuine pleasure. You will return, I hope?'

She smiles. 'I will. It's been really good to talk to someone.' A sudden rush of emotion in her voice. She tries to hide the shake, but has little hope it'll pass by.

Wicktwister lays a hand lightly on her shoulder. 'Indeed. Unusual. Most often I despise company. As does Nubbin.'

Shipwright laughs. 'Can I test her in the field too?'

Wicktwister shakes his head. 'She has been extensively tested over many years, and found lacking in most every department, I regret. So she remains here with me, adorable and useless.' He stops, scratches her ears. Smiles up at Shipwright.

'Farewell, Shipwright. As much speed as you need, and not a drop more.'

41

Imagine! to say the dead have passed away
when you see the birds, the fires,
the smoke that lies so low upon the land

—*The Blue Beyond the Halls*, Hallowfeather

Shroudweaver leaves Shipwright in the street and follows Fallon's broad back through the twisting backstreets of Thriftglow, off the main thoroughfare of the Ghostmarket, towards a shop whose sign is barely visible in the light – a slim silver sigil, high on the dark wood. A birch tree.

The street is warm, the last scraps of morning sun filtered into green by a profusion of plants spilling from the balconies above.

Fallon stops at the door and gestures him inside. 'They don't pay me enough.'

'They don't pay you at all,' Shroudweaver mutters.

He grins. 'My point exactly.'

Inside, the last of the light is muted, only occasionally pushing through slats to illuminate shelves racked with red and silver thread. Bulbous glass jars full of sifted and milled powders, meticulously labelled. Shroudweaver recognises a few symbols from the Aestering; southern work. The rest is a mishmash of arcana – cut marks that might be from the north, beads dipped in the colours of Thell, a spear etched with the script of the Heron Halls.

A couple of furtive customers brush past him as they leave, their hands busy with scarves and wraps that shift in the shadows. They shoot him wary looks, their eyes lighting on the bindings that fringe his wrists.

A high-backed chair sits at the far end of the shop, behind a counter spread with fabrics in neat divisions. Silks, thicker wools, suede; a cloak, maybe.

She's half-turned from him at first, so that he only sees her arms. Long gloves, high above the elbow, fingertips snipped out for dexterity, the thick cinch at the cuffs doubtless to protect against burns, skin-lock, blood contaminants. Not everything in those jars is benign.

She turns to him as he approaches, the profile of her face hanging in the half-light like an eclipsed moon. 'Took you long enough, darling.'

Smokesister hasn't changed – tall, a mess of dark hair in a long, thick braid held with purple ribbon and a fur stole around her neck, white as bone, tipped with black. Perhaps a little more silver in her hair. Perhaps a few more lines at the corner of her mouth when she smiles.

'I was a little delayed.'

'So I heard. You may have raised that daughter of yours too well.' She rises, stalks towards him, boot tapping on the floor, the metal of her other leg knocking gently against the boards.

She stops in front of him, takes his chin in her hands and turns it slowly left and right. 'Let me get a better look at you.'

Smokesister holds his gaze for a moment, large eyes the colour of blackberries lingering on his face and a half-smile on her lips. 'You look old, dear heart.'

'I am old, Smoke.'

She walks around him, trailing her fingers over his collarbone as she moves.

'We're all old, Shroud. You have to learn to work with it.'

He grins. 'I see you have.'

The fur around her neck lifts its head as he draws near, wriggles, bares its teeth, its black eyes neat in a flat, sharp-toothed head.

Shroudweaver starts. 'A holdsnake, Smoke, really?'

Her laugh is as clear as fresh water.

'I couldn't resist. My father used to have one, you know? Proper ship's captain, with one of these beasts slung over your shoulders. I couldn't turn it down.'

She hops up on the counter, ruffling the silks, pats the space next to her. 'Come, sit.'

He levers himself up, edges closer, cautiously. The holdsnake chitters, and she runs a finger along its jaw.

'He's hungry. Pass me the jar by your hand.'

He does, and she unscrews the lid, popping something black, crunchy and multilegged into its mouth. It eats noisily, half-chewed limbs sticking out like a strange little beard.

'He keeps the vermin down, at least. Keeps me company.' She turns to Shroud, arches an eyebrow. 'Did you know they sell them to all the fancy ladies, dip-dyed parti-colour in great vats?' She feeds it again. 'Half of them escape and live feral in the attics by the week's end. They'd be better off hunting rats on the ships where they're supposed to be.' She snorts, 'Of course it does mean that every so often some unlucky thief stumbles on a nest of rainbow murder.' Grins at him, barely keeping the mirth behind her lips.

Shroudweaver glances at the roof. 'The voice of experience, Smoke?'

The laughter bubbles out of her, doubling her over. She thumps the counter, tries to bring it under control. Fails.

Shroudweaver watches her. He's missed that goofy laugh.

Eventually she sighs, wipes tears from her eyes. 'Everything has its little perks.'

The holdsnake slips off her shoulders and undulates off across the floor. Shroudweaver follows its curves, starting at the touch of her fingers on his arm, the faintest thrill along his skin.

'So, darling heart, what can I do for you? I'm definitely old enough to know this isn't just a social call. That would require social skills on your part.'

Shroudweaver looks around. The racks of jars, the roofbeams hung with threads and small skulls. The half-closed shutters.

'This place hasn't changed much.'

Smokesister looks down, smiles softly. 'Change isn't my job, Shroudweaver.'

She slips down from the counter, cocks her head at the door.

'Fallon's cowering outside, I assume.'

Shroudweaver fingers the fabric under his hands. 'Holding down the fort.'

She rolls her eyes. 'Sure.'

A clink from the high shelves as the holdsnake dislodges a jar. She stretches a hand out as it falls, catches it neatly.

'Fast as ever, I see.'

She sets it back in place, coaxes the animal down onto her shoulder. 'Little shit. I stay fit, Shroud. Old habits. I'm bad at staying still.'

He traces his fingers across a few of the jars, marvels at the selection of powders, chemicals, components. 'You've got more stock than ever. How? I would have thought the war would have . . .'

She moves to stand behind him, noticeably close, her scent of peppercorns and soap.

'. . . hindered my supply? Darling, I'm the last one in my business left alive.'

Her fingers drum on his back as she thinks. 'Let's see. There was the nice blonde boy in Astic, and the woman with the hand-thing in the city down south. I wonder whatever happened to them.'

She moves back to the chair, turning it to face the counter. 'Ash and dust and crow fodder I suppose.' The fabrics are cleared to one side; beneath, the wood is marked with intricate sigils, circles upon circles, flowing script threading them like the roots of a tree, or veins in a body. He's seen Smokesister's work before, but it takes his breath away each time.

She places an arm at each end of the counter and looks up at him. 'I suppose this is what you're really here about. The dead, in some respect.'

He gets closer, squints at the patterns, the precise etching.

'Am I that obvious?'

'With you, darling, it's always about the dead, in some respect. So, what is it this time?'

Shroudweaver flicks his eyes anxiously across the room. 'We're heading north.'

'The north is big, sweetheart. Do you mean the actual north? To the blades? Should I pack tea? Beans? Dogfood?'

She watches him for a second, and her face falls. 'Oh, you're going to Thell.'

He nods. 'Yep.'

'Well,' she says. 'That's stupid.'

He winces. 'Thanks, Smokesister.'

She licks a finger, scratches at an errant line in the design.

'Did you come here for help or for me to stroke your ego?'

'Can't I have both?'

'No. Your ego and practical advice are incompatible. We know this. We've known since I helped you design the binding in the first place.'

Shroudweaver's voice is soft. 'Who else was I going to go to? No one's as precise as you, Smoke. Not when it comes to ritual.'

She smiles, genuinely pleased. 'My blessing. My curse.' Her eyes linger on his face for a second. 'Can I make you something to drink?'

'Do you still do that berry fizz?'

Her teeth gleam. 'I've *perfected* it.'

Drinks are decanted from a stoppered demijohn whose valve fizzes and bucks. Poured into tall, smoky glasses where the liquid bubbles light and red.

Shroudweaver sips, tilts his head back, lets out a groan of joy. 'Oh, how I've missed that.'

She turns her glass thoughtfully. 'I'll give you a case not to go.'

He shakes his head. 'We need to reach Thell before Crowkisser. I need to harness the dead to finish her.'

Smokesister twists her lips sympathetically. 'Have things really got that bad?'

'They've been this bad for a while, Smoke.'

She sips again, glances out the window. 'I try not to think about it too much.'

He touches her hand, briefly. 'It's that bad.'

She watches him, dark eyes, elegant brows. 'OK, I believe you. Thell, to harness the dead.'

He nods.

Air hisses out slowly between her teeth. The holdsnake hisses in reply. 'To harness them, you'll need to unbind them.'

'I'm aware.'

'You won't be able to do it partially. We never planned for that. This was supposed to be final. You twit.'

He shrugs. 'Life's full of surprises.'

Smokesister screws up her face. 'I *hate* surprises.'

She moves to the shelves. 'How are you stocked? Sulphur? Powder?' Her voice brisk as she uncorks jars, measures them out into a set of cast iron scales. 'What am I saying? Let me guess. You're running low?'

He nods sheepishly.

She throws up her hands. 'Decades as a grown man and you still can't keep stocked on the basics. It'll be the death of you, mark me.'

She measures, packages, seals. Waves them at him. 'Waterproofed, double-ended, quick release. Don't dunk them in anything for too long or drop them overboard and you'll be fine. Got it?'

He smiles. 'Yes, Smoke.'

'Don't "yes, Smoke" me. Rolling in here without a pinch of powder. Let's see, what's next? Threads – red, and silver.' She pulls on a hank which flows down from one of the beam spindles. Glances over her shoulder. 'You still carrying them all wound around under your sleeves?'

'It makes things quicker.'

She sighs. 'I'd hate to have to undress you.'

He splutters and she grins. Cuts from the spindles with a sharp pair of dressmaking shears, the threads falling like air, gathered and twisted one-handed into neat little hanks. 'Well, you can put them on yourself. More than I'm worth.'

She adds them to the stack.

'So much for supplies.' She puts a finger to her lips. 'Ah, wait, needles.' She slips a drawer open and selects a range, like a magpie in a silversmith's. 'Various gauges. I assume you'll be working with your own body, but just in case.'

She shifts the stack into the middle of a sheet of wax paper, then ties and fastens it with ruthless efficiency, popping it all in a soft leather satchel, red as crushed cherries. It fits perfectly.

She holds it out to him. 'With my compliments.'

Shroudweaver takes it, slips it over one shoulder. 'Thank you, Smoke. Really. It's so good to see you.'

She frowns at him. 'Of course it is, but you should have said that a few decades ago. Still, at least the unbinding will finally take the strain off you.' She steps forwards, rests a hand on his shoulder. 'You were supposed to come back, so I could check on you.'

'There wasn't time, Smoke.'

She lets the hand fall. 'There was near enough twenty years, Shroud. Of all your weak excuses, this is the worst. Just tell the truth.'

He hesitates.

'Go on,' she says. 'It's not like we don't both know it. Why wasn't there time?'

Shroudweaver holds her gaze. 'Because I met her.'

The pain that brushes Smokesister's face is momentary, but it hangs in her eyes for some time after. She lets her breath out slowly. 'Ah, there we are. Nice to hear you finally say it.'

'I'm sorry, Smoke.'

She shoots him a look then, filled with fire. 'The time for sorry was years ago too, Shroud. But then, I've noticed that when it comes to coming clean you like to be . . . fashionably late. I'd work on that, if I were you.'

'I don't know what to say.'

She nods sadly. 'That sounds about right.' Her shoulders drop, her voice softens. 'Well,' she waves a hand. 'I'm not going anywhere. I learnt to hate you a little less directly, over time. Maybe you can learn to like me a little more honestly.'

She brushes a hand across her eyes. 'For now, we need to be grown-ups about this. Besides,' she smiles. 'If I wanted to get my revenge, this would really be perfect.'

His eyes widen.

She laughs, a little sadly. 'I wouldn't. Doesn't mean I haven't thought about it.'

Shroudweaver remains silent.

Smokesister reads the lines of his face. 'Don't get maudlin now, Shroud. This is going to be tricky work. Let me see the state of you.'

He starts, and she gestures impatiently. 'Top off. I need to see what damage has been done.'

He shrugs his robes off and shivers.

She gently runs her hands over his body, the collarbone, the stark ribs, the scars and burns that touch his stomach. 'Could be worse,' she says. 'Some muscle mass still.' She moves closer, presses her ear to his chest. Hears his heart flutter and race. Sighs, the heat of her breath running over his skin.

'Not so good, Shroud. We knew this might happen. Especially if you left it so long without seeing me.'

Shroudweaver lifts her head away gently. 'All bindings need a focus, Smoke.'

She looks back at him, a little flushed. 'Didn't they warn you about this in the Aestering?'

He begins to dress, his reply muffled. 'They warned me about a lot of things. I didn't always listen.'

'That bad boy act's not as cute as you think it is.'

He grins, shakes his head. 'I just mean I had to improvise. I had no idea what the Emperor was doing until I finally met him.'

She raises an eyebrow.

'I mean, I knew he was raising the dead. Modifying them. Infecting the living, maybe. But until I met him, I had no idea *how* he could do it on that scale.' He pulls his sleeves down, shivers at the touch of the wool. 'And I had no idea how to stop it. The binding needed a focus.'

She walks to the counter, lifts the glass, drinks deep. 'Do you know how many nights I spent thinking about how stupid we were?' She stops, raises a finger. 'No, sorry, how stupid *you* were.'

She walks towards him. 'Binding the dead of the Empire, of Thell.' She puts a hand back on his chest. 'Binding them all to your own stupid heartbeat.'

He covers her hand with his own. 'There's nothing stronger than blood, Smoke. A heartbeat's the steadiest rhythm in the world. I needed something I could trust.'

She snatches her fingers back. 'Steady until it breaks. Have you any idea how close you were then? How close you're getting again now?'

She leans against the counter, tips her head back. 'God, I can see you clear as day, staggering to my door. Other peoples' voices spilling off your tongue, other peoples' memories in your head. Half-mad from the hubris of it all.'

Her voice rises. 'You fucking idiot. You think just because it *worked,* it makes it OK? Begging me to help you fix that jury-rigged ritual. Which you did by yourself. *Yourself!* I know for sure your old teachers would skin you alive for that.'

She pushes fingers against her brow. 'How many days was it, Shroud? You and me in here, your head in my lap and your mind in that fucking mountain, running wet with a thousand other souls?'

She glares at him. 'Have you any idea what that was like? Not for you. For me.'

She thumps her chest as she says that, her voice splitting. She drains the glass. 'And now you come back. With another desperate plan stacked onto the back of the first. Fifteen years I swore I'd never touch your bloody magic or your bloodier ego, and here we are.'

Shroudweaver's hands tighten. 'I need your help, Smoke. I know I've handled it all terribly, but this is bigger than either of us.'

She turns the glass thoughtfully. 'You're right, as usual. And as usual that still doesn't make it OK. Do you get that, Shroud?' She gestures towards him with the empty glass. 'It's important to me that you get that.'

Shroudweaver nods. 'I do.'

She grits her teeth, bites down on the urge to go and comfort him. 'That'll have to do. Bare minimum, but it'll have to do.' Smokesister breathes deeply, smooths her dress, adjusts her hair 'OK. One last question.'

'Of course.'

'The unbinding. Why now?'

He looks at her, and the regret that rises in him feels like a black wave. 'Because I can't think what else to do. Because I know this'll work. It'll stop Crowkisser. And because I'm tired.' He stops, looks down. His voice soft, fracturing. 'I can't carry it anymore.'

She holds him at arm's length. 'That's the most honest you've been in decades. Fine. I guess I'm stupid enough to do this.'

'Thank you,' he says, meaning it.

She smiles. 'One last thing Shroud, if you come back, treat me like a person. Not an asset. Not a fucking . . . a fucking *resource*, OK?'

'Yes,' he says, his voice tight, 'I promise, Smoke.'

She rolls her shoulders, loosens the tension.

'Right, nip outside and tell Fallon you're going to be a while. He wouldn't know good magic if it bit him on the nose.'

A moment later, he re-enters, eyes squinting from the light.

'Ready?' she asks.

He nods tersely. 'How long will it take?'

'Hours, at most, breaking's always easier than making.' The sadness hangs in her voice, before it sifts away into the half-light.

Those hours pass in a ritual of fingers and lines, counting the fade into twilight. Magic measured, calculated and twined with precision in red and silver thread. Eventually, Smokesister makes the final knot on his hand, letting her fingers linger only briefly.

A shadow on her eyes. She sounds tired when she speaks. 'There you go. It's all tied to this red thread. Keep it wound around your right wrist. Let it fall when you can see the mountain. The whole damn thing will come down. And you better be ready for it.'

'I will be,' he says.

'I'd like to believe you,' she says, 'but that's cost me before.'

She kisses him on the forehead, her lips light on his skull, and holds him there for a second.

'Die properly, or come back as someone better.'

She pushes slightly, steps away.

Shroudweaver backs to the door, his eyes lingering on the slump of her shoulders, the slight shake in her leg. She doesn't turn around.

When he steps into the street, the moths have fallen to swarm the lamps. In the flickering light, the birch tree looks like it's aflame.

42

AMETHYST
CAT BONE
FLINT

—Graffiti found in the Barrow of the Bells
[Subsequently backfilled, sealed.
By order of the Grey Towers.]

It's a long walk home. The Grey Towers visible across the whole city, sparking with flame as the great globes of oil and pitch that swing from them are lit in advance of the coming night, stringing those thick grey necks with pearls of fire.

Shroudweaver's tired feet carrying him through the hollows of Thriftglow. The streets rise and fall unpredictably, built atop the ruins of older roads. When those buried stones foundered, whole districts sagged, their backs bowing like old mules.

A few turns take him past the closing of the Ghostmarket. The stallholders are folding cloths, bundling rarities and garbage together with equal precision. A few tip their heads or touch a finger to their lips, the wrist of their right hand, half greeting, half warding gesture. He would always be known in this city, for better or worse.

Shroudweaver pulls his hood up, wrapping his scarves tighter. His vision narrowing, the cowl's frayed edges filtering the light. His fingers worrying at the red threads around his hand, his mind worrying at Smokesister's words.

Would he have done things differently, if he'd known the cost? Probably not.

Smokesister was right, as much as it caught in his throat to admit it. He'd rushed from hell to harrow without stopping to

246

catch breath. He'd improvised the binding at Thell. He'd improvised most everything since he'd left the Aestering, but what else could he have done?

He remembered the first stories he'd heard of the mountain, of the Empire of the Dead, and its Emperor. It had been in his first few weeks in Hesper, twenty long years ago, as he'd rolled in determined to ferret out the city's secrets, nose sharp as a bloodhound for the faintest rumour from the north.

There had been rumours aplenty, hanging on the lips of drunkards or purchased for good coin from traders and travellers. Stories sifted from noble parties where the walls shivered with secrets – plenty had heard of the Empire, where it crouched low in the heart of the mountains, quiet and unwelcoming.

Far fewer had heard of its ruler, the Emperor of the Dead. Such a ridiculous title, he'd rolled his eyes at it, the first few times it had caught his attention. Even in the Aestering, when his teachers had warned him with tight-laced hands about the dangers, he'd taken it all with more than a little salt.

That was until he started digging under the skin of the rumours. He'd always been good at piecing together stories, just a different kind of stitching, really. When he'd begun to ask after the Emperor, he'd barely had to work for it at all. The tale had a momentum of its own, something familiar in it that ran like a rat in the back of his mind.

Legend had it that the Emperor had come centuries ago, on the heels of the glacier, as the ice peeled back from the mountains. That he'd slowly brought the people of the Barrowlands into the fold. Whether they were lured or coerced was unclear, for everything Shroudweaver heard had that loose quality of myth.

Some things remained constant, nuggets of truth in that looser soup of muttering. The Emperor was always accompanied by his three lieutenants: the Gem, the Bone, the Stone. That was how one fat old trader had named them, his fingers shaking in the lamplight. They faded in and out of the story like the tides. The closer to the present Shroudweaver got, the more they changed in the telling, becoming symbols, ritual shapes. The Emperor's age was as fluid as his followers. Was he a mortal man, come on the glacier's edge? Or something else, there since the very start of the thaw? Perhaps, some suggested, he was the cause of that great sundering, of the ice falling to cold and mud. Whatever his age, his rule seemed to have barely registered for decades, the southlands and Hesper too concerned with their own bustling trade to push north towards the thaw. Until about half a century ago when rumours grew of villages taken, and of men who wouldn't die whether cut with sword or pierced with bow.

The few emissaries Hesper sent north were received with stern refusal, stolid politesse. No, we have no need for trade. No, we do not wish an alliance.

The south, it seemed, only really took notice when the first caravans were hit, when the northern cities raised a hullabaloo, the heralds flying out of Luss with their long arms trailing gold, and their jewelled mouths flapping. Armies, they cried, ultimatums. Pale faces, and barely veiled blades.

Hesper and the south had not responded. Another northern conflict, wise heads muttered, the ghosts of the bladedrinkers playing on the overactive imaginations of the merchant houses.

Still the heralds had come, with entreaties and boxes of spice and stone. Armies, they had cried, ultimatums.

Treat with them, had been the disparaging response. Shoulders shrugged and turned. Were the northerners not all the same? Cold, stone-gutted men and women. Let them bleed themselves dry, finally enriching that thin and useless soil.

Armies, the heralds had cried, and ultimatums.

And then, nothing.

The silence went unnoticed in the hubbub for a few weeks, until accounts came due, and letters went unanswered. Couriers went out and did not return, save for the odd horse, with ragged bridle and bloodied saddle.

After the couriers, scouts. The first few did not draw too close to Luss, but saw what remained of the city. Empty ruins, they said, smoke curling the sky. The great homes of the merchant houses torn down, the empty sockets of their windows looking out to sea, the birds flying in and out through their ruined walls and unbarred doors.

The next few grew bolder, rode their horses around the walls, or what remained of them, canted and tipped as they were in huge, oblong slabs.

Eventually, they grew very bold. Hallooed over the walls, and crossed inside. They found dogs in the streets, amid the bones and the dried flesh. But not many bodies, for a city the size of Luss, they reported, not many at all.

A few of the bravest stayed overlong, so long they were thought lost. They returned swaying in the saddle and fell abed with fevers, their tongues and teeth clashing on words not their own. Shroudweaver ministered to them, feeling a fire in those bodies too familiar for comfort. On the third day of the fevers, every suffering man and woman tore from their sickbeds into the streets, bursting through windows and doors. Few made it far. Those that did grabbed orderlies and doctors, guards and watchers, scrabbling frantically with nails and teeth. And when they were finally brought to bay, they looked their pursuers in the eyes and drew broken glass and rusted blades across their throats with joyful finality.

No more scouts were sent. The roads north were closed, and new routes were found for people and goods that needed to pass. No caravans moved along the coast-ways, only the occasional large patrol of heavily armed men. The flow of information dried up along with the trade.

The heralds of Luss were not seen again until the battle to retake the north. There, outside the tilted and broken walls of their beautiful city, the gilded and bestoned heralds cavorted once more, in the ranks of the Empire of the Dead. Staring across the field with tarnished lips and bloodied teeth, they met their enemies' eyes and called out, in desperation, once again. Armies. Ultimatums. Blades.

Shroudweaver shivers at the memory, cinching his scarves tighter. The streets have pulled him back up out of Thriftglow and into Peacock's Rest. He can feel the shift under his feet, the cobbles and mud of Thrift smoothing out into the patterned brick that lined the streets and waterways of the Rest.

Evening trade now – hawkers bartering under the awnings. Snatches of music drifting out from beneath porticos as doors briefly swung open onto courtyards, bars, back-alley dives that had slid to the waterfront for a night or two.

Shroudweaver sidesteps the pleading hands of salesmen, lifts his sandals over a few ambitious drunkards already sprawled over the brick. Flinches as an amphora sails out of a second-floor window, painting the street with wine.

'You look nervous.'

She almost falls out of the street-corner light. A brief flicker as a pipe sparks between her lips, her wide hat still low over her eyes. He recognises the hat and the feather first. 'It's Brimlicker now, right?'

She tips the hat back, revealing blue eyes, a lazy, pearly smile. 'You remembered. Cute. A pleasure, Shroudweaver. It's been a while.' She sticks out a hand in greeting, smoothly falls into step next to him. 'Brooding, are we? It's a good time of night for it.'

He laughs. 'Seems like everyone can read me today.'

She waves at a passing couple, blows them a kiss. 'Takes one to know one. At least you've moved to the melancholy wandering stage. That took me a bit.'

He turns to her again, looks closer at her face, the curl of burnt flesh under the hair at her neck. 'You were with us at Luss, weren't you? One of the other captains, first through the breach. Saved my damn life.' He laughs. 'I'm sorry, it took me a moment.'

She shakes her head. 'Not to worry. A lot of water under the keel. It sticks with you though.' She runs a hand under her hat. Laughs. 'Maybe if we'd stuck a little closer to you and Shipwright, I'd have a few less reminders.'

She guides him around a corner, towards a door with a hanging sign, and holds it open, 'Every time I do what Fallon tells me, I get a little crispier. Come in, Shroudweaver, take a load off.'

The room inside is small, a bar running along one side racked with bottles that gleam dully. Shonky wooden steps stretch up to a second level where a band hang like bats, sawing at fiddle and accordion.

Below that, a circle of seats around the fire, familiar shapes. Declan's broad back, Shipwright's golden hair, her head tipped back in laughter.

Shroudweaver feels a pang in his heart as he recognises the room. 'The Harrowed Gull? I thought she'd burnt down long ago.'

Brim moves to the bar, leans over, fills a couple of tankards. 'I think she's too rotten to burn.' She holds the cup. 'Here, drink. Fallon suggested a little reunion.'

He chinks cups, swigs back, grimaces. 'Still swill.'

'Never stopped you before.' The voice harsh as a rusted hinge, its owner rounding the bar, rubbing raw knuckles with a starched rag. His hair fading at the edges into two wild tufts, his mouth home to a few defiant teeth.

Shroudweaver's heart leaps. 'Swallowgut? Is that you? I never thought I'd see you again.'

The old man waddles over to the bar, folds his arms on it. 'You'd have seen me sooner if you'd visited, you young rat.' His face breaks into a pink grin. 'But better late than never. Look at you.' He walks around the bar, reaches up to Shroudweaver's shoulders. 'Tall and thin as a fish-pole. And me remembering you in here, fresh-baked out the Aestering.' He elbows Shroudweaver's ribs. 'Got yourself a lady, eh? And a title. *The* Shroudweaver. Very nice lad.'

'Beats Swallowgut,' Brim chimes in.

'Says you, *Brimlicker.*'

Shroudweaver tilts his head questioningly. 'I did wonder about that.'

She shoots him a look. 'We can't all have cool names, *Shroud-weaver.* And no, I don't really know where it came from.' She pulls her hat down to her chin.

Shroudweaver taps the brim gently. 'Come on, let's go say hello.'

She fakes a pout, plants a kiss on Swallowgut's liver-spotted head. 'Yes, let's.'

Fallon sees them coming and rises up, arms open. Shipwright next to him is beaming.

'Ah, the last of our little party. Bring the good stuff, Swallow.'

Chairs scrape as they make room, and the pair settle down, Shroudweaver running his eyes around the circle. There are a couple of faces he almost remembers, a silver-bearded man, gold jewellery bright against his dark skin. He smiles softly as he catches Shroudweaver's eye. Next to him is a neat little figure, short hair dyed ruddy and cut close against their scalp, hooded eyes half-closed as their head nods to the fiddle's skirl. They raise a lazy hand to Shroudweaver.

Swallow crabs across with the drinks. Fallon sweeps the bottles from the tray, pulling the old man into a space by the fire. 'That's enough, Swallow. Tonight you sit with us. You were there at the start of it all. You deserve warm bones and a sore head in the morning.'

Swallowgut sits, grudgingly, shooting a short smile at Shipwright when she claps him on the back.

Fallon stands again, clearly enjoying the attention. Cheeks flushed enough that he's probably been enjoying it for a while.

'Reintroductions, I think. We might all know each other by reputation, but it's been a long time since Shipwright and Shroudweaver actually stopped in Hesper, and twenty long bastard years since we fought together.' He pours as he speaks, filling tin cups with an amber liquid that smells like burnt peaches. When the last is filled, he raises a glass. 'To the victors of Luss, to all that's left.'

'To all that's left,' they chorus.

Fallon swigs it back, and Shroudweaver follows, his nose burning as the shot races around his skull and down into the pit of his stomach.

The big, bearded man slams the cup down, sighs contentedly. Next to him, the lithe redhead runs their fingers around the inside of the cup, sucking them slowly clean.

Fallon smiles at them. 'Ship, Shroud, you might remember Masthauler and Dropdancer, captain and first mate of the *Hart's Pride*.'

The big man stands, bows at the waist. 'Lord, lady, we were there at Luss. You would not recall us, I suspect.'

Shipwright stands, bows in return. 'I recall your ship, and you.' She glances to the side, 'Along with the *Maiden*. We might not have carried the day without you. Without either of you.'

Dropdancer stretches a leg over the arm of the vacated chair, sniggers. 'Alright. Keep it in your pants. We're glad we won too.'

Shroudweaver coughs. Something in the music drifting down, filling the room, something in the booze. His head feels thick. Might just be Smokesister's words still rattling around in there. He taps Fallon's arm. 'When you say "all that's left"?'

Fallon opens his mouth, but it's Brimlicker who answers. He rolls his eyes.

'He means everyone that stayed in Hesper, that wasn't lost in the south, or that hasn't lit out for somewhere else.'

Shroudweaver nods. 'I guess I owe you all my life.'

Shipwright's face is grim. 'It doesn't seem like time's been kind to Hesper's captains.'

Masthauler leans into Dropdancer. 'How many have we lost, all in all?'

Their slim fingers move over a necklace at their throat, counting beads. 'Twenty-seven.' Masthauler nods. 'Counting the *Volante*?'

Dropdancer shakes their head. 'Shit. No. Twenty-eight.'

Shipwright pours, drinks. 'Ships and all?'

Dropdancer twitches. 'The south was a big old mess.'

'No arguments at this table,' Fallon mutters.

Masthauler leans forwards, scratches at his beard. 'Fallon says you're going north to stop Crowkisser. That true?'

Shroudweaver nods. 'It is.'

Masthauler's eyes are brown as a millpond, wary. 'You need ships?'

Shroudweaver shakes his head. 'No, well . . .' he glances at Shipwright.

She nods. 'We might need you to get people out, if it all goes sideways, or if Crowkisser comes here first.'

Brimlicker's eyes widen. She pushes her hat back. 'Is that likely?'

Fallon shrugs. 'Fuck knows. We don't think so, but that slit loves to be unpredictable.'

'Shit,' Brimlicker says. 'Shit.'

Dropdancer squints at Fallon, refills their glass. 'I hate it when you talk like that.'

Fallon rolls his eyes again. 'She's a slit, Drop. Not a saint.'

Dropdancer drinks, grimaces. 'Still, not a good look on you, Fallon.'

Shipwright steps in. 'We don't have time tonight to cut Declan into a respectable man. But,' she grins. 'We do have time for a game or two.' She produces cards from her shirt pocket with a flourish. Thumps the pack down in the centre of the table.

Fallon bursts out laughing, 'Ship. You dark horse.'

Shroudweaver leans forwards excitedly. 'Deal me in.'

Shipwright arches an eyebrow. 'Are you sure love?'

He nods. 'Deal me in.'

Dropdancer picks up a card, turns it over as Shipwright deals. 'What is this? Martyr's Hook? Blind Piglets?'

Masthauler tuts. 'The art's too nice for Blind Piglets, Drop. Get a grip. Look at these lines.'

They lean over and gnash their teeth at him. He ruffles their hair.

Brimlicker leans back, and pulls her hat down, 'None for me thanks. I get fleeced by these idiots daily. No reason to encourage it.' She waves her glass at Swallowgut, and he refills it absently, then goes back to sorting cards.

'So,' Shipwright says with a grin. 'Here's how you play.'

The next few hours pass in a blur, the pile of coins in front of Shroudweaver shrinking inexorably. He's sure he knows the rules. Sure he knows Shipwright's tells, but somehow, the coins just keep disappearing. Dropdancer folds after an hour or two, curls up in Masthauler's lap, snoring like a torn tin can. He plays over their shoulder, solid and methodical.

Eventually, he's priced out by a beautiful run.

'Mountain to river,' Shipwright smiles, and gathers the coins in.

Swallowgut folds soon after, shifts nearer the fire to pop nuts with his remaining teeth.

Shroudweaver tries to keep pace with Shipwright and Fallon but it's hard to concentrate. The band are still playing, the singer's reedy voice picking up a tune he recognises, worming into his brain. He hums the chorus as the patrons sing along, stomping the boards and rocking the chairs.

. . . the night the bones came tumbling down . . .

Brimlicker tips her head up. 'Sound familiar?'

He nods, 'I'm not sure why.'

She smiles sadly, pours him another drink. 'Because it's our song.'

The singer's voice thin at first, thickening in the smoke as the familiar lines cut through the haze.

> *there's a city by the sea*
> *where bold ship captains dwell*
> *they've seen the shores of old Empire*
> *so, sailors, listen well*

Brimlicker taps Shroudweaver's shoulder, flicks a thumb at her chest and grins. He smiles wanly, trying to pick up the tune. It's changed since last he heard it.

A gaggle of chattering girls barrels past, and he loses some of it. Another snatch drifts down after, and he starts to sing along, softly:

> *oh the night the bones came tumbling down*
> *Old Luss was shining bright*
> *the eyes of all her ladies were like cats caught by the light*
> *the eyes of all her soldiers were a-gleam with blood and hate*
> *and the banner of the Empire flew above its broken gate*

The melody's a little sprightlier than he remembers. Brimlicker joins him, her voice a slightly off-key counterpoint:

255

the night the bones came tumbling down
we danced into the dark
for weaver's thread
and shipwright's hand
had struck the fateful spark

Across the table, Fallon elbows Shipwright. His baritone joins in, a beat late. She winces, buries her head in her hands.

The band picks up momentum and Shroudweaver feels his heart lurch. He hadn't noticed his hands shaking. And the heat in here. Prickling his skin like a cat's tongue.

There's another verse, and a chorus, but it's all filtered through a pulse in his skull like a deep ocean wave:

'gainst Empire's tooth and Empire's bone
we stood in fear and fright
'til shipwright and shroudweaver
drove the dead into the night
and the children of the mountain
sang their name in bloody joy

Dropdancer's voice raised there, the swing of a tankard in their hand, that for a moment, looks like a sword. Shroudweaver flinches.

and the lady of the towers and her darling baby boy
and the lord of all the falcons
with his bold and martial hand
brought our sailors home
to their own beloved land

There's a taste in his mouth, like wet copper. He can see sails. Not coming home though. The sails of the fleet before the invasion. Before the shore. Canvas struck white against the sky, the blue recoiling.

~ *the sea*

~

~ *the ship*

~

~

~ *departing*

It's early morning, they've been sailing all night. Dawn touches the tips of the waves, darkness still hangs on the coast. The walls of Luss are visible even from here, bent and slanted at unnatural angles.

Silence on the sea. The wind swells the belly of the canvas, and the boards creak as the shore rises to meet them. The chink of armour and harness as the captains prepare their crews. The ship a nose in front. Shipwright at the prow, Arissa on deck, a silver spine amid a sea of bowed heads. Fallon back in Hesper, making sure they have a home to return to. Out here, Arissa is the heart of it all. The blade on the deck, the voice at the drill. Moving from soldier to soldier, tightening straps, touching shoulders, murmuring encouragement.

It works, as far as it can, with sixty men and women crammed on to their ship. The same again on the *Maiden of the Forests*, the *Hart's Pride*, the *Volante*. The best on the seas. The smaller ships behind them bringing yet more men, and none of them with a clue what they are up against.

Not that it matters. Hesper marines, all of them, the city's finest – pirates, down in the bone. They're bound tooth and tongue to their captains, their armour marked by little flourishes of defiance. Here a sprig of Burner's wood, there a set of teeth from the slim dreamfish that thronged the Heron Halls. Pirates dressed as soldiers; soldiers playing pirates. There was no standing army for the Grey Towers, so the whole outfit hung on personality, on alliances, on having enough people on your side at the right time.

Economically, it was incredible, practically it was a nightmare. Or it would have been, if Arissa hadn't commanded the respect she did. As she moves on deck, their faces turn to her like flowers to the sun. She speaks to them sparingly, firmly, co-ordinating where and when they would strike.

The whole fleet is poised for some kind of retaliation from the shore. Shields moving forwards and locking together, expecting a hot landing: arrows, catapults, magic. Something. Shroudweaver's teeth itch, his nerves strung tight. And nothing comes.

The shoreline pulls closer; the city, distantly, smokes.

Drums boom as the ships swing into landing formation, picking up speed. The marines crowd the gunwales, lips tight with anticipation.

The sound of horns hangs in the morning air, followed by a great shout from the crews that rolls over the waves. The shore eats the sound, and opens up again to silence, the pull of the waves, the creak of the wood. A shiver runs the length of Shroud-weaver's spine.

Ballistae on the deck swing ponderously around, their crews straining at the winches. Brassy spinners hum along their spans, caging their energy like cats. Still silence. If Luss knew they were there she showed no sign. And if the Emperor waited within those ruins, Shroudweaver couldn't sense him. He runs his mind out across the water, as he'd once been taught, letting it touch the silver thread of the sailors' souls that skipped above the waves, seeking the echo of other souls ashore.

He senses something there. Distantly, within the city walls, but it's far from the gleam of a human heart. Rather, something dull and fractured, spread across the bones of Luss like scum on a pond.

A shout sounds from the tiller, followed by the soft boom of anchors being dropped. The *Volante,* the *Maiden* and the *Hart* a beat behind the ship which rocks to a stop in the last stretch of deep water, before the coast rises to sandbar and shore. The deck lists as bodies crowd to the narrow, sharp-prowed, landing boats, slim and fast as a needle, ten men to a side.

Shroudweaver stumbles in next to Shipwright, threads catching on the rough wood, bundles of powder tucked between his feet. She flashes him a brief smile. Around him, there's a swell of chatter as the marines stow their gear, check their blades, curse each other, place bets – the murmur before war.

A sickening lurch in his stomach as the long boats drop, and the surf rises to meet them. The boats rock briefly as they steady, then regular shouts sound as they scull, oars out, to shore paddle blades digging deep, picking up speed. Shipwright is at the prow of one boat, Arissa balanced lightly on another, the standard of Hesper snapping brightly in her left hand – a grey falcon above the sea.

A beat behind, the other boats follow, prow to stern with grim men and women, silent except for the bark of their skipper's commands, their faces pulled into that tightness before battle. The pirate's quiet, he'd heard it called.

The shoreline drew closer, barren and empty. The wrecks of a few small skiffs are visible, the odd twisted hump of driftwood presenting the only barrier to a coast which rose smooth across dunes and marram before decamping onto the plain outside of Luss.

The strokes of the paddles eat up the sea.

The boats hit the sand with force, their crews staggering. Shipwright is up and over the side before they come to rest, boots down into shallow water, into the kelp that lies thick in the soft waves. Something metal flickers in her hand and she stutters up the beach, a beat ahead of her own shadow.

Shroudweaver runs after her, head low, fingers seeking small souls to work with; dune creatures, beach crabs, sand mice. He pulls them loose, gathering them red-threaded into his right hand.

Not all weavings needed form to be powerful. He remembers the teachings at the Aestering, remembers his tutor stooping low over a pond, reaching down into the water, pulling forth life along silver threads, balling it into his hands; resting it in the wheezing chest of an old man. Watching his eyelids flicker open, even as the water blackened, and the lilies withered from the roots up.

Small gatherings could generate enough power, in a pinch.

A few more steps over scrub, stone and sand, and Luss pulls

into view. As he runs, he catches Shipwright, who has stopped at the head of the rise, her eyes scanning the horizon.

The city's gates not opened, but listing.

Silence shrouds Luss for a moment or two more. Then slow movement from between the riven gates. Bodies, burnt and blackened. At their back, armoured soldiers, the chain at their necks and hearts swimming like fish-scale.

They file onto the plain slowly, raggedly, leaking from the city like blood from a wound. Occasionally, above the ranks, a horse sways like a midnight drunkard, its rider slumped on its back, skin half-cloth, half-bone.

Shroudweaver tries to take count as the crews of the other ships form up on the rise behind him, their bodies pressed low to the dry grass. Companies form up and split off into parties of ten, twenty.

The scouts have misjudged, badly. His eyes run over the bodies blackening the grass in front of Luss. They are outnumbered, two-to-one at least. Perhaps a thousand, he guesses, assuming there aren't more left within the walls.

Arissa ducks low next to him, her hands loosening a dagger in its sheath, her eyes thin, as she performs the same grim calculations.

'Shit. Shit. Your new friends better come through on this. Are they here?'

It's four weeks since they'd received the first message. Shroudweaver startled awake by a voice on the wind as soft and as solid as if it lay on the pillow next to him. That voice had introduced itself as Skinpainter and it claimed to represent a splinter faction within the Empire – rebels.

That was the first Shroudweaver had heard of them. He'd had no idea how they'd found him, or why they'd chosen him out of all the other ears in Hesper. There was something in Skinpainter's tone though, something low and urgent. Bring the Empire to bay at Luss, they'd said, and you won't fight alone.

Shroudweaver had taken it to the Fallons who'd heard him out soberly. They'd paused his tale briefly as an elderly woman rolled in with fresh drinks, bending low to catch her muttered words, before beckoning him onwards. He'd pretended not to notice the pattern her fingers drummed on the cups, or the careful way she arrayed them on the table.

A week later, they'd mobilised.

The voice on the wind had sounded pleased. Relieved even.

Shroudweaver had been unsure about it all. Now it's three weeks later – twenty ships, five hundred men, a city silenced. And he's still unsure.

'*Are they here?*' Arissa's voice is sharp as a wasp.

Shroudweaver squints towards the city. Shipwright nudges his shoulder and hands him a spinner that's buzzing faintly. 'Think about seeing, Shroud.'

Shroudweaver takes it, and does as he's told. His vision clears like mist burning off in the morning. Not perfect, but each body sharpening in contrast to its neighbours. His teeth hum with the effort, and he counts as he hunts for some hint of where their allies might be.

He sees ranks upon ranks of silent soldiers, some blonde-haired, clutching long leaf-bladed spears, stretched tower shields. Their life evidenced only by the racing pulse at their throats and the shifting of their eyes.

In front of them, the people of Luss, or what remains of them. Their flesh is dried and paper thin, torn by sea winds and the teeth of dogs, their cheeks hollow and burrowed through. The elegant robes of their merchants fallen to shreds, hung around their emaciated bones. The dancing legs of their criers still stumbling on broken feet, ceremonial stones gleaming on darkly bloodstained lips. Beyond them gather other dead, many only given away by the fraying silver threads that run from their trapped souls, fracturing at the touch of their cold skin.

Shroudweaver hands the spinner back, relaxes as his muscles untense and his vision clears. 'That's a lot of soldiers. How much do you pay your scouts, Arissa?'

She digs the point of a dagger into the soil, twists it. 'Not enough. But my guess is, they've reinforced since we last sent riders out.' She frowns. 'No matter. We're committed now. Ship-wright, form the lines.'

Shipwright turns, gesturing to the troops drawing up behind the rise. Positions are prepared. Wicked crossbows are cradled and strung. Bundles of gull-feather quarrels staked out neatly. Fifteen of those airborne in a minute would buy them some breathing space.

Arissa straightens her back surveying the lines, and grunts. 'I might have known they'd be expecting us.'

Shipwright looks at Arissa. 'I don't know, my Lady. Thell's not so far. This might just be what they do.' She tightens the strapping on her hands, flexes it experimentally. There's an ache in her wrists. The spinners are taking their toll. 'We just don't know enough.' Arissa flashes her a smile, and she feels it run electric down to her stomach. This is really not the time.

'Declan thinks we should try and parley. Suss them out. Thoughts?'

Shipwright makes a face. 'If you wanted our thoughts, you would have asked a little earlier.'

Arissa sheathes the dagger, grinning. 'True.' She motions, and horses are brought up the embankment. Strong grey beasts, like cut marble come to life. 'Still I'd appreciate the validation.'

Distantly, the criers of Luss yowl like dying cats, wet, feral and looping over the intervening plain and its scattered ruins. Echo-ing over the dregs of what Luss once called its Summer Town, now reduced to broken bricks and splintered tile.

Shipwright frowns. 'We're low on cover out there. As good as dead if they decide to take us out now.' She pauses, 'And I hate horses.'

Arissa swings a leg up over the charger, smiles down. 'Why? Not enough sails?'

Shipwright mounts, unsteadily. 'Not enough space.'

Shroudweaver saddles up, nudges his horse closer to them. 'Do they have horses where you're from?'

Shipwright glares at him. 'Shut up. I don't need to be humili-ated before I die.'

He shakes his head. 'That won't be today.' His eyes study her hands, 'How far can those spinners reach?'

She shrugs. 'Me. My horse, probably. Not big enough for much else.'

'Can I try something?'

She nods. 'Sure.'

He reaches out. 'Give me your hand. With the spinner.'

His fingers are light on her knuckles. Rougher than she would have imagined. Inexplicably, she relaxes. Almost drops the damn thing. His dark eyes are confident as he loops a thin red thread around her palm.

He squeezes her fingers tight. 'When I say, turn it on, let it sing. And push outward.'

She holds his gaze for a second. 'Fine. Don't take my hand off.'

He smiles, sweetly sly. 'I would never.'

Arissa tuts disapprovingly. 'I notice you've both ducked out of reassuring me, but that's fine. Shall we announce ourselves?'

Shipwright glances over her shoulder. Near enough three hundred men and women are tucked against the ridge, with more in reserve. A signal runs down the line and they stand with a shout that sends the sky reeling. She'd never got used to the sound of Hesper at war.

As the drums start, they roll down across the plain. A marching rhythm. A sailor's stroke. Brutal, fast, unrelenting.

Steps match the drumbeat. That mass of men striding forwards, held within a hairsbreadth of a run. Every thirty paces or so, the bright feathers of the first mates and captains, the flash of their pearly teeth, the gleam of gold necklaces and rings. Beards and hair oiled and dyed, shaved and spiked. Monkeys that rode shoulders, screamed in time to the drums, gnashing their filed little fangs.

The three of them a little further ahead on the horses. Not a gallop, not yet, but the long legs of the coursers eating up the salt plain outside of Luss.

From behind them, trumpets rise out of the ranks like breaching fish, silver and slim. The sound is like an unsheathed sword, ringing in the air as it rises and falls with the drums.

The throng ahead of them does not stir. Across the salt plain, only the criers seem to tire, slinking back behind tall shields and long spears.

The walls draw closer. Shroudweaver can count heads now. A thousand at least. Some eyes milky as the grave, some sharp, calculating. Some nervous.

There's a method to it, now he looks. Never more than twenty or so of the living soldiers together. The dead stud the ranks of the army like rivets in a board.

Something in the back of his brain wakes at the thought, but they're moving too fast for him to investigate. Instead, he tries to feel for the threads he's tied to Shipwright's spinners. Keeping them close so he can weave into them, if he has to.

He's never tried it, but it should work in theory.

They ride on.

Shipwright's shoulders tense for a rain of quarrels, of those slim spears. Nothing comes. Yet. These western wars are a mystery. A clash of thousands, with no more planning than an island raid. A confidence she doesn't feel. Her insides are water, and Shroudweaver's esoteric assurances are doing nothing to level them out.

Arissa certainly looks the part, but she's not sure how she ended up a bodyguard for this strange, steely woman. Or how she ended up in her mad city. She can hear her father's voice reproachfully. *Too fond of the tides, little sailor.* Wasn't that the truth?

Here she was, mid-tide. Scared shitless.

She's never seen anything like the army in front of her. Never even knew you could raise the dead. Sure, she'd heard stories from Shroudweaver, but everything he'd told her had sounded gentler, more spiritual. She'd never seen a body get up and walk.

She kept a grip on the reins. Barely.

They stop around a hundred feet from the front line, close enough to see the sporadic rise and fall of breath among the front ranks.

Arissa leans into Shipwright. 'Let me handle this. Pull me out if it goes bad.'

Shipwright winces. 'You're putting a lot of faith in us, Arissa.'

The Lady of the Grey Towers smiles, plants a kiss on her cheek. Violet and steel.

'I'm putting a lot of faith in *you*, Shipwright. You won't let me down.'

Arissa adjusts her helmet, kicks her horse forwards a few steps. Waits.

This close, the smoke above Luss still sings of burning, of hot stone and ash. She can remember when the city rocked with laughter, when she got teenage-drunk in its pleasure gardens. She wonders how quickly the flowers burnt.

Eventually, the crowd parts and a horse edges forwards, black and beautiful. The figure atop it is faceless, shrouded by a mask of milky, shifting stone, its hair bound in thick, dark braids. Shroudweaver shifts to stand beside Arissa as she moves to meet it.

Arissa draws herself straight, feeling her pulse race in her throat. She imagines Declan's big, brash face and tries to keep her voice steady. She takes a breath.

'I am Arissa Fallon. Of Hesper. Of the Grey Towers. We come to the aid of our sister city, at her request.'

The figure watches blankly. Its long fingers fidget with the horse's bridle. She clears her throat and continues. 'We have come to order the immediate withdrawal of the Empire from the city, the surroundings, and all unlawfully ceded territory.'

The figure regards her for a moment. Its featureless head tilts slowly, gloved hands moving softly. When it speaks, its voice is soft.

'The Emperor is here, but will not speak. I am the Gem. I speak for him.'

Arissa composes herself. 'Then we present these terms.'

Its hand raises, palm out. 'There will be no terms. The statement is this. Luss belongs to us now, as she always should have. In time, you will belong to us too.'

Arissa feels her heart lurch. 'So, you will not negotiate?'

Its head moves back and forth slowly. 'We do not negotiate. We claim. We restore all to peace.'

It pauses, gestures to the approaching army. 'You bring us war.'

Arissa takes its measure, but gets nothing from the featureless mask. 'It doesn't have to come to this.'

The thing is briefly silent, then begins to shake. It takes a moment for her to realise that it is laughing.

It points at Shroudweaver. 'Ask your pet, Grey Lady. Ask it how little we care to stand one side or the other of life and death.' Its hand closes into a fist. 'We will kill you in a moment. You may run, if you wish.'

The Gem turns its horse away. Opens its fist, fingers spread wide. Shroudweaver recognises the gesture. Not quite shroudweaving, but close enough. He feels the power pulse from its outstretched fingers into the ranks of the dead and senses something in their tattered souls awaken, something else inside that, dark and hungry.

Fills his lungs. 'Run!'

To her credit, Arissa is as fast as a strung bow, heels into the flanks of her horse, turning towards the shelter of their army.

Distantly, he hears the first creaking hum of Hesper's ballistae as they wind back. The chunk of release, and the sky begins to darken with quarrels. Covering fire. They ride back under falling shadows as the air vibrates like a harp.

The horses' necks stretch out, juking and turning to avoid the jut of shattered buildings.

For a moment, he thinks they might make it – Shipwright crouched low, clinging on white-knuckled; Arissa as effortless as a show rider, spine scalloped against her horse's back.

The front line of their troops approaches, peeling apart to draw them in.

Shields locking. The rough voices of the captains readying their crews.

From behind comes a shriek like an eagle. Those blonde warriors surging forwards, arms lifting, and suddenly the sky is filled with bright, leaf-bladed spears. There's a tearing sound over his shoulder, and one strikes the ground to his left. The next kisses the skin on his cheek with a spatter of blood.

He bites back a yell, calls to Shipwright. 'Now!'

Somehow, she manages to kick the spinner into gear. Her

right hand hanked mercilessly in the horse's hair, her left shifting forefinger and thumb until the buzz of the brass singes his teeth.

Shroudweaver dips to the grass and gathers what power he can, all the little souls of worm and mouse and bug. The earth blackens as his horse's hooves churn it into ash. The spears fall like percussion, like the beaks of birds. The spinner hums, and he saws the reins, pulls his horse closer to Shipwright, to her buzzing hands.

For the briefest of seconds, he can feel all those tiny souls stringing his body like lamps on a wire. Then he reaches for the red thread, and pushes them into the spinner.

The machine screams like a wasp hive, and he feels the force of it expand outwards, like a blossoming flower. The horses stagger with the weight, and Shipwright curses, the palm of her hand blistering to raw strips.

'Damn you!'

'Sorry. Keep it going! Please.'

The next spear hits the spinner's field dead on, ploughing a straight course to Shipwright's skull. Before it gets there, it's lifted, spun, shivered into shards of falling metal and wood, which fray into harmless splinters as the bubble created by the spinner soars to full effect.

Fascinating, if he wasn't shitting himself.

The souls leave him. The spinner whines like a boiled cat.

It's a few hundred yards to their own lines now. Then at his back, a tearing, percussive sound, as if the earth had suddenly learnt to flow like water.

A stark, tall woman sings at the edge of the Empire's line, her voice layering, harmonising with itself, lifting the soil as her lungs rise.

Shroudweaver urges his horse faster.

A splintering behind them as one of the ruined cottages is caught, lifted, the stones tearing with furious noise, arcing down into the ranks of Hesper's marines. Blood. Screams. Where the stones land their line folds inwards in a mess of yelling bodies.

They're a breath away, two, when the rising earth clips the back hooves of Shipwright's horse, lifting them both in a somersault over the lines. Arissa and Shroudweaver follow a second later.

He doesn't have time to disentangle himself, so the only thing he can do is twist to put the horse's body between him and the earth.

When he lands, he can hear the horse's shins snap. He pulls himself free of the screaming animal as the shield from the spinner winks out; rolls to one side as spears land, one through the poor beast's throat, the other just shy of his shoulder.

Staggers to his feet, breath ragged, soaked in hot blood.

Pulls Shipwright free. She's somehow mostly unharmed, buried in a crater under the body of her horse, hollowed out by the dying implosion of the spinner. Her left hand is a blistered, bloody mess clutched in his own.

'We're going to talk about this, Shroudweaver.'

He grins despite himself, picks up a shield from a dying marine, still clawing futilely at the spear through her guts. His head swills with terror and elation.

From their left, Arissa reels to her feet, armour dented and helmet bloody over one brow, her sword coming clear of its scabbard.

She yells for the charge, and the rest is a blur.

Perhaps he remembers his legs lifting, pounding the torn earth.

Perhaps he remembers the shape of that stark, tall woman swaying as a crossbow bolt bows her ribs, her harsh harmonies falling silent, stilling the earth.

The ships' crews diving through that winnowing rain of spears, into the rats' warren of cottages and outbuildings. The skeleton of the Summer Town filling with steel.

The mercy of return fire as the ship's ballistae began to find their mark, skittering off some of those tall shields, punching through others.

The slow advance of the dead, then faster as the Gem's hands rose, stumbling and hurtling over the broken ground. The living soldiers hanging back, locking shields and lowering spears. Letting the dead do the work.

Faster still, some with feet torn and ragged, others only a little paler than the living, tucked inside neat boots that were once embroidered by lovers, punched by the skilled hands of craftsmen.

The marines aren't fazed. Quick economical barks that would normally flit from mast to mast peel their charging groups into neat crescents.

The dead hit them in silence, met with roars and curses. The back of each crescent crumples and the sides sweep in, men and women armed with cruel cutlasses and the single-sided slip daggers so beloved of Hesper's back alleys.

They'd planned for this, for fighting something that might not want to drop with any decency.

'Go for the legs,' Shroudweaver yells. A dreadlocked woman flashes him a wicked smile, 'Whatever you want, Weaver.'

Blades fall, severing sinews, tendons, the backs of knees.

A few of the crews aren't quite quick enough, and get caught by a clumsy blade or a hurled spear, but, somehow, it works. The marines peel back, scattering into the ruins. When the dead follow, garrottes swing out razor-sharp and heads tumble.

Shroudweaver watches it all with a faint vertigo. Pulled up out of his own body, it feels like. He's never really been in a fight like this before.

A man windmills at him, arms flailing, teeth spread wide in a savage grin. Instinctively, Shroudweaver pulls with the silver threads of his left hand, tugs him off-balance, and strikes with the red of the right, sending a clutch of little souls lancing into the side of the man's face. His jaw explodes in white fire and the body lurches sideways and away.

Shroudweaver steps forwards, ducking against a wall as a spear whirs past inches from his face, and reties frayed threads around his shaking hands.

The living soldiers of Thell are advancing in the wake of the dead. Shields locked, spears out.

The marines try to flank them but they're outmatched. Rapidly,

Hesper's frontline is pushed back into the ruins of the outer city. Thrust against walls, speared against the stones.

The fighting is brief and brutal. A shield batters Shroudweaver, knocking him to the ground. Glimpsing a raised spear, a helmet, he tries to roll before the shield explodes from the side, and a whirring, buzzing rain of punches drives his attacker to the ground. Shipwright hauls him to his feet, ducks a thrust from a charging warrior, then recoils as Arissa's sword rises from behind him, cutting into the man's neck, briefly sticking on his spine. She tugs it free, pushing the body off the sword with her boot. Looks at the pair of them.

'This is bad. Where are they?'

Shroudweaver shrugs, heart racing. 'I don't even know who I'm looking for.'

They backpedal as a squad of marines roils past.

'We don't have the numbers for a drawn-out fight like this,' Arissa yells, as they hurry up some broken stairs to crouch on a low roof.

Distantly, the Gem watches the struggle. Shroudweaver can feel its gaze from here, like a sore under the skin.

Shipwright steadies his shaking shoulders. 'We're not done yet, not by a long shot.'

She calls down to the marines below. 'Hellfire, like we practiced.'

Within the press, a few men peel off, digging into satchels to produce clay jars stuffed with the powder for which Hesper is so rightly feared. Ship weapons originally, a gunners' mix that would burn sails, and people, in a pinch.

Thell's shield-bearers advance, implacable. Hesper had tried to plan for this too.

Slings arced up, burly tattooed arms sending the hellfires spiralling over and down towards the centre of the shield-walls.

Shipwright watches them like a hawk, eyes narrow and steady. Not enough in these to break a formation, usually, not enough fire in whatever stones they'd ground down. Not without a little push.

As the pots hit raised shields, bodies, the ground, they splinter. Shipwright opens her spinners at the sound of the first crack, lifting and firing each little grain of dust with energy beyond anything it should ever see.

The shields of Thell light up with scorching flame. It clings to iron, to bone, to hair and lips, and sears until there's nothing left. A head ignites like a flare.

The formation reels, crumples, and the marines surge forwards.

Shipwright falls to her knees, and vomits. Her nose filled with the stink of burnt meat. On the ground below, half-charred voices call out in liquid, looping misery.

Western wars are not the same.

Hesper advances. The captains and marines finish off the injured with merciless efficiency.

The Gem's head tilts, and Shroudweaver feels its gaze on them, before its horse turns and files back into the city. The remainder of its army pulls back with it. The stragglers are unceremoniously cut apart. Hesper pulls no punches once her blood is up.

Shroudweaver watches axes fall to sunder limbs. He feels faintly sick, but professionally, relieved. They've paid attention to his advice.

Arissa vaults to the ground and takes a fresh horse. Her hair's wild and mussed, cheeks flushed, her eyes electric. 'We need to take the gates.'

'It could be a trap,' Shroudweaver replies.

She checks a clasp. 'Of course it is. I have confidence that you and Shipwright can carry us through any surprises.'

Shroudweaver sighs. 'Lead on, I suppose.'

Arissa smiles. 'You're getting the hang of this.' She glances to Shipwright, 'You going to be OK?'

Shipwright nods.

'Sure. Just not used to' – she waves a hand – 'all of this.'

Shroudweaver laughs. 'Me neither.'

Arissa snorts. 'You don't get used to it. You just win it. Otherwise, it happens to you. Mount up.'

They do, the horses picking their way over the remains,

stepping carefully around twisted bodies.

Teams pull Hesper's wounded back towards the boats, cutters already at work. There will be time for the dead later.

Ships' surgeons stalk the battlefield, grim-faced as gargoyles, shepherded by burly men and women moving four-cornered, bows and eyes roving warily.

Shroudweaver watches them. 'Can you do anything for them Shipwright? With the spinners?'

She thinks. 'Possibly, one or two. But I'd need one or two per person. Unless you can pull that trick again.' She flexes her red, stripped fingers. 'And I'd rather you didn't.'

'I need you both here,' Arissa calls over her shoulder. 'Otherwise none of us are getting out of this alive.'

Shipwright shoots Shroudweaver a glance, and he presses his lips tight.

A few clipped shouts and the trumpets pick up a different rhythm. The marines jog towards the walls, some teams with ladders, others with long, whip-thin poles. There's clearer ground before the wall, beyond those outlying ruins.

Here had been the fairground. The feast of Dreaming Flowers. Here the heralds had sung for the great and good of the city.

The ground was churned to mud by dead feet.

The army forms up before the walls, shields raised and cautious. Not too badly hit at all, despite the ferocity of the fighting. Maybe forty, fifty down.

The horses sidestep, whinny. Something rank in the air still, beneath the obvious horror of the city.

Shroudweaver tries to quest out along the threads, but everything's a mess. Battlefields always were, somehow. Too many fractured little deaths. This one was worse than most, though.

As his horse resettles its hooves they crunch down through a mouldered breastplate, worn paper thin by the years. The mace held in the withered hand is like no design he's ever seen, green as a bird's egg, smooth as its shell.

He reaches down, pries it loose, hefting it experimentally. The haft is made of some dark wood, worked as smooth as the head.

He catches Shipwright eyeing him. 'You're an odd fish, aren't you?'

Smiles sheepishly, feeling a flush scorch his cheeks. 'Just a curious one.'

She laughs. 'The fish bit is supposed to be the problem.'

'Oh.' The mace suddenly a little slick in his sweating palm.

She rides a little closer, and elbows him in the ribs. 'We'll work on it.'

Within minutes the army is arrayed, the ships' captains striding the front like peacocks, crowing exhortations to blood and infamy, with a side of bribery. Teeth gleaming, hats trimmed with feathers, and helms tooled with designs of the deep.

Luss itself is quiet, aside from the odd creak of a settling building, or the rattle of stone.

The only quick way in is through the great gates, hewn from gilded whalebone but lying half-fallen now, aslant each other like loose teeth in a spinster's mouth. Beyond that, the walls were a tough climb, still strong on the sea-facing side. According to the scouts, it was only on the inland approach that those vast slabs had caved inwards, as if pushed by a great weight.

A shiver runs down his spine.

'Thoughts, Shroudweaver?' Arissa says.

'I'm not a military man, my Lady.'

She rolls her eyes. 'So what? I'm rolling in those. I want your thoughts.'

Shipwright laughs. 'You sure?'

Arissa shoots her a look. 'Yours too.'

His gaze flits between the two of them. 'I can't sense anything much, but that's no surprise. We know they're in there somewhere. Which means they want to draw us in.'

'Which means they've got something else up their sleeve,' Shipwright finishes.

He nods. 'Quite. But then, so do we.'

Arissa twists her lips sourly. 'Assuming your voice on the wind is to be believed.' She waggles her fingers meaningfully.

'That's not helpful, Arissa. But I trust them. I've never known a magic like it. And the Emperor doesn't seem to be one for guile.'

She nods slowly, reaches up to scratch under her helm. 'So what do you suggest?'

Shroudweaver feels her eyes on him, a twist of fear in his gut. 'If it were me, and I'm not saying it is, I'd draw the tooth. The two of us are enough to punch through and scout the first street or two. And we can get out quickly if they're waiting.'

Arissa looks sceptical. 'Unless they've got something we're not prepared for.'

Shroudweaver looks at Shipwright. 'They're not prepared for us, my Lady, And, respectfully, this is why you brought us along.'

She looks at him, a faint quirk of her lips. 'They train you well at the Aestering, don't they?'

He dips his head. 'Tolerably.' Turns to Shipwright, 'You ready for this?'

She shakes her head. 'No, but I'll do it. Let's not take the horses though. And give us twenty men. I'm good, but I don't want keeping you alive just on my back.'

Arissa nods. 'Done. Brimlicker's crew will go with you. They're the worst pack of street dogs I've ever met.'

She motions a captain over, a tall woman with a ridiculous hat, and a pair of daggers that sit easily on her hips. Her crew follow her, low-browed and bright-eyed, rolling their shoulders and hips.

Arissa points at the pair. 'Brim, don't let these two die.'

Brimlicker's eyes rove over them and she adjusts her belt. 'You got it, lady.'

She steps aside as they dismount. 'Nice to meet you. How do you want to play this?'

Shipwright looks at Shroudweaver. 'Stay behind me.'

He nods.

She turns to Brimlicker. 'Boarding speed, we don't go deeper than a couple of hundred yards, anything less than us that gets in our way, we put it down hard. He's there to take care of anything worse.'

Brimlicker nods, teeth flashing. 'This is fun, isn't it?'

Shipwright shakes her head as they start advancing on the gates, 'Not really.'

Brimlicker pats her shoulder, 'Relax, new captain. I'll buy you a drink after. Never been in a battle that killed me.'

Within minutes they're under the shadow of the pillars, their angles impossibly large, glimpses of bone sheared through the torn metal.

The gates open out into a plaza scoured with dust and swirling wind.

Shroudweaver feels the dead then, in the buildings, alongside the barest flicker of breath. There must be some living soldiers in there too.

He gestures to two houses on the left. 'Troops, waiting.'

Shipwright's voice is low in the drifting ash. 'OK. Follow me.'

They snake to the wall side of the first building. She turns to Brimlicker. 'When this comes down, go in hard.'

The pirate looks puzzled. 'What do you—?'

Shipwright's hands fly out, a spinner in each. The wall in front cracks, whines, and vaporises. She dives in.

To their credit, Brimlicker and her crew follow hot on her heels.

The contingent of soldiers inside is watching the entrances. They turn, but not fast enough.

Shipwright catches a dead man's skull between her fists, the bones vibrating to shards as she brings her hands together. A dagger leaves Brimlicker's hand as she crouches low to take one soldier in the throat, before she ducks beneath the spray to stab another under the ribs. As the rest of her crew engages, Shroudweaver hangs back, trying to pick up some shiver of the Empire's army.

A dead thing swings for his face, another one of those beautiful maces a hairsbreadth from his nose. Absently, he flicks out with the red threads. Pulls its soul from it and binds it to the fingers of his right hand.

The empty flesh totters, wobbles and falls.

As Shroudweaver steps back, arms wrap around him from behind, leathery and thick. He struggles, ducks forwards to shuck them off, but the grip is strong, fingers working their way to his windpipe. Heart hammering. Panic rising in his chest.

The body holding him rocks once, and goes slack.

He turns to watch it slide to the floor, one of Brimlicker's daggers stuck in its skull.

'Don't get relaxed, Shroudweaver,' she smiles, pulling it free with a twisting crunch. 'Relaxed will kill you.'

He nods. 'Thanks.'

She's already gone, helping finish off the last few stragglers. A good first move, all in all, no one down. A couple of nasty wounds, but light and messy rather than fatal. Brimlicker pats one of the injured men on the shoulder and grins. 'Maybe get some good scars out of that. You might finally get laid.'

Shipwright strolls across to Shroudweaver and sits down on a chunk of broken masonry. She dusts her hands and begins rebinding their straps. 'Well, we've made it this far.'

He smiles. 'You're very casual about this.'

She shrugs, 'I'll panic later. I like to bottle things up. Saves time.'

He rests a hand briefly on her shoulder, and she leans her head against his wrist. The touch shocks him, but he fights the reflex to pull back.

'There should be more of them. That was a . . . lot of dead people.'

She nods. 'Well, they're either in here somewhere, or they've left the city.'

He chews his lip nervously. 'Doesn't seem like their style.'

She frowns, 'Do we even know what their style is?'

He toes the ancient body at his feet. Remembers the feel of its fingers on his bruised throat. 'No.'

'I suppose it's clear enough to signal some backup.' She calls out to Brimlicker. 'Captain, can you do the honours?'

The flare that arcs out over the square is red, actinic.

Shroudweaver watches it flame, letting the purple spots kiss the back of eyelids as he closes them for a moment. 'I suppose they'll come now.'

Brimlicker nods. 'We'll keep watch.'

Shipwright glances across at Shroudweaver. 'Are you OK? Your hands are shaking.'

He tucks his hands into his robes. 'It's nothing.'

She frowns. 'Were you always this bad a liar?'

'It's nothing I can't handle.'

She shakes her head. 'Still not convinced.'

The square rapidly fills with the body of Hesper's army, Arissa at the head, still on that horse.

Shipwright eyes her. 'She's got style, I'll give her that.'

Shroudweaver makes a noncommittal noise. 'A stylish target.'

His head's racing, trying to find a trace of the Empire's army. Something keeps pinging his consciousness, like drops in a well, but the ripples and echoes are just too refracted for him to do anything about it.

And she's right. He's not well. Bindings held too long. The shake in his muscles threading his nerves. His ribs jittering with the run of small souls trying to find a way out. He clamps down, hard. It's not the time for it.

Where the hell are they? Where is the Gem, if nothing else?

The marines continue to take up position, working their way slowly outwards, building by building. They don't have the bodies to cover a city this size. It'll slow them down. Perhaps that's the plan. He laughs to himself. How would he know? This isn't his world.

Shipwright's hand on his shoulder makes him start. She smiles. 'Sorry. Deep in thought?'

He nods. 'If I don't find them . . .'

She hunkers down next to him. 'Do you always pile everything on yourself like this?' She gestures. 'There are hundreds of people out there. We'll find them.'

'None of them are me,' he mutters.

She snorts. 'Wow. That's a nice ego.'

He smiles. 'It's not that, it's just this magic, it's . . . familiar.'

A thunderous noise interrupts him as the ground shakes. Brimlicker's curse peels from above, loud and violent, followed by screams.

He rushes to the door in time to see the remains of the square melt and fall into a widening sinkhole. The men and women inside tumble one upon another, Arissa's horse reeling back from the edge as the stones shudder into the ground.

A shimmer like a heatwave and the first thing he hears are the harsh harmonies hauling the earth down into the pit. Another stark singing woman, half-twin to the one on the field, but older, a flare of silver in her hair where age hasn't brought it down to salt. And in front of her, suddenly, the ranks of the Empire, roaring down the spokes of the square, the dead at the front, the living with those wicked spears bringing up the rear.

One of Brimlicker's crew curses, and his crossbow twangs. The bolt takes the silver-haired woman in the throat and her song gurgles into blood. The ground stabilises.

The remaining marines form up around the edge of the pit and take the brunt of the first charge. Shields and bones splinter. Their line buckles, holds, barely.

Shipwright is already moving, a blur as her spinners whine into action.

Shroudweaver follows her, for lack of a better plan, reaching a hand towards the distant body of the silver-haired woman. Her soul is just loose enough for him to snag it, sliding it free past the slick bolt. He lets it shudder down his forearm and releases it to take shape inside the front lines of the advancing dead.

It forms a figure, for the barest moment. Made of light and fury. A new god, that exists for a second amid a tangle of limbs and teeth, before it dies in a detonation of gold light. Limbs rain down upon the marines who flinch backwards. A little slice of Shroudweaver's heart yelps with glee.

Then, for some stupid reason, his legs are taking him towards the front line. He sees Shipwright arrow off towards another breach, and briefly wants to follow her, until the momentum of hammering feet pulls them apart. He's thrown into a gap in the shield-wall and suddenly he's among the press. A hand pulls him forwards, a face yells for help, and he's in the middle of it all.

Bodies thick on either side him. His movement completely

bound to the shift of their muscles, the ragged push of their breath.

Men and women cursing, spitting and gouging.

The space he stands in was created by the woman at his feet. She's holding her guts in, barely. Her wet eyes meet his for a second before her comrades drag her back behind their lines. He chokes down a rising panic that tastes like bile.

The man to his left is bleeding from a cut above his eye, the stink of his sweat still mixed with the wet of the sea.

He grins madly at Shroudweaver. 'They're coming again!'

He's not wrong. There's a ringing in Shroudweaver's ears as he sees the dead of the Empire charge down the street once more, trying to force the survivors back and over into the pit.

Time slick as butter. He can feel the hammer of his own heart, a hundred times faster than the feet rushing towards him. Terror flicks his neck like a rope.

'Shields up!' shouts one of the captains, a brute of a man, silver hair bright against his dark-skin, his voice rolling like a shore tide. The shields lock with a shout.

It takes him about that long to realise he doesn't have a shield.

The woman on his right leans in as their bodies press forwards, her short hair red as blood. 'Duck your skin behind here, weaver.'

He slips behind the curve of her shield, and the man to his left locks the rim of his own against it. 'We've got you.'

The dead are a couple of meters out, close enough for Shroudweaver to feel the drumming of their feet, too many for him to halt completely. But maybe that isn't necessary.

He tries to hold his nerve as they thunder closer, focuses on the small details. The yellow sheen of their bared teeth, the twitch of flies drinking at their eyes. The faded hint of inked designs, chipped paint on nails.

Shroudweaver feels the bodies either side of him tense. The stink of those last few moments, piss and sweat and blood.

He watches the Empire's dead tumble forwards towards the shields held protectively in front of him. Reaches out to the ragged souls of their front line, and pulls.

The first line of the dead drop as the life is wrenched from them. Shroudweaver reels backwards, the silver thread on his wrist burning like fire as unleashed essence thunders into his chest. He falls into the mud with a force that pushes the air from his lungs. The charging soldiers are nimbler than he expected, vaulting over their fallen comrades. The man on his left reaches down to help him, and then the lines hit.

The marines stagger back. A dead man's mace takes his new friend in the side of the skull. The man's face crumples around the socket, and his body lists sideways, his strong hand going limp.

He lands on Shroudweaver. A mess of muscle and armour and sticky fluids. Shroudweaver flails, rolls clumsily from underneath as the red-haired soldier takes the mace-wielding corpse in the neck with a wicked hook blade.

Its head detaches slowly, suspended on strips of dry flesh. Around them, the line buckles. The weight of bodies is relentless. They don't lose many, but with every soldier that drops on the Hesper side they're pushed back towards that terrible pit which used to be the town square.

Shroudweaver can see the remnants of the vanguard scrabbling around down there. Heaped up on each other in a desperate effort to get out, but the sheared walls of the pit are too sharp. The stench of their pain is overwhelming. Silver soul threads fraying and tangling around bodies that yell for help. Help's going to be slow in coming. If they turn their backs for a second on the advancing army, they're all dead.

On the other side of the pit, he can see Shipwright swing like a wrecking ball into the centre of a knot of dead warriors. Maces shudder into splinters as they arc towards her head. Her punches drive through ribcages and detonate spines. The air is cut by the high, thin whine of her spinners, already driven beyond fever pitch. The marines with her cluster in her wake, back-to-back. She can't keep them all safe forever.

A chunk and screech from above, as ballistae fire rains down into the ranks of the dead. The bolt-men have finally, mercifully, managed to take up positions on the twisted battlements. Most of the dead go down if hit squarely, but enough lumber forwards, pinned through shoulder and legs with hideous black barbs.

Shroudweaver ducks another swipe from his right, dodges low and kicks out, scything the legs from under his attacker. Brings that beautiful mace down to crush a skull. Tries not to dwell on the eggshell sound.

Another sound under that, tremors dancing lightly around the edges of his bones and teeth like the first murmurs of a landslide. Trumpets on the south side of the pit, and Arissa's there, still atop the charger, swinging round towards Shipwright's flank on the east. A cohort of marines with her, javelins arcing out to hit the side of the charging dead. As they near the press, she rises up in the saddle and shakes her arms. From her silvered gauntlets blades flow downwards like water. She leans forwards and scythes out. Heads and limbs tumble. The horse rears, and hooves thunder through shield and bone. For a moment, they have respite.

'Weaver!' the red-haired soldier yells and his attention snaps back to their own line. Holding, surprisingly. They might be trained as soldiers, but the men and women here grew up on back-alley squabbles. Shivdancers and blackjack babies the lot of them.

The redhead's having a time of it though, two howling corpses pressing them hard.

Shouts rise from the pit at Shroudweaver's back, and part of him thinks about the ready supply of souls just feet away. He could turn the tide right now. His red right hand twitches.

'Weaver!' the redhead screams again, and he turns from the pit and runs towards the sound, bodily tackling one of the dead to the ground.

Shroudweaver turns his shoulder to it as it falls, hears its ribs creak. Its head rolls madly, jaws gnashing, hollow, shrivelled eyes lining its sockets. He catches a faint smell of the perfume it must once have worn. Mouths an apology as he drives his head into the bridge of its sunken nose.

Too close, too frantic to get a grip on its soul. But he'd learnt a thing or two in Hesper, and in the Aestering before that. As its head lolls back, he swings a fist in from the side and cracks its skull against a cobblestone. It goes limp, and he staggers upright to see the small redhead dusting themself off.

'Bit tardy, Weaver.'

'Sorry,' he smiles.

'Still alive to complain,' they grin, a slight shake in their voice. 'Maybe not for much longer though, eh?'

He follows their gaze as Hesper's diminished line reforms and contracts around the lip of the pit. Another squadron of the dead are marshalling to move down the street. Perhaps a hundred. And behind them, the living warriors of Thell, at least a hundred again, their bright armour and tall spears ready, their blonde hair incongruously beautiful in the mid-afternoon sun. He imagines there must be around the same number on the other side of the square and curses under his breath.

The red-haired soldier nods. 'That's about the size of it.'

The Empire's army advances. At the head of the living soldiers stands a brute of man, heavy-shouldered as if carved from stone, half as wide again as the others, a hammer on his hip like it belongs there.

More worryingly, by his side, a tall woman, iron hair bound back behind her brow, arms festooned with carved wooden charms. Something in the shake of her soul reminds Shroud-weaver of the singer who had collapsed the square. A vibration, deep and strong. A bell in her left hand.

He points. 'We take her out first.'

His short-haired companion nods. 'I'm Dropdancer, by the way. Thanks for asking.'

He opens his mouth to apologise and they nudge him playfully.

'It's OK, you idiot. Just want someone to know my name before I die.'

He grimaces. 'You're not going to die, Drop.'

They put a hand on his wrist, hold his gaze for a second. 'Optimism. I like that. Cute.'

Shroudweaver scans the enemy lines. Something's held them up. The dead are shuffling incrementally forwards, the living soldiers casting around nervously.

Then it arrives. That lean black horse shouldering its way through the ranks of the dead. Atop its back, the Gem, its faceless white stone mask scanning their lines, the quartz gleaming in the sun that filters through the drifting ash.

He feels its gaze alight on him and watches as it slowly unsheathes a black sword.

A shout from behind them. 'Ladders down!'

Shroudweaver risks a glance over his shoulder. Those long ladders and poles they brought to breach the walls have found a better use now, threading down into the pit, forming a web of wood for the injured to scramble up.

Arissa and Shipwright are at the edge, co-ordinating the effort. Slowly, too slowly, the wounded start to wend their way to safety, like dragonflies on a river stem.

Dropdancer follows his gaze. 'We just need to hold long enough to get them out, Weaver. Long enough to get them out.'

They eye the slowly advancing line. 'Can you buy us time?'

Shroudweaver counts the dead, ten upon ten again. More than anyone has ever tried to unbind. In a rush, in the midst of battle. He can hear the dry soft laughter of his teachers. An arrogant boy. A stupid, overconfident, arrogant boy.

He flashes Dropdancer what he hopes is a winning smile. 'Of course. Just keep me alive a bit longer.'

They run a whetstone along the curve of their sword, glancing up from beneath their brows. 'You got it, Weaver.'

As if it's heard his lie, the Gem drops its sword and howls, a thin screech like a vulture pulled from a kill.

As the black sword falls, the dead begin to run.

Hesper's shield-wall locks with a shout once more. Tired. Quieter. Barely echoed on the other side of the pit.

Shroudweaver tries to calm his churning stomach. He'd thought the second charge might be easier, somehow. It's not.

If anything, they're faster than last time. Fifty yards away, then forty, then twenty. He tries to clear his breathing, flush out his body and mind. Find the threads to pull the souls from as many as he can. He can hear shouts from behind him; hear Dropdancer's harsh breath to his right, the muttered curses of the man who has moved forwards to fill the gap on his left. They're depending on him.

He clears his mind, breathes deep and reaches out.

Something hits him like a fist in the gut.

Cold, flinty. He looks down. There's nothing there, but he can *feel* it driving into his stomach, like a stone slowly forced into his intestines, ragged edges tearing.

He falls backwards, vision blurring and catches sight of the Gem as he does, its implacable mask focused directly on him even as that black horse thunders forwards.

The dead are a bare few feet from the front line.

His vision shifts as Dropdancer hauls him up. They're mouthing something at him, but the pain has filled his head like water.

Then the world shifts.

A bell tolls out, light and fierce. Shroudweaver can feel the vibrations lift the hair on his head and run down his spine. That iron-haired woman gestures, and a building in front of their line shears apart, stone and tile thundering down on the advancing dead.

In the same moment, that massive brute unslings his hammer, and calls out: 'For the Republic!' A voice like an unexpected landslide.

Shroudweaver feels Dropdancer's hand on his wrist, their voice urgent. 'What the fuck, Weaver?! What the actual fuck?'

He turns to them and smiles through the pain. 'Turns out I've friends in unexpected places, Drop.'

In front of them the hammer swings like judgement and the dead it meets splinter into fragments. Its wielder laughs with every blow, savage and wild. At his back, the living soldiers of Thell lower spears and charge into the unsuspecting ranks of the dead.

The Gem's head whips around, and immediately the pressure on Shroudweaver's stomach ceases.

It's almost too late. The charging dead are only partially halted, hundreds of them still only a heartbeat or two from thundering into Hesper's line again.

Behind them, the rebellious soldiers are fighting hard, clinically, their spears puncturing skulls and severing sinew.

Their new allies' front rank kneels, and the soldiers behind springboard off outstretched shields to rain down metal upon the dead. That hammer still swings. The iron-haired woman has drawn a slim sword, wielding it and the bell with shattering precision.

For a moment, the momentum is with the living, and before Shroudweaver knows why or how, he's climbing over the rubble, and someone's calling for the charge, and it's him.

Dropdancer follows him laughing, and then like grains of sand tipped down a hill, the marines charge, over the broken building and into the oncoming dead.

Shroudweaver ducks the first incoming blow, reaches with his red right hand and pulls indiscriminately. The worst possible thing to do. Artless. Dangerous. This deep in the press though, there's nothing but the dead in front of him, and he rips their souls from them like meat from a bone.

When they take root inside him, those souls are screaming. There's nothing but bodies pressing on bodies after that. The brutal hack of the marines' blades, Dropdancer's curved sword and the matching arc of their smile.

Somehow, Hesper is gaining ground. Forcing the dead back against Thell's spears.

It's then that the Gem comes for him. That black horse changes, manifesting new joints which pop and twist, angling itself in impossible ways to traverse the rubble and masonry.

Shroudweaver turns to face it, and for a second, he feels the return of that shredding pain in his chest, before his eyes catch sight of a hooded figure in neat robes of red and yellow, battling through the press. The dead claw at their sleeves. Shreds of cloth spin loose, but the grasping hands and swinging maces always seem to miss the bone.

The Gem sees the figure coming at the last moment, rears its twisting, chittering horse and charges, that black sword of rough metal in its hand, studded with the same crystal that hides its face.

The dead try to scramble from its path, some curious terror filling them, but the horse rides over and through them, snapping bone, rib and spine.

As its gaze shifts, Shroudweaver feels the pain fade. He watches with hitched breath as the Gem's sword swings down towards the hooded figure like a talon and somehow, misses. The robed figure leans back briefly behind the shields of the soldiers to either side, and emerges again like a striking snake, a leaf-blade spear in its right hand, haft writhing with markings black as ink.

The Gem raises its blade to intercept, guiding the horse to one side, its multiplied, flexing hooves thundering in the soft soil.

A twitch of the hooded figure's inked fingers, and the spear jukes slightly in mid-air, skims the blade of the sword, and strikes the side of the quartz mask with force, an inch shy of exposed flesh.

Horse and rider stagger sideways as cracks spread in that implacable façade. The Gem unleashes a scream that's more animal than man, turns and runs. Its mount scuttles up the side of the nearest building, its laboured lungs lurching with a wet, bubbling whine. A few bolts whizz after it, peppering the stone.

With the departure of their leader, the dead are lost for a moment, reeling like dreamers half-awakened.

Slowly, methodically, they are cut down.

Soon, there's enough space for the two standing sides to regard each other. They're tattered, war-ragged, bloody.

The hooded figure picks their way across the detritus, towards Hesper's chewed lines.

Shroudweaver is stitching a cut on Dropdancer's cheek. Thread just as thread, for once. He turns as they approach.

Their hood tips back ever so slightly, and finally he can see their face.

Shroudweaver's breath catches in his throat.

They smile, wiping blood from their lips. In the depths of their hood, bright, clever eyes shine.

'You must be Shroudweaver. I'm Skinpainter. I'm the one that's been whispering in your ear, I'm afraid. We have work to do.'

Shroudweaver opens his mouth to reply, when that faint tremor returns, louder this time, roiling up the walls, shuddering the stones and listing buildings.

Skinpainter staggers, and the soldiers behind them look around in confusion.

The sound grows like an undammed river, stones crackling and rolling. It's only when he sees the walls surrounding the sunken courtyard bow inward that Shroudweaver realises what is happening.

This is how Luss fell.

He can hear screams, shouts of caution and panic. Bodies flurry around him. The collapse happens with deliberate, awful slowness. First, a hand at the top of the walls framing the courtyard, then more, followed by an impossible tangle of legs, limbs and teeth. A profusion of ribs and spines. The stones crack as a wave stitched from flesh and marrow hurls itself against them. The shapes of individual people still recognisable within the morass, but the way they move is like nothing human.

Abominations piled against the stones of the city like ants, pushing them down with the sheer weight of their bodies. As they move, a wet rattling accompanies them, like someone shaking a bag of bloody dice, teeth and bones running loose inside their raggedly stitched shapes.

Shroudweaver sees the dead advancing with unnatural speed, heedless and howling, crashing against the hastily locked shields of the marines.

The circle of soldiers backed against the pit draws together, bodies pressing tighter and tighter. The soldiers of Thell scramble into their ranks, adding their own long shields and wavering spears to the thinning defensive line. The conjoined dead roil towards them without the slightest pause, their shifting mouths leaking a sound like a file on bare stone. Shroudweaver feels it dig into his heart, sees the other soldiers shudder, near breaking.

Then, of course, Arissa rides in. A grey banner rises as she pulls her horse back, its hooves striking sparks from stone. A brief shake of her shoulders and she digs her heels into its flanks, driving it forwards. It leaps over the first wave of the dead, as she lashes down with the sword, severing throat, bone, sinew. Heads, hands and limbs tumble.

Her soldiers cheer her, and follow her. Shroudweaver's heart soars with terror, and in that moment he knows they'll die if he doesn't do something. Hesper will fall, and everything else with it.

He stands unmoving as the charge flows past him. His breath stills to shadow within his chest. His mind empties of everything but the pattern of the birch trees by the Aestering. Silver and shadow, dark and light, the rhythm of it.

Absently, he hears the lines hit. The clash of blades. He lets it all fall away, and reaches out to those awful, twisting things. He can sense the Emperor somewhere within all the risen dead, his soul infesting them like a worm in an apple, a sliver of glass in a finger. The only way to stop this is to drive him out.

How though, that's the question. He's never seen magic like this. It's almost like weaving, in a way, but more brutal. Parasitic, dominating. No care, no craft, no symmetry.

Through lidded eyes, he watches Arissa as she's dragged from her horse. That beautiful beast going down beneath an avalanche of teeth and nails. There's no time to plan. The square is slick with blood. The marines have fallen back, cutlasses drawn. The soldiers of Thell marginally fresher, but still driven to their knees, their spears outthrust in a desperate, last-ditch defence. If the strewn bodies slow these things down, he hasn't noticed. Still more come, surging forwards from alleys, battering against shields and blades.

A few familiar faces rail against the tide. Dropdancer wearily at his side, their cutlass falling rhythmically, mechanically, their dodges staggering with exhaustion. At their back, their captain, that dark-skinned, silver-bearded man, pivots with surprising grace, his teeth locked in a grimace. By his side, Brimlicker perches on a piece of shorn masonry, braces herself against a boathook, catches one of the conjoined dead under the armpit, and pulls. It tears wetly. Blood flecks her face and her gleaming teeth as she calls to Shroudweaver across the seething mob. 'Can't hold them forever, Weaver.'

On the other side of the square, a marine is caught and tossed in the air like a dog. The hellfire in his pack detonates, and the thing that seized him screams as half of its body ignites.

A cheer goes up, then turns to shouts of horror as the burning wreck stoops to the corpses below, gathers a welter of limbs to itself, and presses them close to its flesh which melts and reforms. Shroudweaver hears the souls inside it scream.

He can't delay any further. A heartbeat or two longer and he'll be too late.

The fighting swirls around him. He struggles to stay focused, to find the rhythm he needs to weave. Half a hand away, Shipwright reels into view, her hair plastered down with sweat. She catches his eye, reads the worry in his face and shouts over the clamour. 'What do you need?'

'Give me space,' he replies.

She nods, flexes her neck and turns the spinner in her right hand, shuddering into a blur of fists. The first creature to come for her she simply grips at the wrists, and tears. Red rain, and chunks of something warm. The second is faster, getting its jaw around her hand before she hooks her fingers under its teeth, and the spinner burrows out the side of its skull in a spray of bone.

A third takes the legs from under her, before losing its long, undulating neck to a savage blow from a sword – Arissa, still somehow standing, the banner ragged and bloody, her sword-arm shaking with exhaustion. The two women move back-to-back as the creatures circle.

Still more come. Hesper's marines, Thell's soldiers, all pushed back, teetering on the edge of the pit. A glimpse of a hammer swinging. An ink-stained spear. A bell. Shroudweaver can't help them. He has to stay separate. Close enough to the dead to free them.

He rubs powder on his temples, letting the smell of saltpetre push him down into the between spaces. The skin between death and life. He can almost feel his instructors' hands on his forearms, easing him down into that place between the worlds where the silver threads are clearest.

He can see the souls of the dead immediately, snarled and bound to each other, writhing in confusion. And like a spike at the heart of each creature, a barb that gleams bright and slick. The Emperor, he suspects.

He should do something careful, something smart. He doesn't have time. His body rocks as something buffets into him from the side; Shipwright and one of those things battling tooth and nail, Arissa's sword flashing like silvered lightning. He feels it distantly, like thunder under water.

He can release these souls. But if he does so, there will be nothing to stop the Emperor from gathering them in again.

Unless, he thinks, as his heart races, unless they are already claimed by someone else. Someone like him. At that thought his fingers begin to move, weaving an intricate cat's cradle of red thread in his left hand. Striving to keep his legs steady, his heels on the edge of the pit now, the faint sense of stones sliding from under them. Stay balanced, a few seconds more. He presses the twisted bundle of threads to his chest, just above his heart. With his right hand, he reaches to the nearest glimmering soul, and *pulls*. He can feel its edges, cold as mountain ice against his skin. As he does, he releases all those little animal souls, that fistful of charge he's been carrying with him. Scraps of mice and plants. A nothing, a child's cantrip, but, if unexpected, enough. The energy detonates soundlessly inside the first bound soul. It jerks as if lightning struck and its connections unravel like torn wool, like a tugged fishing line, spiralling from one body to another, as the Emperor's barbs are yanked out and cast off.

Freed of those barbs, the souls rush forth in confusion. To leave them in these contorted bodies would condemn them to madness. To set them free would place them back in the Emperor's jaws. Gritting his teeth, Shroudweaver clenches his fists, and pulls the red thread holding the cat's cradle that thrums against his chest.

The cradle unravels. As the threads spiral loose, Shroudweaver brings his left and right hands together, weaves silver to red, and pulls the unbound souls into his body.

The first soul binds to his heart like rain on glass. The second like sweat on skin. The third like lips on ice. The tenth, the twentieth, like flesh on marrow, like moss on the mountain, like bark on the tree.

The fiftieth, like an anchor to a lake. Like tides to the moon. Like the moon to the sun. He gasps, driven to his knees.

The hundredth like spring to winter. The thousandth like a child to its mother. The last few gather like the clouds that make the sea, and pour into him like the ocean.

He can feel them all within him, boiling through his veins, humming under his skin. When he speaks, his teeth shudder with a thousand voices. His limbs shake. His fingers dance. Absently, he knows the creatures have fallen. He can hear cheers wash over his sweating temples like a submerged bell. But he's losing himself in this new sea. This ocean of voices and stolen lives.

For a moment, through closing eyes, he sees Shipwright's shape. Her face registers confusion for a second, until he draws his hand to his temple, taps it. The effort almost kills him.

She nods, lifts a fist and drops it like a hammer. And then, mercifully, empty blackness.

When he wakes, he is back on the ship. Luss hangs in the distance, lit by the red of fire.

He tries to speak, but the words fall out of him in unspent pieces.

Above him on the deck he can hear the sounds of singing, laughter. Shipwright leans across, cradles his head, forces water between his lips.

'What happened?' His voice feels lonely, unechoed, almost a stranger's.

She shakes her head. 'We won, you idiot.'

He swallows, and she strokes his hair.

> ~   *the sea*
>
> ~
>
> ~
>
> ~   *the ship*
>
> ~
>
> ~   *returning*

Twenty years later, she's stroking his hair again – her hands a little more weathered, but still careful, gentle. His head rests on her shoulder as the song fades from the last few tables of drunkards and revellers. The bar is emptying out into the Hesper night, the patrons spilling into the streets to kick cats and swap spit. Cups are drained, bottles swilled. Swallowgut busies himself sweeping up the detritus, his voice a low litany of curses against the heartlessness of his regulars.

Dropdancer and Masthauler say their goodbyes, sway out tucked into the crooks of each other's arms, bickering gently. Brimlicker shoots them a weary look, and ruffles Shroudweaver's thin hair before pulling her hat low and her collar high against the unseasonable chill.

The night air sweeps in with the swinging of the door, hung with the first hint of the ice that must be building thousands of miles away on the edges of the Heron Halls. The cries of seabirds mingle with drunken laughter, fading out into the streets.

The band are among the last to leave, Fallon bowing over the fiddler's flinching back, filling his ears with questions, his pockets with silver. He stoops awkwardly to Shroudweaver's table as he passes, sets down some coins, and winks.

Shipwright raises a lazy hand to trail fondly along his shoulder as he goes and kisses Shroudweaver's head. 'Come on sleepy. We'll stay here tonight. Too long a walk for those ghostly legs.'

He nods softly. 'That'd be nice. I think. That took me back. More than I expected.'

She turns to him, the bones of her face picked clean by the lamplight. 'Funny how a few lines can bring it all back, isn't it?'

He nods again, because he isn't sure what else to do.

A few minutes later, they're tucked up in a small room that sits beneath the tiled eaves like a widow under a shawl.

Decently clean, even if the beams were stained with decades of pipe smoke; salvaged wreck timbers still strung with blackened barnacles. Shipwright is out like a light, her head on the pillow. She'd never met a drink she didn't like, from dark southern wines to herbal spirits that scoured the lining of your skull.

Sleep doesn't come to Shroudweaver. The ticking of the beetles in the eaves, the laughter from outside the window picks at the edges of his skin. Sweat runs in cold waves over his body. He draws his knees to his chest and tries to control his panicked breathing. The song's stopped long ago, but he can't leave the war behind.

Shipwright shifts gently in her sleep. He doesn't want to disturb her, to put any more on her than she's already taken. So he closes his eyes, pulling his knees up tight.

The darkness is unforgiving.

He can see Skinpainter's crooked smile sketched on the back of his eyelids. Hear, clear as the day, that awful question as they stood atop the broken remains of the Empire's unbound army. 'Do you think you can do that again?'

He could. He had.

Over the next few years they'd turned the tide against the Empire, against the legions of its entangled dead. Again and again, Shroudweaver unbound them, taking them into himself, their thoughts and their lives thronging his. Pushing into the space between his bones, threading the meat of his muscles until every breath he took was echoed in a thousand dead lungs.

Again and again, the Empire's forces were pushed back. Without the dead they could not hold, and with the rebellion of Thell's living, they were sore pressed. That motley crew of revolutionaries – Kinghammer, Skinpainter, Belltoller, the Deadsingers – were always at his back. A reminder of what was at stake if he stopped for even a moment.

He performed the unbinding, over and over, until the motions were as familiar as breathing, as chopping wood, as falling in and out of sleep. Fingers dancing raw and aching with thread, with the familiarity of movement. With every burning twist, the patterns became clearer, the feel of the Emperor's sorcery under his fingers, twined round his thumbs, scored beneath his nails, as close to weaving as the out-breath was to the in-breath. The Emperor's magic was the air on the other side of the threshold; a mirror to his own weaving, but bigger and more brutal than anything he could imagine. Spread over so many souls, and over such an age that it terrified him.

It had taken Shroudweaver some time to realise the extent of the Emperor's influence, his ability to thread himself not just through souls, but living flesh.

Battle after battle, with a taste like old ice growing on his tongue, his mouth thickening with stagnant magic, as they drove the Emperor back. Battle after battle. Unpicking, unbinding, all his horrific work. Not a moment to do more than stitch all those souls into his own chest. To lash them to his own feeble heart, his own bowing bones.

At first, Shroudweaver had heard the voices of his tutors, rattling around his skull, deriding the arrogance of it all. The sheer nightmarish scope of unravelling bindings that stretched across half the north, over every blasted furrow of every frozen field. Bright barbs in the hearts of not just the Empire's soldiers, but its farmers, its merchants, its children. Everything that had touched the mountain was corrupt. Infected with the Emperor. Little shards of his essence swimming in the blood. Everything that touched the mountain was corrupt and that included their new allies from Thell, who had followed at his heels ever since the last ash drifted from the walls of Luss.

Shroudweaver's mind had started to unhinge with the horror of it. Every unbinding felt like a conversation with the monster that sat in the heart of every soul from Thell, like a weevil in a boll. Every stitch like they were singing a song together, point and counterpoint.

He'd tried to explain it to Skinpainter, to Shipwright, but his tongue ran loose with the water of other voices. A trickle, then a torrent, until there was little of him left. All these other lives burrowed into him for safety, until his whole body was a hollow, scurrying log, rattling with madness.

What even was Shroudweaver then? A head full of salvaged souls and a heart thudding with the strain of it all. His mornings cursed by blinding headaches that punched through the thin layer of his skull and lanced his brain into insensibility. Shipwright holding him through it all. The touch of her hands on his shoulders. The feel of her lips on his sweat-slick brow.

He tears himself loose from the past and glances down at her as she sleeps, running a hand over her cheek. That nick under her left cheekbone, the curl of hair at the back of her ear.

A sudden ache inside, and a sob that runs the length of him – a sadness lurking under all the souls stitched into his chest. The sorrow just another spirit riding his heart without his consent.

Perhaps their real troubles had all begun back then. By the time he stood outside the mountain, there was barely a shred of him left. His body home to a thousand refugees, and needing space for still more.

The remnants of the Emperor's army were holed up within Thell itself, in the fort they called the Stump. As for the night they'd brought it all down – the siege that lived in the black of his mind, like a scorched wet hole – even tonight, twenty years later, full of drink and guilt and self-loathing, his mind won't throw up the shape of that last battle in its full horror.

A few brief moments come crawling from the pit. Kinghammer, sheathed in blood from the waist up, so thick it seemed like a wet cape. Belltoller bringing the great gate down with a stroke of her hand, falling sideways, streaming smoke from her burning eyes. Skinpainter's magic like a black snake of script, alien and terrifying. The armies of this new Republic and Hesper's corsairs cheek by jowl in the belly of that nightmare.

Of course, the dead had come for them, one last time. And he'd unbound them, taken them into him by the hundreds. Barely noticed; what was a flood to a drowned man?

Then, without elegance or fanfare, they had the Emperor.

Victory. His lieutenants seemingly gone or fled. The mountain finally, dreadfully, quiet.

He shivers, slips his feet under the covers, pressing his calves to Shipwright's back to steal a little heat into his freezing bones. She makes a small noise of protest and flinches away, back into dreams.

He tries to calm his breathing, like Smokesister had taught him, when they'd brought the thing that was his body back to Hesper. Four in, six out, measured like a soldier's drum. Her hands sketching intricate shapes over his heart, as she bound the dead tighter to his shaking ribs.

The Emperor's breathing, that's what he remembered. Not the moment of his capture, or how terribly ordinary he looked, with his heavy brow and sharp nose, hair a little thin on the top. Only his eyes were strange, like flint flecked with gold.

His eyes and his breath: ragged and layered, doubled over and over. Shroudweaver recognised it, how closely it sounded to his own.

Now, in that small smoky room his hands fidget with the covers. His nails pick at the scabs on his skin.

That breath had never changed. Always buzzing and rasping like a cheap lock. Even once they had brought the Emperor to bay, once the soldiers of the Republic had tortured him. Seeking secrets, they said, but Shroudweaver knew the wet sound of catharsis when he heard it.

He remembered that breathing, the way it threaded the first and last conversation he'd ever had with the Emperor of the Dead.

43

a great cleft, black against the water
where light falls through along the path of the moon.

—*Geographical Features of the Farther Reaches*, Vol. IV

Fifteen years ago, and Shroudweaver's down in the guts of Thell, in the near-lightless passages which flee from torchlight deeper into the bowels of the mountain. Miles of rock, ringing with the sound of water slowly dripping out and down into the dark lake that fills the hollowed heart of the Stump.

Skinpainter standing at his side as the Emperor knelt in front of them, a thin, gaunt shape breaking the black sand that framed the lake. This was his final interrogation, the last flurry of questions before the victors of the Republic consigned him to the depths. Shroudweaver hadn't asked to be there. Hadn't wanted it, but the voices of the dead held inside him had grown too loud and he hadn't had the energy to fight the rebels' demands. The newly minted Republic wanted their victory, and Shroudweaver wanted to get home.

The Emperor knelt in front of them. Knees bruised. Naked, and chained. Fingers crushed by Kinghammer's maul so no weaving could take place.

His mangled hands moved slowly, absently, like fronds in water.

'So you're the one.' His voice rusted from lack of use. 'Caused me a lot of trouble, for such a thin little man.'

His hair had grown long, his grey stubbled jaw stark in the half-light. If he was in pain from the ragged cuts that ran across his body, it only showed in his laboured breathing.

From above, the sounds of reconstruction rattled down into the belly of the mountain. The crack of stone sheared clean by belltollers, the bellow of voices shifting carts, men and supplies.

Amid it all, Skinpainter had moved forwards, their voice low as smoke. 'Don't give him a moment, Weaver, we have no idea what he's capable of, even like this.'

A brief laugh from the Emperor then, his smile thin and bright as a rake's dagger.

'That's the first true thing you've said, Skinpainter.' He'd raised his shattered wrists pointedly. 'Your friend with the large hammer made sure of me though.' He smirked as he shot a lidded glance at Shroudweaver. 'Ask *him*, if you don't believe me.'

As he waggled his fingers the bones ground audibly, his smile hanging loose. 'We're not much without our digits, are we?'

Loose fingers, ragged bone, Shroudweaver had seen them in every hand since that day, in every twitching nail. A decade and a half did nothing.

In the smoky backroom bed of the Gull, his ribs ache. He remembers stepping forwards, past Skinpainter's cautioning arm, taking the Emperor's hair and pulling his head back to look into his eyes. He can remember the hatred he had felt.

'We are nothing alike.'

The Emperor had laughed at that. 'Like the sound of that tune, do you? Keep singing it, Shroudweaver. You know what I've done, and you know how I've done it.' His chains shook with the mirth rattling around his gut.

He had grinned at Skinpainter. 'Did you never stop to wonder how your clever friend was able to unpick my work so neatly? I'm almost impressed.' Dark lips thinned over his sharp teeth. 'I'm mostly furious.'

A flicker of rage for a moment, until a smile slid back over the Emperor's tongue like a shark.

'But there's a *price* isn't there?' His crushed fingers jerked pointedly towards Shroudweaver's chest. 'They're all in there now, aren't they? Whispering away. Making themselves at home. All my stolen subjects.'

Shroudweaver had looked away as the voices in his head surged in response, clamouring for revenge.

The Emperor jerked forwards, the burr of his voice delighted, thick with clotted blood, rasping on the edge of that wet, hot breath. 'You'll have to let them go sometime, Weaver. I'll be waiting.'

Hunger slicking his face, until Skinpainter's fist had cracked against his jaw with an audible snap. 'Shut your mouth. You're going nowhere but to the council of the Republic. They'll decide what to do with you.'

The Emperor spat redly on the ground, eyes hooded with fury. 'I bet they will. Won't that be satisfying for them?'

His head rose again, one pupil glinting madly from beneath the ribbons of blood-caked hair and torn scalp.

'Doesn't change a thing, Weaver. You made the biggest mistake. We should never take souls into ourselves. Arrogant. Stupid.'

Shroudweaver had sucked in air, damp, cool with moisture from the lake which lapped the underground shore, somewhere out in the darkness. He'd bitten down on the panic rising inside him and thought of what Shipwright would do: get the job done; deal with the fear later.

Then he'd found his voice. 'So you *are* a weaver?'

The Emperor had laughed, his hunched shoulders shaking, before he turned his head to fix Shroudweaver fully.

His voice a snake's hiss. 'Weaver! Everything you've learnt, everything they taught you in that pathetic birch grove you call an Aestering. *Everything* you think you know is but the briefest sliver of the world I could show you. The world I have walked in since before the ice lay on the stone.'

Shroudweaver recalled his twisted fingers reaching upwards, his eyes wet and luminous in the dim light. 'You have not even begun to know the touch of death, Weaver, the mysteries of the soul.' That smile, pale as bone. 'You're like a blind child lost in a forest. I'm the moon above.'

Shroudweaver had shivered, something in the words lodging under his heart. 'You're talkative, that's all I know.'

A light had gone out in the Emperor's eyes, which turned flat and hard. 'Laugh it off, Shroudweaver.' He'd chuckled. 'How many voices laughing in you now? A thousand? Five thousand?' He shuffled forwards, chain links stretching. 'I was widespread, little weaver, like a seed in the wind, like a lie in the heart, there was a shard of me within everyone, living *or* dead in this mountain.'

He lunged on the chain, his knees striking the wet sand. 'That is where my magic surpasses yours, blind child. I will *always* be in this mountain, in its people, in their blood and bone. I have woven myself into them in their smallest spaces. Every hollow of their heart is a home for me.'

His smile radiant again, a preacher spreading the gospel. 'This brief separation of yours will fail, Weaver. You cannot hold these stolen souls forever.'

Impossible to forget the feral light in the Emperor's eyes as his voice soared. 'And once they are unbound, they will flow forth into every single little shadow, every drop of blood. Every cut, every mouth, every wound will be as a door to me. I ride their souls like skin upon flesh, like wind upon the land, like the buzz in the heart of the fly. You cannot hold me forever. You cannot *hold me.*'

His face twisted with glee, the echoes falling into the black lake, which ate the sound. Shroudweaver remembered the way the words had died, sifting into the black.

Skinpainter had simply rolled their eyes and rubbed their knuckles. 'Are we about done here Shroud? We're getting nothing useful, and I'm growing tired of the sound of his voice.'

The Emperor was now nothing but a grinning, tilting head, hissing into the dark. '*Are* we done here, Shroudweaver? Do you grasp what I am telling you?'

He ran a tongue over crusted lips. 'Such hubris, Shroudweaver. You took them *all* into you. Desperate. Thoughtless. Crude. Taking when you could simply . . . give.' Sand sifted between his fingers. 'They are all mine. *Everyone* in this mountain, in Thell, in that shrieking city called Luss. I bound a shard of my soul to theirs on death, and for those still living I prepared a home in their flesh for me to find them when they died.'

The Emperor's head had tipped back, something close to wonder in his eyes. 'You cannot destroy me. You cannot stop me. I am *forever* in this mountain. And the moment you release those souls I will reclaim them, every one. I will move into their bodies like glass into water. And all it will take will be a single cut. A single tear. One, small, mistake.'

Shroudweaver had watched the man in front of him rant, and heard Shipwright's voice in his head, climbing above his hammering heart. 'Folk are always loudest when they're scared.'

She'd said that the night before the last battle, in camp, as the people of Thell and Hesper fucked and yelled and fought each other just enough to keep the fear of dying away. She'd been right though. He had seen the edges of that fear around the Emperor's eyes.

'Do you buy it, Shroud?' Skinpainter's face clouded.

'Perhaps,' Shroudweaver had said, as he felt a little steel flourish in his spine.

The Emperor had snarled. '*Perhaps*? You know it, Weaver.'

Shroudweaver had thought for a moment. Taken a little of the calm he was taught at the Aestering. The drip of water over stone. The heat of his own breathing. Had felt his mind quiet a little, felt the run of those other voices slow.

He'd looked to Skinpainter, to their broad, expectant face. 'I can't hold these souls forever. That much is true. But we have time to figure out a solution to that.' He had pressed his fingers against his nose, trying to quiet the chattering that pushed on the inside of his skull and pointed to the Emperor. 'His soul might be spread all through the mountain. It might be bonded, somehow, with those that have already died. I don't know. This is seven grades of wrong beyond anything I was ever taught.'

'Lies,' the Emperor had growled, before Skinpainter cuffed him again, then turned to Shroudweaver with bruised knuckles and a heavy brow.

'Speak Shroud, I need your advice here. Before I found you, I had no idea anyone could even play this bastard at his own game. You're our best hope, and you've done right by us. Tell us what needs done, and we'll do it.'

Shroudweaver had smiled sadly. The weight of it all sitting in his gut. 'Even if his soul is spread like seeds on the wind, it's still tied to his body,' he'd pointed, 'to *this* body. Everything needs an origin, and anchor. No one's ever been able to weave without one.'

He'd gazed coldly at the Emperor. 'I don't think he's broken *that* rule yet.'

He paced back and forth flexing his hands. 'We can't stop him reasserting control if he gets back into these people.' Held up his fingers. 'Which means we need to secure three things. The living, the dead, and him.'

The Emperor had watched them sullenly, eyes lidded, as Shroudweaver took Skinpainter aside, an arm around their shoulders. Voice low and confident. 'You'll need to figure out some way of guarding people against this.'

Skinpainter's eyes had widened. The scale of the task blossoming in the silence. 'Is that even possible?'

Shroudweaver sighed. 'Feels like we're specialising in impossible lately. But if that's what it takes.'

Skinpainter spat. 'This is going to be a bastard lot of work.'

'Make it something they want to do then.' Shroudweaver had paused, 'Give them something to believe in.' He'd glanced at the Emperor. 'Give them something to fear.'

He could remember how he had smiled. Confidence roiling in his blood. 'You're building a new world, Skin. No better time to build a new religion. Make it permanent, deep, lasting. Etch it in their minds. Their bones.'

How arrogant. How stupid.

Skinpainter had looked thoughtful. 'What about the dead?'

Shroudweaver had shuddered as phantom bodies moved within him. Kept his face composed. 'I'll take care of them. I can hold together long enough to figure something out.'

'Lies,' the Emperor had snarled. 'Do you not hear it, you painted thief? Your weaver friend's promises are as empty as glass.'

Skinpainter's fist cracked again. 'Quiet. You'll run out of teeth before I run out of enthusiasm.' They rolled their shoulders. 'We *are* winging an awful lot of this, Shroud.'

Shroudweaver had watched the Emperor roll a split tooth around his mouth. Felt that anger rise again. A desperate desire to see this thing over, finished.

'We don't have a choice. We can deal with the consequences later.'

He'd held up two fingers. 'So we can handle the living and the dead, with a little creativity. As for him' – his lip had curled – 'bind him, chain him, lock him up, but take a piece of him. If he's not whole, if the anchor's not whole, then we have some power, we have just a *little* control.'

He'd glanced at the Emperor. 'I have an idea, but not in front of him. Something that'll give Kinghammer his pound of flesh, and give us what we need.'

What they'd done in the end, Shroudweaver's mind hesitated to recall. But there had always been that reminder, swinging in a pouch at Skinpainter's belt. A finger, as pale and thin as his own. The nail still crusted with dark, dry blood.

Tangled under the covers, Shroudweaver sweats, and his skin runs cold. He remembers a show trial, the voices of the rebel mob baying for blood, their teeth white in the light.

The look in the Emperor's eyes as he realised what awaited him. The strength of his fingers on Shroudweaver's wrist. The bruise they left behind as the blood flushed away. The shake in his voice, low and frail and human. 'Don't let them to do this to me.'

Shroudweaver remembered the sickness that had settled in his heart, feels it rising again to choke his throat in that small bed. Remembers turning his back on the council chamber and the mountain, even as the bowl of the Stump filled with a mass of seething bodies, falling on a single, kneeling figure. Like wolves, like eagles.

He'd returned a few days later, from walking the high places, from breathing the ice on the wind. Finding the Emperor after-wards near gone.

Torn by teeth and hands.

He'd driven the guards away in fury. A light in his eyes that sent them reeling backwards, and finally, when he was alone, he'd looked down at the stripped bones of the thing that had been the Emperor of the Dead.

And the first thing he'd said was. 'I'm sorry.' Guilt choking his throat like soft cloth.

He hadn't expected a reply, but he'd got one, falling out of red ribs. That ragged breath still somehow caged within the wreck of the Emperor's body.

It had laughed as it coughed, ratcheting gobbets of spittle and blood out of half-chewed lungs.

When it eventually found its voice, there was still a trace of the man Shroudweaver had come to know. Wry and arrogant, even as the ruin of its face slid and dripped. '*Sorry*. Oh Weaver, they surprised even you, didn't they? That noble Skinpainter, big strong Kinghammer, the Deadsingers with their wide eyes. All of them so hungry for revenge.' The Emperor's breath rattling around hollow ribs, a gouged stomach. 'So hungry.'

Its lung wheezed, wet and laboured, the air sucking through the torn gaps in its throat, its chest.

'Part of you knew though. Part of you knew deep down what I've *always* known.' Its voice rising, catching, hacking on chunks of half-strung meat.

'All order is founded in blood, Weaver.'

It had smiled then, a slash of ruin and glee.

A moment passed, or two, in the heart of the mountain, on stone wet with blood, with nothing but the sound of the Emperor's rattling breath, in and out and in again, like the cascade of sea to shore.

A horror in Shroudweaver's heart so dark, so massive, that for a moment, he had just crouched next to the broken form of the thing he'd once feared, his partner in the dance. He moved a hand next to its body until their fingers were not quite touching, but he could imagine the push and pull of the weave between them. He had stayed that way until Skinpainter arrived, flanked by spears, and horror gave way to ritual, to necessity.

It was then that Shroudweaver had seen the real stone in Skinpainter's soul, the thing that kept them at the heart of the mountain, in the veins of its power.

It was then that they'd taken what remained of the Emperor down into the black, into the deepest hollow heart of the Stump, where a dark lake hung below sharp stalactites.

It was there that they'd bound the Emperor, his thin hair still neat around the long bones of his shattered skull. Bound at wrist and ankle, to hold his magic tight. His fingers and arms stilled. His wrists pinned and shackled, inked with geometries, to hold his spirit back from roaming. Skinpainter watched the Emperor like a hunting cat, and Shroudweaver watched Skinpainter with his heart held between his teeth, until they reached forwards, and snapped off the smallest finger, wrapped it, and stowed it close.

Not even a scream from the Emperor then. His life fading fast, and time growing short.

So there, in the dark, they'd lifted him above the water and lashed him to a stalactite that hung like a black tooth high above the lake. Lashed him there, and Shroudweaver had woven the last scrap of the Emperor's life to his ruined bones, to his tooth-scarred jaw, and ragged legs. Had tied him between life and death, and left him there. Never dying. Pinned like a moth. His spirit held from reaching up into the mountain above. Into its people. Or so they'd thought.

Over time, water had run down the dark tracks of the stalactite, and carried the mountain's stone over the Emperor's wrists and arms, legs and face, until the rock swallowed him, inch by inch. Until there was nothing to be seen of him, but the shape of a thing that might have once been a man, bound in the stone, and the light of a single, mad eye, glaring out from the black.

a great scar, dark against the water
where light falls through along the path of the moon

Fifteen years later, in the thick, hot night of a Hesper summer, Shroudweaver stares into the darkness and shakes, waiting for the blink of that mad eye. Until he finally falls asleep, hearing only the sound of his own hammering heart.

44

West Tide gulls like mealy bread,
and East Tide gulls like marrow,
Astic gulls like little fish,
and corn behind the harrow

—Tannery kids' kick song, Hesper

Morning in Hesper belonged to the gulls. Raucous calls running from roof to roof, the echoes shivering off the whitewashed walls and out to sea. Squabbling over last night's scraps; the fish guts, the spilt food, the washes of bile and beer that tilted down the gutters and pooled in dockside puddles.

Morning belonged to the gulls, crowding the ratlines and rigging. Winkling out barnacles and mussels from the salted ropes, screaming all the while, heads thrown back, orange beaks rattling, the red shock of feathers on the crown of their heads swaying like a laughing dancer.

Fallon sidestepped the gauntlet as best he could whilst bodies swooped low over his head, thick with witless noise. He turned to Shipwright and grinned. 'Something familiar in this, eh? Surrounded by screaming idiots, dodging an interminable rain of shit.'

She smiled stickily, clutching one of the crisp pastries the bakers of Hesper turned out in the morning to ease the ringing heads of the night before. A whole cottage industry based on dealing with drunkards, and the grey ghosts they became come dawn. This one bought for a slip of coin from a small dark-haired woman who moved like a bird in one of the dockside stalls.

Shipwright licks her fingers. 'Aye, something.'

They thread their way portside, beneath the cries of the gulls

306

and the barks of the dock workers as the first ships of morning sail into harbour.

Here, the biggest are anchored and unloaded, pulled into berths by dark-skinned men and women, limbs sanded by the sun.

The smaller boats slip into cut ways leading to the wider locks and canals which will carry them up the cliffs, beyond the seawall and out into the city proper to fill the ice-cellars with spirits, the parlours with tea and spices, the gambling dens with smoke and rumours.

They duck into one of the narrow alleys that slinks between the tall, bright walls of the warehouses. Through an unchained gate and down into the slim warren of shanty homes that cling to the high walls like barnacles hung to rope.

A short haired old woman steps nimbly out of their way, and clicks the gate closed behind them. Fallon flashes her a quick smile.

'Where are we going, Declan?' Shipwright asks.

He presses a finger to his moustache, lets a smile sneak out either side of it. He's clearly enjoying himself.

They duck through a hanging curtain, the wooden beads at its hem clacking softly.

At their sides, small knots of people huddle in a close corridor, a muddle of styles and accents. Shipwright catches a glimpse of the black, tight twists of Heron Halls hair, hands shielding smiling lips that are blunted with eastern dusk-paint. More strangely, a man in armour she recognises as Hesper garrison, perhaps another in the grey weave of Astic, chin tucked into a set of notes being offered by someone whose coffee-coloured hands pick nervously at hair teased into Burners' spikes.

Something wrong with the proportions of this place – they should have hit the back of the warehouse wall by now, she suspects. She gets a dim sense of what might be arch and plaster above for a moment, before they are decanted into a high, wide room, bright with light.

Across its whole expanse, stalls are stacked with the strange and the unfamiliar. Rugs are spread out where traders sift through armour, weapons, creations of terrifying simplicity and complexity and lightness.

But it's the walls that catch her attention. On each whitewashed stretch, maps – four, five times again as tall as a man – their inked curves stretching up and out to the ceiling high above.

Fallon turns to Shipwright and smiles. 'Welcome to the Hall of Loose Tongues.'

As he speaks, she runs her eyes over the men and women that move like water through the light of the Hall, watches the small, hushed knots of their chatter. The trade in words, in silence.

'Spies,' she says.

'Information brokers,' Fallon replies, then grins. 'Basically, yeah.'

She elbows him affectionately, her eyes wandering over a man whistling softly to a bright-feathered bird, which repeats the tune back to him, note perfect. He holds a lock to its beak, and she watches it unclasp as the notes sound out.

Declan appears at her shoulder, the ghost of a smile lingering under his moustache. 'Half the birds are liars,' he mutters.

She shakes her head bemusedly. 'So why am I here?'

'I want you to meet someone. Before you set off for Thell.'

'Why's Shroud not here?'

Fallon twists his lips. 'I asked him to look in on the wife, see if anything could be done to ease her pain.'

He twists to one side to let a gaggle of chattering men past, their fingers moving as fast as their lips. Shipwright catches just a snatch of Katkani . . . *green fire over the halls* . . .

Fallon's eyes track over his shoulder. 'Besides, this might be difficult for him.'

They skirt the left edge of the Hall. Here, separate from the welter of stalls and hawkers and back-of-the-palm whisperers, an elegant dark-skinned woman watches them pass. Her throat is marred by a chalky scar that runs the length of her neck and the cuffs of her jacket are trimmed in gold. Two lean black dogs with long ears curl at her feet, reaching up to take scraps of meat from her manicured fingers.

Fallon turns to look inquiringly at her as they pass.

She shakes her head in reply. 'Too early to read the bones of the year, Lord.'

As she recedes, Shipwright sees a man approach the woman's stall, his face still studded with the grit of the road. He waits as she bends down to one of her dogs, and whispers in its ear. Dog and man leave together, his hand resting lightly on its undulating spine.

The swirl of foreign languages pulls Shipwright deeper into the Hall. She finds her eye drawn again to the massive maps. In each one, the south-eastern corner of the continent has been carved out, or marked with sigils of warning, or simply pried from the wall to leave the bare brick beneath.

On some maps, this torn corner was in the north-west. The world did not look the same to everyone here.

As her eyes wander the curves and lines, Fallon turns her gently, his hands on her shoulders. 'Beautiful, aren't they?'

She nods. 'Incomplete, though.'

He laughs. 'From your perspective, of course. Not sure we have walls big enough for *that* ocean.'

'It's not just ocean, Declan,' she smiles.

You'll have to tell me about it one day.'

'I'll do better than that, I'll take you.'

'I get seasick.'

'I'll keep you drunk.'

'I couldn't leave her.'

Shipwright reaches back, grips his wrist. 'When she wakes up.' Determination in her tone.

She runs her eyes over the maps again, the bold strokes of paint. Mountain ranges as long as a boat. Forests as tall as a man. Almost all of it still so strange to her. A few brief points of familiarity, for better or worse. Hesper, Astic, the Burners' Wood. Thell.

As her eyes run over the walls, Fallon pulls her towards a long, low table stretched in front of the nearest mural, covered by scrolls and maps, staked out neatly, and annotated more precisely still. All of them drawn at different elevations: an eagle's view, a forester's stance, some political, marking out the big cities, the smaller towns, the legacies of older wars, the ruin of the south. Others are more specific – here one for the currents, West Tide and East Tide swirling constantly in teasing parallels, the deep water that pulled off to the Heron Halls, and the shallowing cuts that arrowed in towards where Luss would once have been.

Here was another for herbs: killing, healing, sleeping, dreaming, marked with stunning care and precision. The men and women behind the table move with professional grace, some old, some barely out of their teens, united only by the stain of inks on their fingers, the marks on their lips and teeth from sucked brushes.

'Incredible,' she breathes.

'You'll need a good map for heading north,' Fallon says. 'I doubt you can sail all the way, unless your ship's picked up some new tricks.'

They approach the table. One of the men behind it looks up, eyes owlish from squinting.

'Lord. Come for the latest in herds? Mountain ice? Soil life?' His stubby fingers jab expressively.

Fallon smiles. 'Not today. My friend here needs a map of the routes north.'

The man's huge eyes blink slowly. 'A map north? Yes, of course. Naval and land. But nothing further? No touches upon the azimuth, nothing cadastral or choropleth?'

Fallon shakes his head. 'Just the routes.'

The short man blinks again, his head bobbing like a buoy at sea. 'Not a problem, just unexpected.' He selects one, a beautiful wash of colours, rolls it and stows it in a leather tube, before thrusting it at Fallon. 'My lord.'

Fallon takes the tube, tugs a little as the shorter man's hand refuses to let go.

'Shapetender?'

The mapmaker flashes a smile, his large eyes swivelling. 'Are you sure, Lord? Nothing hypsometric, nothing theodolite-kissed?'

Fallon pulls, firmly. 'Just the map.'

Shapetender's fingers relinquish it reluctantly.

'Your digger will be by later, I expect? For the darkening charts? We have prepared a further one on the movements of the moon. Another on cart roads of the old Empire.'

Fallon looks at him levelly. 'She will, Shape. And don't let that brain of yours get ahead of your lips.' He turns to Shipwright, presses the map tube against her chest. 'Stage one, Ship. A decent map.'

As they walk away, the round-headed man's gaze lingers on them for a moment, before another customer calls for his attention.

'What was that about?' Shipwright mutters.

Fallon laughs. 'Oh, our fidgety little friend? He's a mapmaker of the old school.'

They walk further down the avenue of rugs, the light striped and shaded by awnings stretched far above, against the dusty warehouse glass.

'Cartography was a big Hesper industry, back in the day. No one made maps quite like us.'

Shipwright smiles, recognising his manner, that storytelling style, and eggs him on. 'Oh really?'

'Our maps aren't always just maps. Sometimes, they can hold secrets.'

She raises an eyebrow, 'How?'

He shrugs, sidesteps a sweaty, racing young boy, his face stamped with green ink. 'It can be all kinds of things. The twist with which a mountain's drawn. The stippling on the edge of a swamp. Dots where there needn't be dots. Lines hidden inside other lines. Paper towns that don't exist on the earth, but mean something when they're on a map.' His smile is wicked, his arms conspiratorial around her shoulder. 'Towns that exist on the earth that are just hinted at in a wash of colour, a choice of vellum.' He taps the tube at her hip. 'We're clever bastards.'

She laughs. 'So it would seem. How come no one cottons on?'

'Smart question. The codes change all the time, and only the cartographers know. They'll send them, interpret them, receive them, alter them.'

'That's a lot of trust to place in a few people.'

He nods. 'It is, but they swear an oath, a real serious thing. Can't even break it once they've gone to glass.'

Shipwright sighs. 'You're all so cryptic. "Gone to glass". That's dead, right?'

Fallon nods. 'Almost. Story for another day. Let's leave it at the maps for now.'

Shipwright smiles. 'Agreed. My head's spinning as it is. Impressive though.'

Fallon grins. 'It's one of the reasons Crowkisser's so shit up about us. We have a whole language she can never read.'

Shipwright rolls her eyes. 'You enjoy the idea that she's furious out there somewhere, don't you?'

'Love it,' Fallon grins.

The smile vanishes. 'But seriously . . . Secrets. That's how we survive. That's how we beat her. Not trade. Not weapons. Secrets.'

His blunt face is soft, half-mocking. 'It's not what we're known for. City of ships, right? That's what brought you here.'

She nods.

'City of *secrets*, Shipwright. And you need to learn a few more of them before you go.'

They cut away from the left wall, threading between heaps of merchandise as they push onwards into the Hall. Much of it isn't really saleable, not really goods at all. More like archaeological finds. Relics.

Fallon picks up a helmet, half sheared through. 'I remember seeing these on heads, at Luss.' He hefts the green egg head of a mace, sundered from its haft. 'These in hands. Gives me the creeps.'

Shipwright suppresses a shiver of her own. 'These are all battle plunder?'

He shakes his head. 'Some of it, but most of it's too old for that. Relics, really. Archaeology.' He turns a bent blade in his hands. 'We've been killing each other since we learnt how to try.'

They step further into the press, gingerly, threading around tottering piles of metal, bone, and clay. The ossified arm of some great machine, turned black by a lifetime in the earth.

Fallon's voice pulls at her like a loose thread. 'You wouldn't understand, Ship. Out east, you come from the sea, right?'

'Just above it,' she mutters, but the joke doesn't land.

His smile is perfunctory. His mind elsewhere. 'Here though, on the land, we're on the earth. And it goes down, down and down to who knows where. And it's *all* in the earth. All the history. All the killing. All the betrayals. All the secrets.' He pulls a bent clasp from a pile, turning it gently against the light. 'The land coughs them up every day. Ploughs pull them from the soil, they're cut from the throats of seabirds, hooked from the guts of fish. They're dredged from nets; found in gutters, in attics, in tombs.' He runs a hand across the short wiry hair on his neck. 'Hell, my da used to find them in sheep shit.'

He sets the clasp down, nods at the stall owner.

'We've been selling secrets here since before Hesper was a city. Turning over our past, brushing the dirt off, letting them get a little air. He shakes his head. 'Did you know the rich shits up on the hill used to keep some of this stuff as curios? A status thing.' His lip curls, 'Never mind the people that died to get them there. The ghosts hanging off the edge of their new lamp, their new vase.'

Shipwright frowns. 'Better than it rotting in the earth, surely?'

Fallon shakes his head again, harder. 'It didn't mean anything to them. They took the objects but not the secrets lingering on them, not the history, the *understanding*.' He shrugs, puts a hand in the small of Shipwright's back to guide her around a stack of cages where black, thin-toothed, sleek-furred things squirm and fight.

'Holdsnakes. Used to keep them to clean out the rats from the ships. Nowadays, some nutters are trying to use them to carry messages. Steal little trinkets.' He shudders. 'It's hard to keep them out of anywhere. If their head can get through, the rest of them can. They bend both ways too,' he says, flipping his wrist back and forth. 'Nasty, noodly little things.'

They delve deeper still into the hall, the space seeming to stretch out in front of them. Those vast intricate maps above their heads seeming a little stranger, a little older as they progressed. Surely, Shipwright thought, this couldn't be just one warehouse, more like two knocked together, as the Hall's secrets sprawled out into the body of the city.

There's a brief moment of awning and wood that might be the crossing of a street. The light swells fractionally brighter. She's getting disoriented.

'Where was I?' Declan says, oblivious. 'Right: artefacts; secrets; the bloody rich.' He laughs. 'Not that the poor were any better. If they weren't scurrying around old burial mounds to dig the stuff up, they were setting it up in shrines. Telling people someone's old shinbone or crusty dagger could cure your child, let blind men see.'

His voice softens. 'Of course, that was back when we had hosts, and gods. Maybe some of it was true.'

He turns a corner. 'I guess we can ask someone smarter than I am.'

The tent facing them is neat, brightly stitched from some stiff white fabric. A low wooden table set out in front, covered in copper bowls of some gently bubbling substance.

A man stands behind the bowls, stirring them assiduously with a long tool, half blade, half ladle. He's cutting the liquid into patterns; wax, of some kind, Shipwright guesses.

His arms are thin and twisted as a wind-scorched tree, with skin only a shade or two lighter than the dark wood. His hair is a white shock that seems on the verge of erupting from his skull, like a half-blown seedhead.

One blue eye is alert, the other a mess of scar.

His head tips up, and he nods as he catches sight of them. He flicks the tip of the blade clean of wax, and rubs it dry with a rag.

'Figured it wouldn't be too long before I saw you, Fallon.'

He turns his head. 'Nice to properly meet you, Shipwright.'

Shipwright smiles. 'I'm afraid you're a little ahead of me.'

The man nods, slips the blade into a thin case and pauses to cover one of the bowls.

'It's sort of my job. There's been a lot of talk about you, since you first arrived, all those years ago.' His sunken face softens into a smile. 'Since you charmed the hell out of Fallon's wife.'

She blushes. 'I rather regret that entrance.'

He laughs. 'No need. You made a name for yourself. Hesper likes flash.' He wipes his hands dry, shooting a look at Fallon.

'So, you'll be wanting me to clue her in.'

Fallon's expression is sheepish. 'Am I that predictable?'

The man smiles. 'You only turn up when you want something important, Fallon. Otherwise it's just that vile thief you keep around.' Seeing Fallon's expression he waves a hand. 'Don't worry. I like it. It's honest. Come in.' He pulls aside the tent flap and ushers them in.

It is all neatness inside – neatness in the books, in the journals arrayed in stacks, bound by date and coloured, it appears, by city; neatness in the three clean blackwood chairs that sit in a circle; neatness in the pot that simmers gently next to a set of regimented cups.

He gestures to two of the chairs and waits until they're seated. Shipwright shifts uncomfortably. The chairs are a little small. She wonders if that's deliberate. Fallon looks like a sack on a pedestal.

The slight man sits, neatly.

'You didn't introduce me, Fallon. I'm not that ubiquitous.'

Fallon shifts awkwardly. Crosses his legs, uncrosses them.

'Shipwright, this is Heartshamer.'

The slender man tips fingers to his brow, wryly. 'As billed.'

Shipwright smiles, a little tensely. Something about this space, this conversation, makes her feel out of place.

Heartshamer catches her eye. 'Feeling more foreign than usual?'

She nods, startled.

He smiles softly again, and she notices that one side of his mouth pulls higher than the other.

'I have that effect on people. A legacy of my old profession. Let me pour you some tea.' He rises, passes out cups, and fills them with a light amber brew that smells of flowers.

She takes a cup. Declan takes a cup. He sips. She sips.

Heartshamer drains his tea slowly, sets it down and folds his fingers in his lap. 'I've heard good things about you, Shipwright.'

She watches his face. 'That's reassuring.'

He nods. 'It is. You'd be amazed how few people I hear good things about.'

He gestures to the journals. 'I daresay my notes are more comprehensive than most. It's a point of pride now really. I like to keep track of the notables. The disreputables. The respected.' He looks directly at her. 'The novel. Sometimes, the brave.'

Fallon clears his throat. 'Heartshamer is . . .'

Heartshamer holds up a hand. 'Let her guess, Declan.'

He folds his fingers again. 'What am I, Shipwright?'

Her eyes take in the journals, his posture. That one bright eye. She drinks from the cup. The taste reminds her, a little, of home.

'A spy, perhaps. But I think more than that. A historian maybe or a broker.' She shifts in the chair. 'If I didn't know better, I'd say a priest.'

Heartshamer is silent for a second. Then he laughs. 'She's good, Fallon.'

He turns to fix her with his eye. 'You're good. They're right to talk about you, I think. Would you like to know why Fallon's brought you here?'

'Desperately,' she sighs.

'Always one for cheap theatre, our lord,' Heartshamer murmurs. 'He loves the suspense.' His fingers waggle.

Fallon looks like he's about to object, then shrugs. 'You're not wrong. I get my kicks where I can.'

Heartshamer scratches at his jaw. 'I am or was all of those things, once, Shipwright. I am a historian. And I am certainly a spy, which is why I am not welcome amid those maudlin archivists, with their glass and silence. I believe most information should be free. I merely like to select the channels it travels in with a little care.'

He sighs, fingers massaging the scar tissue by his eye socket. 'However, the reason our melodramatic lord has brought you here, is because of who I used to be. Or rather what.'

Shipwright watches those fingers, the barest shake in the bone. 'I was a host.'

He watches her face. 'It means little to you?'

She looks at Fallon, shakes her head. 'Not much. We had nothing like that back east.'

Heartshamer looks faintly relieved. 'Perhaps a Hesper term. Or a western one. What do you know of the gods?'

She thinks. 'A little. They were a belief system here. Until three years ago. Until the south.'

Heartshamer nods. 'Until Crowkisser. I still haven't solved that mystery. History requires sane sources. But, I'm wandering. A belief system.' His leg jitters. 'A belief system, yes, in the way that a leaf believes in the tree.'

He refills his cup, barely a drop spilt. 'Our gods were close to us. They could be propositioned. For miracles. For healing, or strength, or knowledge.'

His hands steady as he talks. 'Magic, effectively. But not weaving, like your lover. His is a magic of edges, of the between spaces. Of will. The gods.' He sighs, places his fingers against his temples. 'Theirs was magic of the body. Of love. Of partnership. Sacrifice. They were golden. Beautiful.'

Shipwright listens, a suspicion unfurling in her heart like a fern. 'Shroudweaver mentioned a little of this, but you talk about them like you saw them.'

Heartshamer laughs. 'Saw them? I *was* them.'

He reaches for Shipwright's hand, places it against his ribs. 'The gods didn't reach out to everyone. They chose people. People who called to them. Who needed them. Or,' he laughs ruefully. 'Who thought they would never need them. And they entered into them. Into us.'

He lets her fingers fall. 'Host is a literal term, Shipwright. We could feel them in our heads, in our bodies, on our lips. They taste of spice and honey.'

She twitches at that, a jolt of recognition. Remembering tower steps under her feet, light pouring into her. But that had been shroudweaving, surely.

Heartshamer watches her, tilts his head curiously, moves on when she stays silent. 'We lived with them, within our bodies. We gave them our breath and our blood and in return, they gave us whatever they felt we needed.'

He settles back into his chair, crosses his legs. 'For me, that was knowledge. I was full of questions. At first about myself, about the world. Soon, I began to wonder about others. The great. The good. The people who claimed to be great and good.'

Shipwright shakes her head in amazement. 'And the gods— *your* god told you these things?'

Heartshamer smiles. 'I'd like to pretend I used the power responsibly. But I used it like most people, I suspect. I gathered all I could on my friends, my enemies. I asked my god for the secrets of the rich and powerful, and I kept them close against my chest like a hundred sharp little knives, ready to cut and wound.'

He sighs again, refills the cup. 'I like to tell myself I guided things in their correct direction. That I used the sins of the wicked against them, that I gave the good the knowledge they needed to win. I like to tell myself that I was a sword. Ethical when used in the right cause.'

He looks up at her. 'All swords get coated in blood, Shipwright.'

She nods. 'So you were a broker, a blackmailer, a spy. All those things. With the help of this god?'

Heartshamer nods.

'So what happened when Crowkisser killed them?'

His fingers move to the slack side of his face, his ruined eye. 'Initially? I reacted . . . poorly. I don't know how to communicate what I felt. The sense of loss. Many of my friends went mad. Gnawed their own tongues off in the dark of night. Dug their entrails out looking for a missing glow of golden light.'

His eyes tighten. 'Or just neatly dropped themselves into the sea to end the silence.'

He pauses for a second, his breathing ragged. It takes a moment for it to stabilise. Fallon reaches towards him, but he bats it away.

'I was lucky, I suppose. There's a woman that works for Fallon. She found me. Kept me from the worst of it. Taught me how the rest of you lived without a voice in your head.'

He laughs, bitterly. 'In time, I returned to the only thing I knew. Buying and selling information. Gathering those little knives back to my chest.'

He looks at Fallon. 'Recently I've been directing my enquiries more specifically, however. Towards Crowkisser. Towards the world she destroyed.' He waves the cup at Shipwright, his movements loosened with anger. 'You need to know how that world worked if you're going to fix it.'

Shipwright frowns. 'I think Shroudweaver would be better placed than me.'

The cup slams down on the table. 'Hardly. He's rather at the root of the problem, wouldn't you say?'

Heartshamer runs his fingers through his hair. 'My apologies. Rationally, however, he has a southern perspective, influenced by the teaching at the Aestering. I – we, want someone with a more . . . impartial, viewpoint. Will you listen to what I have to tell you?'

She nods. 'OK, but you know that he's my priority. Always.'

Heartshamer's voice softens. 'I do. That's why you need to know this, for his sake, as much as ours.'

He stands stiffly. 'Let me tell you about our kind parasites then, Shipwright. Our strange world.'

His hands move horizontally, one above the other. 'I don't know what they teach you over the sea, but know this. The world falls in layers one atop the other.' His hands move apart. 'Above us, beyond the clouds and the stars, the home of the gods. Our golden gods.'

He sucks his teeth. 'But the gods did not work without symbiosis. They sought something in our souls. Or our bodies. Perhaps our blood. Our life. I've never been able to truly tell.'

'Remora,' Shipwright murmurs.

Heartshamer shoots her a look. 'What?'

'Scavenger fish,' she says. 'They latch onto other, bigger fish, take scraps from them, but they keep their host strong. Keep its blood clean.'

Heartshamer frowns. 'That's distressingly accurate. I may never forget.'

His fingers harrow his hair again. 'So, remora. The gods. They take, but they also give, for they are bound this way.' He holds up a finger. 'One cannot occur without the other.' He shakes his head, 'However, they make no promises not to *change* us in the process. A host for the gods becomes stronger. Age wearies them less. The burdens and failures of the flesh can be made anew.' He sits, scratches at his socket. 'You miss it once it's gone.'

Shipwright nods. 'And you gave back to your god in turn?'

Heartshamer hums affirmatively. 'Every host does. The cost was simple. Your blood, and space within your mind.'

His eye glints. 'This was how I plied my trade. That act of sharing opened my ears to the endless voices of everyone else's gods as they chattered to one another across the miles.'

He smiles. 'A wise person, a canny person might have learnt to play this web of sound, to sift information from it, rolling their attention from conversation to conversation. Learning the thoughts of distant peoples, politicians, kings and beggars and spies.'

He shoots a glance at Fallon. 'A very clever person might use this information to advance their station, their *city*, their nation.'

He coughs. 'The very cleverest would do nothing of the kind, but would hoard their secrets like whispering treasures, waiting for the day when a dagger needed to twist in the hearts of men. The very cleverest would do this. In effect, the man you see before you. Heartshamer. Me.'

'Modest,' Fallon murmurs.

Heartshamer rolls his eyes. 'Like it never benefitted you.'

'Sounds costly,' Shipwright says. 'Draining.'

Heartshamer shrugs. 'It was a fair deal, mostly. A trade, of course, but everyone involved knew what they were giving up.' He breathes out slowly. 'And the god's voices were always there. The power was always there.'

He taps the saucer. 'Until they weren't. Until Crowkisser broke the world and I could hear a thousand heads all filled with the wings of crows.'

Heartshamer's tongue scrapes dryly on his teeth, his fingers fretting with the cuff of his shirt. 'I heard them screaming so loud it tore loose their lips, their tongues, the roofs of their mouths. I could feel their teeth rattle in their jaws and the hair rising on their heads.' His legs shake in sympathy, muscles dancing.

When he looks up, his face is twisted in anguish. 'After that, the power was gone.'

He points at Shipwright. 'And you have to go out there to try and stop the woman that took it away. That killed our gods. Will you try to bring it back? That power? Will you?'

Shipwright shakes her head. 'I don't think we've thought that far ahead.'

'No,' Heartshamer says, his voice bitter for the first time. 'I imagined not.'

He waves the cup towards her. 'But ask yourself this. What becomes of the woman who is used to being cut and broken and cut again without end? Her flesh kept immortal and whole by the god inside her? What happens when she bleeds, when she suffers? Does she recoil in fear?'

He wipes his lips, inclines a finger to his temple. 'Or does a curiosity, lizard-like, begin to stir? To see how much, just how much pain she can take? How much others might take in turn?'

Behind his back, Fallon rolls his eyes theatrically, and picks at a scab.

Heartshamer sighs. 'The death of the gods bred monsters, Shipwright. I'm just the sanest of them.' He shifts uncomfortably. 'Ask yourself what becomes of those who feel the voices gone from a newly silent head? Does peace finally descend? Do they retreat into the simple pleasures of life, do they hold that new silence like a pearl against their chests?'

He laughs. 'Some, admittedly. Lucky bastards. I knew others that found the silence louder than words. Who took themselves to the old places, the holy and highest places and finding *nothing*, despaired. Who scattered their flesh, their broken bones on cliffside and shore, who swung a gallows loop from rafters and branches.'

His head sinks into his hands. 'They were all just trying to flee their own traitor flesh. To find the gods again.'

He smiles sadly. 'Then, of course, the last few of us simply learnt to lie. To make our own voices a replacement for the cacophony the gods had given us. We kept selling wisdom from the tips of our tongues, until we were discovered, or worse' – he gestures to the tent, the chairs, the journals – 'never found out at all.'

His fingers run over the grain of the table. 'What worries me most is that some of us might have been pushed even further, that maybe out there among the surviving few, a bare pinprick of us all, the truly devoted, the truly *driven* will have taken their knowledge, their great whispering of the world before Crowkisser killed the gods and begun to dig. Down.'

His one eye fixes Shipwright's gaze. 'There's another world beneath ours, you know. Bones turned to stone. Faint paintings upon walls that have never seen light. Sketches in caves miles below ground.'

Heartshamer's hands trace the wood of the chair. 'Echoes of peoples and pasts we can't even imagine. And I'm scared that buried world had its gods. Had its voices too.'

Shipwright frowns. 'Other gods?'

Heartshamer nods. 'Or something like that. I gathered all the little scraps I could.' He waves towards the tent flaps. 'Trawled that nest of overpaid jackdaws for months on end.'

His voice is weary. 'We like to talk about the earth, Shipwright. But we've always been afraid of it. Even if most of us don't know why.'

Heartshamer's knuckles are white under the bone. 'I worry that Crowkisser was *not* afraid of the earth. I worry that it called to her.'

Fallon points at her. 'See? Told you he'd know the score.'

Shipwright nudges Heartshamer. 'Did you have to encourage him?'

He rolls his eyes. 'An unfortunate side-effect of long association. The point is, I have a hunch that Crowkisser might be playing with things we barely understand. That we're afraid to even *speak* about.'

He stands. 'Which normally, I would be professionally loath to even mention, but Fallon impresses on me the importance of your mission north to those degenerates in Thell.'

He selects a book or two from the shelves as he talks and leafs through them absently. 'We both felt that it was important that you knew a little more about what you were getting into.' He runs his fingers down a page. 'Twenty years is a small scrap of time to try and get a handle on the fears of this blasted earth.'

Shipwright feels a little grey, a little sick. 'Shroud never mentioned this. The hosts. The earth.' She trails off, uselessly.

Heartshamer raises an eyebrow. 'Unsurprising. Given what happened with his wife, I think he rather wanted to forget about the gods altogether.'

Shipwright's face goes still. 'I think . . . I think he and I may have some things to talk about.'

Heartshamer closes the ledger with a satisfied nod. 'Always advisable to know as much as you can about the people responsible for your life, I find.'

He crosses to Shipwright, lays a soft hand on her shoulder. 'Trust me. Blind faith only gets you so far.'

He turns to Fallon. 'I'll continue to provide you with reports, via our mutual friend.'

Heartshamer pivots back to Shipwright. 'I hope this information helped, Shipwright. More than it hurt, at least. I have the greatest respect for you. For the brave. For the kind.'

She looks at him for a moment. Part of her wants to punch him, for waking that little sliver of doubt in her chest. Instead, she says. 'It's given me a lot to think about.'

A moment later Fallon takes her arm, and guides her towards the tent flap. He turns to Heartshamer as he goes. 'I've always wondered, what's with the wax?'

The one-eyed man laughs. 'I like the patterns. Calms me down. Plus,' he grins, 'it makes me look spooky.'

The trio stand awkwardly for a moment, until Heartshamer sketches a quick bow, and retreats back into the tent.

As the fabric falls back into place, Fallon turns to Shipwright. 'Are you ready to go?'

She takes a moment to reply. Thoughts racing in her head, breath hot in her lungs.

'Just get me out of here. I need some light.'

45

When the forest burnt it was with a single shriek
acres of pale wood sending tongues of flame skyward

—*On Swallowing Gold*, Heartshamer

A few days later, Shipwright stands on deck, watching Hesper sprawl under the heat of a spring sun. The wind off the sea bites her cheeks, leaving salt on her lips. Ropecharmer is at her back, settling the crew. He passes a few words with the cook, an old woman who leaves him with an apple and a smile before he steps up beside Shipwright, his broad, fresh face well-tanned now. 'Ready when you are, Captain.'

Shipwright glances down at him. 'The crew behaved themselves?'

He shrugs expressively, waggles a hand. 'As much as sailors ever do.'

She sighs, blowing her lips out mournfully. 'I'll take it. Get us ready to cast off. We're leaving on the tide.'

Ropecharmer hesitates for just a moment.

A space grows between them, filled with the sound of gulls. 'There's others want to come with us. Afraid of Crowkisser, afraid of war. Chat is, Hesper's next.'

Shipwright narrows her brows. 'I know.' Her eyes roam over the low docks; that last spasmic flurry of activity before the sun rose to a bright coin and work became something to curse in a shadowed backroom. Sailors, stevedores, whores, merchants, soldiers, beggars, and in the middle of them all, Fallon, like a lead weight on a sheet. The hustle of the docks ebbs around him like oily water, the citizens of Hesper leaving a space framed by respectful nods, shoulder dips, the occasional quiet greeting.

The Lord of the Grey Towers is putting on appearances this morning. He's topless, the bruised slabs of his muscles stained with the smoke of forges, discoloured by tanners' dye. His wounds are still easily visible, ragged, broad, but healing. Ostensibly, he's leaning on a cane supplied to him by the physickers, in reality he's propping himself up with something more military than medical – five feet of black ash, with a hammered steel head. Shipwright grins despite herself. The arsehole couldn't even recuperate quietly. Her smile fades as she watches the people milling around him. Busy, noisy, arrogant, she loved Hesperians. But beyond that brassy hubbub, the great walls, and beyond the walls, Crowkisser. The latest reports from scouts put her a week out from the city, at most, moving at a leisurely pace, a grey-cloaked army at her back.

Or so they thought. It was hard to tell for certain. Some of the scouts could remember what they saw only in fragments. Others said Slickwalker moved with the host, in shreds and ebbs of shadow. Another man claimed there was no host, no men, but only a great cloud of wings and beaks.

They'd found him a day later at the base of the walls, twisted and broken.

Seeing her distraction, Ropecharmer makes a soft noise in the back of his throat and moves away, setting himself to meaningless tasks, pacing the boards over the hold. Shipwright glances after him briefly, but there's nothing to say. Nothing to say and too much to do.

War here seemed to be about guesswork. Everything shifting more than the waves under the ship's bow, and without a hint of their rhythm or sense. She was fairly sure of one thing. If Crowkisser came to Hesper, Hesper would fall. If Hesper fell, the people she saw in front of her would be given the same choice given to the people of Astic. Accept a world without gods, under Crowkisser's dubious protection, or die, and see what, if anything, still lay beyond.

Very few had chosen to die. Not after Astic, after the gallowswatchers. After what happened to the temple's priests and the southern weavers. Leaving aside hosts like Heartshamer, shattered at a distance and left to rot.

The solution, it seemed, was to draw her out, to make sure her attention was on anything but Hesper. And nothing seemed to catch Crowkisser's attention like a ship on the sea. Shipwright took a small point of pride in that. Too many months of small, bitter defeats, stinging the back of that mad young girl's mind like salt. If anything, the mess in Fallon's apartments had shown just how much Crowkisser and Slickwalker wanted them dead. Still too many unanswered questions though. Would Crowkisser really kill her own father? There was no question she'd kill Shipwright. As she'd recently been reminded, Crowkisser's mother had left a long shadow, and she stood right in it.

Shipwright got a line, hanked it, stowed it, and tied up the twinge in her heart. Now was not the time.

The hope, then, was that the two of them together would somehow be a more tempting target for the crow-witch than the biggest coastal city on this side of the continent. Threatening enough, for long enough, that her eyes would be pulled past Hesper, along the coast, and up into the grey mountains beyond. Optimistic, to say the least.

Pulling that off meant appearing to have an ace in the hole. And now the closest thing they had to an ace in the hole was Thell.

The last damn place she wanted to go. That ghost-ridden rock calling her again.

Thell had seemed important twenty years ago, when she was young, and the wars had been about anger, and liberty, and blood and sex. Thell had seemed important right up until the point they'd helped the revolutionaries win. Right up to the point where the Empire of the Dead had fallen, its ghosts and spirits apparently scythed out from under it by Shroudweaver and Skinpainter. And then, in one glorious rush, that pair had somehow ushered in the foundation of the Republic with its rituals and its rites, its geometries. So much arcane window-dressing.

And the revolutionaries, the glorious revolutionaries, had

taken the Emperor, and eaten him. Torn him limb from limb, and swallowed him down.

The revolution had seemed a little hollow after that. Of course, they'd had their justifications all ready. The symbolism of the act.

All she'd seen was people drunk on blood. Literally. Her stomach turns again at the thought, and she hears Heartshamer's voice. 'Feeling a little more foreign than usual?'

She twists some more rope under her hands, until the burn pulls her mind away. This is not the time for it.

Down on the docks, she watches Fallon stoop to whisper to Shroudweaver, sharing more of those secrets. Nothing changes. Both of them glance up at her and she waves laconically, before focusing on securing the water casks.

Ropecharmer's done his job well. The ship rides low in the water, her belly full, the hold well-provisioned. There's fresh fruit for the first leg of the voyage, and beyond that, salt meat, hard tack, furs, and black rope.

A corner has been set aside for Shroud's weaving tools. Bright red thread, sharp needles, saltpetre, old bodies stacked like cordwood. She looks at them warily for a moment, like you would a sleeping snake, before she moves to the helm, ducking under rigging strung precisely across a bright canvas sky. Oh yes, Ropecharmer knows his work. The boards of the ship gleam, the brass spinners chuck and worry quietly on the high masts. For a few moments, all is as it should be, and her heart loosens at the thought.

At the prow, Ropecharmer watches her approach, his hair whipped sideways in the freshening breeze, one hand loosely on the ship's wheel; a handsome boy. He smiles at the look on her face. 'The sea's always here.'

Shipwright nods. 'Thank goodness. You have a list?'

'Of people?' he says, surprised.

'Of people. Honestly, Rope, what do you take me for?'

He produces it within seconds. 'Eighty new refugees, give or take.'

She raises an eyebrow. 'I thought there'd be more.'

His shoulders twist awkwardly. 'News got out we're bound for Thell.'

Her voice is flat. 'How?'

He shrugs. 'It's a big city.'

Shipwright thumbs her jaw thoughtfully. 'So they know our heading?'

Ropecharmer is diplomatically quiet.

She moves brusquely, takes the list, runs her eyes over it. 'There's useful people on here. Physickers, soldiers, bloodworkers. Good work.'

Ropecharmer smiles proudly, 'Thanks, Captain.' He pauses. 'There's a lot of others that won't come all the way north. But they don't want to stay here.'

Shipwright watches him. Watches the slow rise and fall of his ribs, the determined set of his shoulders. *Who did you lose?* she thinks. *Where did you leave them? A dock, a doorway, a grave?*

She puts a hand on his shoulder. 'Case the harbour. Anyone waiting draws lots. We take fifty more, that's it. Red stick means you get on.'

Ropecharmer's hand comes up to meet her wrist briefly. She rests her eyes on it until it slinks back into a pocket. 'Rope, listen. Anyone cheats, anyone steals, anyone bribes – they don't get on. You take Fireholder and Cloudwatcher. You give them blades. *Visible* blades. Big, ugly ones. But *you*, you run this.'

A question hovers on his lips. She taps him on the cheek with an open palm. 'Maybe some kids, some families, some old sods that don't deserve to be caught in this, maybe they'll find red dye on their hands. Do you follow?'

Ropecharmer grins. 'Clear as the deep blue.'

She laughs. 'We'll have to do something about that enthusiasm, Rope.'

As she talks, her hands pick carefully at the ship's wheel, flicking the small levers that loosen the brackets and restraints on the rig spirits.

Ropecharmer watches her work. She shoots a lidded glance at him. 'One more thing. Anybody we can't take, you tell the other

Captains that if they ship them out the city, clean and fair, I'll owe them a right-handed debt. We clear?'

Ropecharmer beams. 'Clear as . . . I mean, yeah, got you.' His eyes flick up to the spirits which chirrup overhead. 'Where did they come from?'

Shipwright reaches down and straightens the collar of his shirt. 'I suppose you could say I prayed for them, and then I made them.'

Ropecharmer nods. 'They're gods, then? Amazing.'

She shakes her head slowly. 'No, not your gods. Just me in the end, and a little eastern tradition. I have as little to do with your gods as I can.' The words leave a sweet, sticky taste on her lips, like spiced honey. Heartshamer's voice in her head, *'a little more foreign'*.

Ropecharmer is gone soon after, sliding down a dock rope, fingers curled around a copper hand grip. He's ashore in seconds and off, moving with purpose; awash in errands, that boy.

The docks run a gangplank up and she watches as Shroudweaver embraces Fallon before he makes his way slowly up the thin span. The breeze picks up as he moves and for a second she sees him sway out over the water, the wind lifting his robe and flashing the silver scars on his legs.

In a moment, she is back under the blistering southern sky.

Three years unspooling in the span of a breath, pulling her mind back into the fire, into the desolation, into the first fight she ever lost. She's picking Shroudweaver up, dragging him out of the ruins of the city, lifting him free of that tangle of rock and glass, as the air splits overheard and men burst, burn and boil around her.

The clouds stutter, the stars torn and wheeling and, for the briefest of moments, something that mimics the purple shadow of a second moon, until it blinks.

Shroudweaver's fingers tighten on her wrist, his lips a thin line as she pulls him onwards, the glass teeth of the ruins digging deep into legs which had always been thin, so thin. They run through pulses of golden light in the shattered streets, skirting the howls of dying gods – Crowkisser's gift to world.

The sky's a lurching thing, poorly pinned to the earth, and beneath it, their beautiful fleet burns from its touch. Every crew almost lost in this nightmare of smoke and searing stone, doomed, were it not for Fallon. Even as the sky burns, he's everywhere at once, one arm hanging loosely at his side, writhing with something dark and feathered which worries ceaselessly at the rents in his flesh, exposing pale bone. The other hand holds a brutal club, slick with brain and blood. Behind him are the remains of their army; scared boys, stumbling men and women, hair on fire and eyes lost in smoke-blackened sockets. They're merely bodies gathered for a war that never came; bones thrown onto the pyre Crowkisser had built. There had been no war. No contest. Crowkisser had moved straight to the killing.

A thump followed by a sickening slide, and the earth tears again, buildings disappearing, the planes of the land shifting and sliding. Walls swallowed, towers upthrust.

Shipwright is still stumbling, running for the burning shore, betrayed at some point by the ground, some sudden shifting that swallows a group of cowering sailors, their wails lost in the depths of the air. She's thrown onto her back and Shroudweaver is tipped from her arms to sprawl dazed beside her, his fingers still strung with scorched thread, his lips moving ceaselessly. It takes a moment for her to find herself, breath rasping, looking up at the stars, at the purple belly of the moon, and seeing movement within it like the twitching of a sleeper's lid. She watches it crack like an egg and from inside its parting halves, she again feels the sensation of an eye, vast and alien and suddenly intent on her.

Its gaze is hungry as a fisherman's hook, tugging on her heart, worrying at her like a scrap of meat. Her fingers grope weakly for Shroud even as the ground betrays her again, sliding at new strange angles. Her breath lurches in her throat as he slips inexorably into the depths.

She forces herself up on screaming muscles, dimly noticing a woman spun, caught in the flames of falling stars, her hair a bright white candle, her eyes running like wax.

A jump, a slide, a desperate scramble after Shroudweaver's

tumbling body, a leap that interlocks their fingers with the strength of prayer. Every bone in his hand is a gift and her body curses her heart as she pulls him back, inch by scorched inch, gathering him into her arms like a child, like breath.

In the remains of the city, men tear the teeth from their heads as the sky sings to them. The eye roves over the ground. Where it alights, the gods die and men change. Gold-blooded ghosts sprout eyes, limbs and tails as they are pulled shrieking into the void. Shipwright watches in horror as the moon sheds the last of its lies and becomes the eye it always was. Around her, strong women, brave women, fall to their knees, and rise again twisted and howling in the burnt light.

Still, amid it all, Fallon. Setting his own arm aflame with a burning brand, driving the feathered shadow from it with gritted teeth and curses. He has a sailor under his other arm, her limp body pulled step by gruelling step towards the sea and the ships.

Shipwright feels her mind sliding loose as she hoists Shroudweaver and staggers to join him. She sees Fallon recoil as the air shudders, watches him glance down at the woman under his arm, realising her legs have been left far behind. Sees him kneel, whisper an apology, and break her neck with a swift twist.

The stars spin and list. The eye looks down, and on the shore their ships burn. The great fleet which saved Luss and defeated the Empire burns. Marines throw themselves into a blue sea alight with the heat of dying gods. Even as they touch the water it rises up to meet them, bright and hungry, pulling the flesh from their bones. Great chunks of stars hammer into the roiling ocean, and detonations sound in the deep.

Shipwright sees the ship at the same time as Fallon. Somehow still whole, the fire only just at its edges. They run, a few marines trailing in Fallon's shadow like kicked dogs. She follows them with Shroudweaver slung over her shoulder, limp as wrung cloth. Her legs are meat, but her bones are brass. A spinner hums her nerves to lightning. She thunders across the beach, across the pieces of men who had once been soldiers, women who had once been knights. Men and women who had followed her through the ruin of Luss now burnt to ash in the ruin of the south. Terror pushes her legs onward. As she runs, Shipwright can feel the eye on her, can see it suspended, swallowing the sky, bleak and limitless. Under its gaze, the horses they had brought kick loose their traces and fall on each other, teeth suddenly sharp.

The ship somehow, still waits. It burns, but it does not sink. Another chunk of sky thunders down, and it lists in the smoking swell. Her muscles running on memory and habit alone, Shipwright shins a thin plank up from the shore, and starts up it. Choking down the panic that fills her chest. Tearing her eyes from the wallowing sails, the broken masts and backs of the other ships as they slide into the fizzing water. A few survivors of the *Hart's Pride* and the *Maiden of the Forests* limp at her back. Not much consolation.

Fallon is still behind her, almost alone now, the bodies of the soldiers who'd died in his shadow fallen to ash, or twitching, ready to rise again, swallowing star fire into themselves and staggering upwards. Falling on each other, rending, repurposing arms, legs, fingers, blades; becoming things which could survive under the gaze of that great eye.

Shipwright feels its weight on her. Somehow she gains the deck, her arms shrieking with effort as she throws Shroudweaver over the rail. Fallon vaults after her, pulls bodies in behind him, some still breathing. Something still to save.

For a second, she catches her balance and watches the world dislocate in front of her. Shipwright stands on the ship, looking up at a sky that is no longer a sky. At a moon that is no longer a moon, but rather a great roving eye, and she knows that it sees her. Not the black glass of the burning city, not the melting sea, not the falling stars. The eye sees *her*. And she feels it calling. It wants sacrifice. Something in it moves through her veins, and she knows what she must do, even as she reaches down with blistered hands and hoists Shroudweaver by the scruff of his neck. She can hear the blood in his body, and she can feel the hunger of the great eye calling for him. She knows what she must do. Even as the tears run down her face, even as they evaporate from her cheeks above the burning sea. She knows what must be done. With great care, she extends Shroudweaver's limp body out over the hungry sodium sea – an offering; a farewell. The thundering terror in her heart is shushed by the pulse of blood in her ears, by the call of the eye.

A second before she lets go, Fallon tackles both of them to the deck like a charging bull.

Shipwright's shoulders splinter the boards, and she hisses in pain, but Fallon's warm hands are on her eyes and his voice is in her ear. 'Keep them closed, keep them closed, it's OK. I love you. He loves you. Keep them closed. Don't let it see you.'

She does as she's told. Presses her face to Shroudweaver, pins him to the deck under her aching ribs until he coughs, shuddering into some kind of half-life. And as if by habit, or memory, or hope, his fingers begin to weave. Shipwright feels him call to the dead on the shore and the spirits of the ship. He steals from the stripped bones, the blade-bodied, the torn and the broken, the remnants of their great army, scouring the wreckage of gods and men, taking what he needs.

He steals shreds of hope and life, and feeds them to the ship which bucks like a skittish horse, the spinners whining helplessly, pinned by the weight of the great eye. The sea swirls in strange patterns from the pressure, flat as glass, then boiling like fire. Still Shroudweaver's blackened lips move. Red thread stretches and scraps of the dead weave themselves into plank and caulk, into canvas and mast. The power of their spirits kicks the spinners into a devil's screech, peeling the ship off the shore.

The ship strains. Shipwright feels it in the rise of the timbers, the kick of the sea against the bow, in the grudging scrape of the shallows giving up purchase. It needs a steady hand to steer her home. As if they'd shared the thought, she feels Fallon guiding her, his fingers tight against her eyes, and his strong hands bringing her to the wheel.

'Steer her, Ship,' he'd begged and she had, because she was the Shipwright, and the ship was brightest in motion.

She remembered the sea falling away, a poor shadow to the

grace and beauty moving under her, the beach a spit of jealous sand at her back, thick with smoke. Beyond that the planes of the ruined city still shuddered, slipping, falling shard-like into unseen configurations. Not just dying – evolving, shifting into something alien and new. The sharp smell of stone burning. And above it all, hung the eye.

The eye, twisting and twitching, feral, furious. Its gaze roamed the shuddering streets and where it fell people split and changed, bodies canted into new forms, and there were fingers where there should be teeth, teeth where there should be hands, knives where there should be hearts. And blood, over and over, blood.

In the streets, the gods spasmed and died, beautiful, golden, rent and ragged. The luckiest were dragged down, hamstrung, shredded by weight of numbers. Others lay pinned under flaming rock, writhing and changing. Infected with the weight of the purple sky.

Crowkisser had got her wish. They hadn't come close to stopping her. Their army, their fleet had been an afterthought, an observer to some primal change, to some fundamental murder.

There is enough chaos to drown her head in nightmares, so Shipwright sticks to what she knows. She hauls at the wheel, the sea beneath caustic and hungry against the hull. She steadies her feet, spitting ash onto her hands and gripping tighter as a fury lights in her, pushing the terror aside. Let it come. They are not going to die here. She feels the ship sing to her, feels the vibration of its spinners, and the spirits inside them. She becomes more than a body. She is spar and beam. She is the stretch of canvas, tar-cord, splinter, caulk and keel. She is brass and bright-blue sky. A howl of defiance leaps out of her throat.

The ship hears her and shudders like an old steer in tight traces. High above, the eye is still on them. She feels it at her back, like a cat's tongue against her neck. She grits her teeth until they crack, swallows the acid swilling in her throat and fixes her eyes on the horizon as the sky empties itself of stars. The sea swallows them and coughs forth gouts of bright flame in return. From below, things swarm to the falling light, dark, tentacled, ragged.

Distantly, she feels her hair catch fire.

Distantly, she feels Fallon's hands on her shoulders, slick with blood, blistered. Holding her steady.

His body shakes. She can feel the movement down his arms. She takes it, takes every little scrap of energy she can and feeds it into the guts of the ship as Shroudweaver weaves with scraps of broken gods and dying men, pulling them into wood and sail. And the ship grows faster.

She steadies herself against Fallon's singed frame as they tear over the waves.

He's still shaking. It's a long moment before she realises. He's laughing.

46

He would not talk of the South aflame
but instead told the story of a host
who on watching his temple burn
found himself alight with a wilder fire

—*On Swallowing Gold*, Heartshamer

Three years later, back on Hesper's low docks, Fallon watches the ship cast off. He lets his eyes follow the rise of its keel for a moment and watches Shipwright's hands on the wheel, the sure dance of her fingers, the corded strength of her arms battling against the reluctant helm. It's all a little too familiar.

Memory's a vile dog.

The stone and scut of the docks lurches under him, and in a second, in the flick of a gull's wing, he's back in the south, on the deck of the ship, feeling the flame of a dying city at his back, steadying the tremors in Shipwright's arms as she strains at the tiller above a seething sea. Somewhere overhead the sky tears with a wet shriek. He's got more sense than to look up.

He tries to still the flicker of fear that's running through his bowels. It's not totally unfamiliar; late night in the pastures as a kid, and the glint of wolf eyes on the hills, things that want to eat you hanging just over your neck.

There's a way to deal with it. Get out of your own fucking head. So he does. 'You've got this,' he says to Shipwright, steady as he can manage. She glances over her shoulder. There's something a little unhinged at the edges of her eyes as she mouths a single word. 'Shroud.'

Fallon nods and turns to check on Shroudweaver. He can't

see him at first, among the lashing rigging and the smoke, the magnesium punch of a dying sky. Then there he is, outlined in the first scalpel cut of thunder, one hand on the prow. No, hand not *on* the prow, but lashed to it. Red threads, corded and twined thick, burnt into the flesh of his arm, stuttering with silver light. Weaving. His other hand outstretched to the shore, trailing ribbons like a cat's cradle. And in their wake, a beat behind, the dead.

Hungry, and bright and torn. And his. With every movement, every twist of his wrist, the souls of the dead chase Shroudweaver in a slipstream of loss. Fallon can feel the push of them, the power of them, their hunger. It's terrifying. He fights the urge to leap overboard.

He staggers as the ship bucks with another detonation to starboard, another fallen star. Something massive crests in response and swallows it down. There's an explosion in the deep, the water rosy with fresh blood.

The world is eating itself.

Fallon feels laughter well up inside him again. Dangerous. Keep it together. It's only a few swift steps to Shroudweaver's side. He wraps his arms around the man's sliver of a waist, and whispers in his ear. 'Bring 'em in, Shroud. You can do it.'

Shroudweaver's smile is a thin thing, his eyes closed tight, caught in the shadow and rhythm of his work. But fuck him if he doesn't smile. With a lunge, he hauls backwards, his wrists pulling like a conductor, a fisher, a surgeon.

Fallon braces against his back, feels the immense weight of a hundred stolen lives on the other end of the line, sees the desperate light in their eyes. And then, like a fire kindling in a dark room, he realises what Shroudweaver is doing. The ship rides on the hopes of the dying, like the crest of a wave. And here the dead come, like a flock of birds, bright and chattering. In over the thundering waves, away from the burning beach and its ragged sky.

Fallon watches Shroudweaver sketch their path home, watches his broken, bloody lips murmur the words they want to hear.

*itsokI'llbehereI'myourbrotherI'myourfatherI'myoursonnothingislost-
nothingnothing*

The dead throng him like a flock of starlings, filling the sails, their song bright and beautiful and broken. Fallon watches their silver lines thread the shining waves, ducking and weaving to avoid the falling stars, twisted and guided by Shroudweaver's dancing wrists. Too fast to follow, too fast to stop.

The eye wants them. Wants to hold them and pin them like flies in amber. Fallon can tell that much, can feel it lowering over the fleeing dead like a drunken lover. But who would stand still with someone they love calling them? And Shroudweaver, he loves all these broken souls, he loves them in red thread and silver. In smoke and blood. In something like prayer.

The dead flee the burning shore, and their frail, desperate hope pushes the ship to speeds beyond anything Fallon's ever felt. A surge under his feet. Lifting and filling the timbers. Flaring up through his legs. Filling his hips, his heart with something bright and savage.

Laughter tears loose from his chest and reels off into the sky. Beside him, he sees Shroudweaver's face warm with sudden relief. So when the girl appears on the shore, she hardly seems to matter. A slim, frayed thing. Almost another walking corpse, her grey shift pressed against her bare legs by the scorching wind. She staggers her way to the sea's edge and stops, swaying slightly. Fallon often thought he should have noticed the way the bent and broken vestiges of his army avoided her, circling like hyenas. Should have wondered about the shattered remnants of gods dragging themselves from her path. Should have taken some warning from the great eye twisting to focus on her, from the way it widened in sudden shock. But all Fallon remembered of that day was the swaying girl's upraised hand, fingers spread wide. And then the crows.

★

Memory's a vile dog.

When he comes to, three years and too many leagues later, the dockside cobbles are slick with vomit. His physicker helps him up with a frown and a heave, his soft stubbled face twisting disapprovingly. Eventually, Fallon's feet reel their way back into the heart of the city, but for a time, his mind remains in the past, out on the ocean, on the sea, in the shards of the burning south.

47

a temple may be erected anywhere the gods can see
the home is a temple
and so the cattle shed
and so the skull.

—Meditations on the Vanished Arts, lecture series

The twilight is cut with the first strands of night, the wind low and lazy between the pillars, slinking like a loose-limbed dog over the cobbles of Astic. Lamps gutter, spit and fall to curfew. Shutters are pulled tight, latches dropped. Evenings turned to the spit and crackle of embers.

The hands of the people of Astic are scarred, scrubbed raw. Blistered by forges, scoured by pickling brine. The hands of the people of Astic are methodical as they set coals, stoke fires, turn skillets, push smoky hair from tired eyes.

Hundreds of little grey houses fill with warmth, with the smell of meat and oil, the close-lipped bubble of heavy-lidded pots. Bars fall across doors, feet slip under blankets. Swords lie loosely over knees given up to the whetstone kiss.

In the streets outside, blades walk on long, dark legs. The shadows are filled with the tall, thin strips of men who tend to the city as she sleeps.

As the last lantern goes out, the lights of the gallowswatchers wink on, one by one. The slow swing of their bones against the gibbets. Lambent eyes casting listlessly into the gathering dark.

The long men run fingers over the knots that hold them tight. Murmur instructions to each other. Carve sigils into skin, quick and precise, as Crowkisser's instructed them.

In the warming houses, the timbers stretch and settle as they shake off the evening cold. Strong arms tickle squealing ribs, and small heels kick a frenzy of rushes and laughter and bathwater.

Ladles swim and stir, and steam rises to the eaves which shuffle with rats and owls.

Lips brush each other, stubble against cheek. Quick handclasps are snatched against ranges, by bedsides, beneath covers.

In the streets, the long men climb the winding path to the old temple. It stays open to the sky, its belly boned with pillars which hint at the ghosts of carvings. These are the spaces where the story of the gods used to be told, spaces where offerings could be left to the hosts and priests, in hope of wisdom, or favour, or peace.

Their hands are quite full with different offerings by now. With meat, bones and secrets. Sometimes, they carry them two abreast, their long limbs bowing under the strain.

Above their heads, the moon is a coin in the clouds. Above the clouds, the first black specks of crows begin to spin and fall towards Astic's sleeping heart.

In the cottages, sleep-lidded eyes turn pale faces to flames, to voices, to stories. Small hips are set on tired legs, which become horses for knights and dragons for wizards. Strong hands scratch small skulls, tuck stray hair behind soap-pink ears impatient for the story.

So familiar voices tell a familiar tale, and it starts like this:

'First there were the crows. And then, there was the Crow-kisser.'

She stands at the entrance to the old temple, scrimshawed out of shadows. Her eyes are weary, her body bent back into the smoky sculpt of the Slickwalker. His arms lace her hips like a belt, his fingers tracing small curves on the edges of her tiredness.

The path unfurls down the temple hill, wet with recent rain. Crows chuck and worry over the scraps caught between the canted stones.

The long men lay their burdens at her feet. She sifts them rapidly, methodically. Brutally. Sometimes she cries. Sometimes she screams. Sometimes she tests things with the edge of her teeth.

She is searching for the future.

The long men wait with eyes downcast. Slickwalker moves among them, touching shoulders, murmuring encouragement, balancing blades. Once, he stoops to ruffle the hair of a slimmer shadow, adjusting the tuck of its scarf.

Crowkisser digs, her hands deep in the belly of the city. She sifts rope and leather and flesh. Fishbones and dogsteeth. Glass and clay and piss. Slowly, she feels Astic begin to breathe under her feet.

And the story carries on. Around cupped mugs and crossed legs and waiting hearts.

'First there were the crows. And then there was the Crowkisser. Alone on the bloody beach. And the sand red, red and red again.'

'Red again,' the little ones chant, and giggle with the fear of it all.

'And why was she alone?' The storytellers ask.

'Because there were no ships.'

'And where were the ships?'

'At the bottom of the hungry sea.' Hands sketch shadows of waves, of tentacles and dipping dreams.

The audience wide-eyed and sleepy, torn between the voices stroking their hair and the battening of the wind outside.

High on the hill, the long men draw their coats tight and raise their thick wool collars. The smaller ones cluster together. The smallest hold gloved hands, but quietly.

Slickwalker rubs Crowkisser's back as she searches, his strong hands moving over her sliding shoulder blades, her wriggling spine. If there are words in the sounds he makes, the wind doesn't know them.

Crowkisser is lost to the city. Her fingers are deep inside it. She can feel its thick pulse, hear the words on the tongues of its people, feel the warmth of the small fires that blaze for miles around. For a moment, she feels like a mother. Then the wind gusts, the crows call and she falls beyond the walls and the sky.

To Hesper. To where a ship moves out to sea and slips

northwards into the old grooves of another rebellion. She moans low and long and chews her lip.

Flies onwards.

To Thell where the dead are too quiet, where the people are hungry in their heart of heart of hearts.

She sifts, pushes. Her hand rises against bright light and she sees a mountain fall. Unimaginably vast. Its depths opening up to spill forth a river of mouths that scream and scream. She can do nothing.

She scrapes her nails along wet stone. She is trapped in a fountain, she is broken and hollow and hungry and she needs blood. But there's a wall between her and the world. Shifting, patchwork, unfriendly.

She is trapped inside. The latch will not lift. The doors will not break.

She falls backwards, and Slickwalker's strong hands catch her before she hits the stone.

She is above herself. She is endless and vast and spiteful and blind. There are feathers across the stars. And she needs the stars. She needs their golden light.

Crowkisser's legs scrabble on the slick stone. The long men hold her, soothe her, they straighten her neck and mop at her lips where the spit and bubble of prophecy drips down.

Her bones cannot hold the seeing any longer. The night discards her. She lands in her own weak body with the weight of a falling star. She hurts, everywhere. But she is here.

Everything remains as it was. There is still time perhaps, to save a little blood. If she can hollow out the mountain before her father arrives with his time-worn lies and false promises.

She stands slowly, swaying gently. For a second, she feels the brief hearth fires of the city spreading out around her. The night is studded with fragile hearts flickering against the darkness. She feels the world outside stretching out to snuff them, and something in her stomach aches. She feels like a mother. And she is hunger, and pain and vengeance.

48

hung by their neck, where the wind is howling
hung by the tall bones, the long bones
the ones that stretch close to the gods.

—Headsman's Cant, Mirth

The wind is high on the coastal road, scouring down from the eastern hills and meeting the air off the sea in violent gusts.

The bleached wood of the Teeth list against its force. The base of each signal fire scorched black from the countless flames lit in their depths.

Crowkisser stoops against the nearest pyre, resting her fingers on the cold, damp wood as she lets her lungs snatch a breath from the gale. The burning in her legs is cooling as she pauses from her ascent. She's exhausted. It's her third night of no sleep, her mind skirling with visions, her ears still slithering with voices.

She lets her head lean back and inhales the lingering scent of smoke, only half-tamped by the rain.

For years this shoreline has danced with warning fire, as the fleets of Hesper harried and burnt any ship that tried to bring her people aid. Years of waking to that line blazing in the night. Knowing it meant death in the morning and empty stomachs for weeks after that.

She knuckles the sleep from her eyes. Enough. That ends soon.

All she needs is to break Hesper. To take Fallon, and her father, and that damned Shipwright out of the frame.

Now, there might even be a chance to do that without sinking the world further into death. Thanks to Quickfish.

A brave boy, running all the way to Thell. Stupid, of course. No magic in that mountain would bring his mother back her name half-torn as it was, a lingering ghost between worlds. A half-remembered thing. Stupid, stubborn woman.

But, with Quickfish in Thell, Crowkisser had everything she needed. A few light nudges, a few strings pulled, and the stars had started to align.

Her dad had jumped at just the right moment. The slightest push from Slickwalker, the slightest threat to Fallon and his friends, and he'd run north. Seeking an army in the living *and* the dead, she suspected. A rekindling of that old alliance that had won him the last war, and the electric taste of new souls for the pyre. Predictable. Admittedly, the prospect was worrying, on some abstract level, but she doubted he had the stomach to pull it off, or whether the welcome that awaited him would be as warm as he hoped. And beyond that, she wondered if he'd really turn the dead against her, even if they could be brought to heel. She couldn't quite imagine it. He was still her father. Somewhere, out there, under all the rest of it.

Five years and more since she'd defied him. Left him with the corpse of her mother and his excuses.

All those years, and he'd never lifted a finger against her. Not directly. True, there'd been a lot of noise and fuss around the edges hampering her, holding her back. But nothing direct. He didn't have the guts for it.

Or he hadn't, until now. She wondered if Shipwright would push him to attempt something more final. If Fallon's bitterness would give him enough sway to send some red-threaded death her way, a little bit of payback for his dreaming wife.

She needed something to tip the scales.

And she hadn't found it.

Not that she'd let on to Slickwalker, or to her people. Astic was prepared for war. Slickwalker already yearning to stalk off across the country, living out all his dreams of the bold, lone hero.

And she hadn't found her ace in the hole.

Months of searching, and cutting, and bleeding questions into the dark, and she had *nothing*. Her blood lit with fire at the thought of it.

The prophecies were too vague. The omens could mean pretty much anything. A mess of squawks, of hints that echoed some great defeat for her enemies, and an unsuspected alliance. But nothing *concrete*, just a sense of the change to come, the sense of her own surprise when it would hit her.

All she had for certain was Fallon's son, in that mountain. And if there was a place more foreign to her on this entire blasted earth, she didn't know it. Locked down on land by an army still hardened from their last war, and in the air by the wild, strange warlock that stalked the mountain scarp.

She would have to go there herself, alone, before she dragged her army halfway across the world. She needs to see the mountain, and see what she can use to make its people bow.

She doesn't want them dead. She doesn't want her father dead. However much she hates him for what he did or didn't do, she can't wrap her head around a world without him.

As for the people in the mountain? Thell's "Republic"? They've been ruled before. And she needs bodies. And supplies. It would be a waste to kill them, and she doesn't waste anything.

The solution is to make them bow.

She just doesn't know where to start.

The wind rises to a shriek, driving her into the lee of the Teeth, down onto the trade road.

The name itself is something of a joke now. The carts and drovers that used to come from the north have stilled to a trickle, and the ways from the south are empty of anything beyond the villages she's brought into the fold.

Every mile or so, the road rises briefly to black spars of wood. Old ship timbers and the like, strung up to form sturdy gibbets that even now creak and bend in the wind.

Over those black crossbeams, black rope, and hanging from those ropes by the neck, the corpses of the last idiots to get in her way.

She never wastes anything.

As she draws near the closest spar, its inhabitant turns to watch her approach. The green light of its eyes bright within its hollow

347

skull, shining through the drawn skin of its temples like parchment. Its neck creaks gently, the withered flesh straining as it patiently follows her approaching feet.

Those eyes could see for a mile, two on a good day. Nothing moved on this road that they didn't catch.

One of her better ideas, she thinks.

The corpse's jaw clacks gently as she stops at the base of the gibbet, its teeth nut-brown from rot, knocking together softly, curiously.

The common folk called them gallowswatchers, a little grim, but not inaccurate. Nice, tangible reminders of what happened to anyone that threatened her, and her people.

This man had been a raider, one of the opportunists that had come calling after the burning of the south, thinking the Rim villages were easy pickings, stunned by the devastation that lingered over the horizon. Perhaps the first few villages had been, those that had turned her away, their headmen and women full of bluster and propriety, denouncing her heresy, her arrogance. Her lip curls a little at the memory of those self-important little towns, filled with self-important little people. Once she tore the names from their leaders, their villages became home to nothing much except bleached bones, rotten fruit, and, ironically, crows.

Not many had kept their names after she'd cleansed the south. A few hardy souls, that drew followers to them like a lodestone, like flies to shit. Dangerous, the lot of them. Every holdout she found, she dealt with herself, with as much mercy as you'd give to a rabid dog. For most, the process was also the solution. There weren't many who could survive the stripping of a name. Crowkisser had a lot of respect for Fallon's wife, much as she'd lingered on. For the rest, it was over quickly – a mess of beak and feather down the throat, and the name plucked free like a struggling worm, torn apart and thrown to the sky.

It only took a few, public, examples for the rest of the Rim to come to their senses. Those that accepted her in Dryke, Vantage and Fallow soon found that their highways were watched by the dead. The men who had once stalked their roads now danced a blackwood jig that kept their glowing eyes fixed for any new idiots with knives and ideas beyond their station. When more bandits had rolled down the old approach roads that winter, the Rim villages had known for days ahead. The ambushes had been merciless, the pits deep, and the stakes sharp. And in the spring, the highway had sprouted another crop of vigilant, dangling watchmen.

Nothing was wasted. She idly spun the gallowswatcher by the dried sinew of his legs. Her fingers lingered on the scars at his ankles, the tattoo of a bird that skirted his shoulder. She'd killed this one herself. She remembered the rolling whites of his eyes, the desperate pleading spilling from his lips, even as the barn he'd burnt kindled higher and brighter.

She pats the withered leg consolingly. He didn't seem to hold a grudge. As he spun, his lambent eyes occasionally lilted towards the sea, the bones of his neck grinding quietly in the wind as he turned. So much more useful in death than life.

A slight smile of satisfaction flits across her lips. Raising the watchers now felt like the simplest cantrip. Just the start of the vast whisper of power she'd been given. But it was undeniably effective. Sentries with no need for sleep, no fear in their hearts. Only the salt wind eating away at their flesh, day by day.

She pushes again, watching the twirl of leather, skin and bone. Try to pull one of these down and it would scream to high heaven. Try to hood its face and its weathered hands would pull you close and hold you tight until the long men arrived, faces weary and grim, sad to have been pulled from their dinner tables but glad for a chance to keep their children safe.

The wind gusts as she watches the gallows turn, sending the dead man's thin legs dancing in ungainly spasms, his neck whipped back and forth.

The voice, when it comes, hangs on the edge of the wind, brushing the edges of the corpse's lips like a bird's wing, '. . . kisserrrrr.'

Her head whips around, the spike of adrenaline in her heart setting her pulse racing.

The gallowswatcher's glowing eyes are steady, the dry skin drawn back from its brown teeth in a forced grin. Its head regards her for a moment or two, then tips to the side with a curious rattle. 'Kisser.'

She recognises the voice now. She's heard it before, in the temple, hissing from a mess of meat and bone.

'Again, unclean corpse?' She fingers the knife at her belt, the handle heavy and reassuring. 'I thought I'd sent you out with blade and binding.'

The gallowswatcher laughs, an impossible sound, its frayed vocal cords scratching together like chafer song. 'Oh, you got rid of me just fine. Jointed me up and parcelled me out.' A bony finger digs between its ribs, pulls a maggot out speculatively from under paper skin.

'It's not the first time I've been sundered, crow-witch. I hold no grudge.'

Crowkisser narrows her eyes. Breathes deep, from the belly, counting her heart down into steadiness. 'The dead rarely mean well. What do you want? Who are you?'

The light in the corpse's eye flares like a struck match.

'I'm not dead, dearest crow. Just dispersed.' It laughs again, mirthless and empty.

'I'm the last person that tried to stand up to your father, before you. Or rather, I'm what's left of them.'

Her heart starts at that, but she simply tightens her grip on the knife. 'How do you know my father?'

The gallowswatcher's dry tendons pull its jaws wider. 'The same way you do, more or less. He destroyed my world.'

Crowkisser looks at the corpse for a second. The wind pushing insistently against her shaking legs. 'I don't have time for this.'

She turns and leaves, her feet marching her furiously up and over the wet earth of the coast road.

The scream that tears from the corpse's throat stops her in her tracks. She turns, and the wail slithers wetly down through the gale, before coiling into a laugh that shakes the gallowswatcher on its perch.

'You need me, little Crow. You need into my mountain.'

A spike of shock in her heart. She hides it deep and turns slowly.

The hanged man is silent as she slowly stalks back towards it. Just the faintest glimmer lights the gallowswatcher's scoured sockets.

Her jaw juts as she spits the question. 'How do you know that?'

The corpse twists slowly, its fingers twitching. 'Because I listen to the dark, just like you.' It beckons. 'Come closer.'

Reluctantly, she steps a little further forwards, close enough to see the bones shift under frayed cloth, to hear the rip of old, rotten skin.

Its voice is a rough whisper, soft, confident. 'Listen, child. I understand you. We are both from humble beginnings. Both blessed with incredible mothers.' Its voice dips to a snarl, 'Both betrayed by the weaver.'

Crowkisser watches its dry lips, its cracked teeth. How naïve does it think she is?

She raises a finger. 'I'll not deal with a dead man just because you're crammed full of spite.'

'Spite?' it says. 'Oh, more than that. I've known spite, Crow-kisser. Spite, and rage, and terror, and hatred.'

She shakes her head dismissively. 'I'm not here to help you salve your grudges.' She unsheathes the knife and takes a hold of its leg. 'Time to go, corpse.'

The corpse kicks out, a chipped nail grazing her mouth as she jerks her head back.

'No!' Its voice steadies as it collects itself. 'No. Not yet. Listen a moment.'

Crowkisser watches it warily, her blade hovering between them like a promise.

The gallowswatcher hisses a breath through snail shell teeth. 'You know that your army would break against that mountain even without Shroudweaver set against you.'

It turns a palm outwards as it talks, scratching at the holes and frayed flesh. 'The people of Thell have lived with war forever. I schooled them in it. When they died in service to the mountain,

I raised them up again to fight beside their friends, their families. When their enemies fell against us, I took them, and taught them, and placed them in our ranks, to make a new accord.'

Its eyes flare green in the driving rain. 'Alliances. Brotherhoods beyond death.' Its voice crackles like a banked fire. 'We knew such peace.'

Crowkisser eyes the corpse flatly. How quickly her racing nerves have subsided into curiosity.

'Who are you?'

The gallowswatcher's head flops in the gale, legs and spine dancing a brutal jig as the wind picks up again.

She staggers, leans into it.

'They used to call me the Emperor of the Dead. Now' – it laughs, and a frayed hand traces the length of its body from broken neck to salted feet – 'Now, I'm diversifying. With a little help.'

A nail scratches idly at a desiccated finger, flaking skin down to raw bone. 'I had such loyal subjects. Such harmony, within our mountain, our city. I would have gifted that to the world.'

Its head turns slowly, rattling, as the wind pulls loose wisps of hair across its skull. 'Look at us both. Seekers of harmony. Architects of peace. Unafraid of our tools.' The corpse's jaw widens again, swings loose as a sickle. 'Of course, the world is still adjusting to your gift.' Something that might be a laugh scurries around its empty ribs. It watches Crowkisser step closer, a fish on a hook, her feet bare and blue in the sodden grass.

She runs a hand through her hair. So tired, even if she's trying to hide it behind pulled back shoulders and an upthrust chin. Good. They're so much easier when they're tired.

'All I want is peace,' she says. 'All I wanted was freedom. *Real* freedom. From the gods. From all their whims.'

The gallowswatcher clicks as sympathetically as a corpse can.

'Naturally,' it coos, in its beetle-thick rasp. 'All good rulers do.'

Her face clouds, 'I'm not a ruler.'

Its dry cheeks stretch. 'Are you not? What are you then, to the people in Astic, in Dryke, and Sedge? To all those sleeping babies and careworn fathers? To your dark friend with the beautiful gun? What are you then?'

She shakes her head. 'I'm . . .'

It interrupts. 'You are their ruler. In your own fashion, and through your own methods.'

Crowkisser nods, but the word hanging unsaid on her lips is not ruler. It's mother.

The corpse smiles again, for that's all its stripped jaw can do. 'Are we asking for so much? We want to include all people in our union. A strong union. A safe union.' Its voice drops to a hiss. 'We want to keep them safe.'

She nods slightly at that, and its dead heart rejoices. Its voice rolls on, over the wet cliffs and down the darkened path. 'My people were safe, Crowkisser. We had peace. We had as much freedom as was needed. Until Shroudweaver. Until your father. Until he came to feed the snakes among them. To fatten their restless hearts.'

She takes another step closer. Her hand lingers on the yellowed bone of the gallowswatcher's hip, the ruin of its flank.

'I know so little of the fall of the Empire. The rise of the Republic. He wouldn't speak of it.'

A snarl curls its rotten lips. 'None of them will. Twenty years of trying to scour my triumph from the face of the world and still they fear me.' It pauses, and she wonders what secrets it just hid in the silence.

'We can use that fear, you and I. We can use it to have our revenge.'

She taps the handle of the knife impatiently. 'Well, I'm listening, but only one of us is getting soaked through out here. Make it quick.' Her voice hardens. 'Tell me what I need to know.'

It laughs again, lurching and wet as the rain slowly fills its open throat. 'Very well. But understand this. I knew my people. I knew their every thought, so long as they stayed within my mountain, every whisper filtered down to my ears. And those that escaped, my loyal subjects brought to me like gifts. A trinity of advisers at my heel. Wiser and braver men I did not know.

There were no snakes in my mountain, until Skinpainter came. Until they taught my people to hide dissent in their bodies. In their skin, and their pulses, tapping out messages on collarbones, on wrists, on arms. Hiding betrayal in the count of their breath, and the flicker of their eyelids.'

'That's clever,' Crowkisser smiles.

'Yes,' the Emperor says. 'Unfortunately clever. And Skinpainter was clever beyond that. Clever enough to call out to your father. To lure him into meeting my army at the city of the jewelled lips.'

Crowkisser's mind races, searching the rumours and scraps of history she knows.

'At Luss.'

'Luss.' The word falling from the corpse's lips like a wet rock.

'My greatest betrayal. My own people turned against me. Months of Skinpainter's lies and promises. Bringing some of my best and most treasured into their vile embrace. Elevating rabble to the status of leaders. Secret promises of a better life tapped out on skin.' Its voice drips venom. 'Kinghammer. The Deadsingers. Belltoller. Traitors all. But Skinpainter the worst of them. A thief. A liar. A killer.'

'You were outplayed,' Crowkisser says, a faint smile on her lips. 'You got lazy.'

The corpse's eyes flare again, the green light hissing and spitting where it meets the falling rain. Its voice is bitter. 'I have had twenty long years to learn my lesson, Crowkisser. That's why I've come to you. I don't want you to make the same mistakes I made. I don't want your people to suffer like mine suffered.'

She raises an eyebrow. 'How kind of you.'

It snarls. 'I also want Skinpainter to bleed. I want to see that ink-stained thief in pieces. I want to watch the meat fall from their bones.'

Crowkisser smiles slightly. 'Now, that I can believe.' She taps the hilt of her knife against the gallowswatcher's leg. The corpse shudders in response.

'We still haven't got to how you help me win.'

The Emperor is silent for a while, inside the hanging body.

The rain streams down the man's broken nose, over that bird tattoo, and is whipped off and out to sea.

'You don't want to harm your father. I understand that.' Crowkisser opens her mouth to clarify, and it continues over her. 'Family is hard, and strange. Even I know that. Even if his death meant nothing to you, it would make him a perfect martyr for the thousands who want you dead. This war would drag out for years beyond counting. You can't afford that.'

Her heart stings a little at the truth of it.

'You can't kill Shroudweaver. But you can take away the power he needs.'

It watches her then, and she hates it. Hates the smug green fire in its eyes. Hates that she's leaping at the bait it's dangling.

She presses her lips together, thinking of Slickwalker and of Astic behind her on the road. 'Tell me how.'

The gallowswatcher inclines its head, the skin at its neck tearing to let the knobbed vertebrae through. 'Gladly. When your father and Skinpainter defeated me, they took certain precautions. On the living, Skinpainter tattooed wards, to prevent my reaching out to the lingering trace of me that slept in their blood. And the dead Shroudweaver stole from me, and kept from me. And so, I was diminished.'

Part of Crowkisser admires her father's hubris, admires Skinpainter's arrogance in effecting such a thin, desperate solution. She doesn't say that. Instead she says, 'I thought you were eaten alive.'

For the first time, she hears something close to real pain in the Emperor's reply.

'Your father and Skinpainter were . . . naïve. I suspect they believed their measures to be sufficient in appeasing the mob.' Its voice drops to a lingering whisper. 'They were incorrect.'

Crowkisser winces. 'I'm sorry.'

The Emperor's voice is matter of fact. 'Once you have experienced teeth on your bones, your perspective changes. I saw my skin hanging in shreds off a dozen hungry lips. Yet, I did not die. I saw them swallow my body in red gobbets down pulsing throats.

And somehow, I still survived.' Its voice is almost soft, reflective. 'Magic is a strange thing, girl. All power alters you, and you don't even notice your unmaking until you're forever changed.'

Crowkisser feels her body hum like a struck chord, and bites her lip to stop the tears. Her hand on the dry leathered flesh is suddenly tender for a moment, before she snatches it back, self-consciously.

The Emperor's voice is muted, droning. 'You've felt it, I see. Or the beginnings of it. All knowledge changes you, girl. And all knowledge is power. Do not fight it. Do not even presume you can fight it. There's no point.'

Again, its story cuts in a beat before her choked back reply.

'When Shroudweaver and Skinpainter found me, they gathered the scraps, the half-chewed rags of red bone, and they begged me for answers.' Its brown teeth gleam. 'Men such as these always feel they are deserved answers. Another free lesson – give them nothing, girl. They owe you their world, and they are *nothing* compared to you.'

Crowkisser smiles again, before she can catch herself. 'I'm not in the habit of explaining myself to anyone.'

It croaks approvingly. 'Good. When Skinpainter and your father found me, they could not bring themselves to finish the job the people of Thell had begun.' It pauses. 'Or perhaps they would not. In either case, they were weak, and afraid. And scared people do the most terrible things.'

'What did they do?' she asks, and the Emperor hears the tone in her voice. It has her interest.

Its voice is sing-song, reminiscing. 'In the depths of my mountain, there is a great black lake. Its waters still as new glass. Above it, the teeth of the mountain hang. Growing year on year, drip by drip. Longer and longer. Perhaps one day the teeth will grow long enough that the jaws of the mountain close on the water. I do not know.'

Its voice a sigh, a low undertone. 'Girl. They took what remained of me, that red pile that was nothing but the shreds of a man, and they placed me in the dark, above the lake, in a half-grown tooth. Hollow enough, that for the first few years, my remaining eye could look down on the dark water. Until I was sealed off, drip by drip.'

'That's . . .' Crowkisser, says, and nothing more, her mind struggling with the cruelty of it.

'Quite,' the corpse replies, with a flare of green. 'But, as I said, Skinpainter is a clever thief. Before they left me there, they took a piece of me. A finger bone. Snapped off clean and tucked in a small leather bag. As insurance.'

Crowkisser frowns. 'Insurance?'

Its tone is indulgent. 'Old magic, girl. Bone and body magic. I dream in the blood of everyone born in the mountain. I call to the dead around it. And, it seems, my body never truly died. If Skinpainter keeps my finger clutched to their fluttering chest, they can keep me bound. I can never help you. I can never be free.'

'You want the bone,' she says.

'I want *you* to have the bone,' it smiles. 'Go to Thell. Steal from the thief. Take my finger back, and we will have our revenge.'

Crowkisser looks dubious.

It laughs again. 'Why fret, girl? I told you. We have sought the same songs beneath the earth. When the tooth finally closed over, the only thing left to me was the dark. Within the stone. Within my own head. Days into months into years, until time fell away from my mind like the flesh fell from my bones. And that, girl, that was when the dark started to sing to me. You've heard its songs too. And you've stolen what you needed from them. In the libraries, the forests and the caves, and deep under the earth from the forgotten bodies of the dreaming dead. Perhaps from the singing dark itself. You have been a thief all these years. A thief of power. And you know the only thing that's required to steal is the will, the bravery and the *moment*.'

Crowkisser doesn't bother arguing, just nods. 'Fine. I'll get that bone. Any tips on that?'

The Emperor tries not to rush. This has to seem organic, friendly, unplanned.

'Skinpainter doesn't want a war, and neither, really, do you. You won't even need to lie, much. Get yourself to the mountain, at night. To the high caves that overlook the barrows. They like to walk there most nights, and stew in their legacies. Give them the girl they expect. Naïve, uncertain. Backed into a corner. They will want to see the best in you. They always do. The bone, I suspect, is in a pouch, upon their belt. As always.'

Crowkisser's mind catalogues the details. 'Fine. And your revenge?'

'That will be served when Thell falls in front of you.'

A leathered strip of an arm waves. 'Be wary of Skinpainter. They have taken many things of great power from me. They may have taken more in the years since.'

She shrugs. 'I've taken more from the people of this world than anyone. Maybe we'll have something in common too.'

The corpse twitches. 'That is a worry.'

She smiles. 'Maybe for you. So, once I have the bone?'

'Then you turn it against your father, and his power.'

She scratches at a sudden itch on her wrist. 'Against the weaving?'

The corpse swings back and forth. 'You know your father. If he had access to the numberless dead of my Empire, how would he use them?'

Crowkisser thinks. Scenarios flitting across her mind like flipped cards. Recoiling from some. Stunned by others. 'He'd use them to end the threat. With minimal losses. Or what he considers minimal losses.'

The corpse's yellow teeth gnash around its dry tongue. 'And what is the threat?'

Her shoulders slump. 'Me.'

'And what could end you? No simple weaving, now. Not now you've sung to the dark.'

'A composite,' she murmurs, and suddenly, the shape of the battle to come unfolds before her. A hundred small pieces of vague prophecy, weeks of snatched scraps, suddenly flex and weave into the smooth shape of the future.

'Exactly,' says the Emperor of the Dead, and its skull glows green with the brightest of fires.

'Throw the bone into the heart of the composite, and I'll cut free every single poor soul that your father has bound. We will steal the very ground from under him. And I shall open the mountain to you. You will finally be able to see the world as it should be.'

Crowkisser bites her lip, 'Without my father . . .'

'Only Skinpainter and Belltoller could stand against you. I know this. You cannot kill your father, but you can kill them.'

'Slickwalker,' she mutters.

'A few clean shots from that beautiful gun,' the Emperor replies. 'Belltoller's skull is as weak as any other, if caught unprepared.'

'And Skinpainter?' she asks.

'Mine,' the corpse snarls. 'Mine. In payments of debts long due. Do we have a deal?'

Crowkisser thinks for a moment. Her bones are numb with the driving rain, her skin's beaten blue by the wind. And down the path in Astic, the first lamps of evening kindle.

She clasps the dead man's hand in her own.

'We do.'

49

It is dangerous, to look at the smoke, and imagine the light
dangerous to look at the shell, and imagine a fruit within.

—Archivist Splitwater

At night, when the Stump slept, even the mountains dreamt. Marked by the heavy shadows of ice, the slow drip of water, runs and channels carved out over decades until they became familiar things, a network of veins, neurons, frosted, blackened and sharded by the descent of a thousand winters.

When the Stump slept, when its bright lights dimmed to a fever glow and the sounds of life finally washed themselves into the belly of the mountain, pooling in the drinking halls and sleeping chambers, becoming a softer thread in the tapestry of the mountain's dreaming, this was when Skinpainter liked to walk the halls. In these quieter times, these few brief moments of calm, they walked, one rag-wrapped hand cradling a cup of spiced cider, the other running broad fingered along the curving walls, feeling the Stump's slow breath, listening to the mountain shudder and tick.

It was hardly necessary. The curves and cants of the stone were familiar beneath their shuffling soles. After all, Skinpainter was one of the old guard, a founder of the Republic – a revolutionary. They worry at their lips with their teeth. It's quite the legacy.

The guts of the Stump open up sporadically above the valley and its outbuildings, vast, porphyric, perforated. The humped and shadowed mounds below punctuated by the snap and crack of the cairn banners, occasionally flaring with light snatched from the lamps of cottages and inkworks. The wind roars confidently from the higher peaks, sharpened by the scent of new snow. In spots against the deepened blue of the night sky, night time raptors wheel and duck in pursuit of fast, hot-blooded prey.

Skinpainter watches them for a while, watches their spiral dance down the passes as they dip and weave. Their tattooist's hands tremble in response. Dip and weave. Pluck and turn. Colour and keep. Decades of familiar movements.

The barrows sleep well. The dead of the past twenty years, and the years before those, are quiet, cossetted beneath earth and scree. Skinpainter can relax. The chaos roiling in the south hadn't yet sunk its teeth into the cold ground of the north. They had some time before it stretched this far. Its mother would be here soon enough though. Crowkisser was impatient. They could feel her on the wind, skulking around the low hills outside of the mountain. The witch was riding Quickfish's shoulders like a vulture, poor boy. They sip their cider, feel it sting a mouth grown dry from talking, from the hours upon hours debating with the council, trying to make them see the inevitability of the situation. Trying to turn their gazes outward, for once. For all the levers Skinpainter had, the Council of the Republic was still a weighty rock to shift. Staggering under the burden of everything they had won, now too scared to reach outwards, for fear the world would notice them. For fear of another war.

Skinpainter had been expecting war since the Republic was born, before the blood was even dry. The audacity of what the rebels had done had rung like a bell throughout the cities to the south. Perhaps it had even been heard north of the mountains, beyond the spires. They didn't know. Thell, however, sat on the map like an insult. A reminder of the impermanence of empire. Of the efficacy of a little focused rage.

They sip again, pulling their robes close against the chill wind. They'd been lucky to get the scant years of peace they'd had. Before the south had burnt. Before the southerners' gods had died. Their side aches at the thought, and they run fingers over the shape under their robes.

They shake their head softly. War had always been coming. Since Crowkisser burnt a city to glass, and hollowed out the names of the world. Long before that, if they were honest. Since Hesper had thrown in their lot to free Luss. If they were really honest, since they had first called out to Shroudweaver for help.

Now his daughter gathered her strength on the singed rim of the south. All the traumatised survivors of that nightmare, flocking to her grey banner, just to feel some solid ground under their feet.

Their lip curls. It was hard to welcome another empire founded on fear.

They'd argued the same to the council, until their throat was hoarse. It was no coincidence that Fallon's kid had come here. That old bull wasn't as stupid as his roaring and hollering made him seem. Every ruler leant on their family, consciously or unconsciously.

Blood built kingdoms, Skinpainter had reasoned.

Kinghammer had nodded appreciatively at that. A point scored. Skinpainter runs a finger over their jaw, feeling it ache as the last shreds of tension flee their muscles. There was another strong man who had more in his skull than you'd expect.

The rest of the council had listened too, with varying degrees of fear. Skinpainter understood that. Understood the urge to seal the doors and turn inwards. To wait for the storm to pass, but they were kidding themselves. Crowkisser was not a storm. She was a wave that would never break.

Quickfish was the lever that Skinpainter needed to pry open the door. They had to stand with their allies, for all the thought of picking at those old wounds chafed, because Hesper was not the real target. Crowkisser wanted one thing above all. 'Security,' Skinpainter had said, watching Belltoller's brows rise as she recognised the irony. Everybody wanted to be safe by being free of everybody else.

As long as Thell was independent, Crowkisser would never have control, never be secure. They were doomed by their own success.

Crowkisser had killed the gods and killed their hosts, then gathered their lost flocks in with a smile. That made her a big deal anywhere south of the mountain, but Thell had never had hosts. Never had gods. Because the Empire had never had gods. The Emperor had made sure of that.

That made Thell a threat. They had nothing to fear from her. There was nothing she could take from them. They'd killed their last tyrant years ago.

That meant she could either win them over, or break them. And as Kinghammer had put it, Thell had no patience for foreigners with strange magic on their tongues.

So, they'd agreed, as much as they ever had, on war.

More importantly, they'd agreed that Crowkisser would come to Thell first. The mountain was the real power in the north. That was why Fallon's son was here, whether he realised it or not.

Granted, Hesper was a target, if you wanted to control the sea. A target with walls as high as a gull's eye, sick with metal and weapons. The crow-witch could break herself on those battlements, and without a fleet, the sea would still be there, out of reach.

Thell had high walls, too. But more than anything, it had people. It was the biggest city outside of Hesper. Ten thousand surly souls, stacked tight within the mountain and enough blood and bone to tear the world down, or whatever Crowkisser intended.

Regardless of her desires, she needed to be stopped. Skinpainter hadn't relished turning the screw on Belltoller or the Singers, but this was how the world worked. You did what was needed to drive in the direction of progress. Leant where you needed to lean. Broke what you needed to break.

They shift uneasily as their side flutters. Little legacies dancing in the blood. The question was whether Crowkisser was someone who could be persuaded to bend, or who needed to break.

Skinpainter needed to know more about her, to get a better sense of the pattern that pulled her towards the mountain. They knew in their gut she would come. They could feel her on the air, the cold winds scaling the mountain side touched with the barest hint of black feather.

At night, Thell was not just a mountain. Great black peaks reached up over the dark earth of the Barrowlands. The sky hung with cold, heavy with snow pushing down from the north, snow that had touched the edge of the Blades, that had come in from the east before that, over the chill sea, across the backs of whales and the creaking bows of ships.

The patterns of the world were drawn to that mountain which sat like a dagger in the heart of the weave. They bowed towards its broken rock, towards the stark hollows flickering with flame.

Everything danced along that weave. Everything sought power, and fell towards it like a stone down a well.

Much as rivulets of water traced the mountain's skin from high streams, power slicked the winds that gusted and guttered around the Stump. Learn the movement of that power, and the patterns beneath it would unveil themselves as clear as the rock etched by that cold, mountain water.

Tonight, there is something on the wind beyond snow; something on the lips beyond spiced sweetness. The pattern is eager to be found. Like a lost dog, it noses at the edges of anything seeking it. See, here, in the hiss of windblown grass – the breath of a woman. There in the scut and shadow of clouds, the march of soldiers. In the kiss and cry of pennants, the memories of stolen names.

The wind is thick with the ghosts of names. A wonder it blows so strong.

Some are fiercer than others, exploding on their gums in a riot of taste. The first couple, old and strong. From the south. Always a pair. A particular, personal orbit, neither leaving the other for a second.

Saltpetre, sandalwood, red and burning. Loss and binding. Worn nails and thin legs. Shroudweaver.

Shroudweaver comes to Thell, again, stinking of desperation and hope. Skinpainter does not fret. They know well the shape of his heart – their oldest confidante, their staunchest ally. Others will not accept him so easily. There are survivors of the war with the Empire that remember him less fondly, children born afterwards that have never seen his face. Those holding too tight to power and those that have never known it. Regardless, it will be good to see him again. They've missed him, his smile, his quiet humour, that merciless, dry teasing that seemed to have been a feature of the men and women from the south. Skinpainter shudders – all that humour and joy burnt away in a firestorm of fizzing black glass.

Shroudweaver may have been the best of them. He was certainly the last of them, but charming as he was, not everyone in Thell would be happy to see him return. There were some secrets in the foundations that were not yet ready to see the light. Fretting, they breathe deep of the night wind, cleanse their palate with ice. Best they focus on the wind, for now, and on the patterns of names under the wind.

The shape of the other name that accompanies Shroudweaver has no surprise to it. Would you taste the inhale without the exhale? Polish, canvas, bellows-brass. The scutter and skitter of trapped things. Regret. Love and a stubbornness like lead.

Shipwright. Skinpainter smiles. They like her too. Shroudweaver may have given the Republic its victory, but she gave them something more personal, a taste of worlds beyond their own, a sense of that dark ocean to the east where whales sang. Their fingers pull at their hood, touch their face. Fine memories.

The wind lies a little tonight, though. Skinpainter tastes something else here. Sweet as honey. Gold and gold and gold. God fragments still sifting through the air in eddies from the south. The silty remnants of the great things that had burnt to ash, three long years ago.

The air was never quite clean afterward; always dusty with the dregs of divinity. Contaminants. Crowkisser's last idiot gift. Something must be done about her, and the mess she has left behind. Skinpainter growls deep in their chest and plucks the last little scraps of god from the air, stretching out with their power for just a moment. Filaments of ribboned frost feed shreds of gold into lips pursed with disapproval. Skinpainter chews and swallows, until the sticky sweet taste is gone.

Stone and spit for southern gods. Skinpainter focuses again on Shipwright and Shroudweaver, their names riding the cliff wind like the blue-winged hawks circling above. The pair have always offered such a simple pattern to unpick. Skinpainter has known them too long, too well, has been collecting stories of their adventures over the decades since the fall of Empire. The raid on the black lakes. A summer almost lost in the Midlands swamps, seeking evidence of the Green. Shipwright's years with the Burners, and Shroudweaver's strange, circuitous journeys north beyond the mountains, fancying himself unseen. A few hectic months chasing rumours of bladedrinkers that turned out to be nothing but moonshine. And finally, that doomed mission to the south that near tore Skinpainter's heart from their chest when they lost touch with them both. The surge of relief they'd felt as the whisper of their names somehow returned, once the sky in the south cleared, and the great purple storms ceased roiling across the battered lowlands.

Latterly, the pair had been raiding again and again from Hesper at Fallon's request, punishing Crowkisser and her people as best they could; Shroudweaver starving out his daughter's supply routes with apparently merciless efficiency. A busy life, and wide-ranging, with a conspicuous space around the mountain, the cairns, the Stump. Nearly twenty years and they had never returned in person, sending only a few shamefaced letters laced to the frozen talons of messengers. Absences edged with fear, and hardened by the Councils' insistence on closing their borders with blades, and burning the memory of the gods from Midlands earth. Nearly twenty years they'd stayed away, and yet here the shadows of their names were, drifting slowly north. Skinpainter smiles a little, there was something satisfying in the inevitability of it all. There is only one reason that old pair would risk returning to Thell.

The collection of debts. The reforging of alliances. The harvesting of the dead.

Skinpainter isn't worried. Everything they owe, everything that Thell owes, is long past due, and this is expected. Debts were made to be paid. A satisfying pattern woven tight, closed off.

They shiver as a gust of ice skirls up the mountain from the cairns below, huddling closer to the brazier that gutters on the cliff's edge. Perhaps that's enough questions for one chill evening. Time for more cider, and a high-banked fire. Their side aches, and their brain is weary from jousting with old friends and their hard heads. The world will not end if they raise a cup, and toast a few nuts in the embers. The night has told tales aplenty. They are about to turn in, curiosity satisfied, until something catches at the back of their mind. A little snake's tongue of suspicion. Not quite a hunch, but enough to make their cold fingers reach out and send their curiosity a little deeper into the night. For a moment, the air flashes with the geometrics that mark their body, seeming for a brief moment to hang barely over their skin.

Filaments of power drift on the edge of their fingers, then fray as rock shifts behind them. They curse a little under their breath, and turn. There are no truly quiet spaces in this mountain. Here's Icecaller, Kinghammer's daughter, stalking sleepless again. Skinpainter gestures her to an alcove, placing a finger to their lips and shifting their body between her shadow and the light of the night. It might be useful to have another pair of eyes up here. It feels like something's coming, the night air hangs tense as an uncut string.

They steady their breathing, and reach out again, the shiver of their geometrics touching the ice of the air.

It seems, indeed, that the wind lies a little tonight. Something is hidden beneath its curves. As if it feels itself unmasked, the cairn-wind rises, then drops to nothing. Skinpainter feels it leave. The air at the edge of the mountain goes still with the weight of a held breath. On the cairns, the flags fall flat and listless. The clouds slow and even the ice in the hills sings softer.

Skinpainter waits. They are not worried. They are, for the first time in a long while, surprised.

Slowly, cautiously, they unravel a few slender rags that gently sift the still air. Their arms shimmer with tattoos lifted just off the skin.

There's been another taste here all along, watching them ply their trade. Someone better at the name-magic than they are, by far. Or, someone who thinks they are. Someone confident enough to slink right up the halls of their mountain and try to pluck secrets from their tongue.

Cheeky. Skinpainter enjoys the idea, but not enough to be kind. They grab the edge of that watching pattern, wrench, pull and swallow.

It tastes black on their tongue, thick as ash, smooth as glass.

They sense betrayal, the slow fall of rain. A sky that is not sky. A beach made of burning and blades. A sense of leaving and finding. Love. Hate. Love. Sundering. An eater of golden things. A devourer of gods. A sea that burns the ships that sail upon it. And then wings, wings on the night.

It is a presence, a person. A shape familiar from the stories. From the burning of the south. Skinpainter watches as she rides the ravelling threads into the back of their brain and they sink slowly against the rock to steady themselves.

A sip of cider. 'Hello,' Skinpainter says.

In front of their eyes, cross-legged on the edge of the mountain, a figure breathes itself into life from feather and shadow. 'Hello,' Crowkisser replies.

And in the quiet moments after, the patterns multiply and multiply and multiply.

50

Big fires, little bones, soft petals. The world burns.
The world turns.

—Fireside recitation (apocryphal), Thorndaughter

Icecaller wakes slowly, consciousness tugging gently at the fringes of her body. It's late, the rock heavy around her, the air thick with smoke and drink. She wriggles free from her blanket of legs and arms, trails fingers loosely down a spine softened by low light.

She grabs a pitcher of water, cold from the ice above. Drains one mug, then two. Better. She presses her lips together, shivers, reaches behind her for a blanket. The wool feels scratchy under her fingers. Another scratch in the back of her brain that's pulled her awake

Around her Thell mostly sleeps. Some of the dreamers move slow as snakes, slipping fingers and tongues inside each other, sketching the floor with shadows, sticky and shuddering. She's a little envious, but not by much. All fucked out tonight. And it didn't quite take the edge off the tension inside her. There's a sharpness in the air, something heavy under the smoke.

She traces her tattoos lightly, takes another swig of ice water. There'll be no more sleep tonight. Reluctantly, she swings her legs over the side of the alcove. Her feet flex against the cool stone of the floor as she rolls her neck back and forth, enjoying the subtle clicks and pops her body makes.

Her spear lies just against the wall, and her fingers close over it reflexively. She feels the wood kiss her palm and exhales. Better. The night might have its edges, but, well, so does she.

She smiles slightly at her own idiot humour. Time to find out what the fuck's got her so jumpy.

It's a fast climb through the winding passages of the Stump. Its wide, open loops are made for swift traversal. The sides of each angled spiral are cut with grooved chutes wide enough to fit packages or people and slick with the shine of decades of use. The geometrics along their edges are as good as signs, pointing up and down through the mountain, or laterally to dining halls, sleeping chambers, barracks and markets. Of course, she barely needs them at her age. She knows this mountain like her father's hands, like her lover's ribs. Both of them still snoring below, Kinghammer doubtless sprawled under bearskin, and Steelfinder exactly where Icecaller left her, curled up in the hollow of their bed. It's just her and the mountain tonight. She picks up speed as she moves, the spear in her left hand, the fingers of her right brushing the walls lightly, tracing the shapes and curves which will take her to where she needs to be.

Whatever's bleeding into the Stump is coming from outside. She can smell something feral on the wind. Maybe Fallon's pup had brought it in. God, but he was a worry, so wet; a slip of a ghost of a thin reed of a pup. How he'd even made it here she didn't know. Several hundred miles, past the fucking Midlands swamp cults and flint-eyed merchants that would sell the fingers of your left hand to your right. Skirting the Burners' forests, with their dark eyes and strong snares, through the Barrowlands, where the hills of the dead still lit green with corpsefire on cold nights. Risky enough, if you were a nobody. Mad, if you were the spuff-headed son of the last mardy lord south of Thell to stick it to Crowkisser. A long way for a thin boy and a miracle that he'd made it. That was mostly down to his burly carpenter, she suspected, with his sharp jaw and his clean lines and his suspicious eyes. Although there was something in that scrawny little nit that thrummed like iron.

She'd have had them both, in a different time and a different place. Pretty and lost and handsome. That wasn't the worst mix.

But you didn't fuck a plague dog. You didn't invite it into your house. You filled it with arrows and let it bleed at the gate as a warning to others.

So why, then, had she let them over the boundary? Why had she made them tea, and brought them home, and given them *hope*? She wasn't even sure herself. Curiosity maybe. Curious to see what the south had spat out, to see what the other idiots standing in the crow-bitch's crosshairs looked like. To try and get a sense of what might be coming. More than that – to try and get a sense of what might be possible after.

Her feet hit the stone, faster, harder. She speeds through the corridors of the Stump, leaping gaps and crevices, the old scars of the uprising, swinging one-handed down stairwells burnt and warped by a battle that had ended when she was still a brat.

At the end of the day, she'd wanted to see what Declan Fallon's kid looked like. Wanted to see where his father was hiding inside him.

She'd heard so many stories of Fallon growing up. Fallon, and the others that followed on his heels, like hawks on the storm. When she was a young sprat, she'd crouched goggle-eyed at the feet of the Deadsingers, stilled from her restless fidgeting by tales of the great fleet that sailed north to save them from the Empire, that had broken its hordes at Luss, and sent the Gem howling back to the feet of its master. Heads rocking like moored boats, the Deadsingers had sung of that golden fleet, of that sprawling army of sorcerers and warrior-women and foreigners wielding terrible magic. Most of all, they'd sung of the three at its head: the Lady of the Falcons, Arissa Fallon; the Shipwright, golden-haired and implacable; and the Shroudweaver.

Shroudweaver, who had taken the living and the dead of Thell and parted them at last, who had pulled up the cairns and filled them, taken the halls and emptied them. Put the dead on one side and the living on the other and said to the living. 'Don't look, don't touch, don't even talk about them. Here is the wall that will keep your new kingdom. Let your bodies be the bricks and let your lips hold the key. Keep your wall strong, for I will not preserve you if it falls.'

And he had stood with pride and joy, the Deadsingers said. Pride and joy and contentment, for here was the end of a dark thing and the start of something better. And he had looked at the people of Thell and said, 'Is it not a good thing, to live your own lives, free from the spent and bitter ghosts of the past?'

And the flags on the cairns had flown bright, said the Deadsingers, and bright the blue sky above.

Seventeen years later, that fleet had sailed again, to save the south instead of north, and burnt to ash, save for two or three broken boats. So much for blue skies.

Yet the cairns were still there. The bright flags still flew. That was something, Icecaller supposed, but it was hard to take comfort in it, when the back of her brain itched like an ant's nest. Muttering to herself, she scrambled goat-footed and hot, higher, to the outlooks that would unfold the barrows before her. Something was out there, and she was going to find it.

It was time to see what the bright cairns did in the dark of night.

She had not been surprised at the last twist in the tale of the Empire's fall, the Deadsingers raising their thin-boned hands in mirrored misery above her wide-eyed little face.

For the Shroudweaver, they said, he could not let well alone. He could not rest without knowing the start and the beginning, the finish and ending. So it was with those who worked with death. So, he stayed in Thell when he should have fled. He slept under stone when he should have sailed.

And under the stone he came to know the Emperor of the Dead, reduced to the lowest station. And the Emperor said to him, 'Do not let them do this to me.'

Icecaller recalled the bright whites of the Deadsingers' eyes, their spit-slick lips as their bodies tremored with the horror of the tale.

In the shadow of the mountain, the Emperor said to the Shroudweaver, 'Do not let them do this to me, I beg you.'

And the Shroudweaver, he said nothing.

And the Emperor said to him, 'I don't want to die.'

And the Shroudweaver, he looked away.

And the Emperor fell on bare knees and said, 'I have looked

beyond the world. I have seen the eye. I have seen the void behind the eye. I have felt the gods die. What is there now for me?'

And the Shroudweaver smiled a thin smile and said, 'Only ending.'

And then the Emperor wept, even as the Shroudweaver's footsteps left him in shadow and sorrow.

When the morning came, the revolutionaries came to the Shroudweaver with wet lips, and said, 'It is done.'

And the bright banners on the cairns snapped and cracked.

And the Shroudweaver saw their red hands and their slick teeth.

And who knows what might have happened then beneath the bright sky, with the rage of one man to answer a whole nation.

Until the Shipwright came to him and said, 'Let us away from here,' and took him in her arms. And perhaps it was the Shipwright who had saved Thell then, in truth.

Icecaller remembered the nodding heads of the Deadsingers, the faint smiles as they spun the soft, unsatisfying end to the tale. 'And they went to a place where ships could sail, and where her name meant more, and never more would they return to the cold north.' Horseshit, she knew now. Then, she'd eaten it up like honey.

She still enjoyed recalling the theatrics of it, the Deadsingers placing their heads in each other's open hands, the whispered end to the tale, sliding like a snake into her brain. Never more would the Shipwright and the Shroudweaver return, until the division that was made was to be erased, and the living and dead peoples of Thell united again.

She's jerked back to reality by a blast of chill air that plucks at her collar. She's near the outlook. For a moment, she glances back down into the mountain, at the drowsy spiral of its lights, ten thousand souls, still here, despite it all. The Deadsingers had a good enough story, she supposed. Icecaller didn't much care for its moralising though. People died. People died all the time. People were cunts, all the time. But Thell now was something better than it had been; her city.

Icecaller hoped Shipwright and Shroudweaver would come

back. She had questions for them, but neither of them were the weight of that story. Not even Fallon's wife, as thrilling as her big horse and bright sword were. There was a hole there. A gap noticeable only by its absence.

Declan Fallon. The named and bloody Lord of the Grey Towers.

She wanted to know how he'd done it. Icecaller didn't regret letting go of her old name. It had no claim on her. She was Icecaller and she knew that in her soul, or the meat that clothed it. It made no difference.

She owned herself. Always had.

But Fallon, he'd kept his name, when it seemed as though the entire world was abandoning itself, when the crows had come, and Astic had fallen. But even the crows had no name, and the woman that led them, she was only Crowkisser. Had she ever had a name? And why had she thrown it away?

Only Fallon kept his name, only Fallon. And perhaps, for a time, his wife. She shudders, remembering the whispers of what had happened there. But before her thoughts can finish walking that road, she skids into one of the wide overlooks where the Stump empties out into the cold of the night sky.

She is not alone. A familiar figure rests there, their broad shoulders flush against the rock, nested close to a brazier, in a wealth of coloured rags, checked and ribboned and wound around. Icecaller catches their eye. A brief moment of shock, followed by a sly magpie glint. They slip her the shadow of a smile, and gesture urgently to the alcove.

Icecaller squeezes herself in against the rock, the frost chill against her back. She buries her face against the dark stone, and watches, her breath still in her throat.

A moment later, there's a shudder in the air. It feels like a bubble bursting, as Skinpainter moves to put their body between the light of the fire, and the dark where she hides.

'Hello,' she hears Skinpainter say. And Icecaller stares in wonder as the shadows opposite her grow wings, and reply.

51

Wings even in the dark, in the second sky that sleeps
beneath the skin of the world.
Little things in the black, that know how to thrive
in the absence of light.

—*What Is Born Beyond Blades*, Heartshamer

Crowkisser comes to Thell in the cold shadow of the night, in the dip of the flame. She peels loose from the high walls with a flutter, a scuttling spider-like flowing, quick and economical.

Snow falls with her. Her feet are pale and sure on the stones. She floats the last few inches, landing on the tips of her toes. There's a flicker of feather. In front of her, Skinpainter licks the taste of burnt sugar off their lips, glances up the cold reach of the mountain shaft. Quiet from above, only the last few breaths of summer thaw, and the guards shifting softly at their posts.

She watches Skinpainter, as the last pinions slide back under her bones. Her right hand is twined with scraps of something ragged, red to the wrist. The remnants of a weaver's ribbons. Or a weaver. Her left is spread wide, fingers tense.

Skinpainter nods to her, shifting slowly in front of the fire, before they gesture to an alcove, a carved bench, a gently smouldering brazier with a clay pot suspended above. 'Hello. Sit. I'd wondered if this was coming.'

She does. They busy themselves with the brazier, twisting a wrist and flicking a few dried leaves into the belly of the coals. The smoke is sweet. They beckon it into their hood, breathing deep. It soothes their lungs, their racing thoughts.

Crowkisser sits with her hands gripping the edge of the alcove. Skinpainter joins her, lightly taps a knuckle, offers a cup.

'Drink?'

She shakes her head.

'Suit yourself. It's cold, though.'

They ladle liquid from pot to cup and sip, watching her in the ripples. A flutter of excitement flares in their chest – the godkiller here in their mountain; the name-stealer. Face-to-face at last. She's small, this godkiller.

She turns her head towards them, her eyes light in a face thinned by hunger. Gingerly, she extends a hand. They fill a second cup, pass it.

She leans into the smell of spice and apples.

Skinpainter sips, swallows, 'So, why now?'

Crowkisser smiles, suddenly younger in the firelight. 'You know why. We're marching.'

They snort and set the cup down, turning to face her.

'Hardly a surprise. I felt you fluttering around the edges of the wind nights ago. Feeling out the mountain. A new thing.'

She inclines her head slightly. 'I wanted to get a sense of you.'

Skinpainter runs a hand over their mouth, lips tingling. 'Don't make the same mistake everyone else does, little crow.'

Crowkisser worries at the red bindings on her hand with sharp teeth. Speaks muffled. 'What's that?'

They drink again.

'Thinking that I'm something more than I am.' They grin. 'The power behind the throne.' They shrug. 'I'm not some weaver of destinies. I'm what's left when everyone else tries it.'

She sniffs the cup again, screws up her nose and hands it back. 'But you know things. Old things. From before the south. The tattoos. The shapes. The d—'

They place a hand over her mouth, feel her lips wet against their skin. 'Go slowly, little crow. No need to draw their attention.'

They return the hand to a sleeve. Their hood shifts. 'I do know these things, but they were earnt.' A rueful smile. 'I'm afraid they can't be bought. And neither can I.'

Crowkisser starts to draw breath but they cut her off. 'What are you going to offer me? Money? We don't really use that here.

Power? I already have it.' They laugh. 'Sex? I've never found sex to be of great interest.'

They spread wide palms, tipping them back and forth. 'I prefer ink. If you truly want to understand Thell, you need to understand the ink.'

Skinpainter takes her hand. She flinches. A little part of them is delighted. Finally, some respect. They feel Crowkisser's breath shudder as they pull her fingers across the backs of their hands, along their arms, up beneath their robes.

'Feel how it flows. The angles. The depth of the pigment. We would be lost without it.'

They grin, deep in their hood as they press her questing fingertips to scars, absences. 'Or rather, we would be found.'

It takes her a second to feel the thing that rests against their skin. When it pulses beneath her fingers she snatches her hand back, stifling a scream.

They watch her levelly. 'All power has a price. As well you know.' They readjust their robes. 'But it's an idiot who doesn't shop for a discount.'

She laughs at that. High and bright, almost childlike.

Skinpainter smiles. 'Thank goodness. I thought you were as dry as your father.'

Sudden pressure. The threads on her hands lifting slightly. The briefest flicker of feathers. The coals flare. Ears pop. Skinpainter waves a hand soothingly. 'It's OK. I have no interest in sharing that further. Although more people know than you'd think. Just because you were too young to remember it, doesn't mean it didn't happen.'

She frowns. 'You know about me, and you know him. Yet you still stand with him?'

Skinpainter reaches into their pockets, subtly readjusting the press of their robes. They lean back. A hand cracks a walnut, dancing the shell over quick knuckles. 'You want some?'

She shakes her head. 'You didn't answer my question.'

They smile as they roll the nut between their palms.

'You're a terse girl, as terse as your father. Even if you know how to laugh. And no, I didn't. That's because I don't owe you anything.' The shell is caught, crushed.

'Did you expect something different?'

Crowkisser shrugs, refocuses on their hands as they dust themselves clean.

'You know this is going to lead to battle, don't you?'

She nods.

Skinpainter sighs. 'I knew as much once Quickfish arrived. Too good an opportunity to pass up, wasn't it? A brave boy trying to save his dying mother.'

She flashes them a smile. 'I don't owe you anything.'

They nod, drumming on the floor with a foot. 'You're learning.'

The stone suddenly feels sharp and cold under them, despite the brazier. They shift uncomfortably, rags fluttering. 'You must understand. There are many people I love dearly within this mountain. Now, I have never been a fan of the gods. Or the dead. Or anything that wants us for their own.' They hold Crowkisser's wrist, voice low. 'So, I'm not without sympathy for your actions.'

For a second, she smiles, before they grip tighter, pulling her close into their hood, their lips rough and harsh, clove oil on the skin. 'But, let me repeat. There are many people I love dearly within this mountain. And if it's them or you, it'll be you.'

She flicks her eyes hastily over their shoulder, to the deeper shadows.

Skinpainter smiles ruefully as they let her go. 'Is he here? Slickwalker?'

She shakes her head, laughs, then looks at Skinpainter coolly. 'No. But he will be, soon enough.' Her voice is rougher than expected, husked by the cold and the night.

The back of Skinpainter's neck itches. The air briefly acrid and sharp. They clear their throat. 'Changes nothing. You're a fool if you think I haven't dealt with worse. Permanently.' Their brows are heavy in the shadow of their hood. Keeping the sorrow from their voice is a challenge, even with the softening smoke.

'I understand loss, Crowkisser. More than that. I'm tired of it. I've had my fill. I am sick to my heart of death.'

Their next words are hushed with longing. 'I'd hoped you were too. I don't think either of us wants people to die. Especially not here.'

She's silent for a long time. Long enough for Skinpainter to watch the shadows play over her face, to watch the slight twists and tics she must think hidden, to watch her thoughts running riot over her skin.

Before she even speaks, Skinpainter knows that this only ends in war.

The lie when it comes is obvious, bland. Skinpainter dealt with better in the days of the old Empire, when the only real truths could be communicated by touch, tapped out on skin. Hidden from the ears of the Emperor's spies.

Crowkisser needs a few more decades under her belt before she can sell this one. She tries it anyway. 'What's your suggestion then?'

They pretend to chew thoughtfully. 'Give me time with Shroudweaver. If I can get him out of the walls, away from King-hammer, we could end this without bloodshed.'

All Skinpainter really needs is time. Time to get Thell's army out from the mountain, away from the Barrows. Safely marching south where they can scour this girl and her madness from the earth.

Skinpainter knows the last thing Crowkisser has is time. Years starving in the south, relying on personality alone to hold her people together. They know from experience how hard that is. If they're going to stay here any longer, they need to keep her on the hook.

She tilts her head thoughtfully. 'If my father trusts anyone, it would be you. But if you can't persuade him?'

They shake their head. 'Then bloodshed.'

'And neither of us want that,' her lips say, while her eyes sing out her hunger for it.

Skinpainter's disappointed. As if they hadn't heard the stories of the villages who resisted and clung to their names, of the gallowswatchers raised in their ruins.

Crowkisser shrugs diffidently. 'I'll consider it.'

Another lie, cheap and shallow. They let it wash over them, offering a grateful smile. Perhaps not quite convincing enough to earn her trust, but time will tell. Skinpainter has a moment to try and read her in the flickering light, before she shifts and the spell is broken. As she starts to stand they catch her arm, noticing again that slight, satisfying flinch. 'Thank you. For coming.' And their lie is smooth, and easy, and honest-looking.

Crowkisser pulls away slowly. Her fingers linger on their side for a moment. Skinpainter's too focused on her touch, her face, her words. Misses a slight cut, as a leather strap gives way and a pouch slips into Crowkisser's waiting hand.

The barest weight, a single bone. The last piece of the Emperor of the Dead. As promised.

She fixes on Skinpainter's gaze to hide her hammering heart. 'I had to,' she says. 'I know what happens otherwise.'

The theft hangs unnoticed. Crowkisser holding Skinpainter's gaze steady, even as her hand tucks the bone tight against her skin.

Oblivious, Skinpainter nods sadly. 'High power. The highest prices.'

Something in their voice catches her, and for a moment, the mask slips. Catching the look in her eyes, Skinpainter sighs, and pushes their hood back.

Crowkisser takes them in. The minutes pass; ice melting in the heart of the mountain, sweet smoke, walnuts.

By the time Skinpainter wraps the soft cloth around themselves again, they are both wet with tears.

She leaves soon after. Feathers, burnt sugar, spidering into blackness.

Once she's gone, Skinpainter slowly lets the shells fall into the flames, chaff burnt and consumed. A moment, two. Collecting their breath before they turn again to the shadows. 'What do you make of that then?'

Icecaller steps forwards from the darkness, grim-faced. 'That bitch needs to die.'

Skinpainter puts their arm around her, pulls her close. 'I've taught you well.'

52

every hill is a king
crowned with elder and chestnut
and the birds
the birds sing like jesters

—*The Blue Beyond the Halls*, Hallowfeather

The nest sits fairly high in the tree, cradled in the crook of its branches. A little precarious, a little ragged, a mishmash of twigs and lichen that sways gently in the freshening breeze.

The mother bird dotes on her chicks, swooping down, worm-beaked, her dun wings flicking the leaves aside.

Shroudweaver watches her from the grass, as the tiny orange mouths of the hatchlings pop up in unison. They are almost formless still, little bundles of need and urgency.

Absently, he picks loose blades with one hand, letting his nails work into the warm soil beneath.

It's good to be off the ship. It had been an uneventful voyage for the most part. Four weeks of a jagged coast opening up on their starboard bow in white chalk cliffs, scoured with wiry grass and small, thorny bushes which threw up defiantly pink flowers into the salt spray.

The entire western coastline stretches ragged as a ripped seam. Juts of headland, white as gull shit, slicked in green, struck with the ruins of watchtowers, the furze of low bushes, the gnarled planes of trees bent back upon themselves by the sea.

It's fast travelling near the coast, East Tide tearing up, out and northwards. Its flanks buffeted by West Tide's reverse push, in-wards and downwards to the turbulent channels further south.

Shipwright had schooled him on it once, shown him the charts with their deep, dark lines, the lanes where ships could switch between the two currents without being twisted in half like a hanging nail. She showed him the fish that thrived in the fast flow where the tides met, the backs of their silver heads threaded with purple ribbons. Delicate things which sifted nutrients from the warmer southern streams and from the bones of the shipwrecks that lay in the troughs between the tides.

The Yaw, the Hesper sailors called it – that sickening lurch that could sink a ship like a sucked thumb. It took a smart helmsman to steer this coast, in these seas. Someone like Shipwright.

Still, it was safer than tacking further out, or dragging a shipful of refugees overland.

Alone, they would have been fine. They'd roamed the miles between Hesper and the north often enough in the last few years, pulled this way and that by crisis after crisis. Chasing down rumours, whispers of anything that might give them a handle on what had happened in the south. They'd found too much. Hosts driven insane; short, brutal wars that had sprung up to fill the void; ruins guarded only by the skeletons of past mistakes; villages hollowed out by famine, by panic, by fire.

The Midlands had cooled as time rolled on. The world adjusted. The divisions ossified. Thell pulled even further back into itself. Hesper began its blockade of the sea routes. The south starved itself into fury as the Rim villages banded together, or were pulled into the shadow of Crowkisser's new home in Astic.

Even so, stability was an illusion. There was no way a hundred-odd refugees were getting across the leagues between Hesper and the north without drawing some unfriendly eyes.

So, they'd taken the long way, as fast as they could, riding the lip of East Tide along the teeth of the coast. Less direct, but less deadly.

The refugees were chatty at first, grateful to be out of the city, their shoulders lifted at the thought of living a little further from the threat of war. They tried to make themselves useful, mending nets and rigging. The bloodworkers among them turned their oiled hands to aching muscles and twisted backs. A little hope crept into their movements as time passed, and they drew further from the south. Their heads turned to Shipwright like flowers to the sun and even the lidded gazes they cast on Shroudweaver were leavened with a half-smile.

They had grown quieter as the ship pulled further north, as Hesper faded from the horizon, and they realised what they were leaving behind.

Eventually, they melted away as the ship stitched its way up the coast. A few got off at each village they stopped at, bundled down the gangplank, arms laden with blankets, supplies, pots and pans, whatever the ship could spare. That young man, Ropecharmer, fussing around them like a lean hen, settling them into rooms and garrets, tucking them in under the eaves of these small sea towns and crossing their hosts' palms with silver or stern promises.

Most of the villages welcomed them, if quietly enough. There weren't many up here that would turn away a bloodworker, or a strong pair of hands. There weren't even many that would turn away the old, or children. The folk that clung to the coast were a practical lot, still able to see themselves in the faces of others.

Spaces opened around fires, at the ends of bars and in small, low byres huddled against the wind. It wasn't much in the end, but Ropecharmer seemed to take comfort in it, Shipwright too. Shroudweaver, for his part, was just glad to see people moved a little further from death.

Once they were gone, he missed them. The remainder of the voyage had felt unusually still, marked by their absence. Quiet nights were spent under cooling skies as the north took them in, the coastline hardening with darker rock, like lips pressed too tight. The first glimpse of auroral fire in the distance, followed by the tang of glacier ice and the glow of stranger stars. The water, cool and clear in the day, refracted a white sun which made the boards stretch and creak, and left Shroudweaver drowsy, curled in rough nests of rope and canvas. His fingers moved fitfully in red-threaded patterns, his mind thinking about his daughter, about Thell, and about the dead, worries circling his skull like the rats in the hold.

At night the sea darkened and the depths fell away under the keel, black and endless, spotted with the phosphorescent lights of small jellyfish which rode the tide, ice crystals frosting on their backs.

To begin with, the crew had let down lines, snarling the tiny, glowing creatures, and pulling them up into buckets. Their blood did not freeze, and could be used to keep the spinners and rig charms moving.

They crunched when they died. Shroudweaver couldn't stand it.

As the ship moved north, the lines grew thick with their pulsing bodies. Eventually, something larger surfaced to starboard, and ripped five lures away in a single moment, along with a section of the rail. Shroudweaver hadn't seen it, but he'd heard stories of many eyes, and a great fin which ran slick with rainbow colours.

After a time, they had tacked eastwards, dodging the reefs, and docking at a fishing village where they were greeted with salted palms and cheeks rubbed raw by the wind. They traded iron and spice for news. Fishwives with chapped jaws took Shroudweaver aside, blew on cracked hands and knuckled their aching knees.

There was something on the air, they said. Their tellings wouldn't work – long scrimshawed bones had snapped, twigs lay askant and useless. Their heads itched, their sons lied, and were shiftless about the nets. The shadow of war was on the wind.

The old bones felt restless underfoot. Mountain sons came to town with cartloads of blades and buckles, scavenged stoop-backed from fields which suddenly seemed to be made more of men than mud.

The hills refused their dead.

An old sailor sucked his loosening teeth. He'd brought the bones of his cat for a binding, said the damn thing was keeping him up at night, and he was perilous short of rum.

He'd said more than that, after the scapula were scorched and the reek of sulphur had burnt down to a small stench among the tavern's broader smells. Putting an arm around Shroudweaver like he was a child, he had pulled him close, pipe-smoked and worrying.

Some had seen fires, he said, low on the hills, in from the coast. In the high Midlands, still far from Thell, but near enough to remember the feet of the Emperor's legions.

Later even, with the candles burnt down to stumps, he'd taken Shroudweaver's fingers in his, and rubbed calluses like a warning. 'Those hills only wake for blood,' he'd said, rheum-eyed, as he'd tugged his beard and spat, thick and black into the sleeping fire.

Later than late, in the deep quiet of the night, Shroudweaver had heard a cat yowling at the door and the click of small claws.

There were more villages after the first, the ship pulling in at ports that were barely more than a sunken jetty. A lifted lock. A lamp on a pole. Towns riddled with streets that were explored by the light of tapers, by storm-lamps pulled tight against the wind from the sea. Shipwright had always taken the lead, her heavy boots striking flatly against wet cobbles, the broad sweep of her shoulders picked out in doorframes, against firelight, across suddenly hushed conversation. Forever the first over the threshold with questions, she fell back into the familiar rhythms of her old questing years. Hunting for answers. Always hunting, sifting tales from hands worn thin by the ceaseless pull of the sea, rope-scoured, pitted and pocked with the memory of storms. Filling palms with coin, twice-bit for trust. The questions always the same: what lay ahead? What stirred in the night? Had you, had you *ever* seen a crow?

The answers the same too, for the most part. The Midlands were restless. Rusted blades and emptied graves. Opportunistic men who liked flame and knew several useful knots.

A fear lingered on every hearth, muffled by normality, by the sharp and sour taste of fish stews, fingers crushing leaves into a roiling pot. Pipe smoke and a clear spirit which smelt of blueberries and fell on you like fire.

Shroudweaver stayed in Shipwright's shadow, watched her open palms dance. Her smile, slow and easy, slipping out of the corner of her mouth.

People listened, people talked, sometimes guardedly, some-times not. Once there was the flash of a knife, a quick twist, the soft pop of a joint coming loose.

He had held her close that night, his forehead pressed against the planes of her chest, counting heartbeats, listening to valves open and close, trying not to throw up from fear.

She had been quiet too, in those small towns, even more than usual, keeping her fears tight against her chest, as though let-ting them out would make them real. As though he couldn't read them in the stoop of her shoulders, the shiver of her bones. Neither of them wanted to talk about Thell, which drew closer in their minds, even if it remained only a dark stain on the horizon. Occasionally, heather-hued clouds would flow down the moun-tain passes, rolling over the Midlands in squalling, chill showers. It was then Shroudweaver felt the snap of damp cloth against his skin, heard water dripping into a great black lake, and saw the face of the Emperor turned towards him, high-cheekboned, imploring. 'Don't let them do this to me.'

When those nightmares came, he would wind red threads tight around his hands, until he felt his fingers go numb. Eventually the rest of him would numb too, and he could sleep.

When the sun eventually rose, they began searching again.

As time passed, Shipwright and Shroudweaver grew rumours like a coat, darned and stitched from a thousand loose lips and tongue slips. Eventually, those whispers called them inland, and they had to leave the coast-roads behind.

Cast off, the ship slept in harbour at the last small village, lashed to a grey dock that had never seen anything bigger than a few barnacle-wracked salt scows, Ropecharmer pacing her decks like a lonely cat. He'd sail her south again in a week or two, if no news was forthcoming. Hesper's blockade was thinner than ever without the ship, and he was captain enough to harry what little trade still limped down the coast. Thell was not a place for ships, in any case.

And before Thell, the rivers and rills of the uplands weren't fit for a rowboat, flowing fast and fierce with clear water and small brown fish. It was legs or nothing.

So here they were now, off ship, their tired feet edged against the hills that skirted the cairns of the Barrowlands, wandering into green fields where they could watch small dun birds twist twig and leaf into a shelter against the rising spring rains.

Breathing out a sigh of contentment, Shroudweaver let himself fall back onto the grass, his vision tilting up to the blue bowl of the sky. He loved northern skies, fierce, empty things, scratched by the bodies of hawks, coloured by sudden storms which dropped rain in cold spears.

Southern skies were cluttered, ruddied by sun and muddled with cloud, shadowed by cookfires and bonfires, floated with marsh-light and ghostflame.

The dun bird leaves again, whirring across the sky in a bobbing weave, the soft peeps of its chicks subsiding as they retreat into the nest.

As Shroudweaver watches their mother flit out against the wind, a pair of familiar booted feet obscure his view, setting themselves either side of his hips. He squints up, smiling softly.

Shipwright looks down at him, her hair still mussed from sleep, a mug in either hand.

She offers him one, letting her fingers linger on his wrist for a second. 'Making friends, Shroud?'

He laughs. 'I don't know. They don't seem that interested in me. Lack of worms.'

Shipwright slips forwards on to her knees, the weight of her hips settling over his. Her hand comes up to the side of his face, still warm from the heat of the tea. 'That's grim even for you.'

He frowns. 'Is it?'

She tilts his head to the left gently, her fingers light on his jaw.

The curve of the skull is barely visible beneath the summer grown grass. Bleached and burnished by months of low winter sun, scoured by the freshening winds. Its lower jaw long since gone, one socket cracked and crazed, threaded through with small white flowers.

Shroudweaver looks into its empty eyes and thinks of the weight of the Shipwright above him. His hands find her hips, and his tongue brushes against her lips, sharpened and bitter from tea.

And for a time, he thinks only of her, and of the warmth of the sun. Of a dun bird's wings, and the round stones under the earth.

53

A man cannot hold a lit match without seeking tinder.

—*Proverbs of the Burning Forest*, Heartshamer

Shipwright clicks her tongue softly, the horse moving steadily under her. It's a sturdy little mountain thing, its mane wiry and coarse, piebald flanks working stoically as it climbs the rolling hills of the Midlands.

It whickers gently as it picks its way down the steepening side of another barrow. She can sympathise. This was treacherous terrain that had turned her boots at every step, until in frustration, she'd harried Shroud towards a small Burners hamlet that nestled on the edge of the Barrowlands, and borrowed some sturdier legs to carry them onwards.

The pair of them were exhausted, hammered down by the sheer repetition of travel. The wet socks. The blisters. The aching bones. The rain. Shipwright was used to it. Two decades of it, since the war with the Empire, scurrying over this blasted continent, stamping out fires, or arriving late enough to sift through the ashes. She was used to it, but that didn't take the edge off, didn't stop the lurch in her heart at every near miss, every arrow peeling the air near her head. Every sword blade that bit loam instead of blood. Every time Shroudweaver skipped along the edge of death, and teetered on the brink. He couldn't let well enough alone, whether it was a stranger's war or a friend's mistake, Shroudweaver couldn't stand by. His greatest curse – the heart to not abide suffering and the arrogance to think he could make a difference. It had only worsened with the disaster in the south and with Crowkisser, with the risk that he was somehow personally responsible for every new catastrophe, every loss, every misery his idiot daughter inflicted.

So, he'd kept flinging himself against the world. Swimming in strong tides that most sensible, younger men would steer away from. Even if it tired him out, again and again and again. Every morning, his fingers stiffer, his knuckles swollen in the cold, or the damp, or dried to creaking in the summer heat. Those skinny legs of his shaking as he folded bedrolls, or stooped to drink from creeks.

It tired him out, and Shipwright wearied in return. Twenty years of this, of looking over his shoulder, of guarding his back.

He was already looking worn. Faded and drawn, like an etching washed too many times by the tide. Each night, she gathered his thin hair in her fingers, tucked it behind his ears, felt the porcelain weight of his skull.

He hadn't unwrapped the binding threads since they stepped off the ship. They were the closest things he had to tools of the trade. Frayed lines against the dead, the strange and the unwelcome, pulled red and ragged around his fingers, his wrists twisting fretfully to shift them into new patterns, to keep them moving, keep them ready.

She understood his nervousness, in a way. Thell was always on the horizon, and the closer they drew, the more her mind fell back to those old days, to the dawn of the Republic and the fall of the Emperor. They'd been up to their hands in it, red to the wrists. Stained long after that with the choices they'd made.

The ghost of that war hung like smog. She saw it in Shroud's eyes, reddened from lack of sleep, restless, even when she held his face in her hands, the past lodged in his mind like a rotten tooth. The thought of returning to face that past was a horror that flickered in every shallow breath.

That mountain city had been unkind to both of them. And Shipwright had been so convinced, to begin with, so convinced that they could help, that they were doing a good thing; a great thing.

She bends, cinching the saddle straps tighter and breathing in the soft, sweet musk of the little mountain horse. A quick squeeze of her thighs turns it towards the remains of the old trade road which winds among the cairns like a whitened scar, the earth still chalky from rain. Shroudweaver sways at her back, dozing, for now.

They aren't the only ones moving along that road. Travellers pass in both directions, refugees from the south, still, despite the time gone by. Three long years of watching the sky burn and roil, of breathing that strange smell that drifted north on a warm day, when the winds were high. That smell like fruit soaked in blood, bloating in the sun.

There were no refugees from where the city had been, of course, no reports in or out. It was no longer a place people could walk.

A few survivors came from the northmost edge of the desolation, from the Rim villages, Dryke, Vantage, Fallow. A pair with the lemon hair and freckle-flicked faces of Sedge stroked Shipwright's horse with their gazes as she rode past, their bodies tense as cornered cats, their eyes flicking from hands to blades and back.

Nursing a baby close to their ribs. A little wrench in Shipwright's heart as its small head slowly faded down the path. Born without a name, like so many children in the last three years, and who knew what that meant for them? What Crowkisser could do to them? Its small hands moved fitfully against its mother's scarf, as she drew the edges together to shield it from Shipwright's lingering gaze.

Other refugees were more talkative. Said Crowkisser had finally brought the Rim villages to heel, said they had got out just soon enough, when the first long men began stalking the streets, and the shadows deepened and moved against the sun.

Not many remained in the Rim towns now, a few hundred at most, but some with food, and some with hope, and when had Crowkisser ever needed more than that to encourage her? Shipwright caught Shroudweaver's worried eyes, as stories of his daughter's progress filled their ears, as they cinched the tack tighter, and picked up the pace, fleeing only rumours and tales, for now. Still, these days, rumours and tales were enough.

All these lost souls trickling from the south, into the humps of the Barrowlands, and eventually on into the lee of the mountains, to Thell. Some bringing goods for trade, some bringing news, some bringing relics from the south, salvaged from the city of weeping glass, they said.

Shipwright doubted it. She knew a huckster when she saw one, but she didn't grudge someone trying to earn a coin. Out of curiosity, she bought a few strange pieces of corkscrewed glass, dark as blood.

She crushed them under a stone a day later, when she found they'd burrowed right through her pack, sharp points just near pressing against her skin.

Not much that came out of the south was understood, and not all the people walking that rode had honest hearts. In response, from the north, they began to see patrols of bright-toothed young men and women, the flat, leaf-thin blades of their spears wound around with the snapping, brightly coloured banners of Thell. Their eyes, equally flat and hard, scanned the refugee columns and bickering traders as they pulled the odd cat-skinned man or woman aside for a quiet word. Yet they weren't shy with water, or medicine, helping those that had pushed themselves too far, too fast. That was a mercy, the people of the south had only learnt to run in the past few years, and not all had taken to it well.

Still, Shipwright found it hard to relax on roads studded with blades. She knew from experience that soldiers wanted a reason to draw them.

She says nothing to them, and Shroud pushes his hands deep into his robes as they pass, turning his face to the stones and the damp grass. There's no point in pulling eyes to them yet. She had a feeling that announcing their arrival would only call down trouble. It had been a long time since they'd set foot in Thell. Who knew if they were remembered fondly? To say nothing of how many of these men and women might have more than one master, might spend their evenings whispering tales into the beaks of crows.

Yet, where the patrols walked, people felt the breath of the

Republic at their necks. And maybe it was a comfort for folks that had fled their homes, like a large, muscled brute of a dog. Not one to let into the house, but good enough to keep the wolves from the door.

Shipwright takes solace in the fact that not one of these bright armoured young men and women knows them from the rest of this strange, dusty crowd. Why would they? They were ghosts of another time, and the people of Thell had no truck with ghosts.

She has no idea what they'll find in the mountain these days. Fallon had claimed that the scions of the Revolution held sway there, their mothers and fathers still crouched at the top of the pile, sifting the fragments of the world they'd broken. Dramatic old sod. It was hard to believe that Kinghammer, Belltoller and all the others might still be hale after twenty long years, but if they were, two decades could turn a lot of thoughts around a mind. There was no guarantee of a warm welcome.

She'd asked after them, in that Burners' village, tucked in beneath smoke-stained rafters, sipping barley broth and chewing on loaves of warm, dark bread.

The Burners claimed to know little. They kept close into the forests and trusted the trees more than the hills. Said the roots held down the dead. Said the hills could hold nothing, barren and windswept as they were.

Said they'd seen fires. Not Burners' fires, but low red glows, deep among the cairns, spilling from broken entrances and cracked graves. The people of the Barrowlands taking matters into their own hands, burning the dead before the dead could rise and burn them.

No one had seen crows. Shroudweaver always asked, and Shipwright watched his heart lift with every asking. But there was no answer which would have helped there. He missed his daughter, and he was terrified to meet her. Shipwright wanted to help him so badly, but all she could do was make tea, and hold him and pretend not to hear when he talked in his sleep; the muttered apologies, the anger, the fumbling over the hole where his dead wife's name lay in his head.

Heading to Thell would help him, she hoped, even if he feared it. At the least, it would let him see something thriving from his efforts. Let him see the city they'd saved, the babies that had been born in their absence, and all their friends that were still alive to get fat and grey-haired.

More practically, winning over Thell would mean bodies, and blades for their cause. And beyond that, fuel for a new god. Her heart stumbles at the thought. Her mind flits to worn tower steps, the feeling of light hammering through her bones and the taste of burnt sugar after. She tells herself that it might not happen. That the composite might not need to exist. That the mere threat of its existence might somehow stop Crowkisser in her tracks.

The pony rolls under her and she pats its warm little flank, smelling hot grass and sweat, all the tangled burrs of the road.

She knew better than to hope. If something that horrific could be made, it would be. There wasn't much point rubbing a comforting lie against your lips like a baby's blanket.

A lovely little lie, that all the power of a composite could scour Crowkisser from the earth, and still leave the world untouched, leave Shroudweaver's daughter standing.

The sort of thing they used to sing to the wee ones back home, *Lu-lay, your mother will be safe, and lu-lay, the sun will still shine.*

Still, that was the fiction Shroudweaver clung to and the hope he had sold Fallon. That they could make something that would finally put an end to this, and still be able to look each other in the eye after. Which made it a hope not just for Shroudweaver, but for everyone north of the Rim villages, north of Crowkisser.

Shipwright didn't really have the heart to burst that bubble. She might yet be wrong. She would love to be wrong. And she wasn't surprised Fallon had bitten so readily. To him, the composite was just another weapon, a means of gaining access to the real prize – the mountain. It's people. Allies. She knew that old bull well enough to hope that if he could lay his hands on Thell's steel and see its soldiers arrayed in squares, if he could imagine those soldiers driving that steel into Crowkisser's body, then it might kindle the spark he needed to win this war. *Might.* Blood and brass, that was a long shot. She had a hunch that even if Crowkisser could be knocked on her heels at Thell, it would take more than a miracle to drag Fallon outside the walls while Arissa still faded in a high tower bed.

So, why call down that fire? It was easier if she told herself rousing Fallon would save everyone in Hesper. It was the closest place she had to a home here.

Something in that felt right. Or close enough to right that she could live with it for now. And maybe saving Hesper would . . . Well, she didn't know what it would do, exactly. Slow things down at least. Slow *her* down, Crowkisser. And give Shipwright time to breathe. There wasn't much to be aimed for beyond that at the moment, not in her mind. All of it had happened too fast, over the last three years. The little she knew about this world, the little she'd learnt of its people, its places, its logic, had been ripped out from under her, burnt to glass and ruin in the destruction of the south. All of the years after that nothing but a whirl of sea under her keel. Of sailing from city port to village port, to hidden cove. Trying to help Shroudweaver make sense of it all. Trying to find something to salvage. Some solid ground to build on in the ruins. Something in the shape of a life.

All Shipwright needed was for things to slow down. A beat to figure out what could be done. She was sure if she just had a moment or two, she could do so much better.

The little horse crests a rise, stumbling slightly as scree shifts under its hooves. They're pushing further across the Midlands now, the landscape rumpled like a poorly laid cloth. Beyond the rise, the trade roads cut onwards into shallow curving hills that hold mist against their flanks. The wide, broad plains of the Midlands narrow to shallower bowls of green which shelter villages skirted by knolls and hillocks, small outposts of stone in the great ripple of the land. To the east, the dark scrape of the Burners' forest colours the horizon, and somewhere beyond that, the other sea. Somewhere on that sea, home. Home that she hasn't seen for twenty years or more. Twenty years of being a little more foreign than usual.

Two decades, and she was still struggling to catch up, to under-stand these people, and their hatreds. All of it was still so alien to her; Crowkisser, angry enough to turn half a world to ash and kill its gods. Somehow, that girl had to be stopped. Fallon would kill her in a heartbeat. The wound of losing Arissa wouldn't permit anything less.

And yet she was the daughter of the man Shipwright loved. Shroudweaver would never let Crowkisser be killed, not that child who held the shape of his dead wife inside her bones, her face, her movements. Which left Shipwright, as always, to find some way in between. Her stomach twisted at the thought, the last dregs of that dark Burners' bread threatening to come back up her throat.

The little horse fidgets, and she clucks consolingly. She has no idea how to begin. She needs time, for things to move just a little bit slower, to open up their options. Thell, if nothing else, gave them a chance at a different way out, of defeating Crowkisser without killing her. Threading that impossible needle. A chance at peace.

That's what she really wanted – peace. An end to wars – to *any* wars – just peace. She can barely imagine it, time to get bored, to have your biggest concerns be an unplanted field or an early frost or the cat lost after dark.

But she can't make it happen all at once. So here she is, on the wet back of a tired horse, stumbling north through the Midlands to Thell.

She feels Shroudweaver's arms tighten around her and wonders if he can hear her thoughts. The two of them ride together now. Their other little horse had disappeared in the night, its hitching undone, its trail vanishing in the hard scree which collected be-tween the rolling hills.

He shifts his head against her shoulder blades and murmurs softly. 'Not long now.' His voice is slurred with sleep.

'I know,' she says.

'Skinpainter won't be happy,' he says.

'Won't be happy with what?'

'When I turn them loose.'

She pulls the reins, steadies the horse as it picks its way past the wreckage of a cart abandoned in the road, axel broken, sides scarred.

'What are we setting loose? I thought we were raising a . . .'

She chokes on it again, coughs the feeling of honey from her lips. 'What did you and Skinpainter do in there? Nearly twenty years and you've never really told me.'

There's silence for a while, nothing but the horse's hooves, and the rattle in his lungs. She feels the words form in his chest, feels them fall back unspoken.

She pushes. 'It was bad enough that I had to knock you out at Luss. I remember that. I can still feel your idiot skull on my knuckles.' A tightness in her voice. 'Why does this feel similar?'

She turns her head slightly, so that her cheek is touching his unshorn stubble. 'What happened in Thell? What did you *do* in there? What are we *going* to do in there?'

Still, he's silent. His breath is ragged on her shoulders, stiff with tension.

'Shroud?' her voice low and wary. 'What are we setting loose? I need to know.'

His voice, when it strokes the back of her neck, is the barest ghost of a whisper. 'The dead.'

She turns to glimpse him. 'The dead? Aren't they all buried up there?'

She turns her gaze to the black line of mountains on the horizon, the spill of barrows pocking their skirts.

He shakes his head. 'Not all. Not enough. Half of that is just bones and dark earth.'

She hisses between her teeth. 'So, the rest are somewhere else?'

He nods.

'And we need to loose them to make the composite? All of them?'

He nods again.

Awkward silence for a few moments more. The horse's feet beat damply along the road. Ahead, the Stump presses against a sky which seems to buckle with its weight. Distantly, Shipwright glimpses the first cairn flags, hears them snap in the wind.

'We're setting loose all the dead,' It sounds ridiculous even as she says it and she snorts. 'The Empire's dead.'

'Yeah,' Shroudweaver says. 'If I can.'

There's something far too familiar in his tone. A truth skimmed above a lie. She stiffens reflexively. Tries to hide the frustration in her voice. She needs to know.

'What would stop you?'

He shifts awkwardly. 'Well, nothing. It's keeping the dead bound that's always been the trouble, but . . .'

'But what? Don't be so bloody cryptic.' She jabs an interrogatory elbow.

He flinches, and she regrets it immediately.

He's quiet for a while, his breath flickering against her neck, the rhythm of his ribs playing against her spine.

She gives him room. This is the most he's spoken since leaving the stitched villages of the coast.

The words come slowly, falling against one another. 'The end of the Emperor. The binding of the dead. The foundation of the Republic? Skinpainter.'

She makes a noncommittal noise in her throat.

His fingers tighten in her belt. 'All of it. All of it wasn't what it seemed.'

She tastes it then. On her tongue, even as she asks the question. Tastes it coming. The revelation she never wanted. 'What was it then?'

Shroudweaver lifts his head, looks at the Stump in the distance, watches its shadow fall across the mounded ranks of the quiet dead. 'We needed a victory. Clean and clear. We needed to see our enemies gone.'

She sees his eyes close. The faint lines tight at their corners.

'But the dead were never our enemies.'

His hands tighten, thread flashing bright and red.

He taps her shoulder to slow the horse and dismounts, sandals and thin legs down into the mud. Slowly stoops to wet his fingers in it. The air's cold here, slick with damp.

When he looks up at her, the wind pulls his thin hair across his face.

'All bindings need a vessel, Ship. All of them. Largest to the smallest.'

She watches him. 'Like in Hesper. When we saved Fallon.'

He nods. 'Like in Hesper. You were the vessel then. For the god.'

Shipwright coughs to clear her lips of a sudden sweet stickiness. She's angry, but that's not going to get her answers. She chokes the spite down with the sugar and composes herself.

'I'm with you so far.'

She tugs at the scarf around her head. 'Can we pick up the pace though? It's a hair off freezing out here.'

Shroudweaver takes a few steps to the nearest cairn. Sifting through the broken rock at its base, he lifts out a shard of pottery. 'Every vessel has its limits though, right? You can't pour a wine bottle into a pint glass. You can't drain the sea into a lake.'

She nods. 'Odd examples. But sure.'

He smiles, turns, skips the shard away over the stones. It clacks and rattles into the distance scaring up a few low-dwelling birds that peep across the sky.

'All the dead in that army, all their souls, they were bound by the Emperor, *to* the Emperor. If I'd cut them loose of their bodies, he would have scooped them up like so many fish in a net. Or if they'd flown free, they would have gone mad, and frayed and strange. There was only one place to put them, really. Only one place I could keep them safe.'

She realises it before he says it, and her heart breaks with the swiftness of a spring thaw.

She's down off the horse and her arms are around him, his cold back under her gloved hands and his shaking body pressed tight against hers.

'It was you. You idiot. You stupid, stupid man. The vessel. For twenty damn years. For all those souls. It was you.'

His voice, when it comes, cuts through the wind, the ice and the sky and she shivers.

'It was me. It was always me.'

54

Three sifts of coarse powder for burning.
Two sifts of fine powder for incision.
One man with a hand steady as an oarsman's drum.

—*On the Preparation of Necessary Flames,*
Chapter 6: Burners and Concussives

The gun fits together seamlessly, the pieces interlocking like
snakes. Slickwalker lets his hands fall on the clasps and triggers,
runs them over the buckles, the stock, the long smooth barrel
which rests across his legs. He traces its lines, lets his fingers linger
on the curves, the angles. It hums faintly beneath his gloves.

Astic is quiet in the morning light. He leans back in his chair,
lets the smell of the city fill his ribs. Fish oil and wet wool, tallow
and beer.

It's getting colder. The warm ghost of summer still clings to
the roof tiles, chased by cats who coil through chimney smoke
and washing lines. But it's getting colder.

He can see it in the sea, the green of the coast falling to black.
In the lines of the fishermen, woven tighter, weighted heavier,
plumbing the depths to bring up the thick, grey octopuses that
come to feed on boat scraps. Pots to catch crabs shelled with
barnacles, the wood soured and twisted by fast, harsh currents.

A good season for hunting, on the edge of autumn, the air clear
and cold. Everything that moves pulsing against the landscape,
the hills filled with heartbeats.

He pulls a rag from his pockets, oils it, rubs it over the gun. It
smoulders gently, thin threads eaten by movement, by metal.

He hasn't seen Crowkisser in two days. She's up in the hollow
of the temple, he suspects, on her knees in the ruins, sifting

the rags the long men have brought in and stringing them into prophecy. She'll be cold and hungry, her fingers scraped raw, her nails chipped.

She'll have fallen, and her skull will have hit the slabs wetly. Her eyes will have turned inwards and she'll have thrashed, white and bloody and crying.

The crows will have come to cover her. Soon, he'll go and minister to their marks. The sharp cuts left by their feet. He'll rub the bare spots where they've taken her hair. He'll hold her as she coughs up meat.

She'll be scared. The patterns are filthy, complicated. She can't look too long at them. Makes her feel sick. Makes her scratch at her pale skin. Makes her chew her lips ragged. Makes her hold onto him like a drowner.

He knows she'll pull through, fight through the twisting. She'll pick rope, and rot and blood. She'll swallow it down and cough the world back up to find the patterns they need to succeed. Nothing stays hidden. It'll fill her. Prophecy from bone to tail, until she can flit under the gaze of the eye in the south, like a shadow, like a slip, feet in a stairwell, the click of a door just closed.

Beautiful. Subtle. Unstoppable.

It'll fill her. The hot weight of seeing. She'll come to him later, lambent eyed, black and glowing. Ravenous for skin. Kissing like a cannibal. Arching her back. A priestess of cats, of corners, of secrets.

And he'll hold her. He always holds her. She'll fit against him, all her secret angles that only he knows. His hands against her sides, chasing away the knots and the cold. Dry lips against temples where her pulse runs thready.

Eventually, she'll fall. Empty herself in gasps and heartbeats. Take the space at his side, press her skull into the curve of his arm. She'll sleep. And he'll hold her. Watch her chest rise and fall. He'll tell himself it's worth it. That they're doing a good thing. And for a few ragged moments, it'll be true.

Of course, things are not that simple. There are prices to be paid.

He sets the rag down, takes his gloves off, and presses a palm to the barrel of the gun. As always, it eats him, scorching his flesh, licking at him with terrible, acrid speed. His palm vanishes into a ragged hole, the blood blackening, smoking, swallowed. He grits his teeth against the familiar pain.

The gun purrs and stretches. He watches it realign, becoming sleeker, darker. It pulses with an oil-slick hue, and the air smells of hot metal, copper, lemon.

It eats him down to the bone and he watches it work. When it's done, he turns to the city and raises his hand to his face. He imagines he can see Crowkisser through the hole, between the slats of bone, hung with meat and blood.

She's safe. They're all safe. Because of the gun, the shadow and the crows. Because of him. Because of what he gives.

He flexes his fingers, watching the naked struts dance in his hand. Behind them, people are opening shops, raising shutters, lifting canopies. Children stir, scuff sleep-grit from their eyes, are pulled reluctantly into outstretched jumpers.

Astic wakes slowly, grudgingly, uncharmed by the cold.

With the thumb of his left hand, Slickwalker fingers the gun. It folds in on itself, quick and clever, becoming nothing but a shard of black, a promise. He slides it over his back, feels it nestle into the clasps there. For a moment, its weight feels like her hand and he half-turns, expecting.

Three years now, with her always on the edges of his world, waiting for the next touch, the next word. Crowkisser. What was there but Crowkisser? Slickwalker knew there had been a time before her. Somewhere deep down, he knew it. But his mind was not interested in such things. When he woke, he saw the curve of her cheekbone in the half-shadow. When he slept he felt her breath against his lips. When he killed, he saw her as she wept.

She had given everything for the people of this world. And they cursed her for it. Everything, and they stepped around her like a mad dog.

Everything and they hushed their voices and doused their lights.

Everywhere but here. Over the last few years, the people of Astic had finally come around, finally realised how Crowkisser kept them safe. And after Astic, the Rim villages followed, one by one, as the cost of life alone on the edge of the south became too much to bear.

Behind him, he hears the wet slap of the first boats hitting the morning water as they put out to sea. Rhythm. Astic thrived on rhythm, and so did she. Every night, between those blasted pillars, her hands slick with blood and feather, her hips lifting in desperate hope.

Every night, she tore herself down to find the patterns. Every night she built herself back up from scraps.

And she was winning. She'd gleaned fragments of their enemies' movements, snatched from the wind, teased from the beaks of crows. Plucked from the forest's thorns.

Enough to send him to Hesper at the exact moment Shipwright and Shroudweaver had docked. To menace Fallon and flush them out, after months of hiding and running.

It was a pity he hadn't been able to kill the old bull, but his visit had served its purpose, and confirmed that Crowkisser's visions were true, that the pair were in Hesper. Less pleasantly, it had confirmed that Shroudweaver could still stitch together a god in a pinch.

His side aches at the memory of Shipwright's fists; the bruise is gone, but the guts and bones underneath are slower to mend.

Yes, Shroudweaver could still stitch a god, and it seemed as if he was still as ruthless in his choice of host. Slickwalker smiled a little at that.

Interesting how quickly the pair had rushed to defend their old friend. Crowkisser would use that, he was sure. She had an eye for the weaknesses of others. It had worried him at first, until he'd seen the truth of their work; how much better life was under her, free from the gods.

He watches the boats skim out to the horizon and cast their nets, the arms of their crews slashed against the light. It will soon be time for him to head northwards, on the trail of the crows.

Not that Kisser wasn't confident in her prophecies, but she valued certainty, corroboration; eyes that were still in a human head.

Behind him would come their army. All the able-bodied from Astic, and the others that would join them from the Rim villages, Dryke, Vantage, Fallow. Not much, all told. Maybe three or four hundred bodies, but she seemed certain they would be enough. All of those fisherfolk were confident enough in her, that was for sure.

It didn't mean they could get by alone, however. That's where he came in.

His heart lifts a little at the thought of it. He loved scouting, nothing in his head but his own thoughts, his own body moving at his command. Climbing trees, fording rivers, the earth opening out around him like a puzzle to be solved. The whole army at his back, waiting on his word, for the safe routes, the clear places, the pure streams. It gave him a sense of purpose.

Then home each night, flitting through shadow to her bedroll, her arms. Her approving words.

He checks his supplies one last time. The pain in his hand is already easing, just the steady itch of new flesh creeping across the bone, pulled tight by shadow. A useful gift, another token of Crowkisser's esteem.

He watches the waves a moment more. The light is particularly bright this morning, bright enough that he can almost imagine catching a glimpse out west to the spires and the stilts of the Heron Halls. Not that he's ever seen them, just heard stories. But maybe someday.

In the far distance, something big breaches. A glimpse of white flesh and a finned, sinuous body that slaps the water hard enough to send the echoes racing to shore. The fishermen shout in return, their voices high and eerie, sending their song back out to sea.

His heart thrills from the strangeness of it. The sea both terrifies and delights him. He's glad they won't be fighting on it again; that might be a little too much.

Even taking down the *Volante* had stretched his nerves to the limit, his heart beating like a six-tap drum. No, best they weren't on the sea.

According to Crowkisser, Shipwright and Shroudweaver had already moored that golden monster of a ship, slotted it into the dock of some unsuspecting north coast village and struck out on horseback across the Midlands, skirting the western edge of the Burners' forest and then on into the Barrowlands, into the shadow of Thell.

Smart. The coastline past their anchorage was vile, and the tides were worse. His dad had always told him there was an old sea monster down there, its ragged, broken lungs sucking the water in and out, spitting it up in spumes and whirlpools, ship-breakers all.

Sure, cutting across country would add on a few weeks, but they'd arrive alive, and they'd be able to glean information on the way. Maybe tap into the Burners' networks. The sootfaces might stay in the forest, but their traders ran like lice across the body of the Midlands.

A few weeks, and they'd be in Thell. Where, if you believed the wind and the crows, Quickfish and his lover were too, either hoping to get safe passage through, or somehow leverage the Republic's inkmagic to save his mother.

Slickwalker shakes his head ruefully. Idiots. Romantic idiots. The mistakes people made for love.

He'd fretted about Quickfish too, of course. The possibility of Fallon's son and Shroudweaver together, with Thell's armies at their back, hadn't seemed like an ideal situation. Give them a few months, and they could mobilise, push southwards with a force that would turn Astic and all its brave little satellite villages to dust.

Crowkisser had shaken her head when he told her his worries, a dark little smile on her wet lips.

Not a problem, she'd told him, not a problem at all. She knew all the Republic's sins, she said. And they would come due with just a little push. And then, she'd said, her fingers twining in the soft hair of his chest, then they would have all of them.

All of their enemies, in Thell, like a corked bottle.

Fallon would stay mired in his port city, scared behind his bristling walls, counting his dwindling, useless ships, and in the north, in the mountain, everyone he loved would bend the knee, or burn.

It seemed harsh, but Slickwalker had seen it work over and over again, in every village, with every group of refugees fleeing the south. Given the choice, most everyone bowed. Perhaps they might tell themselves they were rebels, that they were brave, that they would fight. But most fought only to the first broken bone, the first gunshot. At worst, to the first sundered name.

What she'd explained to him, and what he'd come to understand, was that most people simply wanted to get on with things. Almost any change, any loss, could be factored in, ground under the wheel of time and persistence.

Fighting got you killed. Bowing, bending the knee? It might leave you in the mud for a little, but in the end, it let you get on with things. Bar a few empty houses and forgotten names, the cost was slight.

Getting on with things was all that Slickwalker really wanted, too. To get all this over with, to put an end to the last of these diehards, and begin building a life with Kisser, here, or wherever she chose. To have a shape to that life that was more than prophecies and crows and scheming.

He rolls his shoulders; a nice dream. To get it started, he needs to get moving.

His boots carry him down the grey wood of the pier, passing hawkers and traders hollering their wares. Boats coming in now, rather than going out, trade picking up as the years rolled on. People got on with things. War came and death came and people got on with things.

The boats were few now, but given time, people would forget that Astic was a conquered city.

Crowkisser was winning. All she needed was time, and all she had to do was wait. Except she'd always had trouble with that, couldn't let well enough alone.

He juked to the left to avoid a gaggle of boat-jumping children, their shrieks of joy wobbling out over the water. Not much younger than him, now he thought about it. For a moment, his feet long to leap from pillar to pillar with them, to find the swaying trees of the south again, somehow. He contents himself with a swipe at one of the passing lads and a sly wink.

He understood where Crowkisser was coming from. Maybe it wasn't impatience. Maybe what she really wanted was momentum.

And so, boots marched north and west, crossing the hills and bluffs to Hesper, nosing into the Midlands with one eye on the rotten bulk of the Stump; the vanguard of the army that would roll out within the month. Soldiers, nameless and fearless, who remembered what had happened when the gods walked. Good men and women who wanted freedom for their children, whose boots turned old bones and knew that with only a few more they could build a better world.

Slow progress for those grey-clad legions. Sailors and fisherman not accustomed to the land, waiting for the hills to roll, or the valleys to squall with sudden storms. Finding themselves met instead with rain, chill winds, cart roads turned to mud and fields sown with stones.

They'd have an easier time once he left to find them swifter tracks north. He had one or two things to take care of first, then the shadows could slip him away from their dripping noses and numb feet. For now, their ranks were peppered with long men who slunk ahead with noose and rope, clearing the way as best they could.

Apparently there had been little resistance so far. Hesper drew into herself like a bearded boar, her towers hung with fire and fury. She wouldn't fall easily, not with Fallon striding the walls. She didn't need to. They could slip past on the landward side like a wolf skirting the fold. Funny how things changed.

Time was, Hesper had been the only curse on his lips. Near three years of keeping them penned in the south, starving their supplies, sinking their boats with the remnants of that great fleet.

Shipwright and her ship at the fore of every sortie. He curled a lip and spat off the side of the pier. Three years of that golden nightmare harrying their trade routes and their supply lines, trying to either splinter them where they stood, or force Crowkisser into some kind of reckless assault on Fallon's stronghold.

Either the walls or the ships of Hesper could have broken her; they still might.

It was ridiculous how long they'd schemed over how to crack that city. It said something for Fallon that it had taken them years to turn their eyes away.

Then, a few months ago, Quickfish had run for Thell. Nothing to do with them, just an unexpected benefit from tearing out Fallon's wife's name, all that time ago, a panic from a boy who didn't want his mother to die. So, perhaps a little to do with them . . . In any case, Slickwalker had never met the kid, but he owed him one.

Once they knew Quickfish was headed to Thell, all they needed to do was spook Shipwright and Shroudweaver into running there as well. Convince them the people they loved weren't safe, that Hesper wasn't safe, if they didn't do something.

He felt a slight flash of pride. He'd done rather well at that, if he said so himself. Slickwalker smiles as he turns through the market, his boots taking him up the winding path towards the temple.

So, a few fast, lucky months, and almost everyone they needed dealt with was now headed to, or cowering in, that blasted mountain.

Hesper could remain bristling on the Western shore. They'd just march right on by.

Crowkisser seemed to think they'd pull it all off without a hitch. For his part, he suspected there'd be a little more smoke and blood.

To that end, she'd given him a special task, a little something based on his father's trade. Cracking open cliffs to get at the metal inside. He supposed a cliff and a mountain were mostly the same. Except he wouldn't be pulling silver out of the clearing smoke, it'd be blood.

As he climbs the road, he slips into the small house he's kept here and unlatches the door. He peels his gloves off, tucks the gun under an arm, and shucks off the walker's harness onto a peg, then turns at the sound of an insistent hiss.

The small snake twining among the coats, jackets and armour flicks a tongue indignantly at him, the diamond check of its scales loose in the soft light. He chucks it under the chin and reaches for a tin by the door. A couple of unlucky crickets in its jaws and it's much happier.

He runs a hand along its smooth back. 'Hello, hungry.'

Skinsnips, they'd called them when he was small. On account of their little fangs scissoring out bits of finger if you got too close. Docile, and friendly enough once fed.

He'd had this one in his pocket nearly three years ago, had brought it with him unknowingly when the south had burnt.

It might be the last one of its kind, for all he knew.

He throws it another cricket, grinning. 'It's almost your birthday, pal.'

The skinsnip's happy chewing follows him as he moves back through the house; the unused kitchen, the cold fireplace, and then the door with three locks.

He undoes them with practiced speed. His fingers don't shake at all now, he notices.

They're waiting for him in the backroom, stacked in a loose pyramid; almost a full complement. The coarse surface of their rough clay shells holds the light, the briefest glimpse of wicks amid the pile.

It had taken him weeks to get the hang of moving them through shadow – too many variations in speed and momentum. He'd almost lost a hand a few times. And he's still not owned up to the deep midnight detonation that sent chunks of pale rock raining into the ocean and set the seabirds screaming.

His father's legacy, that mix of powders and liquids, held just barely apart with thin walls of clay.

Commonplace enough in the south, they'd been. Common enough that he could remember his grandmother complaining as the explosions would rock out over their village shaking the tea in its cups, rattling the teeth in their heads. The noontime shivers, she'd called them. He'd always thought of the bombs as shivers since then.

Sixteen shivers left now.

Enough to crack the mountain, he hoped. Enough to send him to oblivion in chewable pieces if he got it wrong.

Distantly listening to the crunch of cricket legs, he runs his fingers gingerly over the rough surface of the topmost shiver.

This was a lot of death to bring down on a city. But he understood why Crowkisser wanted it. Thell had to die so everyone else could live. It was cruel, but life was cruel. You had to be hard to make it better.

Still, still, it wasn't what he'd dreamt of as a child. But then, who knew what he'd dreamt of as a child. He vaguely remembered a smaller world, moving stitch-legged among the waists of taller people who dispensed cuffs and care in roughly equal amounts. There had been the flash of jewels, rings and trinkets and deft fingers moving between them. The boom of the rock split open, and the gleam of silver in their hands and hearts afterwards.

There had been boats and sails, yes, but trees as well, their trunks straight and slender. Their branches whip-thin, tempting and treacherous. There had been a fountain he thought, bright with cold water, flecked with gold.

And then, something had happened. The old world had frayed and split and the shadow had come through, and beyond the shadow, the eye. He remembered the fear. Not just fear. He remembered the *terror* as it fell on him. He'd shit himself, and scrabbled limp-legged against the cobbles. Fought. Choked. Gagged. Panic had covered him, swallowed him, filled him. It had slid behind his eyes, into his throat, his heart.

The world had frayed, and he had been a thread left on the seam, curled on the cobbles as men and women screamed around him and golden things with the faces of angels and the voices of lizards split and burst in streets which opened themselves to great depths. Until blackness had yawned under him. Until the whole world shivered.

He'd felt the gaze of the eye eat him. Inch by inch, the whispers of his mind swallowed. He'd stopped there, and given himself up to it, because what else was there to do on the frayed edge of the world?

Given himself up to it. Until she'd emerged from the slanted buildings, smoke-stained and bloody. Given himself up to it, until he'd realised that there was life beyond the shadow.

Years had passed since then. He shifts, setting the gun down. It throbs slowly as he runs fingers over the knots in his neck, feeling the frayed stitching of his collar. He slips the jacket off and finds needle and thread. Wet between the lips and then passed through the eye. Quick, economical loops.

There are a lot of little tears, now he looks, dark spots and blemishes. He moves to the workbench beyond the pile of shivers, reaches up, takes a tin from a box, wax from the tin. Works in small circles, from the inside out. His fingers straighten sleeves and seams, smoothing the lining where it has snagged from sudden, fast movement.

It had been a gift, originally. She'd brought it to him in those early days. A dull grey morning like this, the sky a hammered pan. A bit before they'd taken Astic, in a herder's hut south of here, jam on her lips and her fingers worn raw. The time it must have taken. And there it was, given without ceremony. 'This is yours,' she'd said, and pressed it against his chest. Then pressed herself against him. They'd fallen into rough wool and rushes, the air outside heavy with the scent of hill-flowers, split with the lone piping of a startled bird.

She'd taken him by inches. Teeth running over shoulders, hips. Her body a slim, insistent thing, her legs woven like wire along a branch. Her spine always out of reach, pale in the soft light, until his hands could bring her into him, could lace her with fingers and tongue. Her wrists light against his palms, toes pointed. Her heart a hammer in a bone box. And then her mouth open and a soft, lilting cry, that built like a banked fire. Softness, softness and release.

Leaving the next day, the jacket had felt light and strange on his shoulders, like the touch of a friend just met. The linen tight on his throat, his breath catching when he looked at her. The last scraps of forest falling to the gullies and scree paths of what would become the Rim villages, the people following them picking their way gingerly over stones that turned easily, gave up flints, fossils. The land alive with tall grey grass which shivered white in the breeze, holding tan foxes, and slim, wary deer that emerged at twilight, their coats shimmering with the mock and sway of the grass.

They'd only lost one man on the way to Astic, fallen on the trail, convulsing, spine arched and mobile, his lips bubbling with gold. Crowkisser held him as he talked, her mouth close against his, her cheeks flecked with spittle, thumbed by his desperate hands, her own hands working his body, stopping the worst of the change, until he quieted and she motioned Slickwalker to bring the gun and put a bullet into him.

The gun was hungry even then. Spitting forth death that slunk through the air like a scolded cat, falling on flesh and bone and bubbling gold and burning it all to merge with the rock beneath. Chips of flint, chips of bone.

Over time they moved north and west, seeking the sea, the coast, and the purification of salt before eventually finding Astic. As they travelled, the gun grew sleeker, lighter and the jacket picked up darknesses, blood, tears and blemishes. Still whenever he wore it, he thought of her, with sweetness on her lips and the shudder of silver grass beneath an empty sky.

55

stay warm, beloved ghost
the fire is dipping lower
night still calls you home

—Southern funeral prayer

Digging. So much of power lay in the willingness to dig – in earth, in minds, under skin. Pulling truth into the light, turning it white and slick against the sun and then learning to use it. Crowkisser hadn't had much to go on at first, some vague memory of her father sitting her on his knee, combing tangles from her hair. That birch sap smell he always used to pull home from the Aestering. Light little kisses on her neck. Her mother tickling her toes slyly with an open hand as she passed, making her squirm. She'd felt so safe then, had barely stopped to absorb the tales of ruins, of buried civilisations, sunk down and down into the earth, each more fantastical than the last, sometimes wondrous, sometimes terrible. Legends of hollow cities spun around underground suns, their roofs held aloft by great brass spinners that groaned and shuddered with the weight of the earth above, and the strain of pushing air down into the ground.

She'd had no clue who had lived in those cities, if they had ever in truth existed. Just a vague, confused memory of feeling her heart flutter in her chest at the tales. Watching the excitement and wonder hang on her father's lips before her mother called them out into reality again, to pluck a bird, to rinse bloody hands in hot water, to twine her fingers with her daughter's and play forest princess with the salvaged, prettiest feathers.

No, the great cities were either gone or buried, deep and distant, beyond her reach. She'd never heard a whisper of them,

414

though she'd scoured the libraries of the south for a full year, following hints of names and the half-erased traces of old maps. She took what she needed from those shelves, and then when she could get no further beyond tight lips and tighter attitudes, she'd taken the rest of what she needed on the point of a knife.

She'd never picked up much of shroudweaving, but in those blank wolf years after her mother's death she'd tried to revisit what her father had taught her and found she remembered enough. Red thread for binding; enough of it and you could hold a soul into flesh that desperately wanted to die. Make it tell you anything just for the relief, for the promise of release. But even that small gesture made her so very tired. She had no idea how her father did it. Ten minutes of questions and she'd been racked with the weight of it, every muscle in her body shuddering in protest at the reflected suffering. He must have had a trick or two. Or maybe he just knew how to hold pain.

Not like the hapless targets of her questions. Despite their suffering, she'd felt next to nothing for them, something inside her scoured blank by the thought of her mum long gone. Somewhere deep beneath that memory lurked a hollow loss she didn't ever dare touch. She never dug there.

Her mum, who had loved her curious girl.

stay warm
beloved ghost

A summer's day, years ago, and she's bent over an insect, stretching it out towards Crowkisser; the girl who would be Crowkisser. Whatever her name had been before she'd torn it loose. Her mum points at the creature, delicately. 'See how he turns. See the joints at each angle.' She gives a gentle flick to the insect's bright green head. 'See how he pulls tight to protect himself?'

Crowkisser had pressed her face up close, then screamed in indignation when tiny pincers found the soft part of her nose.

Her mum had laughed, gently wiggled the beast free and sent it into the grass. She'd held Crowkisser tight, wiped her bloody nose on her skirt; hunkered down, knees out and rubbed her shoulders consolingly, with just the faintest hint of laughter hidden behind a sympathetic pout.

'Little bird. There's a lesson there though. What do you think it is?'

Crowkisser had pouted, scuffed the dirt at her feet, not wanting to answer, wanting to stay in that moment, with the dry dust on her shoes, the sun on her back and her mum hanging in the light of her eyes, feeling the warmth of her hands and the blackbird shine of her hair.

She'd answered anyway. 'Don't pester 'em.'

Her mother had shrugged and smiled. A little pit blossomed in Crowkisser's stomach. The wrong answer?

Her mum pulled her close, pressed her forehead against hers. 'Baby, there's always going to be things, people in the world that don't want you to pester them. You know that, right?'

Crowkisser had nodded, even though she hadn't.

Her mum had grinned that wicked grin she gave Crowkisser's dad sometimes, when Kisser had said something cheeky. 'They'll always try to put you off if you get too close.' She'd made her hands into pincers, tickled her daughter's sides. 'Nip you, get you all kinds of nasty ways. But' – and her eyes went wide and serious – 'but tell me something.' She flicked the cut on Kisser's nose.

A squeal. The tiniest bit of blood.

'Did that hurt?'

Crowkisser nodded. Furious. Betrayed. Small hands clenching. Her mum tilted her lowering chin up to meet her eyes. 'But you're still standing?'

She nodded again. Her mum kissed her head, and she felt the fury vanish like rain.

'That's all it takes, little bird. Stay standing after they lash out. That's all you need to do.'

She reached into the grass and dug around, lifted a rock. 'After that, what you do in return is up to you.'

She handed the stone to Crowkisser, rough and too big in her palm. Pointed to where even now the green bug roamed the path, unaware of its crime. Looked at her daughter. 'There he is. And you're still standing. So, what are you going to do?'

Crowkisser bent down to look at the bug, its carapace still emerald against the light, but struck through with colours she hadn't noticed before. Purple, blue, fading again to green. She raised the rock, looked at her mum.

Her mother shrugged. 'If you want, little bird.'

She looked at the rock again, at the weight of it, and then at the bug, and its joints and the sun on the path. As she set it down she felt a brief ache in her muscles as her mum gently took her hand.

'OK, little bird.' She squeezed Crowkisser's fingers and ran a hand over the small of her back. 'Why not? It bit you after all.'

Crowkisser rubbed the drying scab. 'Doesn't matter, Mum. Bugs bite. It's all they know to do.'

Her mother lifted her onto her shoulders. Whispered into her cheek. 'You don't blame them for that?'

She shrugged. 'It's how they are, Mama.'

She'd laughed at that. 'I love you, bird button. But,' she'd said, slinging her piggyback, 'I know what *you* are.'

'What's that, Mama?' she'd asked.

'Hungry,' her mum replied. 'Let's see what your father thinks to fish stew.'

Long strides down the path.

Long strides into her life.

Her mother the teacher.

Her mother the joker.

Her mother the host.

Her mother the memory.

the fire is dipping lower
night still calls you home

The rocks she'd lifted since. For if the great cities had never shown their face, she'd followed their trail through generations before her, following the work of other hunters that wanted to know about the worlds buried beneath their own, and in the process, she'd stumbled on something else, guided by book and map and blade.

Hidden far beneath where the great spinners might have lain. Through structures dug so far under the skin of the earth that she forgot the shape of the sun. Then curving back up to the surface, emerging shyly from under waterfalls, and between clefts in cliffs.

She found herself exploring not cities, but caverns. Networks that hollowed the land. And in them, she'd unearthed more than memories; paintings, relics, traces of people. And when she'd finally found what those people believed in, down in the dark, she'd come away more bloodied than ever before.

But still standing. She'd peeled back the skin of that blasted world, and taken its power.

Crowkisser had known since her mother died what she was going to do. She was going to kill the gods. And the people of the darkness, in the painted caves beneath the earth, had given her the gift she needed to do it.

the fire is dipping lower
night still calls you home

56

night hollows fair the ancient hill
the buried ocean dreaming still

—Embroidery on robe, formerly interred in the
Blue Rest, a day's ride outside of Vantage

Too many years and a week later. The quarry cut into the land like an open sore. A little slice of white bone dug out of the green hills where the burnt earth of the south finally gave ground to the light stone of the Rim. A few days out from Dryke and Vantage, their numbers grown again. Not by much, a couple of hundred more souls, but enough to rattle Crowkisser's head. Enough for her to leave them behind in the lee of the valley while she stalked the quarry ridge.

She'd come for peace, and she'd come for answers.

The sun is high above the white rocks, the air cut with the piercing call of some small bird, floating in looping trills from the spiked bushes that clung to the quarry's edge.

The chalk hewn out in sheer chunks, stepping down to the lake at the quarry's base, its water impossibly blue, picking up the edge of the sun and flicking it back at her eyes as she scours the walls for the path down.

The shore is softer on the southern side, where grass and shrub has started to reclaim the bone-white earth. On this edge, the hillside is stepped like broken teeth. Shallow cuts near the top, where the locals have come for the stone that lines the tops of the ware-dykes, dropping to cyclopean scars further down, the legacy of the Belltollers, brought here by the southern Aestering to shear the chalk into powder for their workings and teachings, and bindings.

419

Crowkisser remembers her dad's dusty fingers, and pushes the image out of her head. This is not the time. She's not here for the folklore, or the weaver's ghosts. She's got a different spirit to hunt.

The path is hard to follow at first, white against bone, the gravel shifting under her feet. She'd light her toes with crow feathers, get a little balance, but that feels wrong here, disrespectful.

She swallows a little retch of bitter bile and feels her hammering heart push against her ribs. She's nervous; she hasn't made this trip for a few years, and never with an army at her back.

About halfway down, the quarry hollows out, pockmarked with windblown caves. Man-made at first, shaped by the miners digging back for the purer rock, then smoothed by the gales which tore up from the south and whirled the bowl of the quarry, lashing the water below, and softening those angular cuts into organic lines, like the inside of an ear, or the curve of a shell.

There are shells here too, buried in the rocks and calcified over time, until only the whorls of their death showed through the stone; the faintest echo of tentacles, rendered into dust. Further back in the rock, she remembers running her hand over paintings, blown like stars around the fingers of a hand. Ochre, yellow as a bird's eye, red as blood.

She hears the house before she sees it, the strung shells clattering in the soft wind. A smell rolls up the path, half the cool kiss of the water below, half a mess of onions and greens, skillet-fried.

The house is barely a house now, more part of the rock, like it was folding itself back into the quarry, year on year, scalloped around a bent lintel and a wooden door bleached close to the chalk by the heat of the sun. A few swoops of those strung shells, scoured, marked with symbols she half-recognises from back in the caves. Maybe an eye, maybe a hand, maybe a leaping fish or diving bird.

She stops at the lintel and knocks, partly out of politeness, partly to let her eyes adjust to the dark inside.

It's a small room, but deceptive, with light coming in from above where the hollow bones of the chalk meet the sky. Sparse;

a chair, a table, a cot; a brazier in the middle where the skillet dances, and bent over it, the Chalkwitch.

Her face like an owl in the half-light, amber skin burnished darker by the sun. She smiles, and the scar on her face pulls upwards. 'Hello, darling.'

Crowkisser starts to reply just as the skillet coughs out a puff of smoke, and a bead of oil ignites black in the pan.

The smoke fills the small room. Chalkwitch curses and shifts the skillet off the stove. She turns back to Crowkisser, tears streaming down her face then bursts out laughing. 'I still can't cook, darling. The gods took that from me too.'

Crowkisser smiles despite herself, and reaches out her hand. 'Shall we get some air?'

Chalkwitch's hand is smooth as sanded wood, the muscles strong over stark bones. Bracelets clack on her wrists as they flee to the fresh air. Crowkisser holds her arm for a moment more in the sunlight, watching the pattern of the beads.

'I made that one for you.'

Chalkwitch smiles. 'When you were seven.'

Crowkisser squeezes her fingers a little. 'It's awful.'

Chalkwitch nods. 'Children's art usually is.' She grins. 'But it reminds me of you.'

She shoots a rueful glance back at the thin wisp of black smoke curling from inside. 'Shall we chat out here today?'

Crowkisser nods. 'I think that'd be best.'

Chalkwitch looks at her critically for a moment. 'You know the rules.' She holds out her arms. 'Hugs first.'

Crowkisser rolls her eyes, and lets out a groan. 'Seriously, Chalk?'

'Seriously, little Crow.'

Crowkisser throws up her hands. 'Ugh! Fine!'

Chalkwitch pulls her close, her grip still strong after all these years. She smells of soap, and chalk, and burnt onions.

'You're crushing me,' Crowkisser squawks.

'Good,' Chalkwitch says, kissing the top of her head. 'Now, take a seat, and talk to me.'

She slings her legs over the lip of the quarry, so they hang over the blue water below. The braids in her hair shift slightly in the breeze coming up off the lake.

Crowkisser settles next to her, lifting the hem of her skirt and sliding in close.

'Missed you,' she says, leaning into Chalkwitch's shoulder.

Chalkwitch ruffles her hair. 'Missed you too little crow. You've been busy.'

This close, the ruin of Chalkwitch's face is unmissable, the burn scar that eats up half her skull tracking across her cheek and jaw like a dried riverbed, pooling in the puckered ruin of her missing eye. The hair on that side is still patchy, burnt to ash in the fires of the south. Burnt to ash when her god tore itself out of her to die.

Crowkisser lifts a hand to her face. 'How does it feel today, Chalk?'

Chalkwitch smiles, the scar stretching, now rough, now eerily smooth.

'It aches. It always does, but I've made my peace with it, little crow.' She frowns a little, 'It's only you that hasn't.'

'I never meant to hurt you. Only the gods, Chalk, only the gods.'

Chalkwitch's face stiffens a little then. 'Killing always hurts, child. You were old enough to know what you were doing. Don't pretend otherwise.'

Crowkisser feels shame burn on her cheeks. She tries to turn away, but Chalkwitch's fingers are suddenly sharp on her jaw, twisting her back to meet the gaze of that ravaged eye.

'Don't. Own your choices. Besides,' she pats Crowkisser's face. 'I've made *my* peace with it.'

'Do you miss it?' Crowkisser asks.

Chalkwitch tilts her head, thoughtfully. 'Do I miss being a host? No.'

'The powers the gods gave were wonderful, but' – she waves a hand – 'they were unrelenting.'

She turns until she's facing Crowkisser squarely, and crosses her legs underneath her. 'Never a night without dreams, never a day without someone battering down my door, asking why couldn't I fix their broken leg, why couldn't I make their fields grow, why couldn't I stitch their husband's limp cock.'

She laughs. 'No, I don't miss it.'

Crowkisser smiles in relief, before Chalkwitch interrupts her, with a raised finger. 'But do I miss the god? Yes. I miss its voice on the cold nights. I miss *understanding*. Or feeling like I understood. I miss knowing that there was a plan. I miss being able to share that plan, and to give comfort.' She leans back, and squints at the sun. 'I don't know what the plan is now. I don't even know how to cook.'

Her voice is flat. 'So yes, I miss the god. It wasn't a friend, but it was a constant.'

Crowkisser picks at her cuffs. 'Do you think that Mum felt like that about her god?'

Chalkwitch thinks. 'Your mother knew what she was getting into, which is more than you could say for a lot of hosts. And she took the god because she wanted to help people, I know that much. But she never told me that much about how she felt about it. Just called it the noisy cricket.'

They both smile sadly at that, and Crowkisser feels an ache like ice around her heart.

'The noisy cricket is chirping, Chalk, fetch the wood. I can't leave the temple today, Chalk, the cricket's too loud. You'll have to go to market.'

She grins. 'Sometimes, I think your mum was just lazy, and liked having a god to blame.'

Crowkisser grits her teeth. 'Did the gods ever help you?'

Chalkwitch is silent for a moment. 'It depends what you mean by help, little crow. They kept us alive. Healed us. Stopped time from touching us. Closed the wound and sealed the scar.' She runs a hand over her face. 'They let us glimpse the future. They let us see the pattern of the past. Was that help?' She shrugs. 'I don't know, but that's not what you're asking me.'

Crowkisser frowns. 'It's not?' An odd feeling in her throat as she speaks, like choking on a stone.

Chalkwitch's face is soft. 'No, you're asking me why your mother's god let her die.'

Crowkisser says nothing, her lips pressed tight, but the tears come anyway as Chalkwitch takes her hands. She nods, briefly.

Chalkwitch makes a low noise in her throat. 'Five years you've been building up to asking me that.'

Crowkisser clears her throat. 'And?'

Chalkwitch shrugs. 'And I don't know, little crow.'

She sees the clouds forming over Crowkisser's face and tries to head them off at the pass.

'I've asked myself the same thing. Perhaps the disease took it too. Perhaps it was so bound up with her body that what she suffered, it suffered.'

'A disease that could kill a god?' Crowkisser asks, sceptically.

Chalkwitch raises her eyebrows. 'Implausible, after what you've done? I don't think so.'

She frowns. 'Perhaps it just didn't understand. They never consciously seemed to feel helpful, when we got sick, or injured. They just fixed it reflexively, like blood filling a wound. Perhaps it just didn't know she was dying.' She pauses for a moment. 'Perhaps it just didn't care.'

Crowkisser's expression is pure fury.

Chalkwitch gently loosens her grip.

'This is what you need to understand little crow, to make peace with this. The gods were always beyond us. We were like pots to be filled, or a coat to be worn. You darn a coat if it frays, but if it rots, you cast it off.'

Crowkisser's breath is a low hiss. 'Parasites. They deserved everything they got.'

Chalkwitch's voice is thoughtful, as she turns her ruined eyes to the sun. 'Perhaps, little crow. But the killing of the gods changed us. The south changed us. We're all just unfilled pots now. Undarned coats, waiting to unravel.'

She gets stiffly to her feet, and holds out her hand. 'But until then, we hunger. Do you want to try and teach me how to cook one more time?'

Crowkisser smiles. 'It's the least I can do.'

Chalkwitch's hands linger on her own burnt skin, and scorched hair. All the deeper aches beneath it, where the fire of her god's death throes seared along her bones as it tore itself loose.

She kisses the girl lightly on the forehead. 'Yes, child. I expect it is.'

57

notgonebutbrokenis
hollowthefluteandthemouthoftheflute
hardthestoneandharderthesky

—memoryhereeyeseaten

She is nothing. She is a heart in the darkness. The sky wraps around her. She is grey and boneless. She dreams of breathing. She sweats. Her legs run wet and hot.

There are edges to her, to the place in which she finds herself. She presses against them. They fill the curve of her neck, her spine, her thighs.

Sometimes they give a little, like the rind on a fruit. She brings her weight against them and they belly outward, rubbery, impermeable.

She turns. She twists. Her spine runs with wet fire. She chokes on nothing. But always there are the edges.

Sometimes, something solid lingers against them, something broad and vast.

The edges are cold. She is cold.

The darkness pushes in. It is not her, and so she can thread it around herself. It tastes of things she once knew words for.

She presses against the ragged scraps of herself, and for a moment, she hears voices.

Something lingers beyond them, waiting. Waiting for her. Her back arches in desperation, and her fingers touch the fraying edge.

She has fingers.

She has a throat. She swallows, spitting the burnt sugar taste of magic, gags and gags again.

Still, the edges hold her back. She presses against them, feels the rind of her skull flex and shift. She is near to something.

Exhausted. Unsure.

The edges fall around her in folds of grey, and she almost sinks back into darkness.

Almost. And then from those edges, a soft golden light, like a kindled lamp.

Gold light, sweet as sugar, humming with its own soft rhythm. Something moving in the light, ambered muscle and burnished scale. It butts against her like a hungry kitten. Then it speaks.

hellowhatis

She struggles to respond, hanging wordless. Language chokes her throat.

hellowhatisneedwant

Desperate, she presses against the edges, seeking the shape of a reply.

hellowhatis

She wants to speak. She can't.

goneis

Rage flares in her, and the golden light flares in response so furiously that she flinches. She *flinches*.

notgoneis

The voice is stronger now, distinctly curious. She moves frantically, trying to hold its attention, battering herself against the edges, until pain fills her. Pain. She's here, and she's hurting. She hurls herself towards the light.

Nonononono. She replies. She *replies*. She is. Not gone.

Its response is quick as a fish in a pond.

hellowhatis

She strains against the edge, presses herself against the gold. She can taste it, bright and warm, sticky and sweet.

hungryisfragmentis

She swallows the gold light down. The edges shudder and purr. The thing inside moves closer. A tendril of golden light. A curious claw.

noteatisbecomeis

She presses herself to it, and it gathers against her gratefully, coiled as a cat, a heartbeat, thrumming as it speaks inside her mind.

shapedisthankis

There is a pause. It waits for her, waits for a response.

She presses against its golden skin and feels that hammering heart.

hellowhatis

What is she? She doesn't know.

The gold pulses, rubs against her wrists. Not just light, but a creature. A sense of bone and scale.

Its voice soft, comforting.

knowingisibecause

She pulls it tight against her. Feels something small and sharp against her ribs. Claws? Teeth?

As she takes in a breath, she feels the wet weight of her lungs move. Lungs. In a body.

hellowhatis

It's insistent now. Buzzing, resonant along the edges.

She presses against them, reaching for the shadows beyond, her fingers edged in gold.

And like silk before a shear, the edges give way.

Its voice is triumphant; jubilant.

whatis

She is lying in a bed, in a room, in a tower.

In her bed. In her room. In her tower. In Hesper.

A lamp gutters nearby.

She throws up in her mouth, feels it run back down her throat. Swallows.

whatiswhatiswhatis

Its voice different now. Closer.

The room seems empty. No edges, except those of the walls, the roof, the door.

Only the quiet hum of the gold remains.

Slowly, agonisingly, she moves her head to glance down at her chest.

The source of the gold curls there, a soft glow against the lamp-light, her blood on its talons.

Its eyes are lazy and amber, its voice familiar, persistent.

whatis

She looks down at her body, at the sores on her legs, and the scabs where she's lain wet and rotting. Her flesh is slung across the remains of her bones.

She runs a thick-nailed hand through her hair, feels it drift away in long grey clumps.

The golden creature shifts, and the barest movement of its weight is agony. She savours it – finally, something real.

whatiswhatiswhatis

She tries to say her name, but she can't.

When she tries to, her tongue slips over it, oily and heavy.

She can't say it.

She can't say her own name.

The scream starts low in her stomach, then coils up through her guts like curdled smoke, filling her ribs, her throat, her mouth, the room.

The lamp gutters, a memory of shadow and light. She shrieks, and lashes out. There's a crash, and for a brief moment the room is shrouded in blackness, before the gilded shape takes form again, clearer in the dark, lucent. A small, twisted body atop her ribs. Golden scales. A steady, buttery light flowing from its bones that pulses to the rhythm of the creature's voice.

namestolenwas

youcanhave

ihaveiknowbecauseknowingis

youwant

It takes her all of a moment to agree. She nods.

Its talons flex painfully, pleasurably.

yesgoodis

herelistenandbuild

It winds its way upwards from her chest. Small precise claws picking their way over her collarbone, along her neck, until its sharp, angled jaw is lying in the hollow of her ear.

Her heart thunders in terror and exhilaration.

listenis
iknowingis
youis
arissa
arissafallon is
arissa

It bites deep, the teeth entering her neck like needles. She moves with it, is filled by it, becomes it.

Slowly, painfully, writhing with the gold in her blood, Arissa Fallon wakes up, and takes back her name.

58

The Gate. The Lock. The Light. The Blood. The Bone. The Dead. The Dark.

> *—A Dictionary of Forms practiced by the wild folk of Thell,*
> Pub: Errant, Glissworm & Co.

It's chill in the belly of the Stump. As the day cools, Steelfinder sits in the debris of the last of the afternoon's sparring matches. Their victors have already slunk off into the depths of the mountain, cut slantwise with booze and adrenaline, their skin itching with fresh marks from their new victories. All of them off to get drunk and loud somewhere else.

And for a moment, there's quiet. Quiet enough for her to practice her trade, and to sneak a little wisdom before the brawlers return. She's not alone – Icecaller's kicking the tar out of some new recruits on the far side of the hall, and closer still, Skinpainter's finished hovering on the verge of the inking ring.

The old mountain warlock has lingered after the last match, obviously waiting for her. Skinpainter was a lot of things, but subtle wasn't one of them. Months now, they'd hung on the edges of the fights, and caught her afterwards, spinning tales about the ink, and the blood and the dark, thrilling her to goosebumps as she worked.

Today is going no differently, in the frozen depths, with the sweat drying on her skin. Skinpainter's thick fingers are heavy against her temples, her brow. Their voice is soft in counterpoint as her needle dips and bites. 'Here, a gate mark, to let all your natural energy pass out. Here, a barrier line to stop the unnatural getting in.'

Steelfinder shivers a little at their touch, tingles running up into her scalp. 'The unnatural? Like the dead?'

Skinpainter nods. 'The dead above all.'

Their face is serious in the flickering light. At their back, Icecaller spins and ducks, sparring with some of the unluckier trainees.

Steelfinder's eyes briefly stray to the lines of her legs, her hips, before Skinpainter turns her face back to them. The old sorcerer's amber eyes are dark and steady within the depths of their hood. 'You have to pay attention, Steel. There are things within you, within your blood and your bone that call to the dead in the air and the ground. That's why you must be tattooed. Why I taught the geometrics to your aunt and the others. Why she passed them on to you. The tattoos keep you separate. Quiet the voice in you that calls out to the dead.'

There's a distant thump, and a yelp as Icecaller strikes home.

Steelfinder ignores her, and catches Skinpainter's wrist, holding it briefly against the gate mark that cuts rigidly across her cheekbone. 'That voice, it's something from the Empire, isn't it? My aunt used to tell me about it. Told me never to listen to the voices in the dark, the ones behind my eyes when I was falling asleep. It's from the Empire.'

Skinpainter holds her gaze. 'What makes you think that?'

'Because I hear it the most when I'm in the depths.'

Her eyes flick to the side, running over the rows of needle and ink, laid out neatly for the work. 'I got turned around once, down in the low dark. Tenth, eleventh level maybe. I was only down there chasing that bastard sister of Icecaller's.'

She shivers again, less pleasantly. 'There's things down there, in the dark. Glowsticks. Those big ol' bugs with a mouth that stretches out. Skittering across the stones. Swinging in the arches. Pale as bone.'

Skinpainter squeezes her fingers. 'That wasn't all though, was it?'

She shakes her head. 'No. I think I got down by that big lake. I could smell the water, hear the drip from the stalactites.' A nervous laugh. 'Those damned bugs were quieter there at least.'

Skinpainter nods. 'They don't go that deep. You really got lost.'

Steelfinder leans in closer. 'Understatement. And I was down there in the dark, inching forwards, because I didn't know if my toes were going to hit water or rock, and that's when I heard it.'

They watch her, the lines of their face unnaturally still. 'Heard what?'

'I don't know if it was weeping, or singing, but it was coming from the darkness. Somewhere out in the black, above the water.' She stops, draws a ragged breath.

'And I swear, I felt it pulling on me. Like I was supposed to swim out into the lake. Or fly up into the black.' She grins nervously. 'Stupid, huh?'

Skinpainter shakes their head. 'No.' They adjust their robes, cross their legs and let out a long, weary sigh. 'The deepest places. That was where the Emperor was strongest. Something about his magic thrives down in the black.'

They pause. Hesitant.

Steelfinder tugs at their hand, gently. 'What, Skin?'

Skinpainter rolls their shoulders. 'It's where we took the Emperor. At the end. To finish it.'

Steelfinder purses her lips. 'Oh.' She shakes her head. 'So, he's haunting the place?'

Skinpainter chuckles. 'Something like that. He lingers.'

Steelfinder frowns. 'No offense, but why not tell everyone this? It'd make things a lot easier.' She glances over her shoulder as Icecaller executes a textbook throw, hammering the wind out of some unlucky sod. 'You know, stay away from the depths. Don't listen to voices in the dark.'

She watches their fists fly for a moment, then laughs. 'Oh wait, that's what my aunt did with me. And it didn't work.'

Skinpainter grins. 'It might work on less stubborn souls, but there's no need. Most people don't feel the call that strongly. Or at all. If they do, maybe they take a drink, or pull someone into their bed.'

Steelfinder scratches at an armpit. 'I do all that, Skin, doesn't help.'

They smile sadly. 'No, it wouldn't. There's a few families, a few bloodlines, I suppose, where the Empire's roots were strongest. Three families, actually, but the way we are now, everything's got so . . .' they tilt a hand. 'Mingled.'

Steelfinder rolls her eyes. 'Because everyone's fucking each other?'

They tip their head in acknowledgement. 'Not everyone, but more than they used to. Understandable. The Empire used to hold us all so tightly. Our lives. Our relationships. Everything was watched. Rigid. Prescribed.'

Their hands disappear inside their hood, pull at their chin. 'Hardly surprising that a lot of us eventually . . . cut loose, when the opportunity came.'

Steelfinder nods reluctantly. 'It's not just like that though, is it? We got all sorts now. Extended families, lovers on lovers. Support networks, Skin. You're never alone if you don't want to be.'

They pat her shoulder. 'Of course, Steel. I'm as happy as you to see it, but there's more of us now, and that means it gets harder to keep us all safe.'

'From the voices,' she finishes. A little lurch in her stomach, cold and wet.

'From ourselves. That's why we need you. All of you ink workers. To learn the forms, the shapes. To tattoo the geometrics that keep our breath and blood apart.'

Steelfinder looks down at her hands, at the scratches and scars. The ink stains. 'That's a lot, Skin.'

'That's why I don't usually explain all this. The catechisms and litanies usually suffice.' They wave a hand. 'Let no man do you harm, blah blah blah.' A sly grin.

She snorts. 'Fuck me for being curious, right?'

The grin vanishes. 'I'm sorry, Steel.'

She raises an eyebrow, her voice slow, unsure. 'No, no, it's OK. But I'm going to need to know more. I want to do my job well.' She glances across at Icecaller, as she twists and darts in the ring. 'I want to keep us safe.'

Skinpainter takes her hand, their grip strong and warm. 'We

have that in common. Now repeat after me. The simplest mark is the gate mark . . .'

Steelfinder's voice gets lost in the litany, as she murmurs the words, and traces the shape of the words on the bone, while behind her in the light, tattooed bodies move and shift and spin.

59

The world is sick with prophecy. In the turning of the stars.
In the movement of grasses.
We seek the present in this abundance of futures.
We eat, dream, act.

—Aestering lecture, Weaver Eelmarrow

Icecaller's hands are fucking freezing. She cups them in front of her, and rubs the tips of her fingers together, blowing on them in short, harsh puffs.

The needle works her shoulders rhythmically, hot and sharp as blood pools along the bone.

She jams her hands in her armpits. It's fucking cold.

'If you keep wriggling you'll tear the lines.'

'You didn't mind me wriggling much last night.'

Steelfinder cuffs her across the back of head. 'I was off the clock then.' Her fingers linger on the back of Icecaller's skull. 'I like your hair short. Feels nice.'

Icecaller stretches, feels the needle bite. 'I like your mouth shut. Sounds nice.' She twists a foot to dig a heel into Steel's thigh. 'Well, shut or full. Either works.'

Another cuff. 'I'm on the clock, damn it. What did you *do* to this anyway?'

Icecaller glances over her shoulder. 'Just a scrape. Took a hard fall in the circle.'

Steelfinder snorts. 'You? Who was brave enough to do that?'

She lids her eyes. 'Jealous?'

The needle lingers, beaded. Icecaller grins. 'Relax, dipshit, it was Dad. Who else is gonna knock me on my ass?'

Steelfinder shrugs. 'I don't know. Nigh maybe? How's she coming along?'

'Full of shit and bollocks as usual. She's great. The other kids don't want to fight her anymore. They're running out of teeth.'

'She takes after her big sister.' The needle dips and runs as angles blossom, black and red and black again. 'You can't leave damage this long. It's dangerous. Anything that gets down to the blood.'

Icecaller shrugs. 'Barely a scratch.'

Steel's voice hardens. 'A scratch is all that's needed. You know that.'

There's a quiet then. The low ceiling of their room filled with smoke, a smudged glow from the lights. The blanket feels tight, twined around Icecaller's feet.

She reaches her hand back, runs it over Steelfinder's stilled arm. 'I know. Well. So Skinpainter says anyway.'

She feels Steel's lips scuff against her hairline. 'You don't think they're right?'

Icecaller twitches her free shoulder. 'Maybe they are. I only know what I know.'

Steelfinder opens her mouth over the nape of her neck and talks down into the skin. Icecaller feels the vibrations run across her collarbone, as Steelfinder tuts softly. 'No sense in taking risks. Let me finish you up.'

Her breath smells of spice and sex. Her fingers are cartographers.

The smoke hangs, the light lowers.

Later, Icecaller's hands are still fucking freezing. She walks the halls of the Stump unsteadily, leaning heavily on her spear. She's out of shape, too much sleeping and fucking.

Sparring in the ring doesn't cut it. One scrape isn't going to keep her strong, not with what's coming. Not now Crowkisser's touched the mountain. She can't shake the memory of her slim body silhouetted against the flame. It doesn't seem right that one girl could destroy everything she loves, it doesn't seem fair.

She needs to get her head right. She needs to head out on

patrol. Taste what's on the wind, and see what the word is outside Thell. The Stump is slumbering its way towards a war and she doesn't like it. All that chat with Quickfish has just made it worse. The world is coming for them, and she needs to move to meet it.

As she winds her way down the spirals that cut through the body of the mountain, she passes forges, barracks, sleeping halls. Metal rings and runs dully. Hawkers shake bones and trinkets, clutches of them running in small gaggles between the traders, crossing palms and ducking curses.

Far below, her father sits in council with Belltoller and the Deadsingers, four survivors of the rebellion against the Empire, stirring the ashes and finding the fires of a new war. They're chewing over the words Quickfish has brought them, picking the thorns from Skinpainter's bold call to aid Quickfish, which is a call to arms in all but name. That sly warlock has put spark to kindling with studied care, sliding the whole mountain towards a confrontation with Crowkisser.

Her da is harder to rile, for all his blood gets hot. Right now, the old man will be a rock in a river, as the councillors drift against him like weeds. She can picture it perfectly.

Belltoller will say little, tall and silent as mountain ash. She will lean against Kinghammer's ear and whisper, and her words will draw his mind to scars she bears from the last war and to the new scars waiting to blossom if they take up arms. To the inevitability of taking up arms, if they help this wild, spuff-headed boy who has come to their door. In the end, she will support him, for she always has, even though it's cost her dear.

The Deadsingers will urge caution, their thin fingers will speak of patterns, ravelling and tradition. They will say that the omens caution patience, that the weight of ice lies heavy on the mountain, that the eagles still haunt the high passes. They'll be happy to remain in the depths, far from the snap and crack of the cairn flags, unable to hear the rattle of the charms in the freshening wind that blows from the south. They will say this, but their eyes will drift to the light slanting into the mountain depths, and their old blood will thrum wild and hot at the thought of turning the high songs loose again, of working a magic strong enough to pull Arissa Fallon back from the edge of death.

Her father will press his great palms to their shoulders. He will consider their words then retreat to that stark cleft in the depths of the cavern, that small room where he keeps himself, his memories, her childhood toys and her sister's cot. He'll pull forth a blunt axe and run a stone along the blade, so that the turn of the stone will fill his fingers and a cup will fill them when the stone does not. Later he will sleep and nothing will change, for now. The idea of leaving the mountain is hard. It's shaped him since he was a boy. He's freed the people in it; built a life inside it. Marching to defend it, to defend his friends, still means leaving it and putting the people inside at risk. You can't rush a decision like that, as much as Quickfish or Skinpainter might want him to.

Icecaller feels a pang of sympathy for him, but her heart and her head still pull her to the world outside. She wants to see what life is like beyond the stone, and the ice. There must be more. And she can always come back to it. Her home will always be here. The thought of staying inside these walls while the world fights for survival fills her with a peculiar kind of frustration, like a fire growing under her toes.

Still, if Crowkisser comes to the mountain, its first daughter will be there to greet her.

The hawkers press closer as she moves through the lower halls. A young boy, pale skinned and strange, thrusts himself in front of her. His hair is strung with feathers, and stream-caught pebbles. He looks the part.

She smiles wearily at him. 'Go on then, Hawkspit. What am I buying today?'

Hawkspit's eyes are wide as he digs feverishly in pockets which overflow with the dregs of prophecy, talons, bear claws, last spring's leaves. His palms are tattooed with thick black rectangles, their hearts lined red – geometrics that warn that he has seen forbidden things and been caught in the act. His eyes flick from his hands, to her face, and back.

'Icecaller. The chief sleeps?'

She laughs despite herself. 'Probably. My dad's an old bear in winter.'

She puts her palms against the side of his face. 'What do you want, Hawk? I love you but I'm in kind of a shitty mood.'

Hawkspit's hands twitch. His pupils drink in the light. The rings in his lips clack nervously. 'I had a dream, Ice. A dream all crows.'

Her hands stay on his face, her fingers against his jaw. A flicker of excitement runs electric down her spine.

She keeps her voice level. 'Tell me about it, Spit. Tell me clear and I'll see you don't have to cast chants for the rest of the week.'

Hawkspit's head bobs, his hands dipping into his pockets, fingertips trailing small white blossoms, dried and crushed. 'Really Ice? That'd be good. I don't sleep since. Can't sleep since. I dreamt a dream all crows. In all the land beyond, coming up against the walls of the mountain. And the steel in the mountain was swallowed in shadow. And the shadow grew teeth from inside itself. And then the crows were the shadows and the mountain was a nest.'

Icecaller lets her fingers drift from his sharp cheekbones down to her hips, pouting sceptically. 'That's it? Hardly inspiring as visions of doom go, Spit. You'll need to do better than that.'

Hawkspit dances back, his feet twisted inwards. He stretches his arms out to either side and, for a second, he looks like more than a scrawny, sleep-deprived kid.

'I dreamt a dream all crows, Icecaller. Crows in the heart of our mountain. Riding in on smoke and ghosts. And beneath the crows a sleeping tooth. And beneath that even, a dreaming lamb, all golden, lost and soft and bloody. And in the land outside all crows. And on the shore by the sea, a shining seed. A sea of feathers. And I cried like a baby. There was a ship on the sea, Ice. A ship that smelt of smoke and saltpetre and smoke again.' His voice grows thin, desperate, the whites of his eyes roll loose in his head. 'How can a ship sail to our mountain? How can crows live in its heart?'

Icecaller quiets her hammering heart and tips a hand at one of the stallholders. Obediently, they fill a mug with water and crush rinds between their palms, let them fall into the brew and pass it to her. She cups Hawkspit's hands gently around it.

'Here, it's OK. Sit. Drink.'

Hawkspit lowers himself into a tiled alcove like a hunted animal. His fingers are tight on her wrists. 'How, Ice? How how how how?'

She presses her forehead against his. 'It's OK, Hawk. What do we do when we're scared?'

He sips, swallows. 'We go to the still water.'

'That's right,' she says and places her lips against his. 'Breathe.'

His mouth parts and she lets air slide from her lungs into his.

He quiets quickly, the fluttering rhythm of his chest stilling into something steadier. Her heart aches for him.

She sits back with the taste of him on her mouth, tongue against teeth. 'It'll be OK, Hawk. There's a lot happens before a war. It's bound to bleed out into your dreams.' She puts a hand on his shoulder. 'I have to go see my sis. You gonna be alright for now?'

Hawk nods slowly. 'Yes, Ice. Sorry to lose it. Sorry, sorry.'

She kisses a cheek. 'We're all losing it, Spit. You're the only one who admits it.' She looks back over her shoulder as she leaves. 'Love you.'

Hawkspit smiles back at her as she heads off. He knows she's right. Knows Ice knows best. Knows his head is stupid stupid stupid full of fret and knowing and crows now, crows crows crows. Maybe he should have told her. Maybe he should have told her what happened when the seeds hatched, or when the lamb bloomed into golden light. Of the eyes that opened in the darkness below the mountain.

Maybe the eyes mean something, he thinks. Maybe the eyes are worse than the crows. He should tell Icecaller. He slips down from the alcove and starts to follow her but there are sharp things in his pockets and he needs to sort them because the order is all wrong.

As he starts laying them out, he thinks there was something that he meant to do, but he can't remember.

It doesn't matter as long as he stays still water. As long as the sharp things are nice and straight.

Keep the fret and the knowing quiet. And the mountain just a dream all crows.

60

There are no monsters, of course. Only wild things that we fail to fully comprehend. It is simply unfortunate that the further we go from civilisation, the more our comprehension fails us.

—*Memories of a Poacher, Beyond the Lickstone Wall*

Her fingers fit neatly in the small of her sister's back. She feels quick little breaths, pushing the ribs up and out. Icecaller catches stray curls of dark hair on sweaty little temples, bright and wet, and, tucks them behind a pair of reluctant ears.

'Good fight, Nigh.'

Nigh buries her nose in her sister's chest, scurries her head back and forth.

A frown. 'Did you just wipe your nose on me? Little shit.'

Nigh chuckles, her whole body shaking with glee.

'I'm going to feed you to the eagles, Nigh.' She makes her hands into eagle claws, strikes from either side of the ribs, merciless.

Her little sister squirms. A lift and a hoist and Icecaller can feel the balls of small feet drumming impatiently on her shoulders. Above, Nigh's arms are eagle wings, dipping and swooping, snatching fruits and sweets from the stalls they pass. Her sister carries herself like a prize fighter, graciously receiving the adulation of the room, dispensing high fives like favours. She smells like milk and mud and meat, little legs covered in bruises, purpling, yellowing as her toes stretch in delight.

Icecaller takes them down through the trade halls, past barrels being caulked, sealed and stored. Fish sleeping in salt beds. Great sides of bloody beef on high shelves of chill stone. Thell has never gone hungry, despite the fervent dreams of her enemies. The cool caverns beneath her feet are stacked with stores enough to feed the mountain for a year; two on thin rations.

She grips her spear tighter as they dip downwards through a practice yard, a barracks. She watches the soldiers for a moment, the shaft in her hand reverberating with memories of strikes blocked, and victories taken over years of sparring in mock battles against imagined fears. Something real is coming for them now, out of the south, on dark wings; that crow-witch at the head of her grey army.

She wonders if they'll be ready — if *she'll* be ready. Half or more of the soldiers in the mountain were born after the fall of the Empire. Most of them were like her, with only a lingering memory, something inherited and passed down. They feared it about as much as you'd fear a night hag, or an ice-witch, a bed-time story.

And yet, her father had never let them relax. Skinpainter had never let them relax. They'd drummed it into them since they were as small as Nigh. Don't disturb the cairns, don't break the skin. Do not spill the blood of a child of Thell within the mountain.

But there was obviously more to it than that. She'd seen cuts and scrapes and broken bones aplenty, had seen a severed finger once. Nothing had come for them. Something else was protecting the people here.

She prayed whatever was watching over her would keep it up.

Still, perhaps they would be OK. In front of her, warriors move back and forth with quick, practiced economy — rhythms and forms coming as easy as breath. Spears and shields interlocking and striking with precision. Her people know war, for all they fear it.

A few of the combatants lift their eyes in acknowledgement, dipping a shoulder to her as she passes. Most remain focused on their dance — blade, foot, hip and thrust.

She watches a little longer, that fire of impatience lighting under her bones again. So close to a change, to something new. She doesn't notice she's biting her lip, keeping her breath tight in her chest, until Nigh's drumming feet push her reluctantly onwards.

As they move deeper into the training grounds, she peels a strip of jerky from a pocket and passes it upwards. 'Did you fuck anyone up today?'

A wide grin. Noisy chewing.

'Did you help them afterwards?'

A nod. Small hands flutter on either side of her head.

'Good girl.'

A lick on her ear. Blown raspberries.

'Ngghhhhh, no. A little gross monster. Killer deadly gross monster.'

Nigh's feet drum happily.

They're in a wider hall now, scooped from the belly of the mountain, more or less at the centre of the training grounds on this level.

The same looming pulse of war beats here on a larger scale. Formations are practiced. Rows of spears are drawn tight against tall shields.

Those same shields are turned and locked to form metal steps, pelted up by lithe young soldiers who explode upwards in a blur to hit targets distantly, impossibly high.

The rhythm of feet on metal pounds a backbeat to the music of tattooists carving geometrics around steel and blood. Alert to torn skin, smudged lines. Ink is armour in Thell, and needs to be maintained in the same way.

Ice feels a tug on her hair. Nigh points.

Skinpainter is here, crouched like a spider over a soldier's spine, their rags and ribbons hanging low, brushing skin and muscle. They see her, nod briefly, beckon. Beneath their thick, careful fingers designs unfold, angles lifting and locking, colour blocked and shadowed. No needles here.

'Hello, Ice,' they say.

She smiles, tips Nigh forwards to pat the rags that wrap Skinpainter's head.

'Hello, killer grossmonster,' they reply.

Nigh climbs off Icecaller's shoulders and onto Skinpainter with surprising speed, twining her hands in their robes. They glance over their shoulder to watch her with eyes brightened by shadow.

'Did you defeat anyone today?'

Nigh makes a blindfold for her eyes and laughs madly.

Skinpainter hisses softly in amusement. 'And did you help them after?'

Rags become bandages wound around. A solemn nod.

The man below Skinpainter's fingers moans in pain. They push down slowly, steadily. Joints pop. Sockets are filled.

'Good, good. We bind if we break, remember. Now, let me work.'

Gently, Skinpainter grabs Nigh by the scruff of her neck and sets her to one side. A moment passes as they straighten limbs, and salve bruises. Nigh watches, bright-eyed. Catching her gaze, Skinpainter reaches forwards, taking her head in their hands. Nigh's jaw disappears into the cut of the broad, brown fingers which frame her face.

They twist her head towards the light, taking in her short shock of mountain-thistle hair, high cheekbones that catch the shadow, and a tongue that wiggles exploratorily.

'No warrior marks on you yet.' Their voice hangs in the wide air.

Behind them, feet beat on steel, the hall hot and noisy with harsh breaths.

'Would you like a warrior's mark, Nigh?'.

She shakes her head, taps on their wrists, sketches a response. For a moment, Skinpainter remembers the last time they had talked only in touch, and shivers, before looking over their shoulder. 'Ice? Translate?'

Icecaller hunkers down behind her sister, hands loose and easy on her shoulders.

Nigh turns, her lips grazing her sister's earlobes, moving fast.

Skinpainter watches them. 'Well?'

Icecaller smiles. 'She wants a monster mark, Painter.'

Skinpainter hisses again, laughter bubbling in their chest and lets their thumb rise to stroke Nigh's cheekbones. 'You're OK with that?'

Icecaller shrugs. 'She's her own snotty little person.'

Skinpainter's eyes flash in the shadow of their hood. 'So be it. Look at me, Nigh. Think of your monster. Think of its shape. Think of its fierceness. Think of its breath.'

Nigh hunkers down in her sister's lap, wriggling furiously, sharp little hip bones stabbing into Icecaller's thighs.

She grunts in pain. 'Stop torturing me and look at Painter.'

For once, Nigh does as she's told, turning her wide, dark eyes up to the hood crouched in front of her face.

'Think of its breath,' Skinpainter repeats.

Nigh holds their gaze and Icecaller, behind her, meets Skin-painter's eyes for a moment. She feels the sorcerer's breath grow slow and steady in the intervening space, watches the hairs slowly rise on their forearms as muscles dance beneath their inked skin. Watches their fingers trace steady, angular shapes on either side of her sister's head.

Tucked between her legs, Nigh goes soft like a rabbit before a snake, her head lolling.

Suddenly, Icecaller feels the weight of her sister's small body hard against her skin, as if an invisible hand was pushing them together.

Between the next inhale and the exhale, the marks appear, sharp-edged, dark against her little sister's temples. Nigh smiles softly, shows her teeth, cheeks flushed.

Skinpainter lets their hands fall. 'That's plenty for a little one, even for a little monster.' They pat her cheek. 'There we go, small fangs.'

Nigh holds a hand out towards their face. For a second, they lean in to the touch. Then from behind them, screams.

A soldier has fallen somehow, stumbled and missed a footing. The side of his face met by the sharp edge of a shield, leaving skin hanging loose, blood flowing. Not deep, but messy, his teeth surprisingly white amid it all.

The tattoos on the left side of his face sheared clean through.

447

A scratch is all that's needed.

A cold flood of fear runs through Icecaller's gut. 'Run home, Nigh,' she says, 'quick as you can.'

Her fingers tighten on the spear, as her sister disappears like a whisper, helpful hands opening paths away from the hall, deeper into the mountain. As Nigh is ushered to safety, Skinpainter moves faster than Icecaller thought possible, each step propelling them across the hall.

The screaming, bloody-faced soldier turns to meet them and is met by an open-handed slap that cracks bone.

For a second, a mist of blood hangs in the air.

For a second longer in that mist, a face, spectral, twisted, in-human. Blossoming in the blood.

Skinpainter's palm is spread wide, red and slick. The ink on their hands stretches out in thin tendrils through the drifting haze, brushing the soldier's ragged skin, holding back something that struggles to flower on the tattered edges of the wound. They step closer to the injured man, pressing ink to blood. And the people of Thell form a ring around them, shields tight, spears out.

The screaming has stopped. The wounded man is forced to his knees, face lit with horror. Spear-points rest at his back, his neck, his shoulders. And Icecaller begins to move before she can control her stupid fucking feet.

Because a scratch is all it takes, one single slip from a sweaty fucking spear.

And she's never really bought the stories until now.

As she runs, Painter's bloody fist becomes a claw lined in black ink. Their fingers hook into a mouth strung wide with terror, driving themselves down a throat that gags and struggles as Skin-painter steadies themselves astride the soldier's body. One wide hand on his windpipe, their feet planted either side of his heaving lungs.

Maybe they chant, maybe they sing. The noise that leaves their lips vibrates the air, a mess of harmonies and tones that drives the ink down off their arms and into the body below.

And underneath that buzzing song, she hears her father's voice berating her, over and over.

Don't disturb the cairns. Don't break the skin.

In her ears, something hums. In her veins, something thrums, even as her momentum carries her to the circle's edge. Inside, beyond the backs of the soldiers, the injured man is hooked to Skinpainter's hand like a fish on a bone line. He flops wildly. His eyes white and white again.

She has no time to go through the circle of shields, so she goes up and over. A hand either side of the shoulders nearest her, a strong push and she's over their heads.

The space between the spears is small. For a second, her brain screams curses as she curls into a roll that misses the spear-points by a shaved hair, and drops her next to Skinpainter's straining form.

When she lands, her breath runs ragged, her tattoos scorching a thin line of fire against her skin. She's shitting herself at how terrible an idea this is. A hairsbreadth from her widening eyes, the soldier's blood dances in the air. It shifts as Icecaller approaches and she glimpses eyes, lips, teeth; a face lined in crimson wetness.

The cold possibility that all her dad's bluster and bullshit might have been true hits her at the same time as the coppery stink of meat. Raw meat.

Underneath it, distantly, she smells cookfires. Against the odds her stomach rumbles fiercely.

Great.

Skinpainter glances at her. They are still chanting. As they chant the swirling blood is drawn to them in red drops, dragged wriggling into inky shapes, writhing across skin. Soon they are penned in, lined in solid black.

She turns slowly to look at the circle of nervous men and women, and chokes down the tremor in her voice, focuses on getting those spear-points the fuck away.

'What are you waiting for? Stitch him.'

A pair of young soldiers run off to fetch medical supplies. Another pair drag the injured man to one side. He leaves a memory behind on the stone, wet and red. Icecaller studies it as he lies curled in on himself, shivering. Blankets are brought, warm water. Herbs. And all she can think is that the myths are real. She can't deny what she's seen, as much as she wants to.

Skinpainter watches Icecaller through eyes hooded with exhaustion. They say nothing, as their blunt nails scratch at a wrist thronging with new geometrics which buzz and shift like drowsy bees.

Icecaller tries to stop the shaking that's in her legs, as she turns to check for Nigh. For a second, she can't see her, and her heart stops. Then behind her, in one of the slip tunnels, she sees Steelfinder standing warily with a familiar snot-scrap on her shoulders. She could kiss her. She will kiss her.

She has to get out of here first. She has a strange hollow feeling in her head, like she's looked too long over the edge of a cliff. As she moves to leave, she leans in close to Skinpainter. 'We bind if we break, remember?'

They catch her wrist. Their hand is rough, callused, wet with a stranger's spit and blood.

She lets herself be drawn in, watches thick lips pull back over squat teeth. 'We bind regardless,' they say. A single nail traces her pulse beneath the skin, as if searching for a second, phantom beat.

Under her fear, she feels the spark of a vague, itchy anger. How dare they keep her in the dark? Secrets upon mouldy secrets. She snatches herself free, crosses the hall. Refuses, bloody refuses to look back. Cryptic twat.

Steelfinder moves to meet her. Icecaller throws her arms around her, and buries her face in her neck; breathes, finally.

A small foot kicks her in the face.

She grunts in pain. 'You were supposed to run home, Nigh.'

Steelfinder shrugs Nigh off and onto her sister. 'I intercepted her I'm afraid. I had to check out those cool new tats.'

Icecaller smiles weakly under a raised eyebrow. 'Not tattoos. Monster marks.'

Steelfinder leans in, scrutinises the small black lines, lifts tousled hair, bends grubby ears, and ignores the furious squirming. 'So I see. Very fearsome. Very cool.'

She looks up. 'Where are you taking this monster?'

'Off to see Dad. Then I'm feeding her to the eagles.'

'Yeah, for the best. Can't have monsters running around.'

Nigh roars and swings. Steelfinder blocks the punch, catches a small fist in her hand. 'Not until they've learnt to keep their claws to themselves,' she whispers in Nigh's ear.

Icecaller runs her fingers along the back of Steel's neck. 'What are you muttering to her?'

Steelfinder bats her away. 'Monster secrets. Not for fancy mountain princesses.'

Icecaller pouts, tightens her grip, leans in. 'I'll interrogate you later.' She reaches up and slaps Nigh on the ass. 'But, we have to get going.'

She's pulled in for a goodbye that runs electric down her spine, her nails tight against the soft prickle of Steel's scalp. It drives the last of the hollow feeling from her head and for a second, she feels herself go tight and hard. 'We *have* to get going,' she mutters. 'You heartless rat.'

'That's me,' Steel grins. 'Say hi to the old bear.'

'Will do, come on, gross monster.' Icecaller runs a hand over her lips as she leaves.

Tastes sweat, sweetness, the copper of a stranger's blood.

61

The hammer is a builder's tool,
the sword for splitting bone
the spear it is a hunter's tool
for feeding hearth and home
yet every weapon ever made
is united by one spark
it is the hope that fits our hand
when there's terror in the dark

—*Little Rhymes for Little Monsters*

In the dark of the mountain, the Kinghammer moves.

Slow, heavy strokes, his wrists turning the weight of the weapon.

The tiled floor of the sparring circle bright under his feet.

What the hammer meets, it breaks.

The air is thick with splinters.

His feet shift his hips through the stances.

The weight of the body, the weight of the weapon.

The depths resound with the sound of movement.

Cold sweat hanging on her brow, Icecaller stands beneath the curve of an arch and feels the blows in her breastbone.

She watches her father move in killing ways, the flat planes of his shoulders tectonic under muscle.

His spine is a map of shattered geometries, sundered glaciers, deep flows and high peaks.

The hammer pulls him. He is the centre of its orbit.

His breath moves his body like a bellows, drags the steel in thick arcs. A shield breaks. A hapless sparring partner is sent staggering into shadow.

Tattoos align in the half-light.

At the edges of the sparring circle, familiar faces watch.

The message is clear. War is coming and Thell is ready. Quick-fish is getting what he wants – the decision has been made.

Icecaller can feel it ringing out with each hammer blow, resonating in the hearts of the onlookers. She wonders if they feel it as deeply as she does.

A warm glow of pride lights in her at the sight of her father, still strong, still unafraid. Someone for the mountain to rally around, someone for her to lean on.

Not all members of her family seem to feel that way. Atop her shoulders, Nigh shifts restlessly. The loops of the hammer can't hold her interest. Icecaller looks around for a suitable distraction.

She spies some likely candidates in the corner, leaning wearily against one other. Her new favourite drips.

Quickfish's dandelion-shock hair struggles with the air down here, and Roofkeeper's neatly clipped beard is starting to run at the edges.

She threads her way through the crowd, pushed and pulled by the current of hammer blows, buffeted by the jostle of shoulders as Kinghammer's most ardent fans vie for room. The pair see her coming and make space.

She slings a leg over a low bench, 'Carpenter, spunkpocket.' A lazy smile. 'How you finding it down in the depths? Adjusting?'

Quickfish glances at the ring, the slow loops of the hammer. 'Some things aren't so different here, truth be told.'

She shoots him a look. 'I suppose you'd know something about showy fathers.'

Fallon's son grins at that, and Roofkeeper elbows him pointedly. Behind them the crowd cheers. Icecaller picks her teeth for a moment, then dumps Nigh onto the table. 'You remember my sister. Somehow worse than me?'

Nigh beams beatifically at the young men, scratches intently at a scab on her knee.

Quickfish smiles at her. 'Hello again, little Icecaller.'

She grins up at him, and excavates her nose in search of something promising.

Icecaller ruffles her hair. 'So, solved any mysteries? Made any plans? Anyone actually got off their arse to help yet? Or has it all just been hot air?'

The room shakes to a thunderous crack and another cheer goes up. A block of stone is split in two. Kinghammer flexes, turns, pushes the pulse of the mountain.

Roofkeeper winces. 'Not really. It's been good to just stop moving for a while. Catch our breath, get our thoughts . . .'

'Have some sex,' she interjects, sniggering.

Roofkeeper lets his fingers run through Quickfish's hair. 'Maybe there was some of that. Not up to Thell standards, I'm sure.'

'We're a mountain of hot cunts,' Icecaller agrees, nodding amiably.

Quickfish reaches out, tucks Nigh's tunic hems. Amazingly, he's left with all his fingers. 'I don't know what I thought, originally. Perhaps that we could send some aid to Hesper. Some help for my father. Or that Skinpainter would cook up some way of bringing my mother back, neat and easy. But there's more going on than that, isn't there? We're running out of time.'

Icecaller blinks, tearing her eyes away from his surviving digits. Nigh has cooried up happily against him, her fingers picking at the buttons of his shirt. She presses her lips together, no point sugarcoating it. 'That's the truth. Word is, Crowkisser's on the march. Chasing after your pretty little bones has set her eyes square on Thell. And we're split up the crack trying to decide how to deal with her. We don't fight so well away from the mountain.' She runs fingers through her hair. 'My head sweats at the thought of fighting here though. Which is what we'll end up doing if Skinpainter decides to help your drowsy mum.' She picks dirt out of a nail and looks at both of them with a flat stare. 'This isn't going to be a safe place for you for much longer. And I think Skinpainter's got bigger fish to fry than just your mother.'

She sees his face fall, and raises a hand. 'I don't mean to be cruel, but we need to get the crow-witch away from our gates before we can start cleaning up her mess.'

Surprising herself, she reaches out, and catches his wrist. 'You know that no one's *ever* come back from having their name torn out, right? Not when the witch has done it personally. Painter told me it's different to whatever she did down in the south. More brutal, less planned.'

Quickfish's face wavers, and she sees him fighting the tears. When he bites them back, her heart gets a little bit warmer towards him.

'I'm not quite ready to give up on her yet.'

She smiles sadly. 'I understand, but you're really going to be in danger if you stay here. If we march out to bloody her nose, we can't protect you. And if she catches you here, you'll be trapped inside with the rest of us. Win or lose.'

Quickfish nods, 'I know, I know. We've been thinking on it.'

She raises an eyebrow. 'And?'

'We don't want to stay in the mountain,' He looks at Roofkeeper.

Roofkeeper mimes with his fingers. 'We want to go beyond it. To the spires. To see if the stories are true. If the magic does linger there. In case Skinpainter can't . . .'

Another crash, another cheer. The bench bows alarmingly as her father bulls his way through and sits next to her, all sweat and steel.

She raises a finger at Roofkeeper. 'Hold that thought.' Turns to her dad. 'Hello. You smell like shit.'

He grins, drapes an arm around her. 'Take a good whiff, dearest.'

A slim young man brings drinks and Kinghammer swallows deep. 'Making friends, Quickfish'? He jabs a finger at Nigh, who is snoring contentedly in the crook of an arm.

Quickfish grins. 'Guess I am. Always been good with kids.'

Kinghammer wipes foam from his lip. 'Teach me your secrets.' He looks at Icecaller. 'Travel back in time and teach me your secrets.'

Quickfish laughs. 'I'm not really the person to ask.'

Kinghammer sips, eyes him over the rim. 'From what I've heard, if anyone's the expert on difficult fathers, it's you.'

Quickfish shrugs. 'Dad's not difficult so long as he's in motion.' He shoots a glance at Icecaller, and she hides a smile behind her hand.

Kinghammer pops his knuckles one by one. 'Is he surviving down there in Hesper? I was down there once or twice after the war. Before the south. It's a nest. A big nest that was rich on southern trade.' Another sip, a raised eyebrow that mirrors his daughter. 'What's to trade now the south is gone?'

Quickfish taps his fingers thoughtfully. 'More than you'd think. We get a lot in from the Midlands. Grain and hedge-trade. Charcoal for the forges, wood, feather, artefacts. Had fish and spice and stone from Astic before it . . .' He wiggles his fingers expressively, takes a drink, sucks his teeth. Roofkeeper's toes nudge his under the table. He taps back reassuringly.

Kinghammer leans forwards. 'Before it fell. Say it, kid. You have to own death.'

Roofkeeper looks down.

'Got something to add, boy?'

Roofkeeper nods.

'Well?' The tankard sloshes expansively.

'They're not dead.' Slowly, almost as if he's figuring out the words as he says them. 'They're not dead. Well, of course, some of them are. The ones that fought Crowkisser, the ones that re-sisted. But most of the folks in Astic are alive. Most of them are marching for her. *Following* her.'

Kinghammer snorts. 'Weak. They might as well be dead. What have they got left once she's done with them? What have they got to believe in? She gutted the damn gods. Split the hosts in the temple from crown to crack and read stories from their bones. What have those poor fools got to believe in?'

Roofkeeper scratches his beard. 'They've got her.'

Kinghammer sketches a sign over his lips. Spits. 'Her. That's the fucking problem. Take her out of the equation and you could go home.' He shoots a glance at Quickfish. 'Take her out of the equation and Skinpainter could set their mind on tending to your mother, rather than reading the wind for every hint of the witch's blood-damned plans.'

Icecaller catches Quickfish's eye, mouths something indecipherable. It looks almost like an apology.

Kinghammer barely notices. 'But of course, she has him.' The handle of the tankard twists and bends. '*Slickwalker*. What I wouldn't give to have that little ratshit on the anvil.'

Icecaller snorts. 'Oh, Dad. Always the way, isn't it? Hammer it hard 'til it's done with. Enemies, metal, women.'

Kinghammer stands and Quickfish remembers again just how *big* Icecaller's father is. For a long moment, he looks furious. Then his face is split by a huge grin. He scoops Icecaller up in his arms. 'You are a *vile* child.'

Two steps take him onto the table, scattering cups. 'Look,' he booms to the assembled crowd. 'Look at my *vile* offspring.' Icecaller beams from her perch in his arms. 'Look at this ungrateful wretch. What shall we do with her?'

The crowd's response is loud, enthusiastic, uncoordinated. Half of them still high on the blood and thunder of the fight.

In Quickfish's arms, Nigh stirs, presses his face to hers with a small palm, gestures emphatically on his cheeks and chest. Quickfish chuckles, pulls Roofkeeper in with his free arm and whispers to him. Roofkeeper pauses, stifles a laugh, and nods.

'What shall be done with her?' bellows Kinghammer.

'Hesper has a suggestion!' yells Roofkeeper.

The room goes quiet.

Kinghammer turns slowly to face Roofkeeper, kneeling until he holds the limp Icecaller at eye-level. She winks.

With deadpan sincerity Roofkeeper points to Quickfish. 'I defer to the noble lord's son.'

Kinghammer looks over his shoulder, playing to the crowd. 'Shall we hear what the Son of Fallon has to say?

The cheers are deafening. Crockery smashes. Hands beat on walls, shields.

Quickfish beckons Kinghammer in and whispers in one massive ear.

The laughter starts in Kinghammer's chest even before he stands. Shaking with mirth, he turns to the crowd and lifts his daughter above his head as he screams, 'Feed her to the eagles!'

The hands of the people of Thell rise like talons and welcome Icecaller as she falls.

62

the high call of the curlew
the sound of the sea carried over land
salt cradled within beating bone

—*What Is Born Beyond Blades*, Heartshamer

Three leagues out from the coast now, heading back towards Hesper. The ship emptied of refugees and filled with nothing but the creak of rope and the crack of canvas. The Shipwright and the Shroudweaver have been set ashore, and this old golden wreck is swaying home to Hesper under Ropecharmer's command. She'd made good time. The sea pulled to dark grey under the stern. The whole ocean stepped in bands of colour, something to do with the corals or the land underneath. He forgets. All the seas were land once, he'd been told, thrown up by fire and shifting. Hard to believe. He didn't really understand it.

Not like the drowned cities inland, in the Hollows. Their towers and chapels still visible clear as day, the torn roofs of their byres wracked by bubbling tones as their pasture bells tolled in slow deep currents, their coppered sides stroked by thick black fish with rot-green eyes and short teeth, blunted and cankered from decades cracking the bones of the dead and drowned.

The drowned cities had been pushed down by men, by clever men and women damming rivers and hewing logs, making clever cuts that pent the water like stallions. Come the signal, the props were cut, and walls of white water were unleashed with a shriek that shook the earth, tearing rock and ground loose, bending and snapping the tops of forests.

With arms raised, those clever men and women took the sound of the roaring waters and tied it to the sounds of life below; to

459

the tolling of bells and, eventually, to screams. It was said that the folk of the Hollows had time to take one deep breath before the wave hit, before their worlds turned to blue and they promised their bones to black fish; before the wrath of the Belltollers struck.

Ropecharmer had asked his mother and father why the cities of the Hollows had been drowned. That was years ago, out on the lakes that covered those lost villages, when he was younger and terrified, watching the swell of their small boat as it was pushed by the heavy curves of those black fish.

'Why?' he had asked, wide-eyed, watching slime slip off black scales.

'Because of the bladedrinkers,' his father had said, his mother nodding solemnly as she swung a barbed hatchet down into the water.

Get enough hooks in and you could lift a fish bodily and plunge a knife into its grey belly, timing your cuts with the pulses of its breath to carve into the first stomach, avoiding the shit and silt of the second.

'Because of the bladedrinkers,' they'd said, but they'd pulled out children's fingerbones along with the rings and teeth. They didn't eat the fishes' flesh.

They'd only had to visit the Hollows over two summers, before his father got boat-trade and his mother was taken back as a cutter, once the ban was lifted. Of course, once their names were taken, they'd stopped working altogether. Crowkisser had scooped them out, left them by the fire, blank-eyed and slack-jawed – still holding hands, fingers gathering with dripped spit.

He'd kept to shipwork, learnt the rope trade, splitting, weaving and binding, strong threads and snap threads. Met Coglifter that way, selling fast-light and stop-light down in the Gutmarket, watching her busy fingers pick and sort and dismiss. Struck up a friendship that was based on cheap deals and cheap booze initially, that became something more when she designed harnesses to keep his parents upright, to lift and turn them at set hours, so they wouldn't choke on their own mucus, so he could work without hearing wet, rattling gasps in the back of his head. She'd helped him bury them too, in clean fresh linen he never could have afforded, their heads tended with meadow-flowers, forever looking out over the cliffs and the sea.

Afterwards she brought him food in glass that somehow stayed hot long past firing. So he ate. She cracked bottles and told him tales of her husbands, wives and lovers. So he drank. She sat a chair by the door and lit a pipe, so he slept. And day after sifted day he fell back into himself. Learnt a little of her trade – the locks and glasses, the acids and tapers. Learnt a little of her thoughts, of what kept the low from the high, and how power moved in the world. Took messages for her when the ships sailed, and brought them to her in her workshop, where she read and nodded and stamped and sealed.

When that last refuge was consumed by fire he had helped her move, dried her tears as she sifted the ash and pretended he'd never seen them. He rigged a rope strong enough to haul a safe the weight of four men up into the Grey Towers, into Fallon's care or perhaps his wife's, before she fell to the Crowkisser.

He'd set that safe on a solid stone and left Coglifter to gather in messages from shore as well as sea; dark-eyed farmers on light-laden carts, weary soldiers with secrets bound between their breasts, toll collectors and tithers, ragged, tattered mendicants and even a grey, tall man, who sounded Barrowlands but walked like Astic. They all seemed to know her, and in return she read and nodded and stamped and sealed. He kept to the ropes, splitting, weaving and binding. Made something that looked like a life.

When the ship arrived in the harbour, he'd felt his heart lift like a hill-bird. Walked the dock to meet its master and saw her at once, a barrel on one shoulder and a sack over the other. Looking at him like the whole hurling hustle of the docks was just canvas.

'You're going to fix her ropes,' she'd said. 'we've come further than we meant.'

He looked down at his hands and saw the rope coiled in them, ready. Behind her the ship had hung like melted bronze on a salting sea. He could taste strangeness on his tongue.

Only seconds had held him back. He'd raced back to Cog and

of course she'd listened and nodded and smiled, given him a seal and a package and dropped some words into his ear that sizzled like stones in a fire. Then he'd hared it back to the docks where Shipwright was waiting with a jug of ale and a raised eyebrow.

He'd smiled at her and that was that. He joined a crew where he played two roles, and kept so many faces he could barely find his own.

Years now, doubling his life. Half lived under sail, half on land. Half at the Shipwright's side as the salt from the sea hit the light of the sun. Half under Coglifter's hand, carrying whispers up and down the coast. Building a web for her to keep the ordinary folk safe, to make sure Crowkisser and her kind would fade into the deep, to make sure no one like her would ever come again. To put an end to hillside graves, and the hollow of wars filled with black fish.

63

we are all little lights
but what a pleasure, what a wonder
to burn so wildly before the greater dark

—Memorial inscription, west shore of the Hollows

The snow still clings to the grass here. Crystals tight against stunted blades, the earth pockmarked with the tunnels of tundra voles, humped by the broader flanks of the first cairns of the Barrowlands.

The earth continued to give up its dead. Shroudweaver stops, digging his fingers into the hard soil, finds some roots and pulls.

Mired amid the thin white strands, clumped in the dark, hangs something that might once have been a wedding band, around something that was definitely once a finger.

He turns to Shipwright, wags the plant disconsolately.

She twists her lips. 'We'll need something a little fresher for dinner.'

He laughs, turns the bone against the pale spring light. 'You might be right.'

She puts her arm around him. 'Remember eating? I'd like you to do that. This extra gaunt look isn't doing it for me.'

Shroudweaver tries to strike a pose, slips. She catches him with both an arm and a meaningful look.

He steadies himself against her. 'OK, point taken. I think we only have a night or two before we reach Thell anyway. I'd rather not do that on an empty stomach.'

'Good,' she kisses his cheek. 'Although, we might not want to look too appetising.'

He groans. 'Please keep that to yourself when we arrive.'

She laughs. 'Isn't that why you keep me around? Shit jokes and great sex?'

'No, it's because you have load-bearing shoulders and you can tell port from starboard.'

He looks around from the top of the outcrop. The black spike of the Burners' woods to the east, the Barrowlands before them, the Midlands behind and Thell on the horizon like a hangover. 'Not that that's much use out here.'

Shipwright nods, wriggles her pack onto her shoulders, stamps her boots. 'It's the worry, isn't it? It's literally eating you.'

Shroudweaver turns his shoulders against the horizon. 'It's not that bad. I'm just fretting about what we'll find. About what we're risking. What I'm risking.'

She raises a sceptical eyebrow. 'Not that bad? I can see the light through you. You need rest. Some food that isn't a herb. Something with fat and life in it.'

He turns, steps gingerly down the slope towards her. 'You're right. I'm hard work just now. Don't think I don't know. But unbinding the dead could destroy so much. Everyone in Thell. Everyone outside. You, me . . .'

He trails off.

'Crowkisser,' she finishes.

He nods.

She strokes the sides of his face. The rough grey hairs that have grown in over the past few weeks. His skin is looser, sallow from lack sleep and his eyes are like smudged pits.

'We could save a lot of lives too. If we stall her at Thell, we can finally stop jumping at our shadows. We can come up with some plans instead of chasing down every move she makes.'

He nods, shivers.

'I just—' he shrugs, rolling his shoulders awkwardly. 'It's all on me. I'm the only one that can do this. If I don't do it right . . .'

She kisses his forehead gently. 'You'll do it right.'

He leans into her lips. 'If I don't.' Stops, clears the tremor in his throat. 'If I don't, you'll have to deal with me.'

She bites down on the flutter of fear that comes in response to that. 'I deal with you every day.'

He smiles. Even now, she can make him smile. A little victory.

Taking her hands in his, he runs his fingers over her knuckles. 'You know there'll be a composite. Like the god in Hesper. But bigger, much bigger. And loose.'

She grips him tighter, feels the old burns from powder, rope and thread. Scars of the trade. 'Loose? I thought . . .'

'That they needed to be inside someone?' He shakes his head softly, shivers again. 'We were always taught that, it was Aestering law, almost. You never bind, you never create outside of blood and bone. So they said.' He tucks into the crook of her arm, and she pulls her cloak over his shoulders to keep off the worst of the wind.

'They? The teachers at the Aestering?'

He nods. 'The other weavers. The older weavers.'

'Nothing outside of blood and bone,' he murmurs, and touches a hand to his chest. The dead still silted around his heart, still just barely held by Smokesister's rituals.

'Well, you fucked that one up,' Shipwright snorts.

He smiles at her, stifles a laugh. 'Wait until you hear my next confession.'

She rolls her eyes. 'When did I get appointed your counsellor?'

He pulls her arm tighter around his shoulders and kisses the tips of her fingers. 'You're never supposed to weave a composite alone.'

She stops walking then, turns to face him fully. 'Oh, another broken rule.' He tenses for a second, until she laughs, and kisses his cheek. 'I didn't realise I was sleeping with a *rebel*.'

He chuckles too, in relief. 'It's more complicated than that.'

Shipwright looks at him wryly. 'Colour me unconvinced.'

They follow the lee of the hill down to where their remaining horse lingers resentfully in the wind. Shroudweaver leans gratefully into its warm flank.

'Let me try and explain.'

'One minute,' Shipwright says, unhitching the horse. 'I'm

going to lead him for a bit. He's had enough for one day.'

He looks at her oddly and she sticks out her tongue. 'It's not all about you, love.'

They pick their way between the rising humps of the Barrow-lands, many of them untended this far out, fallen to ruin, or half-ruin, the grass high on their crowns and the stones loose over the graves beneath.

Shipwright feeds the horse some fruit, picking the berries slowly out of her hand and offering them to its eager lips. 'Explain then. We've got a while yet to go.'

Shroudweaver tends the horse, keeping it steady on the thin, tumbled roads that wind behind the larger green barrows; a mess of rock chips and old bone, broken grave markers and long-rotted flags.

When he talks across its nose to her, the horse's ears prick up, and he wonders if it's learning.

'OK, so. To understand composites, you have to understand souls, and the gods. We always believed that they were basically the same thing. That gods were just big, old lumps of souls that got clever and sentient a long time ago. Impossibly perfect composites, if you believe what the hosts used to say. My wife used to think so.' He shoots Shipwright a look, but neither she nor the horse responds.

'If you follow that logic, souls are like little gods. Or god-fragments. We're not sure. Pieces of something that could be divine. Shroudweavers, we can take those souls, and use them. If I snare one of those fragments, coax it, let it wick along the outstretched thread of my will, guide it with the red thread and the silver, it'll spark into something much stronger, for just a little while. A small god.'

'Lit from somebody's soul,' Shipwright replies.

He nods gravely. 'That's the cost of it. Weaving destroys the soul. It's burnt out like a candle flame, like waxed paper.' His face is wistful. 'The things we can do, though.'

His hands absently move through the motions. 'I've woven that light into bodies, to make them faster and stronger. I've made the sails of a boat leap and the blade of a sword sing with bright, howling speed. All kinds of tiny ascensions.'

Shipwright scratches the horse's ear. 'It sounds like the stuff of stories. By which I mean, horseshit.'

Shroudweaver smiles shyly. 'It's incredibly powerful. And utterly unsustainable. Every one of those little stabs at godhood – the sheer fire of them burns up their source, a person's soul.'

He lifts a leg carefully over a tilted stone. 'At the Aestering, we were raised as caretakers. We're supposed to protect people, protect their souls. We only weave like this in the most desperate circumstances.'

'You weave like that a lot,' Shipwright says, and her tone is wary.

'The last twenty years have been one big desperate circumstance,' he replies. 'Besides, it gets easier.'

They crest another small rise, and Shipwright clucks gently at the horse, who's getting skittish in the gathering dusk. 'I'm not sure that's a good thing.'

Shroudweaver follows, a pale ghost against the setting sun. 'Neither am I. That's why I prefer composites. The effort they take. The skill. It's not something you do lightly.'

She hums thoughtfully. 'So why not just use them all the time?'

His voice comes down from the slope of a barrow. 'Because we're building gods, basically. Clumsy, malformed gods. But gods nonetheless. If souls are just fragments of gods, and composites are woven from souls, then what else do you call the end result?'

She frowns. 'But they're not like the old gods?'

He skids down the side of the hill to join her, pebbles bouncing. 'No, something simpler about them. Something missing. We might just be bad creators. Or there might be a level of craft we can't hope to reach. That's getting a bit too abstract anyway. All this stuff has very real consequences.'

He points out over the Barrowlands. In the gathering dark, small lights kindle haphazardly across the skyline. 'See those fires? They're lighting them against the dead. We're still so scared of it all. And composites are something to be scared of. We were always taught that they needed a vessel. A human body.' He shoots her a pained look. 'But they alter the person that receives them. Placing souls inside someone can change them, permanently, if it goes on too long. All those little shards of god-power stick inside you, like burrs from a hedgerow. We used to think they left hooks for the real gods to get in. To alter your thoughts, your behaviour. It's why the Aestering hated hosts so much. We didn't understand them. We still don't.'

Shipwright picks a stone out the sole of her boot. 'What happens with composites now? Now the gods are dead?'

Shroudweaver shrugs. 'I have absolutely no idea.'

She snorts. 'That's reassuring.'

He pats her on the shoulder. 'The simpler solution, it seems to me, is to take people out of the equation completely. To weave a composite with no body, no vessel, just will. If I could bind all the souls in here' – he taps his chest – 'with all the dead of the Barrowlands, for *just* long enough, I could take out Crowkisser.'

'Take her out?' Shipwright's voice is steadier than she feels.

'Incapacitate her, I hope. I can't think of anything more powerful.' His voice drops, slinks low around the cooling barrow stones. 'I don't want to kill her, Ship.'

'I know love,' she says. 'But this sounds dangerous.' Are you sure there's not a better way? She bites her lip. 'I could do it again, for you. If that's what needed. I could hold the composite.' Even as she says it, her heart lurches with terror, and her lips grow sticky with spice.

He watches her closely, and she can see him run the numbers before he shakes his head. 'Dropping that many souls into someone would change them so profoundly they'd never come back. I could never do that to you. I can't have that on my conscience. There's enough roosting in there as it is.'

He takes her hand again, his eyes bright in the failing light. 'I can do this. Trust me. I'm the best weaver there is. I can do it.'

She squeezes his fingers and chokes down the sadness sitting in her chest. 'You're the only weaver there is.' She holds his gaze for a second, before she looks away. 'What other choice do I have?'

He kisses her softly. 'Well, if I'm wrong, none of us will be around to regret it.'

They stop for a moment, and he leans his back against a way marker, his fingers tracing the carvings. 'Would you look at that? Less than fifty miles now.'

Shipwright nods. 'We're close, but we won't make it before nightfall. The sun's tiring and I'm not keen to travel through the night out here.'

Shroudweaver nods. 'Me either.' He scans the horizon, sighing wearily. 'Can you believe it? Burials as far as the eye can see. No wonder I'm blue. Still, there's a lot of forest out here. Beyond the hills. Not that far away. I'd like to see it sometime.'

Her heart warms a little at that. 'I could take you,' she says. 'I have friends there.'

He grins. 'That'll be our post-catastrophe vacation, will it?'

She tweaks his ear. 'You got it, hot stuff. And maybe after that, somewhere by the sea. Or on it.'

'Either's fine, as long as you're there,' he says, and leans into her.

She's quiet for a spell, as they press on in the last scraps of light, trying to imagine what the future might feel like.

'Do you miss the ship?' he asks, eventually.

She looks at him. 'Only like a limb.'

The driving wind pushes her hair forwards over the angular planes of her face and feeds him strands of his own. He coughs.

'Do you want me to take any of that?' She gestures at his pack, hung with the bones and thread of his trade. Weavers travelled as light as they could, but that wasn't saying much.

'No, I'm good. We won't be walking for much longer.'

She studies the horizon. 'It's getting late, and cold. There's ruins down there, maybe a few miles off. Should get us out of the wind at least. Away from those creepy fires.'

They're there inside an hour, setting up inside the scoured courtyard of a squat tower attached to a number of curved, low-slung buildings that might once have been byres.

The soft glow of a fire on the stones dries out his clothes and a tarp strung between the corners puts an end to the teeth of the

469

wind. The small horse is staked out gratefully with some dry grass and a blanket over its back.

A little of the chill fades from his bones. A little of the weariness from his soul follows it.

Shipwright sits next to him, working her boots from her feet, rubbing the life back into them.

'Here,' Shroudweaver says, patting his lap. She moves them over and he sets to, his fingers tracing calluses and curves.

She sighs happily. 'Now I really know how you bring the dead back to life.'

He shoots her a look. 'A bad place for that kind of chat.'

She kicks to remind him to keep working. 'Why?'

'I'll show you once your socks are on.'

A little later, he hangs the soup over the fire, and pulls a lit branch gingerly out of the larger logs.

Shipwright sits close to the flames, her fingers working over something brass which spins and clicks.

'Come on,' he smiles. 'I'll give you the tour before dinner.'

She grins up at him. 'Give me a kiss before that and you're on.'

He pulls Shipwright to her feet, and presses himself against her. She can taste the desire on the edge of his lips.

'If we keep this up, I'm going to bed hungry and uneducated,' she mutters. 'Plus, you're getting cinders in my hair.'

Shroudweaver steps back. 'Romance is dead,' he intones. 'In its place, we present history.' He moves the torch closer to the outer wall, past a series of small regular hollows. 'See, here, bread ovens. Set around the edge of the house to heat it all evenly. The warmth would have been channelled down through tiles.' He points at her feet. She scuffs experimentally and something clinks.

'Hah, I knew it.' He pulls her back towards the fire. 'Here, living quarters. You see the outlines? Sleeping quarters over there.'

Shipwright turns, waves her arms up at the tower. 'And this?'

He frowns. 'I'm not sure. A watchtower, probably. Times gone by, you'd want eyes on the north. On the forest too probably.'

She watches him explain the finer details, eyes alight.

'Here, a well,' he says, 'and here, if you dug, the midden.' His fingers linger on a wall, a brick scratched with marks. It pulls loose with a little knife work.

In the hollow behind they find some ancient coins, stones worn smooth by the wind. Something that might have been a bracelet once. A cat collar.

She stands behind him as he turns them over slowly in his hands.

He looks up at her. 'So many generations before us.' A soft smile. 'Isn't it a relief?'

She puts an arm around his shoulders. 'I don't know. I'm quite fond of this generation. It has us.'

Shroudweaver leans into the curve of her. 'True. Lucky.'

Her fingers trace the hard lines of his skull as the wind blows down from the sleeping barrows. 'Thell tomorrow?'

He nods. 'Thell tomorrow.'

Shipwright furrows her brow, and harrows a hand through his hair to pick out windblown seeds, hooked as claws. 'And after that, what's the plan?'

Shroudweaver's voice is soft. 'First, we speak to Skinpainter. Get a handle on the situation.'

She works at a particularly stubborn burr. 'And after that?'

'We wait for Crowkisser to come to us. We can't match her on the field, but if I can get her out onto the Barrowlands, we have the advantage.'

'Because of Skinpainter?'

He nods. 'A little. Because of the mountain, and the dead.'

Her fingers stop working. 'And then you're going to try raise a god. One of those composites. Without a vessel. Uncontained.'

He demurs. 'If it comes to that.'

She tilts his head towards her. 'You know it'll come to that,' she says, and there's a shake in her voice. It feels good to say it though, to look it in the eye.

He takes her hands. 'I know it's not ideal, but like I said, we need something big. Bigger than ever before. A deterrent.'

She resumes stroking his hair. 'Because your daughter is so easily deterred.' She sighs, 'I'm sorry, it's just . . . not exactly a neat solution is it?'

He takes the tips of her fingers, squeezes them. 'No such thing as neat solutions.'

She kisses the crown of his head. 'They died in the south, that's what you mean.'

He wriggles his shoulders downwards, settling into the cool grass at her feet. 'If I can unbind the dead, weave them into a composite, even for a few moments, we give Thell a weapon Crowkisser can't fathom. With a little luck she'll struggle to match us, no matter what she has up her sleeve.' He picks blades of grass, splits them with a thumb. 'If we can make it too expensive for her to lay siege, she'll have to rethink. And she can't stay penned in the south forever. The land won't support it indefinitely. She'll starve.'

Shipwright flops down onto her belly, her face close to the fire. 'You mean expensive in bodies, don't you? That scares the shit out of me.'

He splits the blades again. 'It's what she understands. Raw power. It's what'll stop her. She cares about her people.'

Shipwright raises an eyebrow. 'How do you know that?'

Shroudweaver twists his lips. 'Why else try to eke out a living in the south, why not throw everyone at Hesper straight away? Damn the cost? She wants her people alive, and she wants the people of Thell alive.' He sucks his teeth. 'Mostly.'

Shipwright runs her hands through her hair, half-heartedly twisting braids. 'That's an awfully thin assumption to stake this on.'

'I know my daughter, Ship.'

'You *knew* your daughter. How many years since you were both together?'

'Twenty. Twenty-one, though that cuts my heart to say it. Even if I hadn't seen her for a hundred though, I'd know she hasn't changed. She's still clinging on to what she cares about. Regardless of the cost.'

Shipwright frowns. 'How can you know that for sure, Shroud?' It's hard to keep the frustration out her voice.

He splits the grass down to the base, loses it into the earth.

'Because I'm still alive.'

64

Little larks. Tongues of the same. A scattering of hillsheaf. A quart of clear water. The darker berries from beneath the hill. Two hours over a low flame.

—*Good Food for Bad Work*, Coglifter

A day later. Dregs of soup in the pot. Not her finest batch, but it's calmed her down enough to talk about this shit with a full stomach. Hollow blood made her panicky. More panicky. And it was already a panicky topic.

Shipwright clears her throat. 'So, even if we do break Kisser at Thell, what then?'

Shroudweaver laughs. His hands are busy, working small rounds of dough on a flat stone, scattering the tops with seeds, ready to bed down over the embers of the fire.

'Good evening to you too. Small talk out the window then?'

She glares at him, sluicing the pot and tipping it into the grass.

'I've been wrestling a seaspit stomach since you brought this up. Humour me.'

He levers himself up slowly, painfully, feeling the old tightness in his legs again. She can see the stoop in his tendons pulling down his whole body. The road's hard on him.

'Ideally, we capture her. The composite should just hammer her to knees. Along with whatever and whoever she's brought with her.'

Shipwright breathes in slowly. 'So this depends on you raising something more powerful than Crowkisser. Oh. Good. From what I've heard about her since the south fell, that'll be impressive.'

He smiles narrowly. 'I suspect at least some of that is rumour feeding on rumour. She's smart, but young. Power takes time. Always.' He pauses. 'Do you want to get your boots?'

She shoots him a look. 'What?'

'Do you want to get your boots?'

'Why would I want to do that?'

'Because this scares you. And you're happier when you're working on them.'

Shipwright's silent for a minute, jaw muscles working. 'You . . . *ugh.*'

She turns, reaches to unhook them from her kitbag. 'Not a word.' She gets her kit, sets it out neat – boots, rag, polish to keep the rain off – dips the cloth in and sets to.

'Socks could use work too, judging by the state of those toes.'

'Shut it.'

He shuffles next to her, stretches out a hand. 'Give one over then.'

He shoves his wrist inside, coats the cloth and gets to work. 'I can control it. I know I can.' His voice is low, tentative.

She buffs, turns the boot. The moon's an odd one tonight, buttered by rising clouds of summer pollen.

'I'm not saying you can't, but it seems very *final.*'

His nod is curt. 'It has to be, I think. If we don't knock her down hard, she's going to bring to bear whatever tricks she has to hand.'

Shipwright stops, digs in her pack, pops a twist of something fibrous in her mouth. 'And we don't know what those tricks might be?'

Shroudweaver keeps working, the boot buckles chiming softly. 'Not really. I could hazard a guess.'

She chews, shuffles the clump around her mouth with a thumb. 'Go on then. Not like I'm scared witless already.'

He smiles softly. 'Course not.'

He sets the boot down, counts the options off on his fingers.

'Easier to say what they aren't, maybe. Not shroudweaving. She never had the patience for it.' He laughs. 'Never had patience at all.'

Shipwright spits. 'That's not as charming as you think, Shroud. We don't all have the luxury of being her father to keep us safe.'

He holds up a finger. 'Still. Not shroudweaving.'

'Not spinner magic either,' she interjects.

He looks at her. 'No?'

'Definitely not. Not personal enough, not local enough. Whatever magic Kisser's using, she's doing it over miles *and* to herself. Spinners don't work like that. You stick 'em, one or two at a time on people or things. To make a network, or to make one big enough to push the kind of magic she's using?' Shipwright shakes her head. 'Not going to happen. If we ever knew how to do that, we don't now.'

'Plus,' she says, wriggling a sock off, 'Running them for too long on living stuff? There's consequences. Frays things down. You can gallop a horse, but you can't gallop it a thousand miles without its heart going off. Same thing.'

Shroudweaver watches the sock, the sudden appearance of needle and thread. 'I didn't mean you had to do those now.'

She ties off with her teeth, looks at him over the knot. 'No time like the present.'

'Yeah,' he says, 'but . . .'

'But what?' she glowers, her face stark in the firelight.

'You should really just let that pair die.'

She growls. 'They're not the only old, frayed things I could just let die. You watch it.'

Shroudweaver picks the boot back up. 'Ouch. We could get you new ones.'

'Oh, they do good ship socks in 'T hell, do they?' she asks, a spark in her eyes.

'They might do.'

She jabs the needle at him. 'You only counted off one murderous magical option. Stop stalling me. We need to list all the horrifying possibilities. There's still a risk I'll sleep tonight.'

He sets the boot down again, uselessly. 'OK, not shroudweaving, not spinner magic. I don't think it's host magic either, never had a whiff of the gold around her. And she wouldn't touch it after her mother.'

No quips this time. Shipwright nods, moves a little closer. 'So *what* then?'

He shoots a glance at her. 'I can hear you chewing that rubbish.'

She spits into the fire, grins with teeth beetle-red.

'Keep me awake for nights on end in ways that don't involve kissing and I'll cope however I want.'

He sighs. 'It's just a bit . . .'

She leans in, pulls a sticky strand out of her front teeth.

'Distracting? So's wondering if you're going to die in front of that fucking bone mountain. Stop stalling.'

'I hate you.'

'No you don't. *Thoughts.*'

He waves his hand. 'Fine. So if it's none of that, then it has to be something either very new or very old. I'd put my guess on some kind of body magic. Or possession. Those crows either come from somewhere, or she's making them.'

Shipwright frowns. 'Making them? From what?'

He looks at her flatly. 'Meat.'

'Oh.' She stops chewing. 'Gross.'

He nods. 'Probably. But that's just her personal magic. She must have some other stuff going on, to get as far as she's done. To do what she's done.'

Shipwright darns and loops. 'Like what?'

He shrugs. 'Some kind of prophetic skill. She could have picked something up at the temple in Astic, or before. The hosts used to be able to dream the future. Maybe she found something of theirs. Even that's got its problems though.'

Shipwright turns the second sock inside out. 'Course it does. I don't know why anyone bothers with magic.'

Shroudweaver's eyes go wide. 'Says the queen of spinners.'

'S'different,' she says. 'That's just practical. It's a tool. You can put it down once you're done.'

He rubs his eyes, 'You might actually have a point. But anyway, prophecy's not something that comes easy. You have to have it in your bones. Whispers under the skin.'

She shivers. 'You creep.'

'It's true. Unless you're born to it, trained in it, you might not even know you can do it. The hosts used to be the best at it. Something about having a god inside you. Thins you out, gives you a stronger connection between your blood and your soul. Lets your mind slip in and out easier.'

Shipwright shifts uncomfortably. 'Thanks for that news.'

He purses his lips. 'You're fine. The weaving barely touched you. It takes . . . months, years for a god to change a person.'

He finally sets the boot down.

She looks at it with a raised eyebrow. 'That it?'

'What do you mean? It's done.'

She clicks her tongue, picks it up and sets to work. 'So if we're saying Crowkisser would never have anything like a host's power, where's she pulling the juice for this prophecy from? How's she not suffering for it?'

Shroudweaver looks pained. 'I'm not sure she isn't. Suffering, I mean. At the Aestering we were always taught prophecy dislocates you. Pulls you out of your own skin and shoves the future in. Your body sort of soaks up . . . potentialities. Your mind slips free to look at whatever you want. Then when your ritual, whatever it is, ends, your mind and your body slam back into each other. Your mind remembers what it can, and your body absorbs the dregs of the future that are clinging to your bones.'

Shipwright puts the boot down. 'That's messed up.'

He nods. 'Magic usually is. But if you're good at it? Or you don't care about going a little mad? Or you think it's worth it . . .' He shrugs. 'The advantages are pretty huge.'

Shipwright begins unrolling bedrolls, staking their tents in the lee of the wind.

'Could she be watching us right now?'

He shakes his head. 'Not directly. The prophet sees as well as whatever they're using to see. Crows aren't great in the dark.'

'That's a relief,' she says, paying out line.

'Of course, if my darling daughter's actually sifting the future, she might have heard this conversation already.'

'*That's* not. Can we do anything about it?'

Shroudweaver takes a spike, twists the guy rope around. 'If we were talking about something essential, sure. A little pushing out on silver threads can create . . . static. But . . . it's tiring. She can hear us wonder if she wants. I doubt she will though.'

Shipwright smooths cloth. 'Why not?'

He looks up from fumbling with a knot. 'Because prophecy takes you out of yourself. It's a complete loss of control. She couldn't stand it for long. My guess is she only uses it when she absolutely has to. If at all.'

Shipwright nods. 'That's some consolation, I suppose.' She crawls inside the canvas, tests it. Her voice muffled. 'Could someone . . .?'

Shroudweaver steps closer to her shadow. 'Kill her?'

'I didn't want to say it.'

He comes inside, sits down. 'We might need to, at some point.' He shifts until his legs are crossed. 'As to whether we could. Possibly. If it weren't for Slickwalker.'

She grimaces. 'Shit. Of course.' She looks down at him on the bedroll. 'Don't get comfortable, your lordship. The horse.'

She offers a hand, and he takes it grudgingly.

Outside, the little pony is staked close against the wall, its flanks moving rhythmically as it strips the remains of the byre of what greenery it can find.

Shipwright takes out a comb, tosses another to Shroudweaver, laughing at his expression. 'Did you think that this sturdy trooper looked after himself?'

'I thought there might be a charm. From the Burners or something. What was your friend's name, Thorndaughter?'

She laughs again. 'I'll tell her that. She'll enjoy it.' She starts combing and the rough wire of the small horse's mane grudgingly straightens under her steady fingers. 'Come on, this soothes me too, OK? Don't leave me hanging.'

He smiles, starts brushing softly. Shipwright fixes him with a look. 'Harder. He won't break.' They work quietly for a moment, until her courage recovers. She clears her throat. 'So, Crowkisser has some body magic, maybe mixed up with some kind of prophecy. But that's not all, is it? There's what she did down south.'

Shroudweaver flinches back as the pony whickers.

She utterly fails to hide her grin.

He collects himself before he replies. 'Yes, there's that. And that's one thing I don't understand. There's nothing I know of that could have taken a city, an army apart like that. Nothing that could have taken our names.'

Shipwright tries to keep the brush steady. Not too harsh, not too gentle. 'Nothing?' Watches his face as he answers.

'Nothing. Either she's found something very old, or very new. Or she's mixed things that . . . shouldn't be mixed. Broken some rules.'

Shipwright unpicks suckflies from around the little horse's eyes, crushes them between thumb and forefinger. 'Sounds like her.'

Shroudweaver leans forward onto the pony's back. 'It does, doesn't it?'

He stays there for a moment, feeling the warmth of its body against him.

A little spike of guilt in his heart for holding back. A larger chunk of ice as he thinks again about what unbinding the dead means.

'That's why we need the composite. If we can hit her hard enough, we can take her out before she brings . . . whatever else she has to bear.'

Shipwright pats the horse on its flank, reties its stay.

'Take her out. You keep saying that.' She gestures. 'Water into the trough, thanks.'

Shroudweaver stoops over the stone trough. 'How do I do this again?'

'Oh for heaven's. Let me. And you, *tell me* what "take her out" means. I want to puke when you're vague.'

He watches her work, her fingers dancing over a spinner she's pulled from the saddlebags.

'Like I said, hit her hard enough to stun her, or capture her. That would be ideal. She'd be a peerless hostage. That army,

Slickwalker, they're nothing without her.'

Shipwright presses softly on the spinner's hull, and it starts to hum gently before she sets it in the trough.

'And if that doesn't work?'

He watches the brass orb turn for a while, slowly drawing all the moisture and dew from the stone and soil, collecting it in the trough. It takes him a while to get the words out.

'If that doesn't work. I can redirect the composite's power. Pour it into Crowkisser until it burns her out.' He looks away, out across the fields. 'Like I said. That army's nothing without her.'

The trough fills. Shipwright dips her hand and retrieves the spinner, letting her fingers move back and forth on the water's surface for a moment before the horse shoulders her aside.

She walks across to Shroudweaver, hugs him. 'Let's get you to bed.'

He nods.

The tent is warmer once the lamp is lit, and his face softens in the glow. She kisses either cheek, then the bridge of his nose. 'So this composite, it's just *loose*. You're going to be the only thing holding it together? How does anyone hold that many souls? I thought hanging onto those things was killing you.'

He's quiet.

She can smell the night air on his skin, watch the shallowness of his breath. 'I was there when we threw down the Empire. I know just how many dead there were. How can you stand it? Having them all roiling inside you?' When Shroudweaver doesn't reply, she turns his head gently. His eyes are bright with tears.

'I can't. It's why I have to let them out.'

She frowns. 'I thought so. And once they're out, you're the only thing that's going to be holding thousands on thousands of souls together?' She puts a hand to his cheek, holding the tremor from her voice. 'My pale little lover. The only thing holding the shape of a new god? Just you.'

He runs a finger along her hairline, presses a curl straight. 'Yes. Just me.'

She takes his hand, puts it down in his lap, 'You idiot.'

'I can do it.'

She furrows her brow, unconvinced. 'How did they teach it at the Aestering?'

He thins his lips into a line. 'They didn't. But I can do it.'

'Can you?' Her eyes are fire in the half-light. 'Can you really?'

He nods. 'I can. I know I can. I've thought about this for a long time. Since before the war.'

She watches his lips. 'Since then? Why?'

'I thought we might need it to take down the Emperor. In the end.'

'That was more of a group endeavour,' she mutters.

He grimaces. 'I know.'

She takes his hand again, holds it tight between her palms.

'You can do this? Safely? Do it and get out alive?'

'I think so.'

She raises an eyebrow as she gently pushes him down onto the bedroll. 'I could have done with a stronger endorsement there.'

He's thin under her, the sharp, hollow lines of his face picked out by the shadows. Something like the ghost of an owl. Tired. Frightened. Beautiful.

'I can do it.' He says, and she hears the truth in his voice. Somewhere inside her, a knot of fear relaxes.

She adjusts so her head's on his chest, puts an arm over his ribs. Wills her breathing to slow just a notch, the hammer of her heart to drop its drum.

'Do they know? Kinghammer? Skinpainter? Do they know what the unbinding will do?'

He kisses her hair, lets his lips linger, talks down into her skull. 'Only Skinpainter. Only they were there at the end. The real end of the Empire.'

'And they're OK with it?'

'They understand sacrifice. Understand the need to hold the line. Better than anyone.'

She strokes his hair, methodically unbuttons his shirt and shucks him out his robes.

'And my job's going to be what? Stopping Kinghammer from braining you?'

He laughs, slides under the covers with her. 'For starters, yes.'

They're quiet then, taking a moment to be just skin and skin. Part of her heart loves it, this moment of closeness, of peace. The other part of her wonders if her body will betray her. If, somehow, he'll see all the fear, all the worry creep out of her skin.

She holds him tight anyway. It's worth the risk.

'Why have we never talked about this before, love? We're a little down to the wire.'

His fingers stroke her shoulders, finding the knots.

'I . . .'

She shifts, kisses his neck. 'What, string-bean?'

'I didn't want to worry you. I know you worry.'

She doesn't know whether to laugh, or cry. The noise that comes out is somewhere in between.

'So, you just thought you'd not mention it?'

He looks at her. 'There's so much to mention. Sometimes, I just don't know where to start. I don't know how you'd bear it.'

She kisses him again. 'You'd be surprised what I can bear.'

And with that, she turns, and blows out the light.

65

The skull, of course, is nothing but a signifier. The locals, however, will have you believe that it sings. Under the correct starlight. With the correct libations.

—Archivist Splitwater

The morning rises blue, filled with ice. The embers are low and black. Shipwright stirs them with a stick, tin cup against her lips, the tea sharp and hot.

Shroudweaver's still sleeping, curled close to the fire, one hand twined with red threads which fidget and twitch. She thinks about waking him, pulls her boots on instead.

Cracked from weeks of walking. She works grease into the worst of it, kneads the leather until it's loosened enough for her to slip her feet inside.

Beyond the ruins of the squat watchtower, the hills of the Barrowlands push upwards softly, preparing themselves for something more dramatic as they near Thell. The days stay clear, wisps of cloud torn across a sky that wakes blue, and plunges to night with a deep sudden red, flaring orange across the bright tips of the mountains. Blackness follows after, the sky thick with the swirl of stars, sharpened by the absence of lamps. The land below cold, dark and still.

She's grown used to Thell on the horizon. Stark, angular, massive. Close enough that she can see the distant flash of bright pennants. They'll be there by the afternoon. The thought fills her with a fear that sits in her throat like half-melted ice.

She doesn't notice she's biting her lip until blood fills her mouth. She washes it down with tea. Sweeter than usual.

She'll have to wake him, she knows it. But not yet. The sky is still blue. Shipwright scuffs her feet in the grass, and waits.

Eventually, Shroudweaver rouses warily, reluctantly. She stoops to stroke his hair, squatting next to his head. She offers him a mug of something hot and black, bitter and strong, and keeps another for herself.

'Morning, sleepyhead. That's the first good sleep you've had in weeks.'

Shroudweaver yawns, stretches. 'I'm stiff as old sail.'

She ruffles his hair. 'That's because you're decrepit. Get up, I'm bored of being awake without you.'

He smiles, and levers himself to a sitting position, feet still tucked in his bedroll.

Shipwright settles down next to him, taps his knee with finger. 'You look like a grub.'

'I feel like a grub,' he says, knuckling sleep grit out of his eyes. Once he can see clearly, he takes a deep drink from the mug, and sighs appreciatively. 'That's better.' He sips carefully. 'I haven't had this in ages. What's it called again?'

She swirls the leaves in her cup. 'Stillweed. Or that's what my mother calls it. It loses something in translation.'

He drinks, eying her over the rim. 'You'll need to teach me a few phrases sometime.'

She laughs. 'Why? So you can impress my parents?'

He looks away, blushes.

She elbows him. 'Oh my. You want to impress my parents.'

He glares at her. 'Is that so bad?'

She shakes her head, still chuckling. 'No, but you can raise the dead. You saved the world, once. Maybe twice, soon. You'd be amazed how that lowers the bar.'

He grunts. 'Still.'

'Fine, fine. Once we're done in Thell. A holiday in the soft embrace of the forests, then I'll teach you a few choice phrases to make my mother swoon and pluck your cheeks. I promise.'

He grins. 'Thanks. I love you.'

She tips the dregs of her cup onto the half-frozen grass. 'I love you too, grub. Let's get moving.'

An hour later, they're through the outskirts of the Barrowlands, in the low fertile stretch of country that swings east towards the Burners' forests, and west towards the coast, and the ruins of Luss. The Cut, she'd seen it called on maps, but it had other names too. The Furrows. The Lows.

Land that was sparsely populated, but richly farmed. Small clusters of homesteads gathered like gossips around deep wells and fields that seemed bare now, but that would grow lush as the earth turned, thick with the brown and black grain that gave the region its names. The Cut turned out bread as soft and warm as a baker's thumb, and ale that tasted like it had slept in the hollow of a malt mill for years, until it was casked and poured.

She realises she's hungry, takes some dried fruit from her pocket and chews unhappily.

There's more buzz than normal in the sleepy villages of the Cut this morning. The streets that lead from steading to steading strung with bright flags, orange and red and white. Gaggles of young teens, jostling each other for position on the verge, some clutching baskets of petals, some clutching each other, snatching kisses on the edge of the grainfields, running fingers up thighs and necking like swans.

The older villagers gather too, their brown skin baked darker by a life tilling the earth, leaning on sticks or perched on stools. Swapping jugs that still sweated cold beads of water from their time in the root-cellars.

Shipwright nudges Shroudweaver. 'What do you make of all this?'

He shrugs. 'A local festival?' He squints at the lines drawn up either side of the dusty road. 'A race maybe?'

She watches him closely. He never could resist a gamble, but he likes to pretend he can, 'Do you want to stay and watch?'

The smile that lights his face is all the answer she needs.

They hitch their horse outside a fenced field and shoulder their way through the growing crowd, ending up next to an elderly man who nods at them with a grin more gum than tooth.

'Youse are new. Staying for the race?'

485

'Yes,' the Shroudweaver says, quick as a breath.

He grins wider. 'You betting?'

Shroudweaver shoots at glance at Shipwright and she shrugs. 'Like I could stop you. It's your money to lose.'

Shroudweaver smiles beatifically, turns to the old man. 'How does it work?'

The man waves a thick-nailed hand down the eastern road, past where it bends towards the south.

'All the young 'uns goin' to be seen on that yer road soon. Each one's got a colour from their 'stead, fixed on their pennant. And the lead un'll have the singing skull. Clutched in his sweaty mitts. Yis follow?'

Shroudweaver nods. 'I think so.'

The old man grins. 'So yis can bet on colour – who's goin' to be in the lead when they hit t'village line. Or' – he winks – 'Yis can bet on the skull. Who's goin' to take it over village line.'

Another minute of arcanity passes in a whirl of odds and tips and palmed coins, and Shroudweaver eventually walks away with a marked scrip and a vague sense of satisfaction. Shipwright rolls her eyes and slips some coin to a bright young girl for a crisp roll drenched in warm honey.

'Are we going to get rich then?' she asks.

Shroudweaver turns the scrip every which way, frowning at the illegible marks. 'Maybe?'

Shipwright sucks sugar off her fingers. 'Don't lie to me. You never win. *Never.*'

He smiles, waves the scrip. 'There's always a first time.'

They hear the shouts before they see the horses, a rolling wave of cheers and applause that pours out of the south and crashes against the homestead walls like a wave. The livestock in the pens bleat in shock and fear.

And who knew the people of the Cut could make such a noise? These dour, soft farmers suddenly fitted with lungs made of brass, raising cattle-calling voices that fill the air with looping whoops and trills. The shrieks of the girls blend together and fall like a squall of birds as the air rains rice and petals and blossoms ahead of the horses. Shipwright joins in, whooping and hollering. There's something infectious in it, a bright joy that lifts her heart and sends it questing for the first hint of the riders.

She feels them before she sees them, the thundering of hooves raising a hum on the road that makes the stones dance. A cloud of dust boils out of the south, and within the dust, the long shapes of lances, the cut of a bright pennant, and then suddenly, the skull of a horse, clutched in the hands of the lead rider.

Shroudweaver lets out a yell at this, and the distant racers yell in response, a savage whoop that echoes back from the stones of the houses.

The leader is topless, high in the saddle, his chest and face painted with white and yellow bands, streaked like the rising sun. The skull is tucked under one arm as the other cups his horse's jaw, steering its head straight on down the track.

About a mile out, and with the speed of them, Shipwright realises they have a couple of minutes at best. She watches Shroudweaver's delighted face, and an idea hits her.

She grabs his wrist. 'Come with me. Run!'

To his credit, he doesn't bat an eyelid, just turns and follows her pell-mell over the grass. They're both laughing like idiots, breathless, arms windmilling.

She drags him to their horse, unhitches it, and mounts up.

The riders are near now, a minute at most. She takes his arm, pulling him up behind her. 'Come on!'

'What are we doing?' he shouts, his voice muddled with laughter, as their horse picks up pace.

She pulls his hand tight around her waist, gives his fingers a squeeze. A surge of elation in her heart.

'Joining the race!'

Their horse is a little slower with two riders, its stubby coast-cliff legs no match for the horses of the Cut, these white and dappled things that seem to have fallen loose from the hills and dropped, lithe and speeding onto the homestead road.

They have a few moments on the pack though, and they peel

off at an angle that brings them onto the road just as the jostling mob of hooves and dust draws level.

Perhaps twenty riders in all, daubed and painted with bright stripes in varying slashes and swirls. Lean and tough looking, some of them as young as the roadside teens, others with a steel slash of years at their temples and brow.

All of them as one glance at the pair thundering up on their squat brown horse. All of them as one let loose a yell of delight and joy at the strangeness of it.

The lead rider stands high in the saddle, beckoning them, his legs swaying with the thunder of his horse below him. 'Come in strangers, bring your short-legged creature in! Ride your dog with us a while!' He howls uproariously, then jukes as a pennant marked with a white vine swings at him, and hands lash out for the skull. He hollers his horse onward and ducks away laughing.

The pack parts to let them in, the leader's horse skull slipping to one side. He dodges a green pennant with a blue flower couched beneath its rider's arm, as another woman draws level with him, her colours flashing orange and red.

For a moment, Shipwright and Shroudweaver hold their own.

The lead rider shouts encouragement, and the woman with the orange pennant blows a kiss to Shipwright as she sails past.

Over her shoulder, Shroudweaver chuckles. 'I think this invalidates my bet.'

Shipwright whoops in response, her heart surging with joy. For the first time in weeks, her mind is clean, clear of worry, nothing in her body but the rush of speed and the thud of her horse's hooves on the packed earth.

They keep pace for a few seconds more, before their little horse starts to tire, and she chucks gently on the reins to ease its wheezing lungs. The other racers thunder past, their hooves turning the rich, dark earth, the dappled bodies of their horses parting around Shipwright like river water.

As the pack pulls ahead, the dust swirls behind them in a haze of petals. The lead rider turns his head back, eyes alight with speed. His gaze etched into the whitened sockets of his face as he yells a farewell. 'Dog-riders! Grey legions on the march in the south! The crow's got legs. Better hope you're as fast as us!'

His friend's horse barrels into him, sending both animals staggering. For a moment, the skull wobbles, then is caught again. Raucous laughter over the plains, as they cut their necks lower to their animals, striving for every ounce of speed.

Behind them, Shipwright pulls their horse to the side of road. As they dismount, it's mobbed by the crowd, bringing water and garlands of flowers, ruffling its hair and feeding it treats.

She bends to the knees, catches her breath. Shroudweaver rubs her back in soft, even motions. Her head is still buzzing with adrenaline

As she heaves in a lungful of fresh air, a broad-cheeked woman pats her on the shoulder.

'A good race. A brave little horse you've got there. Strong little *mushki*.' She twines her thick black braids. 'I'll buy him from you?'

Shipwright shakes her head. 'No, we need him.'

The woman tuts, reaches into her kirtle for coins. 'Need him for what?'

'To get to Thell,' Shipwright replies.

'Thell!' She scoffs, and makes a sign over her left eye. 'What you want to do there?'

'It's a long story,' Shipwright replies. The woman tuts again. 'Mountain's no place for a horse, and besides,' she gestures over her shoulder. 'You're nearly there.'

Shipwright follows her hand. The mountain *is* closer now. The sweep of the west road must have brought them curving north. Ahead, the true Barrowlands, and beyond that, Thell.

The peaks stand stark on this clear day, the whole black stone range cutting into the sky. It's ten miles, perhaps, no more. The first outbuildings already visible, the painted huts, the flags on the cairns. The familiarity of it all makes her heart sink, the brief lightness of the race draining like rain into rock.

The woman tuts again. 'Mountain's no place for a horse, no

place for you either. How many foreigners it got to swallow in one month, I ask you?'

Shipwright's attention is caught. 'There were others?'

The woman flattens her eyes like a cat, picks burrs from the horse's mane with practiced fingers.

'Yeah, a fluff-head boy and a tree-cutter. Tall, beard.'

Shipwright glances to Shroudweaver. 'It couldn't be?'

Shroudweaver shrugs. 'Maybe I have some good luck after all.'

She shakes her head in wonder. 'Fallon's either going to kiss us or kill us.'

Shroudweaver grins. 'No change there then. It'll be good to see Quickfish though.'

The dark-haired woman grunts and presses her closed fist into Shipwright's chest. 'Talk on your own time. Money for horse or not?' She jingles it meaningfully.

Absently, Shipwright takes the money and hands over the reins.

'Take good care of him.'

The woman gathers the harness and leads the horse away to a chorus of jealous complaints.

As the people of the Cut disperse to their beer and feasting, Shipwright and Shroudweaver stand together, looking at the black mountain. 'The mountain's no place for horses,' Shipwright murmurs to herself.

'No place for us either,' Shroudweaver agrees.

'Still,' she says. 'We should get this done.'

'Shall we then?' he says, offering a hand.

She takes it. 'Sure thing, dog-rider.'

Hand in hand, they walk towards the black mountain, as the fields sleep quiet beneath the songs of their tillers.

66

a bruise which does not heal
a yellow-eyed dog
the sound of oystercatchers before the storm

—*Collected Ill Omens*, Anon

'Visitors, my lord.' Said in almost perfect unison.

Kinghammer levers himself up. The Deadsingers watch him impassively, their eyes flat as snakes, bracelets clacking gently as they straighten their hair and hems.

He grabs a shirt from the floor, glances down at the mess of legs and brown curls beside him. 'Out. I'll see you later.'

The woman in the bed flees with haste, clothes pressed to her chest. The Deadsingers' heads pivot slowly to watch her leave.

Kinghammer pours water into a bowl, knuckles his eyes, runs a hand through his hair, turns. 'It's them, isn't it?' There's resignation in his tone.

The Deadsingers incline their heads. 'The sailor,' the left hisses. 'The binder,' the right adds.

Kinghammer swirls water, spits, and looks at them wryly. 'What would I do without you both?'

The pair don't reply, but tilt their heads upwards like a cat watching a bird. Distantly a bell begins to toll, gathering strength as it echoes down into the depths of the mountain. He hasn't heard these particular chimes for almost twenty years.

'My little daughter's safe?' Another nod.

He lets out a breath. 'And my other daughter?'

The pair turn to look behind them as raucous laughter fills the antechamber. Sly smiles flick across their lips, as they glide to one side. The brown-haired woman's shriek punctuates the space they leave. Icecaller strides in not long after, a grin sloping across her face. 'Morning, Dad,' she says. She glances back over her shoulder. 'Nice choice.'

Kinghammer grunts, laces up his breeches. Above, the bell tolls again.

His daughter skips to his side, ruffles his hair. 'Listen, Dad. They're playing our song.'

And the song is iron and motion.
The song is iron and ice.
The song is iron and air.

Elsewhere in the mountain, Roofkeeper raises his head as the bell tolls again. 'What's that?'

Quickfish turns to him, fuzzy from sleep. 'Who cares? This entire mountain never stops ringing.' He burrows deeper into the blankets.

Roofkeeper puts a hand on his chest, pushes himself into a sitting position. He can see feet by the entranceway. Men and women slipping from beds. Buckles, belts, blades. 'No, Quick. We have to get up. Something's happening.' An edge to his voice.

Roofkeeper pulls on his boots, buttons his shirt. Reaching under the covers he finds his axe. Solid wood in his hands calms him a little, but not much. He readjusts his grip, his palms sweaty. 'I'll be by the door. Come on love. Move.'

Quickfish takes a while yet to come to. He's been caught in the shreds of a dream. Something was pushing insistently against his hand. The scorched heart of a city stretching around him. The taste of smoke on his tongue and the rhythm of a small heart drumming rapid and insistent against his fingers.

For a second, he could have sworn that his mother was there.

The sound of movement pushes him awake, shouts, feet, the persistent clatter of preparation. Roofkeeper stands by the doorway, his jaw set, an axe loose in one hand.

Quickfish dresses quickly, awkwardly. His palm aches. 'So, what is it?'

Roofkeeper shrugs. 'If I didn't know better, I'd say it was war. But there's no way Crowkisser can be here yet.' He pauses. 'Can she?'

A twist of the lips as Quickfish wriggles into his trousers. 'Depends who you talk to. My dad always said she had to drag herself across the land like any other snake. I've heard others say she rides the wind. Moves on whispers, lies.'

He cinches the belt. Roofkeeper grins. 'Plenty of both around here.' Quickfish smiles nervously. 'Maybe, but I don't buy it.'

Another clot of soldiers hammers past, buckling helmets under loose swung chins. Roofkeeper catches one of them by the shoulder. 'What's happening?'

The young man smiles, laughs nervously. 'Visitors out of the Barrowlands. We're the welcoming committee.' He looks over Roofkeeper's shoulder, as he backs up and turns. 'Ask her!' he shouts, before he's lost in the throng.

Roofkeeper pivots to see Icecaller striding through the crowds, slick as a scalpel, the bulk of her father looming behind her. The Deadsingers flutter on the edge of his footsteps, fingers weaving in arcane anxiety.

Icecaller grins when she sees the axe. 'Wood-chopper! I like a boy who's prepared.'

Roofkeeper smiles, turns and catches Quick's wrist. 'Come on. We're safest with them.' Quickfish says nothing, but his expression speaks volumes. Still, they slip into the press and keep pace. The spear blades bob as they weave their way through low tunnels, more and more soldiers joining them from side passages. Whoever's drawing near, Thell is turning out for them, and the city is nervous. The entire throng moves like a chattering steel snake to the high battlements that overlook the Barrowlands, and the gate into the mountain.

Quickfish can feel the weight of Kinghammer behind him as they run upwards. The Deadsingers are quiet and slight in his shadow. Bone charms, polished amber, yellow teeth.

He glances at Icecaller and watches her tattoos move, pulled between arm and shoulder, 'Is it Crowkisser?' He hates how his voice sounds.

She looks across, shoves him with an elbow. 'Chill out spunk, you're not fucked yet. But, we do have guests.'

He lets out a tight breath. 'Who then?'

The Deadsingers hum and click their tongues. 'The debt-collector. The thread-weaver. Render. God-builder.' Their necks sway, their fingers wide in the body-cut light. 'Promise-taker. Voice-holder. Opener. Heart-binder. And his salt-eyed slut.' Their laughter scurries like rats in a hold.

'People we owe a great debt,' Kinghammer interrupts as they reach the upper galleries.

As Thell opens out to the air, sunlight hits Quickfish's face. In front of him, steel upon steel, held against a bright blue sky – the people of Thell painted, armoured, and waiting.

Roofkeeper nudges him. 'We never got any of this.'

Icecaller shoves her face between them. Her skin smells fresh, clean and cold. 'Of course not, pups. We're not nearly as scared of you. *You* didn't save half the people in this mountain.' She winks. 'Now be good. Watch the sky, watch the ground. Fall into the hush.' She turns to go, then moves back to Quickfish, taking his wrists in her hands. 'If you see anything strange. Anything wrong, you tell me.' A hand against his cheek, 'Nigh's down below with Steel. If anything comes for them, kill it.'

Her eyes flick to Roofkeeper. Her fingers tracing a line to his axe blade. 'That means you, hot stuff. Anything moves towards my sis, put that fucking axe in its teeth until it chokes on them.'

Roofkeeper grins. 'If she doesn't get to them first.'

Icecaller bites down on a laugh, and turns to take her place beside her father. Kinghammer nods at them, gazing down to the stretch of the Barrowlands below.

The bell tolls again. The blue air swallows it.

Hushed chatter falls away to the clink and shuffle of restless armour.

Quickfish presses himself up against the parapet, Roofkeeper's arm light around his waist. A thrill of excitement pulses in his chest.

The flanks of the Stump lurch down to the ground impossibly

far below, two hundred feet or more. The grass shows green beneath the fading frost, the brief shadows of hawks and the familiar slender splints of the cairn flags. The outbuildings are empty now, their population drawn up and into the mountain like a startled breath.

Approaching between the abandoned walls, shrunk by distance, come two figures. Hand in hand, one broad-shouldered, walking with a slow, steady roll, blonde hair pulled by the wind. The other leans against her, slight as a shadow, hands loose at his sides, red thread trailing in the wind. Quickfish's heart lurches. He hasn't seen them since he was a child. He remembers those strong hands bouncing him on a toy horse, remembers the soft voice behind the blonde hair and the gentle, quiet man who talked to him as if he was already twenty years grown. Shipwright and Shroudweaver.

The bell tolls again.

The wind drops. The flags hang slack. He can hear the breath of the people next to him, watches it frost in the empty air.

A spear is dropped. Someone's clumsy, nervous fingers. The sound rings out, down, down and down.

The pair draw closer, slowly, slowly.

He can make out their faces now. She is stoic, the blunt lines of her face set against the mountain. His lips are tight, his eyes closed. Perhaps that's why he's holding her hand so tightly.

Roofkeeper leans forwards, murmurs in his ear. 'They look . . .'

'Terrified,' Quickfish finishes.

The bell tolls. The air thick with its echoes. The clouds drag against the sharp blue of the sky.

There is moss growing in the parapet stone, sprouting thin bright alpine flowers. Quickfish picks one, twists it anxiously. He feels Roof's ribs press against his back as he breathes and leans into the soft scratch of his shirt, the smell of his neck. His heart hammers a little quieter.

The bell tolls.

A figure leaves Thell. Skinpainter, alone, their rags hanging slack and lifeless in the still air. The pair stop. Quickfish watches them. Shipwright says something terse, makes a few economical gestures.

In response, Skinpainter stretches their arms wide. Turns to face the mountain.

Shipwright glances upwards, seems about to speak again before Shroudweaver puts his hand on her shoulder. He steps forwards into the space between the two of them, raising his red ribboned right hand.

Slowly, so slowly, he unpicks the threads.

They fall carefully, lazily.

The bell is still.

The air is still.

Thell is still.

The red binding uncoils from his fingers. The grass takes it. The cairns take it.

Soon enough, it's done.

He holds his bare hand to the mountain, fingers spread wide, steady for the briefest moment, before he staggers, curling in on himself like he's taken a punch in the gut. He straightens eventually, but slowly, like a dry leaf uncurling.

Shipwright moves to stand behind him, her feet planted square, her hands on his shoulders. Quickfish recognises the gesture and kisses Roofkeeper's hand appreciatively.

Below, Skinpainter steps towards the pair. Their rags flare, though the air remains hollow and still.

When the trio embrace, Quickfish feels his breath fall through his lungs. He almost drops over the side as the mountain erupts with deafening cheers.

The sky fills with them.

The barrows roil with them.

As the noise swells, Icecaller threads her way through faces mad with relief. She slings her arms around Quickfish, palms wet with sweat.

A long sick laugh slides out of her.

Quickfish looks at her in confusion. He's not quite sure what he's witnessed, but he felt a weight leaving these people. A great fear evaporating, like mist under morning sun. He can read it on Icecaller's face as she collects herself, and grins at him,

'Shipwright and Shroudweaver come to Thell. Fuck me. Never thought I'd live to see that.'

67

Light the hearts that love the sea
Bright the face that seeks the sun
Light the bones that crave the lee
Draw the web until its spun

—Midlands waulking song (trad.)

He slips his hand into hers. It's rough, solid.

His thumb traces the calluses on her palms. Ropework and sea-strain.

The nails of his right hand worry at the red threads around his wrist. Keeping them loose. There's not much worse than a binding ribbon wound too tight. His timing needs to be impeccable. If he unwinds the threads at the wrong moment, he'll tear his chest apart.

The dead are still for now, but he can feel them moving beneath his ribs, coiling around his heart, calling out to the older souls buried in the barrows. He senses a pulse of movement in response, like eels below ground, nudging against the deep-driven cairn posts, flowing over stone, through mud. Following the trail of his footsteps like wolves after spoor. Seeking unity.

In the far distance, the people of Thell line the battlements, high ridges of stone that jut out from the Stump, piled with dry-stone and shale. Parapets that open anyone approaching across the fields below to a rain of spears, fresh from the nervous hands of the men and women above. The stink of their fear is sharp, even from here. A whole mountain brought to bay at the sight of two old fools. He'd laugh if he wasn't so shit scared of dying on those spears.

As they walk closer, Shroudweaver squints against the sun.

He can't make them out from this distance. He sees painted faces, tattooed skin, a bulk in the middle that might be King-hammer. He can't see Belltoller, but he can hear her, the echo of iron bells lingering over the landscape.

No sign of Quickfish, for good or ill.

His head swims. This close to Thell, it's like walking under-water. He's felt the dead at the edge of his mind for a while now. The bound souls of the Empire fill his head like static. Coiling around his heart, squeezing and straining to be free.

Shipwright hums nervously as she walks beside him. An old eastern shanty, lilting and low. Her boots turn stones, clods of earth. The road to the Stump is worn, too many feet coming in and out of Thell, the last flurry before war. She squeezes his fingers gently. 'If they try anything, stay behind me.'

He smiles weakly. 'If they try anything, I'm going to run.'

She pulls him closer, plants a kiss on the top of his head. 'On those skinny pins? Not likely.'

She smells of the road, of grass and grease. There's a tear in her shirt. He puts an arm around her and breathes a little easier.

She watches the horizon as she talks, counting blades lifted against the sky. 'You're worn through aren't you?'

He turns his wrist to catch a stray thread. 'Is it that obvious?'

'Only to me.'

They crest a small rise. A barrow long sunk into the grass. Distantly, a figure emerges from the shadow of the mountain. A thing of rags and ribbons in the deep cleft of the gate. Skinpainter. Shroudweaver's heart soars to see them.

As his mood lifts, the bound souls pulse within his veins, and he staggers slightly. Shipwright wordlessly moves her hand to his waist, creates a hollow for him to lean in to. 'It's the dead, isn't it?'

He nods. When she speaks about them, he feels them push against his skin, and against the skin of the earth in return. His body is the thinnest barrier, just waiting to tear. He winces, pulls the red threads tighter, rubs charcoal between the tips of his fingers. The sensation fades, a little.

She watches from the corner of her eye. 'It's not just that though, is it? You miss her. Crowkisser.'

He shrugs. 'I know it's terrible.'

'Bollocks it is. You're her father. It's not your fault she's . . . tricky.'

He laughs.

She slows her steps. Keeps some space between them and Skinpainter's approach. 'Have you sensed her at all?'

A shake of the head. 'Can't hear anything out here. Except the dead. And you.'

She squeezes his hand again. 'Are you ready for this?'

He makes a soft affirmative noise. 'I'll follow your lead, love.'

Shipwright watches Skinpainter's broad figure stop a few metres away, their cloak hanging tatterdemalion in the still air. A faint flicker of excitement flares in her chest, with just a tinge of resentment beneath, sitting like brine on barnacles. She's not sure how to express it all, so she just nods. 'Skinpainter. All these years and still no new threads?'

A smile splits the shadow beneath their hood. 'I'm comfortable in these, Ship.'

It doesn't lighten her mood. She presses her lips together. 'Are you going to let us in?'

In answer, Skinpainter turns, raising their arms to the assembled crowd on the battlements. Their voice slides over their shoulder, faintly amused. 'That all depends, Ship. Why are you both here?'

She bites down on a reply as she feels Shroudweaver's light touch on her shoulder.

He moves into the space between them. When he speaks it's quiet, careful. 'We're here for unbinding, Skin.'

Skinpainter turns back to them, their hands still spread grandiosely wide. The grin hangs in their face like a key in a lock.

'Are you sure you can handle it?'

Shroudweaver's answering smile is thin. 'As sure as I was that I could bind them.' He straightens. 'Smokesister's work is strong. It's held them until now. But it won't last . . . *I* won't last much longer.'

Skinpainter steps closer, their voice soft, eyes heavy and serious. 'Not here. Not yet.'

Shroudweaver shakes his head. 'No. It's too soon. I'm saving them for Crowkisser.'

Skinpainter's eyes go wide. 'A composite? Unbound?'

Shroudweaver nods.

Skinpainter stifles a laugh. 'You haven't got any more humble, have you?'

Shipwright smiles despite herself. 'They know you too well, Shroud.'

Skinpainter shoots her a grin as they take Shroudweaver's hands, running a thumb over frayed red threads.

'Will this help us win?' They flick their eyes at the mountain. 'Will it keep them safe?'

Shroudweaver tightens his grip. 'It will. I swear.'

Skinpainter holds his gaze for a moment, seems to find whatever they're looking for.

'I've not regretted trusting you yet, Shroud. But what about them?' Their eyes again track along the battlements, stopping on Kinghammer's bulk. 'They're expecting a grand reunion. And they're tense as cats on a griddle.' They pause. 'There's been a few complications I need to catch you up on.'

Shroudweaver sighs. 'Complications. Of course. Well, we'll do what we always do, Painter. Make it look like we've got everything under control, until we have half a clue what's going on.'

Skinpainter shrugs resignedly. 'Fine, I don't have any better ideas.' They roll their shoulders. 'OK. Fuck. Best make it look good.'

'Full theatrics?' Shroudweaver asks.

Skinpainter grins. 'Is there any other way?'

In response, Shroudweaver raises his red right hand, and begins unpicking the outer weaves. Keeps a tight hold of the dead, but throws in a stagger, as best he can. Playing to an audience with life and death on the line. He feels Smokesister's bindings twitch around his ribs, and imagines her wry, disapproving smile. Holds

Skinpainter's gaze as the bones of his hand slide loose from the tight-wound thread. 'Do you think that sold it?'

Skinpainter's posture never changes, only their voice, thrumming deep and soft. 'I think they'll eat you alive unless we do a bit more to convince them.' They cock their head thoughtfully. 'Although, I might be able to help with that.'

The old warlock pauses for a second, as their rags flare around them. Sinuous, hypnotic. 'Don't flinch,' they murmur, stepping forwards. 'Make it look real.'

Shroudweaver feels their broad arms embrace him. The shape of his old friend beneath their robes. Stark, muscular, strangely angled. A brief pulse of unexpected life along their flank.

Shipwright joins them, her arms a light band around his quickening breaths. As she closes the circle, the cheers from above are deafening.

'They bought it,' Skinpainter murmurs. 'Depths and ice, they bought it. Precious little fools.' As their chest begins to shake it takes Shroudweaver some time to realise they're laughing. When Skinpainter speaks again, they lean close, their jaw grazing his skin. He glimpses an eye black as glass, alert, mirthful. 'Come on then,' they mutter. 'Let's help you upend everything. Again.'

68

Split the night down to blue.

—Northern slang for striking an impossible deal

Once they're in, the days drip by like water down a well.

Thell holds itself tense, like a cornered beast.

Its people watch Shipwright and Shroudweaver as they move through the corridors, lean and wary. They eat well, but their food is served by hands that linger too long, or that flee like birds before storm. Their blankets are warm, but they wake to watching eyes in the night, flat and serious.

Curious children come up to them, chewing sweet roots, jaws working furiously, tugging stickily at their clothes and fingers. Their parents sweep them away, apologetically, efficiently. They're not quite taboo, but close enough.

It's no surprise to Shipwright. Thell is as she remembers. Angular, fierce, only partially softened by the steady glow of strange lights. The people are boisterous until she passes, falling silent as she approaches, unwinding into laughter in her wake. She sees no one she recognises, except for Skinpainter, and once, from a high gallery, a tall figure, capped with grey like a spear-point, her hard face lined with sadness. Could Belltoller have aged so heavily? She doesn't get a chance to find out. The mountain swallows familiarity into its depths, keeping her at arm's length. She's the foreigner again. The stranger. The reminder that all is not well.

It's no surprise that she sleeps fitfully, her hand on Shroudweaver's ribs, the other clenching and unclenching next to her, hanking the sheets into fierce lumps. Something in the night won't leave her alone. Her dreams are flecked with gold. She pitches restless. When she wakes, she coughs the taste of spice and honey from her lungs and rinses it from her mouth with cold mountain water.

Skinpainter meets them most mornings. They are quiet, pensive, their barks of laughter slipping out from under long pauses. Kinghammer, they are told, will see them when he is ready. The mountain still keeping them at a distance. The old bear not yet ready to confront his past.

While they wait, Shroudweaver frets, his fingers lingering on rock, on plate edges, tracing the rims of cups. He sleeps with his palms wrapped in red thread, hair smelling like the smoke of a battle. He takes hands when they are offered, turns his head in sadness when they are snatched away. He says soft, kind things to try and make himself sound safer. Shipwright doesn't have the heart to tell him that he is as foreign as she is now. Shroudweaver belongs in the past for the rulers of Thell, and they want to keep him there.

Despite this, the days are bearable, just. They have rhythm, but she wilts from a lack of sky. She presses herself up against the sockets of the Stump and stalks its high ledges, hating it for being solid. Through it all, no one speaks to her, nothing beyond working words.

She tries to get a sense of the place, its sweet spices, the low belly warmth of the deep passages, and the ice of the high reaches. There's more of it than she could learn in a lifetime, twelve storeys, maybe more, and each as high as the tallest halls of Hesper.

Efficient to the core. In the training grounds, she watches warriors move with precision and grace, spears flickering like tongues, shields stark against bare, bright bodies. She hears tongues flicker in other corners. Licking skin, licking rumours. Whispering about her, about Shroudweaver, about the reports of the grey army that marches north under crow-feather wings. The folk of Thell conspire with heads bowed against necks, their fingers tapping out hidden rhythms she doesn't understand. She grows lonelier with every passing day. She misses sex, and closeness, and being held. She wants to relax, for fuck's sake. But for now, that's not happening.

In the evenings, she talks with Skinpainter as they block out the past in easy, economical gestures. The future is painted in starker tones.

'Thell,' they assure her, 'is ready for war.' They play their part. Not a friend, not here. Not the Skinpainter of two decades gone, with their easy confidences, their sly secrets shared with Shroudweaver. Here, they are the mouthpiece of the mountain. They are a decipherer of strange things, and Shipwright has always, always been strange to them.

Still, they run their mouth, and she watches what they don't say. Not a whisper about Hesper, or Crowkisser, or especially the unbinding. Their lips leave more gaps than their words fill. If Quickfish is here, if those wild horse lords spoke true, Skinpainter says nothing. For his part, Shroudweaver doesn't pick it at. Makes excuses. It's a difficult time, a complex situation. Thell's being pulled into something they never saw coming. Shipwright knows better. She's hired on enough crews and brokered enough deals to know the game Skinpainter's playing. They are being vetted. Calmly. Affably. Ruthlessly. She says nothing though. Not yet. You don't tip your hand in a negotiation. You wait for them to come to you.

This morning, Skinpainter is more polite, more formal than ever. Holding them at bay as Shroudweaver picks listlessly at a breakfast of cold, pickled fish.

Their face calm, amber eyes relentless.

'Days at worst,' they say. 'Kinghammer is consulting with his closest advisers. To ensure he has all the facts to hand before he meets you both.'

As they say this, as Shipwright feels herself die a little more inside, a small, dark-headed girl runs up, tugging at Skinpainter's robes. She glances at them all, wide-eyes in a raw-boned little face. Shipwright smiles at her, could hug her when she beams back.

'Who's this?' she says, grateful for the respite.

Skinpainter grins, the first real smile that's graced their lips for days. 'This, honoured guests, is Nigh.'

Nigh nods at the mention of her name and holds her hands out to Shipwright. She picks the little girl up reflexively, sets her on a thigh. 'Oof, hello, little brick.'

Shroudweaver laughs as Shipwright runs her fingers through the shock of tangles on Nigh's head. 'Don't you mind him.' She bends her neck, whispers into a small ear. 'I like strong little girls. They grow up into strong big women. Plus,' she murmurs. 'They're *delicious*.'

She fakes a bite at Nigh's neck. The sprat squeals in mock horror.

'Careful, Ship,' Skinpainter rumbles.

Shipwright grins. 'Please, I'm just happy to find someone here that can stand to be near me.' She goes in for another bite attack, is met with a swivel, a small foot planted squarely in her solar plexus. The air slides out of her.

Shroudweaver and Skinpainter collapse laughing. Nigh looks from face to startled face, joins in, burbling like a brook.

Shipwright turns to Shroudweaver. 'Take this tyrant! She's killing me.'

Shroudweaver reaches for Nigh. As the kid passes between them, for a second Shipwright feels a sharp stab of something. A different moment. A could-have-been, held like a splinter of glass.

Shroudweaver pats the bench next to him, and it's gone. 'I like you already, Nigh. Do you know how many warriors have beaten Ship?'

Nigh shakes her head.

'Three, and one of them's dead.'

Nigh looks worried.

Shipwright leans across. 'Don't panic, little one. I'm not going to fight you.' She lets her lips linger by Nigh's head. 'Just eat you.'

Another spin and a punch.

Shipwright catches it. 'Word of advice, nugget – don't try the same thing twice. Even old salts like me will catch on.'

Skinpainter leans across, laughter lingering on their lips. 'You're holding the fist of the Kinghammer's daughter there, Ship.'

Shipwright unclasps her fingers slowly, plants a kiss on the escaped fist. 'Good. Maybe she can get him to come and bloody talk to us.'

Skinpainter sighs. 'He's afraid, Ship.'

She raises an eyebrow at him. 'So are we. That's why we need to talk to him. To *all* of them.'

Skinpainter nods. 'I get it, I do, but give him time. Last time you were here . . .'

'Last time we were here, we put him on the throne,' Shroudweaver says. There's steel in his voice.

Skinpainter tenses. 'We don't have thrones, Shroud, you know that.'

Shroudweaver waves dismissively. 'The difference doesn't matter.'

Skinpainter grips his wrist. 'The difference is all we have.'

It takes a moment for their hand to leave, a moment more for blood to flow back into whitened spaces.

Thick fingers tug their hood down further. 'Look, Shroud. I'm not trying to be awkward. I've kept an eye on the south. I know what's happening.' They pause. 'And I'm sorry, I really am. But I'm not the final word.'

Shipwright sips her drink thoughtfully. It buzzes on her tongue. 'You're the final line though.' She waves the mug. 'Every skin in this place has your mark on it.'

Skinpainter shakes their head. 'Not all of them. Some notable exceptions.' Shipwright catches the hint. Skinpainter holds her gaze. After a moment, they shove a bowl of snacks across to Nigh, roasted nuts and spiced grains. She grabs a fistful and chews precisely. Skinpainter looks back to the pair, thinking how little they've changed. 'And even if they were, it wouldn't matter. That's not politics. It's survival.'

Shipwright's hands tighten on the mug, 'So's this, Skin, so's this. Crowkisser's on the march. She wants the mountain. She wants your people.'

Skinpainter rolls their sleeves back and rubs at tired arms. 'I know, Ship. I've seen her. Sensed her. Still, we've weathered worse storms. You know that.' They pour into outstretched cups. 'It doesn't mean we aren't breaking out the oilskins. The army is ready. I'm ready. Belltoller hasn't relaxed for twenty years. We're ready.' They stop, hands spread across the tankards. 'But until we know how this is going to play out, we're not going to trust you. And until we trust you – this is how it stays.' They laugh, run hands wearily across their temples. 'For the love of. You know *everything*. You were there on the day we took the Emperor down.' They point a finger at Shroud. 'You were the last to speak to him. Can't you see why that's a problem? Can't you see why that scares them all?' The finger drops. They drink. 'I'm sorry. I'm tired. Drunk. Not drunk enough. I don't know.'

Shroudweaver folds his hands and Shipwright watches his face change into something cold and hard. 'I should think trust is the least of what the Republic owes me.'

The red threads around his wrist follow his pointing fingers. 'You want to know what I want? Kinghammer wants to know? I want to unbind the dead I've carried for you for twenty damn years. I want to save your people. *Again.*'

Skinpainter's fists clench. For a moment, Shipwright sees their jaw working furiously under their hood. Nigh shifts uncomfortably.

'Save us from your own *daughter.*' They shrug expressively. 'Twenty years changes a lot, Shroud. It's not that we don't want to help.'

'It's just more convenient not to.' Shroudweaver is straight-backed, skin flushed, the breath skittering in his lungs. He's furious. Shipwright can read it in every line of his bones.

Skinpainter says nothing, but reaches out to draw Nigh a little closer. She looks plaintively at Shipwright as she reluctantly complies.

For a moment, the silence hangs heavy between them.

'What this then? Three maudlin cunts and a little arsehole.'

Icecaller's voice breaks the quiet like rocks on ice.

Skinpainter's shoulders slump, just briefly. 'Icecaller, meet . . .'

For a moment, Skinpainter tries to use their old names. It slips oily over their tongue. They gesture, '. . . Shipwright, Shroudweaver.'

Icecaller grins. 'Ah yes. Our not-honoured guests. My father's fucking bricking it with you here.' She holds a hand out. 'Nice to meet you. I'm the smart, pretty one. And anyone that can make my father shit frost is fine by me.'

Shipwright takes it. Feels the calluses, the tight muscle. 'You're a warrior,' she says.

Icecaller nods. 'Warrior. Poet. Best sister. Worst daughter.' She wiggles her fingers, 'I've got a lot on my plate.'

She claps Shroudweaver around the shoulders. 'Thanks for looking after this little bratbag.'

Nigh leans her head back, sticks her tongue out. Ice leans down, licks her forehead, covers her in kisses. She screams, scatters back into Shroudweaver's lap.

Icecaller winks. 'See, this is how I help you make friends.' She slings her legs over the bench, sits between them. 'I am the unpleasant alternative.' She takes a flask off her belt and waves it at Skinpainter. 'Fill her up, Hoods. I'm exhausted. Just been chatting to Dad.'

Icecaller looks left, right. 'So,' she says. 'Are you twats going to pull your bloody fingers out and play your hand?'

Shroudweaver takes Nigh's hands in his own, begins winding red thread around her right palm. She watches closely, small teeth tight on her lips. He holds Icecaller's gaze, lets his eyes travel over her face. Bright blue eyes. The same high cheekbones as her sister. Blonde hair shaved close on one side, loose on the other. Marked with geometrics, like the rest of them. Scarred, a little. A pleasant, lazy smile.

Icecaller clicks her fingers in front of his face. 'Not in front of the children.' With a toss of her head, she flicks her eyes to Shipwright. 'What are you? Partner? Lover? Carer?'

'All of them,' Shipwright murmurs.

Shroudweaver shoots Icecaller a look. 'I was just noticing the family resemblance.' He pauses, sits Nigh into the hollow of his stomach, ties off a knot. Icecaller's eyebrows are expectant. He pats Nigh's wrist, shakes his head at her big sister. 'I think given the apparent delicacy of the situation, it's better to wait until we see Kinghammer.'

Icecaller snorts. 'Not the smartest down south are you?' She leans into him. 'I'm his d.a.u.g.h.t.e.r. The one that isn't perpetually covered in snot. That means, I have the connections.' She mimes it, grinning. 'Look, if you level with Skin and me, we can probably speed things along. I don't really want my dad scared. And if there's stuff out there that we should be worried about, let's be prepared for it.'

She leans forwards, shoulders angled. 'It's bad enough with Fallon's kid here mooning about the place. So, lay it on me straight, is your daughter marching to kill us all?'

Shipwright catches her arm. 'Declan Fallon's son *is* here?'

Icecaller's eyes flick from Shipwright, to Skinpainter's aghast face and back again.

'Yes. Right. He is. You didn't—? Oh. Bollocks.'

69

*The shape of it in the dark, like a bird, like a cat
muscle hunting in the black.*

—*The Beast Beneath the Barrow*,
Pub: Errant, Glissworm & Co.

The army moves below him like smoke, filling the valleys, the
gaps between trees. The countryside is noisy with feet, buckle,
harness. Slickwalker watches them from high places, his feet
light on branches. Crowkisser sways at their head, pale and
splintered, a grey horse beneath her, grey men behind. Astic
marches. Alongside them, are the people of the Rim villages;
hard men from Dryke, the outriders and hawk-holders of Vantage, the herders and drovers of Fallow, all moving with stolid
rhythm. Anyone able, anyone angry, anyone with something to
fight for.

An army that isn't really an army. An army that's fisherman and
cartwrights, cooks and potboys. Herbwitches and smoketalkers.
Marshwalkers. Hunters, catchers of frog and fowl.

There's a unity among them that wasn't there before. She's
stitched them together under her care, binding them with their
fears and hopes of a new world. They chat among themselves as
they walk, sing sometimes, their arms around each other. Laughing in the cold mornings, as they piss out campfires and cradle
cups still warm from the embers.

He watches Crowkisser from high places. She talks to them,
walks between them. She brushes hair, rubs ointment into calluses, draws the blood from blisters. She smiles as she works,
hands deft, steady.

People touch their fingers to her lips in thanks, offer up dark bread smoked over fires, strips of fish dried and stored, pungent and herbal.

She speaks in the mornings, on the brow of hills, her fingers light on the horizon. When her nails rest on the silhouette of the Stump, her voice rises, her body tenses. The people cheer.

Afterwards, miles fall away under their feet as they march across a wide and emptying landscape, past the ruins of other wars. As they drum steadily through the skeleton of the Midlands its inhabitants close their doors. The Midlands people know how to survive strife, going to ground and touching their hands to the lintels in hope of a swift passing. All that's left for Crowkisser's army are the ruins of those villages which were not so lucky, those that fell to the Empire. Or the bladedrinkers. Or the riders of Twicefallow. The whole countryside silted thick with old conflicts. They make the best of it, though. Sometimes they gather around old wells to see if they draw clear, or if they pull only muck and bones.

The younger children swarm the wrecks of these old villages, cock-crowing from high towers, scavenging among sherds for old blades, finding corroded clasps that are used to string blankets into ragged banners and heroes' capes.

Their parents gather them up. Show them how to fit straps, where to balance the blade. The old stones hear steel again, run with shrieks and laughter.

The mountain grows closer day on day. The last ghost-acres of the Midlands give way to the rolling mounds of the Barrowlands, with their stands of black pine and sudden outcrops of rock long ago discarded by glaciers. Slickwalker watches Thell from these high, lonely places, sighting along the barrel of the gun, letting its muzzle trace the battlements that lean out over the sleeping earth like a widow's veil. When the land flattens out from rock down to barrows, he climbs the flag poles of cairns, feels them shudder under his touch.

The army's been left a mile or two behind him. He's alone in the wide nights of the north, and he revels in it. The barrows take the evening like liquid, shadows falling from a heavy sun to pool amid the humps and hollows of this land of graves. Some nights, he walks new hewn paths into the bellies of burial chambers, lays his head on slabs slanted from time and listens, heart hammering.

His fingers find traces of other explorers. New ones, at first; a discarded adze, a scrap of chew. The dust moved by wary feet, splashes that might be blood, might not.

Beyond these vestiges of the living, the dead lie in hollows, their legs drawn up to their throats, bound at wrist and knee. He smells the magic on them, tastes it sticky on his lips. He runs his fingers over their old teeth, loosens some, keeps them as charms, as gifts for her.

Once, curious, he lets a blade press against the bindings, and feels his arm throb with a strange deep hunger. Something calling out to his blood. He bites down on it, moves on.

Through mildewed chambers, into long passages which connect one mound to another, fallen far from light into blackness. He draws his own shadow to him, pressing forwards. A joy kindling in his heart, finally the adventurer he'd always dreamt of being – shielded by sorcery, forging into the darkest tombs to find out their secrets.

As he pushes deeper into the last barrow, he realises a battle was fought here. Spear hafts snapped, a point lodged deep within the ribs of a skeleton, the tattered shreds of its bindings still loose on its wrists, tall shields sundered. Another body. Old, dry, its legs torn from the torso, its chest and arms marked with heavy geometric patterns, black and red and black again.

Thell. Even here beneath the earth, Thell.

Beyond even this, another shield split top to toe. Ragged brutal marks across its surface, a withered hand still in the grip. Its owner further up the passage, lips peeled back in death. After these bodies, another low chamber, strung with roots, its alcoves empty save for a few offerings of long-dried flowers, and scattered coins. Not quite the treasures of legend, but at the far entrance he finds a ring of skeletons, fallen one against the other in a jagged circle.

Much more interesting.

The air thick with the burnt-sugar stink of magic. He feels it tugging at him, wraps the shadow tighter against his shoulders in response, unhitching the gun and letting it uncoil. Better than a knightly sword, by far. His feet take him around the chamber's periphery, past deep gouges, a shattered plinth, echoes of some terrible confrontation.

In the centre, beneath the apex of the barrow, stands a small cairn, its top sheared off, the edges melted near to glass.

Curiosity overcomes common sense. He lets his feet cross the space, feels the stones squat in front of him. The plinth is bare, save for a few shards of what might be scorched bone and a little powder that glimmers in the light. Something hypnotic in the debris, like staring into a wasp hive and watching the slow, black dance.

Like hearing a song behind a closed door. Like listening to rock shift in the dead of night.

Something not calling, but pulling.

Gingerly, Slickwalker lays a gloved hand on the smooth edges of the cut shrine. His breath hangs tight under his ribs.

Nothing.

He lets out a laugh that sounds ridiculous down here. Another one follows as he realises that he's almost disappointed not to be struck down, or dumb or blind.

So much for ancient magics. His brow blossoms with cold sweat, all that adrenaline with nowhere to go. A waste of time.

As he turns to leave, his eye hangs on the circle of bones, on those dead men.

Something has settled within the hollow of their fallen limbs – scraps, shreds of fabric, red, yellow, red again. Without thinking, he bends low, takes one and braids it around his wrist, tying it off as he winds his way out from the throat of the barrow, his mind dancing with wizards and warriors, the rat-drum of his heart slowing, steadying.

Eventually the tunnels open up beneath the moon. He shivers at the cold, pulls the shadow to him, and flows back across the hills to the staggered glow of the army's campfires. He slips in next to Crowkisser, takes off gloves and gun, runs a hand over her jaw.

'I missed you,' she says. And he sleeps. Twined with nothing more than a wisp of yellow and red, and a fading memory of the crawling dark.

When the mornings come, they come cold. Crowkisser stretches next to him, grumbling quietly. He kisses her neck, her forehead, smooths tangles from her hair.

'Nearly there,' she says, and smiles. He watches that smile. No longer new, fresh out of Astic, there's something more in it now; a confidence, a certainty he hasn't seen before. It warms his heart. He helps make breakfast, helps make plans.

She speaks again that morning, her eyes bright. Her army listen diligently, shush fractious chatter and nod among themselves. They return to their tents and emerge with blades sharpened, straps tightened. Their pace increases with each passing day.

Each morning Slickwalker takes himself higher, flowing ahead of their tired grey bodies to take the lay of the land. Each morning, he lets the gun unfurl and feed, sees the sky through his own scoured bone, and pulls himself back together with shadow. He returns to the column on tired feet and directs them to water, to game. Later, he sits with Crowkisser by a clear lake as she asks questions. The answers come hard and cold – he watches her eyes kiss the back of her skull as she finds paths further ahead than he can ever hope to look. Stones and sticks falling into clear water, joined now by barrow teeth – a little local twist to the prophecies she tosses in the mud. They are only a week away now, and they need to know how the mountain prepares.

He watches Thell from high places, traces the scars of old ice over its gates. There are plenty of vantage points here, ledges thick with old nests that were home to eagles once. Scavengers now, burrowing amid shell and twig.

It's a bright day, and their soldiers are lined up against the edges of the morning, Kinghammer amid them. Slickwalker lets the gun lick his outline for a while, wondering if it's worth the shot. He's distracted before the temptation to pull the trigger gets too much. Below his perch, a familiar pair move across the open ground like invalids. Shipwright and Shroudweaver, one leaning against the other. He's surprised they've made it, saddened. It would have been better for everyone if they'd died on the road. He lets the gun feel them, mark their muscles. It shivers under his fingers, hungry and impatient.

He shifts his grip, watches carefully as Thell's old emissary comes to meet them, stooped under a cloak of ragged ribbon. Skinpainter. Red and yellow and red again. Slickwalker glances down at the barrow-scraps on his wrist and smiles. Interesting. That mystery makes a little more sense now.

The trio below meet with the sun still high in the sky and embrace. Some cheap theatre goes on. A lot of vague, empty gestures. The people of Thell eat it up, their cheers falling down the side of the mountain.

He watches a little longer, picks at some lichen. Eventually, they retreat inside the gates. The soldiers filter off the battlements. The bear of Thell relaxes, briefly, and sheathes its claws.

Slickwalker follows them in, flowing down the mountainside, where the runs of natural shadow caused by the rock are deep and cool, pulling him smoothly over the sheer surface of the Stump. The barest sensation of limbs as he moves. This is nothing like the descents he used to undertake as a child in the high, broad trees of the south, all burning limbs and thundering heart. To move with the shadow is to fall like thick rain, to drift like blown sleet. Only the briefest of adjustments is needed to swing his form towards his target.

Those old ice cracks, the deep cuts of glaciers positioned so conveniently either side of the Stump's main gate.

Slickwalker takes a minute to catch his breath. The movement may be different, but the exhilaration is the same, the elation of high places and the adrenaline taste of the ground hundreds of feet below. He tries to focus, forcing himself to breathe slowly, precisely, in and out. He lets the shadow slide off him just enough that he can feel his body, the rasp of air in his lungs, the soft burn in his muscles.

Once he's calm, he turns to study those deep grooves. They are almost perfect for his purpose, but perhaps a little sheer to take the shivers securely. Glancing to make sure the battlements are bare, he presses the gun squat against the rock on the left side. It uncoils just barely, pulsing like a lizard's stomach.

The report is muffled, the cat's yowl of the gun driven down into the stone, but the stench of it is the same – acrid, rotten lemon. The rock beneath its muzzle hollowed out and scoured. The gun squirms fitfully. It misses the taste of flesh.

'Too bad,' he mutters, half to himself, before swinging over to the other side of the gate.

He lets his arms take some of the strain, enjoying the exertion, riding the shadow like the cusp of a wave. The same procedure on the right-hand side; a quick press of the trigger and a disgruntled yowl as the gun bores its way into the rock.

Another quick check confirms that the battlements are still clear. Bless Shroudweaver and his magnetic personality.

Slickwalker works quickly. Taking the first shiver gingerly out of his pack, and settling it in the etched niche, before packing the hollow as full as he can, six or seven deep. Enough to level a sailing ship, and then the same again on the other side.

He covers them with a cloth to keep them still until they're secure. His fingers linger a little on their rough shells. 'Don't let me down,' he mutters.

The clink of metal from above ends that one-sided conversation.

Quick as a shudder, he flows away from the gate, back to his perch, to the empty nests and discarded bones. The guards on the battlements are none the wiser, chatting companionably. Slickwalker smiles. Enjoy it while you can.

He lets the gun have one last look at his handiwork before the shadow pulls him back towards Crowkisser. It's enough to make a mountain burn. Enough to open Thell to her armies.

He sighs happily. A week to end this, no more. And if a worry lingers, the shadow claims it, and him, as he flows away from the mountain, and back to her arms.

70

The rain withdraws over the hills
but the hills remain
the hills withdraw over the horizon
but we remain

—Drykesang

They try to kill her in the third week. She stands barefoot on a low boundary wall, moss rough between her toes, her tongue alive with certainty.

The rising sun is warm on her back, her calves ache from walking, her thighs ache from riding. Her teeth are still thick with the taste of sleep, of Slickwalker, of a scorched meat breakfast.

Crowkisser watches her people watching her. Her army hangs on the edges of her words like birds on a branch. They'd hated her at first, god, how they'd hated her. Almost as much as they'd feared her. Kept her cowering behind the broken temple columns, hiding in Slickwalker's protective shadow. Now here they are, choosing to march, to fight; not just for Astic, but for everyone still held in place by the old systems. She couldn't be prouder.

They'd given up their names, but they'd received themselves in return. New people, for her new world, stronger and braver and free from the gods. Free from any authority but her guiding hand.

She wished Slick could see them, could see the world he was helping to build. This morning, like every morning, he was out scouting, tirelessly, flowing over field, hill and hamlet. Ferreting out the secrets of the Midlands, and the Barrowlands after that, always finding a way to make the land cough up enough food to keep them moving. Steering her people clear of the dangers; of the swamps and the scree slopes and the great storms that rolled over the plains like hammers, turning the earth to mud, and pounding the trees down into the soil. This was an unforgiving land. Half his time was spent finding the lees of hills, dry hollows where branches cut the wind into softness and offered up space for fires, for catching breath; they would be in trouble without him.

The locals fled before her army, sealing their doors with unfriendly eyes. Their minds heavy with stories of children lost to older wars, taken by bright-eyed leaders who threw them onto blades and spears, or left them to drown in that rain and mud. They couldn't understand that this was different, that *she* was different. In time, she would make them understand, as she had helped Astic understand. For now, she drove onwards, turning her eyes from their warding gestures and their tense hands. Victory at Thell would persuade them more than days of talking ever could.

For that she needs her people. The people in front of her now.

In the crowd, she sees so many familiar faces, hundreds of miles from the winding Astic streets they called home. Crabflick, with his chipped tooth and easy smile, a boy with mussable hair who used to leave offerings on the temple steps, who now sits and breakfasts with her, complaining like clockwork about fish-bones and dry bread. A bit behind him sits Sandsinger, one of the oldest to march, grizzled and whiskered, her wiry arms loose on the buckthorn club she's taken such a shine too. She was fast with it, too. Before the south, she'd told Crowkisser she'd been a netwife, mending ropes for her husband, mending herself when he drank. Crowkisser had opened him throat to gut one day, took him apart, tore his essence out and let it wither against the sky. They'd been close ever since. Sandsinger was like her grandmother, if her grandmother had drank too much, and licked the sea from her chapped knuckles each morning.

So many more familiar faces. Men and women that she treasured, from their scarred faces to their hopeful eyes. Above all, at the edges of the crowd, her long men lingered, quiet and watchful, palms light on the fishers' knives that gave them their name. Sea men, quiet men, brave enough to find the dangerous voices raised against her and hush them with salt and rope. At home in Astic, she'd felt them gather in the evenings, seasoning their ale with weeping, holding each other close and telling themselves they were doing the hardest, proudest work.

If only they knew how right they were. Her new world rested on the shoulders of brave, uncomplicated men.

Atop the wall, she keeps talking. Exhorting them towards the battle to come. As her voice rises and falls, her mind wanders to the faces that didn't make it this far. There were always a few dissenters. Named ones first, like Fallon's poor wife, her first, most brutal example. A necessary evil, to show the repercussions of clinging to an old name, and old ways. There hadn't been many after the Lady of the Grey Towers, and none of them with her fortitude. Perhaps she'd lost patience with the later ones and dealt with them too harshly. She could still taste the first names she'd taken. The Lady Fallon strongest among them, like a wet, oil-slick hole in her tongue. Of the later ones, those idiot rebels, nothing remained. She'd shredded them like so many strips of carrion. After that, no one clung to their old names any more. Still, other, smarter opponents took new names, and nursed old grudges. She was hated for so many reasons – cartels she'd pushed from business, soldiers and dignitaries she'd cast down, every criminal who felt aggrieved to be punished for a crime. A whole corrupt rats' nest was flushed clean when the south burnt, and still they chittered at her from the wreckage.

Most of them had come around in time. She'd talked to them, over tea, by fires, under temple pillars strung by wet-hung ropes. Most of them came around. Some grudgingly, some dissembling, but that faded over time. Resignation drifted into acceptance. Acceptance into compliance. Compliance into furtherance of her goals.

For those that didn't recant there were the long men, and beyond the long men, Slick. She would have been lost long ago without him. His laugh, his crooked shoulders and slender hands, his steady fingers.

It's the fingers that pull her back to the present. Fingers tensed in the crowd, pushing through knots, past smiling faces. A set face above them, the man's lips white, one hand moving bodies aside, the other unpicking the clasps on a tight-drawn cloak. He moves fast, and as he does, Crowkisser catches just a glimpse of red thread, and a brief flash of gold light. God light.

His head is thrown back as he leaps for her, that light blossoming like a struck flame, spilling from his eyes and mouth, that smell of spice, a taste of honey. The sickly twist of magic on the tongue. Her heart lurches in panic.

She stumbles backwards off the wall, hands raised. She can feel the heat rising against her and the rage of the god inside him. This shouldn't be possible. But he's here, it's happening and she's going to die.

As he leaps for her, her heart is filled with a blind fury. How dare he? How dare he, when she's so close? She bares her teeth in rage. A last defiant scream, as her skin starts to blister from golden fire, as a god who should be dead uses this man to reach out for her.

He never makes it. Instead, he finds hands at his ankle, pulling down hard. Crowkisser winces at the wet sound as his skull strikes stone.

Crabflick's fingers are locked around his foot, straining backwards.

As the young fisherboy hauls with all his might, others crowd in to help. For a moment, the waves of golden heat are submerged beneath a grey-clad tide as her people pile on bodily, swarming to her defence. Axes and clubs rise and fall, as her army strives for their first real blood on this long march.

They're not quite quick enough. As she struggles to her feet, Crowkisser watches the man rise with a ruined face, gold pouring out between the meat and bone, the crushed rasp of his breath strangely loud as he heaves himself upright. As he stands, a knife in his hand rises and falls, and Crabflick's suddenly a slick of red below the chin.

Crowkisser feels a buzzing like a drowsy hive, a pressure in her skull she's not felt in an age. The man shouts something to her, his teeth white, his fingers wet with gore. The words are lost in the light and the pressure, but still she sees the red threads on his knife arm as he charges, weaver's threads. Her heart quails at the buzzing hum of a composite god being unleashed.

'Back!' She screams. 'Back!'

It takes them a moment to react. A moment too long. The long men shouldering through the crowd pause uncertainly.

As they do, light blossoms and the god pushes its way out. The man's eyes boil. His skin burns and runs, then splits at the seams, rays of gold driving his spine and legs into unholy angles.

Crowkisser looks at the low wall in front of her, and knows it's not nearly strong enough.

She looks at the fleeing crowd and knows they're not fast enough.

The grass vibrates under their feet. The pressure builds. The sky is alive with burning, boiling, golden heat.

She has a second to be heartbroken that it ends like this.

The detonation tears the sound from the air, lifting her up and slamming her down until her teeth rattle. She feels a rib snap, hears screams. It's raining in the gold light, soft, drifting wet scraps.

Then a steadier fall. Larger chunks that might once have been fingers, or limbs, or an ear.

Somehow, she's still here to see it all.

She staggers as strong hands help her to her feet. Waves of dizziness crash over her as the colour of the sky slides back from gold, through red to blue.

She spits, tastes honey, spice.

The whole world is ringing.

She slides up onto her knees, peering over what remains of the wall, its stones shattered and twisted into slag.

Beyond it she sees crumpled heaps, staggering, helping one another up. Her people. Her army piecing itself back together. Others bringing buckets of water to douse a circle of burning grass. Astic pragmatism even under a cindered sky.

There's a lump in the middle of that circle, a mess of burning red and gold light, barely in the shape of a man, reeking of burnt sugar and cooked skin. Sandsinger stands at the circle's edge, her arm outstretched.

It takes Crowkisser a moment to see what the old woman has clasped in her blistered hand. When she does, her stomach twists, and she retches the last of her breakfast into the smouldering grass.

Another arm, scorched, sundered at the elbow.

Slowly she sees a second shape atop the pile. Hunched protectively, its spine charred into an arc of bone.

She staggers forwards. The ground is wrong, and the sky is singing.

She falls to her knees beside the flames and sifts the ashes, heedless of the tugging at her shoulders, her arms. Eventually, she finds a few shreds of mussable hair, what might once have been a jaw that once made a smile with a crooked, chipped tooth.

She takes Crabflick's jaw in her hands and turns it slowly, listening to the chimes it makes when it moves the air. After a moment, she looks at Sandsinger. The old woman watches her levelly, holding Crowkisser's gaze as she sets the arm down.

The words don't leave Sandsinger's lips on the first try. Instead, she shoulders her club, runs a blackened hand through her hair, then looks to Crowkisser and tries again.

'This won't stop us,' she says.

Later, her people lift Crowkisser and rinse the pieces of Crabflick from her skin. They miss a few. She finds shreds of boy and bone in her hair for a while after.

In the evening, the army builds a fire to send him on, their grey backs fading into the mist rising off the land. Crowkisser talks to them of endurance, with the heat of the flames on her face. She talks to them of freedom, with the cold of the night behind her.

Eventually, they leave her for the comfort of their tents and the pyre burns low. As she watches the embers wink out, she twines a piece of charred red thread around her fingers. She barely notices when the first crow lands, but by the time the fire is cold she can no longer see the stars.

71

a face haunts me
a face haunts me
sometimes my own
sometimes lying skin
lying bones

—Inscription at the foot of the Waxward Lintel,
above the western cliff drop

It's about a foot long, notched along the blade and the hilt worn
smooth. His palm is drawn to it. The cross-guard's light on his
knuckles like a kiss.

Fallon unlocks the cabinet, runs a finger through the thick
dust. The room at the top of the tower is warm, stifled in the
drip-down light of afternoon. The cabinet's glass is streaked,
muddled by lazy rags. Half his face catches there, hung with scars,
his moustache weird, unkempt, months of growth pushing the
grey out to the edges. He runs the back of a wrist across his
mouth and winces.

His head is ringing with brandy-bells; teeth furred as a cat.
Outside, the endless clattering thunk of war rolls in the streets
of Hesper, metal beats and bites onto metal. The whole city
sweating under the sun: strong backs, worn arms, itchy balls and
stinking cunts. A plague on summer wars. A plague on this one
in particular.

He fucking hated wars. Hated the grime of them.

The blood never washed off, just crusted and dried and scabbed
again. Beneath your nails, your gloves, your gums. Fallon had got
his fill of war long ago. Days and weeks on the march, or cooped
in some stone-walled rathole, skin slick with oil and fat, the smell

of yourself pressing against your armour. The wasp-click of a loose buckle. A sword that smacked the back of your legs in flat, irregular slaps with every step, every stumble over rocks and sand.

A pox on summer wars.

His hands fall off the blade – let it sleep in the dust. He slumps to the desk, toes the bottom drawer open. Uncorks, pours. Peace slopping out in greedy little gobbets. Swilling the bottom of cup. He screws his eyes shut, drinks. Better.

Outside, the ceaseless, dog-breathed rasp of war. Ropes strung tight to the outer walls, lashed to the bed of the rock, thick with tar. Murder to climb, but able to be lit in a pinch, kindling fast enough to wreath Hesper's skirts in flame on the whole landward side. Hot nests for crows; for anyone Crowkisser brought with her. Above the walls, stark, squat towers had grown blades, sharp-nesses, thundering catapults. Balanced ballistae on the coastal edge, bright steel eyes scanning the waves, muttering for blood and blood and blood.

He drinks again, shuffles a hand through maps, manifests, port reports. The only problem being, of course, that she wasn't coming. His whole city set up to crack her like a nut, and that slit had marched merrily pass on the landward side, close enough for his scouts to set his teeth gnashing, but not so close that he could risk reaching out with the marines to pull her back into the city's grasp.

A fucking mess, and he's a sheep-brained shit not to have seen it coming. Of *course* she'd sped right past them, as fast as her rag-gedy skirts could carry her. When had that black-feathered bitch ever not headed straight for the main prize? Thell was the real threat. For all it stung his pride, Hesper was just a dangerous afterthought, clinging to the coast like an angry barnacle.

Of course, Crowkisser would hie straight to the mountain like all the old dogs of the hills were on her heels. She couldn't afford to stay penned in the south, and she didn't have the numbers to pry Hesper open, on salt-side or land.

He swigs again, swishes the booze around his teeth. And of course, she'd follow wherever her father led. They all should have seen that. Instead, they'd all jumped like frogs into the pot.

So not just one sheep-brained shit. Three. That didn't make it any easier to bear.

He's pulled from his sour mood by a thunderous crash from outside. A cart overturned. Pottery smashed. Cobbles thick with curses. A rueful smile curdles on his face. He shoves the bottle back into the drawer. As he does, the ghost of a memory slips into his head. He regards the desk handles ruefully, remembering a small head meeting them, running too fast on quick little feet, wanting to be lifted and spun and whirled.

And oh, the tears afterwards. Barely suppressed laughter rattling in his chest at the melodrama of it all. His wife standing behind them both, mussing the baby's hair. Blowing tiny bubbles into its cheeks until it remembered it was alive. Little Quickfish was always half a breath from tears or laughter, the dearest thing. Declan had soothed him down in an old crib that had lived in the corner of this room. It caught the sun in the mornings, let it go in the afternoon. They'd hung it with ships, spinning around on tiny red masts, forever lost on a non-sea.

He drinks again, tightens his fingers around the handle, feeling that old stiffness in his chest. A familiar heartache, wrapped like soft leather around his hopes. How many more lonely mornings with only the dust and drink for company?

Enough was enough. He could still make himself useful.

He sets the cup down and fumbles clumsily for the tools he needs. Paper and ink, hawk-scrolls to be bound tight. If he's miserable, he's going to make sure the rest of the world is too.

He starts to write, heavy-handed and unsteady:

To Kinghammer and all in the Republic,
To those illustrious in the shadow of the mountain, to that which has risen from the ashes of empire, greetings from the city by the sea. The last great jewel of the West. The Grey Towers. Hear me, Lord Declan Fallon, Lord of Hesper, named and proud.

The quill stops. He writes, scores through, blots, sands. Too fucking flowery by half.

He starts again.

She marches past us. She's coming for you. Wants us out in the open. Thinks if she can pull us across the country, away from our walls and the sea, that she might stand a chance. She wants us to chase her. We can't do that. We'll die. Which just leaves you. She thinks she can break your spine inside its shell. Send in the shadows. Eat you up from the inside out. Scoop out that mountain of yours. Watch for her, she's a tricky one. Watch better still for her ratshit lover. He's got a disregard for gates and walls that twists my gut. Ward everything precious to you.

His hand lingers a moment as he searches for the words. Finally,

Friends are coming. Old friends. If you're smart, you'll trust them. They saved you once. They'll do it again, if you let them.

A pause, a scratch.

This isn't a time to be proud. If they say run, you run. Go west and south. I can have ships waiting. Send a hawk with white wingtips a week before you need them.

There, that's the last dregs of his pride swallowed down. They don't taste as bad as he'd thought they might.

This doesn't mean I've forgotten that you left us alone against her for near twenty years, or forgiven it. But this is close as you'll get. This is a hand of friendship.

A few lines blank, then:

I know you have my son.

He pauses, runs his fingers through his hair. And hadn't that been an awkward conversation, his spymaster's wiry hair brushing his ear as she muttered sotto voce. 'Your boy's in the mountain.'

Just that, then off into the dockside roil leaving him with a singing heart and a burning rage. He steeples his fingers against his temples, and swears quietly. This was what his wife would have called a 'delicate situation'. He wasn't quite sure how to handle it. After a beat, he drains the cup, and writes:

> *Keep him safe. Or I'll kill you all myself. As many times as it takes.*

That was about as much as he had patience for. He finishes off with a few perfunctory stabs of the quill.

> *In greatest salutation, from one proud city to another, in these parlous times, when we are surrounded by murderous cunts.*
> *Fallon*

He folds the letter, seals it. The early afternoon air is clotting around him, thick with tanner's stink and gunpowder smoke. He needs some fucking daylight.

Slowly, he levers himself up with the blackwood cane, stretches. Cocks an ear to footsteps on the stairs, fast and light. He can hear them echoing up through the tower.

Old instincts kick in, images of Slickwalker rattling through his brain. His eyes flick to the cabinet. The blade leaves it easily enough. He switches the cane to his other hand, finds a balance, and waits.

The door bursts open, the messenger's eyes widening at swordpoint before the startled lad skids to a stop and Fallon recognises him enough to compose himself.

They both watch each other for a second. The messenger's breath racing with enough urgency to tangle his tongue.

'Your wife, Lord. Sh-she's awake.'

Fallon's moving before the words fade from his ears, dropping blade and cane and barrelling past startled cries. The stairs are a blur, a shadow. He moves across them like a storm to the high tower, towards the sound of gulls and the low voices of a gaggle of physickers, preening like gannets. One of them moves, placatory, his arms outspread – he goes down like a sack and the others scatter. And there, in the bed, in the light, with open eyes and a smiling face is Arissa, her name as light in his head as a rung bell.

He throws himself on her, knits his arms to her, feels the shape of her. The back of her head against his hands. The angle of her ribs beneath her shift. He kisses her, and the world closes in on itself. Doors shut and the howling gale of worry stops. His mind falls quiet. The shudder of war slides off the walls and for the first time in years his heart knows peace. He twines his fingers in her hair and marks the line of her jaw, tears springing from a deep place he'd forgotten. Distantly, he feels her trace his temples, the new scars, the shaven hair. She laughs. He feels it bubble inside her and presses her face to his neck for the joy of her breathing, peppering her cheek with small, hot kisses.

Her laughter slides to sobbing, great retches of relief.

'It's OK,' he whispers into her hair. 'I've got you, Riss. I've got you.' He holds her, her hammering heart, her sweat-salted hair, her warm skin.

The physickers flock around them like sparrows, fluttering with news.

He waves a hand over her shoulder, gestures. The room clears.

He kisses her again and feels a disordered world slotting into place as she lingers on his lips. They sit. He smooths the tangles from her hair with thick fingers. She rests her fingertips on his lips, his neck, his sides.

'Riss,' he says.

She turns to look at him. She *hears her name*. He only now notices that he can speak it. The oil, the weight on his tongue, gone. He kisses her again. She tastes of spice and warmth. The light hangs golden around them.

He takes her face in his hands. 'I've missed you,' he says. He breaks as he says it, his voice fracturing into something smaller. Relief takes him like a soft wave and he falls forwards into her.

After the relief, sorrow, dug from the heart of him. She cradles him as he weeps, as he comes back from the shadowed places, brushes the dust from his heart and takes it like a bird into the light.

He holds her as if she was a treasure, a gift, a memory. 'Is it real?' he finally asks, and the question is almost too sharp to bear.

She shushes like a lullaby and pulls him close. 'It's real, love,' she says, and her hands run down his broad back. She looks down at him, and smiles. 'I've had the most beautiful dream.'

72

in the end, there is only the blade
and the body that becomes its home

—Bladedrinker's writ, archaic

A week later, the army of the Crowkisser comes to Thell.

Slickwalker watches them advance across the Barrowlands, his whole body alive with tension. Tries to take a headcount.

He flicks his eyes to the mountain ahead. Thell. The last of the old cities to hold any real threat. Hesper, back down there, clinging to the coast, was an afterthought.

The people of Thell had always been godless – conquerors; Empire-eaters. They'd weathered the horrors of the south from deep inside the mountain, washed clean of their names by Crowkisser's ritual, like everyone else, but left free to rebuild afterwards. Unlike most everyone else, they'd seen worse. Bringing them to heel would bring peace, at last.

With Thell, Crowkisser would control the land from north to south, from the blackened glass of the Rim to the great mountain glaciers, and everything in between.

What came after that, he didn't know. He'd heard talk of things beyond the mountains, spires, other cities too, perhaps, off to the west.

Slickwalker shifts numb feet. He didn't need to worry about the future yet. Seeing tomorrow would be good enough.

His eyes move towards the distant gate, tracing the covered holes he's bored in at the glacier lines, the shivers sleeping tightly beneath. He's been watching the mountain day and night for days now, counting heads and memorising troop movements like lyrics. Getting a sense of exactly how many they're up against. That sense is not good.

He feels like a shiver himself, thin brittle skin stretched tight over something explosive. Just waiting for the moment of release. His whole body's itching with it. The adrenaline's enough to make him sick, to double his vision into dizzying spells of excitement and terror.

His attention is caught by the glimmer of metal on the battlements; one of the morning patrols. There are five of them in all, six soldiers in each. They'll switch off with the noon patrol once the sun's high enough. One of them has a cold, sniffling his way around his shield grip. Another, older, has a limp, lifting his hip high every time he turns at the end of his quarter mile route. His counterpart on the western side likes a smoke, arrives early to breathe out a few puffs of something dark against the ice, before her friends join her and she covers her vice with a bluster of orders.

He observes their small vices, small flaws. It's not much, but it's all he needs.

He feels like they've talked this over a hundred times while looking at sketches of the mountain, of the Barrowlands in front. Shaping the course of the assault in their minds.

The Barrowlands themselves aren't the problem. If anything, the swarm of cairns that pocks the landscape gives them more cover than they might have hoped for. Couple that with the outbuildings, those strange cottages with their cauldrons and pits, and the approach to the mountain isn't the death trap he'd originally feared.

That's assuming Thell doesn't have people in the buildings, or between the cairns.

He doesn't think so. His forays into and under the Barrowlands have become more frequent since that first tentative exploration of the burial chambers, still more twisting passages opening up beneath the plain like half-dug trenches. Nothing as wild as that first night, but enough hollow land winding beneath the earth to make for unsteady footing.

The real problem is that the gate is the only way in. They'd considered other options, sending long men up the side of the mountain, to cut throats and create gaps. But that'll only work on the far edges. There are too many eyes on the rest of the mountain, and getting a few blades up on its east and west extremities won't save them if they can't roll the rest of the army in through the main door. Crowkisser was adamant she wanted as little bloodshed as possible. So, they'd tried to find ways to make the siege as quick and clever as they could.

Part of the problem was the scale of the damn thing. He'd seen Thell often enough on maps and charts, but mostly as a symbol, a strange half-scratch that looked like a hooded eye. Nothing to give a sense of its true dimensions. And for all that Kisser claimed to have flown into and over it on crow wings, it turned out crows were slipshod surveyors.

He looked at it again now.

Two hundred feet tall at least, assuming there wasn't more below the earth. Maybe a hundred and fifty wide or more. And those battlements looking out at angles, about halfway up, some kind of natural ledge or cut, he'd guess. It was hard to imagine anything on that scale could be man-made.

Either way, it was more than enough to give anyone on the battlements a clear line down to the Barrowlands below. He'd seen how cleanly Thell's spears flew in their practice drills, and he had a hunch there would be a damn sight more than spears raining from the sky, given Skinpainter still called the mountain home.

If they didn't want to die on their tenth step, they needed a plan.

Now, after three nights of arguing, they have one, but whether Crowkisser likes it or not, a lot of people are still going to die. Slickwalker tries to picture it in his mind's eye as he watches the patrols go through the motions. First, the long men will shin up the mountain on the east and westmost sides, those strong fisherman's arms put to work. They'll be silencing sentries if they can, but more importantly working their way in. Slickwalker doubts whether any of them will survive the night.

The key to getting out of this alive will be countering Thell's heavy hitters. For all Crowkisser thought she was invincible, Slickwalker knew better. All it took was a shot at the right moment. A dagger under the ribs or a falling rock. Sorcerers died the same as everyone else.

He expected four magic-wielders on the field tomorrow, and only one of them was on his side. His skin prickled with cold sweat just thinking about it. Skinpainter skulked inside the mountain and no one knew what they could do when pushed, but they had led a rebellion that tore down an Empire, marking them as one to watch. At their back, Belltoller. Slickwalker hadn't been able to get close to her, though he'd heard stories enough that he didn't care to. The tollers working together had drowned cities. Alone, by herself, who knew what she could muster? Slickwalker had seen enough cornered dogs in his time to tread carefully.

Worse still, Shroudweaver had run to Thell. Crowkisser seemed to think she finally had all the pieces in place to shut him down, but all Slickwalker could see was a powerful, ruthless man with his back to the wall. He knew she wasn't willing to kill her father, but he doubted that mercy cut both ways.

Which left him, and the gun. At the thought, he feels it stir on his back, flexing lazily against his spine. He was willing to do what needed to be done. Killing Skinpainter or Shroudweaver only needed one finger on the trigger to save thousands; to save her.

His fingertips itch at the thought, and his palm absently reaches back to trace the stock of the gun, which pulses impatiently.

Crowkisser was convinced she could handle them both. After her near-death experience she seemed more certain than ever, a light in her eyes he'd only seen once before, when the south burnt.

Someone needed to plan for the worst though. And so, here he was, watching the mountain and thinking about the best division of death.

The patrols shift again, and he counts the seconds in between, the brief span where their backs are all turned to the plain. His eye flits to the gates, and he scratches nervously under his gloves.

Once the gates are blown, the fighting will be close, and brutal, but they have the numbers, close to four thousand now, Astic's own bolstered by the Rim villages. He's not surprised to see so many. Dryke, Vantage and Fallow had been spare, lean towns before the south burnt. Now they sat on the edge of desolation. Leaving to fight for something better was a simple choice.

Slickwalker had been surprised that they hadn't gathered more coming north. The way Crowkisser had talked, the world had been waiting for her. In the end, the world had locked its doors and muttered curses as they'd marched by.

Still, four thousand was enough. From what they'd heard, or bought from the tongues of traders fleeing south, Thell could muster only a couple of thousand at best, and of those, only around half were fit to fight. And of that half, most hadn't seen war in twenty years.

A few dangerous old bears, and an army of unblooded children. No wonder Crowkisser expected Thell to crack without too much strife.

Slickwalker, as always, was a little more pessimistic. Even so, if they could get into the mountain, they'd have the edge, almost four to one. The only trick was surviving long enough.

He starts at the sound of horns, from the eastern battlement first, then rippling along the length of the Stump, until the Barrowlands are awash with noise. He watches as the limper hurries back to her post, as the sniffling boy straightens his helmet on his head. The smoking woman stubs her roll-up ruefully and shrugs her armour tighter across her shoulders.

Slickwalker doesn't need to look to see the source of their panic. He doesn't need to, but he turns to the south anyway, for the sheer pleasure of it.

The army of the Crowkisser has come to Thell. Four thousand men and women, robed in the grey of Astic, the dun green of Fallow, the worked leather of Vantage and Dryke. Appearing in knots and clumps, they form a ragged line that stretches the length of the Stump, then off east and west, half a mile at least.

Knots and clumps, like they'd planned. He smiles quietly to

himself. Groups of two hundred or so, spread out over the field. Only half those groups need to make it to the gate for them to have a fighting chance inside. Split small, they can weave through the barrows and buildings, perhaps get some shelter from the inevitable steel rain.

They'll need it, lightly armoured as they are. Clubs and shields, boat-knives and boathooks, the flat-blades they made in Sedge, and the hooked daggers that stripped the trees in Fallow. They need to move fast. Once they're chest to chest with someone, all blades are the same.

Slickwalker unshoulders the gun, shudders as it unfurls with a rapid hiss. Braces its smooth length against his arm and sights down at the lines.

Crowkisser's there of course, a few feet ahead of the vanguard, far out of spear range and not alone. Four long men flanked her at all times, knives loose in their hands. Good. Another argument he'd won.

There's no theatre to this, no ritual. As the sound of horns fades from the hills, there's silence for a moment, broken only by the piping of mountain birds and the muffled shift and clank of Thell's battlements slowly filling with soldiers.

Then Crowkisser's army gives voice to a shout. High and ragged, washing over the cairns and barrows.

And below him, they begin to charge.

Slickwalker remembers an old salt telling him about battle, once. He'd said that an army charges like a sickness. Bodies clotting into valleys, thickening in choke points. As he watches Crowkisser's people rush forwards, he sees the lie in that. Sure, if you perched yourself high on a mountain ledge, you could almost kid yourself that it played out bloodlessly. Vast human waves, brutal, implacable, crashing against the stone shore of the mountain.

Get a little closer though, and that's when the dying starts.

Beneath him, the first wave of grey bodies roars forwards. Each group peels off into defiles between the barrows, shields up and clubs loose. The army of Thell is silent. The sky is clear. It won't last.

Slickwalker tears his sights from the charge and tilts them towards the mountain. Watching won't keep them alive. It's time to inflict some death of his own.

Slickwalker is just a man with a gun.

Sandsinger is in the lead on the rolling ground below, and fuck, but she does not want to be. Her knees hammering as they charge forwards. A hard spike of adrenaline in her heart, the breath rasping in her lungs like a swilled-out pail. One of the boys behind her screaming already, something high and thin. He doesn't even realise he's doing it. It's just leaking out of him like a pig before slaughter.

A pain in her chest like the one that felled her own beloved boy six year ago, and she's got to get these babes into that bloody mountain alive. She turns her head, bellows, 'Shields up, sprats!' And bless them, if they don't listen to her. Hefting something roughly in the shape of a shield-wall, studded with driftwood and leather. It's a little ragged, their line wavering, but they only need to be strong enough to ward off whatever those stone-dwelling fuckers throw from above. There's not a movement on the Barrowland yet, and gods, she's glad of that. Half of her head's on her own pounding feet, half wandering back to the sight of him keeling over in the kitchen, fingers grasping.

Minds are bastards in the middle of battle. Always wanting to get away. She grits her teeth, lets out a roar. 'Faster, grey darlin's. For Crowkisser.'

'For Crowkisser!'

The shout lifts her back like a following wind.

Crowkisser herself is out in front of them, moving light over the tops of the barrows, nothing around her save a grey kirtle, but even Sandsinger can feel the power gathering on her skin, her limbs writhing with the black edges of feathers. Each leap leaves her longer in the air, drawing her closer to the mountain. The long men at her sides scrambling to keep up.

No leaping for Sandsinger. Just the gentle burn of arthritic bones, and a whispered prayer to keep these sprats at her back alive. Fifty lives under her command, and thousands more spread out across this plain of graves. She can glimpse them drawing level with the first outbuildings, scrambling to keep their heads low and their shields up.

It's as she runs that prayer through her lips again, that Sandsinger remembers she's far from the sea, and the gods are all dead.

So, here's a truth to that old salt's statement. An army *does* charge like a sickness. And it's greeted like a disease.

As they pass the first outbuildings, there's still nothing but long firepits smouldering under copper cauldrons and the knock of loose shutters against stone. The back of Sandsinger's neck itches like it does before a storm. She's halfway through reaching out a hand to bring her boys to a stop, when the ground erupts. Those low firepits covered with old ash rise up in the shape of men, as the doors of the outbuildings are kicked down by bright-eyed warriors who charge, long shields held high, leaf-bladed spears darting out like snakes.

She has a moment to take in tattoos, burning eyes, war cries like an eagle's shriek. Then Thell's soldiers fall on her lads and lasses. One particularly burly bastard sets his lights on her, darting forwards. Some old instinct makes her dip below his spear thrust, but the shield bash that follows takes her full in the chest. The air gushes out of her lungs and she staggers backwards.

To her left, the wailing boy takes a spear through the guts. Sandsinger curses, rolling to the side as a barbed point hammers the mud next to her head. She sweeps out with her club and hooks in at the ankle, is rewarded with a crunch of bone. She throws herself onto her attacker as he hits the ground, putting her whole weight on his spear arm. Down in the mud, she's got the advantage. That bastard blade of his is too long to get to her. She lets out another gust of air as his knee comes for her stomach and just about chokes down the urge to vomit.

Sandsinger swings the club at the side of his head. One, two, three times. Apologising each time. 'Sorry, sorry, sorry,' until she's singing it to a wet mess of metal and bone. She's sick at how much he looks just like one of her boys. Or did, until she'd had her way with him.

As she struggles to rise, another soldier towers over her, spear upraised. Stupidly, she throws up her arms, as if they'll suddenly stop metal. She feels the blood go cold in her veins, as a shot like a scalded cat burns the air above her. A stink of rotten lemon and suddenly the man above her has no head. His fingers lurch up to clutch at the burning stump of his neck for a moment, before his body reels backwards and down into the mud. Sandsinger touches her hands to her heart, and wonders if she's been praying to the wrong gods.

As she stands and looks around, she sees the rest of her silver darlin's haven't been so lucky. Maybe half her boys and girls are still standing. The air is thick with the stink of piss and sweat. One of them is just sat in the mud, crying over the ruined body of his friend. Young men and women stabbed clean through, six or seven times, so she can't even tell where their blood ends and the mud begins.

They've won though. If you can call it that. All the soldiers that ambushed them are down, except those that have fled back towards the mountain. One of them's still half alive, but there's a bunch of lads kicking him with the energy of jackals. There's not much left for him.

She tries to count around her aching head. She figures they've killed maybe thirty, and lost twenty of their own. Those numbers don't work out well. She bends at the knees, takes deep breaths in, lets them slide out. It's war. She's got to be tough as old sail. Even if she can barely breath.

'Form up lads.' Her voice is stronger than she feels. And bless them, but they do, even more ragged than before. Those walls still seem awful far away. There's only one way for them to get closer. She grits her teeth, ignores her aching knees, and picks up the pace.

Down the line, Slickwalker pulls the trigger again, and again, and again. Heads explode, bodies are torn in half. The gun eats through metal and bone alike. He has to keep moving though. He can see faces turning on the battlements, trying to scout his position. Spears fly through the air, peppering his vantage points like rain, and he's forced back into shadow. And every time he's forced back more people die.

All along the Astic line, the story is the same, the first push meeting more resistance than he could have imagined. Thell's warriors emerging from ashpits and outbuildings, the shock and surprise of the assault withering those neat little groups down into ragged bands. They've lost maybe a third of their force in the span of minutes. The ground between the barrows is thick with bodies and blood, the remaining soldiers tripping over their downed comrades. Most are lifting them bodily, dragging them along, or into shelter behind the barrows, reluctant to leave them behind.

They push forwards. They've dented Thell's advance force, but at what cost? Of those ash-covered ambushers, less than a tenth make it back alive. That's not the end of it though. As they run back under the shadow of the mountain, Thell's battered troops reform their lines. The great gates open, and fresh bodies come forth, two hundred more, at least. And as their shields lock, the battlements above let loose in earnest.

Slickwalker's seen spears fall before, but never in these numbers or with this precision. The sky hisses with the speed of their descent.

He watches his army cower in response, throwing themselves into the outbuildings, or behind the humps of barrows. For those not quick enough, death is sudden, at least as spears punch through shields, skewering the men behind, one or two deep. Others are caught by the thigh or arm, nailed screaming to the earth as their comrades scramble to pull them free.

An army is greeted like a disease, the old salt's voice hisses in his head. Sharp metal pierces the most threatening points. Blood flows forth.

Slickwalker spits reflexively in disgust. Fully three hundred dead in a minute or less. There's something dishonourable about it, something deeply unfair. So much lost.

The blue sky holds metal like rain. The people of Astic are a harrowed earth below. It doesn't stop them, somehow. The survivors harden, scab over with shields and leather. He can see commanders reforming their ragged lines, driving them forwards, shields upraised. Some marked with the split tree of Vantage, others slashed with white paint in the shape of a crow's wings. In response, Thell's vanguard closes ranks as they push through the cairns, a solid block of warriors moving out now from the main gate. Maybe three hundred strong, in a wedge at first, then folding into smaller phalanxes to intercept each approaching group.

The gates seem impossibly far. But Slickwalker's counted the breaths to the mountain. They can make it. He knows they can make it. And when they get there, the shivers will let them in.

On the battlements, the remainder of Thell's army set shields, their arms wrapped in bright metal, and beneath that, geometrics – red and black and red again. Slickwalker scans the line for targets, for someone worth more than another common soldier. Nothing yet. Crowkisser hasn't tipped her hand, so neither will they. Instead, more of those damned spears rise and fall. Astic's army are prepared this time. Their grey bodies peel off into huddles, shields upraised, keeping their hands on billhooks, flat-blades, boarding spikes, drawing closer to those phalanxes at the gate. They weather the rain from above with arms around shoulders and waists, those grips getting slicker and slicker as they are torn apart. At this rate, there won't be enough of them to take the gate. Twenty companies had set out for the gate, two hundred men in each, little coveys forging forwards against the storm. Only a ragged stretch are still standing, and some of those just barely, winnowed down to half their number. The Barrowlands are hollow with the sound of chopped meat.

Their screams drift up to Slickwalker's vantage. He grips the gun, sights, pulls the trigger, again and again and again, cursing with every shot. A body pinwheels over the battlements, spun by a slug to the shoulder. Another loses its throwing arm, the spear clattering to the ground. Still they come, flaying his people with steel, over and over again.

Despite the carnage they're causing, Thell's warriors are almost silent. They move metal with precision, adjusting shields and lobbing spears with quiet efficiency. The only sounds are breath, harness, sky, pierced with the occasional satisfying scream. It's then that Slickwalker finds his target – Kinghammer, standing in the center of his troops, hands tight upon the battlements. Can't get to him yet though. Too many bodies around him. When he goes down, it needs to be clean. Slickwalker wants everyone to see him die. The big bastard nods as metal rises and falls. He taps a rhythm on the haft of his hammer, raises a spear in his other hand, throws.

Down on the ground, Sandsinger watches a young girl take that spear in the eye. Her hands don't even have time to flail at the socket before she's driven back into the earth, carried down on six foot of wood and steel. Sandsinger's sprats are in bad shape. So's the rest of their army, from what she can tell. Their shields aren't enough. They weren't prepared for the sheer force of these things hammering through the air.

The only thing that saves them is the dying. She's not sure who has the idea first, but suddenly, they're moving forwards again, their shield-wall strung with the bodies of their friends.

She ducks as another rain of metal clatters off the cairns, wrenches the dead girl free of the spear and levers her to the front, listing wildly.

Their whole front line sprouts the dead, their bodies growing spears like a forest. Sandsinger flinches with every impact. She's almost frozen with fear. Every step is a conscious effort. The boys and girls next to her are shaking something fierce. One of them's saying the old prayers, but he can't find the names, and he's choking on the words. The girl to his left is slick with sweat and blood, her eyes white in a red mask. Every time she moves, she half-falls against Sandsinger, who holds her straight and steady, like a tired animal.

Their shield-wall heaves with one ragged breath, all of them straining together. As they shamble forwards again a spear-point splits the body in front of Sandsinger, and stops just shy of her chest.

Somewhere in that chest, Sandsinger starts singing. Snatches of songs she knows well, quiet shanties that grow and swell and

die, and grow again, old songs of the old sea. The survivors pick
it up, ragged and thin as curlews on the moor, at first. Punctuated
with screams and cries, but Sandsinger hears her voice growing
stronger, and she hears other voices rising next to her. She leans
into the sister on her left and the brother on her right and staggers onwards. Along their whole line, the ragged army of Astic
lurches towards the mountain, shielded by their dead. The gate,
somehow, grows nearer. Its guardians tip spears in response, the
phalanxes of Thell's vanguard barely a hundred feet away.

Near five hundred terrified boys and girls pulling through the
Barrowland in ragged clots of ten and twenty, cowering beneath
the rain of spears, then lurching forwards in the lulls. Above their
heads Slickwalker's gun rings out again and again, its scorched
cat-scream crashing into the howls of the dead and the dying, the
singing, the shouts of command. The noise of it all like a hammer
beating wet on the inside of Sandsinger's skull. Like the breath of
a hunting dog on her shoulders.

She looks up, and prays to her new god, to that strange shadowed boy to keep watch over her.

High on the edge of the mountain, he's doing his best. People
run through the gun's sights like water. Slickwalker's fingers are
burning, shadow eating at their tips as the rifle feeds and pulls.
Still he fires. With every shot, another of Thell's bastard brood
goes down. Through the throat, so a mouth moves uselessly atop.
Through the shield arm and the shield, spinning bodies in pirou-
ettes of sizzling black. Through the guts, eating the whimpers,
the flailing of desperate hands.

Slickwalker takes aim, fires again, his jaw clenching in satisfaction as another spear thrower staggers backwards, the gun
devouring her skull straight from the socket. So many of them
still, at least two hundred on the battlements, spears stacked and
racked enough to kill them all five times over. They just can't
match Thell at range and he's not enough to tip the balance.

As if his worries have found him out, the air tightens near his
head, and he ducks to the side. Too slow. The spear takes him
between scapula and neck, the force of it skidding him sideways

across the rock, his feet skittering in mouldering nests and rotten eggshell. For a moment, the ground looms below him, and he panics.

He trips as he tries to steady himself, hanging for a second on the edge of the precipice, then falls.

The armies below draw closer with frightening speed, as he twists in the air.

The pain in his arm is bad, but the weight of the spear is worse, pulling him off balance. He feels the gun buck in his hand as he nearly loses his grip. It's hard to call out to the shadow through it all, his whole body unstable, hurled by the wind and gravity.

Of course, if he doesn't get out of this, the gates stay closed. And they all die.

Slickwalker grits his teeth, grabs the haft of the spear, and tears it loose.

The agony almost makes him pass out. The spear spirals away below him, red with stolen blood. The ground is far too close now. Close enough that he can make out individual faces.

He closes his eyes, breathes through the agony, and leans into the shadow. It's harder than usual. Gravity wants him, and he's lost a lot of blood. It almost feels like his body is tearing apart. He screams with the effort, and dissolves into blackness, propelling himself into the pockets and hollows of the mountain which the sun never finds.

He hauls himself back up to his vantage, shadows slowly pulling the hole in his shoulder closed, his mouth filling with curses at the lost time.

He has to catch his breath once he's back on the ridge.

The picture unfolding below him almost takes it away again.

The battle joined in earnest.

Both sides moving in. His people are almost through the Barrowland proper, pushing in ragged groups towards the side of the mountain in a slow pincer movement, drawing in to meet the square block of Thell's troops guarding the edge of the Barrowlands. Maybe two hundred of them, crouched low, shields up, spears out. It's odd they're not advancing.

Slickwalker wonders if they've seen the troops to the west and east pulling in to hit their flanks. Dogrunners and Whiteteeth from Dryke and Fallow. Hopefully not – they're fast lads, but lightly armoured. He mouths a little southern prayer to guard their backs. Feels it turn to oil and ash in his mouth. Of course.

Time to get into position.

He flows along the spine of the mountain until he reaches one of the westmost battlements.

The long men there turn to regard him as he reforms from the shadow. One is cleaning his blade on the edge of a ragged cloth. The other moves his knife over the throat of the last soldier. Slickwalker recognises her, the smoker.

She struggles a little, as the long man clamps his gloved fingers over her face, and sketches a wet red line across her neck. No more smokes for her.

Slickwalker looks around. 'Lose many?'

The long man nearest him points to two grey-robed bodies, slumped one against the other, their chests a mess of holes.

Slickwalker shakes his head. 'Get inside. We're close.'

The long man nods, steps closer to Slickwalker. His eyes are pale under the brim of his hat. A seabird skull swings loosely around his neck, beak long and thin as a dagger.

'Deep Fishers be with you, Slickwalker.' A hand on his shoulder, then the pair turn and slip inside the mountain.

As they move from sight, the sky darkens, clouds rolling in, down off the mountains, followed by sudden deep thunder, and the crack of lightning.

Slickwalker tastes the burnt sugar of magic on his tongue, and breaks into a run.

Far below, the people of Astic have gained the last stretch of Barrowland, moving in harrowed grey clots. The spears fall still, as those clots fill the defiles between the barrows with their blood, turn the grass black and weeping.

The wind picks up, the clouds ravelling down off the hills,

a gale building against them. The people of Astic push and are pushed like the sea.

Sandsinger flinches as the thunder rolls. Fucking rain on top of it all. Here she is, dying in the mud, and now it's fucking raining. She doesn't like the look of those clouds. Ship-sinkers, black as a widow's skirt. They don't belong up here.

She claws her wet hair clear of her face. 'Onward, lovers. Just a little more and we get some payback.'

They're all exhausted, reeling forwards behind the bodies of their friends.

Almost under those big battlements now, almost clear of the rain of spears. She glances up, counting steps in her head, her lungs rasping the squall in and out.

Above her, someone odd stands on the edge of the mountain. Stocky, robed. A ragged thing, like an old scarecrow, ribbons of red and yellow streaming off their arms as they raise them high.

She staggers as she's pushed from behind and steps aside absently. Something's fixing her gaze on that figure as they raise up their arms. The hairs on her neck squall a hurricane alarm as she watches their arms reach up and reel the clouds in, their gestures seeming to pull the storm down across the Barrowlands. There's a taste on her lips like burnt sugar, and a pressure building like the summer sky before a squall, lightning coming down the line.

She turns to her boys and girls and screams. 'Cover! Run!'

The figure on the battlements reaches for the thunderheads and she watches those yellow and red ribbons rise from their arms, snaking towards the clouds high above.

Mountain magic.

Sandsinger traces the ghosts of those ribbons as they flicker against the sky, swelling into impossibly huge bands of light amid the storm, red and yellow, ragged and wide as rivers. In response, the clouds pulse, veined with black and red and black again, their angles sharpening to mirror the tattoos on the warriors of Thell. The ship-sinkers move in strange rhythms, against the wind, gathering over her people below. The falling rain hardens into sheets, striking with the force of a breaker's hammer, punishing the land, the people, the dead. She feels her skull bow under the weight of it.

Another rumble of thunder, and Sandsinger tastes its electric edge almost too late. She throws herself low to the ground, dragging her boys and girls down with her.

The lightning arcs red as blood and catches those still raised too high. Across the plain it strikes, six, seven, eight times. She counts under her breath as people explode, as the fire of their screams runs back into the ash sky. She counts to keep herself sane even as the rain develops a thickness, gritty with burnt bone.

Through the cut light of the storm, Sandsinger sees Crowkisser powering forwards, lifted no longer, the weight of the rain pushing her down. She sees the lightning come for her, a twisting red snake, guided through the air by those upthrust hands.

She stretches out her own hands hopelessly, gasping at the last moment as a long man bulls into Crowkisser, knocking her to the ground, his arms still reaching for her even as the lightning sunders his skull, boiling out the tips of his fingers, roiling red in his eyes.

His corpse sways, smokes, falls.

Sandsinger watches Crowkisser stagger to her feet, stare at the body for a moment, then turn and sprint onward.

They don't all have her fortitude, her faith. The sky's against them, the clouds threaded with spears, torn by that red lightning that strikes the earth over and over.

Sandsinger watches hopelessly as the Astic line falters, the right flank breaking entirely, driven apart into swirling eddies. Hundreds lost in a stroke, fleeing the field as fast as their legs will carry them. It's not the end of things though. The rest of her boys and girls aren't done yet, and there's hundreds more at their back. She sees them, all down the line. Pushing onwards with everything they have left, fathers driving the bodies of their children forwards. Brave lads and lasses who have lost limbs are carried, hoisted aloft, urging the others along. All screaming teeth and tongue at the lightning. One last act of faith and defiance before they're all rendered down to ash outside this bloody rock.

If Crowkisser has a plan to save them, Sandsinger would sure like to see it about now. She distantly glimpses their young witch, racing the storm to the mountain, a few steps ahead of the lightning. She doesn't look back at them, doesn't watch her people die.

Sandsinger spits. 'Come on, girl. Be better.'

As if it feels the bitterness in her chest the wind harshens, howling with black fury, picking at the pennants, snapping them in two. The barrow-markers list, tearing the earth beneath. Astic's army staggers towards the mountain. The spears fall through the wet and reddening sky.

Sandsinger grits her teeth, ignores the ache in her knee, her hip, the cuts peppering her forearms. The only way to go is forwards.

The shout that tears out of her lungs is something less than words, but her lads all know it. The swell call. That wild yawp as home comes into view.

They surge into the last of the barrows. That big phalanx of bastards sees them coming. Shit, there's a lot of them.

As Sandsinger's ragged little crew forms up, a group peels off, angling towards them, locking shields with a shout. She feels her guts turn to water.

And of course, as she's shitting herself about the spears, she forgets to watch the storm.

She's sent tumbling as the air tears next to her, another bolt of lightning shearing the arm from the lad on her left. He turns and stares in horror as his flesh catches light. She swings her club upside his head, tears in her eyes. The only mercy she can offer.

Above her, a second clash of thunder as magic roils through the clouds, burning the air, splitting the sound from her ears in punishing thunderclaps. Sandsinger distantly hopes their crow-witch is up to the task. She isn't sure what crows can do against a storm like that, but there's no time to wonder about that now. She tears her eyes from the shuddering sky as another spear buzzes past her ear, haft fishtailing madly. Adrenaline shoots up through her guts and she tries not to piss herself. That tattooed mob from Thell are impatient, a steel bloc of shield and spear creeping towards her, out from under the shadow of the mountain. Sandsinger hefts her club as they advance. There's maybe some sixteen or twenty rolling in, their shields locked like fish scales. Crowkisser might have mentioned this. Or Slickwalker. Some scout he was. There's spears poking out everywhere like tits on a hedgehog. Some kind of ungodly hum comes from behind the shields, as if they're all chanting in unison. Fucking cannibals.

She's not alone though. Glancing left and right along the flattening line of the barrows, she sees others have made it through. Not just her own folk, but all those brave buggers from the Rim. Dark skin, wiry beards and hard eyes. The sight gives her a bit of hope, though they've been cut thin by the approach, only a few dozen left all told. An army of strips.

To her left, she watches a bunch of lads rush forwards, shields out and clubs hurling. Trying to get around the sides of that big block. Stupid, stupid.

She shouts a warning, watches hopelessly as Thell's formation shudders, the front rank dropping to their knees and raising shields, as those behind sprint up that tilted metal, arcing down onto the charging Astic lads.

Screams, the crush of bodies and spear-points driven down like the beaks of seabirds. Then the entire phalanx charges. Those overeager lads and lasses are crushed against shields from above and in front, as spears lick out with terrifying speed. It's over in seconds. Twenty brave boys dead, and the rest crumble and run.

Sandsinger's stomach turns, but she forces herself to run a weather eye over the rhythm of it all. It's deadly, but the more she watches, the more she sees the flow of Thell's formation pulling their soldiers forwards into the barrows. She glances at the woman next to her, raises an eyebrow. 'We could string 'em like we practiced.'

The woman grins, spits out a loose tooth. 'We could.'

Sandsinger taps her shoulder. 'Signal the others. Tell them we're raising ratlines.'

The woman nods, ducks behind a shield and pulls out a ship's whistle. Three short blasts over the field, piercing as a fishwife's call.

'Sounds just enough like a retreat,' Slickwalker had said with a smile, when they'd drilled it out a few days ago. 'They don't know us. They'll expect us to run.'

As Sandsinger's poor battered boys hear the signal they break and run. A beat later, the rest of Astic's line follows, haring back to the barrows like they're done with dying.

Sandsinger runs with them, the lightning at her back, muttering under her breath with every red-lit step. 'Charge, you fuckers, charge.'

For the first time since the gods died, her prayers are answered. She hears the roar of Thell's bloodletters rise behind her, oscillating up to an eagle's shriek, the earth suddenly shaking with the thunder of their charging feet, loud enough that her old bellweather of a heart nearly stops in her chest.

Above the terror though, a glee she's not felt in years. 'Fell for it, you rock-sucking twits.'

She grabs the signaller's wrist. 'Ratlines up on three.'

Sandsinger can feel Thell's soldiers behind her, harrying Astic's front line back into the barrows. A quick glance over her shoulder and she can see their spear-points reaching out for her back. Nearly a full third of the force guarding the gate has pelted off after them, hungry for blood like a dog after a rat.

The signaller's whistle goes up. Three short blasts.

They have about twenty feet on them, just enough.

All along the Astic line, fleet-footed fisherfolk dart back towards the barrow mounds, a couple of men and women from each cadre peeling off and spanning either side of the defiles that thread the cairns, trailing something thin in their hands as they slip low around splintered prayer-flags and outbuildings. Hands held high, steady, feet braced against the rock and earth.

The rest of Astic's troops pelt down the cuts between barrows, Thell's spear throwers a beat behind. As they reach the hump of the cairns, Sandsinger and the rest throw themselves to one side. Then the ratlines are raised.

An Astic ratline is a thin thing, boat-wire, clear as spider-silk, and stronger still. Each strand wound around ten others, thin as baby's hair. Light enough to trick the eye. Strong enough to string sails against the storm.

Strung at head height, just enough to catch the front line of tattooed warriors across the throat, the chest. It doesn't do much to them, but they stumble, skidding in the mud. The lads at their back can't stop fast enough, ramming into them in a tangle of limbs and curses. The wire doesn't give, of course. It's held up to East Tide gales and West Tide whirlpools. So, as they struggle, that's when the other ratline closes in at their backs, dragged forwards by another couple of crafty greycloaks, penning them in, pressing them together with the weight of their own bodies. All down the line, all those forays jammed into the low defiles between the barrows like crabs in a bucket.

Sandsinger watches, crouched in the mud, her nose half-submerged by the torn body of one of her lads. She can smell his blood mixed into melting frost water. These Thell boys are tough. As soon as they see they can't go forwards or back, they start for the sides of the barrows. She remembers Slickwalker's dark little smile, even as she rises. His whisper in her head. 'After the ratlines, the nets.'

A croaked order brings all her good lads and lasses, all of them not hauling with gristle and gut on the ratlines, rising up the side of the barrows and throwing the shoal nets.

Dark things, thick and heavy as a wet wool cloak, weighted with sharp shore rock. Back home, they used them to trap creelbreakers, but they've got a different catch today. The nets settle over upraised spears, heads and arms, tangling everything, pulling inexorably down. Spears can't swing, shields can't raise, all snared up like sprats in a jar. As they realise their predicament, some of the Thell boys start to scream.

Sandsinger steels her heart and gives the order. 'Clubs out, my brave ones.'

Astic's troops swarm the trapped soldiers, covered and camouflaged bodies rising up from the hillside like cormorants. Blackwood clubs smash through the tangled mess of net and rope, crushing bones and snapping fingers. Boathooks come in under the mess, taking out calves and tendons in ragged, howling strokes. Sandsinger swings again and again, dodging blades that flash by her eyes. They're not all so lucky. Overconfident, some of them, eager for payback. A few get caught on spear-points, pulled back into the whole screaming mess. She grits her teeth, spits the blood of strangers out of her mouth and keeps swinging. Slowly, each trapped phalanx is battered to the ground, collapsing in on itself. Deaths by the score, and the punch of broken bone echoing over the Barrowlands.

All along the line, Sandsinger watches the people of Astic take their revenge, Thell's charge foundering in a mess of snares. A full third of the gate guard are down in the mud, dragging themselves helplessly from clubs that fall like wet rocks. The storm doesn't tell friend from foe either. Lightning hammers into the middle of each struggling clot, sending bodies sprawling, filling the air with the stench of cooked meat.

On the battlements, and at the gate, Kinghammer and his generals see what's happening to their army. There's only one way it can go after this. A low, sonorous bell tolls out, and the hail of spears from above stops.

High on his perch, Slickwalker mutters a curse, and darts for the gates. On the ground below, Sandsinger wipes off her club, and turns wearily towards the mountain. 'Shit.'

From outside the gates of Thell, the remaining guards charge. Another two hundred warriors fanning out into a precise line, shields locked, spears levelled. No rash moves this time. They've learnt their lesson. A steady advance, and Sandsinger sees only death at the end of it.

She looks for Crowkisser, spying her for a moment, standing tall atop a barrow, staring fixedly at something on the battlements high above – that ragged, ribboned bastard from before. Then she's not got time for anything but meeting the charge. Dragging her lads and lasses back into formation, straightening shields and propping them up as best she can.

Between her group and the others, they form as solid a wall as half a hundred tired fisherfolk can manage, blocking the low ground between the barrows, keeping the raised mounds of the buried dead to their left and right, plugging the gaps in their line.

Sandsinger counts in her head as Thell's soldiers charge closer. Maybe a hundred of them headed her way, and she makes just fifty of her greycloaks. A few bright slashes as the reserves from Sedge and Fallow come up, and what's left of their second line comes forwards, but that's it. They're near enough evenly matched, which is bad.

Slickwalker's stopped firing, so he must be getting ready to blow the gate, but there's a lot of murderous bastards between them and the mountain.

Fifty feet. The drum of their steps against the plain. She can feel it in her chest.

Forty feet. Their war cries high and bright as eagles. She wants to be anywhere but here.

Thirty feet. She can see their faces. The eyes behind their shields, their tattooed skin.

She calls out, 'Steady!' and she's amazed there's still strength in her voice.

Thell's warriors break into a run, and Sandsinger falls quiet, except for a low murmur she keeps at the back of her lips. 'Not today.' She grips her club tight, hanging in a moment of wood-sweat breath, before the lines meet with a crash that echoes over the mountain.

Bodies are driven into the grass. A shudder goes through their shield wall like a wounded animal. A fisherboy with barely seven-teen summers under his belt finds himself staggering backwards, pinned to the mossy side of a barrow. He doesn't even know why until he looks down and sees the spear shining red in his chest.

In Thell's ranks, a veteran eyes the lad opposite her, as a swung club skitters off her shield. Her bones ache from the impact of the charge. She's been a soldier since the fall of the Empire, but she hasn't seen a war for as long, and she'd forgotten the shape of it, forgotten what it feels like when the bones in your arm near break because your shield's braced wrong. The panic is harsh in her stomach, lit like old coals, rattling out her ribs in panicked gasps.

She can barely breathe, and she has to kill this boy in front of her, who could be her son, if his hair were blonde.

She's not alone. All down the line, the two armies lock, heaving. Grace and tactics gone, nothing but a mess of bodies pushing against one another, sweating, screaming and bleeding into the mud.

Crowkisser's distantly aware of the dying at her back, but her mind's elsewhere, up in the storm, watching Skinpainter's fingers dance as he pulls red-lit death down on her people.

She's trying to sense the shape of their magic, to find her moment to strike back. They're all relying on her. She's the only one in this army that can match Skinpainter, Belltoller, or Shroudweaver. And she will. She won't let them down. She's going to show them all why the south burnt.

That storm's the problem. Mountain magic, but on a scale she's never seen. This is no weather witching, calling a squall down over the fields, or twisting rain towards the brave crops that grow on the rock-side. She has no idea where Skinpainter found the power for something like this, but there's a taste to it that's familiar. Slick as burnt sugar, like honey on the back of the throat. God magic. And she knows how to deal with the dregs of the gods.

Her people need cover, need shelter from that red murder tearing down out of the sky. And there's nobody to protect them but her. She swerves to avoid another lightning strike. The earth near her toes chars, rocks and grass fountaining up. That bastard's after her. She can *feel* them in the storm, directing the lightning like a whip. Wearily, she turns to the long men that are left.

'Cover me!'

They nod wordlessly, moving to defensive positions around the barrow-top. The body of Thell's army is still snarled up on her front line. She has time.

Crowkisser balances on the peak of the barrow, her hands wrapped around the cairn flag, its wet wood rough against her fingers. She lets her mind follow its path, speared down into the soil, reaches for the sorcery lingering on her skin, and calls out. It feels like nothing at first, a shiver across her shoulders, like a door left open to a cold room.

She stretches deeper, further down, seeking the power she needs, the shadow that lurks under the earth.

She pulls it to her, an electric blossoming on her bones, her skin alive with feathers, and something darker, coiling and smoking against the storm.

Crowkisser throws back her head and coats her tongue with rain, calling out into the teeth of the gale. Barely heard above the lashing wind, but loud enough to carry a vibration of counter-magic, sliding like a dagger up into the heart of the storm.

When the crows come, they come quickly, black motes silhouetted against the pulsing ground. She watches as they push through the storm in ones and twos. High above, Skinpainter's no fool. They've sensed her attempts at sabotage. Thunderheads wheel towards the gathering birds, but the storm is an unwieldy weapon, listing like an overloaded cart as their arms strain and pull.

Still the crows come. Crowkisser flinches as lightning picks at the edges of the growing flock. Feathers pinwheel in small explosions as the storm fights for space in the sky. Every strike punches against her heart. She grits her teeth and reaches deep inside herself, wrenching the darkness under the earth upwards, hurling it into the storm, filling the air with crows. The effort drives her to her knees. She chokes, coughing clots of blackness up into the clouds, watches as they grow feathers, talons, beaks. Little black tongues.

The sky grows noisy with wings. The light fades from the day as the sun is pulled behind a thronging mass of birds, the storm muzzled behind their bodies. There are distant flashes of blood and feather as the lightning pounds against the flock like a muffled drum. Crowkisser shakes with each impact, her head tilted to the clouds. A writhing cord of black power shudders from her throat, blossoming into a thousand squalling bodies. A few of Thell's warriors come for her. The long men meet them on the slope of the barrow, bending around spear hafts like ship spars and driving blades deep under ribs. She has time.

Holding the storm at bay isn't enough. She feels it shaking the flock like a wild dog in a hen house. She has to destroy it.

With a scream, she drives the crows inside the thunderheads. A thousand little black bodies riding the lightning, pulling it with their wings. Burning as they fly.

The Barrowland rings to the sound of a skyful of birds on fire. The day grows shadowed. The storm swells like an overfilled waterskin, billowing like a torn sail, writhing with wings and lightning.

Its belly is a mass of beaks and wings and thundering hearts, a clot in the throat of the storm, pulling the lightning inwards, threading it back into the heart of the clouds. Weaving a mesh of static and electricity and bone that hums and screeches.

Crowkisser screams with it. Her own throat chokes with darkness, lightning burning along her veins. Each tiny hammering crow heart igniting inside her own. Skinpainter battles frantically against her, but they're too slow, too cautious, too old. She closes her eyes, thinks of her mother and pushes. The effort nearly finishes her. Dark bruises blossom under her skin.

Miles above, she feels Skinpainter stagger; feels the storm stagger with them.

Overhead, the clouds shift, and realign, turning their lightning inwards. Each jagged stroke dragged back into the heart of the storm on burning black wings. The whole mass glows red as a fired coal. The air is thick as an unstruck match. The armies below reel under its weight. The grass driven flat as cat ears. Every flag on every cairn bowing and splintering as the detonation builds. Pressure, such pressure. Ears bleed. Noses. Soldiers on both sides fall moaning to their knees. The lines waver, too heavy to fight. The weight of storm and sky pressing down into the land. The clouds swell. Wings batter them from the inside. thousands of small bodies filling the space, crows upon crows until the sky is a thing of black and moving wings. The belly of the storm stretches, distended. The sky howls in pain and Skinpainter howls with it. Staggering back, clutching their side, where blood flows fresh under their robes. They lash out with a hand. The air is tattooed red and black and red again, geometric lines of control. Too late, too late. Crowkisser's heart surges with fierce elation.

The pressure builds. On skulls and temples.

Crowkisser feels Skinpainter falter. She has them. She has them all.

She reaches, tries to twist the neck of the storm, to detonate it in the sky.

And just as she holds the thunderheads pulsing in her fist, a tone rings out. A clear bell, light and sharp. She feels it shiver the field, cutting the sweating air like a cold knife, striking like the flat of a great blade. It catches her on the temple, lifts her, rolls her down the side of the barrow. Her head cracks loosely against a rock. Dazed, she loses control of the storm, control of the flock. The sky spins.

Her head lolls to where she can groggily see the two armies locked against one another, straining like tired horses, almost too exhausted to move.

She hears that rolling knell again, and her gaze is pulled back to the battlements. Where Skinpainter had stood, a woman leans into the storm, tall as mountain ash. In her hand, a thick iron bell. Her gaze locks on Crowkisser's crumpled form far below.

Belltoller, stiff-backed, grey-haired, the flat planes of her brow unmoved by the storm. Her eyes are as still as the mountain. Her ribs move in slow, easy exhalations. Crowkisser can feel the steady shudder of her breath from a mile away. She tries to rise, but her head is swimming with chimes, bursting into purple and yellow light behind her eyes.

She stands, staggers, falls against the side of a barrow. The world is tilted, singing, slipping under her feet.

One of the few remaining long men helps her rise. He's mouthing something, but his lips move uselessly in the wet, thick air. He points urgently towards the mountain, and her head turns, just in time to see Belltoller's brown arm swing the bell towards her with a resounding crack.

Belltoller's wrist snaps like whipcord. Her whole body reeling back from the lash of the stroke. A faint smile on her lips. Her eyes locked on Crowkisser.

The sound of the bell travels down the mountain with the speed of a galloping horse. Ice and rock follow in its wake.

When it hits the Barrowlands, the land splits.

The earth fleeing a deep cleft ravine, which tears across the ground with a snarl, the ring of the bell at its back, driving the debris onwards and upwards. Shards of stone flung skywards, fountaining the air.

Crowkisser is trying to run, but her legs are weak, twisted by the bell's echoes, still sick from battling the storm.

The long men haul on her arms desperately. She feels her shoulders pop. Her legs won't work.

A second peal, hard as cracked iron, and the ravine convulses and deepens, as if punched down into the dark earth by a swung axe. Distantly, Belltoller's body jerks and lashes like a struck chord, blood on her teeth, and death in her heart.

Crowkisser watches as the ravine hits the eastern flank of her army, as the earth bucks like a wild horse and throws off the men and women desperately fleeing the spreading darkness. She watches bodies arc through the air. A few beats of horrified wailing, before the steady crunch of stones rising to welcome spines, hips, and skulls.

The earth yawns in front of her as the Barrowlands split like ripe fruit and give up their dead. She glimpses old bones, severed roots. The ground is torn away, and with it the power she needs, the thick might of the old dark draining down these new wounds in the skin of the land.

The speed of it stops her heart. There's nothing she can do. She stays on her knees, rests her hands on the shivering ground and bows her head for the end.

And suddenly, she's moving.

The last two long men lifting her bodily, one at the shoulders, one at the legs, her view jostling as they pelt towards the mountain, always a step or two ahead of the widening ravine, scrambling up the side of a barrow, a heartbeat in front. The whole thing lists as the earth next to it sinks into the depths.

The long men set her down gently. The one nearest her sweeps his hair back from a sweat-stained forehead, smiles in relief, and mouths something that might be, 'Safe.' He offers her a hand.

The crack of the bell behind him rings like a splitting anvil. The tear rips across the land faster than anything she's ever seen. A roar of sundered soil, and the side of the barrow explodes.

The long man's fingers still in hers, the rest of him split by the force of the tolling. She glimpses an eye, drifting loose from the skull and the remnants of a smiling jaw. A brief mess of slithering, wet ropes as his guts arc over her head, then she's in the air, spinning end over end. The earth opens, all those old graves, shuddering to one side, falling into the worm-flecked darkness, making room for her.

Something in her jerks, and she catches the gnarled remains of a root, hanging for a moment over the soft patter of bones and stone sifting into the depths.

The jolt is almost enough to wrench her arm from the socket. Pain flares down her side, fingers scrabbling for purchase. Not now. Not here. Her foot finds loose stone. Enough to kick upwards. The pain is blinding, white fire in front of her eyes. She grits her teeth, yells with the effort and starts hauling herself upwards, arm over arm. Fury on her lips. Not now. Not when she's so close. Not when so many have died.

Hand over hand, Crowkisser climbs.

Above her the clouds chime. Bright, beautiful peals, as the iron bell tolls again and again. Belltoller spins in sharp, precise movements and with every cast of her arms, the peals intensify. For the first time in decades, a Belltoller has taken the field, and Crowkisser sees the horror in the folktales is true. Even alone, she is monstrous. Devastating. The landscape can't withstand her. The grass is bludgeoned, the cairns pressed flat. As the pressure builds, the sound of tolling rolls like a beast across the Barrowlands. It tears the tops from hills and people, shearing barrows and slicing the earth into heaving sheets that pull whole units screaming into the depths.

Crowkisser has lost control of the storm, and Belltoller knows it. She flicks echoes up into the roiling clouds.

In response, the sky rings with purity. The thunderheads shudder and contract. The crows laced inside the tempest becoming less frantic, less urgent.

Belltoller swings the bell, marshals the storm like a wayward flock and draws it downwards. The oldest form of 'tolling. Back from before there was a Thell, or an Astic. The old art of swaying rain low over the fields. Of making the wind come to your beck and call with just clapper and arm. The clouds know it, and they sing in response, pushing the ground percussively, flattening what remains of Astic's bedraggled army. The living are pushed down into the dead, into the rents in the earth and the slick mud between the barrows. Thell's own frontline is too close to disengage now, fighting mechanically, desperately, spears rising and falling. Above it all, red lightning runs ragged along black wings as the cowed belly of the storm approaches Crowkisser's army. And the bells, the great bells of the sky toll, and toll again.

Down on the earth Crowkisser hauls her body over the lip of the ravine, and spits, her fingers scrabbling in wet mud and blood. She's furious. Exhausted. As the breath rasps from her lungs, she digs her hands deep into the earth, gets the stone under her nails and pulls. Beyond Belltoller's cuts, deeper than she's ever gone before. Finds the dark, broken and wounded. Wrenches it up through her body and into the light. The pain of it is incredible, but pain is just pain. The noise that leaves her lips is like a mother giving birth.

She takes the dark, and drops it like a cloak over her people.

It falls like soft feathers, like drifting ash, and beneath it Astic's army rises, linking shattered arms, and singing, their mouths grey with the sea. In front of them, Crowkisser's body contorts in spasms, and the outlines of her people blur, their brows kissed by feathers. Weapons are raised. They move forwards, picking up pace over the shattered ground. The great gates loom.

As Crowkisser works, the Barrowlands grow strong with shadow, thick on their charging bodies. Thell's spears are met with darkness mid-air, stutter through the sky, and are devoured. They reach the ground as nothing but splinters, hollowed metal. Freed from the killing rain, Crowkisser's army is buoyed by blackness. The gates draw closer, Thell's defensive lines wavering in the chaos.

Sandsinger feels magic swill around her legs, feels the kiss of strange winds on her brow. Finally. Finally, her crow-girl has come through. She thinks of Crabflick, and the southern fleets, and those golden bastards, and she raises a club half-snapped from swinging, screaming out a battle cry that's lost to the storm.

That storm is foundering. Even with Belltoller's guidance, it rolls like a wounded animal, seeping sound and light. She battles to keep it within her power, her lips a soft line, her words a secret that she whispers into her bones. The bell rises, falls. Her hands lift, tracing the pulse of the clouds. A rhythm builds. One final strike is all that's needed. She glances at Kinghammer, and he nods.

The people of Thell match the storm's thunder, drumming on their shields. Kinghammer roars and raises his hammer to catch the darkening air. When the haft falls, the sky rains steel. And the steel sings. Belltoller's back arches in response, her fingers curving, catlike. The air reeks of burnt sugar, magic cascading off her in scorching waves. She reaches, casts outwards, and the steel follows her hands. Hundreds of spears twist through the sky like silverfish, hovering, schooling, and striking, piercing Crowkisser's protective shadow to slip steady into bloody homes. The people of Astic are winnowed. The earth takes them. Hundreds fall to their knees, lungs and guts holed by this whirling gale of blades.

They've come too far to stop now. So they try. Still, they try. Shields are raised. Clubs bat aside spear-points in frantic desperation, but Belltoller moves like a windblown flower and kills with every breath. On the battlements, the arms of Thell's warriors rise and fall relentlessly. The sound of the battle swells. The thundering sky, the falling steel of spears, the tolling of bells.

The shot rings through it all, a burnt cat's yowl, that snake-eagle-death cry. It catches Belltoller full in the face. Bone and skull and teeth blown away. She staggers, raises an arm unsteadily and drops the bell. The steel rain wavers. The second shot tears her ribs out and eats her heart. The hissing blackness of Slickwalker's gun pools in her body, devours the stone, her screams, her frantic hands. Shields surround her, raised and hopeless.

A third shot rips the air, catches the raised head of a hammer. Kinghammer staggers, his weapon smoking. A few moments of utter confusion. Here Shipwright's strong hands, there Quickfish's hurried work and Roofkeeper's swift movements. Between them, Belltoller's remains disappear into the depths of the Stump.

The air clears. The storm still squalls with crows and geometries, but it's uncontained. Skinpainter is exhausted, Belltoller a burning husk of blackened skull. And below, the people of Astic pick up their shattered bodies and move forwards. The great gates loom, impenetrable.

Shroudweaver is barely visible high above. A ghost on the battlements, cut from a slip of ice and a scrap of windblown cloud. Unwatched. Unheeded. Unhampered, he begins to weave. Red for binding and silver for sending. The numberless dead of the Empire shift within his chest; pressing against bone and marrow, shaking his veins. Restless in the prison of his hammering heart for twenty years. Eating his spirit by slivers to stay alive.

Smokesister's bindings have been enough to keep them from seeping into every twist of his muscle, every drop of his blood, but not for much longer. He's held them for too long. He should never have taken them in the first place.

It's time for them to come home, briefly. Time for them to become something more. If there's a regret in his heart for what he's about to do, it passes like breath on a mirror.

He squares his shoulders. This is real now. No stage show, no confidence trick. Just a blind stab at halting the inevitable, and righting a wrong held too long against his heart.

He carefully unpicks the first few strands of red thread from around his wrist. Feels a small shudder as the bindings loosen. Like stepping under cool water.

The dead stir under his ribs.

A squad of soldiers thunders past. He pivots and sways absently to avoid them, light on the heels of his feet.

A second red strand unravels. And now there's a chill on the ground, a wave of cold flowing down the mountain. There is saltpetre on body and sulphur on bone.

The Barrowlands ripple, like a pond awoken, like a pulse under skin. Red threads continue to fall. His hands are steady. Relief is the only emotion in his heart. His lips are dry with the words of unbinding, slipping over his tongue like papery scraps. Twenty years, and undoing it all is the work of moments. He could have done it at any time, if he'd been prepared to pay the price.

Now, here, the dead can do something good with their last bright burst of energy. They can stop his daughter, before she makes an even bigger mistake than her last. He can weave them into a composite. Something with enough raw power to bring everything on this plain to its knees. A new god, that will exist for the briefest moment.

And to fuel it, all he needs are the souls he's carried like cargo for the last two decades.

They'll be burnt to nothing. Consumed. The thought gives him a brief ache, although it's gone in seconds – there is no other option. To release them would be to return them to the Emperor. Still twisting down there, in the depths of the mountain.

He watches Crowkisser's army charge below him, closer than he'd ever imagined them getting. Thell's line is retreating, steadily and methodically, but retreating nonetheless.

His errant daughter's certainly pulled out all the stops. The things she's done today have left his mind reeling; magic like he's never seen. And always at her back, the bark of that awful gun.

So much death already. So many souls loose and wandering the plain, tangled with the storm, choking in the mud, strung to the red scraps of their bodies.

His heart aches at it, but clinically, professionally, he sees more fuel for the fire.

Free and ragged, these wandering spirits have little power. They need guidance. They need a weaver. They need him. He breathes deep. There's an order to this. He can't rush. The red doesn't work without the silver. Unbinding requires sending. The souls need a focal point.

What he's attempting is stupid. Impossible. A breaking of the first law. Weaving a composite, raising a new god, with nothing to hold it except the force of his own will. No body to shape its shell. To limit it. But he's seen what his daughter can do. If they don't stop her here, now, they never will. And there's no one to do it but him.

He doesn't want to kill her. So, this is the alternative.

Looked on long enough, a god swallows the mind. That's why hosts only took fragments of divinity into themselves, why composites only tolerate human form for the briefest time. The body can't stand the touch of the gold for long. People aren't built for it.

He doesn't want to kill Crowkisser, but he'll take her mind, if he has to. Hopefully, she'll surrender before that.

He sees her below at the head of her army, wreathed in flickering darkness. The great gate of the Stump awaits her.

Before that, a brief space of blasted grass and rock. Thell's soldiers retreating across it, encircling the passage into the mountain. They can't get caught up in this. He owes Skinpainter that much.

Shroudweaver sights on the empty space in front of his daughter's running feet, and pushes forth with the silver thread.

A lurch like a high dive, and the coldness that follows.

Binding happens with the body, red and raw, in the world we know.

Sending happens elsewhere, in the world of the dead, or close to it. In the between spaces, that place between breaths, where the mind can slip if it's left unguarded long enough.

The voice of his old Aestering tutor echoes in Shroudweaver's head, taking him through the steps, the motions, fluid and precise.

He focuses on the ground in front of his daughter, feels the cold rock under his feet and steps back into the between.

He can still feel his body here, but guiding it is harder. All its pains are multiplied, the harsh rasp of his breath like tin scraps in a can. Light flows down in soft grey ribbons, but the space around him is nothing but darkness, lit by the briefest flecks of silver, strung around bodies, living and dead alike. Soul-thread, the weaver's true material.

He's left it too long, truth be told. He's out of practice, getting old. The pain of it is more than he'd ever remembered. His lips are dry and his teeth feel slight in his head.

On the balcony his body is pushed by running soldiers. Ship-wright catches him as he staggers, her arms around him, solid and real. If she can hold him there, in the real world, he need only take care of himself while his soul hangs in the between.

The ache of his mind is loud in the between spaces, and along with it all the regrets and fears he's held tight 'til now. The reek of them is like a beacon to the dead.

A less experienced weaver would be at risk, but he can use this. He grasps the silver threads of their souls. Shivers them with his fear, his worry, his regret, like a spider plucking a web.

The dead of the plain come for him, invisible and thinned by the rain, heedless of storm or sacrifice. They crawl over his skin. He twists, weaves, and negotiates. Their fury is a quiet thing. They have only recently lost their lives, had them torn away by blade or butchery. Life naturally calls back to them. They're joined by the deeper dead, spirits lurching up from the barrows, casting off the last scraps of burial shroud as they thrill at the memory of old wars, and swim towards his power. They all push against Shroudweaver's jaw, his sternum, his hips. They want in.

He can't allow that. He needs them in that bare space before the mountain, waiting to be joined by the souls within his chest.

He keeps them busy, pulls silver thread in intricate dances that maze them, spiralling them deeper into a nexus of twisting anger and loss.

Every movement in the between is mirrored by his body on the battlements as the fighting rages. Shipwright holds him as he shudders and ducks. Her voice is a hymn and a hollow and a safe place. He sets it like an anchor, squares his back to it, and weaves an offer to the newly dead. He delineates, sketches, trades. His fingers move with frantic speed. The world spins around him. People die around him. And the storm thunders down.

The dead follow his hands, shoal-like fish in front of his daughter's running feet. He has moments, bare moments. In the between spaces though, a moment hangs like a blade of wet glass, held and stretched in the dark. The weaver's secret.

With his right hand he sketches a quick loop of red around the swirling battlefield dead. They complain, distantly, but they are lulled as summer bees, ready to join the throng that swells inside him, that crushes his lungs from within.

His breathing is harsh as a muzzled dog, air vanishing with every twist of his fingers.

As his vison closes in, the gathered dead hang at the end of his gaze. He feels the souls in his chest press forwards, expectant, like calling to like; droplets of rain forming into puddles, pools, rivers, oceans.

All it would take is a word to set them free. They're hungry for it, starving. If Shroudweaver loses his concentration for a second, they'll tear their way out. With Smokesister's wards gone, the only thing holding them back is his patience, his precision. And the powders, the age-old trappings of weaving. So reflexive, he forgets they're there most of the time. Now, as the Empire's restless dead push towards his veins, they butt against the stink of saltpetre and sulphur. It holds them back, just barely, like two fingers on the throat of a hunting dog.

He can't delay any longer. He mustn't.

All it takes is the final unbinding. He mutters a quick blessing and spits the taste of oil from his tongue, pressing his right hand tight against his breastbone. He digs in with his nails, just enough to break the skin and let the red of the bindings touch the red of his blood.

The dead in his heart burst forth like an undammed river – every soul the Emperor had marshalled against them; everyone Shroudweaver has stolen, rescued and kept imprisoned for the past twenty years flows out into the between.

Shroudweaver leashes them with silver, trains their course like willow in a salmon run. Freedom-mad, they rush towards the brightest, nearest thing; that swirling nexus of the battlefield's slain lingering in front of his daughter's charging feet. The dead flow from him like water, down the channels he has carved.

The endless souls of the Empire meet the dead of the battle in a thunderous roiling wave. Their combined energy burns like a silent star. He's in awe. Terrified. The sheer power of the thing he's created already starting to burn the between places, scorching its way into the world.

He closes his eyes, bites his lips, and weaves a red binding, fast and furious, dancing around the hollow of his knuckles, the chipped beds of his nails, around that ache in his wrist that comes with every cold morning.

The dead are pulled together, herded like deer before the beaters, crushed and fused, woven and bound. It is almost a composite. A thing hung with a thousand voices, hopes and fears. Not quite a composite, though. Not yet.

Now comes the hardest part. He has to make it manifest without breaking the binding. A single snag or tear, and all that energy gets unleashed on the edge of the world. He'll make Crowkisser look like a saint.

He weaves, one hand in the between, strung with silver, the other reaching redly out to the real world, inexorably drawing the two together, like guiding a blossom through the eye of a storm. He weaves. Every binding filament is precise, hung with his held breath. Until suddenly, the pattern is complete. The living and the dead are separate no more. The thin skin between places comes down with a whisper. On the plain below, the people of Astic are suddenly no longer alone. The air is thick with forgotten names, and a growing space amid them that hums with golden light.

Shroudweaver feels the heart of a new god start to beat in his hands and his own heart leaps with joy. Then, a gunshot. Screaming down from the high places like a piece of the night aflame. He feels it kiss his head with feral grace. Hears Shipwright's scream. Smells himself burning even as he's pushed sideways, Icecaller barrelling into both of them. She straddles him lithely, smiling.

Her shield is a smoking ruin where the shot's caromed off. With a wink, she levers herself up and takes position in front of him.

He doesn't have the tongue or teeth to thank her. His body is still hung amid the unbinding, outwith his control. At his back, he feels Shipwright's hands lift him. Her mouth making urgent shapes. He nods but it's heavy. He's not here. He's down on the Barrowland. His hands are the god's hands, his lips, its lips. He's thirty foot high and made of love and rage and fire. He can feel it pulling at the edges of his mind.

If he doesn't finish the weaving, the god will eat him, brain and soul. He leans back into Shipwright's chest, hears the steady hammer of her heart, and looks up into her eyes. She reads the panic on his face like a storm-broken sea, smiles down, and kisses him. 'I trust you.'

It's barely a murmur, beneath the squall of blood and battle. But he hears her somewhere deeper and his mind clears, the god's song lessening for the briefest spell.

In that respite, Shroudweaver reaches his hands forwards and finishes the binding. The composite, the new god, solidifies into itself, its form shuddering within each twist of red thread.

For the first time since the world drew breath, a god is strung together from nothing but will. Shroudweaver stitches that god, tethers it. He fetters its form and binds the thousands of souls that fill it into a single thing with a single purpose. With each twist of his wrists the composite brightens and flares until it towers over both armies, lighting the rock and ice of the mountain. Its edges are gold and its eyes infinite. It is full and blossoming with limbs and voices, fire and honey. It is beautiful. Shroud-weaver feels its pull, like a velvet rope around his neck. They all do.

The people of Astic fall to their shattered knees, in the blood and mud and the roiling storm. The composite god stretches its arms wide to them, radiant. Terrible. Perfect.

And yet at its feet, Crowkisser keeps running. She is silhouetted against the bright bulk of the god for a second. Slight, windblown.

His daughter flowing out of the storm on a thousand wings.

Her skin wreathed in blackness that shudders and burns in the golden fire of the new god's radiance.

She does not bow.

The composite watches her. The entire field watches her. Shroudweaver's heart aching for her, at how much it must be costing her to even move in the face of this thing's glory. His lips move, wordless, begging her to give up, to bend the knee.

She does not bend.

The composite is radiant, terrible, beautiful. A patchwork of a thousand, thousand souls fused into a single being that shifts like morning. It is the sun, and the end of things. It is love and dying, spice and mourning, loss and life.

She does not bow.

Stark in the burning light, Crowkisser raises her ragged right hand, clenched tight into a fist, a scrap of the Emperor within. Its voice in her head, triumphant, confident, insistent.

'Now.'

She pauses for the barest moment, then throws.

The smallest scrap of a dead man. A tiny, black speck, against the vastness of a sun, disappearing like a pebble in a pond.

One small, broken finger, kept by Skinpainter all these years. Now lost to gold fire as the composite swallows it.

Crowkisser lowers her hand. There's laughter in her head; the Emperor's voice harsh and delighted: 'Finally.'

A sudden surge of fear spikes her heart. She takes a step back. Turns. Runs.

Shroudweaver watches in horror as the composite shudders and pulls in on itself, the souls inside twisting and distorting, fleeing every which way in panic, like birds in a cage. Something is terribly wrong. There's something new in the threads. Something new but horribly familiar. The caress of a mind he thought sealed into darkness, the touch of the Emperor of the Dead on the back of his neck. Frantic, Shroudweaver tries to pull the composite souls tight, but even as he tugs, he feels something familiar haul from the other side, with strength and conviction. The silver threads burn, lit like flares. His fingers cannot hold them. And in his mind, the Emperor's voice murmurs. 'Hello, Weaver.'

Panic coils cold against his heart. Shroudweaver wrenches, pulling silver fire over his skin. He feels his powders burn away, evaporating in flashes of light and smoke. He saws harder, threads cutting through the meat of his fingers, down to the bone.

He digs his heels in and wrenches again. The silver threads holding the souls to him shimmer, stretch, and snap. Like a cut hawser, the red bindings lash loose and fall away into the mud. Shroudweaver is yanked forwards, staggers to his knees with a crack, teeth punching through his lip. Blood in his mouth, and a hum in the blood as the dead start to hunger. On the plain, the composite shudders, boils and screams. Purest pain, threaded through a thousand throats. And then within the pain, laughter. Deep, delighted and familiar. He last heard that voice in the heart of the mountain, maddened by darkness and torture – the Emperor of the Dead. Loosed, somehow.

What has his daughter done? What has she done?

The composite sways like a drunkard, reaches deep into itself and tears, ribbons of light falling from it like a sputtering lamp. The laughter louder, shriller. Anguished. Spiralling up by octaves.

As the composite crumples, Crowkisser's army seizes its chance. All along the Astic line hands go up, voices holler, and they charge.

They've watched all the old gods die, and now they've watched her kill this new one in front of them.

At the composite's sundering back, the remainder of Thell's line edges towards the safety of the gates. The ravaged god in front of them roils and explodes, the dead inside boiling loose into the air. Crowkisser's army gives chase, a howl of vengeance rising from their grey ranks.

Thell's lines fall back in front of them.

It's then that Slickwalker fires one last shot.

Shroudweaver watches it travel with a sick inevitability. Above the gate, the first shiver ignites with a crack like split ice, spreading into a hissing halo of bright fire that carves into the mountain rock for a second, two, then detonates with a roar that drowns out even the dying god, the mad Emperor writhing inside its splintering form.

The side of the mountain blossoms, black and acrid.

And the gates of Thell fall open.

Slabs of rock slide in great, groaning chunks. Dust billows in clouds. Thell's retreating soldiers scream, lost in fire and ash as the mountain falls above them, all order gone. Those that survive flee over broken rock into the belly of the Stump.

And at their back, over the heads of Crowkisser's running army, between the falling steel and the shouts of dismay from above, the hungry and unchained dead of the Empire pour into the depths of Thell.

73

the black heart
the blood song
the world's only beat
the ceaseless hammer
red rhythm red rhythm red rhythm

—Inscription on the interior of the Gull Barrow
[Subsequently backfilled, sealed.
By order of the Grey Towers.]

Quickfish's ears are ringing. His hands slick with someone else's blood. Belltoller, her face sheared off, chest gone, the black filth of Slickwalker's gun still smoking on her bones. He wants to be sick, but he can't afford to stop moving. As they flee the battlements, Shipwright charges onwards and downwards with furious, unstoppable force, Roofkeeper dragged in her wake, Quickfish following him. Her face is set, one broad arm cradled around Belltoller's shoulders, her left hand working something brass which spins and clicks and chitters. With every twist of her fingers, they seem to move faster, their feet lifting across the smooth rock that slopes down into the Stump.

Wild and strange to see her here, now, as the world melts and implodes, a face from his childhood appearing above the fleeing, screaming ranks. Her broad cheekbones smudged with the light of a dying god, her hair almost haloed with gold, something unreal, almost inhuman in the shape of her. She'd snuck him apple juice from the kitchens, and raised him on broad shoulders to tap the beams of the towers; now she was a stark sketch of relentless fury, holding a burning woman on the edge of death.

She doesn't see him. Her eyes are locked on Belltoller, on the hissing gap in her face that crawls with twitching shadow. She moves with furious speed, the crowd parting before her, reflexively, like starlings before a storm.

Somehow, Quickfish keeps pace, trying not to think about the death at his back, the smell of blood and burning rock wafting up from below. Shipwright has brought the Shroudweaver with her, and the abomination he just conjured has walked straight out of Quickfish's nightmares to die in front of him. He can feel the fire of it washing over him as they run, a burning gloss clinging to his skin. He tries to tamp down the terror, but his body thrums with it, panic rising in his throat, hammering in his heart, holding his head in a vice that threatens to trip his stumbling legs. He slows his breathing into long, ragged gasps and watches Roofkeeper's back as they jog in front of him, his strong hands tight around the axe. Belltoller's body jostles again, wet against his fingers. Quickfish wipes her blood on his shirt, absently watching it eat gently into the threads. The world is unravelling.

They continue to plunge down into chaos. The Stump has been cracked open like an egg. Somewhere beneath them, Crowkisser's army is flooding through the gates, and with them something Quickfish doesn't have a name for. The fragments of that thing that exploded on the Barrowlands. Something Shroudweaver called up. Something Crowkisser tore apart. Swirling, screaming spirits of rage and light. He feels his mind slide loose at the thought, a hysterical laugh bubbling up in his chest. Clamps down on it, and runs. The remainder of Thell's army runs with them and past them, faster than these foreigners by far. They know the mountain like a hound knows its course, speeding by each other, leaping down chutes and funnels in the rock, plummeting downwards to reinforce the gates. The honeycomb of the Stump spits steel. Somewhere, distantly the last dying thunder of Skinpainter's awful storm rages and beyond that Kinghammer's voice beats counterpoint. As they spiral deeper, Quickfish glances outwards, through the passing archways. The Barrowlands are filled with drifting golden scraps, tossed in the driving rain; shreds of the thing Crowkisser destroyed. Between the golden ash, yowling spirits plunge downwards, wreathed in mad laughter. One pauses, meets his eyes for a moment, and Quickfish glimpses a broad, hollow head, hung with sharp teeth. Its mouth splits wide for a second, before it's pulled away and down, following the howling throng towards the sundered gate.

Quickfish has never known anything like it. The madness is beyond anything he's ever seen and they pause for none of it. Shipwright's legs are like pistons, the Belltoller's body rocking in her arms. She never once looks lost, but thunders downwards into the heart of the mountain, to the council chamber. They're not the first there.

Civilians push forwards, filing into the echoing space, ringed by a smattering of scared young warriors, clutching shields and unsteady spears. Quickfish distantly recognises the tattooist, Steelfinder, by her dark hair and strong jaw. Behind her are the Deadsingers, raised above the chattering, panicked heads of the crowd on the first rung of carved stone seats, their hands interlocked and veins blue even against painted skin. Their weathered faces are steady and a soft song is on their lips. Around them the air is unnaturally still. They move slower within it, charms, bones and hair drifting gently as tranquillity radiates from them. Quickfish feels it against his skin like a cool breeze. His racing heart steadies. Around him, the effect is mirrored. The panic slows. The crowd calms.

Shipwright does not slow. She drives towards the Deadsingers, Belltoller's body limp over her shoulder.

They watch her approach. Sway serpentine. 'Leave her with us,' they say, and the syllables fall in unison, hanging in the still air.

Shipwright shakes her head. 'She needs help.'

The Deadsingers glance at each other, their faces shaded with sorrow. 'She is gone. You may leave her with us, for her long walk onward.' They gesture to the milling crowd, 'For now, we tend the living. So should you.'

Another explosion sounds from the gate, dust sifting downwards. Distant cries of pain.

Shipwright doesn't move a muscle. Her eyes are flat. 'I know what you can do. Did you think Shroud wouldn't tell me? Do it.'

The Deadsingers flow towards her, the crowd parting as they slide their mouths either side of her head. 'She is *gone*. Contaminated. As' – their dry hands pluck at her sleeves – 'As are you. Now. *Leave. Her. With. Us.*'

Shipwright's lips sketch a reply but it's lost in the sound of sudden screams. Quickfish turns to see a handful of Thell's soldiers pelting towards them, ragged and blood-smeared, a strange, unhinged light in their eyes. But, for all he knows, there's a similar light in his own. This isn't a day for the sane.

He moves to welcome them, until Roofkeeper steps in front of him, axe ready.

'Easy, Roof,' Quickfish says. 'They're on our side.'

Roof's voice is low, frantic. 'The tattoos, Fish.'

Quickfish looks harder. This troop are a mess, their bodies wet with fresh-cut wounds, torn geometrics crossing their arms. Blood on their teeth. Something is terribly wrong with these soldiers. They shouldn't be walking, much less hurtling towards him at speed.

His mind makes the connection a moment before a spear punches through the woman next to him, a moment before the charging men and women pour into a barely formed defensive line, on all fours, on broken limbs, their teeth red and ravenous. He shouts a warning, and hears it echoed by Steelfinder, high and panicked.

Then all is blades and breaking. Screams rising up the cold walls of the council chamber, as the civilians in the hall realise what's happening.

The people of Thell are met by half-remembered faces, half-familiar voices stretched and torn into something ragged and murderous. The returning soldiers jerk as if filled with fever, twitching and febrile. Their bodies grimed with blood, skin pulsing. The first charge hits the civilians like a punch. Half of them flee up the raked rise of the council chamber, their arms stretching desperately. Others are pulled down by grasping hands, or trampled underfoot. Panic thick as sweat in the air. In response, the Deadsingers' song swells. The charging horde slows, and the fleeing civilians keep their pace, sliding through spaces in the air created by their harmony.

A moment or two for Steelfinder to find herself at the front of a ragged shield-wall, before she's sent reeling backwards under the weight of bodies that throw themselves on her spear arm. Shipwright lurches to her rescue, but picks up another madman on her back. She spins furiously, desperately, hammering a clenched fist into the side of his skull. The brass thing clutched between her fingers buzzes and yowls with every impact. Roofkeeper swings towards the beleaguered women, using the haft of his axe, for now. Quickfish tries to stick close as he forges through the press, but the charging mob are relentless, their voices low and guttural. He staggers under a weight of arms and thighs. Fingers scrabble at his panicking body. He pushes back, feels his knuckles slide off jabbering teeth. A woman that once served him spiced bread, who pulled her child aside shyly when they first met, screams into his face. Her voice is doubled, twisted, wrapped in other whispers that writhe on her tongue like maggots. The strands between her teeth might be the colour of her child's hair.

Quickfish falls hard onto the stone, feels the air rush out of his lungs. Distantly, he watches Steelfinder drive a wedge of soldiers forwards, her fingers hard on the haft of her spear, punching in slow, economical movements, drifting in the spaces opened by the Deadsingers' songs. Quickfish wriggles desperately, pushing upwards with his knees. Another body throws itself atop the first, hot breath that smells of beer and butcher's blocks. Too fucking heavy. He kicks hopelessly, twisting his head to avoid teeth which snap at his throat, his heart a lurching lump of terror.

Steelfinder's soldiers are making space. He can see their feet picking their way through the chaos. Not fast enough for him. The woman's teeth come down again, skittering off his raised forearm. A spike of hot pain flares in his right hand and his palm itches so much he screams. He has a brief memory of a fountain, of sharp little teeth. Part of him wonders if these are the things that a dying person feels. A bigger part of him misses his dad.

Quickfish feels nails dig into his stomach, teeth snapping at his fingers. He lashes out again, watches the frenzied woman catch his wrist in scabbed fingers and raise his veins to her chattering mouth. Something flares in his hand again, hot and furious, a blaze of gold, and a flicker of honey on his tongue. The woman drops his arm with a yelp. Her pupils widen as something shakes loose, beneath the fever. Quickfish pushes away, his eyes locked onto hers. The beer-breathed man scrabbles back to join her. They watch him in unison, mouths open. Slowly, they stretch their arms out towards him. Palms up. Open, hopeful.

The haft of an axe cracks the woman's skull and she drops like a stone, even as a spear swims through the air and pins the wide-eyed man through the shoulder. For a second, Quickfish is furious. Then the noise and the murder floods back in. Roof-keeper leaps forwards and grabs Quickfish's arm, as Steelfinder takes the other. They drag him backwards towards the line of warriors, the screaming civilians huddling behind. He doesn't protest. Just marks the two slumped bodies, and feels his hand burn like a brand.

The infected fall back briefly, the Deadsingers' song sweeping the field like evening shadow. Steelfinder and the remaining few soldiers fan out, forming a thin line of metal against the dark. The chastened, bloody mob skirt their lowered spear-tips, wary of drawing nearer, for now. Shipwright watches them hollow-eyed, massaging her buzzing wrist. In the space, the Deadsingers ghost forwards, falling on the injured, striking them with open palms. They sing to them in thick harmonies that blend and build. Quickfish watches them in confusion, glancing at Roof-keeper who shakes his head wearily, unknowing. The remainder of Thell's soldiers hang back, fearful. Steelfinder scans them with tired, lidded eyes, taking stock.

As he's lowered gently to the ground, Quickfish sees something rise from the bodies the Deadsingers are attending. A drifting haze of red; glimpses of teeth, tongues, eyes. The twins raise the pitch of their song, put it to a glass edge and string it with blades.

The red clouds shudder, burst, disappear. The mob behind the shields bays in response.

The Deadsingers ignore them. Under their hands some of the injured rise, slow and weeping. Cautious comrades help steady them, wiping the worst of the gore from their hair, shepherd them into secluded crevices at the back of the hall.

They don't all get up.

Some curse the Deadsingers in voices that aren't their own, flailing weakly like beached fish. For those, Steelfinder and Ship-wright do what needs done.

It takes Quickfish a while to notice Roof stroking his hair. He buries his face against his chest and weeps.

'Easy, Fish,' Roofkeeper murmurs, kissing the top of his head. 'We're not out the woods yet.'

As he pulls Quickfish closer, Steelfinder approaches them slowly, limping. She offers up a weak smile. 'I don't think they'll hold off for too long. Just waiting for more of their own.' Her voice hitches. 'And if this is what I think it is, there's going to be a lot more. Skinpainter wasn't kidding,' she murmurs, half to herself, before focusing back on Quickfish. She squats down to his level, arms loose on her knees. 'I'm not leaving here without Ice, but this isn't your fight.' She gestures to the back wall as she talks, the dark mass of frightened people. 'There's passages there that'll take you out. The Singers know the way. You could get to freedom, take some people with you.'

Quickfish flicks his eyes to the crevice and back. 'And what about the rest of you?'

Steelfinder smiles. A thin grey line. 'If we don't follow you within the hour, seal us in. This thing travels.' She shakes her head ruefully, 'I've got a friend who lives on the north road. If you see him, tell him Steel hopes he enjoyed the tea. Be nice to his dog.'

Roofkeeper pats her arm. 'Thank you. I'm so sorry.'

He motions to Quickfish, who looks from one expectant face to the other, then at that thin, wavering line of warriors.

His stomach lurches. 'No.'

Roofkeeper opens his mouth to interject and Quickfish hurries on.

'No. We all leave. Together.' He holds Steel's gaze. 'I don't think you'd leave me, if the tables were turned. And I won't leave you.'

Roofkeeper's hand tightens briefly on Quickfish's shoulder, then he laughs. 'Ugh. You're your father's son.'

Quickfish smiles up at him. 'Brave and committed?'

Roofkeeper kisses his cheek. 'Arsey and pig-headed.'

The Deadsingers' song saws up to a fever pitch and Shipwright's voice cuts in from the front lines. 'Steel, they're coming.'

Steelfinder frowns.

Quickfish grabs her wrist. 'Tell me what you need us to do.'

Steelfinder looks to Shipwright, the Deadsingers, then back to Quickfish. He realises how young she is. Not much older than him, really.

'We can't stay here,' she says, finally, shooting a glance at the Deadsingers. 'Can you hold this rock until we return?'

They look at each other, nod. 'For a time.'

Steelfinder straightens her shoulders. Breathes out. 'OK, OK. Then we make our way downwards to the sleeping halls.' She points her spear at the things skulking beyond the shield-wall. 'Before they do.'

As if on cue, the darkness screams, yammers, curses.

Quickfish shudders. 'Why the sleeping halls?'

Her voice is tight with tension. 'Because that's where we sent the children.'

Quickfish loses track of time after that, as the mountain spits out friends turned to killers. Steelfinder and a small cadre of sane soldiers leading them down into the depths of the Stump. Shipwright is by her side, of course, and Roofkeeper too, which means Quickfish follows after, even if he's a hairsbreadth from shitting himself with terror. Whatever Crowkisser has unleashed is tearing through the mountain with ferocious speed; something that slides in through broken skin, spilt blood. The soldiers either side of him more wild-eyed with each step. He can't catch much of their hushed speech, but over and over, one word surfaces like a black fish: 'Emperor.' Always said with a wary glance, a flickering hand over the heart. Quickfish has no idea what Crowkisser's done, but the people around him around are terrified, and it seeps into his bones with every passing second. His feet move faster, fleet with panic, following the others, until they're all hurling through the corridors on a wave of fear. Down and down and down, through the Stump's twisting halls, his exhausted heart hammering like a struck drum, sweat on his lips. The others aren't doing much better, the pace is killing them. They're a half-step ahead of the dead, at first, but losing ground with every slip and stumble. The things behind them are faster, loping forwards, shifting with feral speed. They lose people one by one, dragged screaming backwards by unseen hands.

A few of Steelfinder's small crew plant themselves shoulder to spine. Buying bare moments to keep them ahead. A few brave, terrified faces set against the broken-nailed dark. Quickfish sees those same brave faces lurching after them minutes later, mouths slick with tearing, their catcalls doubled and strung with weeping, their mouths stuffed with each other's meat.

He screams, over and over, until his voice is a husk. The only thing that keeps him moving is Roofkeeper's iron grip around his waist, and beyond that the imagined voice of his father somewhere in the darkness ahead, calling out to him. Fallon's big moon face as incongruous in his mind's eye as anything he could imagine, drifting away as his palm itches like an ant nest around the ghost of golden bitemarks. He retches and spits. Thick, sweet gobbets of honey and spice on his tongue. Somehow, he keeps moving.

He survives because he's kept safe. Steelfinder and Shipwright at the head and heel of their charge, his own tired feet in the middle, and always at his side, Roofkeeper's steady gait. Somehow, he sucks in the burning, blood-thick air and keeps running.

It's all worth it for a second, when they finally reach the sleeping halls, Steelfinder's cadre barrelling through guarded archways to meet a small clot of fearful children and their caretakers. Quickfish recognises Nigh, stepping tousle-headed to the front, her small arms striking martial poses. She holds them for around half a second before she's swept up in Steelfinder's arms, peppered with kisses. Quickfish sidles up to the laughing pair, ruffles Nigh's hair, dodges a batting hand. 'Hello, hair twin.'

Nigh gives him a grave nod in response. Turns to try and lick Steelfinder's neck.

Steelfinder bares her teeth and fakes a growl. 'Monster!'

She adjusts Nigh on her hip, and turns to a worried looking older man. 'We're leaving. Gather the little ones.' She shoots a grin at Quickfish, spits out weary dust. 'Thank you. For coming. I can't believe we got this far. Just have to get these brats up sky-side now. How hard can that be?'

From the darkness outside, the clash of metal. Screams. Resignation falls over Steelfinder's face like a shroud.

At her back, Shipwright's voice is low and breathless. 'We might not get much further.' Stooped over, she points back down the hall. Outside the arch the dead draw closer, slinking along the walls. The remains of the chamber guards glisten on their fingers and teeth. When they see Shipwright, a howl goes up, a swirling, vengeful, thing.

Steelfinder sets Nigh down, and wearily hefts her shield. She looks pointedly at Quickfish, her brown eyes soft. 'She likes you.'

Quickfish nods as he takes Nigh's squirming hand and pushes her gently behind him. He looks at Roof. 'Don't let them take her.'

Roofkeeper winces, running fingers along his jaw. 'Nobody's taking anybody.'

There's something ridiculous in the sound of it. Quickfish grins. 'I quite like you with that axe.'

Roofkeeper shakes his head. 'I don't.'

Beyond the archway something agitates the dead. They glance fretfully over their shoulders, lick their lips like cornered dogs and creep closer.

In response, a shout from Steelfinder's ragged band, as their shields lock with a clatter, filling the entranceway.

Steelfinder moves to Quickfish's side, nudges him backwards

gently with a battered shield. Passes him her spear and draws a long, cruel blade. 'You'll need this.'

Quickfish shakes his head. 'I won't. I can't . . . I'm sorry.'

She purses her lips. 'I don't have time to explain, but trust me, we can't save them. Not without the Singers. Or Painter.'

He nods. 'I know. But . . . I won't. I can't.' He tucks his arm around Nigh's shoulders, 'I'll keep an eye on her.'

Steelfinder's face softens. 'OK. But you better, or Ice'll skin us both.'

Something howls in the black, out beyond the light's glow.

The smaller children start to cry as they cluster behind the thin line of guards. Some of the adults cry too.

In response, the shield-wall tightens like a clenched fist, then loosens again as the air ripples. Shipwright shoulders her way forwards, strong fingers moving over something brass which clicks and whirrs fretfully. Quickfish licks the edges of his teeth. It feels like the air is fizzing. Shipwright shoots him a tight smile as she picks up his discarded spear, and snaps off the blade. He watches as she shucks her shirt sleeves down until she can tear strips to bind her raw fingers. He feels his guts unknot a little as she works. She looks up at him and laughs, 'Your da's going to shit bricks if I let you die here.' Maybe she sees the look of panic on his face, but she steps in close, wraps an arm around him, strong as sailcloth.

'Don't worry. We survive today. We sort the rest tomorrow.'

She smells comfortingly familiar. Pitch and salt and sun.

As he breathes in, Quickfish's heart reels for Hesper. Far from here, with an open sky and an open sea. He looks across at Roofkeeper. Lays fingers on his arm. 'I love you, you know that?'

Roofkeeper smiles. 'Till the ends of the earth.'

Quickfish glances down the corridor. The dead are closer than ever. 'We're nearly there.'

Roof kisses his cheek. 'Just as well I'm in good company.' His voice somehow steady, despite it all.

Quickfish turns to Steelfinder and Shipwright. 'What's the plan?'

The pair look at him levelly. Shipwright's face twists with sadness. 'Keep them from the kids as long as possible.'

He waits for the rest. 'Oh,' he says, finally.

Steelfinder smiles sadly at him. 'I'm sorry, Quick. It's a mountain. The only way out is up.'

Quickfish nods briefly, moves to stand behind Roofkeeper. A hollow feeling in his gut, that leaks into his spine, his shaking arms. Nigh's hand is small in his, sweaty-palmed. She seems calm for now. Quickfish doesn't want to scare her. Instead he presses his face against Roofkeeper's back, feeling the warmth of him, the wool, the sweat.

The dead come after that. Bare feet, faster and faster. It feels like a dream. The rhythms familiar, the beats expected. Quickfish is sick with fear, too frightened to be sick. His stomach churns.

The first few fall as expected, Steelfinder catching them on the flat plane of her shield. Hammering forwards, one, two, down. A swift strike and on to the next. Beside her, Shipwright swings like a pendulum. Bones break. The brass sphere clutched in her fist spins and whines as she shudders through the air like a burning wasp. A kneecap inverts itself. A scapula bends in strange ways. Quickfish can feel the half-moons of small nails as Nigh digs her fingers in, her breath fast and shallow in her chest. He kisses the top of her head. Murmurs the little nothings his mother used to soothe him to sleep.

In front of them, Roof's shoulders twist as he fights, his feet squarely planted to begin with, then slowly pushed back as the dead crowd him like worms seeking rain. His axe rises, falls. His teeth bared, and a shout on his lips. But there is a mountain-weight of them. And beyond the dead, Quickfish assumes, Astic's army and Crowkisser, waiting, grey-cloaked and angry. He retreats slowly as their line is driven back foot by foot, the dead thumping against raised shields like fat flies against glass. Their screams raw and harsh, the air such a frenzied cacophony that Quickfish stops trying to hear words and just lets it beat against his temples. He pulls Nigh close to his chest, and sings to her softly, feels her heart hammering, her fingers fluttering against him like moth's wings.

Steelfinder's down to her last two comrades. The first man caught unawares by a lucky strike that careens off his armour and nicks his neck below the helmet. A blur of red. Something furious and rat-tongued plunging into his arteries as he turns to drive a fist into his friend's face. Again and again until his broken knuckles are a mess of metal and splintered teeth. Steelfinder takes his head off, wet-eyed. She's tackled from the side a moment later, reels into Shipwright, her arms weighted with screaming men and women.

Something barrels into Roofkeeper, and Quickfish catches him. They both go down as the dead swarm them like ants. He tries to keep Nigh in the hollow of his stomach, tries to keep his body between her, and the teeth and the hunger; to give her a second, just a second more.

He feels their nails against his skin and closes his eyes. The air ripples.

The stink of sulphur and saltpetre. Thick as incense.

The air ripples.

Quickfish's teeth whine, his ears pop. His palm burns with golden fire.

The air ripples, and explodes.

Concussions of black and red detonate in his brain and in the room, the air swarming with geometrics which slam bodily against the dead, lifting them like writhing cats, hurling them against the walls. In their midst, back-to-back, hand in hand, eyes closed, Skinpainter and Shroudweaver. The shout that leaves Shipwright is like sunrise.

The pair hang in the air, lifted by the force of their magic. Red ribbon and silver thread billow around their tight clasped, outstretched hands. They sway in strange rhythms. The dead scatter like windblown leaves. In the lull, Quickfish struggles free of the bodies, pulling Roofkeeper and Nigh after him. His breath races. His fingers burn.

A few hectic moments pass before the shapes flow slower, the harsh edges of the geometrics softening and falling to grey. The pressure eases. As the last vestiges of sorcery fade like smoke on water, the bodies of the dead slump, quiet. Shroudweaver's toes brush the ground. He stumbles and staggers.

Shipwright runs to meet him, her arms out and ready even as he falls. And she holds him like a gift, like a memory, like a blessing. Kisses his blackened face. Presses her hands to the small of his back and rocks him like a child.

Behind her, Quickfish sees Skinpainter sink to their knees, their ribs rising and falling in shuddering gasps, flickers of angular red and black wreathing their hands, and a dark stain spreading under their ribs. Steelfinder rushes forwards, raises them up in an embrace. Leans in and mutters a few shadowed words into their cowl. They nod wearily and push her away.

Quickfish finally releases Nigh's hand from a death grip. She looks at him irritatedly, then punches his leg.

'Alright, alright.' He laughs. 'Not my finest move.'

She stares at Skinpainter. Juts her chin questioningly.

'What?' Quickfish says, 'Looking for your sister?'

She nods.

'I . . . don't know, little one. She'll be here soon, I'm sure.'

Nigh looks at him sceptically, sits back down and starts digging at her toenails.

For a few blessed minutes, there's a kind of peace. Injured bodies slowly filling with injured minds. The dead struck down by that brief, furious burst of magic not slain, but stunned. Skinpainter, hung like dark cloth between Steelfinder and Roofkeeper's strong arms, moves from person to person, fingers dancing over slick brows and pushing on bruised flesh. As they make contact, angular tattoos on their arms wriggle to life, ink flowing forth, crossing from body to body. At its touch, skin darkens and bone straightens. The angles tighten and the broken mends.

Fallen men and women push their way back into their bodies with weary effort. The soldiers they killed are not so lucky. All of Steelfinder's cadre down. The gate guards not even in pieces large enough to call a corpse.

In the quiet, Quickfish could swear he hears the slow drip of blood. He might just be going mad. He takes Nigh's small fingers as they pick their way through the dazed and the dying. Whatever Shroudweaver and Skinpainter did here, it cleansed the room like a purging flame. Not even the memory of the dead lingers. Quickfish feels like a banished ghost himself. Lingering light and empty on the edges of things. Nigh tugs sharply on his hand. He's been squeezing too tightly again. He loosens his grip, crouches next to her. 'I'm sorry.'

She rubs her fingers resentfully. Shies a little closer.

Something burns in his chest. A little ache of loss. He runs fingers gently through her mussed hair, tries to remember what his mother would say. 'Hang in, little one. Rough seas, is all.'

Nigh holds tightly, says nothing.

Quickfish wants the mountain to stay quiet, but the battle is far from over. Distant screams still swilling down through the darkness. He wants them to be safe, but there's miles of rock above them, and all of it writhing with things that want them dead. And as if all that wasn't enough, his palm itches furiously. He rubs at it, stretches the thumb out. Nothing helps. A burning like an ant bite, and the choking taste of honey every time he draws breath.

To distract himself, Quickfish watches Skinpainter work, tries to get lost in the steady movement of their craft. The returned dead rest, heads in hands, crying softly. Quickfish can't comfort them. He doesn't belong here, a ghost on the edge of the things. Doesn't understand a single scrap of the murder happening inside this mountain.

And ghost that he is, it takes him a while to notice the sound in his ears. When it begins, it builds slowly, something barely felt. A whine on the edge of his teeth, a weight behind his eyes. Tiredness, he thought. Exhaustion, or something worse. A hangover from so much death and blood. But nothing quiets the sound. It blossoms into a bone-deep hum. Sharpness oscillating up the octaves, until his head rings like cracked glass, growing louder and louder until he feels it in every inch of his body. He looks around wildly. No one else seems to hear it. No one seems to care. Panic builds in his throat, but even that's drowned out by the sound.

He's about to call for help when the nerves in his hand light with feverish fire. His fingers dance of their own accord. The pain spreads up his arm in waves. Two bright lances of fire radiate from where the fountain creature's fangs sank in. He screams out loud. In shock, Nigh echoes him.

From the depths of the mountain, something answers.

Deep-throated, its voice layered and spun with sufferings, echoing back on itself. Furious. Thick with barrows-dust and blood, like a clarion call. A dark beast awakened.

Shroudweaver and Skinpainter's heads snap towards the sound.

Quickfish sees Roofkeeper run towards him, but his vision is slipping, doubling, he can barely see. He's not quite here. There's a city. A square. A cracked fountain. His palm burns.

From far away, he watches Shipwright call to Steelfinder. Hurried, rapid, staccato. Something about the children. Safe. Keeping the children safe. When the words leave Shipwright's lips, they fall edged with gold. Steelfinder nods curtly in response. At her back, Shroudweaver, Skinpainter and Shipwright leave at speed. In sulphur, in red, in shadow. Quickfish watches them go, his head swimming loose in the pool of their departing voices.

He realises he's on the ground, and that's bad.

He's pulled backwards into a circle of rising blades, Steelfinder and Roofkeeper. A few of the clearer-headed warriors. He should help. The danger's not over. He staggers to his feet, swaying. He tries to take Nigh's hand again, but misses and falls, his fingers grinding against stone.

The stone of a cracked fountain. Low in its belly, something golden and broken. Watchers around the rim.

Crowkisser's to his left. Almost familiar now, pale as ever. Thin black hair spidered across her face. The air shudders and suddenly she's Shroudweaver. He raises a red-ribboned hand in salute. To his right, stands something else. Huge and hungry. The thing in the mountain depths. The Emperor. Quickfish doesn't recognise it, but the creature that bit his hand does. The fountain god remembers the Emperor. And now Quickfish does too. He can feel it growing beneath his feet. Stretching up into the mountain, like blood in the vein. As if it can sense his thoughts, the Emperor turns towards him, its body liquid and changing. Many heads sway on its shoulders. Eyes flick in and out, like lit wicks.

Quickfish scrabbles backwards against the stone, bumping against Steelfinder. She mouths something and he tries to follow the lines of her lips, her furrowed brow. Almost manages it, until another wave of fire from his hand sets his arm alight with pain. He reels against Roofkeeper.

Against Shroudweaver, by the fountain. A red right hand on his neck, steadying him. Fingertips that feel like crow's claws. To his right, the Emperor howls, and Quickfish hears it in his head and in the mountain. He wants to focus, wants to help, but everything burns. His head swims, and for a moment, he glimpses someone else, a fourth, a stranger standing dark, and quiet. They are robed and hooded, but he glimpses the briefest flash of a neat, grey beard. They hold something out towards him, glinting, across the cracked basin. A box.
    Their fingers move around it, shining like blades.
    The god in the fountain cries out in rage and fear.

And its voice is Steelfinder's, dragging him back to reality. To the mountain under stone.
    And into the chamber comes Icecaller.
    Child of the Kinghammer.
    Beloved daughter of Thell.
    Her lips red with gore.
    And all the mountain's bloodied, screaming hordes at her back.

74

RISE

It all happens so fast. Icecaller sees Belltoller go down, clipped and eaten by bolts of black fire. Not a heartbeat to draw breath before her skin shivers with an arcane feeling she's never felt before, like a plunge into an icy stream. The whole battle slips slowly out of sync; the movement of bodies past her stilted as twigs against the sun. Shouts of alarm and horror stretch across the sky, blurring like torn cloth. At the heart of it, Shroudweaver is dancing. At least, she thinks he's dancing, his feet sketching loose circles across the stone, his shoulders dipping in fluid, brittle jerks, ribcage thrust out, arms pinned back like a bird's wings. His right hand is sheathed red, and his left shimmers with arctic light, pulling cold out into the world from . . . somewhere, stretching it over the battle like a shroud. She gets the name now.

Icecaller watches him work, the breath hung in her lungs. Out on the Barrowlands, something is forming. Small at first. A pool of gold light that twitches and sings. She imagines she can see faces inside it, bright eyes and wings. A taste on her lips like honey. Shroudweaver's fingers lift like rain, and the thing on the Barrowlands rises, sputtering white fire. It stretches ten, twenty storeys high. Almost as tall as the Stump, as tall as the ledge where Icecaller watches wide-eyed, her heart giddy with terror.

The shape of the thing steadies, Shroudweaver's hands seeming to sculpt its edges. The briefest flicker of red thread catches the corner of her vision, but her eyes are held by the creature growing in front of her, individual faces and features sliding together in a flurry of golden light. The sound that comes from the heart of it is like a song. It turns its face towards Icecaller, and she staggers from the force of its gaze. She touches her own wet face, and realises she is weeping.

The creature stretches the height of the mountain, the Barrowlands' shadows cast into grey whispers by its light, the storm held for a moment behind the clouds.

She lists forwards against the battlements as the army below stops in its tracks. All around her she hears the crash of buckle and steel, as the soldiers surrounding her fall to their knees.

The strain of the summoning is wreaking a toll on Shroudweaver. Icecaller clocks Shipwright stepping up to hold him steady, and shakes her head. It'd be just the thing for that pale little ghost to get himself killed now.

There's never bad luck thought as doesn't make it true. She hears the gunshot a moment before she sees it, ripping across the sky like a torn hawk, dripping something thick and black.

She's moving before she realises how stupid that is, throwing herself over Shroudweaver's waggling legs and scrawny back and bearing him to the ground, shield raised.

The shot catches her shield on the crown and ricochets off, thundering into the mountain side, exploding rock and ice in hissing swirls. Icecaller bites down a scream. Her arm aches like a dropped anvil but amazingly, it's still there. She mutters a quick blessing to Thell's steelmakers, and smiles at the thought of Steelfinder's smug face. She stretches that smile out to encompass Shroudweaver's terrified eyes under her, shoots him a wink, and leaps off. Shipwright can take care of him. She seems used to it.

The marksman must have a perch up high. She skims the mountain's ridges in panic. It's hard to see against the light being thrown off the creature growing down on the Barrowland. Still, she sights something on the western ledge, among the eagle nests, shadow against the black rock, fluid and strange and racing towards the gate.

She tries to follow it but her gaze is taken by the sky. A storm of crows peeling out of it, spiralling down to the ground, forming into a slight girl at the feet of the creature. Crowkisser. It can't be anyone but Crowkisser. And above her, in front of her, all around her, the glowing, living song of glory Shroudweaver has brought forth. A god. It must be a god. This must be what her father meant when he talked about them. He hadn't done it justice. Nothing could do it justice.

As Icecaller looks at it again, it feels like falling in love, like her first kiss with Steelfinder, quick and brave. Like holding Nigh for the first time, as she moved softly against her chest. Like falling into her father's arms.

The Astic army staggers before the god. A few still list forwards, but wending, drunken, as if lost in a harsh storm. Only Crowkisser stands tall before it, her skin still crawling with feathers as the remnants of crows press themselves down into the bone.

At Icecaller's back, she hears her people crying, singing. She's humming something under her breath herself. A song her mother used to know.

Days of fear and panic, all that dying and killing – none of it matters now. They've won. For all his strangeness, Shroudweaver's lived up to his reputation. Crowkisser's finished. Icecaller allows herself a little smile at that.

Below, the composite turns towards the slight girl, and she steps backwards. For a moment, it looks like she might run, but then Icecaller realises she's reaching for something. A scrap too small to make out, hurled overarm into the body of the god, arcing against the seared sky.

A moment later, the world detonates. Icecaller screws her eyes shut against a wash of light. Screams at her back. Wailing. She forces herself to count to five, marking the beats of her hammering heart, despite the feeling that something is very wrong. When she opens them, her vision dances purple. Loss howls in her veins. Something beautiful is gone, the icy calm of Shroudweaver's magic vanished. Below her, the god he made is dead, scattered.

The people of Astic shaking off its spell, swarm forwards. And then, as if in counterpoint, the mountain underneath her shakes, shuddering like a wounded thing. Some kind of detonation from the gate, now weeping black smoke, rock. And between the smoke, in breaths and blood and raindrops, come the dead, blossoming from the corpse of the god, tearing themselves free from its ruined scraps and rushing towards the mountain. They're joined by something older; spirits pulling themselves from the deep barrows, spectral hands breaking the split earth of the mounds. Ephemeral mouths howl in rage and hunger. Ghostly forms move in strands of gossamer light to join the throng flying towards Thell. All her childhood nightmares finally become real.

For a minute she's five again, wide-eyed on her father's knee, listening to his tales of the dead, to his stern warning never to dig on green mounds, never to drink ice water, never to let her tattoos be broken. Or maybe she's nine, sparring with Skinpaint-er, watching their hands as they spin histories of the Empire, of bones, and of slavery only barely escaped.

A cold sweat rides her skin, and her stomach twists with fear. Her eyes linger on the bright lines of the dead arcing towards the smoking ruin of the gate. Beneath them, Astic's army harries the last few soldiers retreating towards the mountain. She shakes herself. She's needed. She's grown and she's needed.

At her back, Shipwright and Fallon's pup disappear into the depths with Belltoller's ragged remains flopping between their panicked hands. Icecaller lets them go, looking for Shroudweaver. The sight of his shocked face and his pale fingers lights a fire of anger in her that burns out the fear. In seconds, her fingers are around his throat, her breath hot and wet against his cheek. His pulse is thready. His skin slick beneath her hands. A stink of saltpetre and sulphur.

She slams him against the rock until his teeth rattle. 'What did you *do?*'

He struggles for breath, kicks.

She slams again, enjoying the wet sound his skull makes. '*What?*'

He winces, then his hands are a blur, tapping on her ribs, her arms. She feels herself go weak, something in those strikes turn-ing her grip to water. He's quicker than she realised. Colder. She staggers back, and he looks at her with twisted lips. 'Not me. Her.'

He starts to refasten the red bindings around his wrists as he talks. Runs fingers over the sticky patch on his skull, grimaces. Soldiers rush by. He sways like a reed. Distantly, there are more explosions, the roar of the storm, screams.

Icecaller shakes the numbness out of her arms, levels her spear shakily. 'You're not going anywhere until I get some answers.'

Shroudweaver gazes down the shaft, and his face softens a little. 'My daughter's done something terrible. I think I can fix this, but I can't do it if you won't let me.' His fingers linger on the engraved tip. Push it gently aside. She lets him. He offers her a small nod, readjusting pouches and belt, as he reapplies black powder to his temples. As he starts towards the tunnels down, he stops and turns. His face is old, and uncertain. 'If I can't fix it, get them out. As many as you can.' He seems about to add something else, but turns and joins the mass of bodies piling into the broken heart of the mountain.

For a heartbeat, Icecaller doesn't know what to do. Then she sees her father, broad shouldered in the storm, slick with the driving rain, barking orders. He smiles at her, backlit by thunder. Even here, amid the rain, the smoke and the dying, he smiles at her.

He's at her side in seconds. One massive arm around her shoulders, his fingers mussing her hair. 'Not quite to plan, little eagle.'

She watches his face and feels five years old again. 'What now, Dad?'

He straightens her spear, kisses her forehead. 'Now we go get your sister, we bottle up the dead and we throw these whelk-fuckers out our mountain.'

She wants to believe him. No, she wants to curl into the crook of his arm and smell the sweat and warmth of him. She wants to fall asleep to his shit jokes and his boozy breath. But before that, she wants to believe him. She has to ask though, and hates herself for asking, 'What about the dead, Dad?'

Kinghammer grins. 'They never got me the first time.' He squeezes her tight. 'And that was before I had you. Now, let's go get your sister, and then we'll be unstoppable.' He turns, bellows over his shoulder. 'Painter, hold the wall as long as you can, then take the rest to the council chamber. We'll make a stand there.'

Skinpainter's hands wave broadly, reassuringly.

Icecaller follows her father and the army into the heart of the mountain in a cacophony of hammering feet, shouted orders, dust and blood. The first clashes with Astic come near the gate, a few hundred of them clambering over the smoking ruins, piling out of the burning haze, tongues alight with curses. In response, Thell spits warriors out of stone sluices, culverts, quick-cut passageways. This isn't the first time the Stump's weathered a war. The city's spears work well down here, filling every corner with blades, taking out eyes, kidneys, throats with snake-quick strikes. It's bloody work, slick with torn guts and stopped breaths, but it seems to be blunting Astic's advance. Icecaller leaves them to it, heading for the sleeping chambers, for Steelfinder and Nigh. They've talked this over. If anything ever happened, that's where they're supposed to go. And things have definitely happened. The chambers are the safest place in the mountain, down in the guts. Big old doors and all the guards already down there on off-shift. Getting there's a challenge, though. Astic's little cutters don't make it easy. One of the grey-clad fucks staggers into her path and swipes, wide-eyed. She ducks, rips him up the middle, doesn't stop to see whether he still looks shocked.

On her left, her father barrels into a clot of scared looking fishermen, his hammer crushing shields, arms, driving rims and shards into shuddering ribcages. Crowkisser's army fold back from their advance. They don't give up though. As they push downwards, lanky men emerge from the press, circling like sharks, their faces grim, large blades loose in their hands. Icecaller catches their thrusts on the haft of her spear, twists the butt to break ribs and knees, stomping down on weakened joints and wrenching the spear-tip deep into startled hearts. Her father doesn't bother with even these small ceremonies. The first few knives simply graze his thick hide as he grabs over-extended wrists, pulls them close, and snaps. Broken bodies are cast into the next charging wave, which crumples under the unexpected weight, before the hammer swings down, to make space and silence amid the blood and chaos.

It gets trickier as they go. There's a lot of Crowkisser's brood, mad for blood. Amateurs, the lot of them, but all they need is luck. Icecaller can sense something worse in the offing too. The dead are thick in the air, calling to her blood. She can feel their pulse in her ears, whispering thinly, touching her neck, her back, her thighs. Her tattoos itch. Whenever it gets too much, her father reaches a thick-fingered hand back for her, guiding her past broken bodies, through whirling knots of violence. The hammer swings in low, brutal arcs and the corridors empty before them. Icecaller follows behind, shield held high, spear darting in fast, economical movements. Her feet move in dancer's patterns, her mind loose. Most of her thoughts are with her sister . . . her sister, who'll be somewhere below, scared, pretending to be brave. Her fierce-faced, fuzz-haired little shit of a sister. Icecaller smiles at the thought even as a gangly ship-boy charges, yelling. She punches a neat hole in his throat, sidesteps, pushes his falling body aside with her shield. Icecaller wonders if Crowkisser's inside yet, if she's here to see her precious army die.

There's a shout at her side as her father lifts a woman by the throat, and dashes her against the wall. Icecaller throws open-armed over his shoulder, piercing a tall knife-wielding man above the hip and kicks his blade clear, crushing his jaw with her boot.

The air thickens with chattering as the dead are drawn to the battle, to the blood and cutting. She slides through a susurrus, eyes locked on her father's back. Soldiers in familiar armour begin to flock towards them. Not far now, a few more curves to the sleeping chambers and Nigh. They've delved deep, fast. Then she can save the little snot and they'll drive these grey rat-fuckers out of her home.

As they push forwards, something skirts Icecaller's spine and she flinches reflexively, ducks low on an ankle and pivots. A spear flicking back. It's a soldier she recognises – Marktamer, young and blonde. She laughs in shock, spreads her arms reflexively, grins. 'It's me, you dumb cunt.'

Marktamer's thrown shield takes her in the mouth. She feels a tooth rattle loose as she staggers backwards. Something grabs her ankles and pulls her down. She scrabbles furiously away from fallen bodies and broken blades, lashes out and connects with a skull, another familiar face, half-pinned to the floor by a spear through the spine and animated by some feverish light. The glow of the dead licks across their skin, their broken tattoos.

A thin whine slides out of Icecaller's lips. She can feel the pieces sliding together in her brain, but it hurts, and she doesn't, doesn't want to think. So, she acts instead. Brings her left heel down like a hammer until she feels the fingers clutching her leg break. Rolls to the left as a blood-wet spear hammers into the ground next to her. Staggers to her feet. 'Fuck you.'

She grits her teeth, straightens her aching spine. Circles, studies the soldiers facing them. All her people. All alight with something wild and hungry in the eyes. The dead hovering at their shoulders, plunging in and out of their broken skin. Icecaller scuffs out space with her spear, loops it in front of their snarling faces as she reaches backwards for her shield and slips an arm through the straps. 'Fuck. You.'

They laugh at her, yipping, loose-jawed, shoulders jutting. She sees ragged cuts in their bodies, the geometrics split, hanging loosely. Knife marks, and spear marks and something worse at the edges, a ragged tearing. Their throats and temples pulse hungrily. She steadies her breathing, lets herself feel her diaphragm rise and fall. Adjusts her weight, calls out, low and easy. 'Dad?'

She feels his back come to rest against hers. 'I see them, love. Steady.'

She is, somehow. She can feel the breath through his body, smell the stink of him, the warm rock of his ribs, the slow shift as the hammer swings back and forth. She leans into him, watching the soldiers. Not *their* soldiers anymore but the dead of the Empire, wearing new bodies; all Skinpainter's old folktales come to life. Faces she knows, pulled into strange angles, sharpened and bloody. They pace outside the range of her spear. 'What's the plan Dad?' Her voice comes out steadier than she feels.

He lashes out, batting a questing blade aside. 'Follow me, foot for foot. We'll hit the sleeping chambers and hold there until the Singers or Painter arrive.'

Icecaller purses her lips, jabs warningly at a questing hand. 'Wish Painter was here right now.'

Her dad hums consolingly. 'It's just us, little eagle. But that's not new.'

They start to move slowly backwards and down, surrounded by a circle of steel and shredded flesh, their former friends, wide-eyed and hungry. Icecaller presses herself into the sway of her father's back and follows his rhythm. Above them, the Stump erupts in a flurry of noise. The cawing of crows tumbles down the tunnels, over the screams and ring of steel.

'Crowkisser's here then.'

'Later,' Kinghammer says. 'We kill her later.'

They shuffle onwards. Below them, echoes of violence swill through the mountain, but stronger still, she hears the sound of singing, tunes she feels in her bones. The Deadsingers, a few storeys beneath her feet, dry lips lifted to the roof, seamed faces held in soft light, voices rising to fill the council chamber with echoes. As they send their song out into the mountain, pushing back the chaos of battle, Icecaller can see them in her mind, hand in hand, harmonising. Twin sisters, always there at the binding of things; barely seen otherwise. Icecaller's never missed them like this.

Because they sound quiet up here, when all else she can hear is the shuffle and drag of her former friends readying to kill her. The slow scrape of blades. The stumbling weight of broken feet. The quiet drip of clotted blood. And under that, something speaking, moving. Rats in the muscles. Scurrying, burrowing lumps that pulse under stomachs, throats, eyes. Brief shapes in the smoke. Chattering on the edges of her hearing. Forming in breathless, snarling gasps before her face. She taps a hand against her father's hip. 'It's them, isn't it, Dad? The Empire's dead.'

He spits. 'What's left of them. Left of him.'

She twists the spear, slaps it down on grasping forearms, shatters ribs. 'The Emperor? I thought you all . . . dealt with him.'

He puts a hand back to guide her over sprawled bodies. The Deadsingers' voices swell from somewhere below, and they sprint forwards into a brief gap.

'The oldest cunts are the hardest to kill,' her father mutters. He swings the hammer. 'You can cut.' Bone breaks. 'You can burn.' Blood pools. 'You can crush.' Soft wet growling. A raised boot. 'You can dig it up by the root. But,' he pauses, his breath heavy. 'There's always, always some fucker *planting*.'

He rolls his shoulders wearily, the haft of the hammer sliding slowly over the bone. 'Look, let's talk about this once we're clear. We're almost there.'

Icecaller believes him. Better, she feels it in her gut. In his calm voice. In the sound of her friends singing below. If she doesn't notice the dead growing closer, who can blame her? If it takes a moment to mark the straightening of their backs, and the sharpening of their teeth, who could judge?

The loss, like all losses, happens in a moment. One breath to the next. The ridden dead are hard to spot in the shadows. Only the light on their broken skin. So Icecaller watches their eyes, their mouths. They snarl before they leap. The gums peel back, their whole fucking mouth like a box of blades. Terrifying, but it gives the briefest clue of what's coming.

Three come for her at once. Icecaller dodges the first, kicks out at the ankles. It tumbles, and she's moving to slide around the blade of the second, her spear down into the calves of the fallen one, using the momentum to vault forwards. Feet into the chest of the third, a sharp blow to its temple with her shield. She can't bring herself to kill them. Not yet. Not when they might still be saved.

Four more go for her father. His hammer arcs out to meet the first two, a crushing pendulum. The other pair latch on to his arms, pulling him down. His knees buckle. She turns to help him. Loses count of the bastards. And before she knows it, there's a flicker, and a weight on her, something hot and stinking inches from her face. A tongue against her cheekbones. Teeth scrabbling for purchase. Thighs on her back pinning her down. Fingers in her hair. Blades skittering off her armour and something, something laughing in her head. Her tattoos flare hot.

She can't lift her spear, there are knees on her elbows, grinding her against the stone. She snaps her head back, yells triumphantly at the crunch of cartilage. She can't move. She arches her hips, scrabbles futilely with her left hand. She can't get loose from the shield-straps. She can't move. Nails start unbuckling her armour with quiet determination. Something wet and heavy snickers above. More of them pile on. She feels teeth skirt her neck and something howls in her own blood in response. She almost wants to bare her throat, to shuck off the weight and let them in. She screams, her voice hoarse as it skitters across the slick stone.

She thinks of Nigh. Pushes herself up hard into the foraging mouth, lets the cusp of her armour crunch their wet teeth. Twists her shoulders till they scream, driving them backwards into wriggling ribs. Spins herself around, somehow. Looks into the face of the thing on top of her. Drives her knees up again and again, until it goes soft and wet and still. Pushes it away with shaking hands.

It pushes back.

It's still not dead. Wrecked and ruined, but still moving. Broken bones realign and scurry under its skin as it pulls itself onto her writhing body, pinning her down. Its friends laugh like jackals. She screams again. Not here. Please not here. Not with Nigh so far. Not with her dad so close. It's so strong. She arches her spine. She can't move.

No. No. No.

She can't move.

She sees hunger light in its eyes, watches its lips curve in triumph.

Two heavy footsteps. Its head vanishes in a spray of gore and bone. The black steel of the Kinghammer. Another swing and the weight on her arm lifts. Bloodied stumps still clinging, but the body long gone. She recoils in horror and brushes lumps of someone from her. And there he is, one hand outstretched. The other swings the hammer again. The dead stagger back, yipping in fear. She takes his hand and grins. 'Dad.'

The blade catches him at the throat. Just barely. He dodges so fast that for a second she thinks it's missed. He drops her hand and presses fingers to his neck. A thin cut, the smallest flash of red.

He reaches for her again, and she feels the air shudder, as his tattoos glow with a bright fire. The air around her father comes alive. In the drifting blood, before the jackal-jaws of their ridden friends, the dead flock to Kinghammer. Their teeth, their fingers, so fast, so fast. Icecaller tries to pull him to her, but she's too slow. The air is thick with spirits. They swarm him like wasps. She has a second to feel utterly, completely helpless. He holds her eyes for all of it. And then firmly, suddenly, pushes her away.

The first of the dead hits him below the cut in his neck, in a sliver of bare skin. Bites, worms in like a maggot. Rippling the flesh above as it moves. Others follow, worrying at the hole like foxes. Kinghammer falls to his knees. Another in from under the ribs, the geometrics flexed apart by a scream of pain. His fingers arch and claw at the stone. His nails rip, bone breaks and blood flows.

More of the dead pile in through the ragged holes, punching through the wet ends of his fingers, forcing their way up through the muscles. His back curves and he vomits. They scurry to his tongue and cheeks, ripping through the clean flesh on the inside of his mouth. When her father screams again, he has so many voices. More of the dead flock to the sound, tearing through his palms, his temples, his eyes. The geometrics try to contain them. Icecaller watches them interlock and shift, red and black and red, red, red again. The dead are too many. The tattoos pull tight in response, crushing arteries, airways. Kinghammer writhes, one massive broken hand groping for his weapon. Icecaller starts towards him, but the dead crowd around her. She feels their grave-rot teeth against her eyelids, sees them picked out in the blood haze and melting ice, seeking an opening. Her tattoos itch like an old burn.

'R-run,' the words fall out of him in lumps, choking their way past rotten air and clotted blood. 'Get your sister.' His face twists, writhes. He says it again. 'Gut your sister.' Jaw hanging loose in a jackal laugh.

Icecaller hefts her spear.

Kinghammer watches her from his knees. Spreads his arms wide. 'Yes,' it says. 'Tear more. Let the others in.'

The swirling mass of the dead roils in joy. Distantly, she can see them punching into struggling bodies, burrowing like ferrets, needle-sharp and hungry. Clumps of soldiers group together, fighting a desperate rearguard. Thell's finest, back-to-back. Alone at first, then opening their ranks to let in fleeing, grey-cloaked figures. The sides of the battle are shifting, the living versus the dead.

No one's coming to save her. There are acres of carnage between her and anything remotely like a friend.

People fall. Briefly listless hands reaffirm themselves to spears and turn on friends and lovers. The thing that was her father shambles closer. It watches her with feral, unfamiliar eyes, then presses against her tattoos, bares its teeth, and shrieks, flicking blood at her face from ragged hands.

Toying with her.

Icecaller casts around the room, desperately getting her bearings. Nigh can't be too far from here, in the sleeping chambers. Which means she's not too far from those solid oak doors.

She takes a breath, and punches outwards, breaking bone. Buys herself about three seconds. Three seconds to turn from the howling face of her father, to duck below the sweep of his hammer, to raise her forearms in front of her face and barrel into the dead. As she runs, she feels their teeth slide off her geometrics, driven back for a moment. She mouths a quick thanks to Skinpainter's work as the dead yowl, incensed. Heart hammering, legs aching but staying a step ahead of the fear, she ducks a spear thrown by the woman who used to bring her breakfast. Somehow vaults a pile of weeping bodies busily devouring one another. Turns, slips on shreds of flesh, falls. Avoids ramming her eyes onto a broken spear-point by a hairsbreadth. The hand holding it twitches.

Icecaller flinches back into familiar arms. The wreck of her father jerks away from her as her tattoos flare, then closes in, purring, gurgling soft and hungry things. Behind her, a man dies screaming as his sister chews her way through his stomach. He's filled from the roiling air and rises again to hunt his wife with a crazed, loose grin.

In front of Icecaller, the arm holding the shattered spear scrabbles, pulling a blood-slick body from under a mound of muttering corpses. It takes a moment for her to recognise Hawkspit. He opens his mouth to speak, but she can already see his geometrics glowing fiercely on his skin. Intact. She grabs, his wrist and screams. '*Run*. The sleeping halls!'

So they run. The loping meat of her father pursues them, sniffing at the edges of their protection, cursing them between smashed teeth. There's a grief building inside her like a stopped river, but she's choked it up with terror. No time to feel. No time to stop. No time for anything other than the mad, aching drum of her feet on stone. Down and down. The halls are in chaos. She glances about wildly for Skinpainter, Shipwright, Quickfish, but if they're there, she can't see them. Always in the front of her head like a pulse is her sister – Nigh, Nigh, Nigh. As they run, her feet draw her towards the sound of singing. The Deadsingers. She'll have to pass the council chamber to get to the sleeping halls. Of course. Perhaps they can help her. Perhaps they can save her father. She sprints faster still, throwing herself towards the arch of the chamber with a yell of exertion, Hawkspit's feet skidding bloodily. His hands pressed to his temples, his mouth a litany of terror and prayer. Her breath is a dagger in her side, the air slipping from her with every minute. As Icecaller collapses against the cool stone of the arch, she sees them. The Deadsingers, driven on to the high speaking stones, back-to-back. Beneath them, a sea of ridden people; herbwives, soldiers, bartenders, all clutching spears and knives and broken things, their bodies bloodied, darkened and torn with the stain of the dead.

The Deadsingers chant resolutely in low harmonised tones. A man leaps for them, and is struck open-handed by the rightmost twin, her hair whipping behind her. He staggers, dazed. His broken tattoos flare and the Deadsingers drag him behind them. It's only then that Icecaller sees the cleft in the rock at their back, and in it, the children. Another ridden woman leaps and the Deadsingers catch her mid-air, singing into her screaming, bloody mouth. She quiets, and they send her scrambling into the cleft to join the others.

Icecaller turns towards them, skirting the milling mass, pushing them back with the flat of her blade, keeping Hawkspit in front of her, between her arms. The closer she gets to the song of the Singers, the more the ridden dead shrink back. But not her father. His roar is close behind her, thundering across the flat circle of the council chamber, scattering bodies in his wake. The Deadsingers see her, see Kinghammer a hairsbreadth behind. Their lips set in a thin line.

'Help him,' she screams.

The leftmost Singer ducks a blade, slaps its wielder between the eyes as he barrels past, and shakes her head at Icecaller, horror cold on her face.

The thing that was Kinghammer laughs, his voice guttural and huge at her back. 'There's too many of us, dearest daughter.'

The rightmost Deadsinger leans back from a thrust chair leg, nods.

Icecaller scrambles up the steps towards them, kicking at grasping hands, hauling Hawkspit's yelping, bruised body behind her. 'Please!'

Something softens in their gaze and a lidded glance passing between them. The twins take Icecaller by her wrists and raise her onto the ledge. They're surprisingly strong, their skin like soft wood, stark with muscle underneath.

She staggers gratefully behind them, Hawkspit flailing after. He shoots her a look and rubs at his shoulder.

The thing inside Kinghammer wastes no time, vaulting out from the mass of the dead, and landing on the ledge in front of them. Unsteady for the briefest moment, its new body and ruined legs conspiring against it. The Deadsingers move quickly, sliding either side of Kinghammer. It screams in rage, flailing the hammer in an arc. They dip like herons striking, as their song hits it from both sides like a vice. Their harmony and resonance shivers through the cavern. Icecaller can feel it against her eyes like a thumb against her veins. Hawkspit falls back screaming, hands over his ears. In the face of the song, the dead are driven back like leaves on a pond. Kinghammer falls to his knees. A jolt of hope strikes her heart, and before she thinks Icecaller runs to him.

The Deadsingers glance at her in horror, raise warning hands. Too late.

Kinghammer meets her eyes. Her father meets her eyes.

'I love you, Ice,' he says.

As she holds his gaze, she watches the wights of the Empire eat his soul between one heartbeat and next. The monster that fills his body blinks, looks at her with the eyes of the hungry dead, and pulls her close.

Icecaller feels a sharp pain in her stomach, and watches her father's hand withdraw, red and dripping. She has a moment to take it in. The broken tattoo, the Deadsingers recoiling. One of them is bodily dragging a shrieking Hawkspit with them, retreating into the cleft just ahead of the yowling teeth of the mob.

The first of the dead hits her like a punch, just above the kidney. She feels it lodge and settle, spreading like fever. Devouring. Her blood sings. She's hungry. And angry. Furious. Her arms take a better grip on her shield. Lifts her spear. Absently, she watches her father's body disappear into the depths, at the head of a howling mob, moving as if hunting. Stalking something down into the depths of the mountain.

He can wait. She has to find her sister. They all have to find her sister. A snarl tears its way down her spine as she throws herself into the mass of her brothers and sisters, and begins to run with them. She is pulled down through the Stump by a hundred eager hands. Her head sings with voices. They chase the sound of steel and screams. Bodies tumble into her path. She stabs, tears. Blood spatters her teeth. She laughs, her tongue hot with the fire of other tongues. Distantly, the mountain thunders. The stone shudders. Rocks fall in great heavy fists. One catches her shoulder, breaks the bone. Her arm ripples with shapes, mouths, eyes that stretch. Her tattoos burn like a banked fire. Voices ahead. Her mind lurches towards them. Close, so close.

Panic in the tones, pitched and shouting. She pushes herself over obstacles. Splintered, charred, bladed and bent. A man reels towards her. She catches his stomach with the point of her spear, reaches into his screaming mouth and tears his cheek off. It slithers wetly down her fingers, which convulse with joy. She runs them over the broad oak side of a door, smiles at the red they leave.

A circle of pale faces swims in front of her, guarding a knot of children, all blades and bravado. A bearded boy with an axe, his free arm stretched defensively over the chest of the man next to him, a scream peeling off his lips. Icecaller swallows meat. Circles. Her spear moves light and lazily in the looped light, as her new brothers and sisters gather behind her. The small defensive circle hold their arms outstretched, placatory, mouthing something that swims slow through the thundering blood in her head, and is lost in the red of her thoughts. Icecaller knows them all. Quick, Roof, Steel.

In her way. All of them, in her fuckin' way.

Behind them, small and tousled, scratched legs and scuffed feet, Nigh. Her head howls with relief. Icecaller howls with it. Her sister. Her sister. Her beautiful, treacherous, delicious sister.

Her legs lope closer. The circle in front of her contracts. Words fly past her in a gabble. The mountain shudders and booms. The air stinks of acid. Icecaller's arms loosen and she charges. And if her tongue runs with other voices, does it matter? The hunger is hers. That buzzsaw, biting hunger. Then, she catches a flicker of movement. The beard and the axe from the left, a drawn blade from Steel on the right.

Icecaller's shield snaps out, hooks the axe edge, lets it bite. She tugs, pulls out and up, drags it free from Roofkeeper's startled hands. Twists, and snaps his arm below the elbow. Laughs. No one fiercer than the Kinghammer's daughter.

Quickfish yells in fury and throws himself at her. She doesn't expect it. Barely sees it coming. Feels his forehead crash into her face. Cartilage pops. The bridge and bone of her nose a smashed ruin. The voices in her blood exult.

She turns the spear, punches closed fist with the haft. Into the throat, once, twice, three times. Feels his windpipe collapse. Spits blood into his gasping face. Shrieks likes an eagle. No one faster than the Emperor's daughter.

She's still howling as Steelfinder's sword takes her in the side, low and subtle under her shield, slipping in like a lover. The blood around it floats, billows, grows the ghosts of teeth and eyes and hands. Icecaller turns on the point of the blade to face Steel. And if she's weeping, they're not her tears. But the hunger is, that black wolf hunger.

The blade hits her again, above the first red mouth. Her spear is held too wide, her shield heavy from Roofkeeper's axe. She lets them fall. Behind the blade, Steelfinder's face, tear-stained and wracked with grief. Icecaller feels something slip inside her. For a moment Nigh's screaming and she's terrified for her baby sister. She wants to pick up her up. To take her.

To take her apart. Piece by piece by red little piece.

And if she's praying, they're not her prayers. But the hunger is, that fat wasp hunger. It fills her head as Steel says something to her, and leans in to push her off the blade. Icecaller sees her moment, and strikes.

The voices rejoice as she pulls Steel into her. Sliding along the blade like a tongue. Taking it deep. Hauling Steelfinder off balance, until her throat tilts against Icecaller's teeth. Until Icecaller's mouth closes on muscle as her hand pushes Steelfinder's chin up and away. Bites down to blood, hot, sweet and flowing. She swallows and bites again. No one sharper than the Emperor's hunger.

Steelfinder's body falls. Icecaller lets it slip in gobbets from her lips. The flesh hangs red and wet. She smiles through it. Crouching, she beckons her sister with a hundred hungry fingers. Then from behind her, curses. Shouts of pain and rage from her new siblings. A trio reel into the room in a mess of fighting bodies. A wrapped fist rising and falling, something brass and screaming between the fingers. Sigils blazing with sulphur and saltpetre. And rags and ribbons, red, and yellow and red again.

Shipwright. Shroudweaver. Skinpainter.

Icecaller's brothers and sisters surround them, fighting with blade, tooth and nail for the Empire. Shroudweaver batters them back with concussive force, a slight man, his right hand wrapped in red, sulphur stink following him like a plague. Behind Shroudweaver, a woman like the prow of a ship. Shipwright, who moves like a wolf, a hammer, a coursing stag. Stringing the two, like a ragged flag, Skinpainter, their eyes wild, skin running with black and red ink. The crowd in front of them roils.

Limbs buffet her, knocking her off balance. While she's distracted, Roofkeeper falls back with Steelfinder's body. Icecaller's sister vanishes in the press, and she howls in rage, staggering as the room brightens around her.

Gold light. Gold light on the brows of her brothers and sisters. Their voices falling silent, red threads wrapped around them. She turns to fight with the anger of a thousand bodies, but there's a pressure on her skull and a twining in her heart. A firm hand grips her blade. A fist smashes her jaw. As the light fails, the last thing she feels is a wash of searing heat and a voice like bellows-brass.

75

REND

Stop. Take a moment, a breath. Watch this horror unfold once
again. Slide back in time to the moment where Skinpainter feels
Belltoller die, a ripping like shorn cloth as she's torn from the
world. An acid edge to the air and then, gone. Skinpainter knows
that behind them her body is falling. Absently, they hear voices,
screams. But there is no time to linger, no space to give to grief.
The sky is wide and swallowing. The wreck of the storm they
summoned lists over the Barrowlands, falling apart as the guiding
mind of the Belltoller dissolves into nothing. The wind drops,
gusts, tears at Skinpainter's ribbons, at red and yellow robes burnt
to blackness from calling down the lightning. Their tendons
underneath lit with fire, fraying as surely as the last scraps of material wound around their straining arms. They spit. This body is
a tool, and they'll use it until it breaks, if needed. The alternative
is unthinkable. Crowkisser cannot win. The mountain cannot
be breached. They tighten their grip, grit their teeth against the
aches blossoming under their skin and spread broad hands across
the shifting sky, to paint it red and black and red again. Geometries opening pathways for the lightning, luring it to the ground
along thrown angles, like water down a rill.

That bitch had lied to them. She had come with a soft face
and wide-eyes and lied to them. They'd known she would bring
death, and she's brought it by the score. They haven't seen so
much blood in years. All across the Barrowlands, people they love
die. Crowkisser was stronger than she had any right to be. The
kind of power that flowed out of her shouldn't be possible. It had
an alien feel to it, something damp and yearning. And strong.
Crowkisser had met them, breath for breath, spell for spell, and

the battle had turned into something worse. A clash of wills, like the old days. The bodies below were barely human anymore. Just a way to keep score. It turned their stomach. By any count, both sides were losing, the Barrowlands thick with slaughter.

It was dangerous, this butchery, ringing out like a bell to the ancient dead of the Empire. Each cut brought them closer to catastrophe, like slaking a dog's mouth with blood and expecting it not to bite. Absently, Skinpainter watches lightning sear the flesh from another huddle of grey-cloaked wretches. It's too late now. This isn't the war they've chosen, but it's the war they're in. There are two options – fight, or die.

At their back, they feel Shroudweaver begin to work, that old familiar pluck and tug, like a nail under a scab. They send lightning down, buying him time for whatever he has planned. Their heart races. The mountain hums along with their sorcery, the angles in its slopes resonating with the geometries. The air grows thick with the cold feel of ritual magic, like ducking slowly under dark water. They've never really understood weaving. Never really understood the between, but they can feel it close to their skin, like a great lake on the other side of their lungs. The dead shoal in its wetness, in hollows created by the weaver's movement.

Skinpainter's chest aches. Behind them, Shroudweaver staggers like a bar-room drunk. He exhales, and on the out-breath come the dead. Abruptly, Skinpainter is not alone; a feeling like a snapped twig, and the air suddenly full of spirits.

They turn in horror. Shroudweaver can't even meet their eyes. His whole mind is lost in the between. His body hangs limp in Shipwright's arms, and flowing from it, the unbound souls of the Empire. Skinpainter staggers against the invisible torrent of the dead, ethereal bodies brushing their face like feathers. A thousand, thousand light limned lives, swelling in murmuration, then arrowing down to where Crowkisser races towards the mountain.

An unbinding. An unbinding of the Emperor's dead. That's what Shroud had proposed, bald-faced, and Skinpainter, fool that they were, had never paused to consider, what, exactly, that might look like. For years, they had wondered how he had freed all the Empire's bound souls. A feat beyond reckoning. A feat that had won them the war. And of course, the explanation, like all explanations, was simple. The weaver hadn't. He'd bound them. Swapped one cage for another. And kept it quiet for decades.

Skinpainter hadn't pressed him on it when the pair had first arrived, far too concerned with keeping face with the entire mountain watching, but now they think about it, they're furious. At the betrayal. At the secrecy. At the sheer fucking idiot risk of it all. It must show in their eyes, because Shipwright catches their gaze and flinches back protectively.

That's all it takes. One small movement of fear.

Skinpainter shakes their head ruefully. This battle needs to be won. There'll be time for recrimination later. It's not like they don't hold secrets of their own. As the indignation fades, it dawns on them they have absolutely no clue how Shroudweaver's planning to pull this off. A small thread of curiosity pulls their gaze from Shipwright, from Shroudweaver's senseless body, and towards the weaver's work. Excitement and terror lights in their heart.

Out on the Barrowlands, above the torn cairns, snapped flags and broken bodies, something forms. A bare space in front of Crowkisser's charging feet, filled with drifting motes of gold, the dead souls of Empire gathered and spun into something far greater. It's at least thirty feet tall, or more. Skinpainter struggles to look at it, to make sense of it. The shapes of the dead within it move like fish under glass, and beyond them, the outline of something else. Eyes liquid as the shifting deep, limbs swaying in drifting shoals. It is beautiful. Terrible. Perfect. It stinks of spice and sweetness. God-magic. Their lip curls in disgust.

All around, the armies on the plain fall to their knees. Even on the battlements, Skinpainter can see soldiers staggering forwards for a glimpse, their jaws hanging slack with wonder.

Skinpainter feels a twitch under their ribs, and places a hand against their side as they run their eyes critically over the adoring crowds. Like watching cattle at market. They look again at the abomination Shroudweaver has raised and feel nothing kind.

Too many short-sighted people always wanting to call something bigger, stronger. Stupid. They sigh. At least this will be over soon.

It takes a second before Crowkisser stutters to a stop before the glowing monstrosity, pulling herself into shape from a squalling mess of feathers. The edges of the flock becoming her edges, crows on crows that are suddenly thin limbs. Skinpainter's almost pleased to see her, so small and so human against this roiling blasphemy, her familiar outline stick-legged and black against the burning sun of the new god.

That empathy lasts for all of half a second, until Crowkisser raises a hand, and in her fingers, they see a small scrap of flesh and bone. Skinpainter has a second to notice its absence among their trinkets. A vertigo spike of panic. A slipped belt-loop. A second to flash back to a moment of closeness, of touching, of betrayal. A second more to see how the pieces of this puzzle fit together before they feel the pulse of its unveiling, feel it calling to them. The Emperor's finger. Rightmost hand, smallest digit. Skinpainter's learnt its shape over the years. Watching it every night, using it to feel out the madness of its owner as he slowly choked down in the dark, his lungs filling with stone and blackness until he fell quiet. The bone shivered every night at first, then every week. Then perhaps every month or so. Eventually, it dwindled to nothing but a reassuring presence on their belt, never shuddering to life, so never noticed. Skinpainter had learnt to live with it, as they'd learnt to live with all their other horrors. Content to keep the Emperor forever separate from the dead.

And now, that grisly little memento is gone. Crowkisser has it.

Crowkisser winds back her arm and throws, the composite exploding even as the curse leaves Skinpainter's lips. The Emperor's flesh touching the souls of the mountain's dead for the first time in twenty years. And as it does, somewhere in the depths, the rest of the Emperor awakens, and calls out. Singing through the blood of everyone who once lived in the Empire. Singing through the veins of their children and their children's children. Skinpainter staggers. Blood bubbles against their teeth. Their flesh awakens, and in response the tattoos on their body blaze upon their skin.

The pain is incredible. But pain means it's working. Pain means the geometries hold. As long as the tattoos remain unbroken, the dead can't get in; the Emperor can't claim them.

They stagger again as below their feet the mountain blooms with acrid black smoke, and the great gate explodes. Their heart sinks. A smaller, less bitter defeat. More expected, more direct, but still deadly. They've badly underestimated Crowkisser. But she doesn't know what they've survived. She is young. Too young to understand that even suffering can be a weapon.

On Skinpainter's body, their geometrics burn. They watch as the mountain shudders, while in front of it, Shroudweaver's new god dies. And from its body, like flies blown from a corpse, through the blood, the gold and the hammering rain, the numberless dead of the Barrowlands flood towards Thell.

After them, armed with knives and hooks and rage, follow the people of Astic. Distantly, Skinpainter hears Kinghammer command them to keep the wall. They wave a hand dismissively. They'll do better than that. Pain is nothing. Crowkisser is nothing. There is only the old equation. People they must keep alive. And people who need to die for that to happen. There are people they love within the mountain. The geometries must hold. Thell must hold.

For that to happen, nothing must get in. Nothing must get out.

Skinpainter grits their teeth and ignores the writhing in their bones as best they can. A twist, a wrench of their hands, and the storm is battened. They can feel the Emperor rising under the skin of the earth; a surge of nausea, a buzzing red fever washing in from the sundered hills and hollows. Years of Skinpainter's work balances on a knife-edge. Ancient things are stirring at their old enemy's call. They stagger as another wave of sickness batters them. The Emperor is growing strong, and quickly, fattened by all the souls Shroudweaver just laid out like lambs under the knife.

They shake their head. Wipe spit from their lips.

Enough of this, they have responsibilities. The mountain has not fallen yet. As they watch, Thell's warriors hammer into the depths of the Stump, following after Kinghammer and Icecaller, clashing with grey-skinned fishermen in narrow passages, dancing the blade-dance. Step, flick, lick, turn.

Skinpainter sweats, curses their churning gut. Mad as it seems, Astic's army is not the real problem. Time is running out.

They feel small salted lives wink out, ten by ten, before they take a deep breath and throw themselves downwards, their bones bouncing gracelessly off the mountain's stone. Dizzy as a drunk dog, eyes full of stars and a skinned knee raw with blood, but still grabbing arms and shouting instructions, until their voice becomes a litany. 'Guard the lines, let no man do you harm.'

Brave bodies fall in line with their tumbling descent. Broad shoulders, wary spears blocking the passages deeper into the Stump.

Skinpainter feels the first few cuts personally. These fishermen are unskilled, but they have something in their eyes. A determination, a steel. They *believe* in that ragged, murderous girl they follow. And every damn cut that breaks a tattoo opens a gate for the dead. Skinpainter reaches the first of the fallen in time, greeting the injured open-palmed, wrenching the dead clear of each shining wound. They reflow ink at speed, mending as fast as their fingers can fly. The dead chatter around them like locusts. They feel nails on their cheeks, teeth on their sweating neck.

They bind, they break. Their heart lurches as they realise they're not fast enough; could never be fast enough.

Around them murder swills, the Stump clotted with people, voices living and dead. If Crowkisser is here, they can't feel her. They have to get deeper. Find the Deadsingers, build something stronger to hold back the dead, to stop the crow-witch making things worse. They beckon a few soldiers forwards to clear a path through the melee. As they run, they stagger into a clot of scared young foreigners who heft clubs uncertainly, every one of them barely as old as Icecaller. The guards at Skinpainter's shoulders lash out. Spear-points punch through sockets and screaming mouths. Wearily Skinpainter ducks a hastily swung club, brushes a billhook aside. Punches, withdrawing an arm wet with teeth and tongue, letting the blood run down into the black geometrics of their arms and sending it back with a flick. Ink follows and scatters briefly across bare muscles. Like cobras at their back, Skinpainter's rags flare, sway, strike. Stripping skin. Flensing down the bone.

It's over in seconds. As the last of the Astic boys gurgles into quiet, Skinpainter steps carefully over the mess, and beckons their own wide-eyed soldiers closer. 'Intact?'

No one misunderstands the question. They nod shakily. Check arms, wrists, legs. One redheaded girl is sick over her shield.

Lightmender. Skinpainter remembers making her first warrior marks. They motion her forwards. She moves gingerly over ripped and broken things that were once men. Skinpainter's heart aches a little at the look in her eyes. They take her face in their hands. 'It's horrible, I know. But it will be worse if we let them win. Breathe for me.' To her credit, she does, shuddering air into her lungs like a skittish horse. Skinpainter busses her cheeks, runs a finger over her mercifully unbroken marks. 'I know you. You can do this.' Her face steadies. They take her jaw, turning it to either side, letting a little ink flow gently over her features, darkening, straightening. 'I'm so proud of you, Light.'

It has the desired effect. She smiles, wet-eyed.

'I need you to do something for me, OK?'

She nods. 'Anything, Painter.'

They raise their voice, so the rest of the little group can hear. Run their eyes over the expectant faces surrounding them. 'You have to hold them here. As long as you can. Nothing gets in. Nothing gets out.' Skinpainter straightens, flings a hand out towards the distant wreck of the gates. 'Crowkisser's brought the dead with her. *She's brought the dead with her.* Most of you won't remember the Empire, won't remember what that means. But mark this, we have to stop her here. We're in between. We're the border. We've *always* been the border. Below you the Deadsingers, below your children.' They pause, pointing a steady finger at the young warriors. 'Only you can keep them alive. They need your time, your breath, your life if needs be. For the mountain.'

'For the mountain,' they murmur.

Skinpainter pauses, their heart aching at the sea of trusting faces. 'I love you all. And I *will* end this. *She will not have us.*'

As the little group mutters assent, Skinpainter pulls Lightmender close, their voice husky against her neck. 'I need you to take something, Light. Keep it safe. It'll keep you safe too.' They glance at the scared faces lingering over her shoulder. 'And them. Come near. And be strong.' Lightmender steps closer still, and Skinpainter pulls her in, hard against their ribs, stomach to stomach. Her breath flutters against their hips. Half a question hangs on her lips, but she's too well-trained to give it voice.

Skinpainter murmurs a quick prayer to all the dead gods, as they dig beneath their robes. Get their nails tight around the gift, its wet little contours, the strange softness flecked with gristle and tendon. Close their eyes against the pain, and pull. Under their ribs something rips, moves of its own accord, drips across the brief space between their bodies and lodges against Lightmender's stomach. She gasps and staggers. Skinpainter remembers the sensation well. They hold Lightmender's head and smile at her, ignoring the tightness in their heart. 'Try to breathe through it. It will get easier to bear.'

She grits her teeth, touches her side tentatively, lifting away fingers flecked with blood, 'This will help?'

Skinpainter nods. 'It always has.'

Lightmender's eyes are wide as she looks up at them. 'What is it?'

They smile tightly. 'Leftovers. A little something I picked up in the south.' They rub her shoulder reassuringly. 'I'll teach you all about it once we're out of here. For now, just know it'll keep you alive. And we need you alive.'

Skinpainter turns Lightmender's head with their fingers, watching the progress of the gift through her eyes. The briefest flare of gold in the sclera, the faintest taste of honey and spice on her breath. 'Hold them here, Light. Hold them here.'

She nods, and her soldiers form up behind her. Skinpainter can already see the gift's effects. The straightening of Lightmender's back, the lifting of her voice. They can already feel the cost too.

They touch a hand to the bloody remnant that still pulses against their ribs, and pray it'll be enough to see them through.

As Skinpainter forges downwards, that thin brave line of young men and women closes behind them. A line against the dark, against the dead. They're thankful for the minutes it'll buy them.

The battle fades to the edges of their mind, as it always does. See enough of war, and the patterns become familiar, pulses of movement like feet on a loom. The warp and weft of bodies. As one cohort stumbles forwards, grey and bladed, another enters from the side, red and blackened. Metal is threaded through muscle with precision. Pulse, push, shift, lock. Another line in the pattern.

Skinpainter moves with it. The ink clings loosely to their body now, crawling over their skin like a cat's tongue, following their outstretched fingers and clenched fists. Waiting to strike down any invaders stupid enough to get too close, but above all warding against the dead that hang in the air on the edges of breath, as they circle, waiting for an opening. They don't have to wait long. Crowkisser has made this a mountain full of openings, more wounds than they can ever hope to stem.

Skinpainter does what they can. Grasping wrists, shoulders, and familiar faces between their open palms and striking hard, purging the dead for the barest second before leaving them hanging in red mists of rage, ink slapping down onto the bone before infection can take hold.

A few are saved this way. Safe until the next rip or tear, at least. Too often, Skinpainter is too late, finding the dead already burrowing in like maggots, lighting the fallen with rage, and filling their mouths with the voices of the Empire's numberless dead.

Skinpainter curses. It breaks their heart, but they can't stop. To fight here is to bail amid the sea. They have to move onwards. The only way to stay sane is to abstract it all. To fall back into the weave of battle, where enemies move like tears along a seam and loved ones are bright knots in the wider pattern. High above them, they catch a distant flare that can only be Lightmender, and their stomach twists in recognition.

And behind it all, Skinpainter feels a weight on the fabric, tugging at the threads, at the edges of their mind – Shroudweaver. They need to find him, he needs to fix his fucking mess, and bring his daughter to heel. Or Skinpainter will. And none of that will solve the problem growing all around them. The dead are loose, and soon, the Emperor. Their old enemy riding the currents of death, stringing together his consciousness, pearl by shattered pearl, from among his former subjects. There might just be time to stop him. For that, Skinpainter needs Shroudweaver. And somehow, they need to reach the Emperor's prison; the black rock, and the lake miles below.

The dead race ahead of them, fast as breath. They feel the Emperor's call too. Skinpainter follows, swirling in the eddies of battle. There's no point in engaging the chaos that wracks the mountain, where there are only their friends to fight now, this far down. Pockets of uninfected soldiers are pressed back into archways, against tables and walls, battling tooth and nail against the dead riding their injured friends, switching sides at the barest cut. Skinpainter keeps their head low, lets the pattern pull them deeper. The only way to salvage this is to get to the Emperor, and somehow bind him again. There's no time to take stock, to gather anything more than an impression of broken chairs and upturned tables, hints of desperate, failed stands.

All of it is just strands in the weave, the whole pattern is so much bigger. This battle just one more in an endless succession. How many loved ones have they lost now? How much time have they spent shaping the larger tapestries, snipping small bright threads with a weary sigh? Skinpainter presses their lips together and rolls their hood tighter across their skull. A whisper of frustration scratches at their spine. This time needs to be different.

Their scalp itches, their short coarse hair prickling with sweat. Close now, they can taste Shroudweaver in the air, breathing in that gunpowder stink that only a southern corpse caller could have.

He's closer than they'd thought possible. Just around the corner, and about to die.

Skinpainter sees red threads flicker in the darkness, and sprints for them, heart surging.

They are not alone.

Blades spring from the shadows. They see a broken thing that was once a stall-keeper, his hands ragged from a thousand small cuts, his face still studded with the smashed bottle that killed him. Shroudweaver has him sighted too. Moving his feet incrementally, he lifts his hands a fraction and red thread licks the poor man's brow, which blossoms with gold fire. The weaver catches his falling body in tight-strung hands and opens his mouth for a benediction, a few words of Aestering grace.

As those half-remembered words fill the air, Skinpainter feels the pattern in their mind blossom with danger and lights their old muscles with fire. From the shadows ahead of them, quiet as a cat, comes one of Crowkisser's long grey men. He's spattered and weary, one cheek torn with a boathook scar that catches wetly in the light. But he's light on his feet and so fast. A damn sight faster than Skinpainter's tired bones, his toes used to climbing rigging and undeterred by mountain rock. A slim, flat blade twirls between his fingers as he dives for the weaver. Skinpainter's not going to be fast enough. They scream a desperate warning and fling a hand forwards. Startled, Shroudweaver turns, his face alert, neck exposed. The long man's blade falls.

Skinpainter winces, arcs their fingers out, and lets the ink leave their skin. Strands of black punch through the air and into the long man's eye. The scream that leaves him is a stretched, thin thing. He drops his blade and falls to the floor, fingers scrabbling against the stone. As he squirms, Skinpainter draws level with Shroudweaver, panic draining from them like water as they feel the pattern knit again.

'You OK?' they ask, although they already know the answer.

Shroudweaver nods. 'Thank you.'

'It's barely a start,' Skinpainter replies. 'I . . .'

Their words fade beneath a second scream from the long man. It's become something animal now, terrified and wordless. The grey-cloaked man spasms onto his back, his fingers tearing at his face until they find purchase around his eye socket and start to dig. Skinpainter catches their wrist. A spark of irritation flashes across their face as they brush their lips against the man's twitching ear. 'Ride it out.'

The long man's eyes roll like a frightened horse. Their voice is a guttural whisper. 'I can *see*.'

Skinpainter winces, anger fading to guilt, 'I know. I'm sorry.'

The man's fingers tighten on his wrist. '*Help me.*' A pathetic sound, thin, writhing with madness. Skinpainter holds him for a second. How many like him in the mountain? How many murderers following the crow-witch? They smile, bloodlessly. 'Very well.'

In one fluid motion, they swing a boot with finality against his skull, before turning back to Shroudweaver's widened eyes. 'I'll deal with him later. For now, we have to find Kinghammer. Ice. The rest.'

There is steel in their voice. 'We have to fix this, Shroud. We have to bind him. Whatever it takes.'

Shroudweaver readjusts his wrappings. 'I know, but first we find Ship. She has to be safe.'

Skinpainter holds his arm for a moment, a flood of bitter responses coursing across the back of their teeth. Eventually, they nod curtly. 'Of course. Of course.'

Shroudweaver smiles. 'I know where she is. Follow me.'

Skinpainter falls into an easy lope at his side. Runs a finger underneath their robes to the torn remnants of the gift. Pulls them back sticky and wet. Running out of time. They nudge Shroudweaver. 'It always seems to end this way, doesn't it? Chasing after the people we love. Trying to keep them safe.'

'It always ends with your damn mountain,' Shroudweaver grins into the brief silence. 'It'll be worth it though.'

Skinpainter's heart sinks as they recognise the path Shroudweaver's feet are following, down to the sleeping chambers and the children. 'Ship's down here?' they ask.

Shroudweaver nods as they round a corner and the noise of battle wells to meet them. 'I could feel her soul anywhere.'

Skinpainter shakes their head slowly. 'Sure. Me, I just look for trouble, and there she is. Figures.'

As if they've conjured her from the shadows, Skinpainter finally sees Shipwright ahead of them, amid a tight knot of familiar faces. Steelfinder, Roofkeeper, Quickfish. Nigh, damnably small. Their heart lurches.

Between them and her, a mass of the bleeding and broken dead, their voices edged as jackals.

For a second, resignation clamps around their heart, but then they shake their head. This time needs to be different. As they roll up their sleeves, they stretch an arm to Shroudweaver. 'Take my hand. We need to colour the weave.'

Shroudweaver's brows rise. 'Really?'

Skinpainter smiles. 'Trust me. They're not taking our people.'

Shroudweaver's silver-dancing fingers lace into theirs and as his power threads their bones, Skinpainter feels the pattern extend, multiply, move beyond worlds. Geometries laid bare behind the skin. They reach out to the weaver's shimmering strands, and feel a jolt of sorcery in their gut. It lifts them into the air, sends tattoos spiralling from their hands to strike into the reeling dead. The power tears loose a surge of emotion they've not felt in years. As Skinpainter's feet leave the ground, their heart cries out in terror, joy and hope.

Then hand in hand with Shroudweaver, they begin to paint.

76

RESURGENCE

The fiercest magic, the powers of a weaver and a painter combined, grants them but the briefest respite. For a few seconds, the dead are pushed back like tide water by geometries, ebbing in blood and teeth.

It can't last. The Empire's unleashed rage is snarling through the mountain. There will be more dead at their back. It's a wild relief to see a small group still standing, Nigh clutching Quickfish's legs, Steelfinder's weary face beneath her helmet.

Skinpainter hadn't dared hope they'd survive, had already half-snipped those threads, already begun to grieve. Yet for the moment, they've held. This time might be different. The relief cuts their legs from under them, and they fall to their knees. Their breath races, as they watch Shroudweaver tumble into Shipwright's arms. Blood thunders in their head, their pulse thready. Perhaps it's not just relief then. Magic howling through them like a storm, scouring them bare.

After a spell, they let Steelfinder's hands raise them from the floor, feel the last traces of geometries fall from their aching skin, feel the nerves underneath blaze into cold, exposed fire. There is no time to linger on the pain. Scant moments to guard the fallen against the dead. Skinpainter grits their teeth and begins salvaging, push, pull and purify. Hard strikes to drive out the lingering taint, quick movements to seal the broken lines of old tattoos. Triage. Mending the injured, as best they can. Salvaging the meat where the rot has not yet set too deep.

For a moment, they think the tide has turned. Some stillness swims in the waters of battle. They've travelled far though. Much as they'd like to fool themselves, they know the real rhythms of the hungry sea – first the calm, then the storm returns in earnest.

As if on cue, Quickfish screams in pain, clutching at his arm, and reels backwards. Nigh wails in shock, and a second later, the mountain is rocked by a shout of rage and horror, an inhuman bellow that roils up through the caverns, vibrating Skinpainter's spine, their guts, the wet absence under their ribs where scraps of the gift spasm in fear.

They watch Shroudweaver and Shipwright pull towards it like fish on a lure. They don't need to turn, don't need to wonder. They recognise that rage, that scream, that boundless madness. The Emperor has finally awoken.

Now he calls out from the spire above the dark lake, a lodestone in the depths. Punishment for Skinpainter's small mercy all those years ago, for that moment of hesitation. Now, this creature brings a final unravelling of all the patterns they have woven to keep their people safe. For all their work, all their care, they have been too slow, always a few steps behind the turn of the world. Skinpainter laughs under their breath. How depressingly *consistent*.

As if summoned, Shroudweaver reaches Skinpainter's side in moments, offering a hand. Skinpainter doesn't meet his eyes. Shroudweaver is the only other person who truly knows what cries out in the mountain's depths. They've been here before, decades ago, on the shore of the lake, as the Emperor was finally sealed in behind black rock, eyes rolling madly. Both of them weak with mercy after the triumph of their rebellion, and sick of killing. Skinpainter can read the recognition in Shroudweaver's eyes, shock falling into a lined face already worn down with the care.

Shipwright is close behind him, calling over to Steelfinder. Beyond her, Quickfish is on his knees, his lover hunched over him. Skinpainter squints at them, briefly. Rolled eyes, but a steady enough pulse at the throat. He has as good a chance as any of them.

Which is to say, not much. At the very back of the room, the children cluster with their guardians. All of them are doomed to rise ravening if something isn't done about the Emperor raging below. At the thought, a fury lights in Skinpainter. This time *will* be different. They're the only one that can fix this. Them, and this southern string-twister they've been cursed with for so long. They grip Shroudweaver's wrist tighter, pulling him close. 'The lake,' they whisper. His assent is nothing more than a short, sharp exhalation, but it's enough. Time for him to make up for what his daughter has done.

The pair leave at speed, aches pushed down into the marrow of their bones. At their back, Shipwright doggedly follows, humming with barely suppressed energy, a brass spinner stuttering to life in her hand. Skinpainter feels it lift them, like the push of a wave moving from fresh to salt water. More use than her paramour by far.

Well, perhaps that's not entirely fair. Shroudweaver too plies quick and clever craft; saltpetred brows and sulphured fingers, strands of red thrown to catch and bind, defend and destroy, clearing their path through the dead.

Yet all of this is performance. It takes Skinpainter only a moment to realise the reality that moves down here in the dark.

The battle is lost.

The dead crowd the halls, wearing the bodies of friends and allies. Skinpainter watches all they have worked for fail, over and over again. All around them, the last few living defenders fall, squirm, rise and rend.

A great heaviness fills their heart, the sadness like a choking weight. Their home is broken. The Deadsingers missing, Bell-toller dead. Kinghammer vanished. Icecaller too. Only they are left from Thell's old guard, and at their back, only Shipwright and Shroudweaver. What can they possibly hope to save now?

Yet despite the carnage, Shroudweaver walks with purpose, his fingers moving in soft tarantellas as the air fills with blood, and the dead things that move through the blood. The red threads around his wrist are wound tight, sulphur and saltpetre smoking at his temples, his lips set in a thin line. When the dead rush them, the threads loosen, gold light pulses on their brows, and they jerk like string-cut puppets and fall.

Behind Shroudweaver comes Shipwright. Like a wall, like a high-roofed church. When the dead pass him, her hands move. A spinner in the left, slicing the air into strips that she slides between, her right hand balled into a fist that swings slow and easy, to catch throats, shoulders and calves. She kills nothing. She shouts as she fights, in a language Skinpainter has never heard. Something fierce and old in a voice like bellows-brass. It lights their mind on fire.

Always, she holds Shroudweaver, catching him when the dead drive forwards, forging like a prow through screaming waves. Still they come. A voice curdled black with hate howls below, the Emperor calling to his subjects. As the trio plunges downwards, the mountain shakes with the aftershocks of Slickwalker's work at the gate. The fire of the shivers is likely dead by now, but the vibrations they've unleashed wrack ice and stone, great chunks of glacier slip and crash into nothing. Shipwright flinches with each battering impact, but drives them onwards regardless. Skinpainter tries to keep pace, their breath harsher with every step, painfully conscious of every small scrape on their body opening to new life as they hammer into the depths of the Stump. The ink on their skin smoulders with constant fire as they hurtle ever downwards, towards the lake.

Distantly, far above, they sense the people of Astic gain the deeper tunnels beyond the gate. Still, still they're singing, the light of their voices bright upon the pattern. Skinpainter would curse them, but they haven't the breath. Some of their own people must still be alive up there, because Skinpainter can sense them striking back, can feel the cut and thrust of their blades, their bodies, their dying.

It doesn't matter who wins above. The dead rule the depths now. Crowkisser's army have no idea what they're cutting their way into.

All of it is far, far beyond their control. The sheer scale of the disaster fills their thoughts, a swirl of panicked voices in Skinpainter's head, teetering on the edge of mad, hopeless, laughter. Sweat beads on their skin as their ink flicks out like a whip. They can't stop. Can't surrender. This time has to be different.

The dead don't give two shits for the hopes of an old mountain warlock. They strike in yowling waves, more careful now, perhaps wary of the power the three of them can bring to bear. Perhaps more closely guided by the Emperor's mind as the fractured parts of his soul slide together amid the growing dead. Still, Skinpainter presses onwards. Shroudweaver and Shipwright follow, uncomplaining, except for the harsh hiss of their breath, shouted warnings and cries of concern. Professionals — that's what's needed to salvage this, hard heads in front and the valuable assets far, far away.

Skinpainter needs to find the other lynchpins. They've seen Quickfish and Nigh, both secure, or as secure as can be. But where is Icecaller? Where is the blasted Kinghammer? The rest of the mountain can be sacrificed in a pinch, but not them. They are too important to Thell, too dear to their old damn heart.

That same heart lurches like a drunken cart-horse as they rush onwards through tunnels wet with killing. The air is thick with the dead, buzzing in red swarms, barely bound to bodies now and growing stronger with every breath the Emperor takes, spasming with delight as his broken throat coughs out a challenge like a cornered lion. Pulling them downwards to the heart of the mountain, to the black spire, and the lake.

The Emperor's magic is still not strong enough to touch the three of them. For a moment, Skinpainter feels the years slip away as the adrenaline spike of battle lifts their heart. A brother on their left, a sister on their right, enemies all around — a simple pattern, solvable. They channel that certainty into their magic, painting as they run. The ink is lithe as a cat, stark geometrics flowing from their hands and back to their skin in a push and pull of interlocking power. Where the dead are caught in its lines, they float like bees sung to sleep by smoke. Chances for a little more salvage emerge down here, still pockets of resistance, hale warriors that greet their coming with cries of shock and joy. They paint the survivors, strengthening them against the burrowing dead, the corpse-call in their blood, the avenues opened by nicks and cuts. The Emperor's legacy.

Shroudweaver guards their back, his threads singed and fraying, bruises blossoming on his arms like puddles after rain.

They're running out of time. Skinpainter feels hollow inside. There are spaces in them where they've forced the ink outwards. It was necessary, but now there are absences. Power has leaked from their body, leaving them bare as the rind on sucked fruit. Worst of all is the bleeding remnant of the gift. An aching space beneath their ribs, scoured empty. As if to mock them, they feel a distant pulse in their veins as Lightmender struggles far above. The first blossoming of the gift as it latches on to its new host. The remnant that clings to Skinpainter spasms in sympathy. Skinpainter bites their dry lips in a strange twist of ecstasy at the unfamiliar sensation, tasting spice and clove.

They have to focus. Down here, Shipwright strides grimly onwards, her hair clotted with sweat and blood, her knuckles split and strapping torn. One hand clumsily works a struggling brass spinner which clunks and stutters. She shoots them a weary smile, blowing a clinging strand of hair clear of her face.

Another brief moment of camaraderie. It's about all that's keeping them alive as the dead press in, the three of them driven closer together by swinging arms and snarling teeth, until they are back-to-back, a small flare of defiance against the dark. They're so close to the Emperor's prison now that Skinpainter can smell the waters of the lake, the damp stone of the spire.

The dead skirt the edges of their small circle. They fear the gold light, the brass stutter, the red and the black. Distantly, selfishly, a little bit of Skinpainter's brain rejoices at being in the heart of battle again. The thrill of dancing just the right side of death. The measured push of bodies moving in rhythm. The ebb and swell of power on the edges of their tongue. Brief flares of victory and consternation. All of it a seductive lie that lasts until they get a good look at the faces which plunge howling towards them. Familiar and beloved and broken. They try to strike them on the temples, the shoulders, to deal only gentle destruction.

Laying them low until there's time to pull the dead loose. To yank the infection from their veins. But there is no time. Rescue isn't coming. Recovery is a joke. Thell's halls sound to the guttural skirl of a dead man's vengeance. The Emperor's voice clearer with every passing moment. It pulls them onwards, a broken dog yelp in the night. Irresistibly drawing their feet down towards the great black lake, the spire that rings with his rage. Thell empties its guts around them, and they bludgeon their way through.

Finally the sloping darkness seeps onto the lakeshore. Their ragged little band spills out on the eastern side of a chamber so large that Skinpainter's eyes can't make out the far shore. Miles of black water, smooth and silent. The mountain's miracle, fed by some unfathomably deep aquifer even further below, and the reason Thell should never have fallen. It's normally home to nothing but pale, eyeless fish who swim the lake, bats with wings like shredded paper that skirl beneath the spire; normally guarded day and night by a few brave men and women Skinpainter had trusted with this greatest, most awful secret, rotated out every few hours lest the blackness and silence drive them mad.

That silence endures, somehow, despite the furore of the battle above, the whole cavern vast and echoing. Shipwright turns to play rearguard as they pelt toward the lake. She's not needed. The dead pursuing them mill at the tunnel entrance, seemingly unwilling to touch the black sand of the shore.

As she takes in her surroundings, Shipwright's gasp echoes off the slick walls and fades into the darkness. Even the dead at her back fall quiet, subsiding into snapping and growling like cowed dogs.

Shroudweaver glances nervously behind them, but Skinpainter's attention is focused on the black spike suspended above. The stalactite still not fully sealed after twenty long years, marred by a jagged crack along a third of its length. They half imagine they catch a glimpse of white bone, the gleam of a madly rolling eye.

The three of them take a few nervous steps forwards, cautious as cats, sand crunching softly beneath their boots, as the pale shells of things that have never seen light are slowly ground into dust.

'All of this down here,' Shipwright murmurs, her voice hushed with awe. 'I never knew.' She shoots a glance at Shroudweaver. 'You never told me.'

In reply, Shroudweaver raises a cautionary finger to his lips, and points.

There's something in front of them, a heap of bodies on the shore beneath the spire, softly twitching. Skinpainter's stomach lurches. They don't need to wonder what happened to the guards any more.

They start forwards, then slide to a halt as the bodies are pushed aside from within, sloughed off as a larger figure hauls itself atop the pile.

Its ravaged, ripped back is turned to them, but even in the half-light of the lake cave, Skinpainter knows that shape, the broad shoulders, the salted hair. Every tattoo on their shifting muscles was painted by Skinpainter's own hand. Kinghammer.

Every one of those tattoos now broken and torn, the body beneath heaving in huge, jagged breaths.

Skinpainter curses under their breath and glances over their shoulder at Shroudweaver who shakes his head, tight-lipped. The dead have filled the passageway behind them. A snarling mass of limbs and steel. There's no way back.

Their mind races. There are other ways out, but all on the other side of the lake, miles distant, which requires passing the pile of corpses and Kinghammer, who remains silent, back turned, bare feet shifting unsteadily on the softly writhing bodies beneath.

Atop the pile, their old friend slowly tilts his head back, until his gaze is fixed on the spire. His hands extend from his sides. The left still clutches the hammer, matted with hair.

'My lord?' Skinpainter says.

Kinghammer's head turns slowly, juddering with the scrape of bone. One eye glints in the half-light, their lower jaw hanging loose on red ropes of tendon.

And from that mangled maw, the Emperor's voice.

'No.'

At that, something breaks in Skinpainter's heart. They should fight. They should raise their geometrics in defence, but the horror hits like a wave, blood rushing in their ears like the sea.

They hear Shipwright's shocked scream, hear their own voice saying. 'How?'

The Emperor laughs at that. A jagged, choking thing that slides over Kinghammer's broken teeth.

'Thanks to his lovely daughter.' A mangled hand waves at Shroudweaver. 'Such an *ambitious* girl.'

Shroudweaver starts forwards, and Skinpainter puts a hand across his chest. 'Not yet.' The barest whisper. 'Please.'

'Let him go,' they say.

The Emperor cocks its head. Kinghammer's puppeted skull listing as it twirls the hammer nonchalantly in slow, long circles. Bits of meat fly off and spatter the sand.

'Let him *go*? No, Painter. I can't do that.' Kinghammer's shoulders roll as the Emperor's voice continues. 'This body is so much better than what you left me with. What you *both* left me with.'

It flicks its eyes up to the spire. 'You do remember what you did, don't you, Skin?' Its voice a guttural hiss. 'Let your people devour me. Shattered the remains piece by piece. Bound even those.'

Skinpainter breathes deep, tries to fight waves of nausea, cold sweat wreathing their skin.

The Emperor continues. 'How clever you thought you were! Painting my own people with your foul patterns. Locking me out of their blood, even as your pale friend locked me away from the dead.'

Kinghammer's head snaps to Shroudweaver, its voice a snarl. '*Thief.*' The hammer swings in an arc, smashing down into the writhing dead. 'A slow death for you, dabbler.'

Skinpainter breathes in, lets it slide out slowly. 'Let him go. I offer you a trade.'

The Emperor's eyes light. It digs a finger deep in its new mouth, pulls a strip of skin loose.

'A trade? From you, Painter?' Its smile is wide. 'How desperate.'

Skinpainter ignores the barb, ignores Shipwright's urgent protest behind them.

'Me. For him.'

Silence for a moment. Kinghammer's eyes wet and limpid. His whole face seeming to writhe as the Emperor's spirit moves underneath.

Then laughter, loud and raucous, splitting the echoes of the cavern into howling shards.

'You.' Its pitch drops. A cat's purr, wet and thick with spit. '*You*.'

A shake of Kinghammer's head. 'No, Painter. No.' Its hand waves. 'If only you'd held onto that last piece of me, you traitorous thing.' A vicious smile on Kinghammer's face. 'The smallest piece of me. Couldn't trust it to anyone else, could you? Couldn't tell anyone else.' Its snarl deepens. 'Didn't think anyone else was capable.'

The Emperor begins to walk towards them on Kinghammer's bloody feet. With every step the dead around him awaken, burrowing like rats in garbage. They see Skinpainter and howl in recognition with a hundred mouths.

As the Emperor's feet hit the sand, it staggers slightly, and laughs. 'New legs. A little tired from all the running.'

Skinpainter tries to summon some scrap of power as the Emperor approaches, but they're spent. The torn gift aches under their ribs, their muscles worn out with a hundred inkings. The stench of the Emperor's magic fills their mind like a black wall, its voice like wolves feasting, 'No trade. No deal. I have this body. Soon, I will have all the bodies within this mountain.' Kinghammer's mouth splits impossibly wide. 'I should thank you, Skinpainter. Without all those years in the dark, I would never have been driven to explore just how *much* I can do.'

The Emperor draws closer, until it's a breath or two from Skinpainter, Kinghammer's massive, ruined chest moving in ragged sighs. The dead coil behind their master, fat as leeches crying out for blood.

At their back, Skinpainter can hear Shroudweaver and

Shipwright shouting, can feel slick fingers tug on their arm, even as the Emperor leans in close, so close they can see the muscles working inside its jaw, can see Kinghammer begin to fray as the body is pulled into new shapes by the spirit within.

'A secret for you, Skinpainter, before you die.'

Its breath is wet against Skinpainter's cheek, its voice delighted.

'Kinghammer's flesh is good. Strong. Perhaps he's still in here, somewhere, but that won't last. And even if it did, I have his daughter too. I have them all, thanks to you.'

Skinpainter's heart sinks, the loss enough to crush them, like the depths of the sea, enough to drown in. But beneath that, a voice, a single thought: this time *has* to be different. They reach a shaking hand towards the Emperor, and push outwards with the last echoes of their power, faint geometries fizzing and burning against cold skin.

Kinghammer's body staggers, and laughs.

As the sparks fade, Skinpainter faces him, steeling the breath within their chest. Their rags float lazily. The air hums. Patterns shift and move, blackening like blood under a bruise. Hiding their treacherous, hammering heart.

'You are dead. A nothing. A relic,' they snarl, lashing out with ink that licks across the surface of Kinghammer's skin. At its touch, his body shudders, and all the dead at his back turn to face Skinpainter as one.

The Emperor replies with a hundred tongues. Smiles with a hundred jaws. The eyes of Skinpainter's friends look back at them from its broken choir with hunger in their hearts.

'I. Am. Whole,' says the thing that was Kinghammer, as its jaw hangs slack and loose. 'I. Am. Whole. And you . . .' It raises a bloody hammer that drips, slow, black clots. 'You. Have. Lost.'

Skinpainter turns their face to Shroudweaver. 'Bind it.' Fury riding their breath.

Shroudweaver's hands move frantically. Red thread spins and loops. The air burns. 'Easy for you to say.'

Skinpainter frowns, a rage kindling in them, cold and hard as ice. Behind them, the Emperor laughs in lurching rasps, as it picks apart a jawbone tooth by tooth.

They retch and begin backing away, painfully slowly, keeping their body between Shroudweaver and the wreck of Kinghammer, giving him time to work.

They glimpse Shipwright at his back, warding the other dead off with slow, buzzing swings of her fists. For a moment, Skinpainter wishes she would let them all through, so they could watch this stupid arrogant man taste a consequence for once in his life.

An indulgence; Shroudweaver can't die yet. He owes them answers at least.

Skinpainter edges closer to his dancing hands, their voice low, furious. 'How did this bastard get loose, Shroud?'

The Emperor laughs thickly inside Kinghammer's skin, the possessed man's eyes rolling in his head. Bloodstained lips quirking in a smile. 'Ask his daughter, inktwister. Wait, no. Ask *him*.'

It waves a hand expressively, small flecks of red flesh dance along the bone.

Shroudweaver tears his eyes away. 'You know I needed the dead, Skin. I needed a composite. To stop her.'

Skinpainter half turns, regards him levelly. 'And you thought she wouldn't have something up her sleeve? Your own daughter.' They shake their head. 'You idiot.'

Shroudweaver's voice is cold, his hands dancing. 'Something that she stole from you, it seems.'

The Emperor chuckles again, throat full, 'As I said, a clever girl, his daughter. Just a little overconfident though. Like her father.' It grins wetly. 'Helpful that she hates you more than she feared me.'

A few steps away, Shroudweaver ignores it all, as best he can. He can't focus on the terror, on how quickly this is all spiralling, on the implications for Crowkisser. For the world.

As if it senses his wavering heart, the Emperor throws its head back and howls, the sound utterly inhuman, feral and hungry, splitting Kinghammer's lips with the force of the shout. The mass of the dead bays in response, loping and lurching ever closer.

Side by side, held in a wary knot, Skinpainter, Shroudweaver and Shipwright slowly retreat, pushed back towards the cave entrance, towards the lakeshore and the freezing cold water beneath the spike of the Emperor's prison. The possessed dead crowd ever closer around Skinpainter, ragged hands stretching as tattoos dance across their broken skin. So much undone in such a small span. And Shroudweaver at the heart of it. Or his daughter, at least. A flicker of rage again. They shrug it away. Useless. A clear head's needed if they want time to sling blame later. They roll up their sleeves. Ink flows down their muscled arms as they turn to Shroudweaver's dancing hands and nervous face. 'Do you want to undo this?'

Shroudweaver shakes his head. 'I wouldn't know how. The binding was hard enough the first time round. Now? With all this?' His shrug is liquid, eloquent.

Skinpainter grins. 'The only regrets that kill you are the ones you don't own, Shroud. Time you southerners took a leaf out of our book.' Their fingers work quickly, sketching patterns on the dark sand. Ink flows into a pulsing square, black and red and black again. 'Get inside.'

Shroudweaver complies, leaning against them gratefully. His ragged little body shakes with the effort.

Shipwright's at his back, her eyes a hard iron. 'What are you going to do?' she asks Skinpainter and they hear the warning in her tone.

They shrug, pushing their hood back as they turn to face the crowding dead. 'I have no fucking idea, but unlike your boyfriend. I didn't spend the last twenty years moping over my bad choices.' Their smile is broad, a little wild. 'I made contingencies.' They glance at Shroudweaver. 'But it's going to hurt.'

As they turn back to the mob, the thing in Kinghammer's skin is suddenly near, pressing to the front of the throng, its bulk waxing with every second. Kinghammer's shape already fraying under the strain, skin splitting and veins bursting as the Emperor's soul takes a firmer hold. Its voice falls into a shuddering drawl as Kinghammer's jaw distends, snakelike. 'Hurt? I'll show you *hurt.*' It shoulders closer, muscles shifting, using the hammer like a massive, wasted limb. Stops just short of the outermost ink and lets out a guttural snarl. 'This won't stop me.'

Skinpainter pretends calm, clamping down on the voice in their head that says it's probably right. Their hands work furiously. Ink flows as geometrics unlatch and dissolve on their body, running like water into the designs on the sand beneath their feet.

Kinghammer's eyes linger on the patterns for a moment, then flick to Skinpainter's face. They can sense its confusion and watch as it scrambles to cover it up. A little spark of hope there, even as the Emperor grins, loose and wet.

'So nice to *see* you, again. Skinpainter. All those years in the dark, and not a glimpse.'

Skinpainter ignores it as best they can, presses their lips together, and paints. Shroudweaver still limp as a beached fish against their side. The spinner in Shipwright's fist screams like a beaten dog as it stutters and fails.

The shriek of it catches at the back of Skinpainter's mind. As their concentration wavers, Kinghammer's ridden body reaches forwards a bloody hand, one ragged sharp nail miming the outlines of their face. 'I'll take all that *off.* Render you back to bone. You'll thank me.'

Reflexively, Skinpainter pushes. The line of ink flexes, catches Kinghammer's hand with a fleck of colour.

The Emperor yowls, snatches its fingers back, circling.

Skinpainter howls in glee as they call over their shoulder to Shipwright. 'See? Contingencies!'

She pulls a face. 'You just pissed it off, Skin.'

As if it's heard her, the Emperor throws itself forwards against the lines in the sand, the dead piling with it. Instinctively, Skinpainter recoils, and raises the barrier. The whole design bursts into shifting light, humming with small frequencies – a little gift from Belltoller, rest her soul. The mob of the dead batters into it and recoils as ink adheres to their skin, peeling like hot wax. The resonance of magic thrums in their heads, clearing their minds. The momentum of their charge broken, for a second. The sheer power of the pattern holding them at bay, pulling the Emperor's contagion from them, like venom from a wound.

All that energy has to come from somewhere, however. Even as Skinpainter pushes the magic outward, even as colours flare against the black glass of the water, they realise how far they've overreached. Something bursts in their guts and they feel blood begin to seep outwards. Stupid, stupid, impulsive, stupid. They grit their teeth, tilt their face towards the Emperor. 'I've walked the barrows since I was born. I sealed you away, and carved you up piece by piece. You don't scare me.'

In response, the Emperor screams in rage, and charges again.

The speed at which it moves is astonishing. Fists crash against the circle like hammers. Kinghammer's skin smokes and burns, scoured down to the bone as the Emperor rides his body past breaking. 'I should!' it bellows. 'I was born before the barrows, in the great ice, when the city below still sang. And you, you hung me in the dark, gave me to the rock above the black water. Thought to keep me penned.'

Its smile is loose, easy. Eyes alight with madness in Kinghammer's skull. 'A child's game. I have sung through the high frost. Through the first dying of the light. Through the splitting of the three. As if you could ever hold me. I swam in blood; the blood of the people, the blood of the mountain.' It quiets, paces, Kinghammer's massive feet kicking up puffs of black sand as the Emperor's voice drops to a low, guttural mutter. 'You'll see, I'll show you. I'll show you what lies beneath the earth. I'll show you the song I found in the heart of the spire, in the blackblackblack behind the rope and the dry blood.' Its gaze fixes on Skinpainter, wet and luminous. 'I'll open up your eyes layer by layer.'

Heart racing, Skinpainter motions softly to Shroudweaver. Their fingers dance Katkani. *Torn door. Sly mouse.*

Shroudweaver smiles nervously.

Skinpainter signals again. *Send from shadow to shadow. The lightest thread is an unknown chain.*

Shipwright watches their flickering fingers, mouthing along with the translation. As Shroudweaver nods his assent to

Skinpainter she catches his wrist. 'No, Shroud. No. You can't. Please.'

There's something cold in Shroudweaver's eyes for a moment; cold or remote. Certain. A ghost of the weavers of old.

Kinghammer's body batters against the circle again. The dead clustered around it peel themselves off the walls, scraping themselves from the floor as they shudder towards that small cage of hissing sparks, backed against the dark.

'Please, love,' Shipwright says. And if she's not begging, she's close.

Gently, carefully, Shroudweaver unpicks her fingers from around his wrist.

'There's no other option.' A little steel in his tone still, a vestige of his training.

Shipwright's shoulders sag even as his hands dance towards Skinpainter.

A quick-closed door?

Skinpainter nods in relief, steps forwards, and embraces him. Their rags flare. The ink beneath their feet fountains in streams, in spikes, pulling Shroudweaver down like a rip-stream tide. Down into the between, and gone.

Shipwright screams in frustration and fear.

Kinghammer's body flings itself against the circle.

The world shakes, blackens and breaks.

77

The weave first, then the world.
The god in the hand, before the god in the mouth.
The god in the heart, before the god in the hand.

—Aestering Knotsong, No. 1

At first, Shroudweaver feels nothing. The memory of Skinpainter's breath hot on his face, the sudden twist of pain in their eyes as they tear a way into the between spaces. He hears Shipwright's fading scream at his back, feels the weight of the Emperor against the sparking wards, the thunder of its fists.

Then the ink reaches his legs, and pulls.

He goes under.

The world shifts, splinters. He lets himself drift loose. It's easy now, the between space opening up to him like a sinkhole, a cenote of darkness. Skinpainter's magic blurs the edges between worlds and yanks him from one to the other with a swift, merciless tug. Shroudweaver's already halfway there from pain and exhaustion. A warhorse stink of gunpowder and saltpetre surrounds him like a corona, and beyond that, the thick taste of rot and the grave. Power lingers in the between like static after rain.

The first thing he sees is his own body, sunk to its knees, head pressed against Skinpainter's stomach, shoulders held in Shipwright's broad hands. When she shouts, the air filigrees her lips, coloured by scraps of spinner magic, the last dregs of the composite's touch. His abandoned body's no better, enmeshed in the remains of the unbinding. Red threads run from his hands, his hair, his eyes. Smokesister was true to her word though. It's all falling apart, fraying as he watches. Time is short if he wants to return. *If* he wants to return. There's a pull here, a call to quietness. It would be easy, so easy, to slip back into nothing, and leave all this behind.

Except, he's not alone here. The unbound dead of the Empire shoal in the grey between, freed as they are from the prison of his heart, from the brief hold of the composite he'd called forth, and scattered by his daughter.

Here, in the space between, they crouch like jackals over the fallen. Shroudweaver can see the souls of Thell's people struggling weakly beneath their touch. Ripped, swallowed, and repurposed piece by piece, ridden like broken horses.

Time is short if he wishes to salvage this, and the dead are not the worst of it.

The Emperor is here, as he had always feared it might be.

Kinghammer's body is only a rough outline in the between, a husk, a half-burst chrysalis. The Emperor's true form blossoms in the void, unbounded by broken meat. Not a man anymore. Not even the pretence of a man, but something stranger, protean, and twisted.

It turns its eyes on him, jaw unhinging, teeth shuddering outwards along it. A tongue unfurls in the back of Kinghammer's torn throat.

'*You.*'

The between place has no distance.

The Emperor stutters across the intervening space with the black buzzing of a wakened hive. A few of Shroudweaver's red threads snag and break loose as he recoils.

Its face presses against his, a chewed ruin pocked with teeth-marks. A stench like a dug-up dog. Its cheeks are torn with half-healed scabs, matted blood. Kinghammer's bones grind when it speaks. 'You let them. *You let them.* You. Let. Them.' Beneath its skin, the pulsing dead of the Empire stretch out in rage, hands, skulls and teeth reaching for Shroudweaver.

The Emperor throws its head back, unleashing a scream that cuts the air like clotted glass. Shroudweaver feels his skin shudder, saltpetre and sulphur blown back into his lungs. There's a terror in his stomach like he's never known. The touch of something utterly alien against his soul. Yet still, distant, he can feel the warmth of Shipwright's hands against his spine, slowing his hammering heart. Time is short, but he allows himself a few panicked breaths. It's all that's needed before his training comes back to him with the speed of long practice. There is a way out of this. The Emperor must be bound, again.

He reaches for a needle, stitches, darns. Threads regathered and woven around the Emperor's grasping limbs. Not the red of the body, but the silver of the soul.

Its eyes lock onto his dancing fingers. 'You dare?'

Shroudweaver ignores it, focuses on his work. Darns, tightens, mends, holding his body tight in the stillness of the between, keeping half an eye on the dead, half an eye on Shipwright, as she dodges and weaves on the black sand of the beach. She reels as Kinghammer swings at Skinpainter's wards. The Emperor has taken the weapon that gave Kinghammer his name and turned it to destroying Skinpainter's work. The great black hammer drips screaming red sparks, smokes, and ricochets off the barrier which flares with every strike. Skinpainter's face twists in a defiant scream, their legs hammering down into ink pooled around their ankles. The wards tighten.

Shroudweaver's mind splits between worlds, half an eye on Shipwright, half an eye on the thing in front of him, the Emperor – or the thing the Emperor has become, riding Kinghammer's body like a sway-backed nag. Here, in the between, Shroudweaver can see its true form, paying only the barest adherence to the outline of the man Shroudweaver had chained over twenty years ago. Its shape is fluid now, roiling with the stress of pulling in the souls of the dead, sprouting eyes, teeth and tongues. Kinghammer's shape shimmers distantly beneath, like fish under water.

Overlaid on his bones, is the Emperor of the Mountain, the Dreamer of the High Ice. He is not doing well, lips blackened and torn from decades chewing weakly in the dark. Skin scarred with a thousand bites, marked by the memory of pain. Shroudweaver imagines he can see the toothmarks of every revolutionary scored deep, down to the bone. Kinghammer. The Deadsingers.

Belltoller. They'd welcomed in their new world with a feast. They'd waited until he'd left to do it.

Not left, but turned his back, Smokesister's voice admonishes in his head. The fire of her broken binding snakes through his chest like lit wire.

There's the briefest flicker in the silver threads as his conviction wavers. Unacceptable. He catches hold of the thought and crushes it. He is not solely to blame for this. Guilt is an indulgence he doesn't have time for.

A binding weave is needed. That and nothing more. His tutors' voices surface like the rill of a river, steady beneath the howling dead, the flash of magic.

The weave first, then the world.

As if his hands remember the lesson, they follow old patterns through the air with speed. Silver thread gathers around him as he moves his body into the first form, darns, stitches, and binds. Spider's web, bat's wing, the very smallest knots at first; a cast net, seeking connections with the soul of Emperor. The hooks are easy to find – memory, hate, the shared experience of pain. Shroudweaver gathers them all in, the smallest fragments of silver at first, teased from the very edges of its shape, then lashed to the mountain. Bound to the air, to the stones, to each other. They are so fragile, a broad mesh, vulnerable to a single tear, but there's nothing else to work with down here. Well, that's not strictly true. Shroudweaver's eyes flash to the struggling souls of Thell's dead, to the bright lights of Skinpainter, and Shipwright. There are stronger materials here, if he's willing to take them. He's pulled up short again by the voice of his tutor.

The weave holds. It takes only as a last resort.

Shroudweaver shakes his head, shifts his feet into the second form. Flowing grass. River top. Wave curl. No, nothing else to work with, just himself and his skill alone. He sews, he stitches, he binds. He'll make it enough.

The Emperor is taken in at first. The slow, silverfish movements of weaving run through Shroudweaver's fingers, a lullaby of hands calling to the monster in front of him. He watches its eyes turn to follow the silver, the gestures, the line of his bones. His right hand unspools red even as his left stitches silver. As he makes the first knot of binding and ties off, the Emperor lurches, the spell broken. Its legs stagger and every one of its eyes snaps to his wary face. 'NO.'

The shout shudders through Shroudweaver's bones. He feels them break inside him. Little shards of white floating into the red.

'NO,' and the Emperor's hand plunges deep into the meat of his shoulder. He feels nails brush against his veins. Feels them. Even here, in the between, where nothing should be felt.

'NO,' another hand strikes on the right, and, impossibly, he *feels* it severing muscle, burrowing deep. He screams as he's pulled forwards.

'NO,' the mouths of the Emperor say, lunging for him, and Shroudweaver's scream is cut off by a foreign tongue, foreign teeth that bite down on his own.

The form of the Emperor is distorting terribly now. The torrent of souls distending the last vestiges of a human shape. Shroudweaver can hear the pop of cartilage, the wet stretch of bone as it struggles to hold. He can feel the hunger of a thousand souls as they clamp down on his jaw.

Another set of limbs tear themselves loose from the roiling mass, plunge in below his ribs, seeking liver, kidneys, finding organs and slicing tendons. Red threads loosen and drift away. He can feel himself dying – all the rules he knows are broken, and he is dying.

'No,' the Emperor says, its mouth full of his, and Shroudweaver feels the word in the heart of him. Beyond the shadow, blood and bones of the between spaces, he sees Kinghammer shatter Skinpainter's wards. His hammer arcs towards their upraised face, and they look, for a second, relieved.

Shroudweaver can do nothing, he's held in the between, pinned like a butterfly as the life drains out of him.

Then, impossibly, a blur of motion, and Shipwright catches the hammer flat in her fist. Brass stutters and whines. The spinner is failing, but something beyond it is giving her strength. Her shout is golden in the heart of the mountain, in the face of the end, the ghosts of new gods lining her tongue.

The hammer holds. And it's then Skinpainter strikes, hitting Kinghammer open-palmed above the heart. Ink spatters, takes hold, lodges deep, as it smokes and burrows against the skin. Kinghammer staggers, and for a second his connection with the Emperor is broken. Shipwright presses her advantage, stepping out of the wards, and swinging a right hook that blurs with a wasp-brass sting. It catches Kinghammer on the side of the jaw, pitching him sideways. Skinpainter's ink flares like a struck match on his chest.

Hung in the between, Shroudweaver watches them fight, his body held in the rot of the Emperor's grasp, his lungs full with the breath of a half-eaten man.

He watches them fight, and he watches Shipwright win. A wild swing from Kinghammer, that she ducks under like a passing breeze. A weave to the left, to the right, and she's inside his reach, a wild grin on her face, teeth bared and flecked with blood. Kinghammer roars with rage, the Emperor's voice hard on his tongue. Shipwright laughs. In the face of it all, in the depths of the mountain, she laughs, then swings her head forwards with brutal intent. Kinghammer's nose collapses with a crunch. He reels backwards, mired in the swarming dead. He tries to raise the hammer, but Shipwright's already there; Skinpainter's ink lashing out to clear her a path that she traces like lightning to grab the hammer's shaft. For a moment, the pair are locked, muscles straining. A hum in the between places, and Shroudweaver sees Shipwright suddenly haloed in gold. There's a sweet taste on his tongue, an explosion of honey and spice, god-magic blazing forth as she leans in, and wrenches. The haft of the hammer twists, screams like a wounded animal and breaks. Kinghammer lurches backward. Shipwright stands there, golden and steadfast, hair a mess, breath heavy, and Shroudweaver's heart sings for her.

As Kinghammer staggers, the Emperor hisses in pain. There's

the briefest loosening of control, and Shroudweaver feels a pin drop in the back his mind.

Now. Saltpetre and sulphur flares, the powders on his skin burning bright into nothing. A brief actinic punch, a last line of defence against the vengeful dead, so simple he'd learnt it as a child. It'll buy him seconds at most, and after this, he's left wide open.

It works though. The Emperor recoils, and as its talons slide loose Shroudweaver raises his red right hand.

'I left you,' he says. 'Because some things have to be left behind.' His fist falls and opens at the last moment to spider red threads in a binding web. They knit fast across a screaming jaw, punch their own ways in, lace tight. 'I left you because you *brought* this on yourself.' A left-handed strike, and the Emperor's side flares in silver. Lancing the wound. Pulling souls loose. As he weaves, its shape shrinks, eyes wink out. Jaws slide together into a single screaming mouth.

Shroudweaver takes its head in his hands. 'I left you *because you gave me no choice.* I would have saved you, if you'd only let me.'

The Emperor watches him with wide eyes, as the red continues to weave up its struggling face.

'I would have saved you, but you chose this, long ago.' A third strike, open palmed, to the forehead.

The Emperor of the Dead falls to its knees, its form shivering and constricting, dwindling towards something more human. It looks up at him, and the writhing threads can't hide the words. 'Please. Don't let them do this to me.' An old echo, twenty years gone.

Shroudweaver kneels next to it. 'They already did. I'm so sorry.'

And he speaks the Emperor's name. He holds its hands. Sends it on.

For a moment, the Emperor's soul slips away, like a lizard under a rock, into the between spaces, almost free, almost gone.

Until Shroudweaver feels something catch it. Something alien and cold.

The Emperor raises its head, slowly, so slowly. The threads

fall from its lips. Something black and acrid eating them into nothing. Its face in shadow. And the Emperor says. 'I'm so sorry, Weaver. I was down here so long. In pieces, so long.' There's a pause, as the battle and the world spins around them. 'I made some promises, down in the dark.'

Its face shudders, rips and melds, until it looks at Shroudweaver with a single, unblinking eye. Here, hundreds of miles from the ruin of the south, the eye that tore the world looks down on him again.

A surge of black-ice terror pierces his heart, before he's pushed with the force of a fallen star. He tumbles through the between spaces as dwindling threads slip through his fingers. Shroudweaver grabs frantically at them, feels them slide over his desperate palms but there's hardly any left. The force of the eye is upon him again, and the weight of what lies behind the eye. Power like nothing he's ever felt, shredding the remnants of his control, devouring the weave. So few threads left, and beyond, only the endless static of the between.

But within this mountain, he remains the Shroudweaver. Within this mountain, somewhere, there is his daughter, and though his bones are tired and hollow, there's a space in them where she lives, where he remembers her first words, her stumbling steps, her mother's fingers on her brow, a silver brush in thin black hair. Laughter, singing, soft sleeps, deep dreams in twined arms and years later, the face of a bold young woman, bloodied, blackened and beautiful. He can't watch his daughter die. He doesn't have the strength left to stem this tide, but he can buy her time. He can buy them all time. He just needs to borrow a little power.

As Shroudweaver falls into the between, he feels emptiness try to claim him, sliding along the edges of his arms, his mind. So he weaves with the only material he has left – hope, memory, soul.

It's hard to tease out at first. Thin, bright threads, barely glimpsed in the growing darkness, the drowning weight of the eye on him. A crushing, deep push, remorseless, heartless and familiar. He can barely see the threads in its darkness; only when he turns and twists and they catch the light for the briefest moment, thin and slight, deceptively strong.

The first strand lodges around Shipwright's wrist as she raises it above Kinghammer. Another thread twines around Skinpainter's waist as they scramble upwards from the black sand, blood on their lips and a curse on their tongue. Shroudweaver feels himself wreathed in their souls, as the silver pulls flecks of their essence into his own. Shipwright is a memory of sea salt and cold heather, woodsmoke and wool. Skinpainter is cider, and nutmeg, worn leather and old medicine. Their essences burn in the heart of him, spreading a fire through the places in his bones where those memories all live, in hollows, pockets and fragments. Shroudweaver takes them all, kindling collated lives and loves, each one gathered to him like birds in a hedgerow, held against his heart; treasured.

He lights them all, and lets them go.

The first time he kissed Shipwright, on the deck of the ship, rocking on a slow swell, the southern sun hot as a hammer, her lips rough and salted, her hand on his back pulling him close and the tightening of her body in response. Lit and gone.

The time he saw her, feet thundering the earth, riding the shouts of their victorious army outside Luss. Lit and gone.

Further back, the sound of his daughter's cries in the cradle, the way they shuffled down the registers into quiet contentment, all of her held against his shoulder, milk-breathed and drowsy. Lit and gone.

Standing at the edge of a cliff, watching her mother's ashes sift down into the water below, a brief dark swirl in the waves, that faded as salt and spume moved onwards, onwards. Pottery shards and smudged hands. Lit and gone.

His dead wife's spine in the moonlight, the curve of her, dark hair between his fingers and wine on her lips. Lit and gone.

Further back. The day he left the Aestering with a fresh spool of red thread and a thumping headache. Saltpetre and sulphur choking his lungs with strangeness. His shoulders still heavy from embraces, laughter, goodbyes. Lit and gone.

The day she took his hand, fingertips brushing with a passed note. Insects under the night sky, teeth against the light and drink from a jar that burnt like varnished fire. Lit and gone.

Further back. The day he arrived at the Aestering, rubbing sleep from his eyes. Fumbling with clasps and catches, straightening a robe over skinny legs. Lit and gone.

The day he awoke, drowsy by the fountain. Low winter sun on the water and golden light swimming lazily in its depths. Spiced pastries and slow songs that spun him to sleep.

The days he's forgotten, of fires and softness and cool water, of strong hands and rocking that ran with the rhythm of a loving heart. Fragments of moon and sun, breath and dreaming. All of them, lit and gone.

Shroudweaver lets all his memories fly free, like little birds out against the darkness, clutching silver threads stitched in their beaks. As they fly, the mountain opens up before him, and he sees all the lives within it, thousands of souls, each cradling countless tiny birds to their breasts, bones and hearts, yearning, dying, fighting. He ties himself to them all, and borrows the smallest fragment of power from each, bright droplets flowing into him as he hangs in the between.

The light that fills him is slow and soft, filled with the lives and deaths of strangers. It lines his bones, his breath, pushes into the between spaces until the darkness fades, and the weight of the eye lifts. Shroudweaver's body floats in silver, buoyed by the wings of a thousand small, shining birds. The whole mountain is spread before him, the struggling lives of its inhabitants flickering in a spiralling weave as the red rage of the Emperor spreads through their souls. Thousands of panicked lives flare in hope, terror and triumph. Shroudweaver gathers fragments of their souls to him along glimmering lines, and then delves deeper, his attention drawn to a ragged, confused thing driving down through the mountain. It takes him a moment to recognise the thrum of Icecaller's hammering heart, to pick out the sound of her soul beneath the fever which roils in her veins. The Emperor's touch has claimed her.

Distantly, abstractly, he watches the red hunger seething in her flesh pull her ever closer to a knot of fears and hopes, to lights he recognises as Quickfish, Roofkeeper, the little girl, Nigh. That last with a few bright birds clutched to her chest, held so tightly their fluttering feathers can barely move. The only way he can help any of them is to borrow a little light from each. To cut the infection off at its source, for a few scant moments. If he can bind the Emperor, even briefly, he can slow the dead.

Above him, the thing that was the Emperor has no birds, no light. Its new eye roves ceaselessly as the mouth underneath it gibbers and curses. The fear Shroudweaver felt fades and a wave of pity crashes over him. The eye is a horror; formless and alien, but the Emperor was a person once, and Shroudweaver knows how to bind a person. He moves towards it slowly, precisely, like a surgeon, like an undertaker; like a Shroudweaver.

He pulls the bright silver light of the mountain's souls into himself, and sends it out again down the threads, attenuated at first, then fiercer, wrapping around the Emperor's rolling shoulders, its broken fingers, and wailing mouth. Quieting, mending, deceiving. It's still too strong. He can feel it bucking against the weave. Whatever shred of a man once filled this body is lost, Shroudweaver far too slow to save him. Too slow by decades, by centuries maybe. He can't stop what's already happened so instead, he does his job.

The shroud he weaves is thin at first, a few scant strands pulled together, but it thickens like lake ice. The Emperor struggles at its touch, but then quietens, until only its eye is left roving and roiling. Eventually, Shroudweaver covers that too, stitching it closed, letting it rest, blinding it for a moment.

Left alone, the fragments of what was the Emperor hang in darkness, the silvered shape of a man, held together and woven into silence as best he can. With a red hand and a heavy heart, Shroudweaver reaches forwards and pushes it into the void, his last kindness to this monster. Let it have a little sense of self, a little piece of commemoration, before the eye devours it whole. Perhaps something will escape.

Even as he humours the thought, there's a flare in the far darkness, as if a smith's hand had struck metal. A feeling of rage and hunger washes over him, and the last silver light from the Emperor's soul goes out. A dull gong of dread hammers in his heart.

There is a moment where the blackness hangs empty in front of his eyes, a moment before the velvet of the between spaces shudders, and a rent splits the dark, before everything he can see becomes the opening of that terrible, merciless eye.

Shroudweaver has to get out, before the thing that devoured the south takes him too. He can already feel the weight of it on him, like a fathomless ocean. With shaking hands, he reaches for the silver threads holding him apart from the world, and tears them loose. In an instant, the between spaces pop like a soap bubble. His body hammers down onto ink-stained sand and he feels a crack as his knees strike rock.

He retches, spitting up silver threads, blood, little black lumps. Shipwright's arms are around him, her hands soft and strong against his spine, rubbing away the convulsions.

'You bastard,' she says, her voice wet with relief. 'You utter bastard.'

Skinpainter reaches around his waist and pulls him up, moving him gently back from the broken circle, the softly twitching body of Kinghammer, the dazed and confused dead, suddenly slumped like puppets with their strings cut.

'I didn't think you'd do it,' Skinpainter murmurs, their voice warm and wry. 'Always got to surprise me.'

Shroudweaver fumbles for a moment, claws at his lips, cleaning the stench of sugar off his tongue. He forces words out through the sweetness. 'It's not gone. Just weakened. Plan's changed. We need to get out of here.'

As if to drive the point home, the dead begin to stir again, slowly reeling to their feet, their eyes lighting as the Emperor's infection once again takes hold.

Shroudweaver grabs Skinpainter's wrist. 'I felt it in Icecaller. We have to get back to them. Now.'

Skinpainter's face folds with sadness. 'Ah. Of course.' They rub their cheek with a broad hand, and glance at Shipwright. 'Need some help with this idiot?'

She grins, kisses the top of Shroudweaver's head. 'Every day of my life.'

And so the pair take him in strong arms, on thin legs, back down into the deep mountain, a hundred new little birds nesting in the hedgerows of his heart.

78

AS CROWN OF GLORY

AS POLISHED STONE

AS HOLLOW BONE

A thousand heartbeats earlier, Crowkisser pulls her arm back and throws. She can feel the composite in her bones, in her brain. It throbs in her veins like a fever. The scale of her father's work chokes her, thousands of spirits, caged into this monstrous thing. She hasn't seen a god since the south, since she watched them tear themselves limb from limb. She had forgotten how beautiful they are, how all-consuming. She wants to fall into its arms, fall to her knees, have it carry her away from here.

The stolen scrap of the Emperor's bone seems to hang in the air for a second, between the lightning. It tugs at her. The rest of her arm wants to follow it, to burrow into the golden skin of the god.

Her skin is wet from the driving rain. She can taste charcoal on her lips. At her back, her people waver. She sees Sandsinger smile like a child, curl up in the drowsy mud like a baby.

The composite regards her with her father's eyes, massive, burnished, beautiful. She hesitates for the briefest moment, as the fingerbone lingers at the top of its arc. Remembers Crabflick's severed hand. Then she turns and runs. The explosion rips the sound from the air. The pressure wave catches her back, lifts her, and for a moment she feels as if she's flying.

She could shift shape now if she wanted. She feels wings at the edges of her skin. Instead, she lets the ground rise, hit her. Her shoulder takes the impact, pounding up and through her bones. She rolls with the pain, sprawling on her back. A spear splits the earth next to her head. She watches it distractedly. A ringing in her ears tolls her skull like a wet bell, her fingers pushed into the soil.

She can feel the ground crawling beneath her. Deep under the mud and bone, and the bits of her friends. The dead, stirred to sudden life.

Lightning thunders down, smokes the ripped earth into stinking craters.

She pulls herself to her knees, spits soil and blood.

There's laughter in the ruins of the god, something mad and wild twitching in the remains of its form, pulling the scraps of spirits to it. Shroudweaver's creation is turning on itself, driving deep into the composite's guts with golden hands, unleashing all the briefly bound dead, and laughing as it tears. Something familiar in that laughter; from the gallows on a salt-lashed road, from a corpse on a temple slab – the Emperor. She has been betrayed.

A scream of rage tears itself loose from her throat, as she punches down into the dark earth. Panic rattles in her heart as her brave, battered army surges forwards. Less than a third of them left, flensed down by steel and sorcery. They think she has done this. They think she *meant* this.

She screams as she straightens a crooked arm in its socket, and mutters a prayer to Slickwalker under her breath. 'Don't let me down.'

The mountain answers in smoke and black fire. Rock thunders loose, and with it, something else. The dead writhing to the surface, likes worms after rain. Rushing to the Emperor, that golden traitor roiling in the body of the composite. Calling to them, pulling them into the mountain. She flexes the fingers of her twisted arm.

Let them come, she has killed gods before.

But she's not alone this time. She can't let her people pay the toll for her mistake, which means she has to move fast, faster than the dead. She needs to call the crows.

She sighs. This is going to hurt. Even as the thought crosses her mind, her spine bucks. She shudders, retches, sprouting feathers and blackness before she leaps into the air, into the between spaces. The colours and sounds of the world wash away as the weight of her body leaves her, draining into a hundred beating wings, a hundred hammering hearts. Distributed, she moves with speed and purpose. The between spaces hum and click, like static, like shell, like bone. They eat at the edges of her. She wants to fall into them, to stop being, but her people need her. She finds Slickwalker by the sound of his heart and tumbles towards him on a hundred small wings. Under her flurrying bodies, she sees the remains of her army helping each other towards the sundered gate, with arms around waists, shields interlocked, singing. Thell's soldiers mounting a defence, but reeling backwards, stunned by the shock of it all, the smoke, the riven god. Astic's army collides with them in a grey wave, pushing them back into the mountain, at terrible cost, death thick on both sides.

As the body of Crowkisser's army charges the gate, she watches long men, brave long men, shin up the cliff face like spiders, into the first breaches on the battlements, heedless of the danger, terrified in their hearts, but deadly. They slide around spear-points, taking off fingers, toes, slipping blades into arrogant throats.

As the first blood falls from those brief exchanges Crowkisser finally sees the dead clearly, as they slip over the shoulders of her army like a bright shroud; the lost souls of the Empire, numberless, liquid. She can't give a shape to them, just a sensation of teeth, nails and hunger. When they reach the gate, they pause briefly, spilling up against the black stone like water from a spilt cup.

She circles them curiously, sends bits of herself towards the wall to harry eyes and tongues. The dead clot and swirl. The side of the Stump flickers with angular magics in a brief hint at Skinpainter's skill, the sheer scale of their wards, black and red geometries as tall as a house flashing in stark patterns against the mountain's flanks. The disembodied horde nips at their edges, yowling as they're cast back. Then, from deep within the mountain, something pushes outwards, a seething wave of rage and purpose. The protective angles fail and power pulses against the flock. Crows scatter, wards shatter and the Empire's unbound souls scream in elation. Crowkisser feels their joy buffet her and shares it for a second, until she sees what they intend to do.

The speed at which the dead move is incredible, pouring forwards towards the frontline of the battle, towards the blades and the blood. The first few carom off the tattooed bodies of Thell's soldiers, before Crowkisser sees a blade flash, breaking a black line stitched across an upraised arm. The injured woman staggers back, but the dead are on her in seconds, worrying at the rent like dogs. When they slip inside her ragged body, Crowkisser realises that she's no longer party to a liberation. This is an infestation, and it spreads with horrific speed. A few heartbeats of writhing flesh and contorted muscle and the battle-wounded light with a feral energy, their bodies fired and moved by the dead.

That ridden woman turns her raised spear on the fisherboy set against her, slides spread fingers along the haft, down into his guts and pulls. Crowkisser watches as she takes the fallen man's knife and hacks into the shocked warrior next to her. With every cut, every rip, the dead pour into opened veins and make them dance. Thell's frontlines collapse in on themselves until Crowkisser's army are left facing only the red teeth of the ridden dead. The ghosts of the Empire are choosing their targets.

If she doesn't do something, no one is leaving this mountain alive. A litany of curses roll through her head. She's so sick of this. She can't believe there's another one, another tyrant, another *thing* trying to rule by taking free will from ordinary folk. Not again. *Not again.*

She has no idea how to fight this. The gods and their hosts had been clear targets, solid and real. The dead are spreading through the mountain like a cancer, like slime across a pond, threading the veins of the living, drawn to the blood of Thell. The flocking spirits are seemingly uninterested in her grey-cloaked warriors, but the things they raise inside those broken bodies are a different story, tearing into anything that crosses their path. Still, she might have time to salvage this. She doesn't feel the dead in the between spaces, yet. But she can hear Slickwalker's heartbeat somewhere below, and she remembers that he has veins, and blood and a heart. Crows arrow downwards towards the battlements where he waits. She veers into herself with a suddenness that makes her stagger and throws herself into his arms.

He pulls her close, his fingers light on the back of her head, small kisses on her temples, 'Did you see the gate?' His voice is afire. 'Did you see it? I wasn't sure it would work. But it did! Every single shiver like a struck match. We did it.'

Crowkisser stays in his arms as the colour, sound and pain of the world floods back in. She can hear screaming and the clash of blades, mingled with strange, long howls which can only be the dead. The battle sounds like the south, right before it burnt. She stiffens against Slickwalker, and he realises in a heartbeat that something is wrong. One gloved hand rests lightly on her jaw. 'What is it, Kiss? We're winning.'

She beckons him to the lip of the ledge, closer to the storm. 'Look.' Below them, the battle rages. The dead continue to stream into the Stump, and Thell's injured continue to rise and dance. Her own army steadily driven back in confusion. Her finger is a weight, down into the heart of the mountain, into the slick of killing.

Slickwalker's fingers grip the stone, her wrist. 'What is this, Kiss?' He sounds young and afraid.

She shakes her head. No time to coddle him. Presses her lips together, runs a hand through her hair, picking out scraps of feather. 'We've been betrayed. I made a deal. To free Thell's dead. To use them against our enemies.'

Slickwalker's face is confused, naïve. 'A deal with who?'

She watches him carefully, decides to risk a little truth. 'With the last ruler of the mountain. With the Emperor.'

From below them comes a welter of screams as another knot of Thell's soldiers collapses in on itself. She's stunned to see some of her own people diving into the morass, pulling the uninjured clear. Shepherding them back behind a hastily formed shield-wall. What is happening here? What can she make from it?

There's a stilted pause as she runs the angles, before she takes Slickwalker's hands, presses her head against his hammering chest. 'I didn't know this would happen. I had to do something. You've seen what my father's capable of.' She waves her hand in exasperation. 'He can raise *gods*.'

Here on the ledge, Slickwalker's not coping. Crowkisser watches the blunt lines of his face process the situation and despairs a little. Predictably, he squeezes her fingers, runs a thumb over her knuckles. 'This isn't your fault. It can't be.'

She refrains from rolling her eyes, barely, but it's hard to keep the frustration from her voice. 'It is. I did this. I made a bad choice, and now we're paying for it.' His eyes are wide, uncomprehending, so she steps forwards, takes his jaw in her hands. 'The sooner you realise I'm not perfect, the better off we'll all be.'

Under their feet, a few storeys down, the tides have changed. Grey cloaks stand next to tall tower shields and levelled spears. Loud, methodical shouts guide the living away from the dead, who roil in snarling masses, still too cowardly to attack the steadier lines forming in front of them. They charge in yapping packs and are cast back by nets, boathooks, leaf-bladed spears. Thell and Astic, working shoulder to shoulder.

Crowkisser watches the lines with narrowed eyes, and a plan begins to form. There's potential here. Nothing unifies like terror. The south had taught her that.

She turns back to Slickwalker, widens her eyes a little, slipping just the hint of a tremor into her voice. 'We have to help them, Slick. I'm not letting my people die to this. I won't let their "Emperor" do this to me. That old ghost doesn't know who he's messing with.'

He winces. 'I'll sound the retreat.'

'No!' Her fingers lace into his armour, pull him close, off-balance. 'We have to help *all* of them. I've no use for a mountain full of corpses.' She starts towards the nearest ramp winding down from the battlements, turns, arms outstretched. 'Please. We can't leave them to this. We have to be better than that.'

'They'll kill you.' His voice is flat. More resolute than usual. Irritating. He needs a push.

She points towards the battle again. 'This is not what we came for. We came to free them. To build a better world. This . . . this is slaughter.'

She lets that hang in the air between them, gives him a moment to listen to the screams and shouts from below. Watches him waver, before she stretches a hand towards him. 'Let's save our people. The old and the new.'

And before Slickwalker can think better of it, he turns and follows her into shadow.

79

Conventional wisdom was that certain elements of the world could not be broken. In the event of the south, we realised that we were wrong. Light can be shattered. The sky can burn.

—*Notes on the Destruction*, Wicktwister

After that, they navigate by the sounds of dying, in a blur of violence and brief, desperate struggle. Slickwalker's gun unfurls, squalls, spits blackness into snarling, distorted faces. Thell's soldiers fall one by one, before rising again, sharp-toothed, yowling, mad. The dead are bolder now, growing in number with every passing moment. Crowkisser's army is driven back into corners and culverts, hauled bodily into the mob, torn limb from limb. Her long men do what they can, fighting the dead and the living, but still dwindling, retreating.

The dead of the Empire are an irresistible tide. Too many of them, too hungry and too fast, infesting the bodies of Thell's injured and casting them back against the living.

Nothing should be able survive this. Nothing, and yet, here in the red belly of the mountain, Crowkisser sees the unity she'd hoped to forge. She sees her new people, Astic and Thell alike, rallying together against the dead, fighting for their lives.

There's too much to take in. Too many souls struggling and snuffed out. Crowkisser thinks she has a handle on it, Slickwalker flowing in her wake like a half-born shadow, but she's wrong. The battle fills the Stump. At every turn, the living clash with the dead, tooth and nail.

Three levels down, Sandsinger's back-to-back with one of the Thell lads. The pair of them are hunkered down behind a broken table as the dead prowl beyond. He looks a little like her grandson who was lost at sea, and a lot like the only friendly face she's seen in a stretch.

His hand finds her shoulder as she reties his shield, his voice low and soft. 'If you get out of this will you tell my da that I tried my best?'

She cuffs him around the head. 'You can bloody well tell him yourself.' As she glowers at him, the howling of the dead swells. They share a glance, heft their weapons and charge.

A drop and a plunge, and deeper in the mountain, a long man faces down the horde. He sketches a thin line with his blade, a weary circle facing the ridden bodies of his brothers as they prepare for a final strike. Behind him, a line of shields and spears seals the passage. Thell's sent fresh troops from below. The long man watches helplessly, they've no idea what they're walking into. The dead go for them with the speed of wolves, and their line crumples. He contemplates using the space to run, to put distance between himself and their teeth, but there's a mountain girl in Thell's front line that looks a little too close to his own daughter, and before he knows it his aching legs are carrying him back to their buckling shield-wall, blade raised against the screaming dead. Minutes later, somehow, they're all down, and he's not the only one of the living left standing. Thell's soldiers lean on their shields, eyeing him warily. He loops his knife into his belt with slick hands, tries not to think about the hair matted down the edge, and shoots them a wild smile.

There are too many lives in this mountain. Even if Crowkisser can't see them all, she can sense them, and sense their potential, all their conflicting loyalties smelted together by necessity. Her beautiful new people. All she needs to do is make them hers. And to do that, she needs to keep them alive. She can't just save them though, they need to *see* her as their saviour.

She smiles in the darkness. That traitor Emperor has handed her all the leverage she could ever need, but she has to move fast if she's going to pull it off. Her feet pick up speed from the shadow, their edges lit with half-formed feathers. They're still so high in the mountain, and every nerve in her body is screaming at her that the magic driving this is down in its guts. If she wants to make a show of this, she needs to go where things are darkest. Nothing changes.

Two more breathless minutes fleeing through the black, down through tunnels swelling with the dead, glowing in the half-light from lamps, the mad look in her eyes bouncing back at her from crystal scars etched into the wet walls. The whole body of this mountain has been marked by the cicatrice of old wars. A few levels later, and they reach the shattered front gate, hasty barricades scattered in an arc around the smoking rock. A resistance has built itself before they even arrived. Atop a spire of crumbled stone, a helmetless red-haired woman shouts orders, her face twisted in pain, one hand clutched to a spreading wound on her side. Her soldiers move with studied precision; her eyes narrow as they approach.

Crowkisser skids to a stop, then cautiously steps closer. The young woman watches her steadily.

'You're her.'

Crowkisser nods. 'I am.' She surveys the blades around her. 'But I'm not your enemy today.' She waves back towards the depths of the mountain, aided by a well-timed scream of agony. 'Do you know what's happening?' Holds her breath, praying for ignorance.

The woman nods. 'The dead.'

Crowkisser exhales, 'I need to get everyone out of here.'

'We're working on it.'

Crowkisser steels herself. 'Can I send them to you? Can you hold the gate?'

The redhead rolls her shoulders. 'For a time.' She frowns. 'I think I'm supposed to kill you, though. Capture you at least.'

Crowkisser gestures at the blood on her hands. 'Haven't you had enough dying for today?'

A murmur of agreement.

Crowkisser smiles softly. 'What's your name?'

'Lightmender.'

'Well, Lightmender, let's be allies for now. If we make it through this, you can kill me tomorrow.'

Lightmender watches her for a second, shifts her weight from her injured side.

'OK, Crowkisser. Send anyone you find up here, I'll get them out.'

Crowkisser nods, and steps back into the mountain before anyone thinks it through enough for things to go south. Back into the battle she goes, back and further down.

Slickwalker follows in her wake, gathering the remnants of both armies; telling them to flee back to the gates, to Lightmender, to the Barrowlands. He stutters through shadow and around blades, collapsing tunnels to stave off the advancing dead, setting charges along rock already scarred to glass by battles long-gone. The toll of the gun makes his hand ache, a feeling like starving as his flesh is swallowed by its magic, and poured back onto his bones by shadow.

He finds a man, leg struck, skin writhing with the dead, and listens as his words change, as his begging becomes imprecations, as the Emperor's madness takes hold. Then he points the barrel of the gun, pulls the trigger.

By his side, Crowkisser takes apart the dead who come at her, turning herself into a devouring torrent of beaks and claws. She births crows in squalls, creating corridors, spaces for movement, pushing the dead back with wings and fury.

Slowly, they salvage what they can from the madness roiling in the mountain's heart, this thing that her broken alliance has unleashed. The Emperor, reasserting his hold. Each moment, no longer a battle, but rather a strange kind of triage, driving their people and Thell's backwards and upwards, sometimes bodily. There's little time to explain, only the stark division of the dead on one side and the living on the other. It takes a while for it to stick, the mountain's defenders are reluctant to welcome the feathered witch and shadow-spitting hunter as friends. It's only when the people of Thell start losing the battle in earnest that Crowkisser can begin save them.

At every turn, Slickwalker sees shield-walls wavering, spears falling, young men and women stumbling backwards into the arms of friends who take them apart piece by piece, rib by rib. He would have rejoiced at this a few days ago. Now, he sees Crowkisser's point. If they let this run its course, they'll be victors over nothing but the dead and they'll have a second war to fight against the Empire's risen horde. Every soul that dies in the mountain is a loss for their cause.

Still, it's not easy to make a difference. His weapon's not made for saving lives. It doesn't help that this place is a warren of tunnels tight around a central well that kills his lines of fire. He's no idea how deep they are now. He's lost count in their haring descent through the Stump.

Four, maybe five levels later, they stagger into the remnants of a marketplace. The gun keens wildly in his hands as it bucks and screeches, every shot scouring flesh and rock with abandon. Everywhere, the injured and ridden dead. Slickwalker tries to target the ones where the madness has set in deep, the most clearly gone, their snarling coruscating up the registers of pain as the gun eats their bones. It's brutal, but enough to get the attention of the survivors cowering beneath sacks and under tables. Then Crowkisser takes her turn, calling crows from the dark places, between the blood-flecked lights and overturned stalls, past makeshift barricades, battering the mad and blood-crazed dead back into one other, creating, for a second, space. Thell's survivors seize their chance, and flee back towards the light.

Both armies merge into a column of refugees, wending shakily upwards. Thell and Astic, both bloodied to red. Slickwalker watches them go, wondering how many'll make it up to Lightmender's barricade alive. Enough to salve his conscience? Unlikely.

They struggle onwards, pulling bodies from the carnage. In ones and twos at first, but foot by foot the form of the battle shifts. Larger groups join them briefly as truces stitch themselves in panicked words. All it takes is a single moment of empathy. A raised shield blocking a falling spear. A grey-clad fisherman hauling a ravening woman off a struggling warrior.

Hands join to reinforce shield-walls, or to pull the wounded loose. And still, at the forefront, her fingers dancing like wings is Crowkisser, filling the tunnels with birds that move in pulses, clots, arrows. Black feathers thick as breath, splitting the living from the dead. Wings. Wings beneath the mountain.

It costs her. God how it costs her, as she pulls meat and air from her lungs in lurching gasps. She stops for the barest second, just to catch her breath, and something scrapes her mind like a struck match. Her father, somewhere down in the darkness, alive somehow, weaving somehow. She can feel his power building like a geyser beneath her feet, the cold touch of the between shivering into her bones.

And as quickly as it builds, it's gone, fading like a struck bell. A release washing through the corridors of the Stump, cool and hollow. In its wake, the dead stumble, a lethargy on them, even if briefly, listless as bees in winter. Just slow enough for her to plunge onwards and downwards.

She shoots Slickwalker a look. 'Now. Quickly. This won't last.'

As they drive deeper Slickwalker sets the gun aside. It hisses resentfully in its holster as he falls back on older techniques, tricks he remembers from a childhood spent scuffling beneath wide branches.

He moves in the rhythm of the green forest, flows through the shadows; trips, stalls, chokes and tries, tries so very hard not to kill. It helps that the dazed dead diminish as they delve further down. Something pulls them still deeper into the mountain, their snarls and yips echoing up through the passages. The Emperor is calling to them, Crowkisser says, with a certain grim satisfaction. Slickwalker can barely believe it. An enemy like something out of a fable, some mad sorcerer he barely understands. And him, here, miles underground, with no one but her at his back. Panic flutters in his hammering heart. His brain pushes it down. He focuses on keeping her safe, driving his bruised knuckles in rabbit punches at the kidneys of a howling man that comes for them, knocking him to the floor. He binds him with leather and moves on.

Crowkisser drives them ever deeper. His arms grow tired.

Mistakes begin to creep in. The darkness is hungry, writhing with grasping hands. Crowkisser can't save them all, and he can barely keep the stumbling dead off her back. They are far too deep now to climb back to the light. The only way onwards is down.

He watches the realisation dawn on her in the stoop of her shoulders, the slowing of her words. Moving to her side, he puts an arm around her waist, steadies the gun on his hip, and keeps his finger light on the trigger.

Driving down and down and down.

Time stretching out into the dark.

Strange shudders of power and magic flowing unseen through the mountain, pressing against his temples like the promise of sudden storms.

The dead around them milling and confused, shoaling towards the frenzied voice from the depths one moment, and hunting them on unsteady feet in the next.

Somehow they push through, clawing their way past bodies and magic and blackness, throwing themselves down the throat of the Stump, running breathless for what feels like an age.

Until below them, at last, living voices. The first like bellows-brass, clear as a bell through the smoke and blood. He'd recognise Shipwright anywhere. She's followed by another voice, softer, dry as paper.

Crowkisser stiffens. Turns to Slickwalker. The crows fall from the air.

Her mouth opens, struggles with the words.

He pulls her close, feels her shake and kisses her softly, on the forehead, the cheek, the back of her neck. 'You can do this. I love you. Stay strong. Be careful.'

Crowkisser's breath slides out of her like broken glass.

The room that opens out in front of them must have been a bunkhouse. Its alcoves filled with colourful blankets, cushions, long, low tables and soft light.

The whole space is now crammed with wailing children and bleeding bodies. And between the children and the teeth of the mountain's dead, a ragged group.

He spies Shipwright first. Of course he does, but even she looks different down here, bruised, pent up, her fingers working at something brief and brass that mutters and clucks. The gun struggles against its harnesses and he tenses reflexively. There's a young woman sprawled at her feet, shorn blonde hair, savagely undercut, matted with gore. Her mouth is cannibal red, the tattoos on her body writhing like worms on a skillet, ink threaded thinly over sharp wounds. She's obviously infected, ridden with the dead. Crouched over her is Skinpainter, their fingers moving lightly against her slumped body. The air is thick with saltpetre smoke-stink. Their red ribbons are scorched beyond reason, and a bruise purples their side beneath torn clothes. Blood under the skin, Slickwalker suspects. Good.

There's so many dead here. A dark-haired young woman with her throat torn out. A tousle-headed young man sprawled immobile across her, his breath a thin rattling gasp. A bearded warrior with the look of the plains people feverishly trying to clear his airways, struggling with an arm broken so fiercely the bone swings from the skin. The dying boy might be Fallon's son. Which would make this a whole new kind of nightmare.

Behind them, others, old and young – bloodstained warriors, children, one little girl who watches him with blackbird eyes, crying quietly with the silent shake of something small and alone.

He starts forwards, is stalled by Crowkisser's hand on his wrist, her nails cutting into his skin. Her arm, her whole body is shaking.

It takes a second for Shroudweaver to see his daughter, and a second more for him to recognise her. A smile flits across his face like a bird across an empty sky. She doesn't move at first, then edges a step or two closer, fingers clenching. Magic flickers along the line of her wrists, flares, and gutters out.

Her shoulders cut in a tense slash, ribs held tight. No one moves. Slickwalker wills her to do it, to put an end to him. Opposite, Shroudweaver does nothing. Leaves his hands slack, threads unwound. He watches his daughter carefully, his eyes tired, softened with sorrow.

Slickwalker can't even imagine what she's feeling. How many years since her mother died? Not long enough for the scars to heal.

Crowkisser steps a little closer in another flicker of feathers, like a torc up her neck, then slithering down her spine. The room flinches. Shipwright holds herself like a greyhound in traces.

Her father opens his arms, and lets the threads fall to the floor; raises his chin a little, eyes wet.

A shudder leaves his daughter, a long tight breath that hangs in her throat like cupped water. Her hands mirror her father's.

She takes a step closer, then another, until something breaks, and she picks up speed in a silent flurry of feet and stifled tears.

Slickwalker watches her father draw her close, press her forehead against his chest, twine his fingers in her hair, and look at her with a face filled with light and longing.

Slickwalker watches her father, and unclasps the gun.

80

The song can be sung again \ and again
the voice changes
the song can still be sung

She's so slight. So thin. Shroudweaver can feel her shake against him, the sharp angles of her shoulders, the line of each rib. She smells just like she should, like she always has, like the salt-sea and heather honey. He remembers the weight of her dreaming against his shoulder, the warmth of her breath rising and falling as he tucked curls behind small ears. The ears the same, the jaw below them grown sharp and strong. His hair. Her mother's beautiful bones.

His little daughter grown to a real person over all these long years, an animate thing that holds him with long-fingered hands, chipped nails. The dark line of her brows presses down on her face, her lungs struggling, struggling with the word.

She turns her face up to him. 'Dad.'

It shakes something loose inside him. He feels an old coiled spring unfurl, a bird fluttering under his bones. She's smaller than he remembers. Slight against the shouting that's filling the room. He tunes it out, focuses on her.

She wipes blood from her face with the back of a hand. 'Hi, Dad.'

'Hello, love,' he says. The words flow out of him before he knows it's happening, like water over rocks. He pulls her closer, kisses her forehead, smooths tangles from her hair, wipes a smudge of something dark from her cheek. 'Hello, love.' Again, more certainly.

She hangs in Shroudweaver's arms for a moment. He rests his chin in the hollow of her neck, looks over her shoulder to see

Slickwalker watching him, eyes flat as a snake. They tilt their head, smiling thinly.

Shroudweaver lets go of her awkwardly. She steps back immediately, the connection broken.

Shipwright moves between them, breaks the last lingering link. 'Shroud? This is not the time.'

A voice from his right. Roofkeeper.

'Please, someone. He's dying. He can't breathe. *I can't make him breathe.*'

Crowkisser turns her back on her father, briskly efficient. 'I'll help him.'

She steps towards Quickfish's body, halts as a hatchet blade brushes her neck.

Roofkeeper lets his axe hang in the air between them. 'Aren't you the cause of all this?'

Her voice when she speaks is not the voice of the girl Shroudweaver remembers. 'Do you really want to force this? Here?' She waves a hand behind her, towards the tunnels filled with dead. 'Now?'

Slickwalker's voice burrs like a sleepy cat. 'She has a point.' He flicks his eyes over Shipwright and Shroudweaver. 'Ship. Shroud. This is . . . unexpected.'

Shipwright tenses. 'Don't make me pull your teeth out.'

Slickwalker tilts his head again, smiles, wide and bright. 'You won't do that. We have people relying on us.' A lazy glove takes in the injured, the children. 'You're not getting out of here without us.'

He places brief fingers on Shipwright's wrist, feeling her back down, inch by inch. Laughing, he slides closer, until his lips brush her ear. 'Of course, once we're out, you can take your very best shot.'

She holds his eyes for a second, curls her lip and then firmly dislodges his hand. 'If it were up to me, I'd leave you in here to rot. You're lucky it's not.'

Shroudweaver watches the pair for a second, heart racing, then gathers himself and crosses to where Skinpainter kneels over

Icecaller, their broad hands pushing and inking in slow, steady rhythm. His old friend's body is marred with wetness. Salt tears beneath the hood, red and copper beneath the ribs. He says nothing. Some trusts must be kept.

He squats beside them, runs a hand along one arm. 'You coming, Skin?' Skinpainter turns their head towards him, holds Shroudweaver's gaze. Their face drawn with pain and sorrow, but still coloured by kindness. Broad, flat cheekbones, heavy graceful brows. That one nicked ear.

They cup Shroudweaver's cheek in their palm as their other hand flows small simple patterns across Icecaller that settle into her wounds like a weary dog.

'I'm so glad you found your daughter, Shroud.' Their voice is ragged, hoarse to breaking, roughening as their grip tightens. 'Keep her safe.' Their eyes flick to his shoulder, to Slickwalker. 'Keep her safe.'

'Come with us, Skin,' Shroudweaver says, because he has to. But he knows the reply before it comes.

'No, Shroud.' They look up to the roof, take a deep breath. 'This is my mountain.' A smile skirts their face, as they turn their head out into the darkness. 'These are my people.' Their hands linger on Icecaller's neck, on her face. 'Take her instead, and the little one. She doesn't deserve to watch her sister die in the dark.'

Shroudweaver fights a tightness in his throat, a catch beneath his ribs. 'We can all get out of here, together.'

Skinpainter's eyes are soft. 'You know that's a lie.' They pat his arm, 'This is my mountain, Shroud. I have responsibilities. I'll buy you some time.'

They stand slowly, painfully, walk to the edge of the group, and begin inking a circle.

The darkness chatters in response, as the dead gather. Backs straighter, gait sharper. Confusion sliding off their bones as the effects of the weaving dwindle into the dark.

Shroudweaver runs after their old friend, his hand light on their shoulder. 'You'll die here.'

Skinpainter pulls him close to their broad chest. 'There now,' they whisper, 'would that be so bad? We all die somewhere.'

They hold each other for a second, until Skinpainter pushes him gently away. Their fingers linger. 'Keep her safe, Shroud.'

They call over his shoulder to Shipwright. 'Keep him safe, Ship.'

She raises a hand, lets it fall slowly.

At their backs, Slickwalker has crossed to where Crowkisser is stooped over Quickfish's body. The boy's unmistakeable up close, he has Fallon's hammered nose, his mother's high brow. At his side, the lad's partner raises the axe wearily, Roofkeeper, he remembers now.

Slickwalker spreads his gloved palms. 'Peace. I'm just here to see the magic at work.'

Crowkisser ignores them both. Her fingers pick their way up Quickfish's crushed throat, along the jaw, over lips and teeth. A brief flutter as she slips her hand deep into his mouth, releasing something. He begins to choke in heaving gasps, his ribcage convulsing. Roofkeeper starts forwards, and Slickwalker catches his arm in a steel grip. 'Don't fuck it up, kid.'

He pulls Roofkeeper back from Crowkisser's irritated gestures and watches as something squirms deep in Quickfish's throat, burrowing and pushing outwards. Crushed cartilage realigns with a wet pop. Like a heron, Crowkisser plunges her fingers down into a gasping mouth, withdraws a crow, fluttering and wet with spit. She steadies herself astride Quickfish's ribs and swallows it whole with a crunch of small bones. A wing spasms weakly against her lips, and Fallon's kid inhales like a surfacing drowner.

Roofkeeper throws his arms around Crowkisser. Her arms stiffen as he pulls back and looks her in the eye. 'Thank you. I owe you.'

She smiles wearily with bloodstained lips, glancing out into the darkness. The dead have gathered just beyond the arch, at the edge of the light. Time's almost up.

Slickwalker moves to her side. 'No sense of timing, have they?'

Crowkisser twists her lips. 'No.'

He kisses her cheek. 'I love you.'

She taps his jaw lightly. 'I couldn't have done this without you.'

Slickwalker turns to a small circle of worried faces. Shipwright and Shroudweaver gradually move back-to-back, adopting old, familiar stances. Roofkeeper leans Quickfish against one shoulder, while the blackbird-eyed little girl slings her arms over his neck, leaving the axe loose in his free hand. His face is white with pain, waxy and drawn, but there's something in his stance. A little bit of iron still upright in the fire. Skinpainter crouches a few feet in front of them, inscribing a rough semicircle before the arch. Ink sputters and lurches from their skin, each twist of their hands wrenching their body forwards.

Slickwalker watches them through narrowed eyes, places a hand protectively in the small of Crowkisser's back. 'Let's go.'

She shoots him a lidded glance. 'We're taking them with us.'

'Why?!' A low, shocked hiss. He can't help himself.

Crowkisser studies him coolly, her eyes flat. 'Leverage. Appearances.'

She half-turns from Skinpainter's ritual, and runs her eyes over the group. 'Hostages, if need be.'

Slickwalker catches her shoulder, spins her around. 'Our people are clear. *Leave them.*' His voice lowers, hardens, threaded with desperation. 'End this.'

She reaches up and rests her palm on his for a moment as the dead yowl beyond the arch. Her grip tightens.

'I will, and this is how I'm going to do it.'

A little harsh, perhaps. As she catches herself, her fingers loosen, tracing over his knuckles. She smiles at him, blood lingering on her lips.

Slickwalker's shoulders slump as he looks from the group to the prowling dead, and back. 'OK, OK. How are you getting them out of here?'

She coughs, something thick and retching, her back curving, shuddering, little movements under the muscle. She grins up at him. 'Crows.'

He frowns. 'For this many people? Is that even possible?'

She shrugs. 'No choice. We've got minutes, at best.'

Slickwalker leans in close to her ear. 'Come on now, I wouldn't say no choice at all.'

The first of the advancing dead test Skinpainter's barrier, stagger back in a welter of red light.

Crowkisser watches them with half an eye, whispers a reply, her lips light against his cheek. 'He's my dad.'

Slickwalker snorts. 'Technically. He's not been around for years.' He pauses. 'Time was, you'd have killed him without breaking stride.'

'True,' she says. 'But I want to know *why* he ran. Does he strike you as someone who abandons his family without good reason?'

Slickwalker watches Shipwright and Shroudweaver, back-to-back, hands entwined, and laughs grudgingly. 'I suppose not, but I think he found a good one.'

Crowkisser shoots him a venomous look. 'I can always kill him later. The blonde bitch too. But I want answers first. And we're close to dying in here. I have to get them out.'

Slickwalker looks at the ragged little group in front of them, at the other wounded soldiers, at an elderly man cradling two crying babies to his chest, at a toothless woman grimly steadying herself on a shattered spear.

He sighs resignedly. 'Fine, but you're going to need time.' He tips his head at Skinpainter. 'And they're not going to give you enough of it.'

As if on cue, the dead hurl themselves against the thin inked lines again. Geometrics pulse weakly against their skin, then sputter and fail. Skinpainter sinks to one knee, clutching their side. Blood seeps from under their robes, thick and black. The dead barely a heartbeat or two from them. Slickwalker utters a curse and begins to run, shadow gathering around him like a thunderhead. He turns his head back to Crowkisser, face ribboned in blackness and flashes a grin she hasn't seen in months. 'I'll see you on the other side, love. Don't leave too many lights on.'

A brief twinge in Crowkisser's heart, perhaps affection, perhaps regret. She reaches out a hand, gathers a few wisps of trailing darkness, and presses them to bloody lips. As Slickwalker runs, the edges of his body slide into shadow, faster and faster, until his feet are a blur.

The dead are already at Skinpainter's face, ink and rags weakly lashing at their grasping hands. Slickwalker leaps, hits the first two-footed and flows off again, pulled into the curves of the mountain. Battering, brutal, joyous. Every strike hissing with a wet, black fire that eats down to the bone.

It's not going to be enough. The tide of bodies is endless. The Emperor's resurgent spirit threads the dead of Thell for miles, up and down through the mountain.

For a moment, Crowkisser loses Slickwalker beneath a swell of limbs and teeth. Briefly she glimpses tattered shadow and Skinpainter's rags. At the final bark of the gun her heart lurches.

She sees Shipwright start toward the melee, sees the stupid, altruistic look on her face and screams. 'No! We're leaving.'

Then she calls the crows. On a scale she's never tried before. From the edges of the dark, from scraps of meat and fragments of blackness, the black bodies of birds peeling off from the edges of her outstretched arms. Her own shape slowing, dissolving, unbecoming, flowing out to embrace them. She becomes one with the flock, her eyes shrunken, doubled, doubled again. The scene in front of her splinters into a nest of scavenged fragments.

The stuttering blur of Slickwalker trying to hold the line. The lemon-slick stench as he throws himself against the dead. Skinpainter falling at last, almost torn apart, then dragged out from under chattering teeth by Slickwalker's gloved hand.

He's bought her a few seconds. She can't waste them, can't waste his sacrifice.

They're leaving.

She sends the first feathered coil of herself to the children and the injured, bringing them into the skirl of the flock, rendering them down piece by piece, stitching them into the hammering hearts of her crows, into the corners of their eyes, under the pinions of their feathers. She feels their tiny thoughts join her own, terrified and confused. No time to quiet them. No time for comfort. The strain of it all almost killing her. Her mind sliding in a thousand overlapping pieces like glass washed by the tide.

She has to focus. She calls the crows, deeper now, muscle flaking off her bones in thick black feathers. Another clot of clamouring birds wraps around Shipwright, Shroudweaver and the broken body of that painted girl. She sees Shipwright struggle at first, a brief flare of something brass and defiant, but Shroudweaver takes her hand and pulls her in. She hadn't expected that. Her da's full of surprises. Those two are a burden though. She senses something coming along with them, not just the touch of their minds, but a taste of their power, flashes of silver and gold exploding in her mind. The flock reels. She strains to bear it aloft. A thousand small wings beat furiously. It's too much, too much, this weight like a ship's keel, and scores of panicking voices. She's never attempted anything like this. Too many minds to move, too many bodies bound to the bone of the flock. It's too much.

Distantly, she sees Slickwalker almost subsumed by the dead. Barely stuttering out from beneath their teeth, hands trailing thick black shadow still clenched around Skinpainter's unconscious body.

It's too much. Then, somehow, she feels her father in the flock. A steady presence at her back, his hands on her arms, her wings. A lacing of soft silver light, a weaving from inside the flock, and she surges with energy. One last push. She calls the crows, deeper than ever before, beyond the bone and down into the marrow, down into the darkness below. The birds rip themselves loose from her flesh in bloody clumps, and she feels the last shreds of her mind disappear into the flock.

She is spread so thin, atomised. She belongs to the mountain, the air, the ice, the glacier; to feather and claw. So thin. Brief flares of herself emerge along the edge of a wing, the tip of a beak. Brief, brief, fluttering, gone. She is a thousand hammering hearts, and she is one. A body that is no body. No bone, no muscle, no marrow.

All of her stripped, fed to the flock. She has no idea if she can come back. Panic thrills her.

One last push, the silver of her father's weaving in her wings, filling her hollow bones. The flock is so heavy with all these salvaged souls, with people weighting the chests of birds.

And still the dead come. Loping and broken and bloody and fast, so fast. Slickwalker is a blur of hands and wrists and fists between them, doomed and desperate. There's a ragged cut on his temple and a gash under his ribs that's writhing with shadows. Still, he fights, but there's just so many of them.

A few stragglers linger outside Crowkisser's reach, a breath ahead of the charging dead. Bloodied hands grasp for the bearded boy with the axe – he's too damn slow. He staggers under Quick-fish's wheezing body, his shattered arm barely fit to shepherd a scared child, as she shrieks with terror. The dead reach for the trio, just moments ahead of the birds driving urgently towards them.

One last push, flensing the last scraps of herself to nothing. The flock screams with a single voice. A final tendril of feathers reaches for the struggling men and embraces them. The small girl wails in terror, slips a desperately grasping hand, and backpedals away from the swirling crows. The dead come for her in their hundreds, in a forest of legs and arms and teeth, swarming over her. The shadows close around her and she's gone.

There's no time for regret. No time for comfort. Crowkisser fills the space of the mountain. Her bodies batter its walls. Scores crushed by hungry hands and mouths as the dead tear into the flock. The pain is unbearable.

She has to go higher. One. Last. Push.

Gaps in the rock above her head, for light, for air. Too small for people, but not for birds. And she is nothing now, nothing but birds.

She leaves, she lifts. The mountain opens up above her, through a hundred howling passages. The flock moves over the battle's embers at the speed of breath, cradled in blackness. The Stump's tunnels writhe thickly with the dead, finishing their bloody work.

She has been betrayed completely. The Emperor has brought her nothing but a charnel house. He will pay for that but first, she needs to survive. And she needs to be a saviour. The flock spirals higher still, up through the wide, tall galleries at the top of the mountain. Hollow halls still chill with the breath of the glacier, and finally beyond even those, an exodus, where the mountain cracks open to the sharp northern sky.

Crowkisser's mind arrows upwards in a hundred black darts, into the cold sky, and the bright air and free, free, free.

The Stump explodes with crows. From every window and crevice, every gap and door. Out out out into a sky that takes them with shrieking calls. The last shreds of storm clouds strung across a blue morning that hums with the scent of fresh rain.

As the flock's shadow paints itself over the wracked earth of the Barrowlands below, Crowkisser sees the mountain's sur-vivors, more than she could have hoped for. Her thousand hearts hammer. A column reels out from the shattered gate, and scat-tered through it, her people, her bold, grey people. Still others with them, Thell's soldiers, dazed and reeling stumbling, side by side with her own army. Lightmender at their head, her lips split, a livid bruise welling across her throat, her shield sundered and something, something beneath her ribs that sings to the flock.

Curious; a puzzle for later. For now, they are leaving, leaving Thell.

The Barrowlands open before them, filling with people that spill out carrying their lives in their hands. Baskets, barrels and carts. Limping, reeling and weaving their way out into a deso-lation still hung with the drifting scraps of a shattered god. The refugees take slow footsteps among the dead, closing eyes, loosen-ing bracelets and necklaces as they shift memories from one skin to another. After that, they make more pragmatic appropriations, weapons, armour, warm clothes. Eventually, they thread their way in clumps to the edge of the battlefield, huddled, shivering half from the cold of the frost-touched day, half from the shock setting in. Those that fall to their knees are lifted, grey cloaks are wrapped around tattooed shoulders and shattered spears become crutches for fishermen's broken feet. Together, the refugees take unsteady steps forwards in the wet mud, until the first scraps of green appear beneath their boots.

Crowkisser should go to them, but she's scattered, slung across a brightening sky that lifts her wings, her tired hearts. She can see the sky! No more dark walls, no more bodies pressed against bodies. She wants to spread herself as widely as possible, to lose herself in the refraction, the ice-light, the silent song of high places. Above her, frost-edged thermals call to her heart, but she can feel the weight of the last refugees within the milling crows, her charges; her insurance. The thought holds her back, barely. They don't belong here. They are needed on the earth, where they can bear witness.

She begins to spiral the flock downwards, stringing herself in dark loops across the air. It's then that she glimpses another huddle of survivors. Almost too distant, on the north side of the mountain, the Deadsingers, leading maybe twenty or thirty ragged souls. Her hearts leap, and she remembers an old pattern, slung in mud and rope and boathook gristle, scraped from the barnacled bottoms of boats by the long men and brought to her high on the temple hill above Astic scant weeks ago. The future's balancing on a knife-edge here.

It's such a small adjustment to nudge it to where it needs to be. With a shiver of effort, the flock splits, and a fragment heads north. Quickfish and his lover's minds borne away on little black wings. Crowkisser feels their confusion as their consciousness peels off from the rest of her stolen souls; she whirls the flock in mad chaos to cover the shock of separation and lets the bird mind bleed in, drowning out the possibility of questions with thoughts of sky sky sky.

Far to the north, the Deadsingers' heads snap to the belly of the clouds, and the refugees following them make a space. A clot of crows plummets to the ground in alpine grass, black against the white flowers. The mountain-witches push to the fore, watching through eyes like burnished stones as feathers shudder, reform, and retract. The discarded pinions are left where they fall. Amid a circle of dark feathers, two confused young men huddle on the grass. The Deadsingers step closer, old eyes wide, old hearts wary, but in their hands are blankets, bandages. Quickfish and

Roofkeeper stagger to their feet, and are drawn into the mass by strong hands. The column turns and heads north, losing itself against the white slash of the horizon.

Crowkisser feels them leave the flock and allows herself a brief flicker of triumph at one more piece set in place. She takes a circling moment to look beyond the Stump to the distant north, the forever green hills, the bright flowers and the blue ice; then further still, slant through the sky, at spires in the ground like the teeth of an old god, an ancient hunter.

Perhaps, she thinks, perhaps she's needed there. But she's heavy, the weight of the minds she carries scratches at her like grit in the eye.

The flock comes in low over the torn barrows, fewer and denser with every fall and plunge. The survivors see her coming and her battered, brave fisherfolk raise a cheer. Thell's people cheer a little too, confusedly.

The earth spreads itself riven and broken before her. The cairn flags snapped and charred, scorched with lightning scar. The ground newly sown with bones. For a moment, her mind shies from it all, and she feels the flock start to scatter. Then she focuses, hauling the scraps together. Further south, she knows the Midlands are wearing the last colours of summer. She falls towards the scent of flowers, letting it call her body home.

As the first few birds hit the ground, Crowkisser feels herself coalescing. Bright scraps of spirit are stitched around hollow bones. Marrow shudders into sinew, spears, spits and scaffolds. Wings stick to scapula that swing wetly. Muscles are strung with nerves. Suddenly she has one body, alive with electricity, convulsant. She grows raw down into the mud. Feathers settle on her scraped flesh, binding the red to the bone.

She squirms. Tiny bodies fill her, deliquescing, blossoming into lungs which shudder huskily. Small black claws tear a space for a stomach which swims with bile. Rows of hollow skulls slot together, punching upwards into a spine which straightens her back in a yell. Her chest is strung with open wings that sink back into the meat and become heaving ribs. The ends of beaks rattle over shins, becoming solid, and sticky as they scuttle down into the mud, straightening in small wet pops, congealing into toes, missing the sky as they root themselves into fingertips.

As she comes to, Crowkisser becomes aware of a space around her, hand-lengths of wariness, while she wiggles her wet feet, muddy and raw. Unexpectedly, her chest heaves and she vomits a scuttering of tiny bones and filth into the damp grass. The remainder of the brood slumps writhing onto the ground, shuddering as it shucks out bodies with umbilical, placental tearing. Crowkisser spies one in particular, and limps over to it. The final piece of her plan.

Behind her, the flock pulls itself into more recognisable configurations, familiar faces emerging from the mess of bone and feather. Shipwright staggers to her feet first, casts about, and runs to Shroudweaver's side, clawing feathers off him in globs and pressing him to her chest. She covers his sticky hair with kisses, ignoring his muffled protests, his fingers fluttering against her sides. 'You, you b— you . . .' Her breath is a collection of catches. She pulls him tighter, trying to shift his bones into her body, to wrap herself around him to keep him safe.

He pulls away gently, coughing over her outstretched arm, softly at first, then sliding into a hack that pushes him over at the hips. Red strands fray from around his hands as the last scraps of thread unwind. There's a shadow of blood under his nails, purpling the skin like wet ground. Shipwright rubs a broad hand along his back, waits for the worst of it to subside as she feels again every notch of his spine, thin and getting thinner. Awkwardly, her brain flashes forth a recipe for soup, something worn and stained and pinned to a wooden wall; she remembers a brassy cookpot, the soft rocking knock of a ladle. Rooks in the trees.

She snaps to. Here amid the mud and grass and stones, there's a murmuring. The people of Astic gather around her like damp dogs, their fingers running over clubs and hooks, buttoning cloaks and strapping helms against the cold wind which continues to blow. Crowkisser is at their head, doubled over Icecaller's body, retching blood and bone as she works. Shipwright shakes her head sadly, struggling to see the point in it. Ice was long gone. She'd seen the ruin Steelfinder had made of her body before the poor girl died.

The crowd draws closer as she watches and Shipwright tenses briefly. She can't take a scrap more fighting. She's so damn tired. Underneath her shaking hands, there's a thin, metallic whine like a squashed wasp, as her spinner shatters and the last pulses of its febrile energy fade from her muscles like spit on skin. Exhaustion hits her like a drowning wave.

She staggers against Shroudweaver, eying the crowd as they draw closer.

It's not just Crowkisser's lot, there's others among them. Thell's people, leaning on broken spears, strapped to shattered shields, black and red and black again. Astic's folk seem to have changed their minds on a few things. She watches incredulously as they gather around their injured enemies in quiet, careful shoals. Heaving shoulders are pinned by grey cloaks. A rough cloth is smeared across a crying face. Poultices of dune herbs and fish-scales are placed on the worst wounds, the saltwitch dance of glass and octopus beaks.

Astic and Thell, or the scraps of both, together. Perhaps it's not so strange. Wasn't that always the way? Blood and knives and murder and then after, meetings and reconciliation. Even in normal wars, the killing brought some sanity, in the end. Enough slaughter always made the survivors weary, on any side. Here, the dead themselves had risen against them. No wonder they were clinging to anything with a pulse and a smile. It wasn't perfect, of course. They were still too close to the mountain to relax, scant hours from the horror that had unfolded. The greycloaks look a little nervous still, their hands torn between hilts and helping.

Best not to make any sudden moves Shipwright thinks, turn-ing to the crowd. She spreads her arms deliberately, tilts her hands forwards, back. Nice, clear empty palms. See? No reason to murder her.

She finds a jut of rock and sits down with a sigh. Everything aches. The hangover of spinner magic is cracking her skull like a hauler's hammer. The crowd hover at the edges of their circle, held in uncertainty, watching and murmuring as Shroudweaver settles next to her, legs stretched. He rubs at his calves, glancing anxiously back over his shoulder at the smoking mountain, which remains mercifully still and quiet. The churned earth is full of potsherds here, scraps of bone and colour thrown up when the land spasmed, and slicked clean by the storm. Just waiting to be joined by the fragments of bodies which now strew the Barrowlands.

He picks up a triangular piece, and thumbs the rough edge, turning it to brush off the mud. The design is simple and bright, blue and white in looping curls depicting the tip of something that might have been a dog's ear or bird wing. He pops it in his pocket.

The pair turn to watch Crowkisser. She's pulled herself together a little. Still busy with Icecaller's corpse, her hands moving like a musician, the thinnest strands of blood threading their way from her fingertips and down into the hideous rents in the girl's flesh, pulling them tight.

Shipwright nudges Shroudweaver, leaning her chin in close. 'What do you think she's doing?'

He shrugs, watching his daughter's fingers dance. 'The spirit's long gone. I felt it go.' He knuckles at his eyes, sighs. 'There's nothing left to save.'

Shipwright rubs her cheeks, winces. 'Awful. I think I could have started to like her.'

He laughs. 'Well, then she was doomed anyway.'

She digs, swishes, spits a piece of tooth into the soil. 'Hey. Not nice.' She slides a bit closer and puts a protective arm around his shoulders, fingers absently working at knots in his neck. Lowering her voice, she asks, 'What are we going to do about your daughter?'

He shrugs. 'I thought I'd have to kill her.'

She kisses the side of his head. 'And now?'

His words are slow. 'I'm not sure. I need answers. She's not what I expected. She's a lot more . . .'

'Human?' Shipwright finishes.

He nods wearily.

She scratches the nape of his neck gently. 'That's the trouble with the real world. We're all human.'

He catches her fingers in his free hand. 'I'm more worried about what she's going to do with me.' He waves at the shifting circle of refugees. 'She's got numbers on her side.'

Shipwright starts absently polishing a scuff on her boot. 'Well, whatever it is, I think we're about to find out.'

Shroudweaver watches Crowkisser raise Icecaller's body into a sitting position, beckoning in an old woman with a face hard as salt tack, her back a mess of mud and blood, her fingers curled to stiffness around a blackwood club. A few business-like words later, and the older woman takes the dead girl's head on her lap like a babe, runs fingers through her hair, crooning something low and warm as a stove fire.

Then Shroudweaver's daughter is walking towards him. Her mother's shoulders on his stick legs and a face above them that's a mix of them both. Hard to read. Sad, maybe, or angry. All he wants is to hug her and take her home, but she's years grown from the girl he knew, and he doesn't have a home to go to.

So instead, he stands and refastens red threads on his hands. As he does, she slows and holds a palm out to him, like he was a wary dog. He risks a smile, and watches it catch her face, pulling the corners of her mouth up. Crowkisser has a different face when she smiles, small bright teeth and a light in her eyes.

For a moment, they stand there. He feels the sharp little sherd in his pocket, watches the mud well up between her bare toes.

She steps up next to him, and hovers there for a second, that tension back in her shoulders.

Then she's in his arms and he hugs her, reflexively, instinctively. Her voice is a soft curl against his breastbone. 'I thought I was going to have to kill you.'

He kisses her brow. 'I know.'

She stiffens slightly. 'I still might.'

'I know,' he repeats.

'I'm so tired, Dad,' she says and the tears come from her like rain.

'I know, love,' he says, and his hands trace the blades of her shoulders in small circles, like ripples on the sea.

81

the little quail of dusk
small minnow of the hedgerow
berrybob, beetlebeak

—*Birds of the Barrowlands*, Chalkwitch

Thirty miles and three days later, there's a brazier, a tent. It's dark and functional, but warm with leather and fur and a fierce little draught that tastes of berries and winter.

Shipwright stays outside, with her usual quiet sense of dignity and timing. If she's sad, she doesn't let it show. She buries it, in fire and drink and jokes that scorch the air with silence before melting into horrified laughter. The old woman, Sandsinger, matches her beat for beat, shadow-puppeting gestures that flicker obscenely against canvas and fall apart into a mess of cackling and flapping for breath.

Somewhere, Icecaller's body lies silent in the quiet dark between the tents. There's been no time for a burial yet. All the rituals for dealing with death were sealed within the Stump. No one wanted to touch the corpses, and there was no one left to perform the rites, anyway. Skinpainter and the Deadsingers were all buried within that mountain. With nothing else to do, Crow-kisser's refugees had fled.

Half a week of walking, a ramshackle slide south, unspoken, and barely directed, just a few hundred tired bodies, sloping seaward in the soft dark, framed by the scents of night-time bush and blossom as the cold hills of the Barrowlands gave way to the warmer plains skirting the Midlands. The smudged shadow of the Burners' forest off to the east brought seeds drifting lazily on the evening air, something in their movement soothing Shipwright's heart. Subconsciously, she steered them a little closer to the trees each day, until the night's camps were struck in the shadow of oak tree and beech hedge, the slender trunks that rose on the forest's western-most edge.

Like a crowd of revellers after a best-forgotten night, the remnants of the two armies travelled south together, incorporated by exhaustion, shepherded by Shipwright. A strange care in it all. Even the most troubled survivors were offered a little companionship around the fires, as if the sound of voices raised in something other than pain might help heal them. Shipwright was too tired to hope for much more than that. She crouched on her haunches, stirring her sadness into the embers, and watching it flare.

At her back, in a small dark tent, Shroudweaver and Crowkisser eye each other like cornered cats, his daughter's face alternately warmed and harshened by the light. Time passes in anxiously knit fingers and half-formed sentences, much as it's done for three days now. Until, eventually, she begins.

'Why did you leave?'

'I thought it was the best thing.'

'Not for Mum. Not for me.'

'You were too young to remember. Twenty years gone.'

'I got older.'

'Did she ever talk about me?'

'Sometimes. Less so as time went on.'

'That's good.'

'I didn't say she was kind.'

'I suppose I can't expect that.'

'You can't expect anything.'

'True. This is all unexpected.'

She sips, eyes him over the rim. 'So you don't want to tell me why you left?'

He shakes his head. 'We're not on the same side in this. Not yet, anyhow.'

She sloshes the glass. 'Fine. I'm too tired to argue. Saving you was hard work. Give me this then. If you won't tell me why you left, tell me why you never came back.' She leans forwards, taps on the table. 'Tell me why, when Mum was dying, you didn't come back.'

Her father's face is hollow. Sadness shadowing his eyes.

'I would have, if I could.'

She snorts. 'And yet, predictably, you didn't.'

He turns the glass against the table-top and drains it. 'I didn't.'

'You let her die.'

'I couldn't have saved her.' There was something raw in his voice, shivering the back of his throat.

She watches his leg dance under the table. 'You could have tried.'

He catches her gaze. Eyes dark and steady. 'I *was* trying. I was trying to save everything.'

She looks away, turns to the lamp where moths dance against the flame.

'Of course. Trying, in the hidden places, doing whatever hidden things you wouldn't trust me with. *Won't* trust me with.'

He laughs a little at that. It irritates the hell out of her.

'Can I trust you, Crowkisser?'

She brushes her hair from her eyes, turns back to him. 'I saved your life.'

Nothing for a moment. The crackle of the lamp wick. Moth wings and the night air. 'Did you now?'

And the tone of him. The disappointment in it.

She chokes down the rage she feels. She can't lose her temper. It's what he expects.

Instead, she refills her glass and imagines leaving him down in the dark.

'It doesn't matter. You wouldn't save Mum. Her god wouldn't save her. Everyone that could have made a difference turned tail and ran. It was just me and her, in the end.'

He opens his mouth, but she waves a hand. 'Spare me. So, it wasn't missing me brought you back. Wasn't the death of your wife. Of my *mother*. Did you even know where I was? What was happening? Or were you too busy trying to save the world?'

The scorn thick in her voice.

'I was— I had to . . .' he stammers.

She smiles, bitterly. 'Oh, of *course*. But something made you give a shit about me. When did I catch your attention again?' She studies the scuffed cuffs of his robes, the stains. 'What made you remember you had a daughter?'

He doesn't answer, at first, his fingers working at the red threads strung over his wrist, half-crusted with blood. He's picked up a lot of little cuts in the mountain.

Eventually, he gets there, with a little prompting.

'When did you first hear about me? When did you start to care again?'

'When we lost the south.'

A little coil of relief inside her. Of course. 'That's diplomatic. Don't lie to me.'

'Fine. OK.' A deep breath. 'After I heard about what you'd done.'

'And what did I do, Dad?'

He winces. 'Do we really need to do this?'

'Yes.' She straightens her legs. 'I want to know what you think of me.'

He reaches for her hand, and she pulls it away, but not far.

He picks his words carefully – hangs them around the rim of his cup. 'You killed the gods. Broke them, at the very least. Destroyed a city in the process. Used our names to hunt us if we kept them.'

She leans forwards, her eyes deep and black, fingers steepled. 'Go on.'

'Left the south with Slickwalker. Took Astic in . . . a night, two. Hung everyone that refused to change for you.' He breathes out, knocks a shot back. 'And now . . . raised an army. Marched north. Destroyed a mountain.'

She blinks, smiles without joy. 'Wow. I'm . . . terrible.'

He reaches for her hand again, misses again. 'I'm not saying that, I just have to know *why*.'

She raises an eyebrow. 'Would you believe me if I told you?'

'I'd try.'

She presses her lips together.

'Why should I? I don't owe you anything.'

He tilts a hand consolingly. 'No, but I owe you a chance to tell your side. Who else do you talk to? Slickwalker?' He reaches, finds her fingers and holds them tight. 'It can't have been easy.'

She tugs a little, gives up. 'What is? Fine. You want to know? Fine.'

She rolls her shoulders, pulls him closer, conspiratorial. 'I did it. I broke the gods. I found their little latches and I snipped them off. Because we shouldn't have to think like they want us to think, or feel like they want us to feel. You know where that gets us. More than anyone, you should know!' Her voice pitches a moment, raises up. She takes a second, gathers herself, 'You should know. Mum did at the end. And it was only me left to see it. To see her starving for their touch. And how many others? How many other mothers and fathers and children? Abandoned.' Her hands wild, agitated. 'They cling. They stick like honey. They never let go. Not really.' She pauses. The glass in her hand creaks. 'So I learnt. I studied. I went places and I dug deep, to find some answers.' She swallows, winces. Reflexively, Shroudweaver puts a hand to the side of her face. She flinches. 'And I found things, in the south. In forests, behind waterfalls. Under fountains. I found things.'

She wipes her lips, her teeth wide and wet. 'And the more I found, the more there was to find. Like something knew I was searching. Like it was calling to me. Scraps at first, then, then . . .' She waves the empty glass. He refills it, watches the oily liquid slosh around the lip. Pours a splash for himself, corks it.

He laces her hands around the glass. 'Scraps.'

She nods. 'About the gods. Where they came from. How to kill them.' She stands, paces, tugging fingers through her hair. Outside there's raucous laughter. She shoots a venomous glance towards the mouth of the tent, then turns and waves the glass. 'The gods. They're not from here.' She chews her lip, worries a thin strip of skin loose. 'We made them, or they came here. I don't know. It's not clear. Not clear at all.' She fixes him with a wide-eyed look. 'And I searched, you don't know how I searched.

In the mud and the bone, and under that.' She slumps. 'I've peeled the skin off this blasted world.'

She swallows and sets the glass down unsteadily. 'And where were you? Where were you? For *years*. When I was lost down there with all that black earth?'

She raises a finger like a dagger, swaying slightly. 'Off *making* them. Making new gods. Stitching them into people. Or with *her*.' She spits. '*Shroudweaver*. You're a parasite. No, worse than that. You're a vector. A dirty, crusted knife.'

He stands slowly, walks towards the tip of her finger. 'I heal people. I give peace and use to the dead.'

Her eyes are flat as stones. 'Some of us can't be healed.'

He shakes his head. 'I don't believe that.'

She steps closer, her fingers clasped around his collar, voice tight and fervent. 'I do. I've seen it. You think you're working with them. Calling them. But it's all a choice. They help because they *choose*.'

'Which means?' he leaves it hanging.

'Which means they can choose not to.' Her forehead presses against his chest.

He holds the back of her skull gently. 'Your mother.'

She looks up. 'Where *were* you?'

He looks at her wide eyes, her flushed cheeks. Finally, he relents. 'In the north. Beyond the Spires.'

'You could have saved her.'

He hesitates. 'Perhaps. I don't think so.'

She steps back. 'But you didn't.'

He shakes his head. 'I had to save something else.'

She glares at him. Her shoulders shake.

'It was the hardest choice . . .' he begins.

'It was the *wrong* choice.' There's something dark and grating in her voice, but she doesn't stop. 'So, I promised her. I promised myself. No more unknown bargains, no more feelings that aren't our own. No more binding our lives to theirs.'

'We're never separate like that, love,' he says, but in his heart it feels more like scripture than truth. The passion in her voice calls to him.

'We are now,' she grins, waving a hand towards the refugees gathered around the campfires. '*They* are. I did it, Dad. I did it for Mum. And I did it for me.' Her knuckles hit her breastbone with a thump. She stares at him defiantly, ribs rising and falling.

He sips, grimacing. 'But something else happened, didn't it? Something must have happened.'

He sees her hesitate. She needs a push. 'In the south.'

She tenses, shoulders heaving. For a moment feathers flicker around the outline of her bones, then she raises a hand, slowly, resignedly. 'The unlatching,' she says, the unfamiliar word hanging in the air between them. 'There were so many locks holding the gods to us. So tightly bound. They needed so much power to open.' She half-glances at him. 'I knew I had it. I could feel all the catches. I had all the keys. But they still held. The gods clung on. Dug in, like . . . like ticks on a dog. But I pushed and I pushed and I pushed.' She turns back to him, eyes wide. 'And on that last push, something pushed back from the other side. And the locks opened, and the light changed.'

Shroudweaver feels something click into place and marshals his face into blankness even as his mind reels in shock. 'The light?'

She crosses back to his arms. 'The light, Dad. And something behind the light.' A breath for fear to grow in her voice. 'An eye. Looking for us, Dad. Looking for us.'

He twines his fingers in her hair, soothes her cheek and tries not to scream.

She looks up at him again. 'It was using our names, Dad. Finding them. Like beacons. Licking down towards the light and pushing it all into darkness.'

She sinks against him, her voice quieter now, muffled by his hammering heart. 'It took so many before I could think. Ripped the names right from them. Ate every bit of who they were, and who they might have been, and who they weren't.'

Her hands are tight against his chest. 'Do you see? Dad, do you *see*?'

'A loss of self,' he says. His voice struggling for calm.

'Worse than that,' she says. 'Every restraint, every border, every limit, ripped out.' Her fingers like claws now. 'Nothing to shape you.' Her voice lowers. 'Nothing to hold you back.' Barely a whisper. 'Nothing to remind you that you're *you* at all.'

Shroudweaver looks at her, at his sweet, scared, terrifying daughter, as it all finally falls into place, and his heart breaks. 'So you did the only thing you could.'

'I took their names, Dad.' Her voice fractures, strings ragged. 'I took them and I flung them as far and as hard as I could. Stitched a ritual to rip them out of the world. Like ripples torn from a pond.' She frowns. 'It wasn't enough though. I had to learn to move faster than the eye hunted and Slick was the only way we could do it. Pulled through shadow and veering into crows. Slicing names off stragglers that dodged the ritual. I wasn't always fast enough to stay ahead of it. But then when I got good enough, I didn't need to be.'

He almost smiles at the genius of it. 'Because we played right into your hands.' He tips her chin up. 'We were so afraid of you. Of the rumours from the south. So afraid of you that we gave up our own names to the echoes of the ritual. Didn't even fight it. Even though you were a thousand miles away.'

She smiles in relief. 'And then you were safe, Dad. You were all safe. It couldn't find you.'

He shakes his head sadly. 'Yes, love. But we weren't us anymore.'

'There was no other way, Dad. No other way.'

'You don't know that,' he says.

'Don't say that,' she screams. 'Don't you *dare!*'

She pushes him two-handed in the chest and he sprawls to the floor. Moves to stand over him, her hips casting sharpened shadows.

'I don't regret it for a second, Dad. I'd do it all again. We're free. And we're going to stay free.'

He looks up at her from the floor, her flushed cheeks and clenched fists.

She glances at her hands, at him, shock flitting across her face, and slowly lets them fall.

He makes a note of that. Levers himself to a sitting position, 'What do you mean, stay?'

She offers him a hand, lifts him with steely ease. Straightens his clothes, brushes imagined dust from his shoulders.

'Stay free,' she says, her voice banked low. 'Stay nameless. We have to.' She sits again. 'It's the only way to be safe.'

He sits next to her, tentatively, leaving a little distance. 'That could be tricky. A lot of people want their names back.' He pauses. '*I* want my name back.'

She shakes her head. 'It can't happen. The eye will find them. Strip them. Strip *you*.'

He shifts his shoulder carefully, opens up a space for her. She settles her head under his arm.

'There are others, you know?' he murmurs. He waits, then decides to risk it. 'Fallon . . .'

'He's already lost,' she mutters. 'If it hasn't taken him already, it will soon.'

He runs a hand down her arm. 'Nonsense, Fallon's fine.'

She smiles sadly. 'You can't prove that.'

Crowkisser turns to face him and crosses her legs. Fumbling for the bottle, she struggles the stopper loose and pours. 'You think it's not patient? Not clever?' She drinks deep with barely a flicker, waves the cup. 'Sure, first it gorges. Fast and messy. Like a starved child. But,' she raises a finger. 'But why rush now? We can't get away. It's filled itself so' – she stops, coughing – 'so incredibly full from the south that it has the luxury of time. We,' she says unsteadily. 'We don't.'

Shroudweaver reaches out his glass, his mind half on her words, half on her mother's mannerisms moving her hands. Outside, the fires have fallen to embers, and the camp is slowly filling with the sounds of people crumbling into sleep. Someone's fucking, hard and low and breathless, and he smiles a little at that sweaty little comfort. Shipwright's shadow lingers briefly against their tent. A moment for her to listen and hearing their voices, move away, but not too far.

Crowkisser pours, empties the bottle down to the dregs and

twists it thoughtfully in the light. 'I used to hate this stuff. All those greasy little fishermen in their fishy little cottages.' She half-laughs, then sits down woozily, holding the glass up between thumb and finger, and sniffing it. 'But now, now it tastes like home.'

Shroudweaver sips. 'It reminds me of my father. He loved this. Loved anything with a fire in it.' He smiles. 'He would've loved you.'

'You're drunk,' she says.

'I have to be,' he replies.

She smiles, and for a little while they let the smoke hang in the air, watching the shape of the flames, the shapes of each other.

Eventually, he forces himself to speak. 'We can't stay like this forever.'

She shoots him a look, half-angry, half-sad. 'Like this?'

He nods. 'Hiding. We can't stay hidden forever. Even if I did agree with you.'

She makes a noncommittal noise.

He forges on. 'People want their names. No, not even that. They want revenge. Fallon's raising an army even now.'

'I can take care of him,' she shrugs.

Shroudweaver feels the stress in his voice for the first time. 'That's not the point. There'll always be another Fallon, another army. The only way out would be to convince people that they're better off this way which is' – he laughs – 'a tough sell, to say the least.' He leans forwards. 'You couldn't do it without telling them the truth. And even if . . . even *if* you get them to believe you, the panic you cause will be like nothing under the sun.' He composes his face carefully. 'I mean, I damn near shit myself. And I just found out.'

She snorts. 'And you my big strong Da?' She grins. 'I know, I know. It's a gift of crabs, this whole thing, but this just makes things clearer.'

Her smile softens. 'I'm glad we talked. I know what I have to do.'

He watches her bright eyes. 'What's that?'

'I'm going to kill it.'

He almost laughs, and then feels a dread set into his stomach like thick green ice.

She steps closer, puts her hands on his shoulders. 'I can do it, Dad. Then we'll really be free. Help me. It'll be easier with you.'

His heart breaks. 'I can't, love.'

Her voice is low, soft, betrayed. 'Why?'

He tries to martial his screaming brain, tries to arrange his words cold and clear as knives on a plate. 'First, to get that kind of power, whatever it might be, you'd need to raise an army. Fund expeditions. Make deals.' His face twists sympathetically. 'They just won't let you.'

She bites off the words. 'Won't *let* me?'

He looks her in the eye. 'People aren't on your side. Not enough, at any rate.'

She gestures out towards the campfires. 'These ones are. More will come.'

Shroudweaver presses his fingers against his temples, fighting the weariness gathering there. 'Do you really think so? Do you think even these poor folk'll stay once they find out the truth of what happened?'

She steps to the tent-flap and peels it back slightly, the freshening of the night breeze lifting the curls at the nape of her neck. 'The truth is what I let it grow into.'

He sets the glass down on a thin, lacquered table, all marquetry and turtle shell. 'That's a dangerous way to think.'

She glances over her shoulder. 'Whereas you think so clearly?' She turns, stretching her fingers until the knuckles pop, little bits of stray bone aligning under the skin. 'How many of your thoughts are your own, anyway?'

She moves her fingers lightly against his temples. 'How do you know they haven't got in there? Some hungry little gods. Making you smile, or laugh, or cry.'

She sits again, long fingers making circles against tired cheeks. 'It scares me. It got so I couldn't trust anyone happy. Couldn't trust my own happiness.' She toys with the hem of her dress.

'Never knowing if my joy was my own. Can you imagine? With Slick, with anyone.' Feeling the sun on my skin, falling asleep, wondering if it was really me, or if something had wormed its way in, burrowed at the back of my brain, sung all its little lies into my ears, day after day.'

He kneels in front of her, takes her fingers in his, straightens them gently. 'The gods were never like that. Not even the ones that took hosts. Not in our time, at least. If ever. They're beautiful, awe-inspiring, sure, but not like that.'

'They're *exactly* like that.' She scratches at her arm, the nails leaving pink welts. 'Tell me. Tell me you've never felt it. That beautiful, thunderous surge. It makes you want to kneel, just lie down in front of them. In the peace and the light.'

'I think that's what healing feels like, love.'

'That's what slavery feels like,' she takes his wrists. 'Help me, Dad.'

'You don't need my help, love. And I can't give it.'

Her head sinks low, her chin touching her ribs. 'I do.' Her voice barely a whisper, a lick of wind from the woods. She looks up. 'I do.'

Her fingers tighten around his, until he can feel bone beneath the flesh.

He leans in. Her breath is hot and sweet against his cheek, her grip like a tired swimmer.

'I do, Da. I want to feel them again. That light. That warmth. I can't get clean of it.'

He holds her hands for a moment longer, feeling her pulse flicker against her wrists. Tears come behind his eyes like unwelcome guests, and he kisses her callused fingertips gently.

'It's OK to be happy, love.'

The wail that leaves her is a brutal and ragged thing, spiralling upwards. The cry of a night-bird. A gaunt, cold thing on the edge of the marshes. She falls against him, the whole of her shaking with sorrow.

After that, time passes in a series of remembered movements – a pot of hot water on the small brazier, herbs that scent of dreams and slow, warm nights, a bed, blankets, furs.

Her head rests on his chest, the ghost of her breath against his neck, slipping and steadying to a sweeter rhythm as the panic and fear leave her. His hand moves softly through her hair, drawing the blankets tighter as cold slides down from the hills.

The coals sink low. Even the loudest and most raucous refugees fall silent as the cool of a late summer night on the edge of the Burning woods sets in. The occasional slink of quiet laughter, of illicit trysts amid the trees. The comforting weight of his daughter's body, and his senses sharpened to something more by the tiredness around him.

The tick of cooling metal, the sough of branches, the irregular slap of wind against the hides. The little songs of the dark. To begin with, Shroudweaver watches the shadows anxiously, but they move as shadows should. The world slips in and out on his eyelids. Smoke twists the ceiling and his thoughts shrink inwards to the song of breath and dream and rest.

He stirs again in the hollow of the night, some sudden thrill jerking him awake. Shipwright is armoured and dozing at the foot of the bed. His world is tilted softly on the horizontal, a muddle of pressures and tastes. Crowkisser's ribs moving against him and the stolen tang of alcohol on his lips, old scars aching beneath the covers. He tries to flex his legs without disturbing her, tries to relax, but it's not just his old wounds keeping him awake tonight. A strange tension presses on his chest, a sense in his head like a chime, an urgent bell. A premonition of something wrong, something watching. For a second, he feels it above them, a weight on the skin of the world, the wing of a bat drawn across an open eyelid, the soft choke of a stifled mouth. It passes as quickly as breathing, leaving him wet with a sweat which has crawled its way under the covers and left his skin alive and itching.

His free hand frets at red thread, but then Crowkisser moves in her sleep, fingers flexing in dreams, and the love that lights inside him washes him clean. A soft glow pushes past his tired bones and frightened skin, sleep comes, and he doesn't wake again until the fingers of dawn.

When he stumbles groggily to his feet, his daughter is nowhere to be seen, though the warmth of her is still in the bed. Shipwright's space at its foot is vacant, a plate of meat and eggs is set conspicuously in her place. He smiles, and reaches for it, staggering slightly. The pain draws tentative fingers along his legs, where the silvered lines of scars ache like spiteful tongues – a little gift from the south. He spends a few moments rubbing life into them, into gaps filled by the memory of tendons.

He eats slowly, enjoying the peace, and the slow reconstitution of the day from the warming morning, as fires are lit and the animals wake to their feeding. The basic joy of eating. Fuel for the body. He brews something dark and strong and sips, the edges of the cup rattling his teeth.

He has no idea what to do next.

Beyond the tent, voices are raised – the burred and clipped accents of Astic mixing with Thell's hammered tones. His daughter's voice threads between them, high and clear, a crystal scalpel. He knows that sound. It's the sound of trouble.

The pieces of the morning shudder as Shroudweaver leaves at speed.

Outside, Crowkisser stands at the centre of an angry crowd who, despite their numbers, don't yet have the guts to turn their tongues on her. He's unexpectedly proud. Around her, a few of the gaunt Astic folk that he recognises as her long men, their confident fingers on slim, flat blades that wave menacingly, like chastened sharks.

Beyond those blades are the injured of Thell, muttering the sort of dire threats which are only valid up to the point of a knife. In front of them, Shipwright, her arms spread. She sees Shroudweaver and rolls her eyes in relief. Crowkisser catches him too, raises a finger to her back. The meaning is clear. He waits.

When she speaks to the mob again her voice is steadier. 'Leave me be if you love her.'

Somehow, grudgingly, they do. As the crowd drift back, he watches the knot of long men part to expose the grass below Crowkisser's legs. There is a coughing at her feet, a sprawled, twitching shape that is retching like a dog with its throat stuck on a bone. Somehow, Icecaller's body is moving, stiff and awkward with the chill of death, but moving, still.

Crowkisser stoops to watch her like she's an exhibit, a specimen. No, Shroudweaver knows this look, she has some trick up her sleeve. His daughter's eyes dart like a craftsman admiring a tricky piece of work, whispers of magic blossoming in the mud. His heart lurches and he starts forwards, but it's too late.

Icecaller's body groans, vomits, and reaches a hand up blindly. Crowkisser takes it by the wrist and pulls her up; not just up, but into her arms. Icecaller hugs her back reflexively. Slowly, deliberately, Crowkisser turns, displaying her to the crowd. The cheer they raise startles birds from the branches. Shroudweaver watches the witch of the south holding the body of the north's treasured daughter, and realises what a beautiful con she's pulled. And as if she senses his gaze, Crowkisser tucks her chin into the returned woman's neck and winks at her father over Icecaller's shoulder, a smile lingering on her lips.

82

hush the babe and crack the branch
send out sound to shore and sea
if the forest was my home
happy I would ever be

—Marriage song, the Cut

A day later, and the sun is haloed like a smudged nail in butter. The refugees are squabbling among themselves as tempers fray in the pollen-hung heat. Divisions are appearing, alliances and fault lines. Crowkisser is at the forefront of the march, the wind driving her cloak back against her shins and shoulders, her thin legs. They forge inexorably southwards in her shadow. The soft turned rocks of the Barrowlands give way to richer Midlands soil, and the rooted edges of the Burners' forests linger to the east, their broad branches soughing in the breeze, the creak and tick of old growth.

No sign of the Burners themselves, but the refugees still clot together in huddles, scanning the treeline with slitted eyes. Wary and weary, but not broken. Stitching each other's wounds, changing bandages, boiling run-off water from the forest's brooks until it sings pure and healthy. They're talking more as the days pass and the numbness of death slowly falls from their lips. Low conversations held in closed huddles, backs to the campfires, eyes off into the treeline, scanning the forest, imagining the mountain behind and the cities beyond.

It's a mixed blessing. Talk was a healer, but tales were a worry. Shipwright caught fragments on the smoke-stained wind. A stew of comfort and questions. Who did this, what happened, who's responsible? If anyone looked to the head of the column where

Shroudweaver's daughter stalked like a hunting dog, she didn't mark it. The bulk of the worrying is confined to cook-fire gossip, cosseted around embers and picking over fish-bones.

Shipwright's not a welcome guest at these campfire meetings. She was a stranger before, and she's a problem now. Both Shipwright and Crowkisser had come to the mountain a moment before it all came down, but Shipwright hadn't had the nous to resurrect the first daughter of the Republic in front of her grieving people. It wasn't surprising that the refugees had a little trouble deciding who to love and who to lynch. Shipwright couldn't bring herself to abandon them though, and Shroudweaver wouldn't abandon his daughter. So, she kept busy each evening, moving from fire to fire, stoking and tending, stirring pots, her mind still ghosted with memories of a ladle rocking back and forth against a copper rim.

She missed home. Here she was, thousands of miles away from her father's soup, over the wrong sea.

There's not much that soothes the ache of it. She talks to Shroudweaver between times. He's the closest thing she has to family here, so she does some work on all the little knots that hold them together, reminding herself of the shape of his hips and the taste of his lips. He unlocks a little as his strength returns. Day after day, flesh slides back onto his frame in slow, steady blooms. She rubs his legs at night when the pain comes, her fingers steady over familiar scars.

He confides in her, as he always has, shares the shape of his conversations with his daughter, with Crowkisser. There's been near a week of talking, on the road south, the pair of them edging closer, nervous as debutantes, and all the while, Shroud's been wrestling with the unspoken knowledge that Crowkisser's caused all this. The bare fact that he's powerless to do anything about it is eating away at him, and at Shipwright too. She can't let it show though. He leans on her like an old cane, burying his secrets and fears deep in her chest. She takes them all, takes him, and holds both afterwards, cooling in the night. He tells her things he won't even tell Fallon, that he barely admits to himself, old anxieties and guilts running like rats around his skull, and out into her heart.

She struggles with it sometimes, the weight of his worries and her own bowing her like a yardarm. On those nights she slips into the Burners' forest and climbs trees, imagining them masts, the windblown leaves a stand-in for spinner and sail, branches cradling crows' nests mercifully free of crows. She breathes in the night air as it races across the tree-tops, watches seedlings and insects ride the currents and strains her ears for the sound of waves on the shores she knows are out there somewhere. Later, she finds strong nooks and broad-armed branches and settles into the rhythms that hold her steady; buffing boots and darning socks. Her fingers and mind focus on needle and cloth, and when that's done, run over the curve and knot of those branches, dreaming of the ships that could be called forth from beneath the bark.

As they march south it becomes harder to chase the worry from her mind. She watches the edges of the refugee column become an army again, as the surviving soldiers form outriders and flank guards. The Burners come to the wood's edge to watch. They are squat, sturdy men and women with lips wrapped around long-stemmed pipes that glow thoughtfully, their wild hair held in raw twists and strung with sweet smoke. The forest's verge is lined with patient eyes alternately haloed and shadowed with the black ash of their trade and their faith. A few spy her, and offer a slight nod of recognition.

The Burners had taught her long ago that sometimes there was nothing to do but endure. So Shipwright followed the old tracks towards peace, pulling her body out onto the coast or up into the forests, finding spaces to stay sane. The Burners' villages were a blessing she had never thought to find again, filled with sly, berry-faced women that reminded her of her own dear mum, though their skin was darker and their jokes filthier.

Fuck, she missed her mum. Shipwright wondered if she was still out there somewhere. She was probably stooped and silvered now, but Ship could just imagine the corners of her smile, still smell butter melting on bread and feel strong fingers combing the tangles out of her hair.

'Little muss-rat,' her mum had called her; the snort of her

father's laughter always burbling somewhere out of sight, and
within the circle of firelight, her mother's hands and a hair brush,
its rhythm smooth and steady. She'd never felt so safe. So safe.
She tried to pass that on to Shroud. Tried not to think of saying
goodbye to her parents, of her father pretending the salt stung his
remaining eye as he brushed her cheek with gruff admonishments
to be careful, to make him proud; her mother never even given
to such pretence, but throwing herself around her only daughter,
her tears wet and wild and her fists gripping the cloth at her
shoulders. 'Come back to me, *esvel*,' she'd said. 'You come back
to me.'

She hadn't come back. She'd sailed out from the east twenty
odd years ago and never come back. Thousands of miles had
drowned under her keel and she hadn't cried since then, for all
she'd wanted to. Because for all she'd wanted to, that would let
Shroudweaver see just how much she hurt, just how lonely she
was. And he would never forgive himself.

She wished she still had her mum and dad. She wished she had
Arissa and Declan, but that was the way the world was now. The
world killed couples. You made your family where you found it,
and you pretended it was only the wind that drew the salt from
your tears.

Ship had always promised herself she'd sail back east, but there
had never been time. The fifteen years since the fall of the Empire
had slipped away, day by day, in running contracts and rebuilding;
in putting bread on the table and keeping him alive. And slipping
more into herself with every passing moment.

She can feel that old isolation washing back over her again.
On the loneliest days, even the forests and the tall trees are not
enough. She follows the Burners along their game trails, mends
their snares, and pulls worrying brown-winged birds from nets.
She builds fires and makes stews of thin bones that peel under the
teeth, placing herself among bodies separate from all the horror
she's felt, admiring their smiles, their hands, their easy movements
and fast rills of laughter.

She drinks deep of foresters' brew, rounded and musked, held within hollow logs and fed with grain roasted over fires, washing down breads studded with nuts and fruits from the trees and black-thorned bushes, their sweet cracked tops decorated in dizzying patterns by old men who placed slivers of heat-honey with the care and precision of craftsmen. She lives, briefly, a gentle double life beneath the branches. For once, she feeds her own heart and bones before anyone else and returns stronger to the camp in the daylight, her fingers quietly stroking a handful of bright flowers, twined around dark thorn.

Carefully, deliberately, Shipwright puts some space between her and the suffering. She swaps tales with women who don't want to kill her; bright-eyed hedgecallers with impish laughs, and faces flushed as half-bit blackberries, enjoying their chat of sex and craft and pride, even as their sticky lips twist wryly over charms scavenged from broken and burnt barrows. She embraces this tree-line witchery in deep earthen culverts, softly lit and hung with herbs, as she helps to braid feathers into sil-vered hair, and rubs warming ointments into tired bones, old and young.

The Burners are safer for their pre-emptive wisdom. The cold currents washed down from Thell pass over these warm, earth-lined homes, coaxed aside with skill and cleverness, fingerbones and needle-punched teeth. This is old magic that pushes on old rhythms, moon to sun, which is not afraid to meet the ghosts of the dead with spread legs and open mouths, rendering them stupid and lost in the sweat that pools between breasts and fingers and shoulders.

On the third night she visits, the younger girls come looking for her, with the message she was expecting. They're two weeks out of Thell now, and almost clear of the forest. There was no way the Shipwright was getting to pass without saying hello to old friends.

There are three of them, hair tangled with thorn and brush, eyes bright as sparrows.

'Thorndaughter's askin' for you,' they say in unison, before dragging her helter-skelter through the tangle of trees to a familiar clearing, a familiar set of tents, a familiar pavilion strung with blossom.

Thorndaughter's there, broad back shifting as she works on garland and green. Her hands deft despite her size. She turns as Shipwright approaches and grins around the stump of a brushwood pipe. Her acolytes release Shipwright's wrist and dart back into the brush.

Shipwright's heart lifts at the sight of her.

She's barely changed, wearing a dun-coloured gown slashed with russet, as befits the season. Her sleeves rolled up and her arms stained with berry juice and ash. The sash at her waist bowing with the weight of bottles, ladle, and knives.

She opens her arms as Shipwright walks forwards, and beckons her in. 'Come by, salt-chuck.'

A strong grip presses her against a chest that smells of the forest, followed by a buss on both cheeks. 'Look at you. Barely remembered your face, tardy girl.'

Shipwright lets out a shuddering sigh, and Thorndaughter tuts as she leads her to a seat under the pavilion, something carved out of an old stump and painted bright by the Burner girls.

'Set down. You've come loaded with sorrow, like always.'

Shipwright slumps in the chair, tilts her head back and watches the red dance of the pavilion's canopy against a mackerel sky. A small brazier smoulders gently next to her, something sweet and lingering.

'Here,' Thorndaughter says, her voice soft. 'Eat. Drink.'

A wooden plate is pressed into her hand – black bread and hard cheese, fruits still holding the dew of the day, followed by cup of clear water, herbs dancing in the depths.

Shipwright hesitates and Thorndaughter waves impatiently, bracelets jangling.

'Come on. I know you and your hollow blood, girl. You'll have been pining by those fires and taking not a drop for yourself.'

Her look is knowing, kind.

Shipwright eats. It's good. The bread dark as a hearth, the cheese sharp on her tongue.

'You knew we were here?'

Thorndaughter nods. 'A'course. Uplanders lighting fires like dogs. See you for miles. Smell you for miles after that.'

She sets herself down in the chair alongside Shipwright, her huge form folding up neatly as she sighs appreciatively. 'Brought a bunch of strange magic down from the mountain, didn't you? Can taste it on the wind.'

Shipwright nods, starts to explain. Thorndaughter waves a hand. 'Lowlander magic. Uplander magic. It's all the same. Hungry. Heedless. It won't touch the forest.'

She refills Shipwright's cup, slips more fruit onto her plate. 'You brought the bone-binder too, didn't you?'

Shipwright nods. 'You can feel his magic too?'

Thorndaughter shakes her head. 'No, salt-chuck, just see the marks of him on your face.'

'He's a good man,' Shipwright says, reflexively.

'Even good men are tiring, dear heart.'

Shipwright says nothing.

Thorndaughter shuffles her chair closer and puts an arm around her shoulders. 'We cope with them by talking about them. Your sea might like it when you play the clam, but not me.'

Shipwright laughs at that, and all the tension of the past few weeks slides out of her. The laughter turns to sobs and Thorndaughter holds her through it, until it eventually subsides.

Shipwright takes a deep, shuddering breath. 'How did you know I'd come?'

Thorndaughter smiles at the question. 'Fifteen year back you first came, and then again every dip of the moon. You were due.'

Shipwright shakes her head, rubs at her red eyes. 'I had no idea we'd be anywhere near here.'

Thorndaughter refills her pipe and draws deep. 'The forest knew.'

Shipwright laughs again. 'Oh, did it now?'

Thorndaughter's eyes twinkle. 'I know what the forest knows. And I knew you were due. You took a trail to get here though. Visited every half-bit black-burner in the forest first, huh?'

'I didn't want to impose,' Shipwright says.

'That's your big problem,' Thorndaughter says, jabbing with the pipe. 'Never wanting to leave a ripple. Idiot girl. The forest always has time for you. And so do I. But not for the bone-binder.' She sucks her pipe. 'That's a tough love you sowed for yourself there, salt-chuck. Forever in the reaping.'

Shipwright grimaces. 'Thanks for the wisdom.'

Thorndaughter snorts and waves her arms expansively at the cluster of tents outside, 'Wisdom, what have I got of wisdom? I have pretty boys with burning hearts and old men that remember being pretty boys, nothing more.'

Shipwright smiles. 'Pretty boys. That reminds me, where's Willowtooth?'

Thorndaughter refills her pipe, tamps it down, her heavy brows lowered. She smiles sadly. 'He was the prettiest.'

Shipwright blushes. 'He was. I always liked his . . .'

Thorndaughter leans forwards. 'Arse?'

Shipwright chokes. '*Laugh.*' She sips her drink, cups her hands around the rim. 'But yeah, that wasn't too bad either, now I come to think of it.'

Thorndaughter nods, her soft chin tucking into the folds of her neck. 'Always a good lad to watch leaving.'

She reaches across the table, bracelets jangling. 'More tea?'

Shipwright holds out the cup. 'You're ducking me, Thorn. What happened to him?'

Thorndaughter fidgets with her bangles. The tea splashes.

She leans back in her chair, turns her head to the side. 'The forest took him.'

Shipwright straightens, her face clouding. 'He *died*? Oh, Thorn.'

'Not died,' she interrupts, eyes flashing. 'Taken. Given. He was the bridegroom of last year gone. Gone to the stag now.'

Shipwright drinks again, the brass hammering around the cup's rim warm as a spinner.

'I always thought that was just a Burner tradition, Thorn. Dress the prettiest boy up, send him off into the green.' She waves a hand. 'Renew the forest. They did a similar thing at the Aestering on the first day of full sun. Green ribbons around the birch trees. Singing.' She grins. 'Shroud never could hold that tune.'

Thorndaughter shakes her head, earrings catching the glow of the fire, her ears briefly dripping gold.

'Not just tradition, salt-chuck. Ritual. Every four year a boy given to the forest.'

Shipwright sets her cup down and studies her hands. Raising her head she asks, 'But they're not dead?'

Thorndaughter shifts. The chair creaks as she resettles. Small embers fall from her pipe onto her thighs, fast patted out. 'No, not dead. But not living as they were. The forest takes them. The god in the forest. The god that *is* the forest. The white stag.'

Shipwright shakes her head. 'I don't totally follow.'

Thorndaughter leans forwards, reaches out a hand, levers herself up slowly, the weight of her whole body against Shipwright.

'You remember fifteen year ago you came. What did I say to you then?'

Shipwright squeezes her hand. 'Thorn. I'm too old for that. My memory's a leaky dinghy.'

Thorndaughter says nothing in reply, but leads her to the side of the pavilion, where red silk curves down to the sod. There's a cabinet there, delicate, beautiful. She reaches into her kirtle, takes out a key and fumbles with the lock.

'I told you and the bone-binder that we could do nothing beyond the forest. That we were bound to the forest. Sheltered by it. That's why we couldn't help, against the thing in the mountain. Against the Empire.'

Shipwright nods. 'Ever since the bladedrinkers. I remember now, yeah.'

The lock clicks, and the lacquered doors swung open. Golden patterns of leaves and thorn.

Thorndaughter stoops, reaches in, and takes out a long thin glass case.

'Our god lives in the forest. And he needs our boys to keep him strong. To keep us safe.' Her large face softens with tears. 'Every four year.' Her voice is as low as the brazier's coals, her fingers moving slowly over the glass and the objects inside.

She turns to Shipwright, holds out the case. 'I keep what I can of them.'

Shipwright gently takes the case and sees curls of hair, each neatly bound, and labelled. The ones on the left faded almost to paleness, those on the right still brown, and russet and black. She looks up at Thorndaughter, and the tears running down the wood-witch's face.

'Oh, Thorn. I'm so sorry.'

Thorndaughter points to a name. 'My own boy, the prettiest ever, gone near twelve year ago. Can't even read his name now. Can't even recall what it was.'

Shipwright squints at the labels as the text on them swirls and blurs. Only the very rightmost remains in clear focus – Willow-tooth.

She hands the case back.

'You can't even remember them, can you? Because of what Crowkisser did. Because of the south.'

Thorndaughter nods, placing the case gently in the cabinet, before she locks it and returns the key to her kirtle.

Her deep voice rough and husky with sadness. 'All those beautiful boys, salt-chuck. And she took even their names.'

Shipwright steps forwards and hugs her, feeling the sobs riding her huge frame, the smell of the forest still in her hair.

'I'm so sorry, Thorn.'

Thorndaughter holds her close like iron.

'That's why I keep you near, salt-chuck. The forest might have taken my boy-child, but spit and bone fore I ever let it take you.'

Shipwright stays with Thorndaughter that night, sleeping in her arms as the forest shifts and rustles beyond the red pavilion. She dreams of bright young boys, a stag whose antlers move like dawn light and of nights aboard the ship, before she was its cap-tain. The dark within her skull is filled with the swell of the sea, with the lights of fires raised and tamed on deck; the call of the long-swimmers in the wake of the boat and the weight of friendly ribs against her side as they swam out into the darkness. And light

706

again, years before even that, in a circle of wagons; the thump of moths against glass lamps, the thrum of badly tuned strings and a voice that might have been her father's raised in song.

All those years held by arms spread against flickering light. And in the light, raised voices, singing off-key, shivering against the cold, or soft and steady in the winter winds. It always came back to singing. Her whole life has been filled with song; she hates to see people silent.

That's why Icecaller worried her so. The girl has been practically wordless after Crowkisser raised her, and who knew how *that* had been done? Every step she's taken in the dwindling shadow of the mountain, has been a silent one, marked only by the hiss of breath, the shift of her body; her eyes flat as wet stone.

She spent her time only with the crow-witch, slipping in and out of living. Whatever magic Crowkisser had worked was struggling to take; death coming for the Republic's first daughter like a cold hound. Every time Icecaller was hauled back from the dark with the same wet wrenching, every time gasping for light like a drowned swimmer. That couldn't be good. Shipwright knew what it was like to drown, to feel water filling your lungs, the weight of the ocean behind it, all the basic rules upended, and breathing your worst possible option. Icecaller's silence felt like drowning, like the girl's world had been tilted upside down.

So, Shipwright had welcomed all the small sounds of change, even the first moans as Icecaller's head inexorably turned back to the north, her feet stumbling bruised over unseen stones. A low, relentless keening that billowed the girl's stomach, and only broke in waves of sickness, starting again as soon as the last drops of bile had spattered the ground.

Shipwright had taken over then, pushing Crowkisser aside with her body and confidence. She was good with words, that one, and a dramatist like her father, but Shipwright had seen better than her slip under the keel; had spent too long wrestling her father's moods to fall for the bluster. More than that, Shipwright had a hunch that Crowkisser was scared of her, and she used it efficiently, controlling the space around Icecaller with her movements.

She fenced her out with the unfurling of bedrolls, the brushing of hair, the feeding of soup, spoon by wretched spoon. The witch of Astic would lurk nervously for a while, then slip away, supposedly busied by forces or fears unseen, but Shipwright knew a flight when she saw it, and stoked the fires in her heart with a little scrap of bitter pride.

In that salvaged space, Shipwright could work. Icecaller was a scared, pitiful thing, mostly compliant, mostly vacant. The stark planes of her face twisted from the inside, her memories surfacing like sharks, but held just beneath the surface. Shipwright sensed pressure on the skin, and the heart beneath the skin; a release was needed, something to break the suffering loose, and soon. Thankfully, there were techniques for this.

Shipwright started slowly at first, moving the physical, her fingers and hands working Icecaller over in steady, relentless rhythms, moon and tide, sea and salt. She heard her father's voice in her head as she shifted the girl's body into healing shapes, recalled memories of sailors' limbs brought straight, of backs unbowed. Later, she turned herself to Icecaller's tortured skin, hauling with the steady pull of an oarsman, gradually unsticking knots and snarls of panicked muscle, grinding them loose. It was like sanding a piece of wood, finding burrs and imperfections half by touch, half by intuition and producing something kinder, more functional with the careful application of force.

But the Kinghammer's daughter was no ship. Something more was needed to call her back from the brink. A little body work had helped Crowkisser's ministrations stick, brutal and raw though they were, but the thing that moved in Icecaller's skin was not yet her. Bringing her back from the dead hadn't returned her to life.

Even this didn't faze Shipwright. How many times had she seen a mind shaken loose? The sharp crack of a swinging boom, a fall from the topsail or the sight of a loved one, gut-stuck and ribboned. The soul's anchor was a strong thing, but it could fray, clinging to the body like a half-torn web.

For that, there were teas, gathered and bound in waxed shells. Some from the Burner's rootwitches, a couple of Thorndaughter's best brews kept close to her kirtle for months. A rare few from the blood-breathers of Astic, taken before the war. Still others gathered years ago from the Hung Forest, from the strange people who dwelt there, long-armed and stilt-legged above the shifting marshes. They were all blended by her own hands, and designed to do one thing – to bring a person home.

She brews them in a broad pot and humours herself by getting a ladle, listening to the shift and clunk against the rim, and breathing deep from the fumes that rise. She tries to make Icecaller drink it at first, holding her as she splutters and coughs and twists. Eventually, she abandons that and drapes her over the pot like ham on a skillet, tenting a blanket around her head and filling her lungs with the fumes. That works a little better.

Shipwright blocks the opening of the tent when inquiries come, answering them all with firm noises. She sleeps with Icecaller at nights, abandoning her excursions to the trees and the Burners for a cot and a vigil. She learns to recognise the sound of nails quietly tearing skin, and becomes attuned to the sound of muffled weeping as she raises the strange, torn child that Icecaller's spirit has become. Time and again, Ship holds her close, just for the sake of warmth, for being there, solid and real, catching her wrists when they curve and stray.

The people of Thell begin to leave gifts, small pieces of foraged food, warm clothes, notes. Shipwright shows them to Icecaller, makes her name each thing and the person who gave it, and then makes her repeat them back. When the night terrors get too strong, she trains her to repeat the list. Gradually, the sound of tearing is replaced by the names of people who love her. This is how mending occurs, through the smallest replacements. It's like caulking a ship, strengthening the vessel piece by piece. It only takes you so far though.

Icecaller barely speaks, barely looks at her. She moves with a tightness, a stiffness. There's colour in her cheeks now, and strength in her body, but a deeper sickness lingers inside, like rot in the hold, pus in the wound, something filling her up and pressing against her skin from within.

In the weeks that follow, Icecaller spends her days by the column, in the light, unsticking wheels and hefting sacks, shuffling with the remnants of her people over the miles. As they move south however, something changes. Shipwright feels it testing her teeth. The sky weighs heavier on her temples. The paths become less safe as the Burners' marks fade out, and their tracks are reclaimed by bramble, thorns and the lumbering bulk of boars. She's never been a country girl, but even she can tell that there's a different kind of space here, perhaps different kinds of spirits.

As the column lurches across the Midlands, the land opens up; the lakes of the Hollows off to the east, eventually fading north and out of view, as they swing towards the west coast and Hesper. The far horizon distantly coloured by the bruised sky that still hangs over the south. Two weeks of this, all the scrapes and cuts she'd picked up in the mountain healing into a lattice of itches.

Two weeks of the same trees, the same damp ground, of the column huddling behind her, hollowed around low fires. Two weeks of new families forming on the road, pooling their supplies and stories.

This feels like the shape of something new for Thell, budding out in the dark, marked by the odd grey cloak around the campfires, or in the bedrolls, the odd chunk of fishbone and fisher-herb tossed into stews with northern spice. Morning after morning, with the familiar fading into the forest, and the half-healed shape of the Republic's first daughter stumbling behind. Shipwright stitches her together, seam by seam and hopes she holds long enough to see her people survive.

83

Shoes, rations for a week.
A name inscribed on the throat.
Charms against crows, against the dead.

—Provisions for the exodus, tallied, Lightmender

The fifteenth morning is dry and unrelenting. He awakes with a taste on his lips like dust, his mouth, dry, dry. The cracked leather of the tent creaks in a parched breeze. Shroudweaver fumbles for a mug, a pitcher. The water is stale and warm, flattened by the night, but still, a gift. The camp outside is unusually quiet, the familiar sounds of the morning being ruggedly manhandled into life conspicuously absent. His eyes struggle to focus on the shape of things, every edge softened and liquid. A thump in the back of his head like meat on a stone. His fingers are numb, his weaving charms hot against his wrist. Odd. He looks for Shipwright and sees her hunched by the remains of the brazier, the palm of one hand pressed against an eye socket.

He stands. A little unsteadily, but for once his legs are mercifully free of pain. Also odd. He walks across to Ship and rests a hand on her shoulders. 'I feel like shit.'

Shipwright looks up, grimaces, 'There's a reason for that.'

She sucks her fingers, reaches into the brazier, and crumbles charcoal into a cup, topping it off with a flask from her belt, then stirs. 'Drink this.'

He takes it. 'What a delightful gift. Why?'

She squints at him, winces against the light. 'What happened before you fell asleep last night?'

He shrugs. 'It's hazy.'

She nods, swigs, swallows, spits. 'Me too. And while that makes sense for you, my little southern flower, it doesn't for me.'

Understanding hits him about the same time as another wave of wet pain in the back of the skull. 'We've been drugged?'

She smiles. 'Well done.' She raises a finger as her face turns green. 'Excuse me a second.'

He watches her reel out of the tent. Damp retching sounds follow and he feels his own stomach turn in sympathy. They stop abruptly and her voice slides its way back in, wired with urgency.

'Shroud. Get over here.'

He does as he's told, his thick head lurching on his neck as he stumbles to the tent flap and throws it back.

His first thought is of death. There are bodies sprawled as far as he can see, around the ashes of cookfires, half out of sleeping furs and bedrolls. The scene conjures brief, horrific, memories of the plain below Thell, of other fields before that. His heart lurches, but Shipwright's already out among them, checking pulses, moving limbs into safer configurations. Even as she works, he sees there's fewer folk than there should be, and the marks on those left separate them, clear as day. Red and black geometrics, stark against the skin, bright against the mud. Thell's people have been discarded. No sign of the grey men and women from Astic, and no sign of Crowkisser. His daughter's gone.

A pang grips his heart, mixed with a strange relief. She's left. Of course she has. He does a quick headcount. Not enough groaning people strewn in the grass to account for most of the column, unless there are others hidden out of sight, and the rolling plains of the Midlands don't offer much cover. The refugees haven't been discarded; they've been winnowed. Sifted for the best and the strongest. If Crowkisser has gone, she's taken over half the survivors of the mountain with her. He smiles thinly into the cold grass. Of course she has. This is what she wanted all along – bodies for the cause.

The next few hours are lost in setting things right. Shipwright crouches over still figures, her laced fingers moving in steady rhythms over the heart or slipping into clogged throats, pulling forth snot and spit, until they shudder back to life.

Shroudweaver's head's a little clearer now, so he staggers a few paces and runs a finger around the lip of the water barrels that feed the camp. A few drops of sticky, brown sap still cling to the edge, lungfallow, most likely. They'd used it in the Aestering to dull pain and encourage sleep. He confirms his theory by flicking a few drops into the ashes, watching as they flare green with bitter smoke. It would be hard to calculate a dosage so large, he supposes, even for an expert. It's inevitable that some would drink too much, be too thin, have sacrificed too much of their fat and strength on the slopes down from the mountain to soak the sap away from their bones.

A flare of anger sparks in his chest. Reckless girl, he thought he'd taught her better. Now's not the time to worry about that, though. Out on the field, Shipwright is still working, splitting the sleepers into those that are just drowsy, and those that are a wet gasp or two from death.

She shoots Shroudweaver a meaningful look, and he wipes his hands off, before turning away from the flames. They're not the only ones out here. Shipwright didn't see her arrive, but Icecaller is prowling the field, ashen-faced and grim, cursing and calling out to her people as she works. She knows them all by name now, thanks to Ship. She stalks the camp, drags them back from sleep, from the cold ground, foul-mouthed and grumbling. There's a change in her, a spark of life back in her eyes, but not sitting quite right, like an unturned gear in a millwheel. Still, she sets fires with brutal, rapid efficiency, and settles the injured close to the flames with care, as she talks to them, quiet and firm.

A few are almost beyond saving, despite the shelters she builds, despite Shipwright's skilled hands. For those ones, Shroudweaver takes his time. Sets his eye on the faint glimmer of their loose-looped souls and stitches them tight to aching, groaning bone with strong silver thread. As he works, his mind flits back to the hold of the ship so many months ago, to the clean, open face of a dead West Tide boy, teeth straight and proud in his head.

He loses not a one.

84

a congregation moves out onto the moss
pale feet on the Green
mist lifts the skin of the world
we wait for the pull of black water

Days pass. There's not much point in marking them, one by one. They accumulate organically, like rings on a tree, or salt on a shell. There are always times when smaller moments slip away beneath larger patterns. Shipwright finds it enjoyable, in a way. Time marches on, they march south with it, and Hesper draws closer. With Crowkisser gone, there's an abdication of worry, of responsibility. She only has one strange, dangerous girl to keep an eye on now, and Icecaller has the decency to feed herself and keep herself busy most days. There's still plenty to do, even with the grey crowds of Astic shucked off, a group this size takes work to feed. Once fed, they shit, fight, wander. Tempers fray and emotions are strung like wire. It's not surprising, with no time for them to grieve, but wearying for all that. She feels like she's picked up a guddle of quarrelling babes and been left to drag them overland to a city that likely doesn't want them.

Land – that's the other problem. She misses the sea with a pang like bared teeth in a keen wind. A sense of loss that burns down to a dull ache in the nights and flares again with each freshening breath of air, each outrider's shout that steals from a sailor's tones. She misses the ship, the feel of its deck under her feet, that cant and buck. The land here feels aggressively static. Farmer's fields, turned by plough, hardened by frost and now soaked by rain. Home to birds that squat amid half-drowned stalks like marsh-wives, fluffing their feathers and preening the damp from their bones. Midland birds, long-legged and dappled, the bright feathers at their throat and neck flashing like signallers as they ee-whit across the fields.

Shipwright spears a few with wet, regretful thumps, sullying breasts with blood, ruddying the water of the fields. They cook up well enough, though their long necks are full of seed, packed with the hard work of farmers, mixed with the occasional fragment of coin and clay and bone to help them digest their hauls. She's fond of them, these ungainly birds. If she closes her eyes, their high preening call could be flitting over the morning waves, or skirting the deck on a twilight watch with the lamps just rising to flame.

She was far from the sea. The land hardened here, nearer to Hesper, the Midlands freeholders resurrecting their old forts as news from the north slid southward. Self-sufficient folk in the Midlands, taking their cues from the ruins of old Luss. Each homestead a fortress, their barn walls turned to outsiders, their thick wood gates bound with iron, and studded with charms and warnings dug from the bone-turned fields outside. They had fewer welcomes as they moved south, and each trade was made with cupped hands and reluctant fingers.

A scattering of little enclaves sealed against strangers and sky. Might it do them more good than it had done Luss; more good than in the stalking times. Shipwright shivered. She'd learnt too many tales of treachery with their roots in Midlands soil, heard all the gory details dripping from Arissa's mouth, years ago, as they split a bottle of wine, and scared each other shitless by digging up the ghosts of their homes. Stories of knives, and dreamers, dark figures on the roads and worse in the ditches.

Every whisper was resurrected now. Every house they passed echoed those same tales. A lamp kept at each threshold and a rod of iron driven deep into the earth, head to stern. They'd never really lost that suspicion of strangers wearing the faces of guests in the moving Green. Gates in the hedgerows and between the trees. Empty cradles. It had left its mark on the landscape. The fields were scored with hedges shorn brutally short, their cut branches and stumps spattered with lambs' blood, layered and dried and spilt again, shrines of cat-skull and flint, shaped around the anvil stones of birds. Splintered snail shells ready to rattle a warning should the Green ever open its hungry throat once more.

Between the binding hedges, the going was tough; the fields of the Midlands drenched by sudden, unseasonable rains, leaving tussocks of grass half-submerged, poking above waterlogged fields. The roads were their salvation, built long ago by people who knew how to play the climate of this country, the odd jut of initially inexplicable rock a legacy of their foundations, where glacier outfall met more stubborn stone. Both were harvested with impunity and folded back into the walls of the homesteads which waited at each split of the raised roads, windows licked with butterlight and gates securely barred.

At the fifth of these the Shipwright decided to test her luck. It was too late in the day to march on through the night, and too sodden on either side of the road to strike anything like a camp. Stray off the path and your feet might call to those sleeping in the wet, their faces wreathed in green. Dreamers, their thoughts floating above the stagnant fields as marsh-light, heavy and drunk in the gloaming. Come the dry heat of high summer, the waters would recede and the Midlanders would seek them out while they were at their weakest, digging down into the damp soil, uncovering weathered skin stained darker still by years of submersion. Making small nicks with copper blades, careful never to drive too deep, decanting the dreamers' rich blood into stoppered vials to be sold and traded for steep prices, steeper by the year. The luckiest and bravest might sever a fingerbone or an ear, flesh dark and strong as leather, and keep it in a root cellar, year on year, producing slow, black blood dripped into long, tall stills.

It was a risk though. There were tales enough of those whose knives and saws had cut too savagely and woken the dreaming revenants. Others still of a finger which had grown again an arm, a set of ribs and a beating, angry heart; an ear which had blossomed a jaw, teeth still studded royal with amethyst. Wake a revenant and let it walk the halls, the tales said, let it drink thirsty and red-lipped. And if the morning brought you family who rose glossy skinned and ruddy cheeked, their limbs supple and their manners strange, best to let them live out their days, dark-skinned, soft-voiced, joyful.

Shipwright fought to get clear of those thoughts as they drew to a halt before the farmstead. The fields on either side were drier, but threaded with the torn stumps and trunks of thin white trees pushed down by the wind. The horizon now only a spare black line, the faint blue of the sky held for a few more seconds by the falling sun.

The column falters behind her as she stops. With a wary look at Shroud she crosses the yard to a great blackwood door, its surface studded with beaten copper. The yard itself shows signs of work in its whetstone and chicken coops. The skulls of something vulpine are speared warningly above. She raises the knocker, lets it fall three strikes, and waits.

When the door opens it does so grudgingly, the wood wet and grown with the sudden rain. The man behind is wiping his hands on a sooty rag and sucking gamely at the thick yellow chunks of his teeth. A weather eye roves over Shipwright's shoulder to the people clustered behind her on the road, slumped in the growing cold.

When he speaks, his breath carries the whisper of woodsmoke and meat, and a slight tang of cheese. He smiles loosely, gums and lips crinkling. 'Be ee bringing army t'door? It's by late for an invading.'

Shipwright laughs despite herself and the old man joins her, stopping suddenly to suck on his teeth and give her a gimlet eye.

'We've come from the north,' Shipwright begins.

'From ee shaytered city,' he interrupts. 'Ken I, seen it in the bone cracks hot from the fire. Took it out ee belly of a dwelling lamb. Ee shaytered city and you all its kitcast babies. You've come a long way and longer.'

Her heart jumps at the prophecy casually tossed off his tongue. She pulls herself together and nods. 'If you have a byre or a building, a floor or a stable we would gladly pay. If you have food, we'll pay again for that.'

He looks at her and waits before finally speaking. 'Both of 'ese I have to hand, but ken your coin is nothing. Only taken in trade these given gifts to ee. Have thee labour, have thee magick? Power? From left or right. Care m'not which. Save I have loose stones and spinners to hold fast, and a body yet to lay.'

Spinners. The Shipwright's mind races. Something in his voice scratches at her, but her mind's alight with this little hint of home. All this shit, all this strangeness, and now *spinners*, here? She catches his worn eyes roving her face, composes herself as best she can. 'We might help with both.'

He beckons, fingers twitching like a sparrow's neck.

She leans in, careful for her feet not to cross the stones of the threshold. His stubble is raw against her cheek, that rancid smell a little stronger, overlaid with turned earth. His voice dry as a marsh frog. 'Cryin' ye a boatbuilder by the sway of airms and brassy snuff.'

'A shipwright,' she murmurs. Her fingers dance Katkani against her back, a warning to Shroud.

Better a snared bird than a hawk in the unknown sky.

Wait, wait, her fingers say, steady, steady.

She feels the refugees gather behind her, a scattered soundtrack of shuffled feet and hesitant coughs. She trusts Shroud to keep them quiet, or to keep them steady if he can't keep them quiet.

Her almost-host nods slowly, the skin of his cheek brushing the side of her face. 'Better a kitcast shipwright than none at all. Long it's been since we heard tell of your kind. There's plenty you could do for me. A good trade, a fine trade, wind it tight with rope and salt and brass.'

He claps her amiably on the shoulder, inhaling deep, then coughs up something brown flicking the rag apologetically across his lips. 'What else ee brought from belly of mountain? Stillbirths? Dead things?' He fixes her with that bright gaze.

She holds his eyes for a second. Says nothing.

He smiles, sticky and yellow, laughs like a toad coughing up a stone. 'No matter. No matter. We trade on the seen and the held. Leave the questions for the dreamers, eh? May they choke on them.' He pointedly scuffs the ash at the threshold, beckons with a leathery palm. 'Come by, come by. I have drink yet. Slung from the white roots, will put a thick on your worries.'

Shipwright smiles and carefully crosses the threshold line, leaving it untouched, before flashing a quick sign back to Shroud.

A taste of meat on strange bones.

Her boots take her deeper into the belly of the homestead. It's surprisingly spacious, with narrow, scalloped corridors opening out into wide domed rooms, fed by fires tucked into the wall like babes, decorated with twists of rushes and thin-slit curves of graceful, bog-bleached bone.

The first of these is a workroom, tools neatly stretched upon shelves, hung in pegs, by size, weight, blade. Jars and stoppers come next, honeycombed, sealed with black wax stamped with year, binding, sealant. Her host's feet are steady, loping among the stones, sped by the gentle suck of air through the corridors as their looping shapes pull warmth down into the belly of the house, pushed along by the contrast of the bitter cold beyond the walls.

His feet are steady, but he runs a broad hand along each wall, tracing the spirals and curves. The stone is softened by carvings, hung with stitched sacks dyed bright with vegetable hues, re-counting the old legends that had crawled and burrowed their way out from the memory of Luss and Rum, John a'Greenshoes, the Maid of Thriceflower, borrowed-Jim's wending. As he relax-es, his chat becomes a low, easy thing, soft as a mole's burr.

After the work room, there's a kitchen, with cheeses stacked and rinded in one corner, shadowed by loops of dark bloody saus-ages. A drain basin is still scattered with sharpened cutting knives and the remains of the last lamb. There's a bucket of hooves, teeth, fragments for charms. She spies brass stamps on some of the flagstones, worn grooves where one might shift and tilt them to allow access to the root-cellars below. Were there stills down there she wondered, waiting copper-necked and thirsty in the blackness, filling drop by drop? Were they waiting for the touch of a slow-grown finger, for something to push up into the warmth from below?

Her host hurries her on, into the warmed centre of the house, the floor thicker with rushes, the walls more richly hung. His family are there, gathered around a pot. An angle-faced wife with lively eyes, a fat baby rocking on the bones of her knee. Two older girls are squawking on the floor, battling dolls made of fox-fur and weaseltooth. She's greeted by the welcome roar of a tended fire and the smell of a stew rendered over days with root vegetables, marrow and patience. The woman tosses a handful of leaves in as Shipwright arrives, shucks the baby off her knee and favours her with a bright, fast little smile that warms her heart.

Her husband beckons Shipwright in and sits her down, smiling. 'A striking deal then. Ee'll come ben with me, coddle the spinners back t'purring, and thy loose-grimmed shroudturner'll see t'body.' He guides one of his daughters away gently with his foot, sending her scurrying to glower balefully from behind her mother's skirts. He looks back to Shipwright. 'In return, I'll turn out the bare walls of my home to ee and ee'r kitcast babies, so longin' as they don't come ben me or mine. I have good straw and the walls tight-laced 'gin spring rains.' He stares into the fire, picks up a branch from by the side of the chair and whittles it into something slim and curving with long, smooth strokes.

She watches his hands, their gathering of hair and burn and scar.

'Mark ye,' he rumbles, waving the stick like a baton, 'you'll not be warded in bare-wall byre. Owt comes for ee, ee'll meet with own steel,' his voice lowers. 'Own flesh.'

A careless toss sends the stick into the flames which swallow it whole, licking the soft white wood down to ash. 'Have thee a deal with me, Shipwright?'

She takes his hand, clasps it, feels the hot blood pulse in his wrist. 'We do.'

He smiles broadly, his broad gums wet in the light. Calls over to the woman. 'Mother, take ee kids behind brass and open the scowrin' barns to them's as out of walls.' His wife nods, gathering the girls in tight wrists and flitting from the room. Her husband turns back to Shipwright. 'You and I ull call on the heart of the house tomorrow. Rest ye. Neither wet nor green'll touch ye here.'

He is as good as his word. In short time, the barns and byres are opened, and if settling down next to the livestock in their hay and grass isn't perfect, it still puts stone and warmth between the refugees and the gathering damp. The people of Thell fall into each other's arms, twined like cats, sleeping with the boneless weariness of folk tired beyond reason. Their hosts bring platters of dried meat, the skin flaked to wafers, scented with berries pulled from the hedgerows and place urns filled with warm stones beneath blankets to bite at the edges of this sudden, unseasonable cold. Icecaller they won't come near. The children shy from her, lacing their fingers across their eyes, while their father only pulls his hood to, pressing brass tight against his eyelids, his offerings fumbling the tension between obligation and terror. Shipwright watches him, and wonders.

Later, they bring Shipwright and Shroudweaver inside. There is work to be done. The children sneak out from behind their mother's skirts, watching wide-eyed as their father leads his guests deeper into the heart of the homestead. The heat from the wall-fires becomes an almost physical thing, thickening in the air, carrying strange, unfamiliar scents of hot fur, vinegar, something sharp on the tongue.

Down deeper still into the narrow corridor which runs the length of the homestead's central chamber, the walls pressing in like unwelcome hands. Shipwright's broad shoulders brush the stone, grazing against the edges. Her mind plays that word, over and over: *spinner*. Shroudweaver is chattering brightly behind her, a light in his eyes, curious and lively, for once. Their host answers sporadically, cautiously, the Midlands burr dragging his answers out into low tones that rumble gently in the positive or negative.

The noise of the house fades as they draw closer to its heated heart. The stones are fiercely warm here, threaded with a sound like soft bellows and something else Shipwright recognises – a brassy spinning, hitched and unsteady.

When their host beckons them into the room, it's with a shrug that is already half-apology, his voice a husk in the rising heat. He gestures regretfully to a body, stretched out black beneath brass.

'She been a-sundered and growin' for nigh on six year now. Fallen to the green in winter, rising dry in summer. She ain't for killin' so I been keepin' her steady on t'spinner. Time was I took it in trade for a full gallon of summer blood. She'm growing strong now though, with all ee wet fallen on field.'

His wide, raw eyes tell Shipwright all she needs to know. Whoever's under that spinner is family. What worse than to keep this at the heart of your home? But where else to hold it? Her heart aches for him. She claps him on the shoulder and moves forwards.

'Let me see what can be done.'

He ducks his head gratefully, shuffles behind her with haste. Shroudweaver slips back with their host into the depths of house, and she gets to work.

The body of the woman in front of her pulses as she breathes, as the forces within her wax and wane. Her body flushes and darkens, clearing and then clouding again, like wine through muslin or blood against a cloth. She looks old, but strong, iron hair scraped back against the skull, muscles corded with a lifetime of use, skin glowing with that tough clarity that only came as a gift from years in the rain, wind, sun and sleet.

She's laid out on a stone slab softened with furs, her wrists and ankles tied securely with hide, strung with charms of hammered brass. Her chest rising and falling in slow, steady rhythms, strengthening as her skin darkens and the colour returns. On the in-breath, her eyelids flutter, and her teeth shine bright in her mouth before they fade again with the hitch and chime of the spinner which hangs over her head, dancing and chucking on the lowest of beams.

The spinner. Shipwright eyes it. Not quite rig-size, but bigger than a hand and old-fashioned, its muttering plates and gears inelegantly holding the spirit inside. Who brought it here, she wonders? Traded it for a gallon of dark summer blood? A fortune at any time. Who else had come from the east? How long had they been coming?

Slowly, carefully, she places her fingers on it, feeling the innumerable rhythms and pulses that run beneath the metal, pushing softly against her touch. It feels like home.

Gently, carefully, she pushes back, and feels its hum run up her skin, over the hairs on her arms, into the threads of her shirt. That little hitch in its tone, like a hiccup in the metal, a swell under steady water. It's an easy fix. Archaic it might be, but its construction is familiar enough that she could bend its fractured harmonies closer to a single, clear tone.

If that's what she wants to do.

Sing the spinner's rhythms into a kinder key and this woman will be kept alive indefinitely, forever, perhaps, until the brass at last pits and fails, unleashing her on the people above. How many summers will it last, she wonders? How many wet, calling springs? How many nights of darkening flesh fading back to a gentler brown as the fields dry or freeze, as the water slides off tanned, weathered bones?

A lot, Shipwright suspects. She feels the weight of the spinner in her hand, the buzz of the spirit inside, like a wasp in a box. An old and inelegant thing, but fierce, fashioned with enough sheer weight of metal and will to keep rattling along until anyone above is too old to care. Probably. Still, there's that strange hitch in its song, and its design is just unfamiliar enough that she isn't quite sure if she will catch any errant clicks or slips. And it would only take one. A single flaw could shred something this size in seconds.

The woman beneath the spinner takes a great shuddering breath as her chest fills like a bellows and her arms raise, dreamlike, grasping. Shipwright jerks away instinctively, and the spinner swings on its perch. As it arcs, the air slides back out of the woman's body, the port-dark swell of blood fading from her face, and Shipwright sighs in relief.

The heat in the room is fierce as a furnace, the struggle between the body and the spinner throwing it off in relentless, battering waves – it's not sustainable. Shipwright exhales slowly and takes the brass sphere in her hands again, resting her head against it, trying to feel its rhythms more precisely as they hum through her bones.

One thing's for sure. The spinner can't be left untended. It's not being used for its intended purpose. All that ancient metal stressed beyond its limits already. Whoever left it was clever, but careless. To leave their handiwork limping like this would endanger everyone, and it would break her promise.

She wonders again who had made it so long ago, who had filled it with a spirit so fierce that it would last, age on age, slipping from hand to hand, from sea to shore to field. There's no way to tell without taking it apart, and that isn't going to happen.

Shipwright sighs. Not all mysteries are meant to be solved. She returns to work, pushing and pulling the spinner's rhythms like wet wool, getting a better sense of it now, as it clicks and buzzes its way through her skull. She feels the spirit inside steady, slipping into a more regular cadence, the shell and gears finding a better fit, a scaffold instead of a prison for its fluttering life. And then, at the spinner's heart, Shipwright finds another option, so unexpected that it stops her dead, partly at finding it and partly at finding herself capable of thinking it. It would be easy enough to tune the spinner to overload. Not immediately, but over time. Shift the resonance up by a single cant, and day on day that hunk of metal would grow in power, until it was uncontainable. And Shipwright could channel it down into the woman below her, giving her an ending, possibly a release.

She wouldn't break free to head above, to find those laughing children and smile hungrily at them with her bright teeth. And she wouldn't be held down here forever, not living, not dying, perpetually coming back to life and being bludgeoned back down. There's a grace in that, a kindness. Shipwright reaches for the spinner and takes its rough curves in her hands. She begins to change the pattern, then stops and looks again at the woman. Her host's mother perhaps? There's something familiar in the bones of her face and the set of her lips. She's not just kept down here, but dressed and changed, her clothes fresh and bracelets on her wrists. There's love there, and tenderness. For a moment, Shipwright takes her hands off the brass, and lays them above the woman's heart, feeling her breath rise and fall. The fierce heat swells and ebbs inside her, moving with the pulse of her blood, her life. Shipwright has no right to end it.

Reluctantly, she removes her fingers, wet with sweat and dries them on her shirt, then fixes the spinner. It's the work of minutes. As it steadies, the scouring heat in the room fades to a hearth-fire glow. Shipwright watches its curve, and smiles. Enough of thinking she knows best. Enough of change and ending without consent.

As she finishes her work, the singing of the homestead's children winds its way down from above, distorted and slowed by the looping corridors. It's an old tune, a Midlands rhyme:

> Come the green, the summer-heat,
> bring copper knife and ruddy meat.
> Come the rain, the growing wet,
> bring calling bird and tight-strung net.

Shipwright shivers as the lyrics fade. She turns as she hears Shroudweaver enter. His face lean and wary, hands fresh with thread and powder.

'Did you fix it?' he asks.

'I did,' she says and smiles. 'What happened with the body?'

'There was a boy,' he says.

She steps forwards, takes him softly in her arms, and they leave. Behind them the spinner continues to sing, steady, constant and strange.

> mist lifts the skin of the world
> pale feet beneath black water
> the pull of green moss
> congregation

They leave after three days. There are no heartfelt goodbyes, no friendships formed. At another time, perhaps, but here their host gathers at the door with wife and children to watch them leave, back down the path. The fox skulls clack mournfully in the wind as Shipwright passes, and a black cockerel shrieks indignantly, pointlessly. She feels eyes on her back until every one of the refugees has crossed the fence-line. Then quietly, finally, gate and door are closed against them. But the Green stays with them. The damp myths of the Midlands seeded like spores in the tales of the train. For days afterwards, the talk around the fires is of damp meadows and their dreamers. The weather is better now, but the fields on either side of the raised stone roads are still wet enough and deep enough that a tired mind can imagine a half-glimpsed light, a hand stained dark as wood, nails crooked above the water.

Strangely durable, those Midlands legends, worming their way into any old brain. For the people of Thell, these stories are hard to resist; strange, foreign horrors washing out their own nightmares for a night or two, as they scare each other every evening in the drifting woodsmoke, relaxing as the monsters, this time, never appear.

Another couple of days, and another handful of miles brings them close to Hesper, the ridged roads of the Midlands fading down to broad traders' tracks, cluttered with travellers. And if she never thought she'd be glad to see that battered squab of a city on the horizon, her heart proves her wrong.

As the road pulls her back towards the sea, the people of Hesper's outskirts come to watch them. Farmsteads and staging inns cough up gawkers who line the verge in clumps, hesitant, wondering, watching hundreds of strangers lurch from the north with narrowed eyes and tense hands.

Shipwright flicks her eyes over their murmuring bodies, digs her heels into the flanks of her weary dray, and rides on into the long shadow of the grey towers.

85

I won't say anything agin' her
I won't
she knows, she always knows

—Last words of Pineye, glimmer, shanksman

Messy little bits. Scraps and shavings. Metal spiralled off with quick, careful movements. Pins held between mummed lips. Fingers quick and deft, livered and blotched. Powerful chemicals and strange acids. Nails chipped and filled full to gumming with oil, rust, picky little grubbings.

A steady, white-powdered hand over stubble. Sucked teeth, hen clucks. Springs teased and poked and tickled. Just so. Wires slimmer than fingers, pushing, prodding, waiting for the click and drop. A surge of adrenaline. Glass stressed. The murmuring creak of an almost crack. Something bitter and burning inside. A twist, hold the pressure in the wrist, run a thumb up the nose and lick the lips.

There, there we go. Easing off, soft, goosey interlockings, downy little leavings. Coaxing sluggish bolts with black oilings. One drop, two, the pull and spin and then the swing. Slow, heavy. Hands through mussy, mussy hair. Little grey wires. Little grey wires. She straightens, runs a hand down her aching spine. Waves a hand.

'There you go.'

Fallon smiles at her, squats down by the opened belly of the safe and digs his hands in. He withdraws oilcloth bundles, bags, papers, a box, Arissa's hands light on his shoulder.

Cog watches them, scratches her neck. A scab comes loose. Messy, messy little bits. She flicks a nail clean, then turns her attention happily back to Fallon, to his ox-thighs and bristle-brush, his back like a slab. A good buck if you could ride it. She scratches her stomach and adjusts her belt hooks. The grey lady's thinner, beautiful like an axe is beautiful. Every edge of her sharp and tidy. Probably worth a finger dip, if you liked the taste of spice and glass.

Finally, Fallon stands, dumps his haul on the desk and shoots her a sweet grin. 'Flawless as always, Coglifter.'

Coglifter snorts, starts sorting the pile. Papers. Oilcloth. Box. 'Flawless isn't the point. It's all about the flaws, Lord.'

Arissa lifts the box, twists it against the light, something strange in its making, like scales that shine in the sun. 'We're lucky to have you, Cog.'

She sniggers, bows. 'The only good thief is the one on your payroll.'

She lopes to the window, presses her breath against the glass. 'Is that your friends coming back?'

Fallon's voice drifts over her shoulder. 'I hope so.'

She presses her mouth against the pane, bares her lips until her teeth grind slowly against the glass.

The thick taste of gunpowder and grease.

Distantly, falling across the fields towards Hesper, winds a train of banners and bodies.

'Can't hardly wait,' she murmurs.

86

Merrywhip
Skindles
Frithow
Beesbump
Mallow

—Horse names catalogued amid the refugees of the
broken mountain

The ribbon around the boy's wrist is filthy, the fabric gritty and stained, soaked through. White once, coloured now with sweat at the edges. He fiddles with it nervously. Above, the air is thick with insects, broad-winged bugs, carapaces thick and black. They've been kicked up in clouds above the waving grass and now float heavy ahead of the hooves and trailing feet of a great grey train which stretches back towards the horizon. Hundreds of people, bruised and bandaged, their skin writhing with strange, angular shapes. Wagons, occasional horses, their ears flicking in irritation, heads lowered from exhaustion.

The bugs die in droves, their fat shells bursting with audible pops, followed by the snap and clack of beaks; seabirds, lured inland on swift white wings, by an unexpected feast. The small dun birds of the Midlands are no match for these raucous, bullying invaders, contenting themselves with discarded legs and wings, the haze of grass seed that hangs in the air.

The riders cough. Rough, ill-favoured waggoneers hunched over haphazard loads of unfamiliar weapons, long boxes twice padlocked, tied with straps smeared white and red.

The crowd behind them coughs too, a long shuddering hack that runs the length of the column like a fly on a horse. Between the coughs, their voices are upraised and unsteady, full of strange songs, snatches of laughter, crying. All of them leaning and listing on each other like drunkards, their feet dragging and their torn soles casting blood on the new-turned earth.

The boy watches them wide-eyed, fiddles with the ribbon at his wrist, and chews his lip uncertainly.

The column draws closer. At its head, is a woman so big he steps back in fear. One of her hands swats at the insects, the other is light on the reins of a roan cart-horse which moves stolidly under her. Her hair is thick, yellow as corn. She watches the pale man riding beside her and her face moves in strange shapes.

He is thinner, like a picture of a ghost, with black hair clinging wetly to his scalp. One hand trails ragged red threads, the other rubs wearily at a leg stroked with the silvered marks of old scars. Their horses come closer. The boy steps back again, stumbles. He feels a hand catch him, heavy on his shoulder. A familiar voice, knotted like old wool. 'Steady chicken.' The hand on his shoulder nothing but a bag of knuckles, veins blue as laces under leather.

He looks up. 'Who are they, Cog?'

Coglifter sucks her gums, spits. Tightens her grip slightly. 'Trouble.'

The column passes them, foot by stumbling foot. The people of his village watch silently, eyes wide. The blonde woman rides closer, hauls the horse to a stop. Hooves like plates thud into the soil. She looks down at the old woman and the boy. 'How goes it in Hesper, mother?'

Coglifter sucks her lips, chews some dirt from under a nail. 'Better than it's gone for you.'

Shipwright narrows her eyes. 'What do you mean by that, mother?'

Coglifter's hands trace the horse's heaving flanks, the burrs and scratches. 'Just saying as I see. You hie on, you'll see the gates soon enough. They might even open for you.'

Shipwright smiles. 'Fallon's an old friend of ours.'

Coglifter tips her head, rolls dirt between her fingers. 'Is he now?' She pauses, smiling slowly. 'That's good. Best of luck to you. Come on, sprat.'

She turns her back, as behind her the column moves on, the heavy beat of the great horse taking the lead again. 'Who were they, Cog?' the boy says.

'No one that matters, boy,' She pauses, narrows her eyes on the wandering column, the tattoos black and red and black again. 'No one that matters anymore.'

She takes his hand in hers, his nails soft in her callused palm.

'Will you be staying for dinner, Cog? There'll be fire-bakes. It's nearly time.'

She squeezes his hand. 'It's not time for me, little man.'

He frowns, fidgets with the ribbon. 'What time is it then, Cog?' She just smiles, taps his rear and sends him home.

Only when she sees the door lock does she turn back to the column, watching its ragged tail fade toward the towers of Hesper.

'What time indeed?' she mutters. A half-cut laugh, as the muscles in her back twitch and sting. Wearily, she takes a pipe, fills, it, fumbles for light and strikes, watching the sparks drift off into the bug-swarmed sky.

'What other time, little man? Time for a burning of ships.'

87

No miracles without the gods. Except the sun. The air. The song that keeps singing itself.

—*Notes on the Destruction*, Wicktwister

Hesper's great gates heave open with protest, followed by a cloud of roiling dust, tinged with gunpowder and sulphur. The city has a reputation: the port of dock rats; fleet-fingered Hesper. Tired shoulders and chipped teeth. It's not a city for strangers, not a city for foreigners, unless they have too much coin and dignity, and are keen to lose both.

The streets throng with traders, the clatter from their throats promising food, water, charms wrought with split steel and bone. In response, the refugees pull together like a worm contracting. At their head, Shipwright lets the roan do the work, hooves thundering without a care for questing hawkers. Her eyes are fixed on the horizon, waiting for the slope of the road to throw up the thin line of a mast, bright against the sky. Not yet. Not quite yet.

Plenty else on the skyline. Above, on the battlements, spikes and cannon have bristled outwards. The song of Hesper stamped out in chain and sweat and fire. Beyond the metal, ranks of solid men and women, their arms loose on blade and bow, their gold armour washed red by the lowering sun, silhouettes rendered slim and sharp by the helms pressed down on their brows. Old seafarers' gear. The mark of the vulture by the ocean.

Brighter than them all, in full regalia, stands the bear of the twin towers, Declan Fallon. Dipped in copper, black and bravado, swilling the streets with curses and commands.

Fallon's horse is as bullish as he is, a scarred charger that drives through the crowds of hawkers and peddlers like the prow of a sweat-flecked ship. The cracked stone of his voice is like a call to home for Shroudweaver. Not so for the merchants. They flinch back like a struck animal, teetering on the edge of the canals.

'Move you scoured gutterfucks. Clear a path, shift your corpses before I make more.'

One of Fallon's broad hands holds a blackwood club to the sky, the tip swooping with promise. He rises in the stirrups, shoulders a broad slant against the spread of the opening road. 'Let's welcome our neighbours.'

A marked change then. The merchants are pulled back, bodily. Into their place step sturdy men and women, their confident hands taking bridles and wrists, pouring fresh water over dusty lips. They slip arms around hips, under armpits, steadying legs too tired of the ground to walk.

Hesper's medicine is almost as aggressive as the rest of the city. Bandages slathered in ointments that glow with a fierce, sinking heat, and blackstick, that Hesper specialty: thick, square pieces of a tacky substance that smells of fruit and tastes of pepper and salt. It's given to sailors too long off land, to horses run too hard. To the foundry workers in the embers of this smoke-strained port.

Shroudweaver rolls the blackstick around his gums, and feels the shaking in his muscles slow and stop. He grins at Shipwright, black and tarry and she beams back, lips the colour of coal.

'Two beautiful Hesper smiles.' Fallon's voice is different for them, warmed like spirits over a fire. 'Hello, you idiots.'

Shipwright edges her horse next to his, leans across. His arm takes her in a fierce embrace and she returns it with a swell of relief in her heart.

Fallon sways slightly, lifts his free hand towards Shroudweaver. 'Come on, skinny. Come here.'

Shroudweaver joins them and for a second, for one blessed second, everything is OK. Sweat and warmth and holding, with the distant sense of the crowd at their back.

After a span, Fallon turns them gently, their horses shouldering against one another. 'You remember my wife.' The understatement in his voice purring like a cat.

Scant metres away, her horse moving under her like weeping stone, her hands light on the reins, Arissa Fallon rides into view. Shipwright stretches a shaking hand out to Shroudweaver and grips his fingers with a fierce heat. He holds her steady, lets his arm move with the sway of the big grey dray. Her breath steadies a little. Arissa grows closer.

Shipwright watches her friend move out of the distance like a memory.

Her face is still long, sharp, scraped with iron where her hair meets her temples; lips a familiar thin line, cheeks the weathered leather that screams Hesper bred. That severe face softens like summer ice when she sees Shipwright, her heavy brows lift in delight and those spare lips slide into a smile bright as a lit knife. Shipwright feels something kindle inside her, a spark of relief on the tinder of her soul. The noise of the crowds and the smell of the city peels back like a turned page.

'Riss?' she says, 'Riss?!' Higher, louder. A name, a real name falling from her lips, word perfect. She can almost see the syllables interlocking.

She's down from the horse in a bound, Fallon and Shroud left at her back. The cobbles under her feet could be the sand of a beach, Luss somewhere on the horizon of her mind.

Two steps and Arissa lifts her in the strongest hug, the steel of her spine softening into delighted laughter. 'Ship, my beautiful girl.'

Her voice is husky, roughened by lack of use. She holds Shipwright in familiar places. One hand in the small of her back, one light on her neck. Arissa brushes her lips against her cheek. 'I missed you.'

Shipwright holds down her racing heart, and squeezes back hard enough to push the air out her lungs. 'Did you miss that?'

Arissa pulls her closer. 'Amazingly, yes.' She pats Shipwright on the cheek. 'Let me get a look at you.'

Shipwright stops, turns a pirouette. 'You see it all.'

'You got tough, beautiful.'

She laughs. 'I got something.'

Arissa smiles. 'I see you've brought us guests.'

Shipwright looks over her shoulder anxiously. 'Yes, a few, what do you think?'

Arissa shrugs. 'I'd have preferred a cake, but . . .'

Shipwright grins.

Shroudweaver alights behind them, walks forwards with his arms open wide. 'You'd have preferred one of Ship's cakes? You *have* been asleep too long.'

Arissa grabs him by the scruff and pulls him into her arms, flashing a wicked smile over his head at Shipwright. 'I see this one's still a jerk.'

Shipwright nods. 'Cute, though.'

Arissa tuts. 'Passably pretty.'

She takes Shroudweaver's chin and twists it each way. 'Still not enough meat on your bones, Shroud.'

'All part of my aesthetic, Riss,' he smiles.

Arissa takes him by the hand, holds the other out to Shipwright, and gestures with her chin. 'Let's get back to that big old bull before he pounds too many heads.'

Shipwright laughs. 'Would you deny him his fun?'

Arissa snorts. 'Mercy on me for having married such a diplomat. I suppose a harried merchant or two is a small price to pay. Declan's quite lively these days.'

'I wonder why that might be?' Shroudweaver murmurs.

Arissa sticks her tongue out at him. 'Such a jerk. How do you endure it, Ship?'

Shipwright shrugs. 'He's useful when he's quiet.'

Shroudweaver rolls his eyes disconsolately.

Arissa pats his arm. 'Oh cheer up, Shroud. You'll love what I've done with the place. By which I mean, absolutely nothing.'

'Might want to cut yourself a little slack on that front,' he murmurs.

Arissa shoots him a look. 'Nonsense. I'm all for a good rest but three years is just excessive.' Her tone light, but her smile a little strained.

Shipwright reaches for her hand. 'Sorry to drop all this at your door, Riss,' she says, glancing back at the milling refugees.

Arissa tuts. 'Nonsense. Where else would you bring them? And besides,' she says, her smile sharpening to a point. 'Anything I can do to rattle that crowslicked bitch.'

Shroudweaver's eyes dart sideways, before he takes a long, slow breath. 'Riss. I need you to know. I tried. I tried so hard to undo what happened.'

She stops him short. 'Not now, Shroud. Give me a moment. Out from under all that. Please.' Her voice is still fragile from years of disuse.

He squeezes her shoulder, pretends not to notice the shaking. 'Of course.'

Shipwright puts an arm around Arissa's waist. 'I like this new husky drawl, Riss. How's Declan taking it?'

Arissa's face lightens, seeming to come back into focus. 'He never could handle me.'

'My ears are burning.' Fallon's voice is light with laughter as he leads the charger across the cobbles, reaching a hand down.

Arissa springs up next to her husband, smiles down at Ship. 'Are you coming back to the Towers with us?'

Shipwright shakes her head. 'No, we have to see the survivors home first.'

Arissa nods. 'I'd expect no less.' She moves to put her heels to the stirrups, then stops and catches Shipwright's gaze again. 'We'll keep the lamps lit for you, Shipwright.'

The crowd parts around her horse like starlings.

Shipwright watches the pair sway into the distance, then mounts up again, trying to ignore the ache in her thighs, the other stranger ache in her heart.

Behind her, the strong arms of Hesper stretch out to enfold the sea. Darkness slinks down from the hills and in the streets above the cold canals, one by one, the lights of evening kindle.

88

Arcs of white stone, shadowed courtyards. The smell of flowers.
Jasmine melting in the sallow heat. Laughter pooling in patios.
Salt climbing the walls toward evening.

—*On Arrival in Hesper,* Hallowfeather

The refugees are taken in with the same haphazard efficiency which colours everything in Hesper. Houses are opened, there are tables, chairs, and eventually beds.

The city barely stretches. Shipwright is unsurprised. Long ago, the people that used to move in and out of the port's great loops were numberless. Nowadays, Hesper is hollow. The ghosts of the men and women who burnt in the south have been left there, and the few that returned don't mind the company. There are beds to spare. The people of Thell sink into them like stones into a lake, they are swallowed and fall silent. Even Icecaller eventually rests, setting her shield and spear down. Exhaustion comes upon her all at once, taking the legs from under her. There have been too many miles and not enough sleep. Hesper's cutters take care of her, straightening cramping muscles, dripping water into her drop by drop, sweetened with sugar and brightened with wine. Whatever nests in her blood doesn't seem to help. Or perhaps Crowkisser's ministrations had their limits.

Two days, they work at her. Two days Shipwright waits for news like a restless dog, the doors closed and the air thick with the scent of Burner's bush. On the third day, the woman treating Ice emerges, ashen faced, eyes widened to whiteness. She brushes past Shipwright and stops at the high seawall. Methodically, she removes her clothes, her shoes, her movements studied, careful. Shipwright watches the shape of her limbs, but doesn't understand

737

their meaning – at least, not until something more familiar strikes the back of her seafarer's skull, memories of pearl divers on the shore's edge. Panic shifts her, her legs a beat ahead of her brain, but still not fast enough. She runs, reaches the wall in time to see the woman plunge, straight and white as a seabird, down into the crashing waves hundreds of feet below. A shout tears loose from Shipwright's lungs and her hands clench the white stone of the wall. Far below, the water swirls, bubbles and coughs forth a pale stretch of tangled limbs that strikes out for shore.

'Only the sea can wash her clean now.'

Shipwright starts at the voice.

The middle-aged man next to her nods in greeting as he digs beneath thick nails, scratching a jaw clouded with stubble, loosened by the wax and wane of starvation.

'She'll be alright?' Shipwright asks.

His face softens. 'She was a gull-girl, back in the day. Never seen one swim so fast and deep.'

They are both quiet for a moment, watching the woman's pale, dark haired shape cut through the rising waves and haul up onto the spar-strewn rocks. Something lingers in the water behind her, a strange play of sunlight that fizzes and fades into the depths.

'A city of birds we were. Pretty little gulls.' He glances back at the Grey Towers. 'Falcons. Mayhap falcons again the way it's going.' His soft, round hands make talons. 'Used to dive right into the deep water. Pull fish up, bright as a smiling eye, huge, huge.' His voice quietens again. 'Don't see them so much no more.'

He turns his body towards Shipwright. 'She'll be alright. I married that little gull-girl and she turned into the strongest, smartest woman you ever saw.' His eyes flick back to the healing house, the door ajar, faint coils of scented smoke still coiling onto the baked clay of the street. 'Your friend is powerful afflicted. We can't change what she's suffered, but we've restored what she lost on the road. A fierce spirit in her.' He laughs, the sound boyish and light in his throat. 'A firewater girl! A gull-witch in another life.'

Shipwright smiles despite herself. 'I barely know her. I wish I did.'

His voice steadies, low and authoritative. 'You will.'

She looks at him curiously. 'What do they call you?' she asks.

'Saltseeker,' he replies, with a soft, slow smile.

She smiles back. 'Thank you, Saltseeker. I'm Shipwright. And I remember my debts.'

He grins. 'We know well who you are. Memory as long as my father's yardarm. Think you we were ordered to this work? No, Shipwright. We *volunteered*. Before I was Saltseeker, I was a sailor. There's no debt here. Never could be. We remember what's been done in our name. Remember the walls at Luss. Remember the south.'

Shipwright laughs wryly, keeping one eye on the pale figure steadily pulling its way up over rock, rope and gantry. 'A pity you can't forget this last venture. Not our finest hour.'

Saltseeker grimaces, takes a nutshell from a pocket, pops it between thumb and finger, 'Finer than most.' He pauses, chews rhythmically, stolidly. 'You think we don't see, but we do. Those of us in the know. Working with salt, spit and sea. You've shown it. Shown it to all of us. Plain as a rotted keel.'

Shipwright holds her hand out for a nut. He obliges. She pops, chews. 'Shown you what?'

He laughs. 'Don't play a fool, ship-mender. Shown us all what Crowkisser's capable of. What she'll do when she thinks she's right.' He glances back at the city, at the refugees propping up the walls, weaving quietly through the streets. 'What it'll cost.'

'We never intended this,' Shipwright says. 'We thought we could stop her.' She picks bits of shell off her tongue. '*He* thought he could stop her.' She spits. 'Even I didn't think she'd go this far.'

Saltseeker's eyebrows raise slowly and he holds her gaze for a long time. 'No, but a silver lining. You're pragmatic. All ship-menders are. Before you treat a wound you have to see the blood.' His face grows grave. 'You've shown us all the blood now. There'll be a waking in the city.'

Shipwright opens her mouth to deny it. The sea air hangs between them, salted and empty.

He smiles sadly, points over her shoulder. 'See? Here she come.

My sturdy gull-girl.' He pulls a robe and towel from his shoulder and starts towards the dripping woman, then stops to rest a hand on Shipwright's shoulder. 'We all pick up the dirt of the world, ship-mender.' His grip tightens, wide face creasing into well-worn lines. 'We can all be washed clean.'

She grasps his fingers, feels them tighten briefly, then slip from her grasp.

The pair link arms and walk away. One dry and wide as the land, the other still a wet strand slipped from the grasp of a scouring sea.

Shipwright winces. The sun is fierce on her head, edged with the last taste of summer. She bends for a moment. Watches the waters push against the cliff, watches the last twist of strange light sink into the ocean. Straightens, shrugs, turns her back on the sea and heads towards the twin grey towers.

89

The horror is not in the fire. The horror is in the ash. Help me.
For it stains, it stains.

—Confession three, execution writ, Mirth

'I know where my loyalties lie.' Ropecharmer waits by the gang-plank, hands braiding a coil of thick hemp which sits like a fat snake atop a barrel.

They've been back in Hesper three days now. The ship lies quiescent in the harbour, lifted on the evening tide, humming with power.

Coglifter chucks his chin. 'Good boy. Now, give me your words.'

He raises an eyebrow. 'Seriously?'

She leans against a barrel. 'I didn't get old by being kind, kid.'

He rolls his eyes. 'Keep your hand upon the tiller.'

She smiles. 'And your eye upon the sail.' Coglifter knocks her pipe against the heel of her boot. 'You're a pretty boy, Rope. If I was half a span younger.' She chews her lip. Looks at him with goose-grey eyes.

Ropecharmer grins, winces as a hawser above squeals like a stuck steel pig. 'I couldn't handle you Cog.' He tucks the wax-paper bundle she's given him into the crook of his arm. It's an awkward shape, the contents sloshing inside their wrapped clay shell.

Coglifter nods, pulls at an irksome chin hair. 'A truth. A pity, but a truth.' She steps forwards, places a hand on the back of his head, her fingers like knots through his short-cropped hair. Her brow hard against his, the sharp chemical scent of her against his skin and the urgent twist of her lips a breath from his own. 'You ca' canny, boy. Dear you are to me. Don't think it doesn't twist my guts to send you down this road.'

He leans his cheek against hers. 'It know it has to be done, Cog. It's for the best.'

'And who else to do it.' Her fingers tighten on the back of his neck. 'Too smart by half, boy.' One thick-nailed finger ticks away at the back of his skull. 'Too smart to be climbing ropes.'

He laughs. 'It's what I like.'

She sits spread-legged on a crate and takes two bottles from the sack on her back. With the palm of her hand she splits the tops off, and pats the splintered boards next to her. 'Have a bit to swill the dust down before you go.'

They chink glass to glass.

She drinks deep, throat flexing. Rope sips, sets it aside. Something fierce with fizz, a guttural alcoholic scrape mixed up with liquorice and seed.

'It's good,' he says.

'Made it myself.'

Ropecharmer nods. 'Of course you did.' He watches a crew of dockworkers load cargo onto a much different ship, a wider, shallow-bottomed thing, with strange lines. Maybe one of those he'd begged, borrowed and bought with Shipwright's coin and promises. His guts twist a little as he turns back to Cog. 'Will this do it? Will it stop things getting worse?'

She smiles back at him. 'Aye, Rope, it'll do what we need it do.'

Rope wets his lips. 'Need and want are two different things, Cog.'

She pulls again, swills the dregs with a critical eye. 'Too smart, like I said. A shame you couldn't just be a good arse on strong pins.'

He nudges her with a shoulder. 'Why not both?'

She laughs, sucks on the pipe. 'We can't always have everything we want.' And the mirth runs out the lines of her face.

He smiles softly. 'This time though. We'll make a better world this time.'

She pats his cheek. Calluses rough against a day of salt and stubble. 'Oh babe, I can tell you're young.' She levers herself down from the crate with a groan. 'Me though, I've got legs like a sucked bone.' She rubs at her thighs one-handed. 'I best get back before the Grey Lords notice I'm gone.'

'Is that likely?' he says.

Coglifter snickers. 'No, but I didn't get old and painful by being lazy.'

She watches the curve of his chest and the fall of his arm across the tight-wrapped package. 'Stay safe, pretty boy. Get it done. Come home.'

His voice catches her on the heel as she turns to leave, 'Cog.'

She pivots, fixes him with a glare.

'The others. Have you heard from them?'

She shakes her head. 'Dead or changed their minds, boy. So far as I know, we're alone.'

Cog doesn't watch him ascend the ship's gangplank. She knows the set of his shoulders like the shape of any planted seed. Instead, she turns and takes Slitters Wynd back into the guts of the city. From the Towers, she hears the distant shrieks of falcons, the hammering of metal. The hot smell of burning rides downhill on the wind, and she keeps her hands tight in her pockets, feeling out the sharp edges of flint, the thinnest sliver of cat bone. Fingers whitened almost to bleeding, Coglifter turns away from the ship and slips on tired legs back into the streets of Hesper.

90

sweet departure
the ocean wide
my one true love
still by my side

—Port song of the *Volante*

'So, that's it then?'

Shipwright grins, ruffles Shroudweaver's hair affectionately.
The port wind is fresh, 'That's it. What were you expecting?'

He shrugs. 'I don't know. Some grander farewell. Arissa at
least, or Fallon. Maybe Icecaller even.'

Shipwright kisses his cheek. 'Bless. Were you wanting hand-
kerchiefs and scattered petals?' She shifts away from him to lean
against the harbour wall, back to the sea, squinting up at the
sprawl of Hesper. 'Let's look at this objectively, huh?'

Shroudweaver grimaces. 'Must we?'

She nods, a half-smile on her lips. 'We must. Ice is . . . recovering. I don't know what she went through in that mountain,
but it's going to take time.' She turns towards the sea, takes a
lungful of good clean salt. 'She doesn't need us for that. I've
talked with her. She knows where we're going, how to get word
to us.' She laughs. 'Enough fat messenger hawks shitting over
the streets round here that she can send one wobbling out to the
Halls.'

Shroudweaver frowns. 'I can't believe we're leaving so soon. I
should stay here. Should help heal them. The damage . . .'

'It would kill you,' she says, a sad twist to her lips. 'There's just
one of you.'

'It's my job,' he says. 'My purpose.' He slides down the wall.

744

'I'm a shroudweaver' – he waves a hand – 'whatever that means anymore.'

Shipwright slips down next to him, amid the lobster pots and nets, and the other, less picturesque things. 'A shroudweaver. One. Fixing this would need the whole Aestering.'

He leans his head on her shoulder. She strokes the thinning strands of his hair, lets kisses run along the sharp angles of his skull. 'You can't fix the whole world's pain.'

'Fix it?' His laugh is dry, joyless. 'I feel like I caused it. Like I missed my chance to stop her. Like I was standing at the top of the hill, just watching the avalanche roll.'

Shipwright shifts uncomfortably, the barnacled stones of the wall sharp at her back, 'That's called guilt, love. It's a human thing.' She turns, takes his face between her hands. 'Think about that mountain. Think about what happened. Now, tell yourself, true – could you have stopped it? Didn't you try? Didn't you try fit to kill yourself?'

'I don't know,' he whispers. 'There must have been something I could have done. There's always something.'

Shipwright kisses him softly on the lips, his skin like warm paper. 'You did everything you could. I was there.' She leans into him. 'I was there at Thell, and I was there at Luss, and I've been there all the times in between. I *know* you. You try. You try so very hard. You want to be more perfect than any of us, and when the world isn't perfect, when you can't keep *everyone* safe, *all* the time, you think you've failed. But the thing is,' she says, and her voice shakes, 'you have no idea how many people simply don't try. You *succeed* by trying.'

Shroudweaver can't meet her eyes. She shifts until she can see him clearly.

'Yes. People died. In Thell, at Luss, in the south. Hundreds, thousands of people. I don't know. But we're alive, because of you. There are so many others alive because of you. They're not going to thank you, because people can't see in front of their own noses half the time. But they'll go on living their ungrateful little lives, because of you.'

He laughs at that. 'I love you,' he says.

'And I love you too. Which is why I need you to buck up. We're not done yet, and I can't be the only one at the tiller.'

He smiles, runs a thumb over her cheek. 'I hear you, I do. Don't worry. I'm far from done myself.'

She kisses him again, deeper, more fiercely. 'We're always far from done, sweetheart. Why do you think it's always us in the middle of this shit?'

Shroudweaver laughs. 'I'd never thought about it that way.'

Birds cut the sky above his upturned head as he looks out over the seawall at the warm curve of the ship catching the rising sun.

'I always just assumed it was because we were too stupid to let well alone.'

Shipwright snorts. 'That explains you, maybe.'

'Are you ready to sail?'

'I've been ready since we docked,' she grins.

He offers her his hand. 'West Tide then, out to the Heron Halls and beyond?'

'Sounds delightful.'

91

sweet departure
the ocean wide

A day later, and the world continues on without the Shipwright and the Shroudweaver.

Distantly, up in the hills, stone peels away in a landslide, the earth raw and red beneath. It exposes the remains of roots, branches. The sky shivers with the half-hearted sighing of shifting pines as the wind pushes through them, the air carrying always from east to west, borrowing the heat from the rising sun and pushing it into the belly of the trees, popping cones and splitting bark. The breath of the forest is painted with sap, pungent and sticky.

The wind freshens as it moves to the coast, its lines ridden by small, swift-winged birds, the tiny stamps of their bodies like punctuation. It gathers the slow heat of fruit groves, the burnt citrus of dusky earth, the scent of herbs hollowed in the sparse soil between warm rocks. It swoops light over the Midlands, and dances on the tongues of tillers, field hands and laughing girls.

Ducking through the white gates of Hesper, it dwindles to dust in the throats of old men, swilled clean by sharp beer and sweetened wine. It chases carts down winding lanes, teasing the hair of back-bent women, keening the edges of ploughs and pushing the stones down into grain fields whipped with life, scattered and tussocked with mice, birds and fattening hawks.

Briefly caught against the morning, it glows afire with golden whispers for a moment, before it swirls under the axles of the first day's trade, picking sweat from the bellies of drays and baking the mud under-hoof, creaking the hinges of wide-flung doors and swallowing the hurling shouts of porters and bakers and long-limbed lovers. It gathers steam from cups and spittle from lips, running the arch of spines and fleeing the clack of shutters quick-clasped against it, running to the salt of the sea.

Picking at chunks of sailor's curses in the freshening light, it skips over cask and barrel and lash, rat back and mule sway, thick thumbs and strong hands and seaweed-slick dock. Along rope-lines and jetties it runs, and over the tops of the waves, called by the shouts of sailors to whip wildly over arms that lash rigging and legs that stride the decks. It brushes over Ropecharmer's dry lips and shaking hands as they stow a package, small, clay-wrapped, twine-tied and wax-sealed. Skirting the replaced board, his quick-turned shoulders and tight legs, before skipping off along sweat-struck skin to twist Shipwright's salt-scoured hair. She feels it cool against her brow, breathes deep – pine and lemon and shore and sea. The ship at long last casts off.

As Shroudweaver slings himself over the rail, the deck flexes under his feet. A last slap of the boarding ladder against the side, and he's offshore, his head turned to the freshening breeze. Hesper's body is square and angular before him as the docks grudgingly relinquish the ship, trailing ropes and anchors into the water like the heavy fingers of a reluctant lover.

The smoke-stained scrape of the great white walls slowly shifts into the horizon. The clatter of metal and the bustle of the docks sifting into the sound of waves and gulls. The stark teeth of the Grey Towers fading into twin lines, iron against the sky.

Above, the rig spirits hum into life, battening against canvas and unfurling their sails out into the sharpening air. Shroud-weaver walks to the bow of the ship, stepping lightly around hanks of rope, quick slung hammocks, the detritus of the refugees coming west with them. There's a smattering of small ports before they strike out for the deep waters and the Heron Halls. They can cling to the coast for a few days and find time to settle the last few of Thell's survivors somewhere quiet, with a soft shore and smoke in the earth. Shroudweaver envies them, a little.

Ropecharmer steps aside as he passes the hold, dipping his head respectfully. Shroudweaver smiles at his broad shoulders and climbs the steps to where Shipwright stands at the helm.

'I'd missed this,' he says.

She turns the wheel slowly, easing the ship out into deeper waters. 'Of course you did, love. This is our home.'

He leans into her as she steers, the warm salt of her skin, the steady shift of her muscles, the faint smell of tar and leather and polish. The noise of the port falls away to the sea, and after that, the noise of the crew, until there's only the crisp song of rising waves.

He places his lips against her ear. 'So, just us then.'

The breath that fills Shipwright's lungs is long and soft, the first real breath she's taken in a long time. She pulls his hands around her waist, and cups her chin into his shoulder.

'Just us, dearest of my heart. The way I like it.'

The ship rides the swell of the waves out under the belly of the sky, and the world recedes.

Shipwright turns the tiller, and kicks the spinners a little higher. The loops of Hesper's docks pull up and into the horizon. Behind them are Fallon and Riss, and Ice, a town of refugees in a city of sailors, the bones of the mountain in the belly of the vulture. Behind them, Thell and the darkness, the tall forests of the Burners and the low dark stone of the Midlands. She breathes out, the shudder of her ribs sounding the timbers of the ship as it turns north, then west again. Above, she hears the snap of canvas as the sails fill with golden light, backed by a gentle hum from the highest spars as the brass of the rig spirits dances up a song. Beyond them, the sea is blue and beyond that there are further places, white spires and the sunken spindles of cities which have never known the weight of land.

The air leaves her lungs and returns to the tops of the waves. Shroudweaver's hand appears in hers, soft and slight, and she holds it for completeness and warmth. She can feel the brush of his bones beneath the skin, the pulse of his blood and the shift of his lips against her ear.

'I love you,' he says, and the ship bucks the crest of a wave.

She puts an arm around him, saves the other for the rail of the ship. Warm wood, warm skin. 'I love you too.'

749

In front of them, the sea opens up to whiteness, the bright light of dawn slipping to blue under the keel.

The ship moves west, and westwards.

The Shipwright holds the Shroudweaver, and the Shroudweaver holds the Shipwright, each lost in the hollow of each other's lives.

92

my one true love
still by my side

Two days later and twenty leagues out from Hesper, the sea pulls
to silver under the stern. Shipwright steps up beside Ropecharmer and claps his shoulder. 'The ropes are singing today, Charmer,
light and easy.'

'I'm glad,' he says, though his heart is hollow. She catches his
tone, pulls him close and kisses the stubble of his cheek. 'Cheer
up, Rope. All these people alive because of you and the open sea
in front.' She presses his shoulder affectionately. 'You did good,
kid. We're all lucky to have you.'

'I know, I know. I'm lucky to be here,' he says.

'Oh, you're so *earnest*,' she says, giving his arm a quick squeeze
before she strides back amidships and leaves him alone at the helm.

He watches the shape of her back pull away and lets the breath
in his lungs drop to the deck like glass, sweat as cold under his
shirt as the first frost of winter.

The sea colours behind him, fading outwards to grey and the
thing beneath the boards calls to his conscience like a slow-tolling
bell.

Time to check on Coglifter's gift.

He takes the steps down to the hold slowly, with exaggerated
care, his legs shaking with the tension.

Making a bomb was a simple business. Firing it is not.

For the moment, the device sits under hessian, nestled behind
the barrels of hard-tack. It smells faintly of spice and herbs down
here, the ghost of the medicinal oils used to repel boatworm and
weevil.

When the ship lists the bomb knocks gently against the casks.

Ropecharmer's hands shake a little as he reaches for it, tucking it in a little more snugly to stop it shifting.

The bomb sloshes as it moves.

He recalls the darkened light of a workshop, a few days ago and Coglifter's gnarled hands tracking the bomb's curves, teasing the wick as she rolled it from palm to palm, enjoying the wet sound as it tipped back and forth.

'Do you know what this is?' she asks him, a grin on her face like a stripped corn cob.

He shakes his head mutely. His heart already sick with the horror of betraying Shipwright and Shroudweaver, the closest thing he's had to family for years; the closest thing except Cog.

'Liquid fire,' she murmurs, her fingers lingering on the bomb's rough edges.

'I had to trade for this one, boy. Had to beg, borrow, steal.' She taps her finger thoughtfully on the bomb's shell, and he winces. 'Mostly steal.' She shrugs. 'Worth it though.' She tosses it to him underarm. He fumbles the catch and she snorts. 'Don't make a habit of that boy, or they'll be bringing you back to me in neat, chewy pieces.'

He eyes her over the bomb's rim. 'I'll do this for you Cog. I swore I'd have your back, and that hasn't changed. But I need to know? Why? The Sh—'

She clamps a dry palm over his face with surprising speed. 'Language, boy. Walls have ears and not all of them waggle for me.'

Ropecharmer swallows, his heart hammering. 'Sorry, it's just, they've always been good to me. To Hesper.' He shrugs helplessly. 'To everyone.'

Coglifter eyes him steadily, her goose-grey eyes serious under heavy brows. 'Have they? Have they *really*, boy?'

She puts a hand on his shoulder, and taps a nail against his throat. 'Tell me. What have they ever made better? What have they actually *fixed*?'

'Thell,' he says.

She laughs. 'Thell's a charnel house. No one won there. Crow-kisser saw to that.'

Ropecharmer feels a spark of anger, a little loyalty to Ship-wright flaring in his chest.

'They got refugees out the city. Asked for nothing. We're taking more on the next leg.'

Coglifter's smile is cold, pitying. 'And why were there refu-gees?'

Ropecharmer frowns. 'Because of Thell. Because of the south.'

'Because of Crowkisser,' she cuts in. 'And who failed to stop Crowkisser? Twice.'

Ropecharmer's shoulders slump. 'They did. But . . .?'

She cuts in faster this time. 'But how could they fail? I don't *know* boy. But that's the point. The pair of them running around with all this power, and they don't know how to fix a gods-damned thing.' She laughs again, short and bitter.

'They let the gods *die* boy. Let her tear out our names. You've seen what that's cost us. Cost your family.'

'I didn't know you had love for the gods, Cog,' Ropecharmer murmurs.

Her lip curls. 'Love? Spit on them. Golden head-fuckers. All their parasite ways. No, we're well rid of them.' She pauses, chews her lip. 'Not like that though, not so brutally. We needed a little skill. A little care. Not a teenage temper tantrum.'

He frowns. 'So you're for Crowkisser?'

Coglifter's fist hits the workbench with a shake. 'No! She's the worst of them all. All that power and not a scrap of understanding. A pissy girl with the power to crack the world and not a shred of sense. Wracked because her mother died? Cry me another, Rope. All our mothers die.'

She keeps her back to him for a moment, her shoulder's shak-ing. When she turns to face him, her eyes are wet with the light, small bloodshot veins spidering across the white. She's not been sleeping.

'We need to get shot of all of them, Rope. It's the only way we get peace. The only way we make sure something like this never happens again. That your parents never happen again. That the south never happens again.'

Tenderly, she folds his fingers over the curve of the bomb. 'And for that to happen, the ship needs to burn.'

Here, in the dark of the hold, as the ship rocks in the swell, Ropecharmer hears Coglifter's words in his head again.

The ship needs to burn.

93

last light
dusk
water moving onto water

Three days later, the sea clear under the keel. A fresh wind in the sails, and treachery in the hold. Shipwright at the tiller and Shroudweaver on deck, his face turned into the salt wind whipping from the east. The last refugees tucked into the small island ports that studded the stark outcrops flung out beyond West Tide. A week at most to the Heron Halls. Shroudweaver twists red threads around his fingers and thinks of his daughter.

Below him, Ropecharmer strikes a match with shaking fingers, sets it to the wick of Coglifter's parcel and mouths something that might be an apology, a prayer or a curse, but ends with, 'I'm sorry.'

His feet hammer up through the decks, a straight turn to the rail and then over, in an arcing dive that cuts the water like a knife, scattering silver fish.

Shroudweaver turns to call after him, before his voice is lost to fire. The blast rips up from the hold like a rising howl, bowing planks and wood, the sides of the ship glowing like split rock and a scream roiling from her depths like a dying whale.

Shipwright turns as the deck pitches, and she sees only flame – flame in the rigging and in the sail, the spinners atop the mast already shrieking in horror and agony as heat splits their skins and sends shards of metal zipping across the deck.

She sees a sailor struck, staggering backwards into the hold, the hold which now yawns as red as the pit of the earth, which has melted into the belly of the ship, which tears her apart from port to starboard. The last thing she has of home is vanishing under the smoke.

Smoke, great black clouds. And steam as the heat of the ship's dying hits the ocean. Shipwright lets it boil on her skin, her mind reeling from a betrayal so huge that she can only stand and watch as her home burns.

The crew rushes everywhere with water at first, and then to the boats as they realise how struck she is.

There's another thunder of fire from below, and the ship gives up the ghost entirely, folding in on herself like a hammered blade, like a crushed flower.

The air fills with screams as the crew disappear into the depths, some afire even as they hit the sea, but still burning on the way down, their bodies plumes of red and orange in the clear water.

Shroudweaver is nowhere to be seen at first, then Shipwright catches sight of him hauling an injured man to one of the boats, half by the scruff of his neck, half by the glowing silver lines that pulse from his hand.

Her heart lurches in terror as she calls his name and his eyes turn to meet hers.

She starts towards him even as the deck under her feet bucks and cants with a third explosion, thick with red flame.

The world spins. Air whipping past her face. The sudden sharpness of the deck under her back.

Shipwright sees the great spar of the mast shear loose above her.

Watches it fall towards her like a lit taper on the wind.

And then, darkness.

Epilogue

first light
stars
stone moving under stone

He lifts the latch and slips the bolts. The door sticks at first, swollen from the damp. Run-off slips down the eaves, past the moss and last summer's nests, dripping into the water butt, slow, steady. He takes a pitcher, dips it, tips his head back and pours, scrubbing at the tangles of his hair, running a critical palm over his stubbled jaw.

Ekk pads out to join him, long-legged and stiff in the dawn chill. He scratches behind the dog's ears, chucks a brindled jaw. The charms in the garden tinkle brightly in a skittish breeze. He reties a few, leaves Ekk to piss on the graves of slow rabbits, then returns inside and sets a fire in the stove. He adjusts the flowers by the windows, brushes their pollen on a trouser leg, and rubs a little under his gums, humming merrily.

Leaves thrown in the pot, followed by the slow hiss of water forced upwards, lively and dark. A gift from the Grey Towers by the sea. He looks at the tin, then sets it down; busies himself by chopping meat, blunts the cleaver on bone, strops it, renders a gamey leg down into manageable chunks. It's half-gone, but Ekk doesn't mind. The clap of his bowl on the flagstones brings him lolling in, damp from morning dew. With a thump on his generous ribs the old dog sets to.

He watches Ekk eat as he pours the brew, sips it left-handed, absently working arms into shirt sleeves, lacing up, and rubbing aching calves. A quiet morning. The soft clack of the chimes outside. A strong smell of herbs as the sun hits the pots on the sill. He finishes, washes his plate and Ekk's, then sets them by the sink. Brushes, spits; a little blood.

757

Heading out back, he checks the pens and the garden, straightens a few stakes, soothes the broodies on their boxes, turns the new plot with a fork. Spits more blood into the earth, straightens.

The highlands are turning bone and blue with flowers, Elsta's Folly and Slipwort starting to show. All worth gathering, if he has time. He rubs fingers over his jaw again, sets his eyes to the horizon. Turning slowly in a circle, he takes in the bowl of the sky, kissed by the mountains to the south, stretching out north and west until it meets the first distant spires. He watches the light play on them for a while, shifting their marble bodies, their sundered edges.

Heading inside, he sets himself carefully opposite a large, lacquered cabinet, and reads. Histories, fantasies, some that are neither and both. He thumbs familiar pages, bent corners, recites the lines in his head before he reads them, savouring the rhythm of it, resting a hand on Ekk's long skull. The chimes tap against each other, against the bent and bowered staves in the garden and the sun stretches across the boards. He watches it make its way, until it toes the cabinet's corners, then raises his eyebrows expectantly – as if on command, the thing inside wakes almost immediately, throwing itself against the doors.

He makes a note in a ledger, under many other notes, then closes it.

Ekk watches him wide-eyed, flat-eared, a low rumble in his long ribs. He murmurs reassuringly as he crosses to the lacquered doors, setting his fingers against the shifting panels, close enough that he can feel the vibration of the thing's rage through the wood. His fingers stray towards the lock, to the deep scratches around the keyhole.

A soft warning growl from Ekk.

He smiles, moves his hand consolingly.

The dog grumbles, whines, quiets.

The thing inside the cabinet throbs, its stench escaping between the joins, spice and sugar, lemon and copper. He thumbs his gums anxiously, and replaces his fingers on the panels, pressing in swift, precise rhythms, his fingers a blur. Tortoiseshell, amethyst, cat bone, flint. The polished squares retreat under his touch. Eventually, the thing inside quiets. He backs away, falls into his chair, takes Ekk's head in his lap, strokes his soft ears and shivers.

A gust picks the chimes outside, drags them against the walls and each other. His head scurries with sound. When it fades, the usual peace doesn't return.

Ekk's ears perk, his spine stiffens.

Footsteps on the path, and voices behind them. He shares a quick look with the dog, who returns it stolidly. It's easy enough to set himself by the door jamb, the rough knots of the wood a comfort against his spine. He runs his fingers over his unshaven jaw again, drums the frame and squints down the path.

There are more of them coming than he thought, and they're in a bad way. A ragged mob of men and women, children, thin babies. A pair of old women at their head, etched like ghosts against the sky. Hand in hand they come, singing so quietly and hoarsely that he only hears it as they draw close. Next to them a young man, his hair a dandelion-shock, his face spattered and muddy, bandages and bloody scarves wrapped around his throat. Leaning on another fellow with his arm in a sling, a wood-cutter's axe at his hip. His face torn and lined with pain. Behind them the rest, maybe forty, fifty more, he can't be sure. Young and old, tired and injured. And tattooed, with red and black geometrics spiralling over arms, shoulders, legs. He feels faintly queasy looking at them.

It takes a little while for them to draw near, stumbling over every rock and tussock. Meanwhile, he thumbs his gums, keeping a wary hand on Ekk's neck. The charms chuck and rattle against the low fussing of the hens in the backyard.

When they gain the first steps up to the cottage, he calls out. 'That's far enough.'

The group draws closer.

He feels Ekk's hackles rise and scratches him soothingly. 'Far enough, I said.'

The old women ignore him, but the young men glance up the

759

path. The bearded one calls out. 'We need water. And a place to stop.' A wave of an arm. 'We have injured.'

He sucks his teeth, shouts back. 'No one stops here. Move on.'

The air hangs still for a moment. He watches the young man look to his axe and weigh his chances, wondering what he sees. He shakes his head ever so slightly and it's then that he feels it in the back of his brain. That bastard itch. Years without, and here, staring at this ragged pair, he feels it. That bastard itch. Curiosity.

He calls out. 'Where you from?'

The young man winces. 'Thell.'

A pause. The chimes, the chickens, the flowers in the high fields.

'It's gone.'

When the young man says it, a wail goes up. A collective shudder of sorrow that he feels in his teeth.

The Lockwatcher runs pinched fingers over his temples.

'Fuck me. You better come up then.'

Glossary

Archivist Primer, for the annealing of new initiates.

Prepared the fourth year after the end. Being known colloquially as Mountain-break or Salt-fire. Marking the arrival of the refugees into our great city. The return of our beloved Lady. The death of our champions.

Burners, The   Primitives, bound to the eastern Forest.

Chek   The city of birdsong. Ruined.

Dryke   A town of leatherworkers and cattlemen. Spit and silence. In service to Crowkisser since the fall.

Empire of the Dead, The   That which dwelt in the northern mountain, prior to the Revolution of Thell.

Errant   The Port of Spirals. Beset by starvation, and the madness that follows. Silent since the fall.

Fallon, Arissa   The Grey Lady of Hesper.

Fallon, Declan   The Bull Lord of Hesper. Lord of the Grey Towers. A shepherd and a shepherd still.

Fallow   A town of sheep-herders and drovers. Wool and wit. In service to Crowkisser since the fall.

Gallowswatcher   A corpse turned watchman by fell magics. Often more useful in death than in life. Spiteful.

Glass Archive, The   A bastion of civilisation. The memory-well of the collected. A library of stilled tongues.

Glimmers   Street children. Gutter rats. Disconnected youths.

Heartshamer	Faithless. A spy. Apostate. A trader amid Loose Tongues. Known to the Grey Lord and Lady.
Heron Halls, The	Those migratory cities that disregard boundaries of country and body alike. Last seen walking West, before the fall.
Hesper	The vulture by the sea. Port of the Fallons.
Lungfallow	One of several plants known as the slight widows.
Luss	The great jewelled city of the Western coast. Ruined by the Empire.
Rom	The city of horses. Ruined.
Sedge	Poachers, eaters of bird legs. In service to Crowkisser since the fall.
Serpent	The Port of Summer. Dying and under blockade. Silent since the fall.
Thell	The mountain republic. Former seat of the Empire of the Dead.
The Hollows	Drowning site. Cf. Twicefallow.
The ~~South~~	The great burning. Site of the crow-witch's murder.
Twicefallow	Drowned.
Vantage	A town of scouts and scavengers. Sharp eyes and sharp tongues. In service to Crowkisser since the fall.
Visage	The Port of Mirrors. Crippled since the White Unveiling. Silent since the fall.

Acknowledgements

This ship was built from many parts, and the list of thanks is long. Much stitching in the sails and much caulk at the seams.

Early thanks should go to Simon Spanton, who was the first person to take an interest in Ship and Shroud, and who was instrumental in helping them sail onward. Simon was generous with time, advice and encouragement, again and again. Look close and you can see his fingerprints upon the tiller.

Similarly, the book would not exist without Jamie Cowen who has been, as well as an impeccable agent, a ferocious support and a guiding influence on the strange, wild MS which first crossed his desk. Jamie *got* the book from day one, and having someone who understood what I wanted to achieve from the outset has been invaluable. As my agent he is to blame for many things, but most of all for having the skill to push the novel farther and wider, and for giving support and steadiness when I was writing after the loss of my father. And of course, Jamie is to blame for more Fallon. You may address your letters accordingly.

At the Buckman Agency, Jessica Buckman O'Connor has been indefatigable in sending Ship and Shroud overseas, and for helping patiently when unpleasant things like numbers and counting intruded on the business of telling stories.

Ship and Shroud have been lucky to attract people who clicked with them from very early on, but no one more so than Bethan Morgan. As my editor at Gollancz, Bethan has been the greatest of good fortune. She has tirelessly championed the book, and I knew she was the right fit from the very first pitch where crows and ancient shipwrecks filled the screen. A deft touch, relentless enthusiasm and a keen eye. Crowkisser would be proud.

The wider team at Gollancz have also been beyond what a new author might hope for, and particular thanks are due to Jenna

Petts, Susie Bertinshaw, Sian Baldwin, Andy Ryan, Ellie Nightingale, Zakirah Alam, Louise Richardson and Paul Stark, among many others.

Ship and Shroud have also had fine champions outside of Gollancz; Molly Powell at Hodder & Stoughton managed to make the process of editorial meetings feel like a fun chat with a friend, and the Gollancz Debut Authors group have been a great source of community and sanity in extremely unusual times.

Lastly the rest of the crew. The witches and weavers who have stayed or shaped the course.

To Cindy Brook for the quiet house and the strong coffee, the whisky and the patient dogs.

To Emma Flint for the twin medicines of a patient ear, and pasta y vino. For helping me keep the heid, as they say in my neck of the woods.

To Helen Boden, Olga Wojtas and Patrycja Kupiec for catalysing and championing and editing.

To James Robertson and Michele Roberts, for teaching me I could write the land well, and monsters better still. To Fiona Benson for firm, smart advice on the alchemy of grief.

To my father and mother again, because how could once be enough? And to Rowan for lifting myself, and the story, with grace, joy and patience.

And to you the reader, for sailing with us. Eyes on the tale and heart on the words.

The list goes on and on. The book is built from more small kindnesses and hard work than I can ever hope to collate.

This is how it should be, and must be. The seas are always dark and wide. The world always stalks onwards in the shadow of the past. So we are kind to each other, and we help each other build and thrive. We must. We sail only once, and the dark comes after. Thank you all.

About the Author

Rafael Torrubia grew up split between Spain and Scotland as the child of a Scottish mother and a Spanish father. They have won a number of awards for their writing and poetry, including Writer of the Year from the National Gallery of Scotland, the Deirdre Roberts Poetry Prize and multiple shortlistings for the Bridport Prize. Their writing has taken a winding route from the Words on Canvas writing group at the National Galleries of Scotland, through the Moniack Mhor and Arvon writing centres. They studied and taught at the University of St Andrews and in Harlem, NYC, exploring the linkages between plantation folksongs and the protest songs of the civil rights movement, and later examining the cultural inheritances of the Black Power movement in America. Like all recovering historians, they have also worked in wine, whisky and at the National Museum of Scotland. Rafael currently supports postgraduate student development at St Andrews and is a Lead Reader with the writing charity Open Book, delivering creative writing workshops to participants across Scotland. When not writing, they can be found lost in a peaty whisky, a muddy allotment or by a wide, dark river somewhere in Perthshire.

Credits

Gollancz would like to thank everyone at Orion who worked on the publication of *The Shipwright and the Shroudweaver*.

Agent
Jamie Cowen,
The Ampersand Agency

Editor
Bethan Morgan

Copy-editor
Andy Ryan

Proofreader
Bruno Vincent

Editorial Management
Susie Bertinshaw
Zakirah Alam
Jane Hughes
Charlie Panayiotou
Lucy Bilton
Patrice Nelson

Audio
Paul Stark
Louise Richardson
Georgina Cutler-Ross

Contracts
Rachel Monte
Ellie Bowker
Tabitha Gresty

Design
Rachael Lancaster
Nick Shah
Deborah Francois
Helen Ewing

Photo Shoots & Image Research
Natalie Dawkins

Finance
Nick Gibson
Jasdip Nandra
Sue Baker
Tom Costello

Inventory
Jo Jacobs
Dan Stevens

Production
Hannah Cox
Katie Horrocks

Marketing
Ellie Nightingale

Publicity
Sian Baldwin

Sales
Dave Murphy
Victoria Laws
Sammy Luton
Group Sales teams across
Digital, Field, International
and Non-Trade

Operations
Group Sales Operations team

Rights
Rebecca Folland
Tara Hiatt
Ben Fowler
Maddie Stephenson
Ruth Blakemore
Marie Henckel

RAISING READERS
Books Build Bright Futures

Dear Reader,

We'd love your attention for one more page to tell you about the crisis in children's reading, and what we can all do.

Studies have shown that reading for fun is the **single biggest predictor of a child's future life chances** – more than family circumstance, parents' educational background or income. It improves academic results, mental health, wealth, communication skills, ambition and happiness.[1]

The number of children reading for fun is in rapid decline. Young people have a lot of competition for their time. In 2024, 1 in 10 children and young people in the UK aged 5 to 18 did not own a single book at home.[2]

Hachette works extensively with schools, libraries and literacy charities, but here are some ways we can all raise more readers:

- Reading to children for just 10 minutes a day makes a difference
- Don't give up if children aren't regular readers – there will be books for them!
- Visit bookshops and libraries to get recommendations
- Encourage them to listen to audiobooks
- Support school libraries
- Give books as gifts

There's a lot more information about how to encourage children to read on our website: **www.RaisingReaders.co.uk**

Thank you for reading.

---

[1] National Literacy Trust, Book Ownership in 2024, November 2024
https://nlt.cdn.ngo/media/documents/Book_ownership_in_2024

[2] OECD. 2021. 21st-century readers: developing literacy skills in a digital world. Paris, France: OECD Publishing.
https://www.oecd.org/en/publications/21st-century-readers_a83d84cb-en.html